Karl Baedeker

South-Western France from the Loire and the Rhone to the Spanish frontier

handbook for travellers

Karl Baedeker

South-Western France from the Loire and the Rhone to the Spanish frontier
handbook for travellers

ISBN/EAN: 9783741193057

Manufactured in Europe, USA, Canada, Australia, Japa

Cover: Foto ©Andreas Hilbeck / pixelio.de

Manufactured and distributed by brebook publishing software
(www.brebook.com)

Karl Baedeker

South-Western France from the Loire and the Rhone to the Spanish frontier

SOUTH-WESTERN FRANCE

MONEY TABLE (comp. p. xi).
Approximate Equivalents.

French Money.		American Money.		English Money.			German Money.	
Francs.	Centimes.	Dollars.	Cents.	Pounds.	Shillings.	Pence.	Marks.	Pfennigs.
—	5 (= 1 sou)	—	1	—	—	½	—	4
—	25 (= 25 sous)	—	5	—	—	2½	—	20
—	50 (= 10 »)	—	10	—	—	4¾	—	40
—	75 (= 15 »)	—	15	—	—	7¼	—	60
1	— (= 20 »)	—	20	—	—	9¾	—	80
2	—	—	40	—	1	7¼	1	60
3	—	—	60	—	2	4¾	2	40
4	—	—	80	—	3	2½	3	20
5	—	1	—	—	4	—	4	—
6	—	1	20	—	4	9¾	4	80
7	—	1	40	—	5	7¼	5	60
8	—	1	60	—	6	4¾	6	40
9	—	1	80	—	7	2½	7	20
10	—	2	—	—	8	—	8	—
11	—	2	20	—	8	9¾	8	80
12	—	2	40	—	9	7¼	9	60
13	—	2	60	—	10	4¾	10	40
14	—	2	80	—	11	2½	11	20
15	—	3	—	—	12	—	12	—
16	—	3	20	—	12	9¾	12	80
17	—	3	40	—	13	7¼	13	60
18	—	3	60	—	14	4¾	14	40
19	—	3	80	—	15	2½	15	20
20	—	4	—	—	16	—	16	—
25	—	5	—	1	—	—	20	—
100	—	20	—	4	—	—	80	—

SOUTH-WESTERN FRANCE

FROM

THE LOIRE AND THE RHONE TO THE SPANISH FRONTIER

HANDBOOK FOR TRAVELLERS

BY

KARL BAEDEKER

SECOND EDITION

WITH 10 MAPS AND 18 PLANS

LEIPSIC: KARL BAEDEKER, PUBLISHER

1895

'Go, little book, God send thee good passage,
And specially let this be thy prayere
Unto them all that thee will read or hear,
Where thou art wrong, after their help to call,
Thee to correct in any part or all.'

PREFACE.

The chief object of the Handbook for South-Western France, which has been re-arranged and expanded from the Handbook for Southern France and corresponds with the fifth French edition, is to render the traveller as nearly as possible independent of the services of guides, commissionnaires, and inn-keepers, and to enable him to employ his time and his money to the best advantage.

Like the Editor's other Handbooks, it is based on personal acquaintance with the country described, which has been specially re-visited with the view of assuring accuracy and freshness of information. For the improvement of this work the Editor confidently looks forward to a continuance of those valuable corrections and suggestions with which travellers have been in the habit of favouring him, and for which he owes them a deep debt of gratitude.

The contents of the Handbook are divided into THREE SECTIONS (I. South-Western France from the Loire to the Pyrenees· II. The Pyrenees; III. Central France, Auvergne, and the Cévennes), each of which may be separately removed from the book by the traveller who desires to minimise the bulk of his luggage. To each section is prefixed a list of the routes it contains, so that each forms an approximately complete volume apart from the general table of contents.

On the MAPS and PLANS the utmost care has been bestowed, and it is hoped that they will often be of material service to the traveller, enabling him at a glance to ascertain his bearings and select the best routes.

HEIGHTS and DISTANCES are given in English measurement. It may, however, be convenient to remember that 1 kilomètre is approximately equal to $^3/_8$ Engl. M., or 8 kil. $=$ 5 M. (nearly). See also p. xxiii.

In the Handbook are enumerated both the first-class hotels and those of humbler pretensions. The latter may often be selected by the 'voyageur en garçon' with little sacrifice of real comfort, and considerable saving of expenditure. Those which the Editor, either from his own experience, or from an examination of the numerous hotel-bills sent him by travellers of different nationalities, believes to be most worthy of commendation, are denoted by asterisks. It should, however, be borne in mind that hotels are liable to constant changes, and that the treatment experienced by the traveller often depends on circumstances which can neither be foreseen nor controlled. Although prices generally have an upward tendency, the average charges stated in the Handbook will enable the traveller to form a fair estimate of his expenditure.

To hotel-proprietors, tradesmen, and others the Editor begs to intimate that a character for fair dealing and courtesy towards travellers forms the sole passport to his commendation, and that advertisements of every kind are strictly excluded from his Handbooks. Hotel-keepers are also warned against persons representing themselves as agents for Baedeker's Handbooks.

CONTENTS.

Introduction.

South-Western France.
I. From the Loire to the Pyrenees.

III. Central France. Auvergne. The Cévennes.

Maps.

Plans of Towns.

Abbreviations.

R. = room; L. = light; B. = breakfast; déj. = déjeuner; D.
= dinner; S. = supper; A. = attendance; N. = north, northern,
etc.; S. = south, etc.; E. = east. etc.; W. = west, etc.; M. = English mile; ft. = Engl. foot; fr. = franc; c. = centime.

The letter *d* with a date, after the name of a person, indicates the year
of his death. The number of feet given after the name of a place shows
its height above the sea-level. The number of miles placed before the
principal places on railway-routes and high-roads generally indicates their
distance from the starting-point of the route.

Asterisks are used as marks of commendation.

INTRODUCTION.

I. Language.

A slight acquaintance with French is indispensable for those who desire to explore the more remote districts of Southern France, but tourists who do not deviate from the beaten track will generally find English spoken at the principal hotels and the usual resorts of strangers. If, however, they are entirely ignorant of the French language, they must be prepared occasionally to submit to the extortions practised by porters, cab-drivers, and others of a like class, which even the data furnished by the Handbook will not always enable them to avoid.

II. Money. Travelling Expenses.

MONEY. The decimal Monetary System of France is extremely convenient in keeping accounts. The Banque de France issues *Banknotes* of 5000, 1000, 500, 200, 100, and 50 francs, and these are the only banknotes current in the country. The French *Gold* coins are of the value of 100, 50, 20, 10, and 5 francs; *Silver* coins of 5, 2, 1, $^1/_2$, and $^1/_5$ franc; *Bronze* of 10, 5, 2, and 1 centime (100 centimes $=$ 1 franc). 'Sou' is the old name, still in common use, for 5 centimes; thus, a 5-franc piece is sometimes called 'une pièce de cent sous', 2 fr. $=$ 40 sous, 1 fr. $=$ 20 sous, $^1/_2$ fr. $=$ 10 sous. The currency of Belgium, Switzerland, Italy, and Greece being the same as that of France, Italian, Belgian, Swiss, and Greek gold and silver coins are received at their full value, and the new Austrian gold pieces of 4 and 8 florins are worth exactly 10 and 20 fr. respectively. The only foreign copper coins current in France are those of Italy and occasionally the English penny and halfpenny, which nearly correspond to the 10 and 5 centime piece respectively.

English banknotes and gold are also generally received at the full value in the larger towns, except at the shops of the money-changers, where a trifling deduction is made. The table at the beginning of the book shows the comparative value of the French, English, American, and German currencies, when at par. *Circular Notes* or *Letters of Credit*, obtainable at the principal English and American

banks, are the most convenient form for the transport of large sums;
and their value, if lost or stolen, is recoverable.

The traveller should always be provided with small change
(*petite monnaie*), as otherwise he may be put to inconvenience in
giving gratuities, purchasing catalogues, etc.

EXPENSES. The expense of a tour in Southern France depends
of course on a great variety of circumstances; but it may be stated
generally that travelling in France is not more expensive than in
most other countries of Europe. The pedestrian of moderate requirements, who is tolerably proficient in the language and avoids the
beaten track as much as possible, may limit his expenditure to
12-15 fr. per diem, while those who prefer driving to walking, choose
the dearest hotels, and employ the services of guides and commissionnaires must be prepared to spend at least 20-30 fr. daily. Two
or three gentlemen travelling together will be able to journey more
economically than a single tourist, but the presence of ladies generally adds considerably to the expenses of the party.

III. Period and Plan of Tour.

SEASON. Most of the districts described in this Handbook may
be visited at any part of the year; though the plains between
Auvergne and the Pyrenees, and the other more southerly regions
are apt to be disagreeably hot in the height of summer. On the other
hand, excursions among the mountains, the Pyrenees especially, are
scarcely possible except in summer.

PLAN. The traveller is strongly recommended to sketch out a
plan of his tour in advance, as this, even though not rigidly adhered
to, will be found of the greatest use in aiding him to regulate his
movements, to économise his time, and to guard against overlooking
any place of interest. The districts of which the present Handbook
treats are not only richly gifted with natural beauties, they abound
also in architectural monuments of great importance, both ancient
and modern, and contain numerous points of artistic and historic
interest.

The special bent of the traveller must be the chief agent in de-
termining the plan of tour to be selected, but the following short
itineraries may at least give an idea of the time required for a visit
to the most attractive points. The tourist starting from London will
find no difficulty in adapting the arrangement to his requirements
by beginning at the places most easily reached from England. An
early start is supposed to be made each morning, but no night-trav-
elling is assumed. The various tours given below are arranged so
that they may be combined into one comprehensive tour of two months
(comp. Maps). The names of the places most worth visiting are
painted in *italics*. The tourist should carefully consult the railway time-tables in order to guard against detention at uninteresting
junctions.

a. Ten Days between the Loire and the Gironde.

	Days		Days
Tours, *Loches*, Tours	1	*Royan*, Pons, Saintes	1
Tours, *Poitiers*, Angoulême	1	*Saintes*, *Rochefort*	1
Angoulême, Bordeaux	1	Rochefort, *La Rochelle*	1
Bordeaux	1	La Rochelle, *Niort*	1
Bordeaux, Royan	1	Niort, Loudun, *Chinon*, Tours	1
			10

b. Ten Days in Central France and Auvergne.

	Days		Days
Orléans (or Tours), *Bourges*	1	Aurillac, *Gorges of the Cère*, St. Denis-près-Mariel, *Brive*	1
Bourges, *La Bourboule*, Mont Dore, *Sancy*	2	Brive, *Périgueux*	1
Mont Dore, *Clermont-Ferrand*, *Royat*, *Puy de Dôme*	2	Périgueux, *Limoges*	1
Clermont, *Arvant*, *Ligne du Cantal*, Aurillac	1	Limoges, *Angoulême*, Bordeaux (or Limoges, Châteauroux, Orléans)	1
			10

c. Ten Days in the Lozère and the Cévennes.

	Days		Days
Clermont-Ferrand, Arvant, Neussargues, St. Flour, *Mende*	1	Montpellier, *Nîmes*	1
		Nîmes, *Aigues-Mortes*, Nîmes	1
Mende, *Cañon of the Tarn*, *Montpellier-le-Vieux*, Millau	2	Nîmes, St. George d'Aurac, Le Puy	1
Millau, *Béziers*	1	*Le Puy*, St. Etienne	1
Béziers, *Montpellier*	1	St. Etienne, *Lyons*	1
			10

d. A Month in Gascony, Languedoc, and the Pyrenees.

	Days		Days
Bordeaux, *Bayonne*	1	*Environs of Bagnères-de-Luchon*	3-4
Bayonne, *Biarritz*, Bayonne	1	Bagnères-de-Luchon, *Toulouse*	1
Bayonne, *San Sebastian*	1	*Toulouse*, Carcassonne	1
San Sebastian, Bayonne, *Pau*	1	*Carcassonne*, *Narbonne*, Perpignan	1
Pau, *Eaux-Bonnes*, *Eaux-Chaudes*, etc., Pau	2-3	*Perpignan*, Carcassonne	1
Pau, *Lourdes*, Cauterets	1	Carcassonne, Castelnaudary, Castres, *Albi*	1
Cauterets and its Environs	3-4	Albi, Capdenac, *Cahors*, Montauban	1
Luz, *St. Sauveur*, *and their Environs*	2-3	*Montauban*, *Agen*, Bordeaux or Périgueux	1
Bartrès and its Environs	2		
Bagnères-de-Bigorre	1		
Bagnères-de-Bigorre, *Bagnères-de-Luchon*	1		
			20-30

IV. Passports. Custom House. Octroi.

Passports. These documents, though not now obligatory, are often useful in proving the traveller's identity, procuring admission to museums on days when they are not open to the public, etc., and they must be shown in order to obtain delivery of registered letters. Pedestrians in remote districts, especially in the mountain frontier-districts, will often find that a passport spares them much inconvenience and delay. The countenance and help of the British and American consuls can, of course, be extended to those persons only who can prove their nationality. A British Foreign Office

passport may be obtained at the Foreign Office, from 11 to 4 (fee 2s.).
on previous written application, supported by a clergyman, banker.
magistrate, or justice of the peace. Application for passports may
be made to W. J. Adams, 59 Fleet Street; Lee and Carter. 440 W.
Strand; C. Smith & Son, 63 Charing Cross; or E. Stanford, 26 Cock-
spur Street, Charing Cross (charge 2s., agent's fee 1s. 6d.).

Sketching, photographing, or making notes near fortified places
sometimes exposes innocent travellers to disagreeable suspicions or
worse, and should therefore be avoided.

Custom House. In order to prevent the risk of unpleasant detention at the 'douane' or custom-house, travellers are strongly recommended to avoid carrying with them any articles that are not
absolutely necessary. Cigars and tobacco are chiefly sought for by
the custom-house officers. The duty on the former amounts to about
16s., on the latter to 7-11s. per lb. Articles liable to duty should
always be 'declared'. Books and newspapers occasionally give rise to
suspicion and may in certain cases be confiscated. The examination
of luggage generally takes place at the frontier-stations, and travellers
should superintend it in person. Luggage registered to Paris is
examined on arrival there.

Octroi. At the entrance to the larger towns an 'Octroi', or municipal tax, is levied on all comestibles, but travellers' luggage is usually passed on a simple declaration that it contains no such articles.
The officials are, however, entitled to see the receipts for articles
liable to duty at the frontier.

V. Railways. Diligences. Carriages.

The network of railways by which France is now overspread consists of lines of an aggregate length of 20,300 M., belonging to the
Government, to six large companies, and to a large number of smaller ones. The districts treated in this Handbook are served mainly
by the lines of the *Orléans*, *Midi*, and *Paris-Lyon-Méditerranée*
railways, and to a smaller extent by the Government lines (*Réseau
de l'Etat*).

The fares per English mile are approximately: 1st cl. 18 c.,
2nd cl. 12 c., 3rd cl. 8 c., to which a tax of ten per cent on each
ticket costing more than 10 fr. is added. The mail trains (*'trains
rapides'*) generally convey first-class passengers only, and the express
trains (*'trains express'*) first-class and second-class only. The first-
class carriages are good, but the second-class are inferior to those in
most other parts of Europe and the third-class are rarely furnished
with cushioned seats. The trains are generally provided with smoking
carriages, and in the others smoking is allowed unless any one of
the passengers objects. Ladies' compartments are also provided.
The trains invariably pass each other on the left, so that the traveller
can always tell which side of a station his train starts from. The

speed of the express - trains is about 35-45 M. per hour, but that of
the ordinary trains is often very much less.

Travellers must purchase their tickets before entering the waiting-
rooms, but, unlike other parts of France, they are then permitted free
access to the platforms, and may choose their own seats in the trains.
Tickets for intermediate stations are usually collected at the 'sortie';
those for termini, before the station is entered. Travellers within
France are allowed 30 kilogrammes (66 Engl. lbs.) of luggage free of
charge; those who are bound for foreign countries are allowed 25 kilogr.
only (55 lbs.); 10 c. is charged for booking. In all cases the heavier
luggage must be booked, and a ticket procured for it; this being done,
the traveller need not enquire after his 'impedimenta' until he ar-
rives and presents his ticket at his final destination (where they will
be kept in safe custody, several days usually gratis). Where, however, a frontier has to be crossed, the traveller should see his luggage
cleared at the custom-house in person (comp. p. xv). At most of the
railway-stations there is a *consigne*, or left-luggage office, where a
charge of 10 c. per day is made for one or two packages, and 5 c. per
day for each additional article. Where there is no *consigne*, the
employés will generally take care of luggage for a trifling fee. The
railway-porters (*facteurs*) are not entitled to remuneration, but it is
usual to give a few sous for their services. — *Interpreters* are found
at most of the large stations.

There are no *Refreshment Rooms (Buffets)* except at the principal
stations; and as the viands are generally indifferent, the charges high,
and the stoppages brief, the traveller is advised to provide himself beforehand with the necessary sustenance and consume it at his leisure in
the railway-carriage. Baskets containing a cold luncheon are sold at some
of the buffets for 3-4 fr.

Sleeping Carriages (Wagons-Lits) are provided on nearly all the main
lines of the *Orléans, Midi,* and *Paris-Lyon-Méditerranée* systems. *Trains
de luxe*, with drawing-room, sleeping, and dining cars (*Wagons-Restaurants*)
run on certain days, during the season, to the Pyrenees viâ Bordeaux;
comp. the *Indicateur*. The fares are about 50°/o higher than the ordinary
first class fares. Déj. is provided at about 5 fr., D. at 8 fr., wine extra
(half-a-bottle 1 fr.).

Pillows and *Rugs* may be hired (1 fr.) at the large stations.

The most trustworthy information as to the departure of trains
is contained in the *Indicateur des Chemins de Fer*, published weekly,
and sold at all the stations (75 c.). There are also separate and less
bulky time-tables ('*Livrets Chaix*') for the different lines: d'Orléans,
du Midi, etc. (40 c.).

Railway time is always that of Paris, shown on the clocks outside the stations, but the clocks inside, by which the trains start,
are five minutes slower. French railway time is 23 min. in advance
of Spanish time, and 56 min. behind Central European time which
is observed by the railways of Germany, Switzerland, and Italy.

Return-tickets (*Billets d'aller et retour*) are issued by all the
railway-companies at a reduction of 20-40 per cent; but on the
Midi system this privilege is restricted to certain fixed routes. The

length of time for which these tickets are available varies with the distance and with the company by which they are issued; those issued on Sat. and on the eves of great festivals are available for three days. The recognised festivals are New Year's Day, Easter Monday, Ascension Day, Whit-Monday, the 'Fête Nationale' (July 14th), the Assumption (Aug. 15th), All Saints' Day (Nov. 1st), and Christmas Day. — Special return-tickets, valid for longer periods, are issued for the variuos watering-places and summer and winter resorts; see the Indicateur.

Excursion Trains ('*Trains de Plaisir*') should as a rule be avoided, as the cheapness of their fares is more than counterbalanced by the discomforts of their accommodation.

Circular Tour Tickets ('*Billets de Voyages Circulaires*'), available for 15-45 days, are issued by most of the large companies in summer at a reduction of 20-35 per cent on the ordinary fares, or even more if a number of tickets be taken together. There are also a number of *Voyages Circulaires à itinéraires fixes* (routes arranged by the railway company) and also *Voyages Circulaires à itinéraires facultatifs* (routes arranged to suit individual travellers), tickets for which must be applied for at least five days in advance. For details, see the *Indicateur des Chemins de Fer*.

The following are some of the expressions with which the railway-traveller in France should be familiar: Railway-station, *la gare* (also *l'embarcadère*); booking-office, *le guichet* or *bureau*; first, second, or third class ticket, *un billet de première, de seconde, de troisième classe*; to take a ticket, *prendre un billet*; to register the luggage, *faire enregistrer les bagages*; luggage-ticket, *bulletin de bagage*; waiting-room, *salle d'attente*; refreshment room, *le buffet* (third-class refreshment-room, *la buvette*); platform, *le perron, le trottoir*; railway-carriage, *le wagon*; compartment, *le compartiment, le coupé*; smoking compartment, *fumeurs*; ladies' compartment, *dames seules*; guard, *conducteur*; porter, *facteur*; to enter the carriage, *monter en wagon*; take your seats! *en voiture!* alight, *descendre*; to change carriages, *changer de voiture*; express train to Calais, *le train express pour Calais, l'express de Calais*.

Diligences. The French *Diligences*, now becoming more and more rare, are generally slow (5-7 M. per hour), uninviting, and inconvenient. The best seats are the three in the *Coupé*, beside the driver, which cost a little more than the others and are often engaged several days beforehand. The *Intérieur* generally contains six places, and in some cases is supplemented by the *Rotonde*, a less comfortable hinder-compartment, which, however, affords a good retrospective view of the country traversed. The *Impériale, Banquette*, or roof affords the best view of all and may be recommended in good weather. It is advisable to book places in advance if possible, as they are numbered and assigned in the order of application. The fares are fixed by tariff and amount on an average to about $1^{1}/_{2}d.$ per mile (coupé extra). — On the more frequented routes the diligences are gradually being superseded by *Brakes* or large waggonettes. — For short distances the place of the diligences is taken by *Omnibuses*, equally comfortless vehicles, in which, however, there

is no distinction of seats. Those which run in connection with the
railways have a fixed tariff, but in other cases bargaining is advisable. — *Hotel Omnibuses*, see p. xviii.

Hired Carriages (*Voitures de Louage*) may be obtained at all the
principal resorts of tourists at charges varying from 12 to 20 fr. per
day for a single-horse vehicle and from 25 to 30 fr. for a carriage-
and-pair, with a *pourboire* to the driver of 1-2 fr. The hirers almost
invariably demand more at first than they are willing to take, and a
distinct understanding should always be come to beforehand. A
day's journey is reckoned at about 30 M., with a rest of 2-3 hrs. at
midday. A return-fee is frequently demanded when the carriage is
quitted at some distance from its home. Tourists may sometimes
be able to avail themselves of return-carriages, which charge not
less than 10-15 fr. per day. — *Saddle Horses*, *Asses*, and *Mules*
may also be hired.

VI. Hotels, Restaurants, and Cafés.

Hotels. Hotels of the highest class, fitted up with every modern
convenience, are found only in the larger towns and in the more
fashionable watering-places, where the influx of visitors is great. In
other places the inns generally retain their primitive provincial
characteristics, which might prove rather an attraction than otherwise were it not for the shameful defectiveness of the sanitary arrangements. The beds, however, are generally clean, and the cuisine
tolerable. It is therefore advisable to frequent none but the leading
hotels in places off the beaten track of tourists, and to avoid being
misled by the appellation of 'Grand-Hôtel', which is often applied
to the most ordinary inns. Soap is seldom or never provided.

The charges of provincial hotels are usually somewhat lower than
at Paris, but at many of the largest modern establishments the tariff
is drawn up on quite a Parisian scale. Lights are not generally
charged for, and attendance is often included in the price of the
bedroom. It is prudent, though not absolutely necessary, to enquire
the charges in advance. The following are the average charges:
room 1½-3 fr.; breakfast or 'premier déjeuner', consisting of 'café
au lait', with bread and butter, 1-1¼ fr.; luncheon or 'deuxième
déjeuner', taken about 11 a.m., 2½-4 fr.; dinner, usually about 6 p.m.,
3-5 fr. Wine is generally included in the charge for dinner, except
in a few towns in the south-east. The second déjeuner will probably
be regarded as superfluous by most English and American travellers,
especially as it occupies a considerable time during the best part of
the day. A slight luncheon at a café, which may be had at any hour,
will be found far more convenient and expeditious. Attendance on the
table d'hôte is not compulsory, but the charge for rooms is raised if
meals are not taken in the house, and the visitor will scarcely obtain
so good a dinner in a restaurant for the same price. In many hotels

visitors are received 'en pension' at a charge of 6-7 fr. per day and upwards. The usual fee for attendance at hotels is 1 fr. per day, if no charge is made in the bill; if service is charged, 50 c. a day in addition is generally expected.

When the traveller remains for a week or more at a hotel, it is advisable to pay, or at least call for the account, every two or three days, in order that erroneous insertions may be at once detected. Verbal reckonings are objectionable, except in some of the more remote and primitive districts where bills are never written. A waiter's mental arithmetic is faulty, and the faults are seldom in favour of the traveller. A habit too often prevails of presenting the bill at the last moment, when mistakes or wilful impositions cannot easily be detected or rectified. Those who intend starting early in the morning should therefore ask for their bills on the previous evening.

English travellers often give considerable trouble by ordering things almost unknown in French usage; and if ignorance of the language be added to want of conformity to the customs, misunderstandings and disputes are apt to ensue. The reader is therefore recommended to endeavour to adapt his requirements to the habits of the country, and to acquire if possible such a moderate proficiency in the language as to render himself intelligible to the servants.

Articles of Value should never be kept in the drawers or cupboards at hotels. The traveller's own trunk is probably safer; but it is better to entrust them to the landlord, from whom a receipt should be required, or to send them to a banker. Doors should be locked at night.

Travellers who are not fastidious as to their table-companions will often find an excellent cuisine, combined with moderate charges, at the hotels frequented by commercial travellers (*voyageurs de commerce, commis-voyageurs*).

Many hotels send *Omnibuses* to meet the trains, for the use of which $1/_{2}$-1 fr. is charged in the bill. Before taking their seats in one of these, travellers who are not encumbered with luggage should ascertain how far off the hotel is, as the possession of an omnibus by no means necessarily implies long distance from the station. He should also find out whether the omnibus will start immediately, without waiting for another train.

Restaurants. Except in the larger towns, there are few provincial restaurants in France worthy of recommendation to tourists. This, however, is of little importance, as the traveller may always join the table d'hôte meals at hotels, even though not staying in the house. He may also dine *à la carte*, though not so advantageously, or he may obtain a dinner *à prix fixe* (3-6 fr.) on giving $1/_{4}$-$1/_{2}$ hr.'s notice. He should always note the prices on the carte beforehand to avoid overcharges. The refreshment-rooms at railway-stations should be avoided if possible (comp. p. xvi); there is often a restaurant or a small hotel adjoining the station where a better and cheaper meal may be obtained.

Cafés. The *Café* is as characteristic a feature of French provincial as of Parisian life and resembles its metropolitan prototype in most respects. It is a favourite resort in the evening, when people frequent the café to meet their friends, read the newspapers, write letters, or play at cards or billiards. Ladies may visit the better-class cafés without dread, at least during the day. The refreshments, consisting of coffee, tea, beer, Cognac, liqueurs, cooling drinks of various kinds *(sorbet, orgeat, sirop de groseille* or *de framboise,* etc.), and ices, are generally good of their kind, and the prices are reasonable.

Furnished Houses. — Furnished Houses and Furnished Apartments are numerous in all the chief watering-places and winter-stations of Southern France, and may be found to suit every purse. In all cases a personal inspection should be made before hiring; and a contract (on stamped paper) should invariably be drawn up, specifying minutely the condition of the furniture, linen, wallpapers, etc., as disputes are otherwise apt to arise. The assistance of a consul, banker, or other responsible person should, if possible, be obtained in drawing up the contract; and in the case of serious difficulty at the termination of the lease, the aid of the public authorities should be invoked. — As a general rule it is advisable to proceed at first to a hotel, and thence direct the search for apartments, though if the traveller's requirements are modest, he may sometimes be able to suit himself at once with a lodging. Not infrequently the hotel-keepers are willing to make special arrangements with travellers purposing to make a stay of some duration.

VII. Public Buildings and Collections.

The CHURCHES, especially the more important, are open the whole day; but, as divine service is usually performed in the morning and evening, the traveller will find the middle of the day or the afternoon the most favourable time for visiting them. In the S. of France, however, it is a not uncommon practice to close the churches from midday to 2 p. m. The attendance of the sacristan or 'Suisse' is seldom necessary; the usual gratuity is $\frac{1}{2}$ fr. Many of these buildings are under the special protection of Government as '*Monuments Historiques*', and the Ministère des Beaux-Arts has caused most of these to be carefully restored. It is perhaps not altogether superfluous to remind visitors that they should move about in churches as noiselessly as possible to avoid disturbing those engaged in private devotion, and that they should keep aloof from altars where the clergy are officiating. Other interesting buildings, such as palaces, châteaux, and castles often belong to the municipalities and are open to the public with little or no formality. Foreigners will

seldom find any difficulty in obtaining access to private houses of
historic or artistic interest or to the parks attached to the mansions
of the noblesse.

Most of the larger provincial towns of France contain a Musée,
generally comprising a picture-gallery and collections of various
kinds. These are generally open to the public on Sun., and often
on Thurs. also, from 10 or 12 to 4; but strangers are readily admitted
on other days also for a small pourboire. The accounts of the collections given in the Handbook generally follow the order in which
the rooms are numbered, but changes are of very frequent occur-
rence.

VIII. Walking Tours. Guides. Horses.

Walking Tours. Many fine points in the part of France of
which the present Handbook treats are accessible to pedestrians
alone, and even where riding or driving is practicable, walking is
often more enjoyable. For a short tour a couple of flannel shirts, a
pair of worsted stockings, slippers, the articles of the toilette, a light
waterproof, and a stout umbrella will generally be found a sufficient
equipment. Strong and well-tried boots are essential to comfort.
Heavy and complicated knapsacks should be avoided; a light pouch
or game-bag is far less irksome, and its position may be shifted at
pleasure. A pocket-knife with a corkscrew, a leather drinking-cup,
a spirit-flask, stout gloves, and a piece of green crape or coloured
spectacles to protect the eyes from the glare of the snow should not
be forgotten. Useful, though less indispensable, are an opera-glass
or small telescope, sewing-materials, a supply of strong cord, sticking-
plaster, a small compass, a pocket-lantern, a thermometer, and an
aneroid barometer. The traveller's reserve of clothing should not
exceed the limits of a small portmanteau, which can be easily wielded, and may be forwarded from town to town by post.

The mountaineer should have a well-tried *Alpenstock* or staff
shod with a steel point; and for the more difficult ascents an *Ice-
Axe* and *Rope* are also necessary. In crossing a glacier the precaution of using the rope should never be neglected. It should be
securely tied round the waist of each member of the party, leaving
a length of about 10 ft. between each pair. Glaciers should be traversed as early in the morning as possible, before the sun softens
the crust of ice formed during the night over the crevasses. Mountaineers should provide themselves with fresh meat, bread, and wine
or spirits for long excursions. The chalets usually afford nothing
but milk, cheese, and stale bread. Glacier-water should not be
drunk except in small quantities, mixed with wine or cognac. Cold
milk is also safer when qualified with spirits. One of the best beve-
rages for quenching the thirst is cold tea.

The first golden rule for the walker is to start early. If strength
permits, and a suitable resting-place is to be found, a walk of one

or two hours may be accomplished before breakfast. It is desirable
to reach the end of the day's walk about midday, but if that is not
practicable, rest should be taken during the hottest hours (12–3)
and the journey afterwards continued till 5 or 6 p. m., when a sub-
stantial meal (evening table d'hôte at the principal hotels) may be
partaken of. The traveller's own feelings will best dictate the hour
for retiring to rest.

The traveller's ambition often exceeds his powers of endurance,
and if his strength be once over-taxed, he will sometimes be in-
capacitated altogether for several days. At the outset, therefore, the
walker's performances should be moderate, and even when he is in
good training, they should rarely exceed 10 hrs. a day. When a
mountain has to be breasted, the pedestrian should avoid 'spurts',
and pursue the 'even tenor of his way' at a steady and moderate
pace ('chi va piano va sano; chi va sano va lontano'). As another
golden maxim for his guidance, the traveller should remember that
when fatigue begins, enjoyment ceases.

The traveller is cautioned against sleeping in chalets, unless
absolutely necessary. As a rule the night previous to a mountain-
expedition should be spent either at an inn or at one of the club-
huts which the French Alpine Clubs have recently erected for the
convenience of travellers. In the latter case enquiry should be
made beforehand as to the condition and accommodation of the hut,
and whether it is already occupied by a previous party or not. The
convenience of arriving betimes at a hotel, so as to secure good
rooms, etc., is well worth an extra effort on the march.

Over all the movements of the pedestrian, the weather holds des-
potic sway. The barometer and weather-wise natives should be con-
sulted when an opportunity offers. The blowing down of the wind
from the mountains into the valleys in the evening, the melting away
of the clouds, the fall of fresh snow on the mountains, and the ascent
of the cattle to the higher parts of their pasture, are all signs of fine
weather. On the other hand, it is a bad sign if the distant mountains
are dark blue in colour and very distinct in outline, if the wind blows
up the mountains, and if the dust rises in eddies on the roads. West
winds also usually bring rain.

It may be added that the particulars in the handbook as to the
mountain-expeditions make no claim to absolute and invariable ex-
actitude. The weather, the state of the snow, etc., no less than the
different inclinations and capacities of travellers, must be taken into
account as variable factors.

Guides. For all important mountain-expeditions guides are indispensable, except where the contrary is expressly stated; and, above
all, a glacier should never be crossed without an experienced guide.
Good guides are unfortunately rare; but they are to be found at all
the principal tourist-centres among the Pyrenees, such as Cauterets,
Gavarnie, Eaux-Bonnes, and Bagnères-de-Luchon. Most of the

guides in the Pyrenees, however, are hardly more than horse-hirers and organizers of parties on horseback, and not only refuse to go on foot but insist also on tourists paying for their horses. The usual fee for a day of 8 hrs. is 6-8 fr., but on longer or more difficult expeditions 10 fr. and upwards are charged. At some of the principal centres there are guide-societies, with fixed regulations and tariffs. Though the usual charges for the various expeditions are indicated in the Handbook, the tourist will find it advisable to ascertain personally the charges beforehand.

Horses and Mules. Riding is more usual and less expensive in the Pyrenees than in the Alps. The excellent little horses of the Pyrenees may be hired for 6-10 fr. per day. On the whole, unless the ascent be very long, it is less fatiguing to ascend on foot than on horseback; while a descent on horseback is almost invariably uncomfortable and fatiguing, and cannot be recommended even to those who are subject to dizziness.

IX. Post and Telegraph Offices.

Post Office. Letters (whether *'poste restante'* or to the traveller's hotel) should be addressed very distinctly, and the name of the department should be added after that of the town. The offices are usually open from 7 a. m. in summer, and 8 a.m. in winter, to 9 p.m. *Poste Restante* letters may be addressed to any of the provincial offices. In applying for letters, the written or printed name, and in the case of registered letters, the passport of the addressee should always be presented. It is, however, preferable to desire letters to be addressed to the hotel or boarding-house where the visitor intends residing. Letter-boxes (*Boîtes aux Lettres*) are also to be found at the railway-stations and at many public buildings, and stamps (*timbres-poste*) may be purchased in all tobacconists' shops. An extract from the postal tariff is given below; more extensive details will be found in the *Almanach des Postes et Télégraphes.*

Ordinary Letters within France, including Corsica, Algeria, and Tunis, 15 c. per 15 grammes prepaid; for countries of the Postal Union 25 c. (The silver franc and the bronze sou each weigh 5 grammes; 15 grammes, or three of these coins, are equal to 1/2 oz. English.) — *Registered Letters* (*lettres recommandées*) 25 c. extra.

Post Cards 10 c. each, with card for reply attached, 20 c.

Post Office Orders (*mandats de poste*) are issued for most countries in the Postal Union at a charge of 25 c. for every 25 fr. or fraction of 25 fr., the maximum sum for which an order is obtainable being 500 fr.; for Great Britain, 20 c. per 10 fr., maximum 250 fr.

Printed Papers (*imprimés sous bande*): 1 c. per 5 grammes up to the weight of 20 gr.; 5 c. between 20 and 50 gr.; above 50 gr. 5 c. for each 50 gr. or fraction of 50 gr.; to foreign countries 5 c. per 50 gr. The wrapper must be easily removable, and must not cover more than one-third of the packet.

Parcels not exceeding 7 lbs. in weight may be forwarded by post at a moderate rate within France and to some of the other countries of the Postal Union. To England, parcels not exceeding 3 lbs. (1500 grammes) 1 fr. 60 c.; from 3 to 6½ lbs., 2 fr. 10 c. These parcels should be handed

in at the railway-station or at the offices of the parcel-companies, not at
the post-offices.

Telegrams. For the countries of Europe and for Algeria telegrams are charged for at the following rates per word: for France
5 c. (minimum charge 50 c.); Algeria and Tunis 10 c. (minimum
1 fr.); Luxembourg, Switzerland, and Belgium 12½ c.; Germany
15 c.; Netherlands 16 c.; Great Britain, Austria-Hungary, Italy,
Spain, and Portugal 20 c.; Denmark, Roumania, etc. 28½ c.;
Sweden 32 c.; Norway and Russia in Europe 40 c.; Greece 53½-57 c.;
Turkey 53 c.

X. Weights and Measures.

The English equivalents of the French weights and measures
in use since 1799 are given approximately.

Millier = 1000 kilogrammes = 19 cwt. 2 qrs. 22 lbs. 6 oz.

Kilogramme, unit of weight, = 2⅕ lbs. avoirdupois =
  2⁷⁄₁₀ lbs. troy.

Quintal = 10 myriagrammes = 100 kilogrammes = 220 lbs.

Hectogramme (¹⁄₁₀ kilogramme) = 10 décagrammes = 100 gr.
  = 1000 décigrammes. (100 grammes = 3⅕ oz.; 15 gr.
  = ½ oz.; 10 gr. = ⅓ oz.; 7½ gr. = ¼ oz.)

Myriamètre = 10,000 mètres = 6⅕ Engl. miles.

Kilomètre = 1000 mètres = 5 furlongs = about ⅝ Engl. mile.

Hectomètre = 10 décamètres = 100 mètres.

Mètre, the unit of length, the ten-millionth part of the sphe-
  rical distance from the equator to the pole = 3.0784 Paris
  feet = 3.281 Engl. feet = 1 yd. 3⅓ in.

Décimètre (¹⁄₁₀ mètre) = 10 centimètres = 100 millimètres.

Hectare (square hectomètre) = 100 ares = 10,000 sq. mètres
  = 2½ acres.

Are (square décamètre) = 100 sq. mètres.

Hectolitre = ¹⁄₁₀ cubic mètre = 100 litres = 22 gallons.

Décalitre = ¹⁄₁₀₀ cubic mètre = 10 litres = 2⅕ gals.

Litre, unit of capacity, = 1¾ pint; 8 litres = 7 quarts.

The following terms of the old system of measurements are still
sometimes used: —

Livre = ½ kilogramme = 1¹⁄₁₀ lb. Pied = ⅓ mètre = 13 in.
Aune = 1⅕ mètre = 1 yd. 11 in. Toise = 1⁹⁄₁₀ mètre = 2 yds. 4 in.
Lieue = 2½ miles. Arpent = 1¹⁄₂₅ acre. Sétier = 1½ hectolitre =
33 gals.

The thermometers commonly used in France are the Centigrade and Réaumur's. The freezing point on both of these is
marked 0°, the boiling-point of the former 100°, of the latter 80°,
while Fahrenheit's boiling-point is 212° and his freezing-point

32°. It may easily be remembered that 5° Centigrade = 4° Réaumur = 9° Fahrenheit, to which last 32° must be added for temperatures above freezing. For temperatures below freezing the number of degrees obtained by converting those of Centigrade or Réaumur into those of Fahrenheit must be subtracted from 32. Thus 5° C = 4° R. = 9 + 32 = 41° F.; 20° C = 16° R. = 36 + 32 = 68° F. Again, − 5° C = − 4° R. = 32 − 9 = 23° F.; − 20° C = − 16° R. = 32 − 36 = − 4° F.

XI. Maps.

The best maps of France have hitherto been the *Cartes de l'Etat-Major*, or Ordnance Maps of the War Office. One series of these is on a scale of 1:80,000, and includes 273 sheets, each 2½ ft. long and 1½ ft. wide, while another, reduced from the above, is on a scale of 1:320,000 and consists of 33 sheets (1 for 16 of the others) or 27 for France proper. These may be had either engraved on steel (2 fr. per sheet) or lithographed (50 c.). The engraved maps are considerably clearer in the mountainous regions, but the lithographs are good enough for ordinary use. Since 1889 the larger scale map has also been issued in quarter sheets (1 fr. engraved; 30 c. lithographed), intended ultimately to supersede the larger sheets.

The War Office has undertaken two new series of maps, printed in five colours; one on a scale of 1:50,000, and one on a scale of 1:200,000. The larger of these has not been published except for a part of the N.E. provinces, but the smaller scale map is already well advanced. The price of each sheet is 1½ fr.

There is also another map in five colours (1:100,000), published in 1881-1894 by the Ministry of the Interior (85 c. per sheet); and yet another (1:200,000) is now in course of publication by the Ministry of Public Works, and is sold in sheets at 40 c. each.

The Spanish slope of the Pyrenees is not included in the maps of the Etat-Major, but is given in the map of the Ministry of Interior (1:100,000; see above) and in that of the *Dépôt des Fortifications* (1:500,000).

All these maps may be obtained in the chief tourist-resorts, but it is advisable to procure them in advance. The following shops in Paris have always a full supply on hand: *Lanée*, Rue de la Paix 8; *Andriveau-Goujon*, Rue du Bac 4; *Dumaine (Baudoin)*, Rue et Passage Dauphine 30, etc.

The catalogue of the Service Géographique de l'Armée (1 fr.) contains key-plans of its maps, including also those of Algeria, Tunis, and Africa generally (parts sold separately 10 c., Algeria and Tunis 25 c.). Barrère's catalogue (gratis) has key-plans of the 1:80,000, 1:200,000, and 1:320,000 maps; and key-plans of the 1:100,000 map may be obtained at Hachette's, Boulevard St. Germain 79; and of the Public Works map (1:200,000) at the Librairie Delagrave, Rue Soufflot 15.

SOUTH-WESTERN FRANCE

I. FROM THE LOIRE TO THE PYRENEES.

1. From Paris to Bordeaux viâ Orléans.

359 M. to the *La Bastide* station, 363 M. to *St. Jean* (see below). RAILWAY in 8³/₄-14¹/₂ hrs. (fares 64 fr. 85, 43 fr. 80, 28 fr. 60 c., or 65 fr. 60, 44 fr. 30, 28 fr. 95 c.). The trains start from the Gare d'Orléans at Paris. — Besides the ordinary trains, there is a service of trains de luxe, in 8¹/₂ hrs., leaving the Gare du Nord in the evening; *viz.* the 'Sud-Express' on Mon., Wed., and Sat., for Bordeaux, Madrid, and Lisbon; and the 'Pyrenees Express' on Tues. and Thurs., for Bordeaux, Lourdes, and Luchon. The fares by these trains are 1¹/₂ times the ordinary 1st cl. fare (*e. g.* to *Bordeaux-St. Jean*, 98 fr. 35 c.); déj. 5, D. 7 fr. in the restaurant-car. — A sleeping-car ticket by the ordinary night-express costs 24 fr. in addition to the fare.

Bordeaux has two principal stations, *La Bastide* on the right bank of the Garonne, the nearest to the centre of the town, and *St. Jean*, in a suburb on the left bank, for travellers proceeding farther to the S. on the main line (comp. p. 46). Travellers with through-tickets are allowed 48 hours in the town on condition of presenting their tickets for examination on arrival, but they cannot remove luggage that has been registered to their ultimate destination.

I. From Paris to Tours viâ Orléans.

145 M. RAILWAY in 3¹/₂-3³/₄ hrs. (fares 26 fr. 30, 17 fr. 80, 11 fr. 65 c.). — For farther details of this route and for alternative routes to Tours, see *Baedeker's Northern France*.

Paris, see *Baedeker's Paris*. — The train ascends the valley of the Seine, on the left bank.

35 M. **Etampes** *(Buffet)*, with 8570 inhab., contains the churches of *St. Basile* (15-16th cent.), *Notre Dame* (12th cent.), *St. Gilles* (12th and 16th cent.), and *St. Martin* (12-13th cent.; with a leaning tower); also the old *Mansions* of Diana of Poitiers and Anne de Pisseleu (16th cent.), and the *Tour Ginette* (12th cent.), near the station. — The train then ascends a steep incline to the plateau of *La Beauce*, one of the granaries of France.

74 M. *Les Aubrais* (Buffet). The day-expresses halt here for déjeuner. Passengers by the express-trains change carriages here for Orléans, as only the slow trains enter the station of that town.

75 M. **Orléans** *(Buffet; Hôt. St. Aignan; d'Orléans; du Loiret)*, with 63,700 inhab., on the *Loire*. We reach the town by turning to the right at the boulevards, then to the left by the Rue Bannier leading to the Loire. To the left is the Gothic church (almost

entirely modern) of *St. Paterne*, and in a square farther on is an *Equestrian Statue of Joan of Arc*, the Maid of Orléans. The Rue Jeanne d'Arc, a little farther on, leads to the left to the Gothic cathedral of *Ste. Croix*, near which is the *Hôtel de Ville* (16th cent.). To the S. of the Rue Jeanne d'Arc, in a small square with a Statue of the Republic, is the *Musée* (paintings, sculptures, etc.), and more in the direction of the Rue Royale is the *Musée Historique*, in a fine 16th cent. mansion. The new *Musée Jeanne d'Arc* is in the Rue du Tabour, to the W. of the Rue Royale. The walk should be continued as far as the Loire.

From Orléans to *Clermont-Ferrand*, see R. 35; to *Nevers*, see R. 34.

The Bordeaux railway now follows the course of the Loire (to the left).

91 M. **Beaugency**, with 4300 inhab., has a Renaissance *Hôtel de Ville*, a mediæval *Keep*, and a *Château* of the 15th cent. (now a poor-house). The *Tour de l'Horloge* is one of the old town-gates. The church of *Notre Dame* dates from the 11th century.

110 M. **Blois** (*Buffet; Hôt. de Blois; de France; du Château*), with 23,450 inhab., possesses a celebrated *Château*, the finest part of which was built by Francis I. The *Church of St. Nicholas* (12-13th cent.), the *Cathedral*, and the *Statue of Denis Papin* are also interesting. — The *Château of Chambord* lies 11 M. to the E.

120 M. *Onzain*, beyond which, on the left, appears the *Château of Chaumont*.

133 M. **Amboise** (4480 inhab.). The historic *Château* is seen on the left. We cross the Loire three stations farther on.

144 M. *St. Pierre-des-Corps* (Buffet). Passengers to Tours by the Bordeaux expresses change carriages here; the ordinary trains run into the station of Tours.

145 M. **Tours** (*Buffet; Gr. Hôt. de l'Univers, de Bordeaux*, near the station; *Faisan, Boule d'Or, Négociants*, in the Rue Nationale), with 60,335 inhab., is situated between the Loire and the Cher. Turning to the right on quitting the station, and then to the left at the boulevards, we reach the handsome Rue Nationale, which leads to the Loire. The *Cathedral*, a fine Gothic edifice of the 12-16th cent., lies some distance to the right. Near the end of the Rue Nationale is the church of *St. Julien* (13th cent.), and near the bridge are statues of *Descartes* and *Rabelais*. To the right is the *Hôtel de Ville*, containing the *Musée*. Not far from the principal bridge, downstream, is *Notre-Dame de la Riche*, a church of the 12th and 16th cent.; and farther to the S.E. are the *Towers* of the old church of *St. Martin* and the new *Basilica* of that name.

From Tours to *Les Sables-d'Olonne*, see R. 2; to *Vierzon*, p. 35.

II. From Tours to Poitiers.

61 M. RAILWAY in 1³/₄-3¹/₄ hrs. (fares 11 fr. 40, 7 fr. 65 c., 5 fr.).

Tours, see above and *Baedeker's Northern France*. — Trains in connection with the express proceed to the (2 M.) station of *St.*

POITIERS
1 : 12.500

Pierre-des-Corps on the line from Paris (see p. 4). Slow trains make use of a loop-line.

South of the town the lines to Nantes and Les Sables-d'Olonne (R. 2) diverge on the right. Then, after crossing the *Cher*, we pass over a viaduct from which there is a fine view and cross the line to Châteauroux (p. 35). To the left is the fine *Château de Candé* (16th cent.). The valley of the *Indre* is next crossed by a viaduct, ¹/₂ M. long and 89 ft. high, which affords another fine view. — 7 M. *Monts.* Beyond (12¹/₂ M.) *Villeperdue* is another viaduct, 102 ft. high, over the *Manse;* on the right, the *Château de Brou.* — 20 M. *Ste. Maure,* a little town 2 M. to the left. — 27 M. *Port-de-Piles.* Branch-line to Chinon, see p. 16.

From Port-de-Piles to Le Blanc, 41¹/₂ M., railway in 2¹/₄ hrs. (fares 7 fr. 50, 5 fr. 5, 3 fr. 30 c.). The line first ascends the valley of the *Creuse,* then that of the *Claise.* — 8 M. *La Haye-Descartes,* the birthplace of Descartes (1596-1650), the celebrated philosopher, to whom a statue has been erected here. — 13 M. *Le Grand-Pressigny,* with a keep of the 12th and a castle of the 17th century. About 1¹/₂ M. to the W., at *La Doussetière,* numerous flint celts have been found. — 22 M. *Preuilly* has a very fine Romanesque abbey-church. — Our line then quits the banks of the Claise, and returning to the valley of the Creuse, is joined at (31¹/₃ M.) *Tournon-St. Martin* by the branch from Châtellerault (see below). — Beyond (36 M.) *Fontgombault,* which also has a very remarkable old abbey-church, we rejoin the Poitiers line. — 41¹/₂ M. *Le Blanc* (p. 10).

We cross the *Creuse* and ascend the valley of the *Vienne.*

40¹/₂ M. **Châtellerault** (*Hôt. de l'Espérance; de l'Univers*), a town on the Vienne with 22,522 inhab., famous for its cutlery and for its *Arms Factory* (no admission). The Boul. Sadi Carnot, to the left from the station, and then the Rue de Berry, to the right, bring us to the *Boulevard Blossac,* at the other end of which is the Square Gambetta, with the tall *Monument of the Revolution.* The Rue des Mignons (before the Square), and its continuation, lead to the church of *St. Jacques,* of the 13th cent., with a rich modern west front. — Line to Loudun, see p. 17.

A branch-line runs hence to (28¹/₂ M.) *Tournon-St. Martin* (see above), viâ *La Roche-Posay,* a little town on the Creuse, with a 12th cent. keep. In the neighbourhood is a mineral spring, with a bath-establishment.

We next cross the Vienne and ascend the valley of the *Clain.* — 46 M. *Les Barres.* In the neighbourhood is the site of *Vieux-Poitiers,* and farther on, also on the right bank, is *Moussais-la-Bataille,* the probable scene of the famous battle of Poitiers (see p. 6). — Beyond (49 M.) *La Tricherie,* on the left, is the castle of *Baudiment,* a curious edifice of the 15th cent. (restored). — 51¹/₂ M. *Dissais-sur-Vienne,* with a fine castle of the 16th and 18th centuries. — On the right is the line to Loudun (see p. 17).

61 M. **Poitiers** (*Buffet*). — Hotels. Hôtel du Palais (Pl. a; B, 3), a large house near the Palais de Justice, R. 2¹/₂, D. 4 fr.; de France (Pl. b; B, 4), R. 2, D. 3 fr.; de l'Europe (Pl. c; B, 4); des Trois-Piliers (Pl. d; B, 4); the last three in the Rue des Halles, near the Place d'Armes. — Cafés, in the Rue des Halles and in the Place d'Armes. — Cabs. Per drive ³/₄, per hr. 1¹/₂ fr.; at night 50 c. extra.

Poitiers, with a pop. of 37,500, the ancient capital of *Poitou* and now the chief town of the department of the *Vienne*, is the seat of a bishopric and possesses also a university, with a school of law, founded in 1431. It is situated on a hill at the confluence of the *Clain* and the *Boivre*, and most of the streets are narrow, tortuous, steep, and badly built. The limited trade of the town and the fact that it is largely occupied by religious foundations combine to make it rather a dull place, but it has some objects of interest which every tourist should endeavour to see.

Poitiers first appears as a Celtic town, the capital of the Pictones or Pictavi, whence its modern name. To the Romans it was known as *Limonum*. About 353 St. Hilary (not to be confounded with his namesake of Arles) became its first bishop. Poitou was included in the Visigothic kingdom of Aquitaine, founded in 419, but after the defeat of Alaric II. by Clovis at Vouillé, in 507, it was added to the Frankish dominions and constituted a countship whose holders afterwards made themselves dukes of Aquitaine. One of these dukes is said to have invited the Saracens into this part of the country, but be this as it may, it was within 20 miles N.W. of Poitiers that Charles Martel in 732 finally broke the power of the Moorish invaders. By the marriage of Eleanor, sole heiress of Poitou and Aquitaine, to Louis VII. of France these important provinces became part of the royal dominions. On her divorce and re-marriage to Henry Plantagenet in 1152 they passed, unhappily for France, into the power of England. The most important event in the two centuries of strife which succeeded is the Battle of Poitiers (or Maupertuis) in 1356, when John the Good was defeated by Edward the Black Prince and lost more than 11,000 men. By the treaty of Brétigny (1360) Aquitaine, and with it Poitou and other counties, passed in full sovereignty to Edward III., but the country between the Loire and the Garonne was finally won back in 1372 by the Constable Bertrand du Guesclin. The Protestants under Coligny unsuccessfully besieged Poitiers for seven weeks in 1569. Since then its history has been uneventful.

Quitting the station (Pl. A, 4), which is situated in the lower part of the town, carriages reach the centre by a long circuit to the left viâ the Boulevard Solferino. Pedestrians go direct by the Rue de la Visitation, the first street ascending to the right from the boulevard. Turning again to the right at the first cross street, they reach the square in front of the *Préfecture* (Pl. A, B, 4), a large featureless building. Hence the Rue Victor-Hugo leads to the *Place d'Armes* (Pl. B, 3, 4), a large square forming the centre of the town. On the right side of the Rue Victor Hugo is the *Collège de la Grand' Maison* (Pl. B, 4), with an elegant chapel; on the left, No. 9, is the new *Musée des Augustins*, of the Société des Antiquaires (p. 7).

The Museum contains tapestry, furniture, enamels, porcelain, etc., besides the former Chevlères collection of 175 paintings, including a landscape by *Hobbema*; a Holy Family by *Giulio Romano*; St. John the Baptist by *Jan van Leyden*; Witch-scene by *Teniers*; Battle-scenes by *Bourgsignon*.

In the Place d'Armes is the **Hôtel de Ville** (Pl. B, C, 3), a fine building, completed in 1875, in the style of the French Renaissance. It contains the *Musée des Beaux-Arts* and the *Musée d'Histoire Naturelle*, the former open on Sun., the latter on Thurs. from noon to 4 p. m. (except when it rains), but both accessible to strangers on other days, at the same hours.

The Musée des Beaux-Arts contains an important collection of paintings by French artists, also a fine portrait by *Tintoretto* (No. 114) and works by *Titian* (118), *A. del Sarto* (117), *Van Dyck* (113, etc.), *Masaccio* (109), *Guido Reni* (104), etc.; besides sculptures, antiquities, furniture, enamels, coins, etc. — The STAIRCASE is adorned with caryatides by *Barrias* and frescoes by *P. de Chavannes.* — In the SALLE DES FÊTES the stained glass and the ceiling-painting (Duguesclin freeing Poitiers from the English, by *Brunet*) should be noticed. — The SALLE DES MARRIAGES is decorated by *Léon Perrault.*

The SOCIÉTÉ DES ANTIQUAIRES DE L'OUEST has also in the neighbouring Rue des Grandes-Ecoles (Pl. B, 3) an important museum of Roman and other antiquities.

On the right, behind the Hôtel de Ville, is the pretty *Hôtel Bauce* or *Gaillard*, in the Renaissance style. In the vicinity is the *Lycée* (Pl. C, 3-4), with a painting by Finsonius and 17th cent. woodcarvings. From the Hôtel Bauce we follow the street on the left to the Rue d'Orléans, the second on the right, by which we descend.

The *Temple St. Jean* (Pl. D, 3), in the next street, is a curious structure, now identified as a baptistery of the 7th century, partly built of Gallo-Roman materials. In plan it is an oblong of about 42 ft. by 26 ft.; the floor is for the most part below the present level of the street. On the longer sides are additions made in the 12th cent., and at either end are apses. The interior (apply to the concierge of the bishops' palace to the left) contains a font in the centre and sarcophagi etc. of the 6-9th cent., and some 12th cent. frescoes.

The **Cathedral** (*St. Peter's*; Pl. C, D, 2) was begun in 1162 by Henry II. of England, husband of Eleanor of Aquitaine or Guienne (p. 6), but the west façade only was completed and the church consecrated in 1379. Some parts are Romanesque, but the Plantagenet-Gothic style predominates. The façade is comparatively poor; it is too wide and too low and the unfinished towers which flank it increase its heaviness. The interior is imposing on account of the boldness of its proportions and the width of its aisles and bays. To make it appear longer than it actually is the architect has increased the effect of the perspective by lessening the width of the nave and aisles and by a corresponding lowering of the arches towards the choir. Some of the stained glass dates from the 12-13th cent., while the fine choir-stalls are assigned to the latter half of the 13th. Behind the choir, on the left, is the modern tomb of Monsgr. Bouillé.

From the rear of the cathedral we descend to the right to *Ste. Radegonde* (Pl. D, 2), a church founded about 560 by the queen of that name, wife of Clotaire I., who retired hither to her convent of Ste. Croix. It was, however, rebuilt in the 11-13th cent. in the same style as the cathedral, except the main entrance, which belongs to the 15th or 16th century. A fine Gothic steeple rises from the façade. Specially noteworthy within the church are a *Crypt* containing the sarcophagus of St. Radegonde (an object of pilgrimage), and a marble statue of the saint (a portrait of Ann of Austria), attributed to Girardon. On the left of the nave is a kind of niche called the chapel of the Pas-de-Dieu, with two poor statues, between which,

on the pavement, is a foot-print made, according to the legend, by
our Lord when he appeared to St. Radegonde. Fine stained glass.

This church is near the Clain, which is spanned by the *Pont
Neuf*, to the right, and by the old *Pont Joubert*, to the left.

On the opposite bank are the colossal gilded statue of *Notre Dame des
Dunes* (Pl. D, 3) and a barrack. A little lower down a Gallo-Roman *Ne-
cropolis* has been discovered, and a *Champ des Martyrs*, with the remains
of a hypogæum.

In the suburb of St. Saturnin, 1/4 M. from the Pont Neuf, vià the third
street on the left, is a dolmen known as the *Pierre-Levée*.

We re-ascend into the town by the street which begins at the
Pont Joubert and is continued by one which leads us straight to —

*Notre-Dame-la-Grande (Pl. B, 2), a very interesting monument
of Romanesque architecture dating from the end of the 11th cent.,
with additions of the 15th and 16th. This church is noted for its
* West Façade*, which, like that of Angoulême cathedral (p. 11), has
all the elaboration of detail which we associate with the repoussé
work of the goldsmith. It is composed of three tiers of arches, in
the lowest of which are inserted a round-headed door and two ob-
tusely pointed blind ones subdivided into two semicircular arcades.
The uppermost tiers, broken by a large window, contain mutilated
statues of St. Hilary, St. Martin, and the Apostles, and in the gable-
end is one of Christ in the act of blessing, surrounded by the em-
blems of the Evangelists. There are also bas-reliefs with subjects
drawn chiefly from the life of the Virgin. This façade is flanked by
turrets with conical tops and fish-scale ornamentation. The steeple
of the church, with a similar top, is at the entrance to the choir.

The Interior, disfigured by modern paintings of coarse tone, is divided
into nave and aisles, the former having a barrel vault, the latter being
groined. The side-chapels were added in the 15th and 16th centuries.
There is no transept, but the aisles are prolonged round the choir. The
latter contains a 13th cent. fresco on its vault and a fine modern high-
altar in the Romanesque style. In a chapel on the right is a 'Holy
Sepulchre' of the 16th century.

The Palais des Facultés (Pl. B, 2), near Notre-Dame, was
altered and enlarged in 1892-94.

It contains the *University Library* and also the *Municipal Library*, of
nearly 400,000 vols. and 389 MSS., including a Life of St. Radegunda by
St. Fortunatus (6th cent.) and other early specimens.

The Palais de Justice (Pl. B, 3) a little beyond Notre-Dame, on
the left, includes, behind some late additions, remains of the old
castle of the counts of Poitou (14th cent.). The *Salle des Pas-
Perdus*, the old guard-chamber, 160 by 56 ft., recalls that of the
Palais de Justice at Rouen. At one end is a carved triple chimney-
piece, surmounted by a gallery and five windows, all in the Gothic
style of the 15th cent., between two staircase-turrets.

The Provost's Court (*Prévôté*; Pl. A, B, 2), a building of the
15-16th cent., now a school, has a very remarkable façade, with
four turrets and some fine pediments over its windows.

At the N. end of the town stands the church of Montierneuf
(*Moutier-Neuf*; Pl. A, 1), an ancient church of the Benedictines,

of the 11th cent., and of exceptional width for that period. It has a little cupola above the crossing, surmounted by two bell turrets which are connected by three arches.

Between the Palais de Justice and the Place d'Armes is *St. Porchaire* (Pl. B, 3), a church of the 16th cent., with a Romanesque tower, dating from an older building. — To the S. is *St. Hilary* (Pl. B, 5), a monastic church founded, it is said, before the 6th cent., rebuilt in the 11th and 12th, and partly in the present century. It consists of a nave and six aisles and has 6 cupolas, but no steeple.

The PARC DE BLOSSAC (Pl. B, C, 5, 6), at the S. end of the town, a promenade laid out in the 18th cent., commands a fine view of the Clain valley, on which side it is bordered by the remains of the old 14th century *Ramparts*, which extend some way westward between the town and the railway. At the entrance from the Rue des Capucins are two marble groups by Etex, representing the Joys and Sorrows of Motherhood. A military band plays in the park on Sunday and Thursday.

From Poitiers to *Loudun* (Angers) see p. 17; to *La Rochelle* and *Rochefort*, R. 3.

BRANCH LINE from Poitiers to (35¹/₂ M.) *Parthenay*, identical with the Loudun line as far as *Neuville-de-Poitou* (p. 17).

FROM POITIERS TO LIMOGES viâ *Bellac*, 87 M., railway in 4¹/₂·8 hrs. (fares 15 fr. 80, 10 fr. 85, 6 fr. 80 c.). — The Angoulême line is followed as far as (3¹/₂ M.) *St. Benoît* (see below), beyond which a short tunnel is passed. — 7¹/₂ M. *Mignaloux-Nouaillé* (branch-line to St. Savin and Le Blanc, see below). 10¹/₂ M. *Nieuil-l'Espoir*; 13¹/₂ M. *Fleuré*. Beyond (18¹/₂ M.) *L'Hommaize* the line crosses the Vienne. — 25¹/₂ M. *Lussac-les-Châteaux*, which has only one old castle, through the ruins of which the railway passes. Branch to St. Savin, see p. 10.

33¹/₂ M. **Montmorillon** (*Buffet; Hôt. de France*), a small town (pop. 5268) on an eminence, ¹/₂ M. to the left, at the foot of which flows the *Gartempe*. In its lower part is the Gothic church of *St. Martial*. *Notre-Dame*, on the left bank, is partly Romanesque, partly Gothic. Near it is a modern tower, surmounted by a *Statue of the Virgin*. The *Petit Séminaire*, an ancient convent of the Augustines, comprises a curious building of the 11-12th cent., called the *Octagon*, consisting of two chapels, one above the other. A branch-line runs hence to (25 M.) *Le Blanc* (p. 10), viâ (11 M.) *La Trimouille* or *La Trémouille*.

51¹/₂ M. **Le Dorat** (*Hôt. Bordeaux*), a small town with an interesting Romanesque church and remains of fortifications of the 15th century. — An alternative line to Limoges (Gare d'Orléans) runs hence viâ (12¹/₂ M.) *Châteauponsac* (*Hôt. de la Promenade*), a small town (3270 inhab.) on the Gartempe, and (23¹/₂ M.) *St. Sulpice-Laurière* (p. 98).

59¹/₂ M. **Bellac** (*Hôt. de la Promenade*), a town with 4000 inhab., on the *Vincou*. Beyond (60 M.) *Chapterie* the *Monts de Blond* (1800 ft.) appear on the right. 64 M. *Blond-Berneuil*, followed by several other small stations. After passing (81 M.) *Couzeix-Chaptelat*, the train rapidly descends, traverses a tunnel 750 yds. long, and joins the line from Paris (p. 39). — 87 M. *Limoges* (Gare de Montjovis, p. 39).

FROM POITIERS TO CHÂTEAUROUX viâ *Argenton*, 89 M., railway in 5¹/₂-9¹/₂ hrs. (fares 18 fr. 25, 11 fr. 5, 7 fr. 15 c.). — Diverging from the last-described route at (7¹/₂ M.) *Mignaloux-Nouaillé*, we proceed N.E. over a dull plain. — 20 M. **Chauvigny** (*Lion d'Or*), a small town of 2129 inhab., prettily situated on the *Vienne*, with two fine churches of the 12th cent., and the ruins of four castles, richly repays a visit.

31³/₄ M. **St. Savin** (*Hôt. de France*), a small town of 1805 inhab., on the Gartempe, with an interesting *Abbey-Church of the 11th cent., a cruciform

building with three aisles, a transept, and ambulatory. Over the porch
is a fine steeple with a Gothic spire, and over the transept a square
tower. The height of the interior is exceptional for a Romanesque church.
The columns are 59 ft. and the main vaulting 69 ft. high, although the
total width of the building is only 55½ ft. and its length 180 ft. Among
the interesting features of this church are some *Wall-Paintings* of the
12th century. One series consists of subjects from Genesis, Exodus, and
the Apocalypse; the others represent the patron saints of the abbey and
of the neighbouring district.

45 M. **Le Blanc** (*Buffet*; *Hôt. de la Nouvelle Promenade*), the *Oblincum*
of the Romans, with 7539 inhab., stands on the Creuse. The chief object
of interest is the church of *St. Génitour* of the 12th, 13th, and 15th centuries.
— Line to *Port-de-Piles*, see p. 5; to *Montmorillon*, see p. 9. Another
line is under construction to (31 M.) *Buzançais* (p. 31) viâ (16½ M.) *Mé-
zières-en-Brenne*, which has a fine 14th cent. church, with a later chapel
(15·16th cent.) adorned with good stained glass.

The line to Argenton is a continuation of that from Port de Piles,
and follows the valley of the *Creuse*. — 55 M. *Ciron*. — Beyond (64 M.)
St. Gaultier we join the line from Limoges (R. 5). — 69½ M. *Argenton*
and thence to (59 M.) *Châteauroux*, see pp. 33-35.

III. From Poitiers to Angoulême.

70 M. RAILWAY in 1½-4¼ hrs. (fares 12 fr. 75, 8 fr. 55, 5 fr. 55 c.).

The line passes through a short tunnel into the picturesque
valley of the *Clain*, and crosses that river several times. — 64 M.
(from Tours) *St. Benoît*, the junction for St. Sulpice-Laurière and
Limoges (p. 9), and also for La Rochelle and Rochefort (R. 3).
— 66 M. *Liguge*, with an old Benedictine abbey founded by St.
Martin. Farther on, on the right, is the castle of *Bernay*, of the
15th century. — 19½ M. *Iteuil*; 73 M. *Vivonne*; 79 M. *Anché-
Voulon*; 82 M. *Couhé-Vérac*, situated 3½ M. to the W. (omnibus);
87½ M. *Epanvilliers*. — 93 M. *St. Saviol*.

A branch-line runs hence viâ (4½ M.) *Civray*, a small town on the
Charente, with a Romanesque church with an interesting west front,
(10 M.) *Charroux*, with the remains of an abbey, and (14 M.) *Persac*, to
(29 M.) *Lussac-les-Châteaux* (p. 9).

102 M. **Ruffec** (*Buffet*), with 3527 inhab., also has a Romanesque church with a remarkable façade. The town is celebrated for
truffled pies. Line to Niort (p. 23).

A short tunnel is passed through. 108 M. *Moussac*, beyond
which the *Charente* is crossed. 11 M. *Luxé*; 119 M. *St. Amand-
de-Boixe*; the town, 1¾ M. to the S.-W. (omn.), has a curious
church, a mixture of Romanesque and Gothic. 123 M. *Vars*.

As we approach Angoulême, a fine view of the town and its principal buildings is presented, the most prominent being (from left to
right) the steeple of St. Martial, the tower of the Hôtel de Ville,
and the cathedral with its square tower.

131 M. **Angoulême.** — Hotels. *HÔTEL DU PALAIS (Pl. a; D, 2, 3), Place
du Mûrier, in the centre of the town; DE FRANCE (Pl. b; D, 2, 3), Place des
Halles Centrales; GRAND HÔTEL, Avenue Gambetta 54. — Cafés in the
Place du Mûrier and the Place des Halles Centrales. — *Buffet*.

Stations. *Gare d'Orléans*, for Bordeaux, *Gare de l'État*, for Limoges
and Saintes (pp. 12, 13), facing each other in the Avenue Gambetta (Pl. F, 1);
Gare de Rouillac, for the unimportant line to (23 M.) *Rouillac*, next the
Gare de l'État.

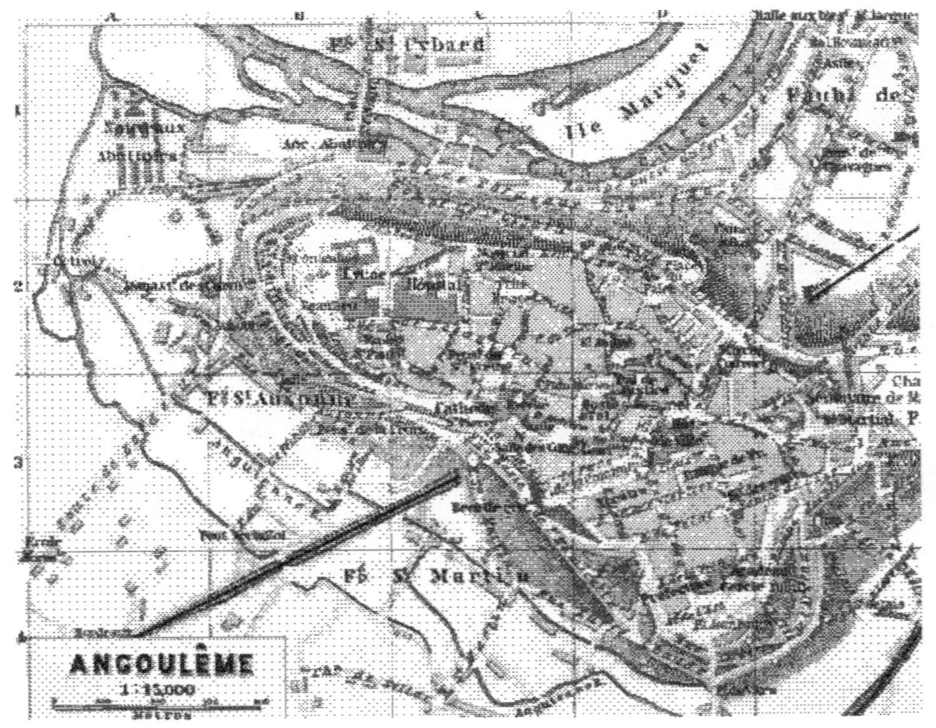
ANGOULÊME
1:15.000
Mètres
Ile Marguet
Fg St Cybard
Fg St Ausone
Fg St Martin
Nouveaux Abattoirs
Lycée
Hôpital

Angoulême, with 36,690 inhab., the ancient capital of the *Angoumois*, is now the chief town of the department of the *Charente*, and an episcopal see. Like Poitiers, it occupies an eminence between two rivers, the *Charente* and the *Anguienne*, but it is a little better built and is encircled by promenades which afford very fine views. The cathedral and other public buildings deserve a visit, and may be seen in a few hours. The town is noted for its paper-mills.

The town existed in the time of the Romans, who named it *Ecolisma*. It was included in the kingdom of Aquitaine, but at a later period became the capital of a county which was handed over to the English by the treaty of Brétigny in 1360. It revolted in 1373, and as a reward for its fidelity to the crown, it was constituted a duchy and made the appanage of one of the royal princes. The town was several times taken and sacked in the Religious Wars, notably by Coligny.

From the stations we ascend to the right by the Avenue Gambetta. On the left is the seminary and church of *St. Martial* (Pl. E, 3), a fine modern building in the Romanesque style, with a steeple over the façade, by *Paul Abadie* (d. 1884). The Rampe d'Aguesseau, a street diverging to the right, leads to the *Halles Centrales* (Pl. D, 2), on the site of the old prisons.

A new street beginning at the Halles leads to the *Hôtel de Ville (Pl. D, 3), a very remarkable structure, in great part modern (1858-66), which is also the work of *Abadie*. It is in the style of the 13th cent. and occupies the site of the castle of the Counts of Angoulême, of which there remain two towers on the left, one of the 14th, the other of the 15th century. The small *Picture Gallery and Archaeological Museum* in the interior is open free on Sun., Thurs., and holidays from 12-4; to strangers also at other times. — In a small garden on the left side are a marble *Statue of Margaret of Valois*, or Angoulême, sister of Francis I. and queen of Navarre (d. 1549), by Badiou de la Tronchère (1871) and a *War Monument* for 1870-71, by R. Verlet.

In the Place du Marché-Neuf (Pl. D, 3), to the right of the Hôtel de Ville, is a bronze statue, by R. Verlet, of *Dr. Jean Bouillaud* (1796-1867). The *Theatre* (Pl. D, 3) is in the Place de la Commune, a square abutting on the *Ramparts*, which command a comprehensive view of the valley of the Anguienne.

The *Cathedral of St. Peter (Pl. C, 3), a short distance to the right, is one of the most interesting Romanesque-Byzantine churches in France, recalling Notre-Dame at Poitiers (p. 8) and St. Front at Périgueux (p. 43). It belongs, as a whole, to the 12th cent., but was thoroughly restored and even partly rebuilt between 1866 and 1875 by Abadie. It comprises a nave without aisles, surmounted by three cupolas; a transept with a cupola forming a lantern in the centre; a north transept tower (see below); the remains of a south transept tower; and an apse with four chapels. — The *Façade*, which recalls on a large scale that of Notre-Dame at Poitiers, is also the most

curious part of this church. Exclusive of the gable, it is composed
of four tiers of arcades, divided from top to bottom by columns
into five bays. The lowest tier has five arches, of which the largest
and central one contains the sole door in the façade. Above this
door is a large window and above that, between symbols of the Evangelists, is a Christ in Judgment, to which event most of the many
sculptures of the façade refer. Below the Christ, to the right and
left, are angels sounding the last trump, the dead rising from their
graves (the blessed distinguished by the *nimbus* and the reprobate
accompanied by demons), the Doctors of the Church, the Apostles,
symbolic representations of Faith (St. George), Hope, and Charity
(St. Martin), etc., and numerous beautiful ornamentations.

The splendid **Tower* at the end of the N. transept, 103 ft. in
height, is the next striking feature of this church. It was necessarily pulled down at the time of the restoration, but rebuilt exactly
in its former shape and, as far as possible, with the same materials.
It has six square stages, diminishing in size, and four of them present open bays. The corresponding S. tower, of which only the base
remains, was destroyed by the Calvinists in 1568; it had a Gothic
spire. — In the *Interior* the cupolas of the nave (which has slightly
pointed arches) and the lantern of the transept, pierced by twelve
windows, merit special notice.

The pile of buildings to the left of the cathedral is the *Bishop's
Palace*, of the same age as the church and also restored by Abadie.

Continuing to follow the ramparts beyond the cathedral, we arrive at the *Jardin Vert* (Pl. B, 2), a fine promenade on the side of
the hill. To appreciate the view, the best plan is to make for the
top by the *Promenade de Beaulieu* (Pl. B, 2), which skirts the spacious buildings of the *Lycée* and commands the valley of the Charente.
In the valley, on the right bank, lies the suburb of *St. Cybard*.
The return may be made, by the edge of the hill, as far as the Place
des Halles Centrales (p. 11).

From Angoulême to Saintes (Rochefort, La Rochelle), 48½ M., railway in 3¼-2¾ hrs. (fares 7 fr. 95, 5 fr. 90, 3 fr. 85 c.). — From the Gare de
l'Etat (p. 10) we pass through a tunnel under the town and cross the Bordeaux line. — 3 M. *St. Michel-sur-Charente*, with a curious octagonal church.
The line then follows the valley of the Charente.

14¼ M. Châteauneuf-sur-Charente (*Soleil d'Or*), a thriving little town,
once a stronghold in the hands of the English, and only recovered from
them after a siege of four years (1378-80). A branch-line runs hence to
(12 M.) *Barbesieux* (Boule d'Or; Hôt. de France), a town of 4100 inhab., on the
slope of a hill, with the remains of a castle of the 15th cent., a church
of the same period, and another of the 12th century.

18 M. *St. Amant-de-Graves*; 20½ M. *St. Même*. — 23 M. Jarnac (*Hôt. de
France*), a small town chiefly known for the victory of the Catholics under
the Duke of Anjou, afterwards Henri III., over the Protestant army of the
Prince of Condé in 1569. The country to the left of our route and to the
N. of the Charente, as far as beyond Cognac, is the *Petite Champagne*.
Farther south is the *Grande Champagne*. They are so called because they
are of the same geological formation as Champagne and, like it, produced
excellent white wines of which highly-reputed brandies were made, those
of the second being called 'Fine Champagne'. — 27½ M. *Gensac-la-Pallue*.

31³/₄ M. **Cognac** (*Hôt. de Londres; d'Orléans; de France; Café du Chalet*), an old town of 17,400 inhab., the centre of the brandy trade of the Charente, the products of which are sent to all parts of the world. Its chief object of interest is the church of *St. Léger*, mainly of the 11th, 14th, and 15th centuries. The façade has fine florid Romanesque details. Cognac contains an *Equestrian Statue of Francis I.*, a modern bronze by Etex. The large brandy distilleries and the vast store-houses should be seen. One of the latter is on the site of the castle in which Francis I. was born (1494).

36 M. *Le Pirat*; 38¹/₂ M. *Brives-Chérac*; 42 M. *Beillant*. — 48¹/₂ M. *Saintes* (p. 30).

From Angoulême to Ribérac, 42 M., railway in 2-2³/₄ hrs. (fares 7 fr. 60, 5 fr. 15, 3 fr. 35 c.). We start from the Gare de l'État (p. 10). — 3³/₄ M. *Ruelle*, with a large cannon-foundry established in 1750. — 6¹/₄ M. *Magnac-Touvre*. The copious springs of Touvre are at the foot of a hill which is crowned by a ruined castle. — 21 M. *La Roche-Beaucourt*; 25¹/₂ M. *Marcuil-Gouts*. — Beyond (38¹/₂ M.) *Celles* we pass the *Tour de la Rigale*, said to be the 'cella' of a Roman temple. We cross the Dronne. — 42 M. *Ribérac* (*Hôt. de France; du Périgord*), a prettily situated commercial town with 3700 inhabitants. — The line goes on to *Mussidan* (p. 45), *Bergerac* (p. 14), *Marmande* (p. 72), etc. — From Ribérac to *Périgueux*, see p. 45.

From Angoulême to Limoges, 73 M., railway in 3¹/₄-3³/₄ hrs. (fares 13 fr. 30, 8 fr. 90, 5 fr. 80 c.). — To (6¹/₄ M.) *Magnac-Touvre*, see above. — From (10 M.) *Le Quéroy-Pranzac* a branch-line runs to (39 M.) *Thiviers* (p. 42), viâ (8 M.) *Marthon*, where are the remarkable ruins of a castle of the 12th cent., (21¹/₂ M.) the little town of *Nontron* (*Hôt. Michaudel*), and (26¹/₂ M.) *St. Pardoux-la-Rivière*, on the *Dronne*, whence a tramway runs to Périgueux.

17¹/₂ M. **La Rochefoucauld** (*Hôt. du Commerce*), a little town (2800 inhab.) on the *Tardoire*, with the remarkable *Château of the family of that name, founded in the 9th or 10th cent., but dating chiefly from the 12th and 16th. The finest parts, dating from the Renaissance, are the magnificent staircase built by Fontani (1528-38) and the galleries, surmounted by arcades, which surround the inner court, by the same architect. — 25 M. *Chasseneuil-sur-Bonnieure* has a castle of the 17th cent. and iron-mines. — From (33 M.) *Roumazières-Loubert* (Buffet) a branch-line diverges to (10¹/₂ M.) *Confolens* (*Hôt. Chaboussant*), a town with 3188 inhab., a castle, and two ancient churches. We now reach the valley of the *Vienne*. 40¹/₂ M. *Chabanais*. 45¹/₂ M. *Saillat-Chassenon*. Chassenon, 2¹/₂ M. to the S.W., is the *Cassinomagus* of the Romans. A branch-line runs hence to (29 M.) *Bussière-Galant* (Périgueux, see p. 42), viâ (4¹/₂ M.) *Rochechouart* (*Hôt. Mary Valasade*, below the town), a little town (4500 inhab.) with a remarkable castle situated on a lofty rock and rebuilt in the 15th cent., and (23¹/₂ M.) *Châlus*, with two keeps of the strong castle in attacking which Richard Cœur-de-Lion was mortally wounded in 1199, at the rock Maumont.

50¹/₂ M. **St. Junien** (*Commerce*), an industrial town of 9378 inhab., containing a remarkable abbey-church of the 12th cent. with the richly sculptured tomb of St. Junien, of the same period, and a beautiful high-altar. Near the station is a bridge of the 13th cent., with a chapel of the Virgin to which Louis XI. was a pilgrim. — Beyond (66¹/₂ M.) *Aixe-sur-Vienne* (*Hôt. du Pêcheur*), an industrial place with 3838 inhab., we pass through a tunnel ¹/₄ M. long. — 73 M. *Limoges* (Gare de Montjovis, p. 39).

IV. From Angoulême to Bordeaux.

82¹/₂ M. to the Gare de la Bastide, 87 M. to that of St.-Jean (see p. 46). Railway in 2-5 and 2¹/₄-5¹/₂ hrs. (fares 15 fr., 10 fr. 5, 8 fr. 50 c., or 15 fr. 80, 10 fr. 70, 6 fr. 90 c.). Best views to the right.

The line passes under the town through a tunnel ¹/₂ M. long. — 136 M. (from Tours) *La Couronne*, with a large paper-mill and the remarkable ruins of a Gothic abbey-church of the 12th century. — 139¹/₂ M. *Mouthiers*; 144³/₄ M. *Charmant*. We now pass

from the Charente to the Dordogne basin by a tunnel nearly 1 M.
long, and enter the valley of the *Tude*. The country assumes more
and more a southern appearance. — 152 M. *Montmoreau*. — 162¹/₂ M.
Chalais (Hôt. de France), a small decayed town, with the ruins of a
castle of the 14th, 16th, and 18th cent. Hence we pass to the valley
of the *Dronne*. Two small stations.

182 M. **Coutras** (*Buffet*; *Lion d'Or*), a small commercial town,
with scanty remains of its ancient castle. In 1587 Henri IV. here
defeated the Leaguers. Line to Périgueux, see p. 45.

From Coutras to Cavignac, 16 M., railway joining the line from Bordeaux to Nantes (R. 4). The *Isle* is crossed. 4¹/₂ M. *Guîtres*, a small town on a hill to the right, with a fine Romanesque church. 13 M. *Marensin*, junction of a line to Libourne. 16 M. *Cavignac* (p. 32).

We next cross the *Isle*. — 197 M. *St. Denis-de-Piles*.

192 M. **Libourne** (*Buffet*; *Hôt. de France*, Rue Chanzy; *des Princes*, Rue de Guîtres), a commercial and industrial town with
17,867 inhab., at the confluence of the *Dordogne* and the Isle. It is
of ancient origin (Condate), but has been to a great extent rebuilt
since the 17th century. The Rue Chanzy leads from the station to
the Place Decazes, with a *Statue of the Duc de Decazes* (1780-1860).
Thence the Rue Gambetta descends to the 16th cent. *Hôtel de Ville*,
beyond which, straight on, are the *Prison* and the church of *St.
Jean Baptiste* (15th cent.), with a fine modern steeple 233 ft. high.
The bridge over the Dordogne affords a beautiful view. The *Tour
de l'Horloge*, on the Quai de l'Isle, is a relic of the 14th cent.
fortification.

About 1¹/₂ M. to the W. is **Fronsac**, on a hill (233 ft.) which affords
a fine view. The town was fortified since the time of Charlemagne, but
the castle is now destroyed.

From Libourne to Marcenais (see above) a branch-line of 12 M.,
joining the line from Bordeaux to Nantes.

From Libourne to Le Buisson (*Cahors*), 81 M., railway in 3-4 hrs.
(fares 13 fr. 45, 10 fr. 25, 7 fr. 75 c.). This line ascends the Dordogne valley.
5 M. **St. Emilion** (*Hôt. Gare-Dussaut*), a curious little town famous for its
wines. It occupies a picturesque site on a hill, and still retains a great
part of its mediæval ramparts, with large ditches dug out of the rock.
In the hill itself are immense quarries still worked for building stone.
Here, too, is a *Monolithic Church*, scooped out in the rock in the Middle
Ages, and measuring 104 ft. in length, 48 ft. in breadth, and 52¹/₂ ft. in
height. It is at the side of the hermitage of St. Emilion, or rather St.
Emilien, who lived here in the 8th cent., and on a terrace above stands a
fine tower of the 12th and 15th centuries. The neighbouring collegiate
church and cloister (12th and 13th cent.) are also remarkable. Of the
Castle, to the W. of the town, there remains little more than a square keep.
11 M. *Castillon* (Boule d'Or), memorable for the defeat which definitely
cost the English Guienne, in 1453. John Talbot, Earl of Shrewsbury, was
among the slain.
Beyond (22¹/₂ M.) *St. Antoine-Port-Ste. Foy*, the Dordogne is crossed.
24 M. **Ste. Foy-la-Grande** (*Messageries*), a town of 3242 inhabitants. 32 M.
Lamonzie-St. Martin. Then the Dordogne is recrossed.
38 M. **Bergerac** (*Grand Hôtel*; *Hôt. des Voyageurs*), a town of 14,735 inhab., on the Dordogne, was one of the Calvinist strongholds of the 16th
century. *Notre-Dame* is a fine modern church in the style of the 13th century. A large business is done here in wines and truffles. Line to Marmande, see p. 72; to *Angoulême* viâ Mussidan and Ribérac, see p. 13.

42¹/₂ M. *Creysse-Mouleydier*, with paper-mills and the ruins of a castle. After a tunnel we see a canal rendered necessary by the rapids of the Dordogne. From (49 M.) *Couze* a diligence plies to (7 M.) *Beaumont*, with ramparts and a fortified church dating from the English occupation. — 51 M. *Lalinde*, an ancient little town (Diolindum); 53¹/₂ M. *Mauzac*. Then a tunnel, two bridges over the Dordogne, and a second tunnel. 56 M. *Trémolat*; 58 M. *Alles*. We cross the Dordogne for the last time. 61 M. *Le Buisson* (p. 102). Thence to *Monsempron-Libos* and (126 M.) *Cahors*, see pp. 102, 103.

Quitting Libourne, we cross the Dordogne, already a very large stream. 195 M. *Arveyres*; 197¹/₂ M. *Vayres*, dominated by a castle partly of the 13-14th centuries. 201 M. *St. Sulpice-d'Izon*; 203 M. *St. Loubès*. At a distance, on the right, are the bridges of Cubzac (p. 33). 205¹/₂ M. *La Grave-d'Ambarès*. A little farther on, to the right, the line from Nantes is approached (R. 4), and the *Garonne* now appears on that side. We pass through a series of cuttings, over three viaducts, and through three short tunnels. — 210¹/₂ M. *Lormont* (3236 inhab.), on the Garonne, with shipbuilding yards. Two more tunnels and then, on the right, a splendid view of Bordeaux and its harbour.

213¹/₂ M. **Bordeaux** (*Gare de la Bastide*; see p. 46). Trains in connection with the line to the South, at the *St. Jean* station (p. 46), back out a little way and make a détour to cross the Garonne by the bridge mentioned on p. 48.

2. From Tours to Les Sables-d'Olonne.

156 M. RAILWAY in 7¹/₂-8³/₄ hrs. (fares 25 fr. 70, 19 fr. 10, 12 fr. 45 c.). The trains start from the Gare de l'État, beside the principal station.

Tours, see p. 4 and *Baedeker's Northern France*. — The line, after passing above that to Nantes, crosses the *Cher* and traverses marshy tracts. — At (3³/₄ M.) *Joué-lès-Tours*, the line to Loches-Châteauroux (p. 37) branches off on the left. 6¹/₄ M. *Ballan*. Pope Martin IV. (Simon de Brion, d. 1285) was born in the neighbouring *Château de la Carte*, the chapel of which has some fine stained glass of the 16th century. 10¹/₂ M. *Druye*; 13¹/₂ M. *Vallères*.

16 M. **Azay-le-Rideau** (*Hôt. du Grand Monarque*), with 2175 inhab., has an interesting Renaissance *Château (visitors admitted).

A branch-line runs hence to (12 M.) *Crouzilles-St. Gilles* (p. 17), for the *Camp du Ruchard* (5¹/₂ M.), established in the 'landes' of that name.

The line crosses the *Indre*, and beyond (20¹/₂ M.) *Rivarennes* traverses the forest of Chinon. 24 M. *St. Benoît*; 27 M. *Huismes*. Before Chinon, which is seen on the right, a tunnel of 1000 yds. is passed through.

31 M. **Chinon** (*Hôt. de France*, Place de l'Hôtel-de-Ville; *Boule d'Or*, on the quay; *de l'Union*, Place Jeanne-d'Arc; private carr. dear), is a commercial town (pop. 6120), prettily situated on the eminences of the right bank of the *Vienne*, and celebrated for its history and its castle. It consists almost entirely of narrow and tortuous streets in which are still seen houses of the 15th and 16th centuries.

Chinon already existed in the Roman period, under the name of *Caino*. Subsequently it was occupied by the Visigoths, belonged to the kingdoms of Paris and Austrasia, then to the Counts of Touraine and to Henry II. of England, who was fond of the town and died here in 1189. Reunited to France early in the 13th cent., it nevertheless changed hands frequently up to the beginning of the 15th century. It was here that Joan of Arc sought audience of Charles VII. in 1429 to induce him to march to the relief of Orleans.

The Rue Solférino leads from the station to a square in which is an equestrian *Statue of Joan of Arc*, by Roulleau. — Farther along the quay is a *Statue of Rabelais*, born at or near Chinon about 1495, a modern bronze by Em. Hébert. Opposite is the Place de l'Hôtel-de-Ville, whence the Rue St. Etienne leads to the right to the Rue du Puy-des-Bancs, the principal approach to the castle.

The CASTLE of Chinon really consisted of three distinct castles. The *Château de St. Georges* (the least ancient), of which only the base of the curtain-wall remains, lies to the right of the entrance to the two others, whose ruins are surrounded by a fine promenade, public from noon till dusk in summer on Sundays and holidays. The *Château du Milieu* was built on the site of the Roman castrum in the 11th cent. and was often repaired. Its chief parts are the Pavillon de l'Horloge, at the entrance (ring), the Grand Logis, and the donjon or keep. The *Château du Coudray* has still a fine tower with a chapel of the 13th cent., and two round towers.

Near the foot of the approach to the castle is the church of *St. Etienne*, of the 15th cent., with a beautiful doorway, some fine stained glass and a handsome modern gallery. It also still possesses a cope, said to have belonged to St. Mesme, which dates from the 10th or 11th century. Farther on, in a continuation of the Rue St. Etienne, is the ruined church of ST. MESME, of which two Romanesque and Gothic towers are the chief remains. Adjoining is a tasteful modern Gothic *Chapel*.

On the opposite side, at the end of the Rue St. Maurice, which also starts from the Place de l'Hôtel-de-Ville, and in which there are some interesting old houses, is the church of *St. Maurice*, of the 12th, 15th, and 16th cent., with a steeple partly Romanesque, and fine vaulted arches. Among the paintings are a large fresco by Grandin and a Madonna attributed to Sassoferrato, on the first pillar to the right.

BRANCH LINE to (9¹/₂ M.) *Port-Boulet*, on the line from Tours to Nantes; see *Baedeker's Northern France*.

FROM CHINON TO PORT-DE-PILES, 23¹/₂ M., railway in 1¹/₂-2 hrs. (fares 3 fr. 85, 2 fr. 85, 1 fr. 90 c.). This branch diverges to the left from the line to Sables beyond the bridge and ascends the valley of the Vienne. — From (3 M.) *L'Igré-Rivière*, a branch-line runs to (10 M.) *Richelieu* (pop. 2344), the birthplace of the famous Cardinal (1585-1642), who made a handsome town of it and built in it a splendid castle of which nearly nothing remains. At *Champigny-sur-Veude*, the preceding station (3 M.), there also stood a magnificent castle, of which the chapel is still extant, built in the early Renaissance style, and adorned with beautiful stained glass by M. Pinaigrier. — 10¹/₂ M. *Ile-Bouchard*, a small town containing the ruins of an 11th cent. priory, and near which is a large dolmen. — At (12¹/₂ M.) *Croutilles-St. Gilles*, we join the branch-line from Azay-le-Rideau (p. 15). — 23¹/₂ M. *Port-de-Piles* (p. 5).

The railway crosses the Vienne at Chinon and affords a striking view of the town. — 34 M. *La Roche-Clermault*. Beyond (38 M.) *Beuxes* the keep of Loudun is seen on the left.

45¹/₂ M. **Loudun** (*Buffet; Höt. des Iles*, near St. Pierre-du-Marché), the *Juliodunum* of the Romans, is built on an eminence (pop. 4652). It played an important part in the Religious Wars and gave its name to an edict favourable to the Protestants in 1616; but it is still better known for the trial of the curé Urbain Grandier, who was burnt alive in 1634, on a charge of sorcery.

Loudun has still many old streets, narrow and dark. Turning to the left at the end of the Rue de la Gare, then to the right into the Rue Sèche, we reach *St. Pierre-du-Marché*, a Gothic church with a Renaissance portal, and a lofty stone spire. The street on this side of the Place leads to *Ste. Croix*, a fine Romanesque church with nave and aisles and a transept, with ambulatory and little apses. This church now serves as a market-house. — Turning to the right on the other side of St. Pierre-du-Marché, we reach the *Palais de Justice*, in front of which a bronze statue, by Alf. Charron, was erected in 1894 to *Theophraste Renaudot* (1586-1653), physician of Louis XIII. and founder of French journalism (1631). Behind the Palais is the lofty square *Keep* of the old 12th cent. castle which is in a close. — The street to the left, beyond the close, leads to *St. Pierre-du-Martray*, a church with some good details in the Flamboyant style. — Still farther is the *Porte du Martray*, the chief remaining portion of the old fortifications of the town.

From Loudun to *Angers* (Saumur) see *Baedeker's Northern France.*

FROM LOUDUN (ANGERS) TO CHATELLERAULT (p. 5), 31¹/₂ M., railway in 1¹/₂-1³/₄ hr. (fares 5 fr. 20, 3 fr. 85, 2 fr. 50 c.). The principal intermediate station is (20¹/₂ M.) *Lencloître*, a town which has sprung up around an abbey of which the Romanesque church is still extant.

FROM LOUDUN TO POITIERS, 43¹/₂ M., railway in 2-6¹/₂ hrs. (fares 7 fr. 25, 5 fr. 35, 3 fr. 50 c.). — 5 M. *Arçay* (see below). 12¹/₂ M. Moncontour, a village famous for the victory of the Duke of Anjou (Henri III.) over the Protestants commanded by Coligny in 1569. It has a ruined castle and a keep of the 13th century. Branch to (10 M.) Airvault (p. 18), viâ *St. Jouin-de-Marnes*, with its celebrated abbey. — 23¹/₂ M. *Mirebeau*, with the remains of fortifications; 33 M. *Neuville-de-Poitou*, the junction of the Parthenay line (p. 18).

The railway skirts Loudun on the side of the Porte du Martray.

61 M. **Thouars** *(Buffet; Hôt. du Cheval-Blanc*, Grande-Rue; *de la Gare)*, with 5169 inhab., on the *Thouet*, was the capital of the powerful viscounts of Thouars, almost always partizans of the English, until it was taken by Bertrand du Guesclin in 1372. Afterwards it was long held by the Ducs de la Trémouille.

The *Castle* is a spacious structure of the 16th cent., built on steep cliffs above the river, 1 M. from the station. It is now a prison and cannot be visited without a special order; but visitors may obtain admission (after 10 a. m.) to the chapel, called *Ste. Chapelle*, a fine example of the Gothic style, finished in 1514. It has a crypt cut out in the rock, with the vault of the Trémouille family. Fine view of the valley of the Thouet from the terrace in front of the castle.

The *Church of St. Médard*, on the right of the main street as we return, has a fine Romanesque *Portal. *St. Laon*, on the left of the same street, dates from the 12th and 15th cent.; interesting interior.

From Thouars to *Saumur* (Paris) viâ Montreuil-Bellay (Angers), see *Baedeker's Northern France*.

From Thouars to Niort, 55 M., railway in 2¹/₂-4¹/₄ hrs. (fares 10 fr. 90 8 fr. 25, 6 fr. 5 c.). This section of the line from Paris to Bordeaux viâ Saumur quits the Sables line beyond the viaduct (see below) and ascends the valley of the Thouet. — 15 M. Airvault *(Hôt. des Voyageurs)*, a little town in which the church of *St. Pierre*, an old abbey-church, is a very noteworthy example of the Romanesque style of the 10th cent.; it was repaired in the 12th. Here, too, are the remains of a strong castle. — The Thouet is crossed, ¹/₂ M. higher up, by an 11th cent. bridge with eleven arches, called *Pont de Vernay*. Branch to Moncontour, see p. 17. — 17¹/₂ M. *St. Loup-sur-Thouet*, with a château of the 17th century.

28 M. Parthenay *(Buffet; Hôt. Tranchant)*, a picturesque place of 7300 inhab., is still surrounded with ramparts of the 12-13th cent., which formed three lines of defence. It played an important part in the wars against England in the Middle Ages, in the Religious Wars, and in those of the Vendée. The *Church of St. Laurent*, in the Romanesque and Gothic styles, has a modern spire and a 12th cent. tower. *Ste. Croix* is Romanesque. The ruined *Château*, the *Porte St. Jacques*, and the ruins of *Notre-Dame-de-la-Couldre*, in the Romanesque style, are also noteworthy. — Line to Poitiers, see above.

50 M. *Echiré-St. Gelais*, where the *Sèvre-Niortaise* is crossed. About 1³/₄ M. to the right are the impressive ruins of the *Château du Couldray-Salbart*, built in the 9th century. — 55 M. *Niort* (p. 31).

The Sables-d'Olonne line now makes a great curve and crosses a viaduct 125 ft. high and 650 ft. long, which affords a fine view, on the left, of Thouars. The railway ascends nearly to Cerizay and the pasturage of the district grows like that of the Bocage (see p. 19).

68 M. *Coulonges-Thouarsais*; then *Luché*, with an agricultural colony. Beyond (74 M.) *Noirterre*, we rejoin and follow the line from Nantes (Angers) to Poitiers, noting on the left the fine steeple of Bressuire.

79 M. **Bressuire** *(*Buffet; Hôtel du Dauphin)*, with 4723 inhab., occupies a hill on the left. Like Thouars, it played a part in the wars with England, and it was taken by Bertrand du Guesclin in 1371. It has a very curious *Castle* of the 12th and 15th cent., half in ruins, half restored, and visible to the right of the via-

duct before entering the station. It has two lines of defence with
48 towers. — The church of *Notre-Dame* belongs chiefly to the
12th and 15th cent., and has a steeple finished in the style of the
Renaissance.

Lines to *Clisson* (Nantes) and to *Poitiers*, see p. 27.

FROM BRESSUIRE TO NIORT, 48 M., railway in 2-2¼ hrs. (fares 7 fr. 95,
5 fr. 90, 3 fr. 85 c.). — This line traverses part of the *Bocage* (see below),
with coal-mines. — 9½ M. *Moncoutant*, where flax is cultivated and a
woollen stuff made which is called breluche. 18 M. *Breuil-Barret*, junction
for La Rochelle (see below). — 31 M. *Coulonges-sur-Autise*, with a castle of
the 16th century. — 39 M. *Benet*. Line to Velluire, see below. — 41½ M.
Coulon, beyond which we cross the *Sèvre-Niortaise*. — 48 M. *Niort* (p. 21).

FROM BRESSUIRE TO LA ROCHELLE, 56½ M., railway in 2½-4¾ hrs.
(fares 11 fr. 60, 8 fr. 55, 5 fr. 55 c.). To (18 M.) *Breuil-Barret*, see above.
— Beyond (21½ M.) *Châtaigneraie* we follow the valley of the *Mère*.
24 M. *Antigny*. 28 M. *Vouvant*, with a fine church (11-12th cent.) and a
ruined château (tower of the 13th cent.); 31 M. *Bourneau-Mervent*. —
36 M. *Fontenay-le-Comte* (*Hôtel de France*), a venerable town with 8884
inhab., situated on a hill on the right bank of the *Vendée*, which here
becomes navigable. It suffered greatly during the Religious and Vendean
wars, and almost all traces of its strongly fortified castle have disappeared. The churches of *Notre-Dame* and *St. Jean* have each a fine Gothic
spire. The town also possesses a handsome Renaissance *Fountain* and
some interesting old houses. Branch-line to *Benet* (11 M.; Niort), see
above. — 39½ M. *Fontaines-Vendée*. — At (43½ M.) *Velluire* we join the
line from Nantes to *La Rochelle* (p. 28).

82 M. *Clazay*; 89 M. *Cerizay*, with a modern château on the
right. We cross the *Sèvre-Nantaise*. — 92½ M. *St. Mesmin-le-
Vieux*. We are now in the *Vendée* and in the *Bocage* district famous in the annals of the Revolution. The land here is divided
into square plots, each 5 to 7 acres in area, fenced in by hedges 6
to 10 ft. in height, ornamented with trees.

97½ M. *Pouzauges*. The large village, beautifully situated on
the slope of a hill, 2½ M. to the N., boasts of the ruins of a large
and picturesque keep of the 13-14th cent., which once belonged
to the famous Gilles de Laval, called 'Bluebeard' (p. 27). In the
neighbourhood are several interesting castles, picturesque ruins,
and fine points of view.

104 M. *Chavagnes-les-Redoux*. The line crosses the *Grand-
Lay* on both sides of the station. — 112 M. *Chantonnay* (pop. 4300).
The line, which intersects a very hilly tract, makes a wide curve
to the left, followed by two cuttings and a viaduct affording a fine
view. — Beyond (120 M.) *Bournezeau* is a forest. 125 M. *La Chaize-
le-Vicomte*, with 2740 inhabitants. Crossing the *Yon* we then rejoin the line from Nantes to La Rochelle and Bordeaux (R. 4).

133 M. **La Roche-sur-Yon**, formerly *Napoléon* and *Bourbon-
Vendée* (*Buffet*; *Hôt. de l'Europe*, in the Place; *Hôt. des Voyageurs*, at the station), with 12,215 inhab., the chief town of the
department of the *Vendée*, on a hill washed by the Yon. There
was formerly a strong castle here which was a place of importance
both in the English and Religious wars. The town having become
the chief place of a prefecture, Napoleon I. erected numerous build-

ings which are anything but remarkable. It is now a modern town, regularly built and almost without interest. The large Place Napoléon, in the centre, which is reached from the station viâ the boulevard on the right, and the Rue des Sables, to the left, is adorned with an equestrian bronze *Statue of Napoleon I.*, by De Niewerkerke. Here also is the *Hôtel de Ville*, with a garden behind it containing a small museum of paintings and antiquities and a small monument to *Paul Baudry* (1828-1886), the painter, a native of the town. On the other side of the Place is the *Church*, the interior of which is in good taste and shows some fine modern stained glass. A little farther to the right, in a small square, is the *Statue of General Travot* (1767 - 1836) 'pacificator of the Vendée' during the Hundred Days, an indifferent bronze by Maludron.

From La Roche-sur-Yon to *Nantes* and *La Rochelle* see R. 4.

Beyond (138½ M.) *Les Clouzeaux* and the small station of *Ste. Flaive*, to the right, in the distance, is the Château de la Bassetière. 145 M. *La Mothe-Achard;* 151½ M. *Olonne.* To the right lie salt marshes, with large heaps of salt, and a succession of sand-dunes.

156 M. **Les Sables-d'Olonne.** — **Hotels.** GRAND-HÔTEL DE LA PLAGE & SPLENDID-HÔTEL, HÔT. DU REMBLAI, GRAND-HÔTEL DU CASINO, all on the beach; R. 2½-5½, B. 1, déj. 3, D. 3½, omn. ½-¾ fr.; HÔTEL DE FRANCE, DU CHEVAL-BLANC, JOUET, in the town.

Cafés. *Café de la Plage;* *Grand Café*, Place du Minage, near the Remblai. — **Sea-Baths.** Machine and towel 30 c.; bathing-dress 30 c. — **Casino**, adm. 1 fr.; per month 30 fr. — **Donkeys**, 50 c. per hour.

British Vice-consul: *Mr. Théophile Lelièvre.*

Les Sables-d'Olonne is a much-frequented sea-bathing place, with a small harbour and 11,550 inhabitants. Its magnificent sandy beach, sloping gently towards the S. and stretching in a semicircle for a distance of about 1 M., is flanked by a wide esplanade called the *Remblai* and *Quai Franqueville*, with a carriage-road and numerous handsome villas. Near the end is an *Aquarium* (½ fr.). The town, however, is badly built, and the church is its only object of interest.

To reach the beach from the station we turn to the right, into the Rue de l'Hôtel-de-Ville, and then follow the Rue Travot, the first street to the left. Carriages turn to the left farther on, at the *Church*, a Late-Gothic building, with fine vaulting. To the W. of the Remblai *i. e.* to the right as we reach the shore, is the *Casino*, and farther on is the narrow *Channel* leading to the harbour. Beyond the latter rises the *Arundel Tower*, a modern erection with battlements and machicolations, which serves as a lighthouse. Adjacent are the ruins of a château of the same name. Here, too, lies the unimportant suburb of *La Chaume*, near which the shore forms a promontory bearing a small fort.

The *Harbour*, to the N., between the town and this suburb, comprises a dry dock, a floating dock, and a graving dock. Near it there are *Oyster Parks*, and farther off, some *Salt Marshes* which may be reached viâ La Chaume (ferry 5 c.).

On this side the shore is bordered by dunes; to the S.E. are curious rocks, some ruins, and a wood of evergreen oaks.

On Sundays and festivals the varied head-dresses of the country-women at Les Sables will attract the visitor's attention.

3. From Poitiers to La Rochelle (and Rochefort).

00 M. RAILWAY in 3¹/₂-5¹/₃ hrs. (fares 14 fr. 90, 11 fr. 6, 7 fr. 15 c.). — The line to Rochefort (88 M.) diverges at Aigrefeuille, 11 M. before La Rochelle (p. 23).

Poitiers, see p. 6. The Angoulême line is followed as far as (3 M.) *St. Benoît* (p. 9). Beyond (12 M.) *Coulombiers* we cross the pretty valley of the *Vonne* by two lofty viaducts.

16 M. **Lusignan** (*Hôtel de la Mélusine*), a picturesquely situated little town, partly on the bank of the Vonne and partly on a hill crowned with the inconsiderable remains of the *Château* of the illustrious family which gave kings to Jerusalem and Cyprus. This stronghold is fabled to have been built by the fairy Melusine, whose name is probably derived from the earliest châtelaine, the 'Mother of the Lusignans' ('mère des Lusignans'; Merlusina, Mélusine). The château was destroyed in the Religious Wars. The interesting *Church* dates from the 11-12th centuries.

From Lusignan a diligence (75 c.) plies in 1³/₄ hr. to **Sanxay** (*Hôt. du Bienvenu*), a country-town 9¹/₂ M. to the N.W., in the valley of the Vonne, where considerable Celtic-Roman remains of the 1st cent. of the present era were discovered in 1881-83, including a temple, baths, a circus, and several large hostelries. There seems to have been a town of some size on this spot, though its name has not come down to us.

20¹/₂ M. *Rouillé*; 25 M. *Pamproux*. In the neighbourhood is the *Roche Ruffin*, a grotto with an underground lake. — 29 M. *La Mothe-St. Héraye*, a small town, most of the inhabitants of which, as of many other places in this district, are Protestants. We then enter the valley of the *Sèvre-Niortaise*.

34 M. **St. Maixent** (*Ecu de France*), a town of 5036 inhab., on the Sèvre-Niortaise, has an interesting church of the 12-15th cent., in great part destroyed by the Calvinists in 1562 and 1568, but rebuilt in 1670-82 on the original plan. The fine tower over the W. front, with its truncated spire, dates from the 15th century. The oldest part is the crypt, which contains the tomb of St. Maxentius (d. 515), the second abbot of the monastery round which the town grew up. This monastery, rebuilt in the 17th cent., now serves as a barrack. At St. Maixent is a *Statue of Denfert-Rochereau* (1823-1878), defender of Belfort in 1870-71.

The line now ascends and then descends rapidly to (38 M.) *Ste. Néomaye*, (40 M.) *La Crèche*, and (44 M.) *Arthenay*.

49 M. **Niort.** — **Hotels.** *HÔTEL DU RAISIN DE BOURGOGNE, Rue Victor-Hugo 38; DES ÉTRANGERS, Rue des Cordeliers 8; DE FRANCE, Place du Temple 11; DE LA GARE, unpretending, good cuisine. — Buffet, at the

station, well spoken of, déj. 3, D. 3½ fr. — **Cafés**, in the Place de la
Brèche.

Cabs, 1 fr. per drive, 2 fr. per hr. (at night 1½ and 3 fr.).

Niort, with 23,225 inhab. on the Sèvre-Niortaise, is the chief
town of the department of the *Deux-Sèvres*. Handed over to
England with the domains of Eleanor of Aquitaine (p. 6), it was
several times taken and retaken in the Hundred Years War, on the
last occasion (1372) by Bertrand du Guesclin. Its Calvinist sympathies also led to considerable suffering in the Religious Wars.
The chief industry of Niort is in hides and skins, and gloves are
largely manufactured here.

We enter the town, to the right, by the Rue de la Gare and the
Rue St. Hilaire. Near the end of the latter street is the large modern church of *St. Hilaire*, in a debased style. Adjacent is the spacious *Place de la Brèche*, adorned with flower-beds and statues
in bronze and marble. Turning to the right (W.) and following
the Rue Ricard, we next reach the Rue Victor-Hugo, the chief street
of the town. The Rue du Pilori, on the right, leads to the so-called
Palais d'Eléonore, the old Hôtel de Ville. The present building,
flanked by two round machicolated towers, dates from 1520-30.
It contains the *Musée Départemental*, a collection of antiquities
and casts (open on Sun. and Thurs. 12-4 or 5, to strangers on other
days also; concierge at No 11, opposite the entrance). Farther on, to
the left, is the church of *St. Andrew*, lately rebuilt in the style of the
15th cent., and still farther on is the beautiful *Jardin Public*, laid
out on a slope by the river-side and affording pleasant views.

We now return by the Quays to the *Halles*, a tasteful iron structure at the end of the Rue Victor-Hugo. On the other side is the
Keep (Donjon) of a castle built by Henry Plantagenet, which con-
sisted mainly of two large towers with turrets. Beyond the keep
are the *Préfecture* (rebuilt in 1893), the *Palais de Justice*, and
Notre-Dame, the chief church of Niort, rebuilt in 1491-1534. The
N. portal is embellished with a curious balustrade, and the tower
has a stone spire surrounded with turrets bearing statues of the
Evangelists. In the interior are a Gothic pulpit, 'Stations of the
Cross' in carved oak, an elegant Renaissance gallery, etc.

The Grande Rue Notre-Dame leads to the right from this church
to the Rue St. Jean, which leads back to the Rue Victor-Hugo. At
the corner of the Rue St. Jean and Rue du Musée rises the handsome new *Ecole de Dessin*, behind which is the *Library* (open daily
1-5, except on holidays; closed in Aug. and Sept.).

In the Rue du Musée is the *Musée de Peinture*, occupying an old
convent and open to the public on Sun. and Thurs. from noon till
4 or 5, to strangers on other days also. The first floor is devoted to
sculptures, drawings, casts, and Natural History collections, while on
the second floor is a picture-gallery, containing about 200 paintings,
including some good works of the Italian School, for the most part

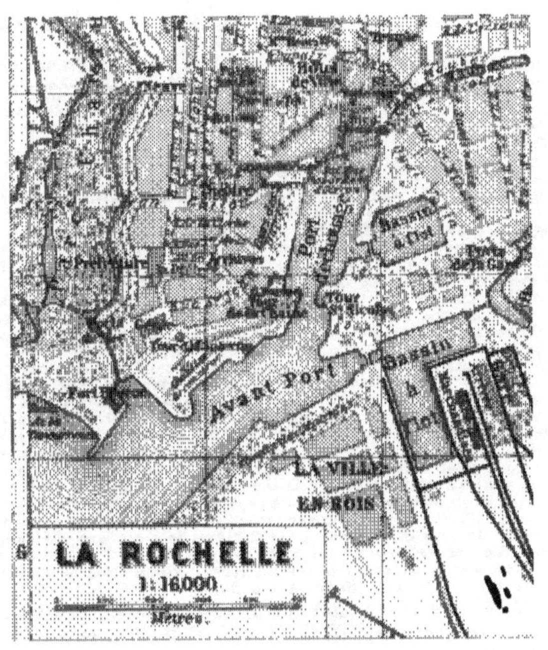

Hôtel de Ville
Avant Port
Port Marchand
Tour St. Nicolas
Bassin à Flot
LA VILLE
EN BOIS
G LA ROCHELLE
1:16000
Mètres.

by unknown masters, and several works of the early French School. On the landing-place of the first floor are 76 painted wood-carvings of the 16th cent. in the Flemish style, representing Biblical subjects.

From Niort to *Bressuire* and to *Angers*, see p. 16 and *Baedeker's Northern France*.

From Niort to Saintes, 48 M., railway in 1¹/₂-2¹/₂ hrs. (fares 7 fr. 95, 5 fr. 90, 3 fr. 85 c.). — Beyond (3³/₄ M.) *Aiffres* the line to Ruffec (see below) diverges to the left. — 18 M. *Villeneuve-la-Comtesse*, with the interesting remains of an old château. — 30 M. **St. Jean-d'Angély** (*Hôtel de France; des Voyageurs*), a town with 7300 inhab., on the right bank of the *Boutonne*, which here forms a small harbour. The town owes its origin to a Benedictine abbey, destroyed in 1568 by the Calvinists, who had made the place one of their chief strongholds. It was taken the following year by the Duke of Anjou (Henri III.) and in 1621 by Louis XIII., who levelled its fortifications. Among the objects of interest are some remains of the abbey and its church, rebuilt in the 18th cent.; a tower of the 15th cent.; an old market-house; and the bronze statue, by Bogino, of *Regnaud de St. Jean-d'Angély* (d. 1819), a distinguished politician and father of the marshal of that name. — At (41¹/₂ M.) *Taillebourg* we join the Rochefort line (p. 30).

From Niort to Ruffec, 51¹/₂ M., railway in 2¹/₄-4¹/₂ hrs. (fares 8 fr. 45, 6 fr. 25, 4 fr. 10 c.). — 3³/₄ M. *Aiffres*. On the right diverges the line to Saintes (see above). — 20¹/₂ M. **Melle** (*Hôtel Ste. Catherine*), an ancient town (*Metallum*) with 2848 inhab., built partly on the bank of the Béronne and partly on a steep hill, which contained a silver and lead mine worked by the Romans. The chief building is the *Church of St. Hilaire*, in the lower part of the town, dating from the 12th cent. and containing some interesting sculptures. *St. Pierre*, in the upper part of the town, is of the same period. — 23¹/₂ M. *Mazières-St. Romans*. Near Mazières is a modern château, with the fine *Tour de Melstard* of the 15th century. We now ascend the valley of the *Boutonne*, a tributary of the Charente, which rises near (34¹/₂ M.) *Chef-Boutonne*. — 51¹/₂ M. **Ruffec**, see p. 10.

54¹/₂ M. *Frontenay-Rohan*; 57 M. *Epannes*. The train traverses a marshy district. 62 M. *Mauzé*; 67 M. *St. Georges-du-Bois*.

69¹/₂ M. **Surgères** (*Hôt. du Commerce*), a small town with a Romanesque church of the 12th cent. and a ruined Château (14th and 16th cent.). — 73 M. *Chambon*; 79 M. *Aigrefeuille*.

From Aigrefeuille a branch-line runs to (9¹/₂ M.) *Rochefort* (p. 28), passing *Ciré*, with a 16th cent. château.

83 M. *La Jarrie*. The line describes a wide curve to reach La Rochelle, which is seen in the distance to the right, and joins the Nantes and Bordeaux line (R. 4).

90 M. **La Rochelle.** — **Hotels.** Hôtel de France (Pl. a; B, 3), Rue Gargoulleau 28; Hôt. des Etrangers (Pl. b; C, 3), Rue Thiers 12; Hôt. du Commerce (Pl. c; B, 3), Place d'Armes; Richelieu, du Mail, at the sea-bathing place (see below). — *Buffet* at the station. — *Cafés* in the Place d'Armes. — *Post and Telegraph Office* (Pl. B, 4), Rue du Palais 12. — Sea-Baths at the Mail (p. 21): *Bains de la Concurrence*, unpretending; *Bains Louise*, similar, for ladies; *Bains du Mail*, *Bains Richelieu*, with hotels, casinos, cafés, etc. — British Consul: *Mr. R. S. Warburton*. — Steamboat to the *Ile de Ré*, see p. 26.

La Rochelle, a seaport with 26,808 inhab., a fortress of the second class, and the seat of a bishopric, was the ancient capital of the *Pays Aunis*, and is now the chief town of the department of the *Charente Inférieure*. It is situated on a bay in the Straits of Antioche, sheltered by the islands of Ré and Oléron.

Whether this town was the *Portus Santonum* of the Romans is uncertain. It first appears in unquestioned history at the end of the 10th cent. under the name of *Rupella*. Incorporated with England together with Aquitaine, it was permanently restored to France in 1372, after which it enjoyed two centuries of commercial prosperity, brought to an end by the outbreak of the Religious Wars. Protestantism already counted many converts here when Condé and Coligny made the town their headquarters in 1568. It was the chief stronghold of the Huguenots, and the cruisers of La Rochelle were well-known in the Atlantic and the English Channel. In 1572-73 the town successfully withstood a siege of upwards of six months. The re-awakening of religious bitterness in the reign of Louis XIII. hurried it into fresh contests (1622, 1626, 1627-28) in which it was less successful. In the last of these it had taken advantage of the hostilities between France and England, and the latter country despatched more than one expedition to its relief, the chief of which failed through the blundering of its commander, the Duke of Buckingham. Richelieu succeeded in completely investing it, closed the port by a mole, part of which still exists (see below), and, after a siege of 15 months, starved it into surrender. The fall of La Rochelle destroyed the political power of the Huguenots, who never recovered from this blow. Richelieu, however, did not abuse his victory. In 1809 the English made an unsuccessful attempt to destroy the French fleet at La Rochelle. The chief articles of the trade of La Rochelle, which suffered greatly from the loss of Canada by France, are timber, coal, brandy, wine, vinegar, salt, preserved meats, and grain. Fishing is also actively pursued and forms a staple industry. Among famous natives of the town may be mentioned Réaumur (d. 1757), Bonpland, the naturalist (d. 1858), and Admiral Duperré (d. 1846).

From the station the town is entered by the PORTE DE LA GARE or *St. Nicolas* (Pl. C, 4), erected in 1857. The fortifications were constructed by Vauban in the reign of Louis XIV., the old works, except those on the seaward side, having been demolished after the siege of 1627-28. They form an unbroken line about $3\frac{1}{2}$ M. in length, strengthened with bastions, redans, and a hornwork (near the station).

The **Harbour** (Pl. B, C, 4, 5), a little to the left of the entrance to the town, is partly within and partly without the walls. Outside are the *Outer Harbour*, and a *Floating Dock*; inside are a *Careening Basin*, a *Dry Dock*, a *Canal*, and the *Reservoir of Maubec*, the waters of which serve to scour the harbour. — Port de la Pallice, see below.

The COURS DES DAMES or *Richard* (Pl. B, 4), on the other side of the dry-dock, is embellished with a bronze *Statue of Admiral Duperré*, by P. Herbert. Opposite is the *Porte de la Grosse-Horloge*, the only old gate remaining, a large square tower with round turrets of the 14-15th cent., altered in the 17th and 18th centuries.

At the entrance to the dry-dock are two old towers (Pl. B, 5): the *Tour St. Nicolas* (1384) to the left, and the *Tour de la Chaine* (1476) on the right (facing the sea). The first is square with four round turrets, and the interesting interior has been recently restored for the reception of an antiquarian museum. The second tower is round and was at one time 110 ft. in height. The harbour was formerly closed with a chain, and the Tour St. Nicolas seems to have been united with a 'small chain-tower' (now vanished) by a Gothic arch under which the ships passed. A little farther on, in a straight line, is the

Lantern Tower (Pl. B, 5; 1445-1476), deriving its name from having served as a lighthouse. It is round, flanked by two turrets, and surmounted by a stone spire. In the distance, by the Outer Harbour, rises the black and white *Richelieu Tower*, with a bell rung by the waves, which warns vessels of the mole above mentioned. The mole itself is seen at low-tide.

The *Porte de Mer*, or *Porte des Deux-Moulins* (Pl. A, 5), near the Lantern Tower, leads to the *Outer Harbour* and to the *Bathing-place* (p. 20), the arrangements of which are good, though the bottom is covered with pebbles and shells. Above the bathing-place extends the *Mall*, a promenade planted with trees and affording a series of fine views. The new *Parc Charruyer* (Pl. A, 5-2) skirts the fortifications.

At the Porte de la Grosse-Horloge (see above) begins the wide Rue du Palais, flanked, like several others, with arcades. At one corner, to the right, is an interesting house, built in 1554. Farther on stand the *Bourse* and the *Palais de Justice* (Pl. B, 4-3), buildings of the 18th and 17th centuries. The Rue du Palais is continued by the Rue Chaudrier, from which the Rue des Augustins diverges to the right. In this last, No. 11, at the end of a court, is the *House of Henri II.*, the most quaint and interesting of the ancient houses of La Rochelle.

The **Cathedral** (*St. Louis* or *St. Barthélemy*; Pl. B, 3), farther on, at the corner of the Rue Chaudrier and the Place d'Armes, was rebuilt between 1742 and 1762 in the Greek style, after plans by J. Gabriel. Behind it is a *Tower* of the 14th cent., a relic of the original church. The cathedral contains modern stained-glass windows and paintings, among which we may notice the ceiling of the Chapel of the Virgin, in the apse. In the same chapel is the monument of Mgr. Landriot (d. 1874), with a fine marble statue by L. Thomas.

The **Place d'Armes** (Pl. B, 3), the largest square in the town, extends hence to the W. as far as the ramparts.

The Rue Gargoulleau, to the E., leads to the former bishops' palace, containing the *Library* (Pl. B, 3), which is open on Tues., Thurs., and Sat. from 12 to 4 or 5. The *Museum*, in the same building, is open on Sun. & Thurs. from 12 to 4 or 5, and on other days also to strangers. Its chief contents are some modern French pictures by A. de Pujol, Antigna, Bouguereau, and Fromentin; a painting of the great siege of La Rochelle by Van der Kabel; and works by Giordano and Vien.

The Rue St. Yon, diverging to the right at the end of the Rue Gargoulleau, leads to the **Hôtel de Ville** (Pl. B, 3), the most interesting building in La Rochelle. It was erected in 1486-1607, partly in the Gothic and partly in the Renaissance styles, and has lately been restored. Its most remarkable external features are a richly sculptured gallery with a parapet, and two projecting belfries with corbels.

On the larger, to the left, is a recess with armorial bearings. The façade towards the court, consisting of two distinct parts, is still more interesting. The smaller part, to the left, is of the time of Henri II. and has a modern staircase in front, with a painted statue of that monarch. The ground-floor of the part to the right is formed of an arcade with fine semicircular arches and a sculptured ceiling. The two upper stories are adorned with four niches containing allegorical statues, between eight fluted columns, a dormer window, pediments, and other ornaments of the time of Henry IV. (1607). Inside is the Council Hall in which Guiton, the mayor and intrepid defender of the town during its blockade by Richelieu, swore to stab any one who should suggest surrender.

Beyond the bathing-place, 3 M. from the harbour proper, lies the Port de la Pallice, a new harbour, constructed 1883-90 in the deep bay of that name, opposite the Ile de Ré. It consists of an outer harbour, about 30 acres in area, between two long piers, and a dock-basin, 26 acres in area, with quays 5000 ft. in length, and a depth of at least 28 ft. The works, which can be enlarged if required, have cost about 80,000*l.* Mail-steamers for South America leave La Pallice every fortnight.

In the neighbourhood of La Rochelle are numerous *Salt-Marshes*, a visit to which is interesting. Most of them lie just beyond the hornwork mentioned at p. 24.

From La Rochelle to *Nantes* and to *Rochefort* and *Bordeaux*, see R. 4.

The Ile de Ré, about 10 M. to the W. of La Rochelle, but not more than 2¹/₂-3 M. from the little port of *La Repentie* (Inn) at the W. end of the roadstead, is about 18 M. long and 2¹/₂-3 M. wide. It is populous (9500 inhab.) but of little general interest, consisting to a great extent of productive salt-marshes. A steamer plies daily from La Rochelle to St. Martin-de-Ré in 1¹/₄-2 hrs. (fares 2¹/₂ or 2 fr., return 3³/₄ or 3 fr.). Intermediate station, *La Flotte*. Or we may proceed by omnibus to (3 M.) La Repentie (60 c.) and take the steamer thence (four times daily; fare 75 c.) to *Rivedoux*, whence another omnibus runs to (5¹/₂ M.) St. Martin (1 fr.).

St. Martin-de-Ré (Hôt. du Bateau à Vapeur) is a small town and port on the N. side of the island, with 2600 inhabitants. It suffered much in the English wars; its fortifications are the work of Vauban. St. Martin is the depôt from which convicts are shipped to New Caledonia.

4. From Nantes to Bordeaux.

a. Via Clisson and La Rochelle.

232 M. RAILWAY in 9-15³/₄ hrs. (fares about 37 fr. 90, 28 fr., 18 fr. 35 c.). The trains start from the *Gare de l'État*, but call at the *Gare d'Orléans* 18 min. later. At Bordeaux they arrive at the *Gare St. Jean*, not at the Gare de la Bastide (p. 46). — Breaks on the journey, see p. 3.

Nantes, see *Baedeker's Northern France.* — The line crosses three arms of the Loire, of which, as well as of Nantes itself, it affords a striking view. — 4¹/₂ M. *Vertou*, a country-town, picturesquely situated 1¹/₄ M. to the right. — 9¹/₂ M. *La Haie-Fouassière*; 12 M. *Le Pallet*, the birthplace of Abelard and of Astrolabe, the son of Héloïse. Beyond it the *Sèvre-Nantaise* is crossed. — 15 M. *Gorges.*

17 M. Clisson (*Buffet*; *Hôtel de l'Europe*, R., L., & A. 2-2¹/₂, B. ³/₄, déj. 3, omn. ¹/₂ fr.), a town with 2916 inhab., prettily situated on two hills at the confluence of the Sèvre and the *Moine*. The

latter river is crossed by a handsome viaduct. The best view of the town and ruins is obtained from the hill (on which is the hotel) on the opposite bank of the Sèvre, reached by following the road to the left from the station. The old feudal *Castle* (13-15th cent.) and the town itself were destroyed in 1793-94 in the wars of the Vendée, so that nothing ancient now remains except the interesting and picturesque ruins of the castle. On the capture of the latter many of the inhabitants are said to have been thrown alive into the castle-well and left there to perish miserably. The town was rebuilt in a somewhat peculiar style, mainly after the plans of the sculptor Lemot (1775-1827), the owner of the ruins. Both the rivers are bordered with attractive 'Garennes' or parks, the finer of the two being the Garenne Lemot, on the right bank of the Sèvre, while the Garenne Valentin occupies both banks of the Moine. Clisson has given its name to a family of which the most famous representative was Olivier de Clisson, Constable of France (d.1407), one of the most distinguished champions of France in her wars with England.

From Clisson a BRANCH RAILWAY runs to the S. E. to (109 M.) Poitiers. — 11 M. *Torfou-Tiffauges.* Tiffauges, a country-town on an eminence on the left bank of the river, is dominated by the extensive ruins of a *Castle* of the 11th, 14th, and 15th cent., which belonged to the infamous Gilles de Laval, the original of the nursery hero Blue Beard (Barbe-Bleue; p. 19). — 16³/₄ M. *Evrunes-Mortagne.* Mortagne is another little town in a picturesque situation on the right bank of the Sèvre, possessing a ruined castle. We then quit the valley of the Sèvre. — 24 M. *Cholet (Hôt. de France; de l'Europe)*, see *Baedeker's Northern France.* — 37 M. *Châtillon-St. Aubin. Châtillon-sur-Sèvre*, 1¹/₄ M. to the S. E., was named *Mauléon* until 1736. — 44¹/₂ M. *Nueil-les-Aubiers; 47 M. Voultegon.* We now ascend the valley of the *Argenton.* — 53 M. *Bressuire*, see p. 18. — 60 M. *La Chapelle-St. Laurent* is an important cattle-market. — 74 M. *Parthenay*, see p. 18. Several small stations are passed. 94¹/₂ M. *Valliers-Vouillé.* Vouillé, where Clovis defeated Alaric II., king of the Visigoths, in 507, lies 2¹/₂ M. to the S. — 109 M. *Poitiers*, see p. 6.

The train now enters the *Vendée*, traversing that part of it which is called the *Bocage* (p. 19). — 24 M. *Montaigu-Vendée*, a small town, prettily situated on the *Maine*, which is crossed here, was the birthplace of Laréveillère-Lepeaux (1753-1824), one of the five members of the Directory. A monument was erected to him in 1886. — 30¹/₂ M. *L'Herbergement;* 40 M. *Belleville-Vendée.*

48 M. **La Roche-sur-Yon** (see p. 19).

53¹/₂ M. *Nesmy;* 61 M. *Champ-St. Père.* The hedges separating the fields now disappear and are replaced by trenches. — 66¹/₂ M. *La Bretonnière.*

71 M. **Luçon** (*Hôtel de la Tête-Noire*, near the cathedral, R., L., & A. 1¹/₂-2 fr., B. 60 c., déj. 2¹/₂, D. 3 fr.), a town with 6535 inhab., is the seat of a bishopric which Richelieu held from 1607 to 1624. The *Cathedral*, an old monastic foundation of the 11th cent., was not finished till the 17th and has been lately restored. The most noteworthy object in the interior is the pulpit, ornamented with paintings. Adjoining are *Cloisters* of the 15-16th centuries.

Luçon stands on the N. border of the Marais, a swampy part of the Vendée, which extends in the direction of the *Breton Straits* as far as the *Bay of Aiguillon*, with which it communicates by a canal 9 M. in length. Down to the 8th cent. of the Christian era this district was a gulf, one of the arms of which extended on the E. as far as Niort, which is now 37 M. distant from the sea. The gradual elevation of the district, to which this metamorphosis is due, still continues. The entrance of the gulf, once upwards of 18 M. in width, is now not more than 8 M. across. The marshy tracts are drained by innumerable canals. The Marais affords excellent pasturage and contains numerous productive salt-marshes, while near the mouth of the Sèvre-Niortaise are extensive 'bouchots', or 'parks' in which mussels and other shell-fish are reared for the markets of La Rochelle. This district and the other marshy regions fringing the sea-shore beyond it are all more or less unhealthy.

77 M. *Nalliers.* Beyond (80 M.) *Le Langon* we traverse a corner of the Marais and cross the river *Vendée.* 86 M. *Velluire;* line to *Bressuire* and *Niort* viâ *Fontenay-le-Comte*, see p. 19.

88 M. *Vix.* The large village of this name lies 2¼ M. to the left, on a hill, which was formerly an island in the gulf (see above), as was also (93 M.) *L'Ile-d'Elle*, beyond which we cross the *Sèvre-Niortaise.* On this river stands (97 M.) *Marans*, a well-built little town with a large grain trade. At (102 M.) *Andilly-St. Ouen* we quit the Marais, and farther on we skirt the *Niort and La Rochelle Canal*, which passes through a tunnel at (107¹/₂ M.) *Dompierre-sur-Mer*, the next station. To the left lie extensive salt-marshes.

112 M. **La Rochelle** (p. 23; *Buffet*). Line to Poitiers, see R. 3.

The direct line to Rochefort and Bordeaux now skirts for a considerable distance the *Pertuis* or *Straits of Antioche*, bounded by the Ile de Ré on the N. and the Ile d'Oléron (p. 30) on the S.W. — 115¹/₂ M. *Angoulins;* 117 M. *Châtelaillon* (Hôt. des Bains), a small sea-bathing resort. The ocean is steadily encroaching on the land here, and has already engulfed the two towns of Montmeillan and Châtelaillon. To the right is the small *Ile d'Aix* (see below). — 121 M. *Le Marouillet.* 125 M. *St. Laurent-de-la-Prée.*

A branch-railway runs hence to (3³/₄ M.) **Fouras** (Hôt. des Bains; de l'Océan), a sea-bathing place at the mouth of the Charente, with a castle of the 14th century. — Near the Pointe de l'Aiguille, the extremity of the right bank of the Charente, is the small *Ile d'Enet*, connected with the mainland at low tide. About ³/₄ M. from the Pointe is the *Ile d'Aix* (3³/₄ M. in length, and 1 M. in breadth), which was the last refuge of Napoleon I. before his surrender to the British. Both islands are fortified.

At (126 M.) *Charras* the train crosses the canal of that name.'

130 M. **Rochefort** (*Buffet*). — **Hotels.** HÔTEL DE FRANCE (Pl. a; B, 3,4), Rue du Rempart; DE LA ROCHELLE (Pl. b; B, 4), Rue Chanzy; DU GRAND HACUA (Pl. c; B, 4), Rue des Fonderies et de l'Arsénal. — **Cafés.** *Café Français*, Place Colbert; *des Voyageurs*, corner of Rue Thiers and Rue Audry de Puyravault; in the Rue des Fonderies, etc. — *Post and Telegraph Office* (Pl. B, 3), Rue des Fonderies.

Rochefort, a town and fortress with 33,334 inhab., situated on the right bank of the *Charente*, 9 M. from the sea, is a modern and regularly built place, containing little to interest the traveller. It possesses a naval as well as a commercial harbour, which, like the town itself, were first established by Colbert in 1666.

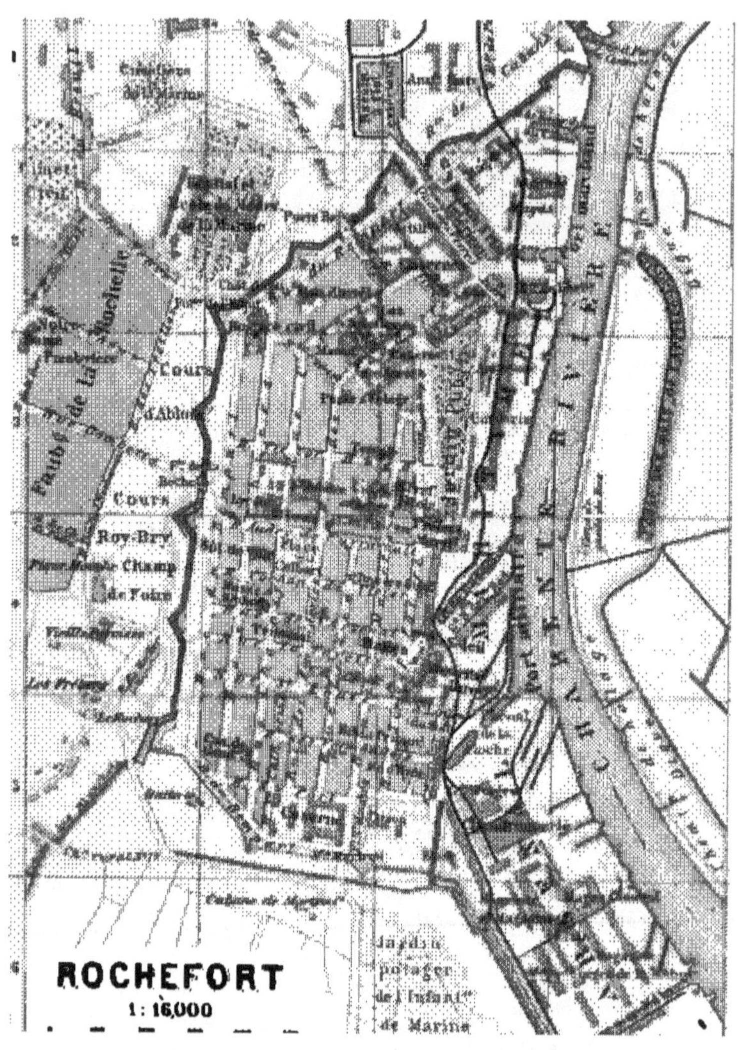

ROCHEFORT
1:16,000

The naval harbour and its vast arsenal are the 'lions' of Rochefort. To reach the entrance, which is near the end farthest from the station, we turn to the right on entering the fortifications and follow the Rue du Rempart and the Rue Thiers to the Rue de l'Arsenal. Or we may follow the Rue Begon in a straight direction, and then turn to the right into the Rue La Touche-Tréville, whence the Rue Chanzy leads to the Rue de l'Arsenal, at the corner of which is a small *Picture Gallery*, with a library. Between the Rue Thiers and the Rue Chanzy are the *Lyceum* and *Church of St. Louis* (Pl. B, 3), two modern buildings, the latter containing some fine stained-glass windows. Adjacent is the *Place Colbert*, the centre of the town, with a fountain.

The *Arsenal and the Dockyard (Pl. C, D, 2-6) cannot be visited without permission, to obtain which foreigners usually require a letter of introduction from their government countersigned by a French minister.

The visit takes at least 2 hours. The departments are not always taken in the same order, and some of the magazines and workshops are not shown. The *Porte du Soleil* (Pl. C, 4) is a handsome structure in the form of a triumphal arch. To the right are the *Offices*, eighteen *Building Slips*, for vessels of the first rank, an interesting *Model Room*, several *Store Houses*, the *Sail* and *Rigging Workshops*, etc. To the left are *Repairing* and *Graving Docks*, *Anchors* (some of which weigh from 5 to 6 tons), *Projectiles*, *Torpedos*, *Cannon*, and a large *Salle d'Armes*, decorated in a very ingenious fashion with arms or groups of arms arranged as trophies, columns, etc. A *Man of War*, too, is often shown.

Above this part of the arsenal, but outside the enceinte, is the *Naval Préfecture* (Pl. C, 4), which contains nothing of special interest, and behind it is the *Jardin Public*, a fine promenade.

Farther on, to the N.E. of the town, is the *Commercial Harbour*, or *Cabane Carrée* (Pl. C, D, 1). It has two floating basins of moderate size, and a much larger one (completed in 1890) higher up the river. The chief articles of trade at Rochefort are wine, brandy, grain, cattle, salt, timber, coal, and salt-fish.

On the N. side of the town, outside the fortifications, is a large *Naval Hospital* (Pl. A, B, 2; 800 beds), with a *School of Naval Medicine*. There is also a very deep artesian well, the water of which has a temperature of 100° Fahr. In front of the hospital extend the *Cours d'Ablois* and the *Cours Roy-Bry*.

From Rochefort to *Niort* and *Poitiers*, see p. 21.
From Rochefort to Le Chapus (*Ile d'Oléron*), 25 1/2 M., railway in 1 3/4 - 2 1/4 hrs. (fares 4 fr. 20, 3 fr. 10 c., 2 fr.). — To (7 M.) *Cabariot*, see below. — 21 M. *Marennes* (*Hôt. du Commerce*), a small town (5415 inhab.), famous for its oysters, of which about 25,000,000 are annually exported. The church has a 14th cent. *Tower*, and there are numerous quaint old houses in the town. About 3/4 M. to the S. is the small harbour. — From the town an omnibus (1/2 fr.) plies to (2 1/2 M.) *La Cayenne*, whence a steam-

ferry (25 c.) crosses the Seudre to *La Grève*, united by railway with Pons
and Royan (p. 59). — From (25¹/₂ M.) *Le Chapus* a steamer (45 or 60 c.),
crosses to Le Château in the Ile d'Oléron.

The **Ile d'Oléron**, which with the Ile de Ré (p. 26) bounds the straits
of Antioche, and is separated from the mainland by the *Straits of Maumusson*, is a flat, fertile, and populous island, measuring 18 M. in length
by 2¹/₂-6 M. in width. *Le Château-d'Oléron* (Hôt. de France) is a small fortified town with 3458 inhabitants. About 7 M. farther (diligence) is *St.
Pierre-d'Oléron*, a town of 4556 inhab., with a cemetery containing a pretty
little beacon-tower ('lanterne des morts') of the 18th century.

On quitting Rochefort our line describes a considerable curve
to regain the valley of the Charente, leaving the Poitiers line (p. 23)
to the left. — 133¹/₂ M. *Tonnay-Charente*, a small town with a
harbour on the Charente. — 136 M. *Cabariot* (branch-line to Le
Chapus, see above). — 140 M. *Bords*; 146¹/₂ M. *St. Savinien-sur-
Charente*. Farther on, to the right, on the opposite bank of the
river, are the châteaux of *Crazannes* (13-18th cent.) and *Paulou*.

151 M. **Taillebourg** *(Hôtel de France)*, a little town where St.
Louis defeated the English in 1242. By the treaty of Brétigny (1360)
it was assigned to the latter, but was recovered from them by Bertrand
du Guesclin in 1372. It is overlooked by the ruins of its *Castle*,
built on a sheer rock. We here join the line from Paris to Bordeaux
viâ Niort (p. 23).

157 M. **Saintes** *(Buffet; Hôtel des Messageries, Hôt. du Commerce*, both in the Rue des Messageries, to the left of the Cours
National), a town of 18,481 inhab., the ancient capital of the *San-
tones* and afterwards of the *Saintonge*, is prettily situated on the
left bank of the Charente. It was in great favour with the Romans
after their conquest of Gaul, and still possesses the remains of
several structures erected at that period.

Leaving the station we turn first to the left and then to the right,
and follow the Avenue Gambetta, crossing a suburb in which, within
a barrack-yard, stands the old and interesting monastic church of
Notre-Dame, dating from the 11-12th cent., but now in a dilapidated condition and no longer used for service. Over the crossing
rises a fine steeple, composed of a square tower, with three arcades
on each face, which is surmounted by a drum with twelve double
arcades, the whole ending in a conical roof with fish-scale ornamentation. The church of *St. Palais*, at the entrance to the barracks,
with its main portal concealed by a porch, dates from the 12-13th
centuries.

The town proper is entered by a stone bridge, to the left of
which is a marble statue, by F. Talhuet (1868), of *Bernard Palissy*, who was born at Saintes in 1510. The old Roman bridge,
which formerly crossed the river here, was pulled down in 1844;
and the *Triumphal Arch* which stood upon it was removed and
re-erected lower down, among the trees. The arch, erected in the
reign of Augustus in honour of Germanicus, consists of two semi-

circular archways, each 13 ft. in span, and is decorated with pilasters and engaged columns with Corinthian capitals.

On the other side of the bridge begins the Cours National, the principal street of the town. The Rue d'Alsace-Lorraine, on the left, leads to the old cathedral, the great tower of which is conspicuous. On the way to it we pass, on the right, the *Old Hôtel de Ville*, a Renaissance building with a small tower, containing the *Public Library*.

The *Church of St. Pierre*, the ancient cathedral, is supposed to have been founded by Charlemagne, but it has been twice rebuilt, and dates in its present form from the end of the 16th century. The tower, however, with the exception of the cupola at the top, is a remnant of the second building, dating from the 15th cent.; and the arms of the transept are of the 12th century. Below the tower is a fine doorway in the florid Gothic style. The nave, with its large round pillars without capitals and its flat arches, is somewhat heavy. The small cupolas of the transept also belonged to the old building.

Farther to the right is the *Hôtel de Ville*, with a small Musée of paintings (adm. on application). The concierge of the Hôtel de Ville also opens the *Musée d'Antiquités*, containing fragmentary sculptures, inscriptions, etc.

Retracing our steps to the Cours National, we continue to follow it towards the centre of the town. On a hill to the left stood a Roman building called the *Capitol* (?), which was destroyed during the wars with the English. Its site is occupied by a hospital, and nothing remains of the Roman building but some fragments of the walls. We now turn to the left into the Cours Reverseaux, which leads through the hollow with the amphitheatre (to the right; p. 32).

The *Church of St. Eutropius*, farther to the right, is of very ancient foundation, but was rebuilt in the 11th cent. and altered in the 15th, and again, like the cathedral, after the Religious Wars. The fine stone spire was also added in the 15th century. Nothing has been left of the old nave; the present one being made up of the old choir, in the Transition style, and part of the transept. The capitals of the columns and the vaulting of the aisles should be noticed. The present choir is of the 15th cent. and contains some modern statues of the Apostles under old canopies. Below the church there is a large and fine Romanesque *Crypt* of the 11th cent., consisting of a nave and aisles with three chapels, the central one of which has been rebuilt and transformed into a sacristy. This crypt is lighted by windows and is entered directly from the street. Behind its chief altar is the tomb of St. Eutropius, the first bishop of Saintes, who suffered martyrdom here in the 3rd century. It has recently been restored. The capitals in the crypt also deserve notice.

In a hollow near St. Eutrope, to the right, are the ruins of the
Roman Amphitheatre, dating from the 1st or 2nd century A. D.
They are reached by the street in a straight direction, or (better) by
a lane near the church, at the end of which we turn to the left. The
amphitheatre was oval in form, measuring 436 ft. by 354 ft., and
was capable of holding 20-22,000 spectators. There was but one
tier of arches, inclined towards the arena, and one 'præcinctio', or
lobby, with three flights of steps. Of its 74 arches nine only remain
in more or less good preservation. The services of the guide are
not needed unless the visitor wishes to inspect the interior of the
arches and galleries. A street on the other side of the hollow takes
us back to the Cours Reverseaux (p. 31).

From Saintes to *Niort*, see p. 29; to *Angoulême*, p. 12.

161 M. *Chaniers*, with a Romanesque church, visible to the
right. The train now crosses the Charente, quits its valley, and ascends that of the *Seugne*. — At (162¹/₂ M.) *Beillant* (Buffet) the line
to Angoulême diverges (p. 13). — 167 M. *Montils-Colombier*.

172 M. **Pons** *(Buffet; Hôtel St. Charles)*, a town of 4615 inhab.,
is prettily placed on a hill rising from the Seugne, ¹/₂ M. to the
right of the line. It has still some remains of ancient ramparts and
is dominated by a *Keep* of the 12th century. The adjacent *Hôtel
de Ville* was formerly the château; it dates from the 15-16th cent.
and is partly built on semicircular arches. There is also a pleasant
Jardin Public. The river banks here are very picturesque.

From Pons to Royan, 29 M., railway in 1¹/₄-3¹/₄ hrs. — From (23¹/₂ M.)
Saujon, the sixth station, a town with 3132 inhab., on the *Seudre*, a branch-
line runs to (13¹/₂ M.) *La Tremblade* (see below). — 29 M. *Royan*, see p. 58.
From Pons to La Grève *(Ronce-les-Bains)*, 38 M., railway in 2-2³/₄ hrs.
— To (23¹/₂ M.) *Saujon*, see above. — 37 M. La Tremblade *(France; Cheval
Blanc)*, a small town surrounded by salt-marshes and sand-dunes, 1³/₄ M.
from which is the sea-bathing place of *Ronce-les-Bains* (Hôt. du Grand
Chalet). — 38 M. *La Grève*, port of La Tremblade, on the Seudre, facing
Marennes (p. 29) and not far from the Straits of Maumusson (p. 30).

177¹/₂ M. *Mosnac-St. Genis*; 180 M. *Clion-sur-Seugne*.

183¹/₂ M. **Jonzac** *(Ecu)*, a town with 3431 inhab., on the Seugne,
with a castle of the 14-18th centuries. — 189 M. *Fontaine-Ozillac*;
192 M. *Tugéras-Charluzac*, in a barren sandy district. 197 M.
Montendre, a country-town situated on a hill to the right, with a
restored keep of the 12th cent.; 205 M. *Bussac*. — From (208 M.) *St.
Marlens* (Buffet) a branch-line runs to (15¹/₂ M.) Blaye (p. 59).

Beyond (210 M.) *Cavignac* the line to Coutras (p. 14) diverges
to the left. 214 M. *Gauriaguet*; 217 M. *Auble-St. Antoine*.

219 M. *St. André-de-Cubzac*, a small industrial town with a
handsome modern château.

From St. André-de-Cubzac to Blaye and St. Cibard-Lalande, 33 M.,
local railway, on the right bank of the Dordogne, then of the Gironde.
— 8 M. Bourg-sur-Gironde, an ancient little town, with quarries and
celebrated vineyards. 15 M. *Plassac* is also noted for its wine. 18¹/₂ M.
Blaye (p. 59). — The line now quits the Gironde and runs viâ *St. Martin,
St. Seurin, Eyrans-Cartelègue*, etc., all noted for wine, to (33 M.) *St.
Cibars-Lalande*.

Beyond (220 M.) **Cubzac-les-Ponts** the train traverses a viaduct, 1¹/₂ M. in length, including a *Bridge over the *Dordogne*, 620 yds. long and 72 ft. high. The piers on the banks of the river go down 95 ft. below high-water mark and 75 ft. below the river-bed. The road from Paris to Bordeaux also passes near this point, to the left, crossing the river by a splendid iron and stone bridge nearly 1 M. long, which replaces a suspension-bridge, partly destroyed by a hurricane in 1870. The Dordogne joins the Garonne a little way to the right, at the Bec d'Ambès (p. 59), and the two together form the Gironde. The tract between the Dordogne and the Garonne is known as *Entre-deux-Mers*. — 223¹/₂ M. *La Grave-d'Ambarès.*

Crossing the line from Paris to Bordeaux (p. 15) we pass (226 M.) *Carbon-Blanc* and (230 M.) *Bordeaux-Benauge* and cross the *Garonne* by the bridge mentioned on p. 15, obtaining a fine view on the right of Bordeaux and its harbour.

232 M. *Bordeaux (Gare St. Jean)*, see p. 46.

b. Viâ Challans and La Rochelle.

233 M. Railway in 10³/₄-16¹/₂ hrs. (fares same as viâ Clisson). The trains start from the *Gare d'Orléans*, but stop also at the *Gare de l'État.* Arrival at the *Gare St. Jean*, p. 46.

Nantes, see *Baedeker's Northern France.* — The train crosses several arms of the Loire. 3³/₄ M. *Pont-Rousseau;* 4¹/₂ M. *Les Landes;* 5¹/₂ M. *Bouguenais;* 9 M. *Bouaye.* To the left is the *Lac de Grand-Lieu*, in form almost oval, 5¹/₂ M. long by 3³/₄ M. wide, but very shallow, in the midst of meadows which it overflows in winter. — 13 M. *Port-St. Père.*

At (16³/₄ M.) *Ste. Pasanne* the line to Paimbœuf and Pornic diverges on the right (see *Baedeker's Northern France*). 25¹/₂ M. *Machecoul.* Near (30 M.) *Bois-de-Céné* we enter the Vendée. — 33¹/₂ M. *La Garnache.*

37 M. **Challans** *(Gautier)*, a small commercial town.

A Diligence plies from Challans to (23 M.) Noirmoutier (5¹/₂ fr.), passing (11 M.) *Beauvoir-sur-Mer*. — The flat and sandy Island of Noirmoutier, 5¹/₂ M. from Beauvoir, is separated from the mainland by a narrow channel (2 M.) which is dry at low tide. The greater part of its surface is below the level of high tides and requires to be protected by dykes, but there are some picturesque rocks at its N. end. It is 11 M. long and 4 M. wide at the widest part, and contains some fertile ground and several salt-marshes. In 1793-94 the possession of the island was vigorously disputed by the Vendeans and the Republicans, and it was here that D'Elbée, the commander-in-chief of the former, was taken and shot.

Noirmoutier (*Hôtel du Lion-d'Or*), the chief town of the island, has 6120 inhab. and a small fortress. About 1¹/₄ M. to the N.E. is the sea-bathing resort of *La Chaise*, near which are woods of pines and evergreen oaks. La Chaise is only 10 M. distant from Pornic (see *Baedeker's Northern France*), which lies opposite it, on the mainland.

A Diligence (2¹/₂ fr.) also plies from Challans to *La Barre-de-Monts* and (15¹/₂ M.) *Fromentine*, the starting-place of the steamer for (2 hrs.) the Ile d'Yeu. — The Ile d'Yeu or *Dieu*, a small fortified island, 6 M. long and 2¹/₂ M. broad, with 3428 inhab., lies 16 M. from the mainland. The coast is very rocky on the W., but easily accessible on the E., where lies the harbour of *Port-Joinville* (Hôt. Camaret). The chief town is *St. Sauveur*, in the centre of the island.

41 M. *Soullans*; 44½ M. *Commequiers*, a large village with a castle, a menhir, and two dolmens.

A branch-railway runs hence to (8 M.) *St. Gilles-sur-Vie* (Maisscot), a small seaport and bathing-place. Opposite is *Croix-de-Vie*, a small fishing port.

Our line now crosses the *Vie*. 47 M. *St. Maixent-sur-Vie*; 51 M. *Coëx*; 58 M. *Aizenay*, a town with 4170 inhabitants. Beyond (63 M.) *La Genétouze* we join the line from Nantes viâ Clisson (p. 26), and that from Tours to Les Sables-d'Olonne (R. 2).

69 M. **La Roche-sur-Yon** (p. 19). Hence to (253 M.) *Bordeaux*, see p. 27.

5. From Orléans (Paris) to Bordeaux viâ Périgueux.

313 M. RAILWAY in 14¾-19½ hrs. (fares 61 fr. 40, 46 fr. 10, 33 fr. 75 c.). — From Orléans to Bordeaux viâ Tours, see R. 1.

I. From Orléans to Limoges.

173 M. RAILWAY in 5-8¾ hrs. (fares 31 fr. 70, 21 fr. 40 c., 14 fr.). — From *Paris*, 248 M., in 7-13¾ hrs. (fares 44 fr. 90, 30 fr. 35, 19 fr. 80 c.).

Orléans, see p. 3 and *Baedeker's Northern France*. — Beyond (1¼ M.) *Les Aubrais* we quit the Paris and Bordeaux line, skirt the N. side of Orléans, and cross the Loire (good view of the town to the right). 7 M. *St. Cyr-en-Val.* — 13½ M. *La Ferté-St. Aubin*, on the right, a very ancient town of 3341 inhab., with a church of the 12th cent. and a château of the 17th century. — 19 M. *Vouzon*. — 23½ M. *La Motte-Beuvron*, on the *Beuvron* and the *Canal de la Sauldre*, possesses a château of the 16-17th cent., which has been converted into an agricultural station. Branch-line to *Blois*, see *Baedeker's Northern France*. We now enter the plateau of the *Sologne*.

The *Sologne*, which occupies an area of about 2000 sq. M., was down to 1860 a sterile and marshy region. The number of ponds in it was reckoned at 1200, and the total number of inhab. did not reach 100,000, less than 50 per sq. M. Previously it had been a flourishing and well-peopled district; its ruin dates from the Religious Wars and the Revocation of the Edict of Nantes, which caused numerous Protestant families to leave it. Government and an agricultural association for the purpose have done much to render it healthy and to restore its ancient prosperity, especially by the planting of pines on an extensive scale and by the construction of roads and canals. The population has already increased 50 per cent.

Beyond (27½ M.) *Nouan-le-Fuzelier* we cross the *Grande-Sauldre*. — 35 M. *Salbris*, a commercial and industrial town containing a church with fine stained glass. Beyond (42½ M.) *Theillay*, the train passes through a tunnel 1345 yds. long, with 34 air-shafts, and traverses the Forest of Vierzon.

49 M. **Vierzon** (*Buffet*; *Hôt. des Messageries*; *du Boeuf*), an industrial town of 10,559 inhab., situated on the *Cher* and the *Canal du Berry*.

From VIERZON TO TOURS, 70 M., railway in $2^{1}/_{2}$-$3^{1}/_{2}$ hrs. (fares 12 fr. 65, 8 fr. 55, 5 fr. 55 c.). This line (for details, see *Baedeker's Northern France*) descends the valley of the Cher. Best views to the left. — 10 M. *Menneton-sur-Cher*, with ramparts of the 13th century. — From ($15^{1}/_{2}$ M.) *Ville-franche-sur-Cher* a branch-line runs to Blois, passing (5 M.) *Romorantin* (*Lion-d'Or*), a cloth and linen manufacturing town of 7800 inhab., on the Grande Sauldre. From (26 M.) *Selles-sur-Cher* (Lion-d'Or) a diligence ($1^{3}/_{4}$ fr.) runs to *Valençay* (*Hôt. d'Espagne*), noted for its magnificent Renaissance *Château, which belonged to Prince Talleyrand, and was the place of retirement of Ferdinand VII. of Spain from 1808 to 1814. — 35 M. *St. Aignan*, a little town, $1^{1}/_{4}$ M. to the S., with a château of the 13-16th centuries. — 46 M. *Montrichard*, a small town, with a fine church of the 13th century. Beyond it, to the left, is the Château of Chenonceaux.

50 M. **Chenonceaux** (*Hôtel du Bon-Laboureur*), a village with a cele-brated *Château, in the Gothic and Renaissance styles, built on piles in the bed of the Cher. To reach the latter, we pass through the village which is $1/_{2}$ M. from the station (omnibus). Beyond the first court we reach a *Keep* of the 15th cent., where we apply for admission (open Tues. and Thurs., 2-4). The chief façade (beginning of the 16th cent.) is elabo-rately and tastefully ornamented. The most interesting parts of the interior are the *Dining Hall* and the *Chapel*, on the ground-floor, and the *Store-room* and the *Kitchen* in two large piers of the bridge. A less ancient *Bridge* supports a two-storied building of very singular appearance erected by Diana of Poitiers at a somewhat later date. The first story is fitted up as a picture gallery.

$66^{1}/_{2}$ M. *St. Pierre-des-Corps*, where we join the Orléans line. — 70 M. *Tours* (see p. 4 and *Baedeker's Northern France*).

We now leave the Bourges line (R. 35) on the left and cross the Cher and then the *Arnon*. $58^{1}/_{2}$ M. *Chéry*. Among the numerous châteaux seen on the right the most striking is that of *La Ferté-Reuilly* (17th cent.), beyond (61 M.) *Reuilly*. The line now follows the valley of the *Théols* to (87 M.) *Ste. Lizaigne*.

71 M. **Issoudun** (*Hôtel de France*), a town of 13,564 inhab., situated on a declivity to the left, and surrounded by vineyards. The town sustained several sieges by the English in the Middle Ages and one by the army of the Fronde in 1651, which have left very few of its houses standing.

Turning to the left on leaving the station and then to the right, we reach the Place du Marché, in which is the modern *Palais de Justice* and a 16th cent. *Town Gate*. A little to the left is the *Hôtel de Ville*, in the garden of which is the *Tour Blanche*, a keep of the beginning of the 12th cent., 88 ft. high. The *Musée* in the Hôtel de Ville is open daily 9-4, except Mon. and Frid.

The Rue de la République leads from the Place du Marché to *St. Cyr*, an uninteresting Gothic church with a fine large ancient stained-glass window. — *Notre-Dame-du-Sacré-Coeur*, a little farther on, is a modern and tasteless Gothic building (closed).

A branch-railway runs hence to (15 M.) *St. Florent* (p. 225) viâ the little town of ($7^{1}/_{2}$ M.) *Chârost*.

79 M. *Neuvy-Pailloux*. Before reaching Châteauroux, we cross the *Indre*. To the right are the fine towers of Déols (p. 36) and Châteauroux.

88 M. **Châteauroux** (*Hôtel Ste. Catherine*, Place du Marché; *de France*, Rue Victor-Hugo; *de la Gare*, unpretending; *Grand Café*,

Rue Victor-Hugo), the chief town of the department of the *Indre*,
with 23,924 inhab., is situated on the right bank of the Indre. It
is now a manufacturing town of some importance and has been
much improved in recent years. Its chief products are woollen stuffs
and coarse cloth.

The *CHURCH OF ST. ANDREW, a few minutes walk to the right
of the station, is a fine reproduction of 13th cent. Gothic, built in
1864-75 from the designs of Dauvergne. The W. front is flanked
by two towers with stone spires. The aisles have galleries above
them and side-chapels opening off them. The interior contains
some fine stained glass by Lobin of Tours and others; a large wrought-
iron chandelier by Larchevêque, of Mehun, near Bourges; and a
stone organ-loft.

A little farther on, to the right, is the Place Lafayette (see below)
and, to the left, the Place Gambetta with the *Theatre*. The Rue Victor-
Hugo, behind this building, leads to the Place du Marché and the
Hôtel de l'Ville, the latter containing a small *Museum*, open to
the public on Sun. from 1 to 4, and to strangers on other days also.
The entrance is on the other side.

Room I. Engravings, drawings, etc. — Room II. To the right: 46.
Molenaer, The fortune-teller; 35. *Van Goyen*, Sea-piece; 15. *Le Bourguignon*,
Cavalry-charge; 49. *Van der Poel*, Conflagration; 8. *'Velvet' Brueghel*,
Holy Family; 28. *Franck the Elder*, Scenes from the story of Esther; 10.
Bys, Sea-shore; 88. *Unknown Master*, Virgin, on a gold ground; 70. *Flemish
School*, Sea-piece; 39. *Largillière*, Portrait; 6. *Boats*, Procession; 60. *Un-
known Artist*, Descent from the Cross; 8. *'Hell-fire' Brueghel*, Temptation
of St. Anthony. — Room III. To the left: 85. *Unknown Master*, Esther.
At the end of the room is a cast of the *Tomb of St. Ludre* (original at
Déols, see below). A glass-case contains souvenirs of Napoleon I. and
his friend General Bertrand, a native of Châteauroux. In another glass-
case in the centre are some fine enamels and medals.

NOTRE-DAME, in the street that descends in front of the Hôtel
de Ville, is another handsome modern church in the Romanesque
style, with a dome surmounted by a gilt figure of the Virgin, a
tower over the W. front, and fine stained-glass windows.

Near this point is the CHÂTEAU RAOUL (Châteauroux), an edifice
of the 14-15th cent., now used as the Préfecture. It occupies the
site of an earlier castle which gave its name to the town. To see
it properly we must descend to the bank of the Indre by the Rue
de la Manufacture, passing in front of Notre-Dame.

The Rue Grande, beyond the Hôtel de Ville, leads to *St. Martial*,
an old church of little interest, and terminates at the other end of
the Place Lafayette. The latter is adjoined by the Place Ste. Hélène,
which is embellished with a *Statue of General Bertrand* (1773-
1844), in bronze, by Rude.

Déols, ³/₄ M. from Châteauroux, reached by a pleasant road beginning at the Place Lafayette, possesses the ruins of a once notorious
abbey, consisting of the fine *Tower* of the interesting Romanesque church
and some fragments of sculpture (to the right on entering the village).
Farther on, to the left, is a *Gateway* of the 15th cent., with two round
towers. Beyond this stands the *Church of St. Stephen*, the crypt of which,

to the right of the choir, contains the *Tomb of St. Ludre*, with bas-reliefs
dating from the earliest centuries of the Christian era (copy in the Châteauroux Museum, see p. 36). The church also possesses some paintings,
which, though of no intrinsic value, are interesting as giving views of
the ancient abbey.

FROM CHÂTEAUROUX TO TOURS, 73 M., railway in $2^3/_4$-$3^1/_2$ hrs. (fares
13 fr. 30, 8 fr. 80, 5 fr. 80 c.). — This line follows the valley of the Indre. —
16 M. *Buzançais*, which is to be connected by another line with Le Blanc
(p. 10). — 21 M. *Palluau-St. Genou*. The former contains a ruined château,
seen in the distance to the right; the latter, an interesting *Abbey Church*
of the 11th century. Near (28 M.) *Le Clion*, to the right, is the *Château de
l'Ile-Savary*. The Indre is then crossed several times. — 31 M. *Châtillon-
sur-Indre*, which has also a ruined castle, with a keep of the 12th century. As we approach Loches we have a fine view, to the left, of its
keep and château. To the right is the steeple of *Beaulieu* (see below).

44 M. **Loches** (*Hôtel de la Promenade*), a town with 5132 inhab., picturesquely situated on the left bank of the Indre, possesses a celebrated
castle, the ancestral home of the Plantagenets. At the entrance to the
town rises the *Tower of St. Antoine*, a fine remnant of a 16th cent.
church. Following the Rue de la Grenouillère in a straight direction,
we see on the left the *Porte Picoys*, an erection of the 15th cent., through
which we pass to the *Hôtel de Ville*, a pleasing building in the Renaissance style. Farther on, to the right, is the Rue du Château, containing
some interesting houses of the Renaissance period.

The castle, which had a fortified enceinte of about $1^1/_4$ M. in extent,
resembles a little town. The first street on the left leads to the collegiate
*CHURCH OF ST. OURS, a very interesting relic of the 12th century. The
nave consists of two square divisions, divided by a plain Gothic arch,
and each surmounted by a lofty octagonal cupola without windows. The
Romanesque W. doorway is richly moulded and sculptured, and under
the porch in front of it is a holy-water basin made out of an old altar,
also adorned with sculptures. Adjoining the church is the ROYAL PALACE,
a building of the 15-16th cent., with a fine façade, now the Sous-Préfecture. In one of the towers of the façade is the *Monument of Agnes Sorel*
(d. 1450), mistress of Charles VII., formerly in the church, and in another
part of the palace is the pretty *Oratory of Anne of Bretagne* (d. 1514),
wife of Charles VIII. and of Louis XII. — The ancient *KEEP or DONJON,
at the other end of the enceinte, is the most interesting part of the
upper town. To the left, on entering, is the *Keep* proper, a rectangular
tower of the 12th cent., 83 ft. long, 46 ft. wide, and 130 ft. high, of which
the walls alone remain. To the right of the keep is the *Martelet*, in one
of the dungeons in which Lodovico Sforza, Duke of Milan (d. 1510), was
imprisoned for nine years by Louis XII.; it contains some inscriptions
and his portrait done by himself. Still more to the right is the *Round
or New Tower*, which contained the famous iron cages in which Louis XI.
confined Cardinal de la Balue, the inventor, the historian Philip de Com-
ines, etc. — In the street below, by the side of the Indre, near the tower
of St. Antoine, stands the *Porte des Cordeliers*, of the 15th century. On the
opposite bank of the river is *Beaulieu*, with its fine Romanesque abbey-
church. — A branch-line runs hence to *Montrésor* and *Ligueil*. The former
contains a Renaissance château and a fine church of the same period.

$56^1/_2$ M. *Cormery*, with a fine spire. — 63 M. *Montbazon*, dominated
by the huge keep of a castle which dates back to the 11th century. On
the top is a modern statue of the Virgin. — $69^1/_2$ M. *Joué-lès-Tours*
(p. 16). — 73 M. *Tours* (see p. 4 and *Baedeker's Northern France*).

FROM CHÂTEAUROUX TO MONTLUÇON, 66 M., railway in 3 hrs. (fares 11 fr.
85, 7 fr. 85, 5 fr. 15 c.). — Ascending the valley of the Indre we reach
(6 M.) *Ardentes*, a little village to the right, with a partly Romanesque
church. — 15 M. *Mers;* 20 M. *Nohant*, with a château formerly inhabited by
George Sand (see p. 38).

23 M. **La Châtre** (**Hôtel St. Germain* or *Descrosses*, Rue Nationale), a
commercial and industrial town with 5048 inhab., on the left bank of the

Indre. In a square 1/2 M. from the station is a fine marble *Statue of George Sand*, the famous authoress (Baroness Dudevant, 1804-76), by A. Millet. Proceeding thence to the left, we reach the *Church*, which contains some fine modern glass and a painting by Helm. To the left, beyond the church, is a square *Tower*, a relic of the château of La Châtre, and farther on lies the fine *Promenade de l'Abbaye*, overlooking the valley.

Beyond La Châtre, on the right, we pass the *Château de la Motte-Feuilly*, which dates from the 12th century. We then quit the valley and ascend towards a plateau where chestnuts are extensively grown. — 31 M. *Champillet-Urciers*, a large station where a branch-line to (23 1/2 M.) *Laraud-Franche* (p. 228), viâ (20 M.) *Boussac*, diverges on the right. — 35 1/2 M. *Châteaumeillant*, a town with 3802 inhab., with an interesting château and church, situated in a finely wooded district. Beyond (42 M.) *Culan*, to the left, is a small lake. The train then crosses two viaducts, the second of which is very high. — 48 1/2 M. *St. Désiré*, with a noteworthy Romanesque church (to the left); 51 1/2 M. *Courçais*. Extensive view to the left. Farther on, in the valley of the Cher, we join first the Bourges, then the Guéret line. — 65 M. *Montluçon*, see p. 227.

95 1/2 M. *Luant*, in the *Brenne*, a district in parts marshy and sterile. Beyond (99 M.) *Lothiers* the train passes through some cuttings and a tunnel 2/3 M. long and crosses a viaduct, which affords a striking view of the valley of the Bouzanne, which we soon cross, and of the magnificent 15th cent. château of (104 M.) *Chabenet*.

107 1/2 M. **Argenton** (*Duffet*; *Hôtel de la Promenade*), a little town (6270 inhab.) on the *Creuse*, the *Argentomagus* of the Romans. We turn to the left on quitting the station. The Creuse is here spanned by two bridges, near the second of which are several quaint old houses. Of the castle, destroyed after the war of the Fronde, only a few scanty remains are now extant. — Branch-line to *Le Blanc* and (76 M.) *Poitiers* see p. 10.

About 1 1/4 M. to the N. is *St. Marcel*, a small town of 2570 inhab., formerly walled, with an interesting church of the Transition period. — In the pretty *Valley of the Bouzanne*, which is traversed by the road from Argenton to Châteauroux viâ St. Marcel, about 4 M. from the latter town, are several castles, some in ruins, but others still inhabited. About 1/2 M. below the road, on the right bank, is the *Castle of Rocherolles*. At the same distance above the road, also on the right bank, are the ruins of *Prunget*; 1 1/4 M. farther on, on the left bank, are those of *Mazières*, on the site of a Celtic-Roman town. Still farther on, on the right bank, are the castles of *Broutay* (2 M.) and *Plessis* (1/2 M.).

The *Valley of the Creuse*, above Argenton, also displays some fine scenery. The village of *Gargilesse* (*Hôtel Chambiant*), 7 1/2 M. from Argenton, by the right bank of the Creuse (a fine walk), possesses a Transition church, with a fine crypt, wall-paintings of the 13th cent., and a curious old tomb. Adjacent is a ruined castle. About 2 M. to the W., on the left bank of the Creuse, are the remains of the castle of *La Prune-au-Pot*.

Near (113 1/2 M.) *Célon*, to the right we see an old castle with machicolated towers. — 120 M. *Eguzon* (Hôt. de France), about 1 1/2 M. to the E. Omnibus to Crozant (see below), 6 M. to the S.E. About 3 M. to the N. is the ruined castle of *Châteaubrun*, on the right bank of the Creuse. — Station of *La Chapelle-Baloue*.

About 2 1/2 M. to the E. lies Crozant (*Hôt. du Rendez-Vous des Touristes*). On a rugged and sheer promontory, at the confluence of the *Sédelle* and

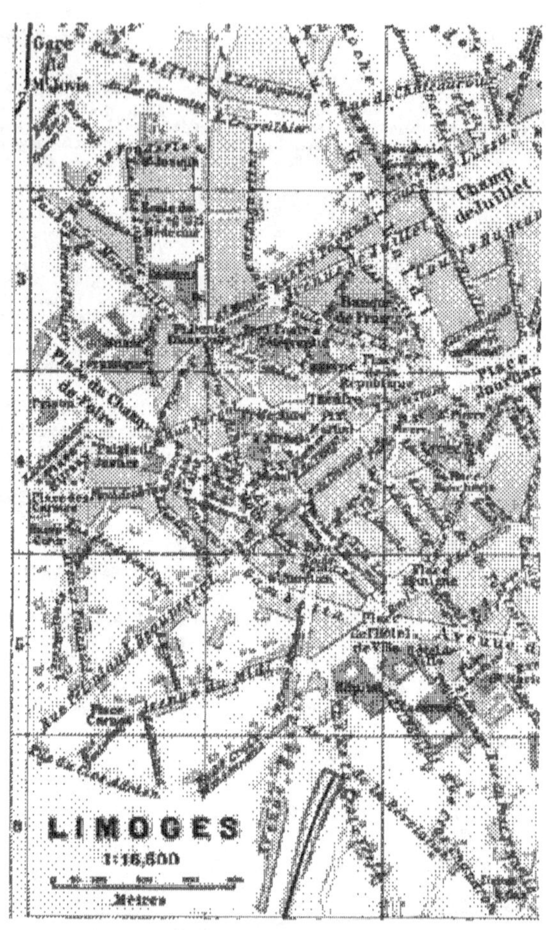

LIMOGES
1:16,600
Metres

the Creuse, stands the picturesque ruined *Castle (adm., 50 c.), a mediæval fortress the history of which is almost unknown.

From (125 M.) *St. Sébastien* (Buffet), a branch-line runs to (28½ M.) Guéret (p. 228). — 129 M. *Forgevieille.*

136½ M. **La Souterraine** (*Hôt. de France*), a town with 4770 inhab., still possessing a fortified gate of the 16th cent. and a very interesting Romanesque and Gothic church. In the cemetery is a *Lanterne des Morts*, a kind of tower in which a lamp was formerly kept burning through the night.

We next pass through a tunnel, ²/₃ M. long, piercing the granite rock which forms the groundwork of the plain extending from Argenton to Thiviers (p. 42), about 40 M. beyond Limoges.

142 M. *Fromental*, with a château. Farther on our line is joined on the right by that from Poitiers (p. 9) and crosses a viaduct, 615 ft. long and 174 ft. high, with two tiers of arches. Fine view of the valley of the *Gartempe.* — 149 M. *Bersac.* The railway skirts (on the right) the wooded hills of the *Echelles* (2250 ft.) and threads a tunnel piercing the central chain of the Limousin.

153 M. *St. Sulpice-Laurière* (Buffet), a picturesque village surrounded with mountains, ¹/₈ M. from the station. From St. Sulpice to Poitiers, see p. 9; to Guéret, Montluçon, etc., see p. 229.

Our line next passes through a tunnel, ¹/₂ M. long, into the valley of the Vienne. 157 M. *La Jonchère.* — 162 M. *Ambazac*, with 3670 inhab. and a church, in the Romanesque and Gothic styles, containing a beautiful *Shrine of St. Etienne de Muret* in gilt and enamelled copper (12th cent.) and a dalmatic (deacon's garment) given by the Empress Matilda, wife of Henry V. of Germany (d. 1125). — The train now passes through two tunnels and reaches (166 M.) *Les Bardys-St. Priest*, beyond which it crosses a viaduct 111 ft. high. — 173 M. *Limoges* (Buffet).

Limoges. — **Railway Stations.** *Gare des Bénédictins* (Pl. D, 2, 3), the central station; *Gare de Montjovis* (Pl. A, 2), for the line to Angoulême, communicating with the former.

Hotels. *GRAND-HÔTEL DE LA PAIX (Pl. a; C, 4), Place Jourdan, R., L., & A. 3-6, B. 1¼, déj. 3, D. 3½, omn. ½ fr.; RICHELIEU (Pl. b; A, 4), Place d'Aine; HOULE D'OR (Pl. c; A, 3), Boulevard Victor-Hugo; GRAND HÔT. VEYRIRAS (Pl. e; A, 3), Rue Montmailler 29-33, near the Gare de Montjovis, well spoken of, R., L., & A. 2¾-3¾, B. 1, déj. 2½, D. 3½, omn. ½ fr.; CAILLAUD, Place Jourdan, next door to the Hôtel de la Paix, R., L., & A. 2, D. 3, omn. ½ fr.

Restaurant. *Taverne du Lion-d'Or*, Place de la République. — **Cafés.** *De la Paix*, etc., in the Place de la République; *de l'Univers, de la Division*, Place Jourdan.

Cab for 1-2 pers., per drive 1 fr., per hr. 1½ fr.; for 3-4 pers. 1½ or 2 fr.; at night 1¼, 2, or 2½ fr. — **Tramways** traverse the Boulevards.

Post and Telegraph Office (Pl. B, 3), Boulevard de la Pyramide 7.

American Consular Agent: *Mr. Walter T. Griffen.*

The *Churches* are closed from midday to 2 p. m., according to a custom common in the S. of France.

Limoges, the ancient capital of the *Limousin*, now the chief town of the department of the *Haute Vienne*, the headquarters of the 4th army corps, and the seat of a bishopric, rises in the form of an amphitheatre from the right bank of the Vienne. Pop. 72,697. Although the town has been greatly improved since its fortifications were demolished in the last century, especially of late years, during which its population has more than doubled, the older quarters still contain numerous narrow, crowded, and tortuous streets, impracticable for carriages and unfavourable to health. Many old timber-built houses still exist.

At the time of the Roman conquest this town was the capital of the *Lemovices*, a powerful Gallic tribe, able to send 10,000 men to the succour of Alesia. After its incorporation with the Roman empire it had a senate and abounded in fine buildings, such as temples, theatres, palaces, public baths, etc., of which, however, scarcely any trace remains. St. Martial, the patron-saint of the Limousin, first preached the Gospel here. The town preserved a part of its importance down to the Middle Ages, but unfortunately it formed two distinct towns, often at rivalry with each other, and it suffered much during the English wars, especially in 1370, when it was taken and sacked. The Religious Wars, plague, and famine desolated it afresh in the 16th cent., and in 1630-31 it again suffered from a terrible visitation of the plague. Under the administration of *Turgot* (d. 1781) it began to revive, but a terrible fire consumed nearly 200 of its houses in 1790. Of the numerous other fires from which it has suffered the most disastrous was that of 1864.

Limoges is well known as the birthplace of the greatest masters in the art of enamelling, which seems to have flourished here as early as the 12th cent. and reached its culminating period in the second half of the 16th century. The most famous masters were *Nardon Pénicaud*, *Léonard Limousin*, *Jean* and *Pierre Courtays*, *Pierre Reymond*, and *Noël Laudin*. At the present day the porcelain of Limoges is highly prized, and the kaolin, or china-clay, prepared here, is exported to America and other countries. Admission is easily obtained to one of the numerous porcelain manufactories in the town, which employ about 5000 workmen and produce about 20 million pieces a year. Limoges has also thread and textile manufactories, large shoe and sabot-making workshops, etc.

The Gare des Bénédictins or d'Orléans (Pl. D, 2, 3) is in the lower part of the town, near the Place Jourdan and the cathedral. On the right, above it, is the *Champ-de-Juillet* (Pl. C, 2, 3), a large square, to the N. and W. of which lies an extensive modern quarter.

The *Place Jourdan* (Pl. C, 3, 4) is adorned with a bronze *Statue of Marshal Jourdan*, a native of Limoges (1762-1838), by Elias Robert. The first street to the left leads hence to the —

Cathedral of St. Etienne (Pl. D, 4), the most important and interesting building in the district, only recently completed. It occupies the site of a Romanesque church, of which the crypt (see below) still exists. The foundation dates from 1273; the choir was finished in 1327; the S. portal a little later; the N. portal and two bays of the nave in the latter half of the 15th century. The remainder of the building is partly of the 15th cent. and partly modern. To the left of the main portal, recently completed, is an octagonal *Spire* (200 ft.) rising in three stages from a square and massive lower story. It is partly Romanesque and partly Gothic in style and is surmounted with turrets. The *N. Portal* is very richly ornamented, but has no statues.

The INTERIOR presents a very imposing appearance. Beneath the organ is a magnificent *Rood Loft*, executed in 1533 and placed here in 1789. Its ornamentation, which is of the utmost delicacy, includes, curiously enough, six bas-reliefs representing the Labours of Hercules. Some of the *Stained - Glass Windows* date from the 14th cent., but have been restored in the 18th cent. and again more recently. In the choir are the interesting, though somewhat dilapidated, *Tombs* of three bishops: to the right is the tomb of Raynaud de la Porte (d. 1325); to the left those of Bernard Brun (d. 1349), and Jean de Lanjeac (d. 1541). The last has lost its bronze statue, but retains fourteen bas-reliefs representing the visions of the Apocalypse. — The *Crypt*, under the choir, is at present inaccessible. — In the *Sacristy* are some magnificent *Enamels* by Noël Laudin.

The streets to the W. of the cathedral lead to the *Hôtel de Ville* (Pl. C, 5), a fine structure in the Renaissance style, built in 1878-1881 by Alfons Leclerc. The *Museum of Painting and Sculpture* installed here is not very important though it contains some interesting antiquities. It is open to the public on Sun., 12-2; to strangers on other days also.

The Boulevard Gambetta, which ascends hence to the W., marks the limits of the ancient town. — The old *Rue de la Boucherie* (Pl. B, 4, 5) is still exclusively occupied by the butchers, whose guild was formerly very influential in the town. In front of the little church of *St. Aurélien* is a fine stone cross (15th cent.).

The church of *St. Michel* (Pl. B, 4), the spire of which, surmounted by a ball of disproportionate size, the visitor will have noticed on arriving, is of the 14 - 15th cent., with nave and aisles of equal height and width. It contains some stained-glass windows and modern paintings.

To the W. of this church in the *Place d'Aine* (Pl. A, 4) with the *Statue of Gay Lussac* (1778-1850), the chemist, erected in 1890. Here also is the *Palais de Justice*. This building and the *Place d'Orsay*, behind it, occupy the site of the Roman amphitheatre.

Adjacent, to the N., lies the extensive *Place du Champ-de-Foire*, on the other side of which stands an old hospice, containing provisionally the **Musée Céramique** (Pl. A, 3), one of the chief objects of interest in Limoges, now belonging to the State. It is open to the public on Sun. and Thurs. from noon till 4 or 5 o'clock, and to strangers on other days also. It occupies five rooms and consists mainly of a collection of porcelain and modern fayence, in which the ware of Limoges itself is represented to great advantage. — A special building is to be erected for the museum.

The adjacent *Place Denis-Dussoubs* (Pl. A, B, 3) is named in honour of a Limousin advocat, who was killed in Paris before a barricade at the coup d'état of 1851. His statue was erected here in 1892.

The Rue Turgot, to the E. of the Place du Champ-de-Foire, leads back to the Place Jourdan, passing near the *Place de la République* (Pl. B, C, 3, 4), on the S. side of which stands the *Theatre* (Pl. B, 4).

The *Church of St. Peter* (*St. Pierre*; Pl. C, 4), in the Rue Porte Tourny, to the S. of the Place de la République, dating chiefly from the 13th cent., is of irregular shape, with nave and double aisles

all of the same height. At the end it terminates in a flat wall. The
interior contains at the E. end a fine stained-glass window of the
16th cent. by Pénicaud, representing the Death and Coronation
of the Virgin (to the right), and some good modern windows by
Oudinot.

To the N. of this church, in the Rue du Collège, is the *Lycée*
(Pl. C, 4), dating substantially from the 17th and 18th centuries. The
chapel contains an Assumption ascribed to *Rubens.*

An interesting excursion may be made from Limoges to *Solignac* and
the *Castle of Chalussel*, see p. 105.

From Limoges to *Angoulême*, see p. 13; to *Le Dorat* and *Poitiers*,
see p. 9; to *Périgueux*, see below; to *Toulouse*, see R. 12.

From Limoges to Ussel (Clermont-Ferrand), 71 M., railway in $3^3/_4$-4 hrs.
(fares 12 fr. 75, 8 fr. 60, 5 fr. 60 c.). — The train starts from the Gare des
Bénédictins (p. 39) and ascends the valley of the *Vienne.* $15^1/_2$ M. *St.
Léonard* (Boule d'Or), an old industrial town of 6000 inhab., has a Romanesque church of the 11-12th centuries. — 32 M. *Eymoutiers* (Hôt. Pintou),
a busy little town on the Vienne, has a Romanesque church (Gothic choir),
with fine old stained glass. — About 3 M. to the S.W. of ($35^1/_2$ M.) *Viam*
is the *Saut de la Virole*, a very fine cascade formed by the *Vézère.* — The
railway now crosses the Vézère, and attains its highest level (3015 ft.). —
At (63 M.) *Meymac* we join the line from Tulle to Clermont-Ferrand.
71 M. *Ussel*, see p. 230.

<h2 style="text-align:center">II. From Limoges to Bordeaux viâ Périgueux.</h2>

Railway to *Périgueux*, $61^1/_2$ M. in $2-2^3/_4$ hrs. (fares 11 fr. 30, 7 fr. 55,
4 fr. 95 c.); from Périgueux to *Bordeaux*, 79 M. in $2^3/_4 \cdot 5^1/_4$ hrs. (fares
14 fr. 30, 9 fr. 60, 6 fr. 25 c.).

The line passes under the town by a tunnel 1115 yds. in length.
7 M. *Deynac;* $12^1/_2$ M. *Nexon,* a place of 3155 inhab., with a church
of the 12th and 15th and a château of the 16th century. Line to
Toulouse viâ Brive, see RR. 15, 16. — $17^1/_2$ M. *Lafarge.* Fine view
to the left. From ($23^1/_2$ M.) *Bussière-Galant* a branch-line diverges
to Saillat (p. 13). Beyond (30 M.) *La Coquille* we traverse moorland
and pass through a short tunnel.

$38^1/_2$ M. Thiviers (*Hôtel Lambert*), a small and prettily situated
commercial town (pop. 3765), with a Romanesque church of the
12th cent. and the fine Renaissance *Château de Vococour.*

Branch-line to *Angoulême* viâ *Nontron,* see p. 13. This line is being
extended to (49 M.) Brive, viâ ($12^1/_2$ M.) *Excideuil* (p. 45) and (20 M.)
Hautefort, with a château of the 16-17th centuries. — *Brive,* see p. 108.

After passing through another tunnel we reach (45 M.) *Négrondes*
and ($51^1/_2$ M.) *Agonac,* the latter with a Romanesque-Byzantine
church. — 56 M. *Château-l'Évêque,* so named from its château, a
building of the 14th cent., which was once the residence of the
bishops of Périgueux.

Tramway viâ Chancelade to *Brantôme* and *St. Pardoux,* see p. 45.

The train now crosses the *Beauronne* several times, describes
a wide curve to the left, and enters the valley of the *Isle.* The line
to Bordeaux runs to the right, crossing the Isle.

$61^1/_2$ M. Périgueux. — Hotels. Hôtel de France (Pl. a; D, 3), Place
Francheville; des Messageries, same Place (Pl. b). R., L., & A. 4-5, déj.
$2^1/_2$, D. 3, omn. $1/_2$ fr.; de l'Univers (Pl. c; D, 3), Rue de Bordeaux; de

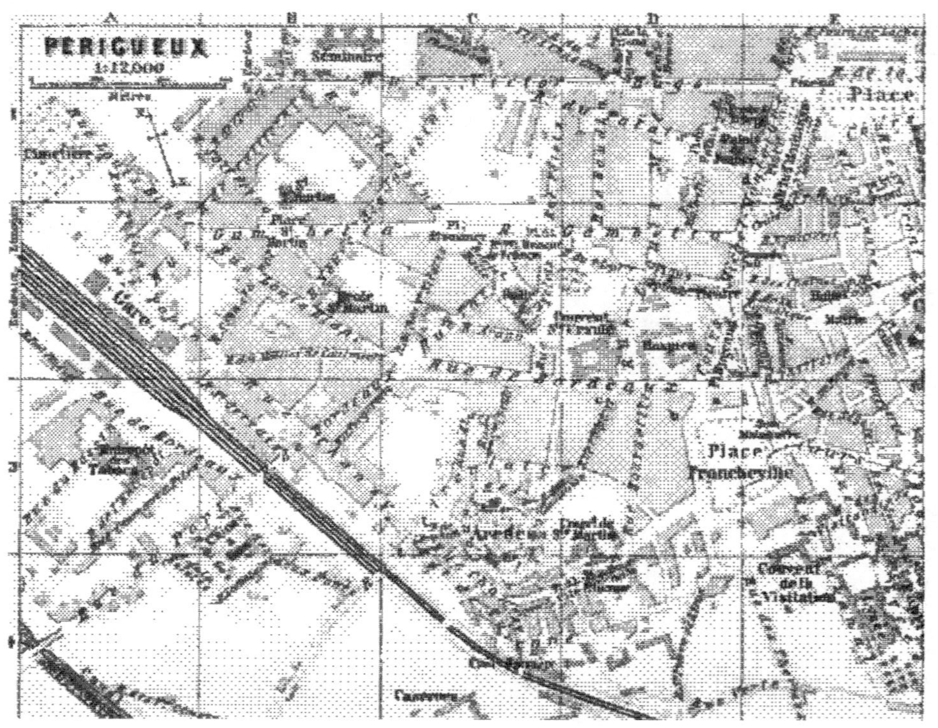

PERIGUEUX
1:12,000
Mètres
A B C D E
Séminaire
Place
Place
Francheville
Couvent
de la
Visitation

PÉRIGORD (Pl. d; E, 1), Place du Palais-de-Justice, DU COMMERCE, Place du Quatre-Septembre (Pl. D, 2). R., L., & A. 1½-2½, B. ½-¾, déj. 2½, D. 3 fr., omn. 30 c. — *Buffet.* — *Cafés* in the Place Bugeaud and Cours Michel-Montaigne. — Périgueux is noted for its pâtés of partridge and truffles ('Périgord pies').

Périgueux, the capital of the department of the *Dordogne*, is a town with 31,430 inhab., conspicuously situated on the right bank of the Isle. It is the ancient *Vesuna*, the capital of the *Petrocorii*, or rather it has taken the place of that town, which was situated farther to the S., to the left of the station. To the right, on the high ground, is the modern town, *Le Puy St. Front*, and below lies the *Cité*, or mediæval town. Under the Romans Vesuna enjoyed considerable prosperity, and it became the capital of the countship of *Périgord* in the time of Charlemagne. The English besieged it three times but did not take it till 1356. It was afterwards sacked by the Huguenots, who occupied it from 1575 to 1581.

Turning to the right at the station and following the Rue Papin, and then following to the left the Rue des Mobiles-de-Coulmiers and the Rue de Bordeaux, we reach the *Place Bugeaud* (Pl. D, 2), which is adorned with a bronze statue of *Marshal Bugeaud* (1794-1849), a native of Périgord, by Dumont. A few paces to the right is the Place Francheville (p. 44); to the left, the Cours Michel-Montaigne (p. 44). The Rue Taillefer leads in a straight direction to the old *Place Marcillac* (Pl. E, 2) and (left) to the —

Cathedral of St. Front (Pl. F, 2), an old abbey-church dedicated to the patron-saint of Périgord. The entrance is on the N. side. This church was formerly one of the most remarkable in France, but the restoration, or rather reconstruction, which has been going on since 1853 and is now nearly completed, has seriously disfigured it and deprived it of much of its interest. Thoroughly Byzantine in design, presenting the form of a Greek cross with cupolas, but having slightly pointed arches instead of round ones in the arcades below, it was looked upon as the first church in which the pointed arch had been systematically introduced. Now, however, the pointed arches have almost throughout been replaced by semicircular arches, so that St. Front resembles, still more than before, St. Mark's at Venice, with which it is contemporary (984-1047; St. Mark's, 976-1071). It does not, however, rival that church in lightness and richness of ornamentation. The interior measures 184 ft. both ways, and its five cupolas, resting on pendentives and carved square piers, are about 90 ft. in internal height. In the S. transept is the monument of Mgr. G. Massonais (d. 1860).

Adjoining the cathedral on the W. are the remains of a basilica of the 6th cent., above which rises a curious *Tower*, 197 ft. high, the oldest in France and said to be the only one extant in the Byzantine style. It dates from the beginning of the 11th cent., but has undergone some modifications. It is now being thoroughly restored, not to say reconstructed. It is composed of two square

stories (the first with pilasters, the second with columns), a circular
story surrounded by a colonnade, and, lastly, a kind of dome covered
with fish-scale ornamentation (like Notre-Dame at Saintes, p. 30).

The Rue St. Front, which leads to the right, passing in front of
the *Freemasons' Lodge*, a noteworthy modern edifice, ends to the
N. of the cathedral at the *Cours Tourny* (Pl. E, F, 1), a fine promenade planted with trees, and containing the Museum, the Préfecture,
and a statue of Fénelon.

The **Museum** (Pl. F, 1), to the right, is open to the public on
Sun. and Thurs. from 1 to 4 p. m.

GROUND-FLOOR. Room I. Roman sculptures, inscriptions, and archi-
tectonic fragments; modern sculptures. — Room II. Antique inscriptions,
vases, glass, etc.; prehistoric remains; mediæval arms; bronzes; fine
Renaissance chimney-piece. — FIRST FLOOR. Chief Room. Paintings:
111. *O. Venius*, Conception of the Virgin; 22. *Bronzino*, Portrait; 16. *P.
Bouillon*, Œdipus and Antigone; 108. *R. Fleury*, Death of Montaigne; 51.
Guet, Troops returning from the Crimea; 316. *Venetian School of the 17th
cent.*, Venus and Adonis; 104. *Rugendas*, Fox-hunting; 39. *J. L. David*,
Mars disarmed by the Graces; 106. *H. Scheffer*, Virgin and Child; 368. *J.
K. Lafon* (of Périgueux), Mary Magdalen at the Sepulchre; 32. *Daurass*.
Toledo; 69. *Labbé*, Friday on the Asiatic shores of the Bosphorus; 86.
Maratti, Nativity; 52. *Giordano*, St. Paul on the way to Damascus; 12.
Bloemaert, Landscape; 58. *Guesnet*, Roland at Roncevalles. — 135. *J. B.
Debay*, Bust of Montesquieu; 147. *Maillet*, Young huntsman (bronze). —
The glass-cases contain enamels (78. *Laudin*; 84. *Nouailher*) and small.
works of art. — 130. Bust of Attila, an Italian work of the 16th cent.;
335. Portrait of Brantôme (p. 45). — The Cabinet contains engravings,
drawings, porcelain, and a few paintings: 24. *Carpaccio*, Arrival and
Adoration of the Magi (sketch); 83. *Fil. Lippi*, Virgin and Child; 54. *Giotto*,
Virgin and Child, with saints.

Farther on, at the end of the Cours Tourny, we obtain a fine
view of the valley of the Isle. To the left rises the *Préfecture*, a
modern building in the Italian style. At the opposite end of the
Cours is a bronze *Statue of Fénelon*, a native of Périgord (1651-
1715), by Lanno (1840).

To the left lies the **Cours Michel-Montaigne** (Pl. D, E, 1, 2),
which extends from this point to the Place Bugeaud (p. 39) and is
the most animated part of the town. It is embellished with statues
of two other illustrious natives of Périgord: *Montaigne*, the
essayist (1533-92), also in bronze by Lanno, and *General Daumesnil*
(1776-1832), in bronze after Rochet.

Returning to the Place Bugeaud, we descend to the left to the
Place Francheville (Pl. D, E, 3), near which, on the left, rises the
Tour Mataguerre (Pl. E, 3), a relic of the 15th cent. fortifications.

The street on the other side of the Place Francheville leads to the
church of **St. Étienne** (Pl. D, 4), in the Cité. This church, which
was the cathedral until 1669, is of almost the same period as St.
Front and resembles it in style, but it has now only two cupolas.
In the interior is a carved oak reredos, 30 ft. high and 36 ft. wide,
executed by a Jesuit in the 18th cent. and representing the Assumption. The pulpit and the frescoes by M. Brucker deserve notice.

The street to the right, in front of the church, leads to the N.W. to the ruins of the **Amphitheatre** (Pl. C, 3), a Celtic-Roman erection of the 3rd cent., the only remains of which are a few arches and fragments of walls, in the middle of a square. The amphitheatre was about 440 yds. in external, and 290 yds. in internal circumference.

The street running to the S. from the Amphitheatre crosses the railway by a bridge, whence there is a view of the *Château Barrière* (Pl. C, 4), dating from the 10-12th cent., and built on the Roman fortifications, of which two towers still remain. It was burned by the Protestants in 1575. The entrance is on the other side. Beyond this bridge is the *Tour Vésone* (Pl. D, 4), another relic of the Roman period. This is a cylindrical building, open on one side, which is supposed to have been the *cella* of a temple.

From Périgueux to *Agen* and *Tarbes*, sec R. 14; to *Brive*, *Tulle*, *Clermont-Ferrand*, etc., see p. 105, and R. 36 B. — *Grotte de Miremont*, see p. 101.

From Périgueux to Ribérac, 23 M., railway in 1-1¹/₂ hr. (fares 4 fr. 15, 3 fr. 80, 1 fr. 80 c.). — 12¹/₂ M. *Lisle*, 5 M. to the N.E. of which, in the valley of the Dronne, is *Bourdeilles*, which has a curious castle of the 14th and 16th cent., with a keep 130 ft. high. — The line then follows the valley of the Dronne. 14¹/₄ M. *Tocane-St. Apre*, 3 M. to the N. of which is *Le Grand-Brassac*, boasting of a Romanesque-Byzantine church of the 13-14th cent. with cupolas and very remarkable sculptures in excellent preservation. — 18 M. *St. Méard.* — 23 M. *Ribérac* (p. 13).

From Périgueux to St. Pardoux (*Nontron*), 33 M., steam-tramway, starting from the Place Francheville (Pl. D, E, 3). — 4¹/₂ M. *Chancelade*, with an old abbey-church. — 7 M. *Château-l'Evêque* (p. 42). — 20¹/₂ M. Brantôme (*Hôtel Chabrol*), a town of 2422 inhab., prettily situated on the *Dronne.* It possesses the interesting remains of an old Benedictine abbey, dating from the days of Charlemagne, and once owned by the chronicler Pierre de Bourdeilles (1527-1614), who assumed its name. The Romanesque *Tower*, standing on a sheer rock honeycombed with caverns, is one of the oldest in France. The *Church* is partly Romanesque and partly Gothic. Adjoining are portions of the 16th cent. *Cloister.* The abbey itself was rebuilt in the 18th century. — Bourdeilles (see above) lies 5 M. to the S.W. The château of *Richemont*, 5 M. to the N.W., was built and inhabited by Brantôme. — 33 M. *St. Pardoux*, on the line from Angoulême and Nontron to Thiviers (p. 42).

From Périgueux to St. Yrieix, 46¹/₂ M., steam-tramway from the Place Francheville. The chief station on this interesting route is (22¹/₂ M.) *Excideuil* (p. 42), with a château of the Talleyrand-Périgord family (13-16th cent.). — 46¹/₂ M. *St. Yrieix*, see p. 108.

The Bordeaux line now follows the valley of the Isle as far as its confluence with the *Dordogne*, crossing the river several times. Many picturesque castles are seen on the banks. 67¹/₂ M. *Razac*, in a hilly district. — 72 M. *St. Astier*, with a domed church of the 11-12th cent., afterwards rebuilt. — 77 M. *Neuvic*, with a château of the 16th century. From (83 M.) *Mussidan* a branch-line runs to (20 M.) Bergerac (p. 14). — 88 M. *Beaupouyet*; 93 M. *Montpont*. About 3 M. to the N. of the last is the Carthusian convent of *Vauclaire*, dating from the 14th cent. and lately restored. — 98 M. *Souble.* Beyond (104 M.) *St. Médard*, we join the line from Paris to Bordeaux.

108 M. *Coutras*, and thence to (139 M.) *Bordeaux*, see p. 14.

6. Bordeaux.

Railway Stations. Bordeaux has three railway stations: (1) *Gare de Paris* or *de la Bastide* (Pl. E, 4, 5), the central station, on the right bank of the Garonne, facing the town; (2) *Gare du Midi et de l'État* or *de St. Jean* (Pl. E, 7; buffet), to the S., on the left bank of the Garonne, 1½ M. from the centre of the town, communicating with the Gare de Paris (see p. 3); (3) *Gare du Médoc* (Pl. D, 1) at the N. end, for the line of that name and for trains to Lacanau (R. 7). — The *Gare de la Sauve* (Pl. F, 6) is no longer used for passenger-traffic. There are no hotel-omnibuses, but the trains are met by railway-omnibuses and cabs (see below).

Hotels. HÔTEL DES PRINCES ET DE LA PAIX, Cours du Chapeau-Rouge 40, near the Grand Theatre (Pl. C, 4); DE FRANCE ET DE NANTES, Rue Esprit-des-Lois 11, close to the Bank (Pl. C, 4), R. (3rd floor) 3, L. ½, A. 1, déj. 5, D. 6 fr.; *RICHELIEU, Cours de l'Intendance 4, near the Place de la Comédie (Pl. C, 4), R. from 3, déj. 3, D. 3½, served separately, 4 and 5 fr.; DES AMBASSADEURS, Cours de l'Intendance 14 (Pl. B, C, 4), similar charges; MÉTROPOLE, Rue Condé and Rue Esprit-des-Lois, near the Theatre, R. 3-15, L. & A. 1½-2, B. 1½-2, déj. 4, D. 5 fr. (or à la carte), pens. 12-15 fr.; DE BAYONNE, Rue Martignac 4, near Notre Dame (Pl. C, 4); no table-d'hôte; DE NICE, Place du Chapelet 4, refitted; DES AMÉRICAINS (commercial), Rue Condé 8, déj. 3, D. 3½ fr.; DES QUATRE-SŒURS, Cours du Trente-Juillet 6, restaurant à la carte; LANTA, Rue Montesquieu, 6, near the Marché des Grands-Hommes (Pl. C, 4; restaurant, dear); DE TOULOUSE, Rue Vital-Carles 6-8, and Rue du Temple 7; GR. HÔT. CENTRAL, GR. HÔT. & RESTAURANT FRANÇAIS, Rue du Temple 8 and 12 (Pl. C, 5); NICOLET, Rue du Pont de la Mousque 10 (Pl. C, 4, 5), R., L., & A. 2½ fr., good restaurant; D'AQUITAINE & DE LA GIRONDE, Place St. Remi and Rue du Pont de la Mousque; MONTRÉ, Rue Montesquieu 4, NORMANDIE, Rue Gobineau and Cours du Trente-Juillet, DELARC, Rue de Grassi 18 (Pl. C, 5), these three hôtels meublés; DU PÉRIGORD, D'ORLÉANS, third-class houses, in the Rue Nautres. — HÔTEL DU PRINTEMPS, R. 2 fr.; DU FAISAN (R., L., & A. 2½-5½, déj. 2, D. 3 fr.), Rue de la Gare, and the other hotels near the Gare du Midi are all 3rd class houses.

Restaurants. At most of the hotels; *Chapon-Fin*, Rue Montesquieu 7, déj. 2½, D. 3 fr. (also à la carte); *Comédie*, at the Grand Theatre, déj. 4, D. 5 fr.; *de Paris*, Allées de Tourny 26; *de Tourny*, same street No. 16; *Café Bibent*, same street, No. 1; at these three déj. 2½, D. 3 fr.; *Parisien*, Rue Mably 7 (Pl. C, 4), déj. 1½ fr.

Cafés. *Café de Bordeaux*, Place de la Comédie 9; *Café de la Comédie*, in the Grand Theatre; *Grande Taverne Anglaise*, etc., on the E. side of the Allées de Tourny; *Café de l'Opéra*, Cours du Chapeau-Rouge 50; *Cardinal*, *Tortoni*, *Montesquieu*, Cours du Trente-Juillet 2, 8, and 12; *Bibent*, Allées de Tourny 1; *Turc*, Place Gabriel, at the Exchange. — There are several *Brasseries* (beer-houses) in the Allées de Tourny.

Cabs.	From 6 a. m. to midnight.			From midnight to 6 a. m.		
Voit. de Place.	Drive	1st hour	Each addit. hour	Drive	1st hour	Each addit. hour
One-horse . . . . *Voit. sous Remise.*	1 fr. 75	1 fr. 75	1 fr. 50	2 fr. 25	2 fr. 25	1 fr. 75
One-horse (coupé)	2 : —	2 : —	1 : 75	3 : —	3 : —	2 : 25
" (fiacre)	2 : —	2 : —	1 : 75	3 : —	3 : —	2 : 50
Two-horse (closed)	2 : —	2 : —	1 : 75	3 : —	3 : —	2 : 50
" (open) .	3 : —	3 : —	2 : 50	4 : —	4 : —	3 : —

In hiring by time the first hour must be paid for in full, after which the time may be reckoned by spaces of ¼ hr. — *Luggage*: 50 c. for 1 or 2 packages, then 25 c. per package. — Outside the barrier the charges are somewhat higher. — *Per Day* (12 hrs.), 15, 20, and 25 fr. according to the carriage.

Tramways and Omnibuses. There are eight lines of tramway (see Plan) and five lines of omnibuses with 'correspondances' as in Paris. Fares inside

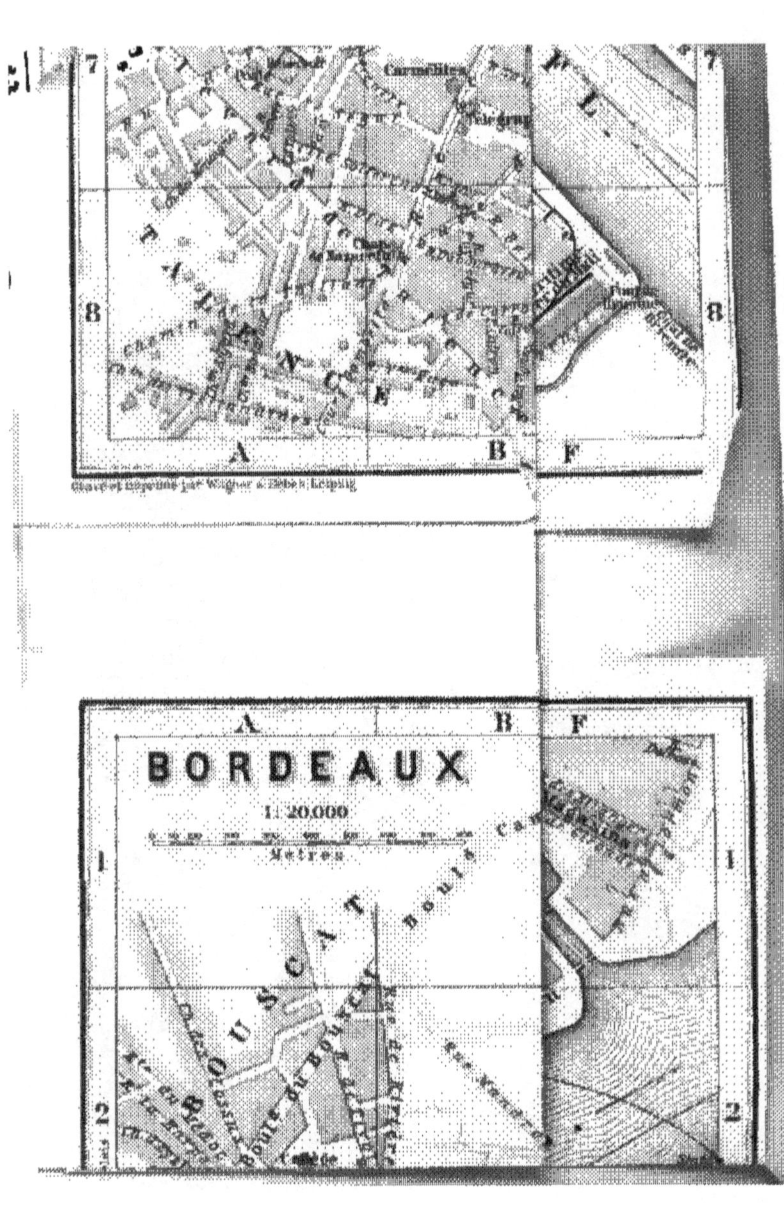
BORDEAUX
1:20.000
Mètres

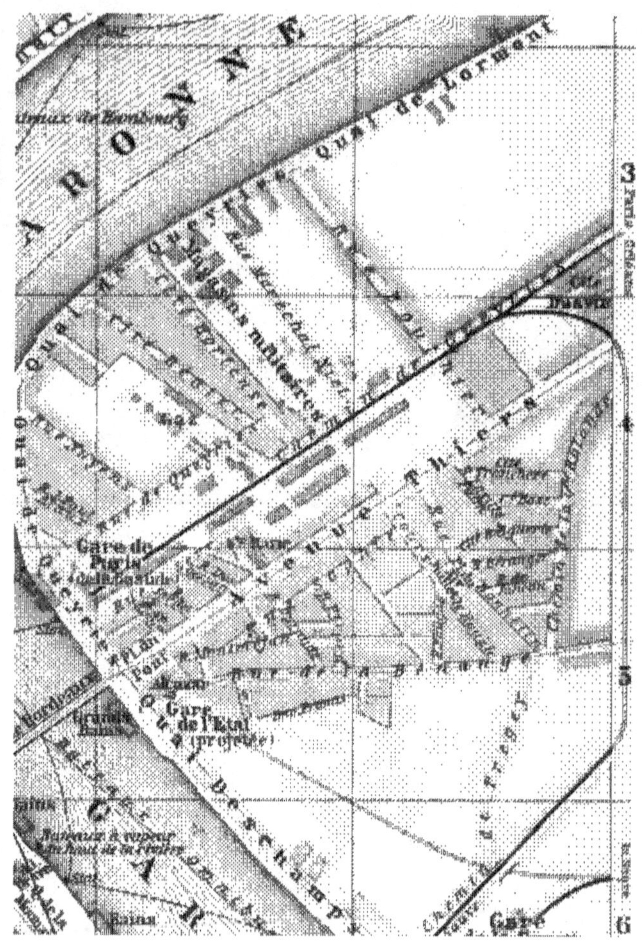

GARONNE
Quai de Lormont
Quai
Rue Maréchal Niel
Avenue Thiers
Gare de Paris
(de la nature)
Gare de l'État
(projetée)
Quai Deschamps
Gare
Bateaux à vapeur
Bordeaux
3
4
5
6

20 c., outside 15 c. (including correspondance); return, 30 c., 25 c. — Tramways (managed by a British company). 1. *From the Boulevard Jean-Jacques-Boscq* (to the S. E. of Pl. F, 8) or *Footbridge* (Pl. E, 7) to the *Rue Lucien-Faure* (Pl. F, 1). — 2. From the *Place Magenta* (Pl. B, 6) to the *Bastide* (Pl. F, 4). — 3. From the *Gare du Midi* (Pl. E, 7) to the *Gare du Médoc* (Pl. D, 1) or *Rue Lucien-Faure.* — 4. From the *Place de Bourgogne* (Pl. D, 5) to the *Boulevard du Tondu* (to the W. of Pl. A, 6). — 5. From the *Place Richelieu* (Pl. C, D, 4) to the *Boulevard du Bouscat* or *de Caudéran* (Pl. A, 2), viâ the Allées du Tourny. — 6. From the *Place Richelieu* to the *Boulevard de Caudéran*, viâ the Rue Judaïque (Pl. A, B, 4) or Rue de la Croix-Blanche (Pl. A, 4). — 7. From the *Place Richelieu* or *Croix de St. Genès* to the *Boulevard de Talence* (Pl. B, 8), viâ the Rue de St. Genès (Pl. B, 6-8) or Rue de Pessac (Pl. B, 6, 7). — 8. From the *Place d'Aquitaine* (Pl. C, 6) to the *Boulevard de Talence* (Pl. B, 8), viâ the Route de Toulouse (Pl. C, 7, 8), or viâ the Route de Bayonne (Pl. B, C, 7, 8) — Omnibuses. 1. From the *Rue Lucien-Faure* (Pl. F, 1) to the *Passage Lormont* (to the N. E. of Pl. F, 1). — 2. From the *Quai des Chartrons* (Pl. D, 2, 3) to the *Cours d'Albret et d'Aquitaine* (Pl. B, 6). — 3. From the *Place de la Comédie* (Pl. C, 4) to the *Place Nansouty* and *Boulevard de Bègles* (Pl. C, 8). — 4. From the *Place de la Bourse* (Pl. C, D, 5) to the *Boulevard du Tondu et de Caudéran* (Pl. A, 3-5). — There are other omnibus services in the environs.

Railway Omnibuses. These ply from the following offices in the town. For the *Gare de Paris*: Rue Gobineau 2, at the Allées de Tourny (starting 3/4 hr. before the departure of the train). For the *Gare du Midi*: Cours du Trente-Juillet 18 (starting 35 min. before the departure of the train). For the *Gare du Médoc*: Rue Gobineau 2. Fare from the office 25-30 c., from a private house 50 c.; each article of luggage 20 c.

Steamers. *Hirondelles*, *Gondoles*, and *Abeilles* ply in the harbour and to places in the immediate vicinity. Larger steamers run to Castets, La Réole, Agen, and other places above the town, and to Pauillac, Royan, etc., below (see p. 58). Ferry to La Bastide every 5 min. (10 c.). — For the steamers of the *Messageries Maritimes*, of the *Pacific Steam Navigation Company*, and of the *Compagnie Générale Transatlantique* (South America, etc.), see the Indicateur or the Livret Chaix.

Commissionaires. Per 1/2 hr., with a letter, 25 c.; per hr., with a parcel of any weight 50 c., or 60 c. if a barrow is required.

Post & Telegraph Office, Rue du Palais Gallien 7-13 (Pl. B, 4), near the Place Gambetta; several sub-offices. — *Telephone* to Paris, 5 min.'s use 3 1/2 fr. by day, 2 fr. 10 c. at night.

Theatres. *Grand Théâtre* (Pl. C, 4), for operas (prices 1-5 fr.); *Théâtre Français* (Pl. B, C, 4); *Des Arts* (Pl. B, 4, 5; 1/2-4 fr.), Rue Castelnau-d'Auros 1-7; *Casino des Lilas*, Boul. de Caudéran. — *Cirque Bordelais*, Quai de la Grave, above the stone bridge; *Hippodrome*, Boul. de Caudéran. — Bands play in the *Jardin Public* (p. 51), *Parc Bordelais* (p. 56), etc.

Baths. *Hot Baths*, Allées de la Place des Quinconces (1 1/4 fr.); *Cold Baths*, Ecoles de Natation, above the Pont de Bordeaux, etc. *Hydropathic Establishment*, Place Longchamp 4 (Pl. B, 3; from 60 c.).

Consulates. British Consul, *Mr. William Ward*, Cours de Gourgues 9; Viceconsul, *Mr. W. J. Norcop*. — American Consul, *Mr. John M. Wiley.*

English Church, Cours du Pavé-des-Chartrons (Pl. C, 3); Chaplain, Rev. *J. W. L. Burke.* — *French Protestant Churches*, Rue du Hâ 52 (Pl. C, 5), Rue Notre-Dame (Pl. D, 3), Rue Barennes 19 (Pl. B, C, 3), and Impasse St. Jean (Pl. D, 7). — *German Protestant Church*, Rue Tourat 31 (Pl. C, 3).

Bordeaux, the ancient capital of *Guyenne*, the chief town of the department of the *Gironde*, the headquarters of the 18th army corps, and the seat of a bishopric and a university (5 faculties), is a town with 252,415 inhab., situated on the left bank of the *Garonne*, 16 M. from the Bec d'Ambès at the confluence of this river with the Dordogne (p. 59), and 60 M. from its mouth on the Atlantic.

It is the fourth largest town in France and also one of the leading
towns in the republic in virtue of its commerce (p. 49), its splendid site, and its imposing appearance. The Garonne furnishes it
with an excellent harbour and with a safe and convenient water-
way to the ocean.

Burdigala, the capital of the *Bituriges Vivisci*, was one of the chief
cities of Gaul in the Roman period. It became the capital of *Aquitania
Secunda*, endured the devastations and the yoke of the Vandals, Visigoths,
Franks, and Normans, and became part of the Duchy of Aquitaine or
Guienne, which passed to England on the marriage of Eleanor to Henry
Plantagenet (see p. 6). More fortunate than other towns of the province, it
suffered little from the wars for supremacy between France and England,
and it became loyally attached to its new masters, who did much to
encourage its commerce, and retained it in their hands for 300 years (down
to 1453). The imposition of the salt-tax, under Henri II., caused a
serious insurrection here, for which the town was cruelly punished by
the Constable de Montmorency in 1548. Contests also arose between the
Catholics and Protestants of Bordeaux, and 264 of the latter were massacred after St. Bartholomew's Day. The district was again disturbed
by dissensions under Louis XIV., who regarded the town with particular
favour. From the reigns of Louis XV. and Louis XVI., when Bordeaux
had for its governor the Marquis of Tourny, date its principal embellish-
ment and the construction of its spacious thoroughfares. The ambition
of its 'Parlement' was easily repressed; but it did not so easily escape
the consequences of revolting against the Convention after the proscription
of the Girondins, at the head of whom were Vergniaud, Guadet, Gen-
sonné, Grangeneuve, Ducos, and Fonfrède, the deputies of the department. The town could not reconcile itself to the rule of Napoleon, who
ruined its commerce, but its attachment to the Bourbons was also luke-
warm. In 1870-71 it was for three months the seat of the Provisional
Government, and then of the National Assembly, which here accepted the
preliminaries of peace with Germany.

The traveller who reaches Bordeaux by the Paris line, quitting
the train at the Gare de la Bastide, at once gains an idea of the
imposing character of the town, as he enters it by the *Pont de
Bordeaux* (Pl. D, 5). This bridge was for a long time without a rival
and it is still one of the most remarkable in the world. An attempt
made in 1810 to build a bridge of timber was abandoned, and the
present permanent one of stone and brick was erected (1819-21) by
the engineers Deschamps and Billaudel. It is 532 yds. long and
16 yds. wide, and has 17 arches, the central and widest of which
have a span of 87 feet. Inside, between the arches and the roadway,
are passages, which lighten the structure and facilitate its being
kept in a proper state of repair without interruption to the traffic.
The interior may be visited (9-11 and 1-5) by applying to the custodian, who lives at the Bastide end of the bridge. The bridge commands a splendid *View* of the town and harbour. Higher up the
river we see the *Railway Tubular Bridge*, which is 546 yds. long
and is connected with a viaduct 110 yds. in length. The railway
bridge also has a passage for pedestrians. Near it, on the left bank
of the river, is the *Gare du Midi*.

The **Harbour** is one of the chief attractions of Bordeaux. The
Garonne here describes an almost complete semicircle, the arc of

which measures $3^1/_2$ M. and the radius about 2 M. Along this crescent stretches the town, which is in the shape of a half-moon and is barely $1^1/_2$ M. across at its widest part. Although Bordeaux is 60 M. from the mouth of the Gironde, the tide comes quite up to it and vessels of 2000 or 2500 tons easily reach the port. The ordinary depth of the river here is 20 ft., and this is sometimes doubled at spring-tides. From 1000 to 1200 ships can anchor in the harbour; and a vast floating basin, 25 acres in extent, has lately been constructed lower down, at the end of the quays, for the accommodation of the largest vessels, of which it can hold seventy or eighty. Spacious quays, dating, like most of the adjoining buildings, from the end of the 18th cent., extend from one end of the harbour to the other. Bordeaux, which now ranks as the third seaport of France, has regular communications with most of the ports of the Atlantic, the English Channel, the North Sea, and the Baltic, with N. and S. America, with Africa, and with India, and its shipping amounts annually to nearly 2 millions of tons. Its commerce is chiefly in wines, colonial produce, metals, English coal, timber from N. Europe, vinegar, grain, brandy, and manufactured products. It is at the same time an industrial town, and has a large number of dockyards and establishments for the supply of everything connected with shipping.

The *Cours Victor-Hugo* (Pl. C, D, 5, 6; see p. 54), which forms a continuation of the Pont de Bordeaux and bends to the right towards the cathedral, marks the limits of the old town, which in the other direction (down stream) did not extend beyond the Place des Quinconces (see below). The *Porte de Bourgogne*, at the beginning of the Cours, was erected in 1751-55, but altered in 1807. From the Quai de Bourgogne, the first below the bridge, the *Cours d'Alsace-Lorraine* (Pl. C, D, 6), a wide and handsome new street, leads to the W. direct to the cathedral. Farther along the quay, to the left, is the PORTE DE CAILHAU, called also *Porte Royale* or *Porte du Palais* (Pl. D, 5), the ancient gateway of the Palais de l'Ombrière, pulled down in 1800, once the residence of the Dukes of Aquitaine, and afterwards the seat of the governors of the district and of the Parlement of Bordeaux. It is a fine Gothic structure flanked by two round towers dating from 1495.

The Quai de Bourgogne is adjoined by the Quai de la Douane, with the *Hôtel de la Douane*, or *Custom House* (Pl. C, D, 5), built by Jacques Gabriel at the end of the 18th cent., under the Marquis de Tourny. Adjacent is the *Place de la Bourse*, adorned with the fine bronze *Fontaine des Trois Grâces*, executed by Gumery, after Visconti. The *Hôtel de la Bourse* or *Exchange* (Pl. C, 4, 5), which is a counterpart of the Hôtel de la Douane, built at the same time and by the same architect, has lately been restored, and the N. façade in the Place Richelieu, and the W. façade, towards the Cours du Chapeau-Rouge (see below), are new. The old allegorical sculp-

tures on the pediments of the Bourse are due to Franclu, the new
to Coueffard (Place Richelieu) and to Jouandot.

A little farther on is the **Place des Quinconces** (Pl. C, 4), the
largest in Bordeaux, occupying the site of the Château Trompette
(Tropeyte), built at the same time as the Fort du Hâ (p. 55), by
Charles VII., after the submission of Bordeaux in 1453, to ensure
the obedience of the town. This château was destroyed in 1789.
The Place is 425 yds. long and 360 yds. wide, without reckoning
the semicircle with a fountain, which forms an addition to it on
the side opposite the quay. On the side next the river are two
Rostral Columns, 65 ft. high, surmounted by statues of Commerce
and Navigation, by Manceau, and serving also as lighthouses. To
the right and left of these are two *Bathing Establishments*. Nearer
the middle of the square, among the trees, are colossal marble statues of *Montaigne* (d. 1592; to the S.) and *Montesquieu* (d. 1755;
to the N.), two celebrities of the province, by Maggesi (1858).

In the centre of the place a *Monument to the Girondins* (p. 48),
by Dumilâtre and Riche, is to be unveiled in 1895. The design
includes a column surmounted by a gilded bronze statue of Liberty
and surrounded by groups of the leading Girondins; and two foun-
tains with figures of Concord and the Republic seated in cars drawn
by sea-horses.

The Rue Foy leads to the N. from the Place des Quinconces, passing
the vast warehouses of the *Entrepôt Réel*, to the church of *St. Louis*
(Pl. C, 3), a fine modern Gothic edifice in the style of the 13th cent., with
stone spires, and an elegant porch.

The Cours du Trente-Juillet, which runs along the W. side of
the Quinconces, ends on the N. at the Jardin Public (p. 51) and
on the S. at the Allées de Tourny (see below) and the **Place de la
Comédie** (Pl. C, 4). The last, which owes its name to the neighbouring theatre, is the busiest point in the town, of which it may be
called the centre. To the E. runs the handsome Rue Esprit-des-
Lois, and to the S. is the busy but narrow and crowded *Rue Ste.
Catherine*. The S. side of the Place de la Comédie also joins the
main line of thoroughfare which intersects the town from E. to W.,
beginning at the Quai de la Bourse with the *Cours du Chapeau-
Rouge*, which is continued towards the W. by the *Cours de l'Intendance* and the *Rue Judaïque*.

The **Grand-Théâtre** (Pl. C, 4), to the S. of the Place de la Comédie, built in 1755-80 by Victor Louis, but lately restored, has long
ranked as one of the finest theatres in Europe. It is in the classical style and is 290 ft. long, 154 ft. broad, and 82 ft. high. In front
is a portico of twelve Corinthian columns, above which is a balustrade with twelve colossal statues. At the sides are spacious
colonnades. The most noticeable features of the interior are the
vestibule, with its sixteen Ionic columns; the grand staircase,
which ascends in two flights; and the circular auditorium, which
is embellished with twelve composite columns. Above the vesti-

bule is a concert-hall. — It was in this theatre that the sittings of
the National Assembly were held in 1871.

Behind the theatre is the *Préfecture* (Pl. C, 4), also built by
Louis, in 1775, for the 'Avocat Général' of the Bordeaux Parlement. The façade, towards the Cours du Chapeau-Rouge, was restored in 1873.

The *Allées de Tourny* (Pl. C, 4), an oblong 'Place', formerly
embellished with trees, now offer one of the most bustling scenes
in Bordeaux. Most of the cafés (p. 46) are situated here. At each
end is a monumental fountain. In the middle formerly stood a
bronze statue of Napoleon III., by Debay, on the pedestal of which
might be read the words from his famous Bordeaux speech (1852):
'L'Empire, c'est la paix'; but this was removed in 1870.

A little to the left is the church of *Notre-Dame* (Pl. C, 4), founded in the 13th cent., rebuilt in 1701 in the style of the period, and
restored in 1834. The internal decorations are elegant and luxurious. We note especially some paintings by Romain Cazes, the
chief of which is a large fresco representing the Madonna enthroned
(1874).

To the right of the church, in the Rue Mably, is the new *Public
Library*, open daily, except holidays, 11-4 and 8-10 in winter,
11-5 in summer; during the vacation (Sept. and Oct.) on Wed.
only, 11-4. The library comprizes upwards of 150,000 volumes and
250 MSS. The chief curiosity is a copy of the 'Essays' of Montaigne,
covered with annotations in the handwriting of the author. There
is here also a *Collection of Arms and Antiquities* (open on Sun. and
Thurs. from 11 to 4 or 5). — Behind the library is the *Marché des
Grands-Hommes*, a circular market-hall of iron and glass.

On the N.W. the Allées de Tourny end in a small circular Place
with a *Statue of Tourny*, of no artistic merit, erected in 1825.
To the left diverges the Cours de Tourny, leading to the Place
Gambetta; to the right is the Cours du Jardin-Public.

The **Jardin Public** (Pl. B, C, 3), which was originally laid out
by the Marquis de Tourny, but completely transformed in 1859, is
the finest promenade in Bordeaux. It consists of two parts: an
English Park, with a large number of splendid magnolias and other
exotics, and a well-stocked *Botanical Garden*, with large conser-
vatories. A grove of China palms (Chamærops excelsa) flourishes
here in the open air. The park is much frequented on Sun. and
Thurs., when a military band plays here at 8 p. m. in summer and
2.30 p. m. in winter. — On the S.W. side of the garden, and with
a direct entrance from it, is the *Museum*, open on Sun. and Thurs.,
11-5 in summer, and 11-4 in winter, and to strangers on other days
also. It comprises natural history, ethnographical, and prehistoric
collections; the first being much the largest.

Leaving the Jardin Public by the gate at the S.W. corner, beyond
the Museum, and taking the Rue du Colisée, the fourth cross-

street to the right, we see in front of us the main part of the ruins
of the **Amphitheatre** (Pl. B, 3), generally called the *Palais Gallien*
because the Emperor Gallienus (d. 268) is supposed to have erected
it. The arena proper was oval in form and measured 84 yds. by
60 yds., while the whole structure was 144-149 yds. long and 114-
124 yds. wide. A great part of the building was still standing in
1792. The four arches under which the street passes formed the W.
entrance. The ruins at this point are still over 60 ft. in height.

From the amphitheatre we may proceed to the S. to the old
cathedral of **St. Seurin** (Pl. B, 4), built in the 11th cent. on the site
of a much more ancient church. Parts of the building, however,
are not later than the 13-15th cent., and a few additions have been
made more recently still. The W. façade, which is surmounted by
a spire, is of the 11th cent., but it was masked in 1829 by a poor
porch. On the S. side is an interesting *Doorway of the 13th cent.,
with a Renaissance porch in front of it. The principal subject of
the sculptures, which have been restored, is the Last Judgment.

The Interior is very low and dark. The roof is borne partly by enormous
round pillars, and partly by pillars grouped with half-columns. The church
is throughout embellished with fine modern stained-glass windows. To the
left, in front of the choir, is a large new Gothic chapel, near which is
a chapel of the 13th cent., with graceful arches and a handsome altar.
The choir contains an elaborate episcopal throne in the Flamboyant style.
On an altar in front of the throne is an ancient alabaster altar-screen,
part of which is in the Chapel of the Virgin. Its sculptures, comprising
about 40 groups, represent the Crucifixion and scenes from the life of St.
Seurin, Bishop of Bordeaux in the 5th century. Under the choir is a very
old and interesting *Crypt*, divided into three vaulted aisles with semicircular vaulting (for adm. apply to the sacristan). It contains a Renaissance cenotaph, placed over the tomb of St. Fort, first Bishop of Bordeaux, the tomb of St. Veronica, and six marble sarcophagi, of the
4-6th cent., adorned with sculpture.

Crossing the Allées Damour, to the S. of St. Seurin, and following the Rue Judaïque, to the left, we soon reach the Rue St. Sernin, in which, to the left, is the *Institution Nationale des Sourdes-
Muettes* (Institution for Female Deaf-Mutes; Pl. D, 4), a handsome
classical building, with a statue of the Abbé de l'Épée at the entrance. Nearly opposite, to the S., is a large *École Professionnelle.*

A little farther on the Rue Judaïque ends at the *Place Gambetta*
(Pl. B, 4, 5), a fine square from which the Cours de l'Intendance
and the Cours Tourny diverge to the E. and N.E. From its S.E.
corner we enter the Rue Porte-Dijeaux, so named from an old town-
gate, and turn at once to the right into the Rue des Remparts,
which takes us to the Hôtel de Ville, the new Musée, and the
Cathedral. The **Hôtel de Ville** (Pl. B, 5), formerly the archiepiscopal
palace, was built in 1770-81 for the Prince-Cardinal de Rohan-
Guéménée and was restored after a fire in 1862. It is a handsome
building with a conspicuous entrance between two colonnades.

The **Musée** (Pl. B, 5), at the back of the Hôtel de Ville, and
facing the Cours d'Albret, consists of two wings, one on each side

of a small garden. It is open to the public daily, except Mon. and Frid., from 12 to 5 in summer and 12 to 4 in winter; and strangers are admitted on Mon. and Frid. also.

The **Right Wing** is devoted to the old masters. — The Vestibule contains a few sculptures: 706. *Hoursolle* (of Bordeaux), This age is pitiless; 712. *Lemot*, Apollo. — Room I. To the right, 223. *P. Grebber*, Bathsheba bathing; 233. *Holbein the Younger*, Portrait; 508. *Monrousie*, Battle of Denain (1712); 80. *School of Murillo*, Virgin and Child; 41. *Lorenzo di Credi*, Annunciation; 148. *Titian*, Triumph of Galatea; 32. *L. Carracci* (?), Dance of Amoretti; 78. *Murillo*, St. Anthony of Padua in an ecstasy; 23. *P. Veronese*, Holy Family; 117. *Sabattini*, Holy Family; 664. *Dutch School*, Portrait; 22. *P. Veronese*, The Woman taken in adultery; 75. *Moya*, Portrait of a painter; 125. *Solimena*, Joseph in prison; *12. *Pietro da Cortona*, Virgin and Child; 138. After *Andrea del Sarto*, Holy Family; 113. *Salvator Rosa*, Ajax; *147. *Titian* (?), The Woman taken in adultery; 643. *Italian School*, David before Saul; 78. *Murillo* (?), Portrait of Don Luis de Haro; 21. *Paolo Veronese*, Adoration of the Magi; 2. *Correggio* (?), Ganymede; 108. *Seb. Ricci*, Love jealous of Fidelity; 103. *Ribera*, Conventicle; *143. *Vasari*, Holy Family; 63. *Liberi*, St. Apollonia and an angel; 15. *Moretto*, Virgin and Child; 8. *Fra Bartolommeo*, Holy Family; 84. *Palma Vecchio*, Holy Family; 138. *Perugino*, Virgin and Child, with SS. Jerome and Augustine; 87. *Palmezzano*, Crucifixion; 77. *Murillo* (?), A philosopher; 648. *Italian School*, Ecce Homo; 42. *G. Poussin*, Landscape; 99. *Guido Reni*, Mary Magdalen; 133. *Tiepolo*, Eleazar and Rebecca; 64. *Giordano*, Venus asleep; 98. *Bassano*, Jesus with Martha and Mary; 148. *Titian* (?), Tarquin and Lucretia; 3. *School of Allegri*, Venus asleep; 95. *Il Calabrese* (*Preti*), Guitar-player; 120. *Spada*, The four ages of life; 40. *Cesari*, Jesus washing the Disciples' feet; 96. *Cam. Procaccini* (?), The Annunciation; 150. *School of Titian*, Mary Magdalen. — Room II. To the left: 128. *Tarella*, Mary Magdalen with two angels; 92. *Bassano*, Leaving the Ark. — Room III. To the right: 264. *De Momper*, Landscape; 311. *Teniers the Younger*, Village festival; 296. *School of Rubens*, Adoration of the Magi; no number, *Weerts*, The exorcism; 320. *O. van Veen*, Marriage of St. Catharine; 293. *Rubens*, Bacchus and Ariadne; 157. *Bakhuisen*, Sea-piece; above, *J. Coudray*, Copy of the Hunt by Delacroix (see below); 248. *Lingelbach*, Flemish topers; 288. *Moucheron*, Landscape; 254. *Maes*, Portrait; 218. *Govaerts*, Landscape, Diana resting; 253. *Maes*, Portrait of a man; 213. *Franck the Younger*, Christ on Calvary; 214. *School of Franck*, Different ways of attaining immortality; 186. *Benj. Cuyp* (?), Interior of a barn; *292. *Rubens*, Martyrdom of St. Justus; 304. *J. van Steen*, Tavern-scene; 185. *A. Cuyp*, Landscape; 187. *B. Cuyp* (?), Interior; 237. *Karel du Jardin*, Landscape with animals; *Snyders*, 305. Fox-hunting; 302. The aged lion; 182. *Ph. de Champaigne*, Joseph's dream (injured); 212. *Franck the Younger*, Christ on Calvary; 166. *N. Berghem*, Landscape; 316. *Tilborgh*, Interior; *291. *Rubens*, Martyrdom of St. George; 310. *Teniers the Younger*, The Incantation; 263. *H. Mommers*, Landscape with figures; 283. *School of Rembrandt*, Adoration of the Shepherds; 231. *Hobbema*, Landscape with figures; 301. *Siberechts*, Landscape; 178. 'Velvet' *Brueghel*, La Rosière; *Rubens*, 294. Villagers dancing, 295. Crucifixion; 265, 266. *Momper*, Landscapes; 217. *Oedom*, St. Jerome; 200. *Van Dyck*, The penitent Magdalen; several Flemish and Dutch landscapes. — Room IV. 729. *Raggi*, Bronze statue of Louis XVI., 21 ft. high (1829).

The **Left Wing** is devoted to modern works. — The Vestibule contains sculptures: *Carmelo*, Mozart dying. Paintings: *Gigoux*, Baptism of Clovis; *Rosa Bonheur*, Five dogs (sketches). — Room I. To the right, 543. *Lehoux*, Louis IX. visiting the plague-stricken; 385. *Bouguereau*, Bacchante; 408. *Français*, Landscape; 300. *Bellangé*, Cuirassiers of Waterloo; 631. *Troyon*, Oxen ploughing; 441. *Eugène Delacroix*, Lion-hunt (a fragment, the picture having been partly destroyed by a fire; copy see above); 510. *Jouy*, Execution of Urbain Grandier (p. 17); 473. *Claude Lorrain*, Landscape; 563. *Mignard*, Louis XIV.; 45. *Ferrandis*, Judgment of the Syndics of Valencia (Spain); 348. *Antigna*, Image-seller; 415. *Cogniet*, Tinloretto painting his dead daughter; 591. *Pils*, Trench before Sebastopol; 378. *Fr.-Aug. Bonheur*, Return from the fair; 350. *Antigna*, Mirror of the wood; 808. *Restout*, Presentation in the Temple. Sculptures: *Blanchard*, Discovery; 701. *Cambos*, La Cigale; 384. *Bouguereau*, All Souls' Day. — Room II. To the left: 479. *Gérôme*, Bacchus and drunken Cupid; 308. *Rosa Bonheur*, Fox; 384. *Bouguereau*, Jour des Morts; no number, *E. Buland*, The heirs. In the middle: 714. *Lemoyne*, Bust of Montesquieu; *Chapu*, Bust of Carayon-Latour; 698. *Is. Bonheur*, Cow defending her calf, in bronze. — Room III. To the right, 159. *A. Achenbach*, Sea-piece; 508. *Isabey*, Burning of the steamer Austria (1858); 365. *Baudry*, Toilette of Venus; 432. *Daubigny*, The banks of the Oise; 548. *Luminais*, Gallic scouts; 495. *Gros*, Embarkation of the Duchess of Angoulême (1815); 359. *Beaulieu*, Duel; 579. *Pallière*, Bazeilles (1870); no number, *Roll*, The old carrier; no number, *Delacroix*, Boissy d'Anglas; no number, *Corot*, Landscape; 496. *Gudin*, Captain Desse saving the crew of a Dutch vessel (1822); 300. *Schenck*, Réveillé; no number, *Auguin*, Summer on the Grande Côte (p. 60); 440. *Delacroix*, Greece expiring amid the ruins of Missolonghi; no number, *P. Quinsac*, Fountain of youth. — Sculpture: *Longepied*, Neapolitan fisherman. — Room IV. contains pictures and sculptures of little interest.

The *Cathedral (St. André;* Pl. B, C. 5), a few yards to the S. E. of the Hôtel de Ville, is one of the finest Gothic churches in the S. of France. It consists of a large nave, destitute of façade and aisles, dating from the 11-12th cent., with Romanesque arches; a transept; and a choir with double aisles of the 14th century. The principal portal, on the N. side, is flanked with two towers surmounted by stone spires. The sculptures in the tympanum represent the Last Supper and the Ascension. In the trumeau is a statue of Bertrand de Goth, archbishop of Bordeaux, afterwards Pope Clement V. (d. 1314), who contributed largely to the building. The S. portal is of the same character, but its towers have no spires.

The Choir is the most admired part of the interior. Among the chief works of art are the monument of Cardinal de Cheverus (d. 1836), with his statue, by *Maggesi* (near the pulpit); opposite, the monument of Mgr. Donnet (d. 1882), with his statue and figures of Faith and Charity, by *Delaplanche;* a Resurrection, by *Alessandro Veronese* (opposite the pulpit); a Crucifixion, by *Jordaens;* a Raising of Lazarus, by *Jalla* (1877); two large bas-reliefs of the Renaissance, below the organ, originally part of a rood-loft and representing the Descent into Hell and the Resurrection; a Bearing of the Cross, attributed to *Ag. Carracci* (at the side); the monument of Monsgr. d'Aviau in the second choir-chapel to the right; a statue of St. Anne, of the 16th cent., some fine wood-carvings, and the monuments of Aut. de Noailles (1662) and Mgr. de la Boullerie (d. 1882), in other chapels. — Richard II. of England was christened in this cathedral.

About 30 yds. to the right of the choir of this church, opposite the end of the Cours Victor-Hugo (p. 49), is the CLOCHER PEYBERLAND, built in 1440 by Archbishop Pierre Berland. It was sold at the Revolution and partly pulled down, but was bought back in 1850 and restored. Unfortunately, however, the spire has been left in a truncated condition, with a gilded statue of the Virgin at the top. This tower contains a bell weighing about 10 tons.

To the S.W. of the cathedral rises the *Palais de Justice* (Pl. B, 5, 6), a vast building erected in 1839-46, with a heavy façade, upwards of 150 yds. long. In the centre is a peristyle portico of the Doric order, and the projecting wings are crowned with seated figures of Malesherbes, Aguesseau, Montesquieu, and l'Hôpital.

Behind the Palais de Justice is the *Prison*, which occupies the site of the Château du Far or Fort du Hä, built at the same time as the Château Trompette (p. 50).

To the S. of the Palais de Justice is the extensive *Hospital of St. Andrew* (650 beds; Pl. B, 6), rebuilt in 1825-29, with a handsome entrance. A little farther on, to the left, is the church of *Ste. Eulalie* (Pl. B, C, 6), of very ancient foundation but rebuilt in the 14-15th centuries.

The Rue de Cursol (Pl. B, C, 6) leads to the *Cours Victor-Hugo*, which extends from the cathedral to the Pont de Bordeaux. At the bend which it makes near the Rue de Cursol are the new buildings of the *Faculties of Theology, Science, and Literature* (Pl. C, 5, 6). The vestibule contains a monument to Montaigne, who is interred in the basement. Farther on, to the left, is the *Grand Marché*, a recent erection of iron and glass, and almost opposite is the new *Lycée National*. In a short street to the right stands the *Porte de l'Hôtel de Ville*, a fine relic of the old Hôtel de Ville, dating in its lower part from the 13th cent., while the upper half, with its three turrets, was rebuilt in the 16th century. Above the arch, through which the street runs, is a curious clock in the Renaissance style. Higher up is another arch with a bell, and on the top of this is a lantern surmounted by a lion. — Adjoining this gate is the modern entrance of the church of *St. Eloi*, which itself dates from the 15th century.

The church of St. Michel (Pl. D, 6), near the Quai des Salinières, a little above the Pont de Bordeaux, is a fine Gothic edifice, founded in the 8th or 9th cent., but rebuilt in 1149 and in the 15-16th centuries. Its three portals are adorned with interesting sculptures, representing the Nativity, the Adoration of the Shepherds, the Sacrifice of Isaac, Abraham (to the N.), and the appearance of St. Michel to the Bishop of Sipontum. The choir is lower than the nave, and the wall above the arch by which it is entered is pierced by a window. In the fourth choir-chapel to the left is a Descent from the Cross, carved in the 16th century. The chapel of St. Joseph dates from the Renaissance period.

The Bell-Tower of St. Michel, standing apart like that of the cathedral, 32 yds. from the W. front of the church, was built in 1472-92. The spire, destroyed by a hurricane in 1768, has recently been rebuilt, and the structure has also been strengthened by the erection of six buttresses, crowned with statues, round the base. The total height of the tower is 354 ft.

The soil of the old cemetery which once occupied this spot had the singular property of preserving the dead bodies committed to it; and a guide is at hand to conduct strangers into a *Vault* where about forty natural mummies of this kind may be seen (adm. 1 fr.). The melancholy aspect of this exhibition is made almost fantastic by the attitude of the mummies, placed upright against the walls. The guide recounts a more or less true history of several.

Ste. Croix (Pl. D, 6, 7), in the midst of the populous artizan quarter which lies to the S. of St. Michel, is also one of the most interesting churches of Bordeaux. It was originally founded in the 7th cent., or even earlier, but it was rebuilt in the 10th cent. in the Romanesque style and has been restored several times since. Its most striking part is the W. front, which recalls those of Notre-Dame at Poitiers and the cathedral at Angoulême. No satisfactory explanation of the sculptures of this façade has been given, the only recognizable details being the signs of the zodiac and a knight slaying a dragon at the feet of the Virgin. The interior, part of which is in the Gothic style, contains a noteworthy tomb of the 15th century.

Adjoining this church is the *Ecole des Beaux-Arts*, in an old Benedictine abbey, with a Renaissance gateway.

The street to the left of Ste. Croix leads back to the Quays, which it reaches not far from the railway-bridge mentioned at p. 44, and the *Gare du Midi*, rebuilt in 1891-94.

The *Boulevards* of Bordeaux are noteworthy for their extent, their fine trees, and their handsome buildings. Beyond the Boul. de Caudéran (Pl. A, 2, 3; tramways) is the *Parc Bordelais*, a new public park, still somewhat bare and dusty (band 4-6 on Sun. and holidays). Cafés-restaurants in the vicinity.

From Bordeaux to *Paris* see R. 1; to *La Rochelle* and *Nantes*, see R. 4; to *Périgueux* and *Limoges*, see R. 5; to *Royan*, see R. 7; to *Arcachon*, see R. 8; to *Bayonne* and *Biarritz*, see R. 9; to *Toulouse* and *Cette*, see R. 10; to *Tarbes* (Pyrenees), see R. 14.

From Bordeaux to La Sauve, 17 M., railway in 1-1½ hr. (fares 3 fr. 30, 2 fr. 5, 1 fr. 35 c.). The trains start from the Gare de la Bastide (comp. p. 48). — The intermediate stations are of no interest to the tourist. Near La Sauve (*Hôtel Français*) are the ruins of an abbey founded in the 10th cent., and rebuilt in the 13th cent., with a beautiful church. — This line is to be continued to join the railway from Marmande to Bergerac (p. 14) at (42 M.) *Eymet* (p. 72), and will pass *Duras*, a town with a château and fortifications of the 16th century.

7. From Bordeaux to Royan.

a. By the Médoc Railway.

Railway to (62½ M.) *Le Verdon* and Steamer thence, in connection with the trains, to *Royan*, at the mouth of the Gironde. The whole journey takes 4⅓-4½ hrs. Tickets to Royan allow the holders to break the journey at Soulac and Le Verdon. Fares 11 fr. 40, 8 fr. 50, 8 fr. 20 c.; return-tickets, available for 8 days, 13 fr. 65, 10 fr. 30, 7 fr. 45 c.; cheap excursion-trains run in summer (return-fares 6 fr. 85, 5 fr. 95 c., 5 fr.). The trains start from the Gare du Médoc (p. 48). The sea is sometimes rough at the mouth of the Gironde.

The whole journey may be made by railway (92 M., in 3-5 hrs.; fares 13 fr. 75, 10 fr. 30, 8 fr. 85 c.), viâ the State line (Gare du Midi) and branch at Pons (p. 32).

Bordeaux, see p. 46. — From (2½ M.) *Bruges* a branch runs to (30 M.) Lacanau (p. 61). — At (5 M.) *Blanquefort* there is an old castle.

Here begins the **Médoc**, a district of the Bordelais occupying the tongue of land between the Gironde and the sea (Medoc = 'in medio aquae') and long celebrated for its wines. The vineyards extend along the left bank of the river in a band 5-12 M. in width reaching as far as (48 M.) St. Vivien (see below). There is a great variety in the growths, but as a rule, only five kinds are distinguished as 'crus classés' (classified growths). The first-class growths are confined to Upper Médoc, which extends from Ludon to a little beyond St. Estèphe. Most of the Médoc wines are red, but excellent white wines are also produced, though the best of these, the Sauternes, are grown higher up on the left bank of the Garonne (see p. 71). Some of the white wines are called 'graves' because produced on the gravel deposits ('gravier') at the confluence of the rivers. The soil of the vineyards elsewhere consists mainly of siliceous deposits, quartz, etc., brought down from the Pyrenees by the Garonne. These deposits are particularly suitable to the vine because they are very loose and retentive of the heat. In consequence of the ravages of the phylloxera and a series of bad harvests the wines of Bordeaux are becoming more and more expensive, and those of the first growths, which are generally exported, are extremely dear. The vintage generally begins after the middle of September and lasts till nearly the end of October.

Beyond Blanquefort, to the right, lies *Parempuyre*, with vineyards and ponds in which the breeding of leeches is carried on on a large scale. Fine modern *Château.* — 9½ M. *Ludon* produces wines of the third class (Château de la Lagune). — 11 M. *Macau*, with a small harbour on the Garonne, which the line touches here. The Bec d'Ambès (p. 59) lies to the S. E., but is hidden by an island. To the right lies *Cantenac*, producing Brane-Cantenac, a wine of the 2nd class.

15½ M. *Margaux* produces wines of the 1st, 2nd, and 3rd classes. The finest, known as Château Margaux, is the best Médoc wine but one, being surpassed by Château Laffitte alone (see below). — 17½ M. *Soussans*; 20 M. *Moulis.*

25½ M. *St. Laurent-St. Julien. St. Laurent*, a small town 1½ M. to the left, produces wines of the fourth quality. The wines of *St. Julien*, 2½ M. to the right, are mostly of the second class, and are widely known under the names of St. Julien, Château Léoville, etc. — Farther on, we pass on the right the domain of *Château Latour*, the wine of which ranks next to Château Laffitte and Château Margaux. The line again approaches the river.

29 M. **Pauillac** *(Grand-Hôtel)*, an old town of 4564 inhab., lies on the left bank of the Gironde and possesses a harbour used by vessels which cannot get up to Bordeaux. Its wine-district, reckoned the second of the Médoc in general importance, includes the domain of *Château Laffitte*, which produces the finest wine of all. This domain (170 acres) was purchased in 1868 for about 180,000 *l.* by the Rothschilds. The wine is worth 80-120 *l.* per 'tonneau' of 198 gallons. Over 60,000 bottles are stored in the vaults. The domain of *Mouton-Rothschild* (170 acres) produces wine of the 1st and 2nd classes.

32 M. *St. Estèphe*, with the largest vineyard in the country. Its chief growth, Cos-Destournel, ranks among the second class wines.

— 35 M. *Verteuil* has an interesting Romanesque church. — 38¹/₂ M. *St. Germain-d'Esteuil.*

42 M. **Lesparre** (*Lion d'Or*), a town with 3972 inhab., has a tower of the 14th cent., a relic of an old castle, and a fine modern church. It is the junction of a line to Facture and Arès (Arcachon; see p. 62). — 47 M. *Queyrac;* 50 M. *Vensac;* 51¹/₂ M. *St. Vivien,* where the vines give way to marshes. This large village has a church belonging partly to the 14th cent., with a fine modern spire. — 54 M. *Talais.*

58 M. **Soulac-les-Bains** (*Hôtel de la Paix, Hôtel Fontêtes,* both expensive), a small watering-place, with a fine beach and surrounded by pine-woods. Near the village, which lies ¹/₂ M. from the station, is the curious Romanesque church of *Le Vieux Soulac,* buried after the middle of the 13th cent. by the encroaching sand-dunes, which have once more uncovered it in their advance inland. An interesting walk may be taken at low tide along the foot of the dunes, towards the Pointe de Grave (see below). The sea, which is extremely violent in this vicinity, has swallowed up the harbour of Soulac and various other localities, including the Roman town of *Noviomagus.* Extensive dykes ('epis'), constructed with great difficulty, have been raised at the *Anse des Huttes* (1¹/₂ M.), the *Pointe de Grave* (5 M.), and elsewhere, to resist the encroachment of the waves.

63 M. *Le Verdon* (Hotels), the terminus of the railway, is at present of little importance, but possesses a small harbour of refuge.

From the station we proceed by tramway (no extra charge) through a fine pine-forest to (¹/₄ hr.) the steamboat. To the right of the pier is a fort. To the left, in the direction of the Pointe de Grave, appears Royan, with its conspicuous casino. Directly opposite us is St. Georges-de-Didonne (p. 59).

The voyage usually takes less than ³/₄ hour. In the distance to the left, is the *Lighthouse of Cordouan* (p. 60). Good view of Royan as we approach. — *Royan,* see p. 59.

b. By the Gironde.

Steamers ply from Bordeaux (near the Quinconces; Pl. D, 4) to Royan in 4¹/₂-5¹/₂ hrs., twice a day in summer (July, Aug., Sept.) and thrice weekly (Tues., Thurs., and Sat.) during the rest of the year. They start in summer at 8 a. m. and 2 p. m. (returning from Royan at 7 and 2), in winter at 8 or 8.30 a. m. Fares 6 fr., 4 fr.; return-tickets, available for 8 days, 9 fr., 6 fr.; fare by Sun. excursion-steamer in summer 3 fr., 2 fr., return-ticket (valid till Mon.) 6, 4 fr. Restaurant on board.

The scenery is dull and monotonous, but the great width of the Gironde, amounting at places to 7¹/₂ M., makes it impressive, though the water is generally turbid. Numerous islands are passed. The passage is sometimes considerably protracted when the tide is rising or the sea at the mouth of the river rough. It is not possible to make the excursion both ways by steamer in one day (except by excursion-steamer in summer), but those who are much pressed for time may go by water and return by railway, or *vice versâ.*

The steamer at first threads its way through the harbour of

Bordeaux, which is fringed by warehouses, manufactories, and ship-building yards. To the left are the docks and a floating basin. To the right rise the heights of *Lormont* (p. 15), with its picturesquely situated château; l. *Parempuyre* (p. 57); r. *Montferrand*; l. *Macau* (p. 57); r. *Ambès* and *Le Bec d'Ambès*, the latter a low and narrow tongue of land stretching for some distance between the Garonne and the Dordogne.

The *Mascaret*, a tidal wave similar to the Barre on the Seine and the Bore on the Severn and sometimes 8-10 ft. high, advances as far as this point in August and September. It appears on a rising tide and is, partly at least, the result of the two opposing currents in the bed of the river.

We next pass some long islands on the left, while to the right are several quarries.

r. 25 M. **Blaye** (*Hôtel du Médoc*), a town of 5015 inhab., which existed under the Romans and to this day retains a certain importance as a stronghold. It is prettily situated, partly on a hill, but offers nothing of interest to the tourist. Its *Citadel*, on a rock beside the river, is supplemented by the *Fort du Pâté*, on an islet, and the *Fort Médoc*, on the left (opposite) bank. A branch-railway runs hence to (15¹/₂ M.) *St. Mariens* (p. 32); another to (14 M.) *St. Ciers-Lalande* (p. 32).

The steamer now heads for the left bank, on which are the *Château de Beychevelle*, the slender spire of *St. Julien*, and several vineyards (p. 57). The right bank is now, in its turn, hidden by islands. To the left lies (37 M.) **Pauillac** (p. 57), and farther on are the hospital of Pauillac or *Trompeloup*, and *St. Estèphe* (p. 57), the latter on a knoll. Still farther on, to the left, rise the towers of *St. Christoly* and of *Valeyrac*. Near this point the Gironde is at its widest. In mid-channel there is a sandbank about 8 M. long, beyond which we again steer for the right bank, on which little is seen but chalk-cliffs. Lastly, on the same side, lies *St. Georges-de-Didonne* (p. 60), a small river-port and bathing-place surrounded by woods, 2¹/₂ M. short of Royan. On the left off the mouth of the Gironde stretches the *Pointe de Grave* (p. 68). Out in the open sea rises the *Lighthouse of Cordouan* (see p. 60). On the right bank stands —

Royan. — **Hotels.** HÔTEL DE BORDEAUX ET DE FRANCE, DE PARIS, D'ORLÉANS (R. 2-3 fr.), all in the Boulevard Thiers, near the harbour; DU COMMERCE, Boulevard Lessore. RICHELIEU, Boulevard Botton, both near the baths; DE LA CROIX-BLANCHE, Rue de Rochefort and Boul. Botton, déj. 2¹/₂, D. 3, pens. 8 fr.; DE FRANCE, Rue Gambetta 45 and Boul. Lessore, D. 3 fr.; HÔTEL-RESTAUR. DU CENTRE, Rue Gambetta 52, R., L., & A. 2-3, B. ¹/₂-1, déj. 2¹/₂, D. 2³/₄, pens. 7¹/₂-8 fr.; HÔT.-REST. DES VOYAGEURS, Rue de la Plage. — At Pontaillac: GRAND-HÔTEL, R., L., & A. 3-8, déj. 3¹/₂, D. 4¹/₂ fr.; HÔT. D'ANGLETERRE, DE PONTAILLAC, DE L'EUROPE, on the beach. At the Parc: GRAND HÔTEL, on the beach.

Cafés. *Des Bains, de France*, Boul. Thiers, at Royan; *de la Plage*, at Pontaillac.

Sea Baths, with bathing-box and dress, 60 c. to 1 fr. — **Casino**. Adm.
by day 1-2, in the evening 3-4 fr.; subscription, per week 21, per fortnight 35,
per month 55, per season 100 fr. (families at a reduction).

Cabs, per hr. 3 fr., each additional 1/4 hr. 1/2 fr.; donkey-carriage,
2 fr. — *Horse*, per hr. 2 1/2, *Donkey*, 1 1/2 fr. — **Steam Tramway** (Decau-
ville) to *Pontaillac* (see below), to the *Parc* and *St. Georges-de-Didonne* (see
below,) 25, 40 c. — **Steamboat** to Le Verdon (p. 58), 2 fr., return-ticket 3 fr.
This boat starts very punctually.

Post and Telegraph Office, Boulevard Botton 54.

Royan, a modern town with 7247 inhab., is one of the chief
sea-bathing resorts in France, being frequented by about 40,000
visitors annually. It is well built, partly on the rocks which
overlook the mouth of the Gironde, opposite the Pointe de Grave,
and it offers to visitors all the usual amenities of a fashionable
watering-place. Its four *Conches*, or beaches, are covered with fine
sand and afford admirable facilities for bathing. At Royan itself
the sea is generally calm, even when the waves are breaking furi-
ously at *Pontaillac*, 1 1/4 M. to the W. (hotels, see above). Between
the two lie the *Conche de Foncillon*, and the small *Conches de Chay*
and *du Pigeonnier*, beyond a small fort. The *Grande Conche* lies
to the left of the harbour. A new bathing-establishment has been
built here, near which is the handsome new *Casino Municipal*
(opened in 1895). The *Statue of Eugène Pelletan* (1813-1884), by
Aubé, commemorates a benefactor of Royan. Near the quay where
we disembark is a fine park, which we may enter also from the Rue
du Casino, near the harbour, between the Boulevard Thiers and the
Rue Gambetta. The last-named street leads to the church of *Notre-
Dame*, a handsome modern Gothic structure. — The *Railway
Station* (line to Pons, see p. 32) is about 3/4 M. distant in the same
direction.

About 2 1/2 M. from Royan by road (tramway, see above) and nearly
3 M. by the beach is St. Georges-de-Didonne (*Hôtel de l'Océan*), another
sea-bathing resort.

The chief excursion from Royan is to the **Lighthouse of Cordouan**,
to which steamers ply during the season, usually on Sun. and Thrsday.
The lighthouse stands on a rock 7 1/2 M. from Royan, accessible from the
shore at low tide. The islet was formerly, it is said, attached to the
Pointe de Grave (see p. 58), which is now more than 3 M. from it. The
tower was perhaps originally constructed by the Saracens or by Louis the
Pious, but it was rebuilt by Edward, Prince of Wales (the Black Prince)
in 1370, and again in 1584-1610 from the plans of Louis de Foix, one
of the architects of the Escurial. The present tower, however, dates
from the beginning of this century. The lighthouse, with its basement,
rises to a height of 212 ft. Such is the violence of the sea at this spot,
that the waves, though broken by reefs, still rise more than 40 ft. against
the tower. The light is visible for 30 M. In the second story of the
tower is a chapel of Notre-Dame-de-Cordouan.

Another excursion may be made to the *Grande Côte* (omnibus there
and back 1 fr. 60 c.; see the bills), about 6 M. to the N.W., where the chief
attraction is the spectacle of the stormy sea dashing on the rocky coast.

From Royan to *Soulac* (p. 58); fares 2 fr. 70, 2 fr. 45, 2 fr. 35 c.; return-
ticket 4 fr. 50, 4 fr. 15, 3 fr. 95 c.

Railway from Royan to *Pons* and to *La Tremblade*, etc., see p. 32.

8. From Bordeaux to Arcachon.

35 M. Railway in 1½-2¾ hrs. (fares 4 fr. 25, 3 fr. 25, 2 fr. 25 c.;
return-ticket 6 fr., 4 fr. 50, 3 fr. 50 c.). Excursion-trains at reduced fares
on Sun. and holidays in summer (return 3 fr. 50, 2 fr. 50, 1 fr. 50 c.). The
trains start from the Gare du Midi or de St. Jean.

Bordeaux, see p. 46. This line diverges to the right from the
Toulouse railway (R. 10), and passes, partly in cuttings, through a
wine-growing district, the finest product of which is the *Haut-
Brion*, a wine of the premier cru (p. 57). 3¾ M. *Pessac*.

The disappearance of the vineyards and the appearance in their place
of plantations of pines now indicate that we have entered the singular
district known as the Landes (waste lands). The name is given to a vast
triangular plateau, 150-200 ft. above the sea, and bounded by the Atlantic
and the valleys of the Garonne and the Adour. On the side next the
sea it is upwards of 120 M. in length, its maximum width is about
60 M., and it covers an area of 2300 sq. M. The soil is composed of a
layer, about 1½ ft. deep, of sand and *alios*, *i. e.* vegetable detritus solid-
ified by a ferruginous cement, which renders it unfit for cultivation.
Even after the great improvements of modern times the district is still
dried up in summer and marshy in winter, the alios rendering the soil
impervious to moisture, while the sand-dunes (200-300 ft.) along the coast
hinder the escape of the surface waters. These dunes moreover used to
invade the country, advancing about 20 yds. every year, but the attack has
been arrested by the planting of sea-pines (*pinus maritima*), begun in 1786.
The circulation of the waters, too, has been regulated, and the forests, already of great extent, are daily gaining on the bare ground. There still
remain, however, vast stretches of country, almost entirely waste, over-
grown with heath, furze, reeds, bracken, and broom, and presenting a
unique but monotonous appearance. It will be noticed that the trunks of
the pines are scored with gashes, below which small tin vessels are
placed. The purpose of these is to collect the resin, which forms a very
important article of commerce here. The sea-pine is not, however, the
only tree which thrives in the Landes: the acacia, the ailanthus, the oak,
and the cork-tree are successfully grown, the last chiefly near Bayonne.

In order to traverse the sands and the marshes, the inhabitants of the
Landes have had to adopt the custom of walking on stilts, 4-6 ft. high,
supporting themselves by a pole which serves as a walking-stick. It was
formerly no uncommon sight to see the natives, often clad in sheepskins,
traversing the Landes with the speed of a horse at full gallop, or
supported on the end of their long poles, tranquilly watching their
flocks and knitting the footless stockings peculiar to the district. Now-
a-days, however, the tourist, or at least the railway-traveller, will see
nothing of this kind, for there are fewer marshes and fewer pasturages
than formerly, and many roads have been made throughout the Landes.

6¾ M. *Gazinet*; 11 M. *Pierroton*; 14 M. *Croix-d'Hins*; 17 M.
Marcheprime; 20½ M. *Canauley*; 23 M. *Facture*.

From Facture (Arcachon) to Lesparre (Royan), 56½ M., railway in
2¾-4¼ hrs. (fares 9 fr. 40, 7 fr. 5, 5 fr. 15 c.). This line, which traverses
the Landes of the Gironde, skirts at first the N.E. side of the Basin of
Arcachon (p. 63). — 8 M. *Taussat*, a small sea-bathing place; 13 M. *Arès*,
a country-town and bathing-resort. The line then turns to the N., skirting the W. side of the *sand-dunes*, which here attain a height of more
than 200 ft. and have several times necessitated the removal of the neighbouring hamlets. — 28 M. *Lacanau* (Hôtel Caupos), to the E. of the pool
of the same name, which is 5 M. long and 2 M. broad. It is the junction
of a line to Uruges and Bordeaux (see p. 56). — Beyond (35 M.) *Carcans*,
we pass the *Étang de Carcans* or *d'Hourtin*, 11 M. long and 2½-3½ M.
wide. — 43 M. *Hourtin*. — 56½ M. *Lesparre*, see p. 58.

The railway just described is continued to the S.E. of Facture by a line running through the valley of the *Leyre* (see below) viâ *Hostens* (junction of a line to Beautiran, p. 70) and (31 M.) *St. Symphorien* (p. 71) to (45 M.) *Luxey*.

We now cross the *Leyre*, a navigable river flowing into the Basin of Arcachon, and at (25 M.) *Lamothe* diverge to the right from the Bayonne line (p. 64). — 26¹/₂ M. *Le Teich*; 29 M. *Gujan-Mestras*; 31 M. *La Hume*.

33 M. **La Teste**, a town of 6480 inhab., represents the ancient capital of the Boii, which the dunes have driven back to its present site. In the Middle Ages it was the residence of the famous Seigneurs of Buch, whose castle has disappeared.

La Teste is the junction of a branch-railway to (8 M.) **Cazaux**, a village on the lake of the same name, which has an area of 17,000 acres and is more than 150 feet in depth. It formerly communicated with the sea, but is now 80 ft. above the sea-level. Steamboats ply on Thurs. and Sun. to *Sanguinet* and *Navarrosse*, with their picturesque woods. Farther on is the similar *Lake of Parentis*.

35 M. **Arcachon**. — **Hotels**. Grand-Hôtel, R. from 3, B. 1¹/₂-2, déj. 4, D. 5, pens. 9 (B. extra; less in winter), omn. 1 fr.; Continental, with dépendance in the forest, R., L., & A. 4-15, B. 1¹/₂, déj. 4, D. 5 (both incl. wine), pens. 12-20, omn. 1-1¹/₂ fr.; Richelieu; de France; all in the Boulevard de la Plage, with verandahs on the side next the Bassin; Jampy, in the same Boul., but not facing the sea, pens. 10 fr. — Grand-Hôtel de la Forêt, near the Grand Casino, R., L., & A. 4-9, B. 1¹/₂, déj. 3¹/₂, D. 4¹/₂, omn. 1¹/₂ fr.; Legallais, Boul. de la Plage, at a distance from the centre; Royal Hotel, in the Ville d'Hiver, etc. — *Furnished Houses:* Chalets from 100 to 2500 fr. per month; Villas in the forest.

Cafés. *Grand Café*, *Molière*, *Central*, Boulevard de la Plage.

Sea Bathing. Three establishments: *Grand Hôtel*, *Grands Bains*, near the centre; *Eyrac*, to the E. Bathing-box ³/₄-1 fr., with bathing-dress.

Casino. Adm. 1 fr. (50 c. when there is no concert or theatrical representation), children half-price. Adm. to theatre: 1, 2¹/₂, 4 fr. Subscription, including the theatre: for gentlemen, per week 18, fortnight 30, month 50, season 100 fr.; for lady accompanying her husband, 14, 25, 40, or 90 fr., from July 15th to Sept. 15th; about half these charges in winter. — *Club des Etrangers* and *Yachting Club*, at the Grand Hôtel.

Carriages. Per drive 1¹/₂ fr.; with two horses 2 fr.; per hour 2¹/₂ or 3 fr.; 50 c. extra on Sunday and at night. Carriage without driver, 3 or 4 fr. per hr. *Saddle-horse*, 3 fr. per hr. — *Boats* 3 fr. per hour. — *Steamer* to Cape Ferret and the lighthouse (p. 63), there and back 2 fr.

Post & Telegraph Office, Avenue Gambetta, near the Place Thiers.

Musée-Aquarium, 161 Boul. de la Plage, beyond the Château, adm. 12-6, ¹/₂ fr.

English Church (*St. Thomas's*). *Rev. S. Radcliff*, B. A., Chaplain. — British Vice-consul: *Mr. C. P. Wember*.

Arcachon is a charming sea-bathing and winter resort, which has recently come into vogue and is now annually frequented by 100,000 visitors. The resident population is 7910. On Sundays and holidays it is inundated with excursionists from Bordeaux. It consists of two parts, the town proper, situated on the lagoon of the same name (see below), and the Ville d'Hiver, or winter-town, in the forest planted on the dunes to the S.

Opposite the exit from the station is the *Château Deganne*, an elegant modern mansion in the Renaissance style. Thence we take the Boulevard Deganne to the left, then the Boulevard Gambetta to the right, and reach the *Place Thiers*, almost the only spot in the town where there is free access to the beach. Arcachon still lacks a promenade-pier.

The *Bassin d'Arcachon* is a capacious gulf or lagoon, nearly 50 M. in circumference and 60 sq. M. in area, of which, however, two-thirds are dry at low-water. Its form is triangular, the apex being to the N., near Arès (p. 61), and the base extending from the mouth of the Leyre on the N.E. to the strait which connects it with the open sea, on the S.E. The shore is a very safe one for bathing, of gentle slope and of fine sand. The water is as strongly impregnated with salt as that of the open sea, but vigorous bathers will miss the buffetting of waves.

In the centre of the Bassin are the *Oyster Parks* (see below), and on the opposite side extends a tongue of land consisting of sand-dunes and ending to the S. in *Cape Ferret*, on which stands a lighthouse of the first class (8 M. from Arcachon). The roadstead protected by the cape is broad and safe, but access to it is made difficult by banks of shifting sand. A scheme has been mooted of narrowing the channel by means of dykes and so establishing a refuge on this part of the coast, which is dangerous and offers no other shelter.

The long Boulevard de la Plage runs in front of the houses fringing the Bassin, and is continued towards the W. by the Boulevard de l'Océan. Arcachon extends to the E. and W., with its pretty houses of every style scattered amid gardens and parks.

The street nearly in front of the Grand Hôtel, a handsome edifice to the W. of the Place Thiers, ascends to the *Casino*, a large building in the Moorish style, comprising a concert-hall, reading and conversation rooms, card-rooms, and cafés in the Oriental style. At one side is an iron *Observatory*, or belvedere, commanding a fine view (10 c.). — Farther to the W. is the church of *Notre-Dame*, built in 1856 by Alaux, in the Gothic style.

The *Ville d'Hiver* is snugly ensconced among the pine-woods, the resinous emanations of which combine with the bracing sea-air to make it a peculiarly healthy resort. The temperature is at the same time very favourable to invalids, the mean of the whole year being 59° Fahr. and that of winter 48° Fahr. The villas of the winter-town are even more luxurious than those on the beach. — Arcachon, however, is far inferior to the Mediterranean winter-stations; the monotony of the woods and the absence of view are apt soon to pall upon visitors.

A pleasant walk may be taken as far as *Moulleau*, a village about 3 M. to the W., with an institution and a chapel founded by the Dominicans. It may also be reached by the beach, by a route passing, to the right at the end of the Boulevard de l'Océan, the *Parc Pereire*, a private park to which the public are not admitted.

Oyster Parks. Those parts of the Bassin which are left dry by the tide, called 'Crassats', are utilised for the breeding of oysters, which is the chief industry of the district, supporting about 20,000 persons. The oysters of Arcachon are in high repute and 300 millions of them are sold annually, representing a value of about 180,000*l.* A visit to the oyster-beds is interesting if time permit. Fresh oysters may be obtained there and in the town for about 15 c. per dozen. In the middle of the Basin, reached by boat in $^3/_4$ hr., is the *Ile des Oiseaux*.

The steamboat trip to *Cape Ferret* (p. 63) is not recommended to visitors pressed for time. It takes at least 3 hrs., and presents no special attraction except the view of the open sea. The walk from the steamboat quay, over fatiguing sand-hills, may be avoided by using the tramway (return-fare 40 c.). The lighthouse is too far from the landing-place to be conveniently visited. — The excursions to the lighthouse and to the open sea, at the entrance to the bay, are scarcely more interesting. To the *Etang de Cazaux*, see p. 62.

9. From Bordeaux to Bayonne and Biarritz.

RAILWAY to (128 M.) *Bayonne* in 3-5$^1/_4$ hrs. (fares 22 fr. 30, 15 fr. 5, 9 fr. 75 c.). — LOCAL RAILWAY from Bayonne to (5 M.) *Biarritz* in $^1/_4$ hr. (fares 75, 45 c.). — Through-tickets to Biarritz convey the traveller to *La Négresse* station (p. 129). — The trains start from the Gare St. Jean (p. 48).

From Bordeaux to (25 M.) *Lamothe*, see p. 62. The line then runs straight across the Landes for a distance of nearly 30 M. — 32 M. *Caudos*; 39 M. *Lugos*; 47 M. *Ychoux* (branch-lines to *Parentis*, 7$^1/_2$ M. to the W., and to *Pissos*, 9$^1/_2$ M. to the E.); 50 M. *Labouheyre*, a small industrial town (branch-lines to the W. to *Mimizan*, 17 M.; to the E. to *Sabres*, 12 M.); 60 M. *Solférino*, a modern place, with large plantations.

68 M. **Morcenx** (*Buffet; Hôtel du Commerce*), a large village, 1$^1/_4$ M. to the S. of the railway.

FROM MORCENX TO TARBES, 85 M., railway in 4-4$^1/_4$ hrs. (fares 15 fr. 35, 10 fr. 35, 8 fr. 75 c.).

24 M. **Mont-de-Marsan** (*Hôtel des Ambassadeurs; des Voyageurs*), a commercial town with 12,030 inhab., the capital of the department of the *Landes*, is pleasantly situated at the confluence of the *Midou* and the *Douze*, which together form the *Midouze*, an affluent of the *Adour*. It possesses little of interest to the tourist. A branch-line runs hence to (61 M.) *Marmande*, see p. 72. Another branch-line runs to (10$^1/_2$ M.) *St. Sever* (Hôt. des Ambassadeurs; de France), a town of Roman origin with an old abbey-church (10th cent., altered in the 15th).

We now reach a more fertile country and gain our first sight of the Pyrenees, on the right, the Pic du Midi d'Ossau (p. 147) being the chief summit visible. — 33 M. *Grenade-sur-l'Adour*. About 3$^1/_2$ M. distant is *Eugénie-les-Bains*, a small watering-place with warm sulphur baths.

44 M. **Aire** (*Poste*), a very ancient town with 4551 inhab. and the seat of a bishopric, also on the Adour. The cathedral and the church of Mas d'Aire (13-14th cent.) are interesting. Beyond (50 M.) *St. Germé* the line crosses the Adour. — 59$^1/_2$ M. *Riscle*, the junction of a new line to Condom (p. 72). — 71$^1/_2$ M. *Vic-en-Bigorre*, with 3840 inhab., is the junction for Agen and Périgueux (see p. 105). — 85 M. *Tarbes*, see p. 135.

From Morcenx a branch-line, devoid of interest, crosses the Landes to the W. via *Sindères* to (14 M.) *Mézos* and (16$^1/_2$ M.) *Uza*.

76 M. *Rion*; 83 M. *Laluque* (branch-lines to *Linxe*, 16$^1/_2$ M. to the W., via *Castets*; and to *Tartas*, 8$^1/_4$ M. to the E., on the Midouze). In clear weather the Pyrenees now come into view on the left. — 87$^1/_2$ M. *Buglose*, a hamlet belonging to *St. Vincent-de-Paul* (formerly *Pouy*), the birthplace of the saint of that name. A handsome chapel has recently been erected here to the saint, and at Buglose is a pilgrimage-chapel, with a wonder-working statue of the Virgin. — We now quit the Landes and enter the valley of the Adour.

92 M. Dax. — **Hotels.** Grand Hôtel des Thermes, pens. 8-11 fr. in summer, 10-13 fr. in winter; Gr. Hôt. de la Paix, R., L., & A. 2-5, B. 1-2, déj. 3, D. 3½, pens. 8 fr.; de l'Europe. — Invalids find accommodation at *Les Baignots*, 5¼-8 fr. per day, incl. treatment. — *Café de la Renaissance*, Promenade des Remparts. — *Baths*, ½-3 fr. — *Cab* from the station ¾, per drive 1½, per hr. 2½ fr.

Dax, a town with 10,240 inhab., on the left bank of the *Adour*, ¾ M. from the station, is the old capital of the *Tarbelli*, called by the Romans, in honour of its thermal waters, *Aquae Tarbellicae*, afterwards *Civitas Aquensium*, and then simply *Aquae* or *Acqs*. After submitting in turn to the Goths, the Franks and the Vascons, the town was reconquered by Charlemagne, destroyed by the Normans and the Saracens, and held by the English from 1177 to the end of the 15th century.

In spite of its antiquity this town has no noteworthy monuments. It is, however, of importance as a thermal station, and even as a winter-resort. The waters (108° Fahr.) are used in baths of every description (including mud-baths) for rheumatic, surgical, neuralgic, and uterine diseases. Some of the baths are fed by the bed-water of a mine of rock-salt.

A bridge leads over the Adour from the station to the (½ M.) town. To the right, on the opposite bank, are the well-managed *Thermes de Dax*, with rooms for boarders. To the left, above the bridge, is the copious *Fontaine Chaude*, the chief spring, which supplies the *Thermes Romains* and the *Bains Lavigne*, etc., while the water is also used for domestic purposes.

The site of the old walls beside the Adour is occupied by the pretty *Promenade des Remparts*, and in the former moat are the mud-baths of *St. Pierre*. — The former *Cathedral* was rebuilt in the 17-18th centuries. In the adjoining square is a statue, by Aubé, of *Borda* (1733-1799), the mathematician, a native of Dax. The neighbouring *Hôtel de Ville* contains a small Museum of antiquities and natural history. — Farther down the left bank are the *Thermes Séris* and the *Baignots*, both unpretending but well-managed. — Behind the Establishment is a pretty *Promenade*, with the *Tour Borda*.

About ½ M. to the W. of Dax is *St. Paul-lès-Dax*, with an interesting church. — At *Tercis*, 4 M. to the S.W., are warm baths containing chloride of sodium.

Steam-tramway from Dax to (21½ M.) *Moliets*, viâ (10 M.) *Magescq* and (18 M.) *Léon*, near the *Étang de Léon* (36 sq. M.), under construction. Cork-oak plantations; cork-manufacturing, etc.

comes into view on the right , as we emerge from the forest. The
Adour reappears at the next station. — 121 M. *Le Boucau*, not
far from the outlet of the river.

The *Adour* has not always had its mouth at this place. Down to 1360,
or even later, it flowed along the dunes and entered the ocean 8-9 M.
farther N., at the small port of *Cap Breton*. This outlet having been choked
by a storm, the river was forced to seek another at *Vieux-Boucau*, 10 M.
farther on. This change having proved very prejudicial to the navigation
of the river and particularly to the trade of Bayonne, Louis de Foix,
architect of the Escurial, was commissioned in 1578 to create the present
outlet, which owes its continued existence to strong embankments cutting
the river off from its older and natural channel.

We now follow the right bank of the Adour and pass the foot
of the citadel of Bayonne, skirting the quarter of St. Esprit, in which
is the principal station. For the line to Biarritz, see p. 68.

123 M. **Bayonne.** — **Hotels.** *GR. HÔT. DU COMMERCE, Rue Thiers 21,
moderate; PARTIER-FLEURI, Impasse Port-Neuf, well spoken of, D. 3¹/₂ fr.;
DE PARIS & BILBAÏNA, Rue Thiers 13; ST. ÉTIENNE, Rue Thiers 4, R., L.,
& A. from 4, B. 1¹/₂, déj. 4, D. 5, omn. ¹/₂ fr.; DE L'EUROPE ET ST. MARTIN,
Rue Thiers 12; DE LA PAIX, at the station, unpretending. — Café du Grand
Balcon*, Place d'Armes. — *Omnibus* from the principal station to the Biarritz
station, 20 c. — **British Vice-Consul**, *Capt. R. P. Leeson.*

Bayonne, a town and fortress with 27,192 inhab., is prettily
situated at the confluence of the Adour and the *Nive*, 3¹/₂ M. from
the Bay of Biscay. It is badly built and presents few objects of
interest, except its fine cathedral; but its situation gives it a quaint
and interesting appearance. The population consists mainly of
Basques and Spaniards, whose types, manners, language, and dress
form a striking contrast to those of the other inhabitants.

Bayonne, which is probably the *Lapurdum* of the Romans, acquired
some importance in the Middle Ages by its whaling fleet, its trade with
Spain, its tanneries, and its manufactures of arms. The bayonet is said
to have been invented here. Acquired by England along with Aquitaine,
the town remained faithful to that country till 1451, thanks to the privileges granted to it. It offered a vigorous and successful resistance to
Spain in 1523. Here, in 1565, amid great rejoicings, took place the inter-
view between Charles IX. of France and his sister Elizabeth, Queen of
Spain, in the presence of their mother, Catherine de Médicis, and the
Duke of Alva, when the Massacre of St. Bartholomew is said to have been
planned. In 1814 Bayonne made a brave resistance to the British and
Spanish troops under Sir John Hope and was still untaken when peace
was declared. The name Bayonne is Basque and means 'port'.

The suburb of *St. Esprit*, in which the station lies, formed a separate town until 1857. It is dominated by a *Citadel*, built by Vauban
(1674-79) and considered one of his best works. It has never been
taken , and over the entrance is the inscription 'Nunquam polluta'.
It commands a fine view, but admission is not easily obtained. The
'Cimitière des Anglais', at the N. base of the citadel, owes its name
to the total defeat of three English regiments.

Turning to the right on leaving the station, we soon cross the
Adour by a bridge from which there is a striking view. At the end
of the bridge is a fortified gate, the *Réduit*, near the mouth of the
Nive, which divides Bayonne into two parts. *Petit-Bayonne*, the

quarter adjoining the Adour, is chiefly occupied by the working-classes. It contains the *Military Hospital*; the *Château-Neuf* (15th cent.), converted into a barrack and military prison; the *Arsenal;* and the *Church of St. André*, a modern Gothic building in the style of the 15th century, containing (in the last chapel on the right) an Assumption by Bonnat.

The *Pont Mayou,* the first bridge over the Nive, on the other side of the Réduit, leads us to the Place de la Liberté. The large building here comprises the *Town Hall*, the *Theatre*, the *Public Library*, containing some important records, and a small *Museum*. On the other side of the town is the *Place d'Armes*, at which the Rue Thiers (see below) begins; farther on, outside the fortifications, is the *Gare de Biarritz* (see below).

The Rue Victor-Hugo, the principal street of the town, and its prolongation, the Rue de l'Argenterie (on the right), lead from the Pont Mayou to the —

CATHEDRAL, originally founded in 1140, but rebuilt after a fire in 1213. The choir was first taken in hand, and the work was continued till 1544, when the great portal was left unfinished. In 1847 a citizen of Bayonne, M. Lormand, bequeathed a sum of 35,000 fr. a year for the restoration and completion of the building, and the work is still going on under the direction of M. Boeswillwald. Both spires are modern. The usual entrance is by the portal on the N. side, which is preceded by a vestibule. On the S. side of the church, which is hidden by other buildings, stands a cloister of the 13th cent., formerly used as the burial-place of the chapter. The fine *S. Portal adjoins the Sacristy, which contains beautiful and well-preserved sculptures of the 13th cent. (entr. from the interior of the church). — The internal proportions of the Cathedral are vast and harmonious; the transepts project very slightly beyond the aisles. Among the most noticeable points are the triforium (with stained-glass windows of the 15-17th cent.), the handsome high-altar (modern), the marble pavement of the sanctuary (modern Italian work in imitation of an Oriental carpet), and the modern mural paintings on a gold ground in the apsidal chapels.

In the Place de la Cathédrale is a small *Fountain* in memory of two Bayonnais killed at Paris in 1830, with the inscription: 'Les révolutions justes sont le châtiment des mauvais rois'. Near the cathedral, to the N.W., stands the *Château-Vieux*, of the 12th and 15th cent., which is supposed to have been built on a part of the Roman enceinte. It is now occupied by military offices. Descending farther we reach the *Rue Thiers*, with the principal hotels (p. 66) and the Place d'Armes, near the fortifications. Outside the town is the *Allée de Paulmy*, a promenade skirting the fortifications (adjacent is the small *Biarritz Station*, see p. 68); and opposite are the *Allées Marines*, a fine promenade about 1¼ M. long, on the left bank of the Adour.

Bayonne has a handsome modern *Amphithéatre* in the Moorish style,
for bull-fights and other entertainments; it lies a little to the W. of the
town. — *Race Course*, see p. 69.

FROM BAYONNE TO BIARRITZ, $^1/_4$ hr. by local railway (see p. 64):
trains every hour, or oftener, from the station near the Allée Paulmy
(p. 67). There is also a tramway-line from the Place d'Armes at
Bayonne to the beach at Biarritz, in 35 min. (fares 50, 35 c., return-ticket 90, 55 c.). Travellers are advised not to go to Biarritz
by the Hendaye line (p. 123), the station of which is about $2^1/_4$ M.
from the Baths, as omnibuses do not always meet the trains.

Biarritz. — **Hotels.** HÔTEL D'ANGLETERRE, Rue Mazagran, beyond
the Casino; GRAND HÔTEL, Place de la Mairie and Place Bellevue, before
the Casino; DU CASINO, at the Casino; these three overlook the beach;
VICTORIA, in the lower town, near the beach, R. from 5, L. & A. $1^3/_4$,
B. $1^1/_2$, déj. 4, D. 6 (both incl. wine), pens. in winter 10-14, in summer
15-20, omn. 1 fr.; CONTINENTAL, adjacent; DU PALAIS, in the former Villa
Eugénie (see below); DE PARIS, Place Ste. Eugénie, at the end of the Rue
Mazagran, also with a sea-view; DES PRINCES, Rue Gambetta, to the left
of the Mairie; DE L'EUROPE; DE FRANCE, Place de la Mairie; DE BAYONNE
ET DE L'OCÉAN, Rue Gambetta, R. 2-4, A. $1/_2$, B. 1, déj. 3, D. 4, pens. from
7 fr., etc. — *Furnished Houses* and *Apartments* abound.

Cafés. *Anglais, de Paris*, Place Bellevue; *de l'Europe*, Place de la Liberté.

Baths at the Bathing Establishments (see below) 35 c., with dress 50 c.

Cabs. With one horse $1^1/_2$ fr. per hr.; with two horses 2 fr.; $1/_2$ fr.
more outside the town; 1 fr. more at night (10 p. m. to 7 a. m.). — BATH
CHAIRS drawn by donkeys, 1 and $1^1/_2$ fr. — OMNIBUS to La Négresse station
(p. 123), 1 fr.; particulars at one of the offices in the Place de la Mairie.

Casino. Adm. 1 fr.; 3 fr. after 7 p. m. Subscription for a week 15,
for a fortnight 25, for a month 40 fr.

English Church (*St. Andrew's*); Chaplain, *Rev. W. G. Sharpin.* — British
Vice-consul; *Mr. E. H. W. Bellairs.* — English and American Physicians:
Dr. Macken, Dr. Welby, Dr. Malpas.

Biarritz, a town of 9177 inhab., situated on a line of cliffs
facing the Bay of Biscay, is one of the most frequented bathing-
places in France, especially during September. The court patron-
age of the Second Empire undoubtedly contributed to this result,
but the reputation of the place is also founded on its real merits,
such as its singular situation and its magnificent beach. The climate is mild and free from extremes, so that Biarritz is now in
vogue as a winter-resort. On the other hand, the parks and woods
which constitute the charm of Arcachon are altogether wanting
here. The tone of society, too, is very different, Biarritz being
specially frequented by the upper classes, by the aristocracy of
Southern France and by Spaniards in summer, and by the English
in winter.

The station is now in the Place de la Liberté, near which, to
the right, is the *Place Bellevue*, between the Casino and the Grand
Hôtel. From the Place we obtain a fine view of the sea and of
the beautiful situation of Biarritz.

The *Grande Plage*, which is more than $^1/_8$ M. long, extends

on the N. to *Cape St. Martin*, on which is a lighthouse of the first
class. It is divided into two parts by a small promontory on which
stands the former *Villa Eugénie*, a large and massive building erected
by Napoleon III. for his wife, converted into a hotel in 1894. Opposite is an elegant new *Russian Church*. At the beginning of
the Grande Plage is the principal *Bathing Establishment*, in the
Moorish style, with a terrace which always presents a scene of great
animation. The fine sandy beach is safe and pleasant for bathing,
and the force of the waves is slightly broken by a barrier of rock.

The road passing the base of the Casino leads to the *Atalaye*, a
promontory crowned by a ruined castle and surrounded by a picturesque chaos of rocks called *La Chinaougue*. On one side of it is
a small fishing harbour, on the other (reached by a tunnel 82 yds.
in length) a harbour of refuge, the half-ruined pier of which affords
a fine view of the Spanish mountains near the mouth of the Bidassoa. From the tunnel, a road descends to the *Port-Vieux*, a
narrow and perfectly sheltered creek between rocks. Here stands
the *Bathing Establishment* for persons who are weakly or unaccus-
tomed to the sea. — Farther on we reach another beach, the *Côte
des Basques*, where the waves, with nothing to arrest them, attain
extraordinary force. There is a third bathing establishment here.
On the second Sunday in September the Basques resort to this
beach in vast numbers, and bathe all together, affording a very
curious spectacle.

In 1893 *Saline Baths*, connected with a hydropathic establishment, swimming-bath, etc., were opened at Biarritz, on the Bayonne
road. They are supplied by the saline springs of Briscous, 12 M. to
the E., whence the water is brought by means of subterranean canals.

The *Race Course* is at *La Barre*, near the entrance to the harbour of
Bayonne, reached by the road followed by the tramway, then by the
Avenue du Phare, and the Chemin des Pignadars.

From Bayonne to *St. Sebastian*, see R. 18; to *Pau, Toulouse*, etc., see R. 10.

From Bayonne to Cambo, St. Jean-Pied-de-Port, and Roncevaux.
To (12 M.) *Cambo*, Railway in 35-40 min. (fares 2 fr. 15, 1 fr. 45, 95 c.);
thence to (24 M.) *St. Jean-Pied-de-Port*, by rail to (13¹/₂ M.) *Ossès*, whence
a diligence (1 fr. 20 c.) plies in connection with the trains, pending the
completion of the railway; from St. Jean to (18¹/₂ M.) *Roncevaux*, interesting carriage-road. — The railway ascends the left bank of the Nive,
passing (6 M.) *Villefranque*, (8 M.) *Ustaritz*, a small industrial town, and
(10 M.) *Halsou*. — 12 M. Cambo (*Hôtel Angleterre* or *St. Martin, de Paris*,
both near the Baths; *de France; des Basques*) is a picturesquely situated
village, partly on a steep eminence on the right bank of the Nive (*Haut-
Cambo*) and partly in the valley (*Bas-Cambo*). About ³/₄ M. farther (station, see p. 70) is a bathing-establishment, with iron and sulphur springs.
The climate is hot in summer, but pleasant in spring and autumn.
A great gathering of Basques takes place on St. John's Eve (June 23rd),
when each tries to drink the greatest possible amount of water whilst
the clock is striking twelve (midnight), in order to insure his well-being
until the following anniversary. They also take away with them a supply
of the water for those who have not been able to come. The *Church* at
Haut-Cambo, in the style peculiar to the country, contains three galleries
for men and a blue ceiling with silver stars. — The environs are pretty.
The railway continues to ascend on the right bank of the Nive, via

(12½ M.) *Cambo-les-Bains* and (15½ M.) *Itxassou* or *Itsatsou*. About 1 M.
from this village, in the rocky part of the Nive valley, is the *Pas de
Roland*, a rock through which the road passes by an opening made,
according to the legend, by a kick of the Paladin's foot. The chief
eminence near Cambo is the *Pic Mondarrain* (2460 ft.; to the S.), which
is easily climbed in 2 hrs. from Itxassou. The top, on which is a ruined
fortress, commands a very extensive view. — The next stations are (18½ M.)
Louhossoa and (21½ M.) *Bidarray*, 3 M. from which is a small grotto containing a stalactite, regarded with superstitious veneration by the peasants. — 25½ M. *Ossès*, the temporary terminus of the railway, at the
confluence of the *Nive de St. Etienne* and the *Nive d'Arnéguy*. A diligence
(1 fr. 25 c.) plies hence to (7½ M.) *St. Etienne-de-Baigorry* (Hotel), a town
of 2343 inhab., in the valley of the Nive de St. Etienne.

The road to St. Jean ascends the valley of the Nive d'Arnéguy, viâ
(7 M.) *Irouléguy* and (9½ M.) *Ascarat*. — 10½ M. (38 M. from Bayonne)
St. Jean-Pied-de-Port (*Hôtel de France*), a small town fortified by Vauban
in order to command the passage of the *Port* or *Col de Roncevaux* (see
below). St. Jean, the old capital of Basse-Navarre, has belonged to
France since the Treaty of the Pyrenees in 1659. — A diligence plies
hence to *St. Palais* (p. 127).

Beyond St. Jean the road runs to the S., on the right bank of the
Nive, which forms several picturesque gorges. At (5 M.) *Arnéguy* we quit
French territory by crossing the river. — 7½ M. *Luzaide* or *Valcarlos*
(Hôtel de Barcelone) is a Spanish village with a hydropathic establish-
ment. The road now ascends in windings (short-cuts for walkers) to the
Port de Roncevaux (3470 ft.; fine view) in about 3¼ hrs. from Valcarlos.
From the col, on which is an ancient chapel, we descend in less than
½ hr. to Roncevaux. — 18½ M. (50 M. from Bayonne) **Roncevaux**, Span.
Roncesvalles (3200 ft.; *Posada*) is situated in the valley famous for the
defeat of Charlemagne's rear-guard in 778, and the death of Roland, better
known in poetry than in history. Eginhard is the only chronicler who
mentions the famous paladin as among the slain. The village contains
an ancient *Abbey*, with a Gothic church enriched with a costly statue of
the Virgin and several interesting paintings. The *Chapel of the Holy Ghost*,
near the church, is said to mark the spot where the companions of
Charlemagne were buried. — The road goes on to *Pampeluna*, 28 M. from
Roncevaux.

10. From Bordeaux to Toulouse.

159 M. RAILWAY in 4¾-8½ hrs. (fares 28 fr. 90, 19 fr. 55, 12 fr. 75 c.).
The trains start from the Gare du Midi or St. Jean.

Bordeaux, see p. 46. The line diverges to the left from that to
Bayonne and ascends the valley of the Garonne. — 3¾ M. *Bègles*;
4½ M. *Villenave-d'Ornon*; 5½ M. *Cadaujac*; 8¾ M. *St. Médard-
d'Eyrans*. — 12 M. *Beautiran*.

From Beautiran a branch-line runs to (20½ M.) *Houéins* (p. 62). The
chief intermediate station is (4½ M.) La Brède (*Hôtel du Grand-Montes-
quieu*), a small town containing the château of Montesquieu (1685-1755),
a building of the 13-15th centuries. The chamber of the famous essayist is
kept as it was in his lifetime (visitors admitted). A statue of Montesquieu,
by P. Granet, was erected here in 1895.

13 M. *Portets*; 15 M. *Arbanats*; 17½ M. *Podensac*; 18½ M.
Cérons. About 1 M. to the E. of the last station, on the right bank
of the Garonne, is the small town of *Cadillac*, still surrounded by
walls of the 14th cent. with fine gates. The *Château d'Epernon* at
Cadillac, an edifice of the 16-17th cent., has been converted into a
prison for women. — We now traverse a district famous for its

white wines, those of (21 M.) *Barsac* and (23 M.) *Preignac* being specially esteemed. *Sauternes* (p. 57), which lends its name to the whole class, is about 4 M. to the S.W. of the latter place.

26 M. **Langon** *(Cheval Blanc)*, a town of 4733 inhab., on the left bank of the Garonne, with a suspension bridge, has a small harbour at which the tide is perceptible.

From Langon to Bazas, 12¹/₂ M., railway in 40-55 min. (fares 2 fr. 25, 1 fr. 50 c., 1 fr.). — 4¹/₂ M. *Roaillan*. — About 2 M. to the N. of (7¹/₂ M.) *Nizan* is the *Château de Roquetaillade*, built in the beginning of the 14th cent., with six towers and a keep more than 100 ft. high.

[Nizan is the junction of a branch-line to several industrial places, including (4¹/₂ M.) *Villandraut*, the birthplace of Pope Clement V. (Bertr. de Goth; d. 1314), whose large *Château* still exists, though in ruins; and (11 M.) *St. Symphorien* (junction of the line to Facture and Arès; p. 62).]

12¹/₂ M. **Bazas** *(Cheval Blanc)*, a town with 4948 inhab., on a rock washed by the Beuve, belonged to the ancient *Vasates*. It played an important part in the Religious Wars, when it was the scene of excesses of all kinds committed both by Catholics and Protestants. Down to 1790 it was the seat of a bishop. The *Cathedral* dates from the 13-16th centuries. Some of the 13th cent. *Town-Walls* and a number of old *Houses* are interesting. — The railway is to be extended from Bazas to Auch (p. 104).

The main line now crosses the Garonne by a bridge succeeded by a long viaduct.

29 M. **St. Macaire** *(Hôtel de l'Alma)*, a town of 2250 inhab., to the right, the ancient *Ligena*, suffered considerably in the Hundred Years'War and the Religious Wars. It still possesses the remains of three lines of defence of the middle ages, the principal feature being a gateway of the 13th cent., and many quaint old houses. The handsome church of *St. Sauveur*, in the Romanesque and Gothic styles (12-15th cent.), has transepts ending in apses, and contains some ancient mural paintings which have recently suffered considerable injury. About 3 M. to the N.W. is *Verdelais*, with a pilgrim's shrine of the Virgin. — 39 M. *St. Pierre-d'Aurillac*. A little farther on the river is joined by the *Canal Latéral à la Garonne*, 120 M. long, which meets the Canal du Midi at Toulouse (p. 80). — 32¹/₂ M. *Caudrot*; 35 M. *Gironde*, beyond which are two short tunnels near La Réole.

38 M. **La Réole** *(Grand Hôtel)*, a town of 4177 inhab., on a hill rising from the Garonne, was built in the 10th cent. round the Benedictine abbey of *Regula*. We turn to the right on quitting the station, pass the end of a suspension-bridge, and ascend to the right. The church of *St. Pierre*, at the other end of the town, dates from the 13-15th cent. and has a modern Romanesque steeple. Adjoining is the former *Abbey* (17th cent.); and behind the church is a *Terrace* with a modern Collège. Near the church are the ruins of a *Castle* built by the English during their rule; it is now private property and is still partly inhabited. From the end of the Grande-Rue we keep to the left by the Rue Gensac and Rue Brumard to visit the Romanesque *Halle*, with its row of fine columns.

41¹/₂ M. *Lamothe-Landeron*; 45 M. *Ste. Bazeille*.

49 M. **Marmande** (*Hôt. des Messageries*, near the station; *du Centre*, Rue Nationale) is a commercial and industrial town (10,341 inhab.) on the Garonne. The Boul. Gambetta, to the left, then the Rue Puyguéraud, to the right, bring us to the Place Nationale, whence the street of the same name leads to the *Church*, of the 12-15th cent., adjoined on the right by a ruined cloister, in the Renaissance style.

From Marmande to Bergerac, 46¹/₂ M., railway in 2¹/₄-2¹/₂ hrs. (fares 8 fr. 40, 5 fr. 65, 3 fr. 70 c.). The line runs viâ (5 M.) *Seyches*, (15¹/₂ M.) *Miramont*, a town of 2000 inhab., with trade in 'prunes d'Agen' and containing a statue of Martignac (1778-1832), the statesman, by Foyatier; (21¹/₂ M.) *Eymet*, proposed terminus of the new line from Bordeaux viâ La Sauve (p. 56); and (35 M.) *Issigeac*, etc. — 46¹/₂ M. *Bergerac* (p. 14).

From Marmande to Mont-de-Marsan, 61 M., railway in 3-3³/₄ hrs. (fares 11 fr. 10, 7 fr. 40, 4 fr. 85 c.). — This line diverges to the left from that to Bordeaux, and crossing the Garonne and the lateral canal by means of a viaduct over 1000 yds. in length, ascends the valley of the Avance. — 18 M. *Casteljaloux* ('Castelgelos'; *Hôtel Giral*), a town of 3710 inhab., with a ruined *Château*, remains of *Fortifications*, an old *Commandery* of the Knights Templar (now the Mairie), and chalybeate springs. — Farther on the scenery is monotonous as the line traverses the extremity of the *Landes* (p. 61). — 42 M. *Retjons-Lugaut*. — 46 M. *Roquefort*, a small town with a ruined château. — 61 M. *Mont-de-Marsan* (p. 64).

55 M. *Fauguerolles*. — 60 M. **Tonneins** (*Hôt. de l'Europe*), with 7090 inhab., on the Garonne, formerly consisted of two towns, which were destroyed in 1622 by Louis XIII. on account of their attachment to Protestantism. Branch-line to *Penne* viâ *Villeneuve-sur-Lot*, see p. 103. — 64¹/₂ M. *Nicole*, beyond which we cross the Lot, not far from its confluence with the Garonne.

67 M. **Aiguillon** (*Tapis Vert*), the *Acillo* of the Romans, on the left bank of the Lot, contains 3120 inhab. and possesses ther uins of a castle of the Dukes of that name, and a modern Gothic church.

72 M. **Port-Ste. Marie** (*Hôt. de l'Europe*), a small and ancient town on the Garonne, with two Gothic churches of the 14th century.

From Port-Ste. Marie to Riscle, 72 M., railway in 4³/₄-6¹/₃ hrs. (fares 10 fr. 25, 7 fr. 35, 4 fr. 50 c.). — The line crosses the Garonne. 3³/₄ M. *Feugarolles*; 6¹/₄ M. *Vianne*, a small walled town; 8 M. *Lavardac*, a small industrial town on the *Baÿse*, with a trade in cork.

12 M. **Nérac** (*Hôtel de France*), a commercial town of 6800 inhab. on the Baÿse, belonged to the Sires d'Albret from the 14th cent. onwards, and was often the residence of the court of Navarre in the 16th cent., before the accession of Henri IV. to the French throne. Taken and dismantled by Louis XIII. on account of its Protestant sympathies, it has never regained its former importance. Only a part of its 16th cent. *Château* remains, but the park still exists, forming the beautiful *Promenade de la Garenne*, which contains various points of interest. In one of the squares of Nérac is a statue of Henri IV., by Raggi. The *Sous-préfecture* contains a small Musée. — A branch-line runs hence to (9¹/₂ M.) the little town of *Mézin*, and is to be prolonged to Mont-de-Marsan (p. 64).

Several small stations are passed. — 25 M. **Condom** (*Hôtel du Lion-d'Or*), a town with 7405 inhab., on the Baÿse, carrying on an important trade in Armagnac brandy. It was formerly the seat of a bishopric, which was held by Bossuet. The handsome Gothic *Cathedral* (1506-21) is adjoined by remains of a cloister, now containing the *Hôtel de Ville*.

Several small stations are passed. — 40 M. **Eause** (*Hôtel Soubeyran*), a town of 4110 inhab. on the *Gelise*. It is the modern representative of *Elusa*, an important town in the time of Cæsar, which was completely

destroyed about A. D. 810. The old town was at *La Civitat* ('City'), about
1/2 M. distant, on a plateau above the right bank of the Gelise, and many
antiquities have been discovered on its site. Eauze has a fine Gothic
Church of the 16th century.

49¹/₂ M. *Gaillon*; 53¹/₄ M. *Manciet.* — 58¹/₂ M. *Nogaro*, a town of 2364
inhab., with a trade in brandy. Its old Romanesque church is interesting. — 61¹/₂ M. *Sobrets*; 64 M. *Fustérouau*; 68 M. *Thermes.* — 72 M. *Riscle*,
p. 64.

76 M. *Fourtic*; 79 M. *St. Hilaire*; 80¹/₂ M. *Colayrac.* As we
approach Agen, we see to the right a fine aqueduct, carrying the
canal across the railway (see below).

84 M. **Agen** *(Buffet).* — **Hotels.** Des Ambassadeurs et de France,
Cours Voltaire 22; Gr.-Hôt. Baran, Place du Marché-au-Blé, good, R. 2,
déj. 2¹/₂, D. 3 fr.; Petit-St. Jean, Cours Voltaire 35, expensive; George,
Rue Jacquard; Jasmin, at the station. — Cafés in the Cours and in the
Place de la République; *Grand Café*, near the Place Jasmin. — *Post & Tele-
graph Office*, Place de l'Hôtel-de-Ville.

Agen, a town with 23,234 inhab., the capital of the department
of *Lot-et-Garonne*, and the seat of a bishop, lies on the right bank
of the Garonne. As the capital of the Nitiobriges, it was a place of
importance under the Gauls, and it afterwards became the chief city
of the Agénois. The executions of Albigenses and Huguenots form
bloody pages in its history. It was the birthplace of the philologist
Joseph Scaliger (1540-1609), and of the naturalist Lacépède (1756-
1825). It has a large trade in dried plums.

Most of the town is badly built, and the older streets are
narrow and inconvenient. The wide new Boulevard de la République
(begun in 1885), however, has been constructed through the middle
of the town, from E. to W., and this is to be crossed at right angles
by another, beginning at the station.

In front of the station is the *Steeple of Ste. Foi*, a modern Gothic
tower marking the site of a former church. — A little farther on,
bending to the right, we reach the *Cathedral of St. Caprais*, with
a fine apse and transept of the 11-12th cent., and a nave rebuilt in
the 14-16th centuries. The interior is richly decorated with polychrome paintings and frescoes. Among the most noteworthy features
are the left arm of the transept and the huge piers which formerly
supported a dome, adorned with shafts ending in singular capitals.

The Rue St. Caprais and the succeeding one lead from this
church to the *Market Hall*, a handsome modern building in the
centre of the town. In the E. part of the Boulevard de la République
(see above) are a modern *Bust of François de Cotète* (d. 1567), an
Agenais poet, and a *Statue of the Republic*, by Fumadelles.

In the opposite direction, the Boulevard descends to a small
square adorned with a bronze *Statue of Jasmin*, author of several
poems in the Agenais dialect (1798-1864). The statue, by Vital
Dubray, represents the poet, who was a barber by profession and
has been styled the 'Last of the Troubadours', in a quaint French
costume, and reciting the following verses, which are inscribed
on the pedestal : --

'O ma lengo, tout me sou dit,	O ma langue, tout me le dit,
Plantarey uno estelo	Je placerai une étoile
A toun froun enerumit'.	A ton front renibruni.

In front of the Place Jasmin runs the wide Cours Voltaire, which a little farther to the E. skirts the *Promenade du Gravier*, on the bank of the Garonne, here crossed by a *Suspension Bridge* for foot-passengers. Higher up is a *Stone Bridge*, while lower down is a *Canal Bridge* or aqueduct, over which the Canal Latéral is carried, and which also serves for foot-passengers. The last-mentioned bridge is a fine specimen of engineering skill. On the same side, to the right, not far from the Cours Voltaire, is the *Church of St. Hilaire*, a building of the 15th cent., with a modern façade and a handsome modern tower. The interior is adorned with polychrome paintings and contains some good modern stained-glass windows and a handsome stone organ-loft.

The Rue Loudrade, the second in ascending the Boulevard de la République from the Place Jasmin, leads to the *Eglise des Jacobins*, a brick building of the 13th cent., adorned with polychrome paintings and modern stained-glass windows. — Hence we proceed by the Rue du Pont-de-Garonne to the *Hôtel de Ville*, adjoining which is the *Maison de Montluc*, a building of the 16th cent., with a fine winding staircase. It contains the *Municipal Museum*.

The Museum, which is at present of little importance, is open to the public on Sun. and Thurs. from 1 to 4 or 5, and to strangers on other days also. — On the ground-floor are Roman antiquities and sculptured and architectural fragments, mosaics, small bronzes, etc. — The rooms on the first floor contain paintings (most of them modern), faïence and pottery, antiques, curiosities, and objects of natural history. Among the pictures may be mentioned Clytemnestra, by *Toudouze*; Le Rabouteux, by *Carteron*; the Massacre of Machecoul, by *Flameng*; Emp. Henry IV. at Canossa, by *Darant*; Battle-field in Lorraine, by *Bettannier*; and the Valley of Pralognan, by *J. Desbrosses*.

The Rue Montesquieu, which begins at the Market and is joined by the streets which pass the Hôtel de Ville, leads S. to the *Promenade de la Plate-Forme*, in which stand the *Préfecture*, originally the Bishop's Palace (18th cent.), the modern *Palais de Justice*, and other large buildings. In front of the Palais de Justice is a small bronze *War Monument* ('Round the flag'), by Campagne. The Rue Palissy, to the right, leads back to the Gravier (see above).

From Agen to *Périgueux*, to *Auch*, and to *Tarbes*, see R. 14.

87 M. *Bon-Encontre*, the station for the pilgrimage-resort of that name, 1¼ M. to the N.E., and the junction of the line to Auch and Tarbes (p. 103). — 90 M. *Lafox*; 93 M. *St. Nicolas-de-la-Balerme*; 97 M. *La Magistère*; 100 M. *Valence-d'Agen*; 105 M. *Malause*. The Garonne is crossed by numerous suspension-bridges, one of the finest of which, near Moissac, is prolonged by a viaduct, carrying the road over the railway.

111 M. **Moissac** (*Hôtel du Nord*, mediocre), a commercial town with 8797 inhab., on the Canal Latéral and the right bank of the *Tarn*, owes its existence to an ancient abbey, believed to have been

founded in the 7th century. To reach the interesting remains of
the abbey, which adjoin the hotel and consist of the church and
the cloisters, we turn to the left at the end of the avenue issuing
from the station.

The *Church*, dedicated to St. Peter, was rebuilt in the 15th cent.
but retains a magnificent, though somewhat mutilated *Portal of
the 12th century.

The portal consists of a deeply recessed archway forming a kind of
porch. The central pier is adorned with lions and statues of the Prophets in high relief, while on the lateral piers are similar statues of
Isaiah and St. Peter, and sculptured bands of rats and birds. The inner
walls of the porch are also lavishly embellished with groups of statues
(the Annunciation and the Visitation on the right; Avarice and Luxury
on the left) and bas-reliefs (Infancy of Our Lord, Dives and Lazarus). The
tympanum group represents Our Lord surrounded by the Elders of the
Apocalypse, with symbols of the Apostles and two Angels. Both statues
and reliefs are framed in bands of decorative sculpture, of great beauty
and delicacy, and at each side are three attached columns, the capitals
of which are adorned with griffins, arabesques, etc.

The chief objects of interest in the interior are the Renaissance screen
enclosing the sanctuary, the organ, and a Merovingian sarcophagus (below).

The *Cloister*, adjoining the church on the left, and entered from
the little Place in front of it (custodian), dates from 1100-1108 and
is one of the finest in France. Its arches, which are very slightly
pointed, rest alternately on single and clustered columns, the capitals of which are embellished with scenes explained by inscriptions.

Beyond Moissac the railway passes through two short tunnels,
after which we see on the right the church of St. Pierre (see above).
It then crosses the Tarn by a tubular bridge, and reaches —

116 M. **Castelsarrasin** (*Hôtel de France; de l'Europe*), a town with
7772 inhabitants. The name has nothing to do with the Saracens,
but is supposed to be a corruption of 'Castel-sur-Azin' or 'Castrum
Cerrucium'. The brick church of *St. Sauveur* (12-15th cent.) is
interesting; the tower over the nave is modern.

Beyond (121 M.) *La Villedieu* the lines to Cahors and Limoges
(p. 112) diverge to the left.

128 M. **Montauban** (*Buffet*). — The *Gare du Midi* lies about ¼ M.
from the centre of the town, in the suburb of Ville-Bourbon, and the
Gare d'Orléans about as far on the opposite side, in the suburb of Ville-
Nouvelle, but the two stations are connected by rail, and the trains which
arrive at the latter go on to the former.

Hotels. Du Midi, Place d'Armes, of the first class; de l'Europe,
Place de l'Horloge and Rue de l'Hôtel-de-Ville; Quatre Saisons, Rue
Bessières. — *Café de l'Europe*, Place de la Préfecture.

Montauban, a prosperous town with 30,388 inhab., the capital
of the department of *Tarn-et-Garonne*, and the seat of a bishop,
occupies a plateau on the right bank of the Tarn, the sides of
which are washed by two small affluents of that river.

Montauban was founded in 1144 by Alphonse I., Count of Toulouse,
on the site of the Roman station of *Mons Albanus*. It embraced with ardour the doctrines of the Albigenses, partly through hatred of the monks
of Le Moustier, which is now its N.E. suburb, and the Inquisition wrought
terrible havoc here, without, however, preventing the Reformation from

making such progress that the town was one of the chief strongholds of
the Huguenots. Louis XIII. failed in his attempt to capture the town in
1621, but the struggle could not be continued after the fall of La Rochelle,
and the town, submitting to Richelieu in 1629, had its fortifications levelled. Even now it is partly Protestant, and it has a Faculty of Protestant Theology.

Quitting the Garo du Midi, we traverse the suburb of *Ville-
Bourbon*, with a fine modern Romanesque church, and cross the
Tarn by a lofty brick *Bridge*, built in 1303-1316, with pointed
arches; it was formerly fortified. The water of the Tarn is even
more turbid than the waters of the Gers and the Gironde.

The *Hôtel de Ville*, a brick building on the other side of the
bridge, is the old château, begun by the Counts of Toulouse, added
to by the Black Prince in the 14th cent., and finished by Bishop P.
de Berthier in the 17th century. The MUNICIPAL MUSEUM, on the
first floor, is chiefly interesting because it contains the collections
as well as some paintings and souvenirs of *Ingres*, who was a native
of Montauban (1780-1867). It is open to the public on Sun. from
1 to 4, and to strangers on other days also.

First Floor. — Room I. Above the door, 34. *Ingres*, Dream of Ossian,
unfinished; to the right, 259. *J. Jouvenet*, Descent from the Cross, a
smaller replica of the picture in the Louvre; 297. *Sturler* (pupil of Ingres),
Procession of Cimabue's picture of the Madonna; 378. *Italian School*,
Adoration of the Magi, with the Ascension as predella; 278. *Mignard*,
Portrait of a prince; copies of *Correggio*, *Giulio Romano*, *Titian*, and *Ingres*.
— The glass-cases contain small antiquities, miniatures, medals, bronzes,
drawings, etc. Busts in bronze. — Room II. To the right, 291. *Rigaud*, Portrait; 193. Copy of *Murillo*, St. Augustine; 187. *Van Dyck*, Portrait of a
monk; 350. *Italian School*, Cæsar Borgia; 199. *Jordaens*, Silenus and the
four Seasons; 192. *Coello*, Coronation of Charles V.; 365. *Von Calcar*, Portrait of a man; 292. *Couder*, The Levite of Ephraim; 249. *Glaize*, Faun
and Bacchante, painted on wax in imitation of the antique; 202. *Pourbus
the Elder*, Portrait of a woman; several other portraits by unknown hands;
384. *Bellini*, Circumcision; 227. *Cambon* (of Montauban), The Republic
(1848); 341. *Albani*, Allegory. — *44. *Ingres*, Jesus among the Doctors in
the Temple; no number, *French School*, Pastoral; 178. After *Titian*, Venus
crowned by Cupid; 200. *Jordaens*, Head of a faun; 363. *Bassano*, Country
scene; 247. *De Gironde* (of Montauban), Judith; 50. *Poussin*, Landscape;
248. *Valentin*, Singers; 349. *Italian School*, Crucifixion; no number, *Spanish
School (Murillo?)*, Singing-lesson; no number, *Salvator Rosa*, Guard-house;
204. *Pourbus the Elder*, Portrait of a man; 376. *P. Veronese* (?), Madonna and
Child. — In the centre: to the right, *Cararaggio* (?), Portrait; *Vasari* (?),
Judith; *Cambon*, Sleeping nymph, Roland and Olympia; to the left, *Cambon*, Artist's portrait; *P. Veronese* (?), Doge and Dogaressa; *De Gironde*,
The Sleeper. — Behind the pictures on the right: 205. *Rubens*, The Thinker;
288. *Lawitzki*, Catherine of Russia; 191. *Flemish School*, Writer.

Room III., the first room of the *Musée Ingres*. In the middle is
the easel of the artist, with an unfinished picture. To the right of
the door, 182. *P. Veronese*, Head of a woman; 4. *Velazquez*, Portrait of a
woman; 124. *Unknown Master*, Head of Christ; 109. *Giottino*, Triptych;
41. *Ingres*, Ruggiero delivering Angelica, a variation on that in the Louvre;
191. *Byzantine School*, Ten Saints; 1. *Holbein the Younger*, Portrait of a
monk; 13. *G. Poussin*, Landscape; 9. *Phil. de Champaigne*, Monk per-
forming the operation of trepanning; 21. *H. Flandrin*, Portrait of Ingres;
118, 116, 117. *Unknown Artists of the 17th cent.*, Saints, Christ; 16. *Chardin*,
Dead game; 10. *Pourbus the Younger*, Portrait of a man. This room also
contains several copies, small antiquities, a glass-case with souvenirs of
Ingres, and a mantelpiece with sculptures by the father of the painter

Ingres. — Rooms IV., V., VI. contain an important collection of drawings (many of them copies by Ingres himself), antiquities, casts, pictures (15. Portrait of Molière, attributed to *Seb. Bourdon;* copies of Raphael), sculptures (Cupid bending his bow, attributed to *Praxiteles*), bronzes, etc. The ceilings of the 4th and 5th rooms deserve notice.

The *Basement* contains a *Museum of Antiquities and Objects of Art* of the Middle Ages and the Renaissance. — The *Public Library* (25,000 vols.) and archives are also deposited in the Hôtel de Ville.

Opposite the Hôtel de Ville stands the *Exchange*, containing a Museum of Natural History (second floor; open on Sun., 1 to 4).

The Rue de l'Hôtel-de-Ville leads towards the Place d'Armes and the cathedral (see below). In the meantime, however, we turn to the right and proceed to the *Church of St. Jacques*, a brick building in the Gothic style of Toulouse (see p. 81), with an octagonal tower adorned on the outside with faïence. The pulpit and the fine modern stained-glass windows are noteworthy. — A little farther to the E., behind St. Jacques, is the *Place Nationale*, bordered by double arcades and with gates at the corners (17th cent.).

In the Place d'Armes (see above), which we reach by turning to the right on the other side of the Place Nationale, stands the *Cathedral*, a commonplace building of the 18th cent., but containing a fine painting by *Ingres* (in the sacristy), representing the Vow of Louis XIII. — A little farther on, to the left, is the *Préfecture*, a modern edifice in stone and brick.

The Promenade des Acacias, to the right, on this side of the Préfecture, in front of a convent, leads to the *Promenade des Carmes*, at the end of which stands the *Monument to Ingres*, by Etex. It consists mainly of a bas-relief in bronze, reproducing the picture of the Apotheosis of Homer, with some modifications by Ingres himself, and of a marble statue of the artist seated in front of his work. In clear weather the Pyrenees are visible from this point. At the beginning of the promenade is the entrance to the *Jardin des Plantes* (25 c.) which occupies the slope on the right bank of the *Tescou*, an affluent of the Tarn, and also part of the left bank in the suburb of *Sapiac.* — The church of Sapiac, which is reached by the street descending at the end of the promenade, possesses a second-rate picture by Ingres, representing Ste. Germaine (second chapel on the right).

From Montauban to *Limoges* (Paris), see RR. 16a, 16a; to *Montpellier* viâ *Castres*, see R. 13; to *Lexos* (Limoges line), see p. 115.

The railway now returns to the side of the Canal Latéral, leaving on the left the line to Castres, and passes through a fertile but uninteresting district. — 135 M. *Montbartier;* 139½ M. *Dieupentale;* 143 M. *Grisolles;* 146 M. *Castelnau-d'Estretefonds;* 150 M. *St. Jory;* 155 M. *Lacourtensourt*, where we join the Paris line (R. 16; to the left).

159 M. *Toulouse* (Gare Matabiau), see R. 11.

11. Toulouse.

Railway Stations. *Gare Matabiau* (Pl. F, 1, 2; Buffet), the central station on the N.E. side of the town; *Gare St. Cyprien* (Pl. A, 5), to the S.W., about 1¼ M. from the stone bridge over the Garonne, for the line for Auch (p. 86). — There are no hotel-omnibuses at the stations, but the trains are met by railway-omnibuses (25 c. for each pers. and for each trunk) and cabs (see below). The town-office of the railway-omnibuses is at Rue Lafayette, 21.

Hotels. Hôtel Tivollier, Rue d'Alsace-Lorraine 17 and 19 (Pl. E, 3); du Midi. Place du Capitole 1 and 2 (Pl. E, 3). R., L., & A. 6-10, déj. from 4, D. from 5, pens. 15 fr.; Souville, Place du Capitole 20, with baths, R., L., & A. 8-10, B. 1½, déj. 3, D. 4. pens. from 9 fr.; all these of the first class. — Or. Hôtel Meublé des Arcades, Place du Capitole. — De l'Europe, Square Lafayette 16 (Pl. E, 3), R., L., & A. 4-7, B. 1/₄-1½, déj. 4, D. 5, pens. 10-15 fr.; Capoul, Place Lafayette 12, R., L., & A. 2½-4, B. 1, déj. 3, D. 3½ fr.; Haichaux, Rue des Arts 7 (Pl. E, 3, 4), R., L., & A. 3-7, B. 1, déj. 3, D. 3½ fr.; Grand Hôtel Central, Rue St. Pantaléon 1, behind the Hôtel Tivollier, R., L., & A. 4-7, déj. 3, D. 4-6 fr. (à la carte); de la Poste (Maison Meublée), Rue d'Alsace-Lorraine 35, R. 2½-6 fr. — Domerg'e. Rue Gambetta 33 (Pl. D, 3); de Paris, Rue Gambetta 66, near the Place du Capitole, R., L., & A. 2½-5, B. 1, déj. 3, D. 3½, pens. 6½ fr.; du Grand Balcon, Rue des Lois and Rue Romiguières (Pl. D, 3); *Hôtel Meublé, Rue Neuve-St. Aubin 5; Hôtel Chaubard or du Buffet, opposite the Gare Matabiau, with restaurant, R., L., & A. 2½-3, B. 1, D. 3 fr.; Bayard, close by.

Restaurants. *Tivollier*, see above; *Café Albrighi*, Allées Lafayette, déj. 3 fr.; *Café de la Paix* (Hôt. de Paris), déj. 2½, D. 3 fr.; *Hôtel Chaubard*, opposite the Gare Matabiau; *Buffet* at the Gare Matabiau. — A speciality of Toulouse and other towns in S. France is Pâtés de Foies de Canard aux Truffes (pies of duck's liver with truffles), and they are also famous for their ortolans, mushrooms, and fruits.

Cafés. *Tivollier*, see above; *Café de la Paix*, *Bibent*, *Baric*, *des Deux-Mondes*, Place du Capitole; *Albrighi*, *du Midi*, *des Américains*, *de Toulouse*, *de la Comédie*, in the Allées Lafayette, and the Boul. de Strasbourg and Lazare-Carnot; *Gr. Café Fagot*, Allées Lafayette, near the station; in the Place Etienne, etc.

Cabs (*Citadines*). One horse: per drive within the town 80 c. by day, 1¾ fr. after midnight, per hr. 1½ and 2½ fr. Two horses: per drive 1 fr. 10 c. and 2 fr., per hr. 1 fr. 80 c. and 3 fr. Drive to hirer's address, 25 c. more. Each package of luggage 20 c.

Tramways (comp. the Plan). From the *Place du Capitole* (Pl. E, 3) to St. Cyprien (Pl. C, 4), to the Gare Matabiau (Pl. F, 1), to the Minimes (N. suburb; Pl. D, 1). From the *Allées Lafayette* (Pl. E, F, 2) to Les Amidonniers (Pl. C, 2), and to St. Michel (Pl. D, 5) by the boulevards. From the *Rue des Tourneurs* (Marché; Pl. E, 4) to the Gare Matabiau. From the *Place Extérieure St. Michel* (bridge; Pl. D, 5) to the Place St. Cyprien. Fare 10 c.; 'correspondance' 5 and 10 c.'— *Omnibuses* also ply in the city and suburbs.

Post and Telegraph Office (Pl. E, 2), Rue de la Poste 6; Place de la Bourse (Pl. D, E, 3), etc.

Theatres. *Théâtre du Capitole*, at the Capitole (Pl. E, 3), for operas and comedies (tickets 75 c. to 5 fr.); *Théâtre des Variétés* (Pl. E, 2), Avenue Lafayette, for dramas and operettas (75 c. to 3½ fr.). — Circus, Allées Lafayette 64, near the Canal.

Cafés-Concerts. *Casino*, Rue Dutemps and Place Lafayette; *Pré-Catelon*, Allées Lafayette 60.

Music. At the *Allées Lafayette* (Pl. F, 2; p. 80) and the *Grand-Rond* (Pl. F, 5; p. 84) on Sun. and Thurs.; in the *Place du Capitole* (Pl. E, 3; p. 80) on Thurs.; and at the *Cours Dillon* (Pl. C, D, 4, 5) on Sunday.

Baths. *Dutemps*, Place Lafayette 1 and 2; at the *Hôtel Souville* and the *Hôtel du Buffet*. — River Baths, *Gayton*, Quai de Tounis (Pl. D, 4, 5).

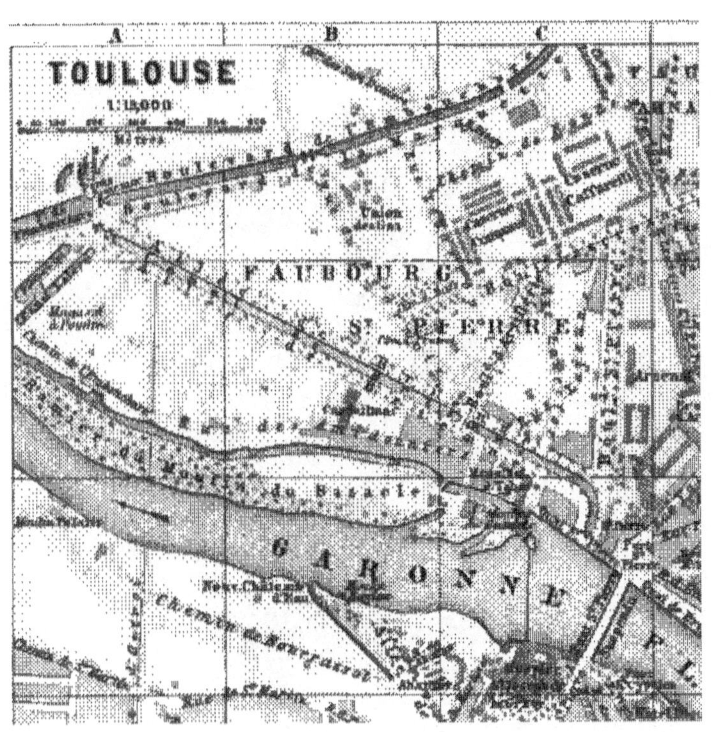

A
B
C
TOULOUSE
1:15,000
FAUBOURG
St. PIERRE
GARONNE

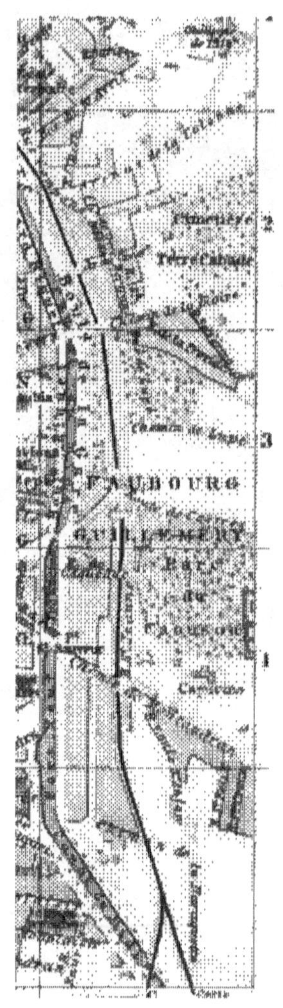

Cimetière 2
Terre Cabade
Chemin de Anglè 3
FAUBOURG
GUILLEMERY
BAC
DE
L'EMBOUQ.
4

Protestant Church, Rue Deville (Pl. D, 3). — **Synagogue,** Rue Palaprat 2 (Pl. F, 3).

Toulouse still maintains night watchmen who cry the hours ('minuit passé, dormez en paix').

Toulouse (460 ft.), the ancient capital of *Languedoc*, the present capital of the department of the *Haute-Garonne*, the headquarters of the 17th army corps, and the seat of an Archbishopric, a University, and a School of Medicine, is a city with 149,791 inhab., situated in a fertile plain on the right bank of the Garonne, at the junction of the Canal du Midi with the Canal Latéral (pp. 72 and 64). It is a large and wealthy town, enjoying great importance from its position as the centre of Southern France, and from the extent of its industry and commerce. The greater part of it, however, is irregularly laid out and meanly built, while its badly paved streets combine with its excessive heat in summer and the violent winds to which it is subject all the year round to make it a fatiguing place for the visitor. Considerable improvements and embellishments have, however, been undertaken and partly executed of late years, and the town has a character of its own and a sufficiency of historic remains to recommend it to the notice of strangers.

Toulouse, the ancient *Tolosa*, was an important town some centuries before it was conquered by the Romans. It was the capital of the Tectosages and possessed a temple which was celebrated for its immense treasures, partly stored in sacred tanks. Having allied itself with the Cimbri to shake off the Roman yoke it was taken, in B. C. 106, by the consul Quinius Servilius Cæpio, who seized the treasures of the temple. Cæpio was, it is true, utterly routed by the Cimbri in the following year, but he was succeeded by Marius, and Toulouse was reduced to submission. In 419, after the fall of the Roman empire, Toulouse became the capital of the Visigoths, and in 507 it passed into the power of the Franks, after Clovis had vanquished Alaric II. at Vouillé. Subsequently it recovered its independence, and in 778 it was made a county governed by hereditary princes till it was united to France in 1271. Under its Counts the city enjoyed a long period of prosperity, but the Albigensian wars brought upon it great calamities. Count Raymond VI., too tolerant in the eyes of those who had just instituted the Inquisition, and accused of the assassination of the Papal Legate, Peter de Castelnau, tried to save the town by a most humiliating submission, but had notwithstanding to see it besieged by Simon de Montfort, leader of the crusade, to whom his dominions had been adjudged. Raymond successfully defended the town on the first attack, but he was dispossessed of it in 1214, after the battle of Muret (p. 138). Toulouse did not, however, tamely accept the rule of De Montfort, and till 1229 its history was little more than a succession of revolts and sieges. On the succession of Louis VIII., King of France, to the claims of Amaury de Montfort, son of Simon, Raymond VII. had finally to submit, and the Inquisition extinguished with the utmost cruelty what was left of heresy. Thereafter the town became so oblivious of the principles it had so bravely defended that it repeatedly made itself notorious by violent acts of intolerance. Thus in 1562 a civil war broke out between the Roman Catholics and the Huguenots, and 4000 of the latter perished, while 300 more were massacred on St. Bartholomew's Day in 1572. Dr. Vanini, accused of Pantheism, was burnt alive here in 1619, after having his tongue cut out, and an aged Protestant, Jean Calas, unjustly accused of murdering his eldest son in order to prevent his becoming a Roman Catholic, was broken on the wheel in 1762. The generous exertion of Voltaire in behalf of the last-named victim is one of the brightest gems in the great author's crown. In 1815 General Ramel, confidant of Louis XVIII., was assassinated here by the Verdets, volunteers more royalist than the king himself. In 1862 the authorities had to interfere to prevent a festal celebration of the tercentenary of the massacres of 1562. — In 1814 the final battle of the Peninsular War took place at Toulouse between Wellington and Soult, some days after Napoleon's abdication.

The *Gare Matabiau* or central station (p. 78), which has become too small for the traffic, lies to the N.E. of the town. On quitting it we cross the *Canal du Midi*, turn to the left, and soon reach the *Allées Lafayette* (Pl. F, 2). At the beginning is a marble *Statue of Riquet*, the creator of the Canal du Midi, by Riffoul-Dorval, erected in 1838.

The **Canal du Midi** or *du Languedoc* was made in 1666-81 by Paul Riquet de Béziers entirely at his own expense (17 million francs, which would to-day represent a sum of 34 million francs, or about 1,300,000 *l.*). It connects the Atlantic and the Mediterranean with the aid of the Garonne. It begins at the Bassin de l'Embouchure (Pl. A, 1), a little below Toulouse, and ends at the Etang de Thau, beyond Agde (p. 85), after a course of 148 M. It is 33 ft. wide at the bottom and 65 ft. at the surface and its depth is 6½ ft. Its highest point is 8 M. to the N.W. of Castelnaudary (p. 87), and it has 100 locks, 26 on the side of the Garonne, with a fall of 200 ft., and 74 on the other side, with a fall of 426 ft. It is fringed by a double row of trees, those on the side next the Mediterranean being cypresses, as those trees are particularly fitted to mitigate the Mistral, which often blows on this side. The *Canal Latéral*, not finished till 1838, was made in consequence of the obstacles to navigation presented by the Garonne in its upper course. The Canal du Languedoc was at one time regarded as a perfect marvel of engineering skill; but lately it has been proposed to replace it by a ship-canal.

On the other side of the canal and the railway stands a huge edifice containing the *Veterinary College* (Pl. F, G, 1), one of the three veterinary colleges which exist in France, the other two being at Alfort (near Paris) and at Lyons. It is not interesting except to professional men. Beyond it stands the *Observatory* (Pl. G, 1; not accessible to the public), adjoining which is a brick *Obelisk*, erected in commemoration of the Battle of Toulouse, which was fought on April 10th, 1814 (see above). In clear weather the Pyrenees may be seen from this point.

At the end of the Allées Lafayette, the Boulevards, which form a ring round the old town, diverge to the right and left. Crossing these we next reach the *Place Lafayette*, an oval Place with a garden embellished with a bronze group ('The Wrestlers') by Labatut. Hence the Rue Lafayette leads to the Capitole, crossing the *Rue d'Alsace-Lorraine*, a new street which traverses the town from N. to S.

On the E. of the Place du Capitole, the centre of the town, rises the **Capitole**, or *Hôtel de Ville* (Pl. E, 3), a building of the 16-19th cent., almost entirely rebuilt in recent times (interior still unfinished). The commonplace Ionic façade, rising directly from the square 'Place' used as a market, scarcely justifies the classic name. That, however, is due to the magistrates of the town before 1789, who were called 'Capitouls'. In the first court, which has a fine Renaissance doorway, by *Bachelier*, with a statue of Henri IV, Duke Henry II. de Montmorency, Marshal and Governor of Languedoc, was beheaded in 1632. He had shared the revolt of the Duke of Orleans against Richelieu because the title of High Constable was refused to him. Visitors are shown the sword with which he is said to have been executed, though in reality he was beheaded by a kind of guillotine, used at that time in Italy. The Capitol is also the seat of the Académie des Jeux-Floraux.

The *Académie des Jeux-Floraux*, perhaps the oldest literary institution in Europe, was founded in 1323-27, under the name of the 'Collège du Gay Scavoir', and observed the custom of distributing flowers of gold and silver to its laureates. Clémence Isaure, a noble dame of Toulouse, left a legacy at the end of the 15th cent., which enabled it to increase the number of these flowers, and the Flower Fête is held every year with great solemnity on May 3rd. The flowers distributed are nine in number: the amaranth of gold, the violet, marigold, primrose, eglantine, and lily of silver, all for poetry; the violet or eglantine and immortelle or jasmine of gold, for prose compositions, and the carnation of silver, a 'consolation prize'. The Academy consists of 40 'Mainteneurs' and an indefinite number of 'Maîtres-ès-jeux'. The former are so called because it is supposed to be their duty to 'maintain' the Provençal language and literature.

The Capitole is also the seat of an *Academy of Science, Inscriptions*, and *Belles-Lettres*, founded in 1640, and of an *Academy of Legislation*, dating from 1851. The town numbers many other learned societies. The former *University* of Toulouse, founded in 1229, was the oldest in France after that of Paris; at present the town possesses only an *Académie Universitaire*.

To the S. of the Capitole is the *Théâtre Municipal du Capitole* (p. 78), and behind the two buildings is the *Donjon*, a square keep of the 15th cent., restored by Viollet-le-Duc in 1880, and now the depository of the archives.

We may now either visit the Musée (p. 85) or proceed to the N. from the Place du Capitole, following the Rue du Taur, which owes its name to the *Eglise du Taur* (Pl. E, 2; to the right), built on the spot to which St. Saturnin, the apostle of Toulouse, was dragged by the bull which he had refused to sacrifice to Jupiter. It is a building of the 14-15th cent. and possesses a façade with triangular arches and battlements. The interior contains some modern paintings.

The church of **St. Sernin*, or *St. Saturnin* (Pl. D, 2), at the end of this street, is the chief monument of Toulouse and one of the finest Romanesque churches in existence. The choir was begun at the end of the 11th cent., and the building was extended westwards in the 12-13th cent., the great W. portal remaining unfinished. A thorough restoration took place under the direction of Viollet-le-Duc (d. 1877). The church is cruciform and has a nave with double aisles. It is 330 ft. long, and 104 ft. wide; the transept is 210 ft. across; and the nave is 70 ft. high. The **Apse* is flanked by five semi-circular chapels, and each arm of the transept has two similar chapels adjoining its E. side. These chapels group picturesquely with the apse, the choir, and the transept, and above the crossing rises a fine octagonal **Tower*, of later date, with five tiers of tri-

angular arches in the Tolosan style and terminated by a gallery
and a spire, 210 ft. above the ground. An *Outer Porch* of the
16th cent., by Bachelier, stands in front of the S. transept-porch,
facing the Rue du Taur. This portal and the one on the N. are both
more interesting than the unfinished Gothic portal at the W. end.

The Interior is of large dimensions for a Romanesque church, but
the general effect is somewhat marred by the strengthening of the central
pillars supporting the tower. Under the choir is a crypt containing the
relics of six Apostles, St. Saturnin and three of his successors, and several
other saints, whose names are inscribed on two marble slabs on the stairs.
In a chapel of the N. transept is a singular Byzantine figure of Christ,
on a colossal scale, and the aisle of the same transept contains a votive
offering of 1525, representing the church as it then was surrounded by
defensive works. The 16th cent. stalls also deserve attention; on the first
to the right is a pig in a pulpit, intended to represent Calvin preaching.
Behind the choir are some interesting bas-reliefs of the 12th cent. and
a Holy Family attributed to Correggio. The sacristy contains two magnificent mediæval copes. The organ is a fine modern instrument.

Opposite the façade of St. Sernin is the former *Collège St. Raymond* (15th cent.), restored by Viollet-le-Duc, and converted in 1892
into a *Museum of Industrial Art and Antiquities*.

On the ground-floor are collections of foreign art and ethnography
and objects of the 17-18th cent., etc. On the 1st floor are Greek, Egyptian,
Roman, and Gallic antiquities; a collection of coins (5000 in number);
mediæval and Renaissance objects; furniture, arms, medals, seals, enamels, ivories, etc.

Returning to the Place du Capitole and following the Rue
Romiguières towards the W., we pass, at the corner of the Rue Deville, the *Protestant Church* (Pl. D, 3), some paces to the right of
which, in the Rue Deville, are the remains of the *Eglise des Cordeliers*, a building of the 14th cent., burned down in 1871.

To the left, opposite the Protestant church, begins the Rue Lakanal in which stands the Lycée. The *Church of the Jacobins* (Pl.
D, 3), which is attached to the Lycée, is a tasteful building of the
13-14th cent., chiefly noticeable for its 13th cent. brick tower,
which, however, has lost its spire. This is a typical Tolosan tower,
with triangular arches. — The *Lycée* (Pl. D, 3) occupies a part of
the large building at the end of the street, originally the house of
Bernuy, the Spanish merchant who guaranteed the ransom of
Francis I. (2,000,000 fr.) after his capture at the battle of Pavia
(1525). It has fine details in the Renaissance style. In the same
building, on the side next the Rue des Balances, is the *Town Library*, containing 70,000 vols (open daily, except Mon. morning,
9-11 and 1-5; closed Aug. 15th to Oct. 15th).

The Rue Lakanal joins the Rue Gambetta, following which to
the right, and again turning to the right we reach **La Daurade**
(Pl. D, 3) a church rebuilt between 1764 and 1810, which owes its
name ('dorée', Lat. de aurata) to the richness of its original decorations. The present edifice, which is partly shut in by houses,
is of no architectural merit. The usual entrance is by the side-
doors in the Rue de la Daurade or on the Quai (No. 1). The choir

is decorated with scenes from the life of the Virgin, painted by Roques the Elder. Clémence Isaure (p. 81) is said to be buried beside the high-altar. The flowers destined for the successful candidates in the Jeux-Floraux (p. 81) are blessed here on 3rd May.

The old tobacco-factory, beside this church, is the *École des Beaux-Arts.*

A little above the somewhat dull quay on which the Daurade stands the Garonne is crossed by the *Pont-Neuf* (Pl. D, 4), a fine stone bridge of seven arches, built in 1543-1626 by Nic. Bachelier and his son. The roadway was lowered in 1867.

On the *Garonne* within the town are two extensive mills, each having 34 mill-stones. Below the Pont St. Michel, at the end of the Ile de Tounis, is the *Moulin du Château*, so called because it belonged to a château now replaced by the Palais de Justice (p. 84). It is mentioned as early as 1182. The other, the *Moulin du Bazacle*, founded in the 9th cent., is below the Pont St. Pierre and may be visited by permission. Its weir dates in part from 1719. Farther down are several other industrial establishments, which make use of the mill-lead. — Close at hand, on the right bank, is a *Tobacco Manufactory*, which gives occupation to more than 1200 persons. — From the N. side of the river, near the last-named mill, issues the small *Canal de Brienne*, which unites with the Canal du Midi and the Canal Latéral at their junction, in the *Bassin de l'Embouchure*, at the W. end of the Faubourg St. Pierre.

The vast pile of buildings to the right, on the other side of the Pont-Neuf, in the Faubourg St. Cyprien, is the *Hôtel-Dieu St. Jacques* (Pl. D, 4), founded in the middle of the 12th cent., but repeatedly rebuilt. — Farther down is the *Hospice St. Joseph de la Grave* (Pl. C, 3), with a dome-covered chapel. On the left, near the Hôtel-Dieu, stands the old *Château d'Eau*, whose tower, 90 ft. in height, together with the new one near it, supplies the town with water from the Garonne, purified by underground filters in the meadow between the Garonne and the Cours Dillon (Pl. D, 4-5).

To the E. of the Pont-Neuf is the Place du Pont (Pl. D, E, 4) whence the Rue de Metz (still unfinished) runs across the town in the direction of St. Etienne (p. 84), intersecting the Rue d'Alsace-Lorraine. On the left, as we enter it, at the end of a short cross-street, is the *Hôtel d'Assézat*, a building of the 16th cent. with an interesting court, but unfortunately very dilapidated.

To the S. of the Place du Pont we follow the Rue des Couteliers, which leads to **La Dalbade** or the church of *Notre-Dame-la-Blanche* (Pl. D, E, 4), rebuilt in the middle of the 15th century. It has a fine square tower and an elegant portal of the Renaissance, by Nic. Bachelier, with a modern tympanum in enamelled terracotta, representing the Coronation of the Virgin, after Fra Angelico. The interior, consisting of a nave without aisles, is distinguished by its bold proportions.

A little farther on to the right, in the Rue de la Dalbade (No. 25), is the *Maison de Pierre* or *Hôtel de Clary*, a fine mansion of the early part of the 17th cent. lately restored. Next come, on the right the *Hôtel Felzins* (No. 22). on the left the *Hôtel St. Jean* (No. 32).

houses of the 16th and 17th centuries. — A street to the left leads
to the Place des Carmes, where we see on the opposite side, at the
beginning of the Rue du Vieux-Raisin, another fine Renaissance
building, the *Hôtel Lasbordes* or *de Fleyres*, which is considered
the masterpiece of Nic. Bachelier (1515).

The Rue du Vieux-Raisin descends to the S.W. to the *Place du
Salin* (Pl. E, 5), a small triangular Place where the autos-da-fé of
the Inquisition took place. Adjacent, to the W., in an unpreten-
tious house occupied by nuns, is the *Chapelle de l'Inquisition*, open
to visitors, but no longer containing any relics of the Holy Office.

A little lower down is the *Palais de Justice* (Pl. E, 5), the old
Palais du Parlement, a plain building, containing some richly decorated rooms. · To the N. rises a statue of *Cujas* (1520-90), the
celebrated jurist, a native of Toulouse, in bronze by Valois (1850).

To the S. of the Palais is the *Allée St. Michel*, near the end of
which, on the right, is an ornamental portal of eight marble columns
forming the entrance of the *Jardin des Plantes* (Pl. F, 5), one of
the finest promenades in Toulouse. In this neighbourhood is the
seat of the *Faculty of Medicine*, beyond which is that of the *Faculty
of Science*, a handsome building opened in 1890. At the entrance
of the Botanic Garden is a *Museum of Natural History*, founded
in 1864 (open on Sun. and Thurs., 1-5 in summer, 1-4 in winter).

Nearly opposite the entrance to the Jardin des Plantes is the
Jardin Royal (Pl. F, 5), in which is a bronze, by A. Fabre, of a
Shepherd playing with a panther. Adjoining is another promenade,
the *Grand-Rond* or *Boulingrin* (bowling-green), the focus of five
avenues. This also is embellished with statues. Band, see p. 78.

We proceed through the short avenue to the left, and then through
the Rue Ninau, and the Rue Ste. Scarbes, to the —

Cathedral of St. Etienne (Pl. F, 4). This church, which is partly
concealed by the adjoining houses, consists of three distinct and
somewhat inharmonious parts. The *W. Front*, flanked on the left
by a huge square tower, and now much mutilated, dates from the
15 - 16th century. It has taken the place of an earlier façade, the
rose-window of which (13th cent.) has been retained, though its
position is no longer central with regard to the main doorway. The
Nave, which is the oldest part, is a wide and rather low structure
of the first half of the 13th cent., without aisles. It is evident that
it was meant to be rebuilt after the completion of the *Choir*, which
was taken in hand in 1272 on a larger scale and with a different
axis. The work went on till the 16th cent. when so many churches
were left unfinished. The choir is a handsome and imposing structure with aisles, though it was partly spoiled in the 17th cent.
when restored after a fire. It is surrounded with seventeen chapels
and is adorned with stained-glass windows of the 15-17th centuries.
The metal screens and the stalls are noteworthy. Above the high-
altar is a Stoning of St. Stephen in marble and stucco, by Gervais

Drouet (1670). The walls of the nave are hung with paintings of little value.

The Rue St. Etienne, in front of the Cathedral, takes us back to the Rue d'Alsace-Lorraine, where we turn to the right.

The **Musée des Beaux-Arts** (Pl. E, 3), the enlargement of which has been going on for some time, occupies an old Augustine convent, of which some interesting features remain, and a new and massive brick building of doubtful taste, on the side next the Rue d'Alsace-Lorraine. Founded in 1742, this Musée is particularly rich in antiquities and pictures. It is open to the public on Sun. and Thurs. from noon till 5 in summer and till 4 in winter, and to strangers on other days also. The entrance is on the N. side, in the Rue du Musée, whence we first reach a *Small Cloister* in the Renaissance style (1626), containing some fine bas-reliefs and other works of art of the period. To the right is the *Large Cloister, a picturesque structure of the 14th cent., the trefoil arches of which, supported by double columns, recall the Moorish style. This cloister contains a large portion of the collection of antiquities, while the paintings occupy the old convent church.

The **Museum of Antiquities** consists mainly of objects found in excavations in Toulouse itself, or at Martres-Tolosane (p. 115) and other places in the environs. In the chief cloister and in a tasteful 15th cent. chapel, parallel to one of its galleries, are a series of votive altars dedicated to the divinities of the Pyrenees, some antique, mediæval, and Renaissance sculptures, inscriptions, and casts.

The **Picture Gallery** contains nearly 400 paintings, which are all furnished with names. As the present arrangement is temporary, and as there is no catalogue, the most noteworthy works are here mentioned in alphabetical order.

ITALIAN SCHOOLS: **Baroccio*, Holy Family; *Bellotto*, The Rialto; *Caravaggio*, Martyrdom of St. Andrew; *Carracci*, Madonna; *Guercino*, Martyrs, Patron saints of Modena; *Guido Reni*, Apollo flaying Marsyas; **Perugino*, St. John the Evangelist and St. Augustine; **Procaccini*, Mystic marriage of St. Catherine; *Raphael* (?), perhaps *Giulio Romano*, Head of a woman; *Salv. Rosa* (?), Neptune threatening the winds; *Solimena*, Portrait of a woman; *Tempesta*, Cavalry skirmish; *Vanni*, Madonna and Child, with saints; *Unknown Masters*, Madonna, the Saviour, Holy Family (15-16th cents.).

SPANISH SCHOOL: **Murillo*, St. Diego at prayer.

FLEMISH AND DUTCH SCHOOLS: *Van Bloemen*, Horsemen; *Bril*, Venus and Cupid; *G. de Crayer*, Job; *A. van Dyck*, Miracle performed at Toulouse by St. Anthony of Padua (at his command an ass falls on its knees before the Holy Sacrament rather than eat the oats that are presented to it, although it has been three days without food), a copy of a picture in the Museum of Lille; *Van Dyck*, Christ with angels; *Jordaens*, Madonna; *G. de Lairesse*, Crucifixion; *Van der Meulen*, Louis XIV. before Cambrai; **Mierevelt*, Portrait; *Quellin*, Martyrdom of St. Lawrence; *Rubens*, Christ between the two thieves, unfinished; *S. van Ruysdael*, Landscape; *Seghers*, Adoration of the Magi; *Verelst*, Head of an old man; *Van Wittel*, Piazza S. Pietro, at Rome; **Unknown Master* (15th cent.), St. John the Baptist, triptych; **Unknown Master* (16th cent.), Descent from the Cross.

FRENCH SCHOOL: *Boucher*, Bather; *Brascassat*, Sorceress; *Chalette*, The 'Capitouls' (p. 80) on their knees before the Saviour; *Phil. de Champaigne*, The Virgin and the Souls in Purgatory, Descent from the Cross, Crucifixion, Annunciation, Louis XIII. bestowing the Order of the Holy Ghost; *Benj.*

Constant, Mahomet II. entering Constantinople (1453); *Corot*, Landscape; *Couture*, The thirst for gold; *Eugène Delacroix*, Muley Abd-er-Rahman, emperor of Morocco; *Duveau*, Deposition of the Doge Foscari (1457); *Gérôme*, Anacreon, Bacchus, and Cupid; *Gros* (of Toulouse), Hercules and Diomede, the last work of the artist who had not the courage to bear the criticism which it aroused; *Gros*, Portraits of Mme. Gros and the artist himself; *P. Guy*, Presentation in the Temple; *Henner*, Mary Magdalen; *Isabey*, Harbour of Boulogne; *Jourenet*, Foundation of a town by the Tectosages, Descent from the Cross; *Lafosse*, Presentation of the Virgin; *Largillière*, Portraits, the first of the artist himself; *J. P. Laurens*, Pool of Bethesda; *Mme. Lebrun*, Portrait; *Lesueur*, Sacrifice of Manoah; *Lucas*, A Christian Martyr; *J. Michel*, Marriage at Cana; *Mignard*, Ecce Homo; *Oudry*, Hunting; *Pils*, Death of a sister of mercy; *Poussin*, John the Baptist; *Protais*, Diana; *J. Restout*, Diogenes; *Rigaud*, Racine; *Rivals*, Foundation of Ancyra by the Tectosages; *Robert-Fleury*, Pillage of a house on the Gludecca; *Rixens*, Death of Cleopatra; *Stella*, Marriage of the Virgin; *Subleyras*, St. Joseph and the Infant Jesus; *Tournier*, Descent from the Cross; *De Troy*, Dream of St. Joseph; *Aubin Vouet*, Deliverance of St. Peter.

The Museum also possesses a few SCULPTURES, among which are a Chloris, by *Pradier*; model of the Tarcisius, by *Falguière* (a native of Toulouse), and a cast of his Victor in a cock-fight; Cast of the statue of David, by *Mercié*, also of Toulouse; a Shepherd teaching a kid to dance, cast by *R. Barthélemy*; bronze reproduction of Mercury inventing the caduceus, by *Idrac*.

On issuing from the Museum, we turn to the right along the Rue d'Alsace-Lorraine in order to regain, on the left, the Place du Capitole, or, on the the right, the Square Lafayette, etc.

For the principal lines starting from Toulouse, see p. 78. To *Bagnères-de-Luchon*, see pp. 134, 137, and R. 26; to *St. Girons*, see R. 27; to *Foix, Tarascon, Ussat*, and *Ax*, see R. 28.

FROM TOULOUSE TO AUCH, 55 M., railway in 3 hrs. (fares 9 fr. 95, 6 fr. 75, 4 fr. 40 c.). There are four trains, one of which starts from the *Gare St. Cyprien* (p. 78), which those from the Gare Matabiau take 25-30 min. to reach, having to make a circuit of 6 M. The line passes through a picturesque and diversified country, crossing several valleys. — 14 M. (from Toulouse-Matabiau) Pibrac, birthplace of Germaine Cousin, a young shepherdess (1578-85), who was canonized in 1867, and whose tomb has become an object of pilgrimage. — 26 M. L'Isle-Jourdain, a town with 4440 inhab., beyond which we cross the *Save*. — Near (30 M.) Gimont-Cahuzac we cross the *Gimone*. Gimont is a small town with an interesting Gothic church, of brick, visible on an eminence to the left. — 44 M. *Aubiet*, beyond which the line crosses the *Arrats*. 49 M. *Marsan*, with a fine château. — 55 M. *Auch* (p. 104).

12. From Toulouse to Cette.

138 M. RAILWAY in 3³/₄-7 hrs. (fares 24 fr. 75, 18 fr. 75, 10 fr. 85 c.). To *Carcassonne*, 55¹/₂ M., in 1¹/₄-2³/₄ hrs. (fares 10 fr. 40, 6 fr. 85, 4 fr. 55 c.). The trains start from the Gare Matabiau.

Toulouse, see p. 78. — Leaving on the right the lines to Tarbes and Auch, we ascend the wide, fertile, and well-cultivated valley of *Lhers*, which is also traversed by the Canal du Midi (p. 80). — 8 M. *Escalquens*; 12 M. *Montlaur*; 14 M. *Baziège*; 16¹/₂ M. *Villenou-velle*; 20¹/₂ M. *Villefranche-de-Lauraguais*, a small town on the Canal du Midi, possessing a church of the 14th cent., with a portal in the Tolosan style; 25 M. *Avignonet*, another small town with a

14th cent. church. Beyond (28 M.) *Ségala* we cross the low watershed and begin the descent to the basin of the Mediterranean. — 31 M. *Mas-Stes. Puelles.* On the left the Cévennes appear.

34 M. **Castelnaudary** (*Buvette; Hôtel de France*), a town with 10,059 inhab., situated to the left on a hill adjoining the Canal du Midi. It was burned and several times besieged in the Albigensian wars, and was again burned by the Black Prince in 1355.

About ¼ M. to the E. of Castelnaudary lies the large village of St. Papoul, formerly the seat of a bishop and still possessing a fine abbey-church, part of which, including the cloisters, is in the Romanesque style.

From Castelnaudary to Castres, 34 M., railway in about 1½ hr. (fares 6 fr. 15, 4 fr. 15, 3 fr. 70 c.). The line skirts the town on the E., with the Montagne Noire (p. 80) to the right. — 12½ M. *St. Félix*, a small town, 2 M. to the W. — About 2 M. to the S. E. of (16 M.) *Revel* (Lune) is the Bassin de St. Ferréol, the most important feeder of the Canal du Midi. It is formed by a dam about 2600 ft. long, 230 ft. thick, and 100 ft. high. It holds 1400 million gallons of water, and when full has an area of 160 acres. — About 3½ M. to the E. of Revel (diligence) and 2½ M. to the N. E. of the basin, lies the small town of *Sorèze*, long famous for its Benedictine abbey, converted into a college in 1682 and acquired by the Dominicans in 1854. Father Lacordaire (d. 1861), the famous preacher, is buried here, and a statue (by Girardet) was erected to him in 1888. — 29½ M. *La Crémade*, where we join the line to Montauban. — 34 M. *Castres*, see p. 97.

The Cette line continues to descend through a fertile and well cultivated plain, traversed by the Canal du Midi. — 39 M. *Pexiora;* 43 M. *Bram;* 47 M. *Alzonne;* 51½ M. *Pezens.*

56½ M. **Carcassonne.** — **Hotels.** Bernard (Pl. a; C, 2), Rue du Marché; Bonnet (Pl. c; C, 2), Rue de la Mairie 41, R. 3-6, L. & A. 1¾, B. 1½, déj. 4, D. 5 fr.; du Commerce (Pl. d; C, 2), Rue du Port 16, déj. 3, D. 3½ fr.; *St. Jean Baptiste (Pl. b; C, 1), Rue de Tivoli and Rue de la Gare, similar charges; de Paris (Pl. e; D, 2), Boulevard de la Préfecture 16; St. Pierre, Rue de la Gare 58. — *Restaurant* at the station. — **Cafés.** *Grand Café*, Place aux Herbes; *Ambigu*, Boul. de la Préfecture, near the Square Gambetta; others in the Boul. Barbès and near the station. — **Café-Concert.** *Alcazar*, Rue de Belfort.

Carcassonne, the capital of the department of the *Aude*, and the seat of a bishop, is a town with 28,235 inhab., situated on the river *Aude*. It consists of two distinct parts: the *Lower Town*, on the left bank, near the railway, and the *Cité*, some way off, on a hill on the other bank. The latter is one of the most interesting spots in Southern France.

Carcassonne was in existence in the Roman period, but its importance began during the three centuries ending with 713, when it was in the possession of the Visigoths, and reached its climax in the 11-13th cent., when it was ruled by a series of viscounts, the Trencavels. It suffered greatly in the Albigensian war, when it was taken partly by a ruse and partly through treachery. The viscounty was united to France in 1239, like the rest of the territories to which the Montforts had laid claim after the crusade against the Albigenses. Carcassonne made a desperate but unavailing resistance, under the last of the Trencavels, to this absorption, and King Louis the Saint isolated the Cité and founded the Lower Town (1247). This latter was pillaged and burnt by the Black Prince in 1355. In 1560 many of the Huguenot inhabitants of Carcassonne were massacred for having dragged a statue of the Virgin through the mire.

The LOWER TOWN, which is well built and regularly laid out, is encircled by green and shady boulevards. A long street beginning opposite the station, beyond the Canal du Midi, traverses the whole town, passing the Place aux Herbes in the centre. The Rue du Quatre-Septembre leads to the Gothic *Church of St. Vincent* (Pl. C, 1; 14-16th cent.) with a massive unfinished tower, from which Méchain and Delambre calculated the site of the meridian of Paris, which passes only 46″ to the W. This church, like many others in the S., is remarkable for the width of its nave. It is lighted by rose-windows above the chapels between the pillars, and contains some fine stained glass.

The PLACE AUX HERBES (Pl. C, 3), to which the Rue du Port leads from St. Vincent, is planted with fine plane-trees and contains a marble *Fountain* of the 18th cent. with a figure of Neptune, by Baratta. — Continuing to follow the same direction, by the Rue des Halles, we reach the *Cathedral of St. Michel* (Pl. C, 3), a Gothic church of the 13th cent. which seems to have served as a model for St. Vincent's. There is no portal at the W. end, but the wall is adorned with a fine rose-window. The church is entered from the Rue Voltaire by a small doorway on the N. side. The interior is painted in grisaille.

Near the church passes the Boulevard Barbès, which, however, can be reached only by a detour to the E. or to the W. To the E. is an old gate, known as the *Porte Barbès* (Pl. C, D, 3), at the end of the cross-street leading from the station. In the boulevard, to the right, is the bronze statue, by Falguière, of *Barbès* (1809-70), the revolutionary, with a musket curiously placed between his legs.

At the other end, the boulevard passes the base of an old bastion, and assumes the name of Boulevard du Musée. Farther on, to the right, is the *Square Gambetta* (Pl. D, 2), the handsomest in the town.

Near this point, in the Grande-Rue, is the MUSÉE (Pl. D, 2), open to the public on Sun. and Thurs. from 12 to 4. It contains chiefly paintings.

STAIRCASE. *J. P. Laurens*, The Immured of Carcassonne (copy); *Lehoux*, After the battle. — ROOM 1: to the right, 85. *Jos. Vernet*, Landscape; 32. *Desportes*, Game; 22. *Curtois (Le Bourguignon)*, Cavalry skirmish; 163. *Subleyras*, 149. *Rivals*, 146, 145. *Rigaud*, Portraits; 129. *Maurzaisse*, Louis Philippe at Valmy; 88. *Girodet*, Man meditating on death; 19. *Chardin*, Still-life. Also a small geological collection. — R. II: to the left, 183. *Weenix*, Still-life; 59. *Jordaens*, The temptation; 185. *Teniers the Elder*, Alchemist's study; 166. *Salvator Rosa*, Head of a soldier; no number, *C. de Vos*, Portrait; 121, 122. *Locatelli*, Landscapes; 160. *Seibolt*, Portrait of a painter; 4. *Guercino*, St. Matthew; 137, 136. *Panini*, Ruins; no number, *Ribera*, St. Peter; *Dirck Hals*, Merry company; *H. Martin*, Francesca da Rimini (copy); *O. Venius*, Descent from the Cross; etc. *Moreau-Vauthier*, Shepherd quenching his thirst (bronze). Continuation of the geological collection, and some prehistoric antiquities. — R. III: to the left, 115. *Laloir*, St. Cecilia; no number, *A. Perret*, The sower; *La Prade*, Pygmalion; 12. *Brigubowl*, Tubal-Cain teaching his children music; 135. *Ouvrié*, Eaux-Bonnes. Also medals, seals, weights, and small bronzes. — R. IV, to

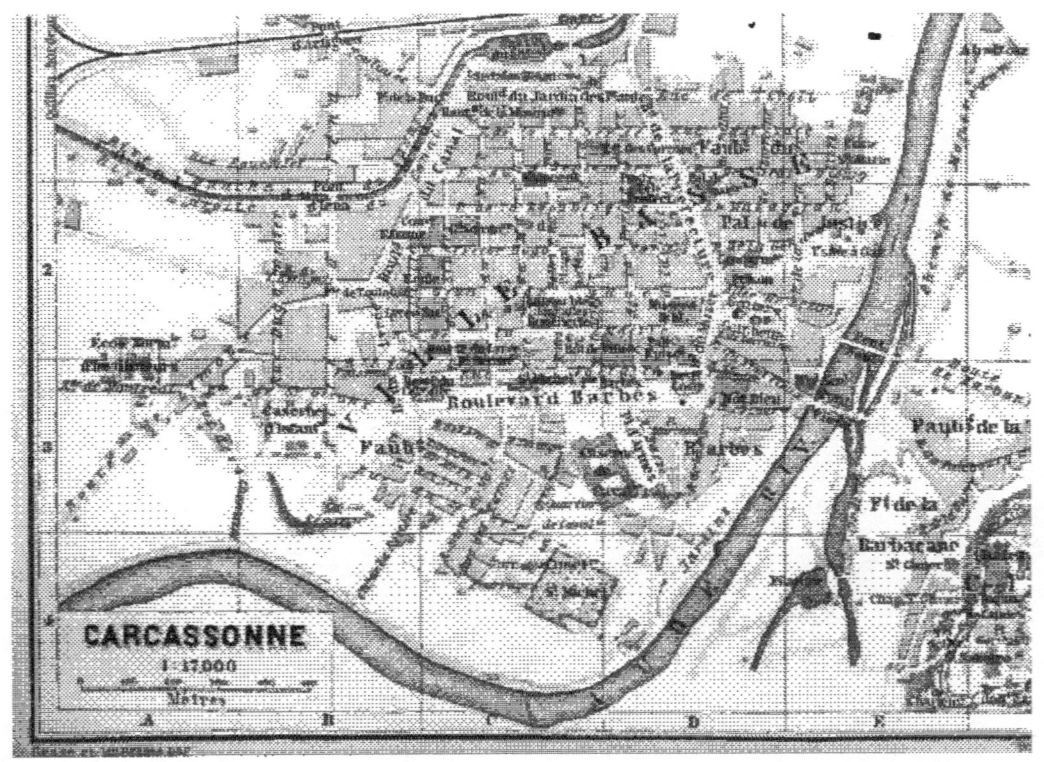

CARCASSONNE
1:17000
Mètres
Boulevard Barbès
Palais de Justice
Faubg de la
Pl. de la
Barbacane

the right of R. III: Small paintings, including a sea-piece by *Van de Velde* and other Dutch works, etc. Faïence and curiosities. — R. V: to the left, 20. *Coignet*, Lake and Cascade d'Oo (p. 179); 143. *Beaumetz*, 'They shall not have it'; 112. *Laverges*, Genius extinguished by Pleasure; no number, *Pelouze*, Floods in Holland; 187. *F. Thirion*, Eleazar and Rebecca; 16. *Caband*, Christian martyrs. *Diebolt*, Meditation (statue). In the glass-cases, natural history objects and curiosities. — R. VI. to the right of R. V: to the left, 9. *Falguière*, Cain and Abel; 60. *B. Constant*, The Cherifas; 5. *Cheral*, Girls on the beach; 84. *Van Ruysdael*, Landscape; 229a. *Guillaumet*, Wolves devouring a horse; 28. *Van Dyck* (?), Madonna; 2. *Bassano*, Disciples at Emmaus; etc. — R. VII: to the left, no number, *Lerolle*, Arrival of the shepherds; *P. Colin*, Moonlight; *G. Laugée*, First steps; *J. Aman*, St. Julian Hospitator; *Lansyer*, The reef; *Chartran*, Vision of St. Francis d'Assisi; *Luminais*, Last of the Merovingians; *Rossel-Granger*, Orpheus. — R. VIII, to the right: Drawings, engravings, bas-reliefs, furniture. — R. IX: Modern landscapes, genre-scenes, still-lifes, and flowers; to the left, *Baduel*, Still-life; to the right, *Pelouze*, Grandcamp; to the left, *Em. Boutigny*, Boule-de-Suif, scene from the war of 1870; to the right, *H. Bertaux*, Joan of Arc; *Cousin*, Pacification of the Vendée; *L. Deschamps*, On a day in spring. In the centre, *Champard*, Cato of Utica (marble).

Here, too, is the *Town Library*, containing 20,000 volumes.

The *Cité or Old Town of Carcassonne is on the S. E. side of the town (Pl. E, F, 3, 4). It is reached by crossing the Pont Neuf over the Aude, near the Square Gambetta, or the Vieux Pont, a little higher up, and traversing the suburb of Trivalle. Anything more curious or unique in appearance than this town of the Middle Ages, with its double line of fortifications, furnished with fifty round towers and dominated by a citadel, can hardly be imagined. A good distant view of the finest part of it is obtained from the side of the valley. The fortifications date back to the days of the Visigoths (5th cent.), but were frequently reconstructed or altered before the 14th cent., and they were also renewed in 1850-1879 by Viollet-le-Duc, who considered them the most complete and the most formidable example in Europe of fortifications of the 6th, 12th, and 13th centuries.

The outer line or enceinte is more than 1600 yds. in circumference, the inner one 1200 yds. The whole of the N. part was built by the Visigoths on the ruins of Roman fortifications, which are still visible at several points. There are only two entrances, the *Porte de l'Aude*, to the W., beyond the fortress, and the *Porte Narbonnaise*, to the E. To visit the principal points of interest the services of the custodian, who lives near the Porte de l'Aude, should be secured. Specially noteworthy are the numerous defences of the Porte de l'Aude, the *Bishop's Towers*, one of which adjoins both enceintes, the *Tower of the Inquisition*, *Charlemagne's Tower*, the *Tower of St. Nazaire*, the *Treasury Tower*, and the Porte Narbonnaise. The squalid interior of the Cité contains a few ancient and badly preserved houses. The small street which begins at the Porte Narbonnaise leads to the *Citadel*, in which very little restoration has been effected. It is now used as a barrack.

Next to its fortifications the chief building of the Cité is the church of *St. Nazaire, formerly a cathedral, founded in the 5th cent., but rebuilt in the 11-14th, and restored by Viollet-le-Duc. The portal has disappeared and we enter by a Romanesque doorway on the N. side. The nave, in the Romanesque style of the 12th cent., with Gothic side-chapels, is heavy and massive when contrasted with the transept and the choir, both of which are splendid erections of the 14th cent., containing magnificent stained-glass windows. In a chapel to the left of the nave is the monument of Pierre de Roquefort (d. 1321), the bishop who finished the church, with three fine life-size figures in high-relief. To the left of the choir is the tomb of Simon Vigorce, archbishop of Narbonne (1575), with a fine marble statue. A coarse bas-relief on the S. side of the nave represents the siege of Toulouse in 1218. In the small sacristy on the same side is the interesting tomb of Bp. Radulph (1266). A tablet of red marble near the high-altar is said to mark the original resting-place of Simon de Montfort, the persecutor of the Albigenses.

A good view of the Pyrenees is obtained from a point outside the fortifications, near the Porte de l'Aude.

From Carcassonne to *Quillan* (excursions), see R. 29.

Resuming our journey from Carcassonne, we cross the Canal du Midi and the Aude and, after getting a fine glimpse of the Cité on the right, enter a short tunnel. We follow the valley of the Aude, at some distance from the river. 61 M. *Trèbes*; 64 M. *Floure*; 67 M. *Capendu*. To the right rises the *Montagne d'Alaric* (1950 ft.), on which the Visigoth king is said to have had a castle, with some ruins of the 14th cent. and marble quarries. — 72 M. *Mour*.

A branch-line runs hence to (17½ M.) *Caunes*, with valuable marble quarries.

Diligence (80 c.) to *Fabrezan*, a country-town, 8 M. to the S., on the Orbieu, with a castle dating in part from the 12th cent., the tower of which is nearly 100 ft. high.

From Fabrezan and from *Lagrasse*, also finely situated on the Orbieu, 6 M. to the S. W., picturesque excursions may be made among the Corbières, a small chain of mountains which strikes out from the Pyrenees near the Pech de Bugarach and runs from S.W. to N.E., between the Aude and the Agly (good roads). About 3 M. to the S. of Fabrezan we join the road from Lagrasse to Narbonne, whence diverge several of the most interesting routes across the Corbières, the finest those to Estagel and La Nouvelle.

To Estagel. There are two roads from Fabrezan. The first, the shorter (31 M.) and less interesting, diverges to the right from the Narbonne road, and joins the second at Tuchan (see below). The latter (34 M. from Fabrezan, 32 M. from Lagrasse) quits the Lagrasse road at *St. Laurent-de-la-Cabrerisse* (1½ M.) and rejoins it 4 M. farther on. — 11 M. (from Fabrezan), *Villerouge-de-Terménès*, with a château and iron mines. 18 M. *Palairac*; 20 M. *Maison*; 24 M. *Tuchan*, a large village and the centre of a coal-field on the S.E. slope of the *Montagne de Tauch* (2850 ft.). At (27 M.) *Paziols* we reach the valley of the Verdouble. — 34 M. *Estagel*, see p. 197.

To La Nouvelle. The road leaves that to Narbonne on the right 2½ M. from the Fabrezan road. About 1 M. farther on is *Thézan*, where the scenery begins to be very picturesque. Farther on (12½ M.), a road on the right goes off to (3½ M.) *Durban*, with its ruined château, and beyond this point we enter the valley of the Berre. 19½ M. *Portel*, beyond which is the Pont de Tamaroque, 65 ft. high. 23 M. Sijean (*Hôtel du Midi*), a small town near the lake of the same name (p. 172), with salt-works which produce annually about 2500 tons of salt. — 71 M. *La Nouvelle*, see p. 196.

Beyond (79 M.) *Lézignan* the train crosses the *Orbieu*. 84 M. *Villedaigne*; 87 M. *Marcorignan*.

93 M. **Narbonne** (*Buffet*). — **Hotels.** HÔTEL DE LA DORADE, DE FRANCE, Rue de la République 44 and 7, near the Hôtel de Ville; GRAND HÔTEL, Boul. Gambetta; DE L'UNIVERS, new, at the station. — *Cafés* in the Place de l'Hôtel-de-Ville. — *Post and Telegraph Office* in the Place du Tribunal, beside the former cathedral.

Narbonne, a town of 29,566 inhab., is situated in a dusty plain, 5 M. from the Mediterranean, with which it is connected by the Canal de la Robine. Though still carrying on a number of industries (distilling, coopering, etc.), it has emphatically seen its best days, and its streets are badly built and far from clean. A handsome new quarter has, however, been laid out near the station, necessitating the removal of the interesting old fortifications. It is a disappointing town to those who bear in mind its former importance, as its only lions are the old Cathedral and the Archbishop's Palace. Even the Museum is poor in antiquities.

Narbonne, *Narbo*, was a flourishing town as early as the 5th cent. B.C. It was colonized by the Romans B.C. 118. At that time it was surrounded by lakes which were connected with the Lake of Sijean (p. 172) and so communicated with the sea, thus making the town one of the first ports of the Mediterranean and the rival of Massilia. It gave its name to Gallia Narbonensis, a part of Gaul conquered by the Romans before the time of Cæsar. Martial, in A. D. 96, speaks of it as a beautiful town, and Sidonius Apollinaris (d. 484) praises its theatre, temple, capitol, warm baths, triumphal arches, and other buildings, of which nothing remains but fragments discovered in the walls of the enceinte, which were demolished in 1867. The Visigoths established themselves here in 413 and kept possession of the town till 719, when it was taken by the Saracens after two years' siege. So strongly did the latter fortify it that Charles Martel failed to take it and the troops of Pepin only effected their entrance through treason in 759. In 817 the town became the capital of the duchy of Septimania or Gothia, adjudged to Lothaire, but it afterwards had its own viscounts, passing subsequently first to the Counts of Auvergne, then to those of Toulouse, with whose dominions it was finally united to France. The decay of the town dates from the beginning of the 14th cent., when the Jews, who had been established in a quarter of their own by Charlemagne, were expelled, and the port became silted up through the bursting of a dyke, by which the Romans had diverted to it a branch of the Aude. — The honey of Narbonne is considered the best in France.

The best way from the station to the centre of the town is to follow the Boulevard de la Gare to the right, leaving the old town to be visited on the return. The Rue de la République leads to the left from the end of the boulevard, on this side of the Canal de la Robine, direct to the Place de l'Hôtel-de-Ville.

The CHURCH OF ST. JUST, formerly the *Cathedral* (closed from noon till 1), on one side of the Place, is a fine but unfinished Gothic edifice dating mainly from 1272-1332. The work was resumed in the 18th cent., and again in recent years, but has once more been

interrupted. The choir, the only ancient part, with towers added
in the 15th cent., is a vast pile 131 ft. in height, rivalling the
churches of the North in boldness of style, if not in richness of
ornamentation. The exterior is crowned with a double range of
battlements, and the flying buttresses end in turrets.

INTERIOR. In the ambulatory are some interesting tombs of bishops
of the 14th and 16th cents.; in the 3rd chapel on the left, that of a
general of the time of Henri IV. The organ-case dates from 1741. The
treasury contains MSS., missals, ivory carvings, portable altars, a cross,
a chalice, etc. (7-16th cent.). Fine view from the towers. — Adjoining
the church are some remains of the *Cloisters* (14-15th cent.).

The chief remains of the ARCHIEPISCOPAL PALACE, which was
fortified in the Middle Ages, are three towers on the façade, the
largest (on the left) dating from 1318. The Gothic *Hôtel de Ville*,
between this tower and the next, was built by Viollet-le-Duc.

The *MUSEUM, in the same building, chiefly contains paintings
and a fine ceramic collection (Sun. and Thurs., 2-4; to strangers at
other times also). We enter by the door to the left, at the end of
the court, or by skirting the building to the left to the Jardin Public
at the back of it. The garden contains sculptures, inscriptions,
architectural fragments, and other antiquities found at Narbonne;
the rest of the antiquities have been deposited in the old Eglise
de Lamourguié, beyond the canal, and may be seen on application
to the keeper of the Museum.

Room I. Gallic and Roman antiquities; fossils from the quarries of
Armissan, 5 M. to the E. of Narbonne; six pictures representing aldermen

lion; 284. *Velasquez*, Portrait; 208. *Unknown Artist*, Portrait of an archbishop; 41. *Ph. de Champaigne*, Nativity (a copy by his nephew *J. B. de Champaigne*); 59. *Despichel* (ca. 1588), Holy Family; 287, 288. *Antonissen*, Landscapes; 318. *J. van Eyck* (?), Triptych; 240. *C. Dolci*, and no number, *Baroccio*, Descent from the Cross; 263. *Palma Vecchio* (?), Marriage of St. Catharine; 268. *Veronese*, Madonna, with the donor and saints; 179. *Unknown Artist*, Still-life; 282. *J. de Valdès-Leal*, Hearing of the Cross; 261. *Seb. del Piombo*, Portrait; 232. *Bassano*, Adoration of the Shepherds; 234. *Pietro da Cortona (Berettini)*, Massacre of the Innocents; 254. *Titian*, Vinc. Capello; 148. *N. Poussin*, John the Baptist; 258. *Salvator Rosa*, St. Jerome; 298. *Jordaens* (after *Rubens*), Bacchanalian scene; 243. *Giotto* (?), Holy Family; 242. *Garofalo* (?), Jesus and the Woman of Samaria; 245. *Guercino*, Judith; 91. *G. Poussin*, Landscape; 274. *Bassa* (Spain), Holy Family; 290. *Ribera*, St. Andrew; 273. *J. de Arellano*, Flowers, fruits, and birds; 292. *G. de Craper* (?), A Doctor of the church.

Room VII. (*Galerie l'ayre*; adjoining R. IV.). Above the door, 284. *Fyt*, Kitchen (figures by *Jordaens*); to the left, 30, 40. *Ph. de Champaigne*, Portraits; 330. *G. van de Velde*, Sea-piece; 140. *Nattier*, Portrait; 129, 128. *N. Mignard*, Portraits; 127. *P. Mignard* (?), Portrait of a queen of France; 89. *Greuze*, Head of a girl; 314. *Van Dyck*, Honoré of Savoy; 126. *P. Mignard* (?), Mme. de Sévigné; 262. *Seb. del Piombo* (?), Study; 279. *Juan de Ribalta* (?), Monk; 149. *Primaticcio*, Rape of Europa. — Room VIII. Casts from the antique. To the right, between the windows, 529. *Silenus*, an ancient marble statue found in constructing the railway. — The Gallery parallel to the large hall, contains furniture, engravings, etc.

The Rue Droite leads from the Place de l'Hôtel-de-Ville to the station. In the Rue Michelet, running parallel to the Rue Droite, is the church of *St. Vincent*, in the florid Gothic style. The chapel to the right contains a fine stone reredos. — Archæologists may visit the church of *St. Paul Serge*, a Gothic building of the 13th cent., near the outskirts of the town, beyond the Robine.

From Narbonne to *Perpignan*, see R. 30. — A branch-line runs from Narbonne to (13 M.) *Bize*, a manufacturing town on the Cesse, with some prehistoric caves. — Tramway to *Coursan* (see below), hourly; 60 c.

97 M. **Coursan** (*Maison-Dorée*), a town of 3847 inhab., on the Aude, with an artesian well yielding an aerated and ferruginous thermal water. We cross the Aude. Farther on, to the left, is the *Lake of Capestang*, which is to be drained. — Beyond (102$\frac{1}{2}$ M.) *Nissan*, we thread a tunnel of 550 yards, partly under another tunnel through which the Canal du Midi passes. Reaching Béziers, we cross the Orb, which a little lower down is also crossed by a fine aqueduct of the Canal du Midi.

108$\frac{1}{2}$ M. **Béziers**. — Hotels. Grand Hôtel de la Paix, Paul Riquet, des Postes, du Commerce, all in the Allées Paul-Riquet, the first near the theatre, the second nearest the station; du Nord, Place de la Citadelle, to the left of the Allées. — Cafés. Several near the theatre, well fitted up. — Buffet at the station.

Béziers, with 41,475 inhab., finely situated on a hill to the left, is a town of very ancient origin, having been colonized by the Romans under the name of *Biterra Septimanorum*. Like most of its neighbours, it suffered severely in the Albigensian wars, and in 1209, about 20-30,000 of its citizens were massacred or burned. Béziers produces good red wines and carries on a large trade in brandy.

Quitting the station we have before us the *Jardin des Poëtes*, embellished with a monumental *Fountain*, surmounted by a bronze Titan, by Injalbert.

Across the garden foot-passengers ascend to the *Allées Paul-Riquet*, the central and finest part of the town, forming a shady promenade 550 yds. long. In the first half of it stands a statue (by David d'Angers) of *Paul Riquet*, the constructor of the Canal du Midi (p. 80), who was a native of Béziers. Adjacent is the large *Place de la Citadelle* (band twice or thrice a week), with a tasteful marble *Fountain*. At the end of the avenue rises the *Theatre*, adorned with fine bas-reliefs in terracotta, also by David d'Angers.

The Rue de la Promenade, diverging to the left on this side of the theatre, leads to the *Hôtel de Ville*, a building of the 18th century. It contains a small *Musée*, on the second floor (open on Sun. and Thurs. 2-4), consisting chiefly of paintings, mostly of the French school.

Among others: 4. *Domenichino*, Portraits of Gregory XV. and his nephew Ludovico Ludovisi; 5. *Titian*, Tobias and his son burying the dead; *Guercino*, 'La Femme aux trois couronnes'; 11. *Bon-Boullongne*, Miracle of St. Benedict; 12. *Van Hoeck*, Portrait; 13. *Fyt*, Wild cat and game; 14. *Maas*, Horses; 15. *Goyen*, Landscape; 17. *Brekelenkam*, Concert; 47. *Vien*, Samson; 50. *Diaz*, Women bathing; 51. *Glaize*, Cupids at auction; 68. *Cabanel*, Druid priestess; 69. *Daubigny*, Banks of the Oise; 71. *Isabey*, Sea-piece; 73. *Corot*, Dutch scene; 78. *Giulio Romano*, after *Raphael*, Holy Family; 80. *Francia*, Head of a monk; 89. *Glaize*, Mona Belcolor; 107. *Van Dyck*, Portrait; 132. *Tiepolo*, Our Lady of the rosary; 146. *J. P. Laurens*, Obsequies of William the Conqueror; 147. *Ribera*, St. Sebastian; 154. *Luminais*, Gallic hunter resting; 157. *Glaize*, Flower-girl.

Hence we proceed to the old cathedral of *St. Nazaire*, the principal building of Béziers, at the S. W. end of the town. It dates from the 12-14th cent. and is in the Gothic style peculiar to the district, partly fortified and showing little adornment. The windows of the choir retain their old glass and iron scrollwork. In the W. façade is a fine rose window and over it a large square tower. The S. transept is adjoined by Gothic cloisters of the 14th century.

The terrace by the church affords a magnificent view, comprising the valley of the Orb, the Cévennes to the N., the Corblères to the S. W. and the Mediterranean to the S.

About 1/2 M. to the S.W. are the interesting *Locks of Fonserannes*, by which the Canal du Midi descends 80 ft. within 330 yds. to reach the level of the Orb. — At the mouth of the Orb, 6³/₂ M. to the S. E., are the modest *Sea Baths of Sérignan*, 3 M. beyond the little town of that name, served by a steam-tramway (1 hr.; 75 c.) starting from the bridge above the railway-bridge.

From Béziers to *Neussargues* and to *Rodez*, etc., see RR. 17, 42.

From Béziers to Montpellier viâ Paulhan, 47 M., railway in 2³/₄-3³/₄ hrs. (fares 8 fr. 50, 5 fr. 75, 3 fr. 75 c.). — The direct line is quitted at *Vias* (p. 95), whence we ascend to the N. through the valley of the *Hérault*. — 22¹/₂ M. *Pézenas* (*Hôtel de la Paix*), the Roman *Piscenae*, a very ancient town of 6720 inhab., with an important trade in cognac. During the 17th cent. this town was frequently the meeting-place of the Estates of the large and wealthy province, and it still retains several buildings dating from that period of prosperity. Among these are the *Hôtel d'Alfonse* (16th cent.); the *Theatre*, formerly a chapel and the scene of the meetings of the Estates; several old *Mansions*, *Gates*, etc. Here Molière made his début in 1655-56 and composed his 'Precieuses Ridicules'. The town has also another station, on the line from Béziers to Montpellier vià Mèze (see below). The *Château de la Grange-des-Prés*, once belonging to the families of Montmorency and Conti, lies ³/₄ M. to the N. — 29 M. *Paulhan* (Buffet), on the line from Castres and Montauban to Montpellier (p. 100). — To *Lodère*, see p. 100.

FROM BÉZIERS TO MONTPELLIER VIÂ MÈZE, 50 M. This line, starting from the *Gare de Pézenas*, opposite the main station (¹/₂ M. from the theatre; omn.), is longer than that above described and is almost without interest to the tourist. — 16¹/₂ M. *Pézenas* (p. 94). 27 M. *Mèze* (Hôt. Eustache), a town of 6326 inhab., on the Lake of Thau, with salt-works. — 37 M. *Montbazin* (p. 100). — *Montpellier*, see p. 100.

FROM BÉZIERS TO ST. CHINIAN (St. Pons), 16¹/₂ M. This line also starts from the Gare de Pézenas (see above), and runs vià (8 M.) the little town of *Cazouls-lès-Béziers*. — 16¹/₂ M. St. Chinian (Hôt. du Grand-Soleil) is an industrial place of 3424 inhab., in a picturesque situation. A public conveyance plies hence to *St. Pons* (p. 88).

112¹/₂ M. *Villeneuve-lès-Béziers*, beyond which the Mediterranean comes into view on the right. — 119¹/₂ M. *Vias*, with an interesting church of the 14th century. To Montpellier vià Pézenas, see p. 94.

About ¹/₂ M. to the S. E. is a curious *Aqueduct* by which the Libron crosses the Canal du Midi. It consists of two movable parts, which open and shut for the passage of boats along the canal.

122 M. **Agde** (*Hôtel du Cheval-Blanc*, on the quay), the ancient *Agathè*, founded by the Massiliots, a town of 7389 inhab., is situated on the Hérault and the Canal du Midi, 3 M. from the sea, and has a harbour carrying on a brisk trade with Spain and Italy. Like most of the towns in S. France, Agde was taken and sacked in the early Middle Ages by the Vandals, the Visigoths, the Saracens, the Franks, and the Crusaders in the Albigensian wars. The Calvinists also held possession of it from 1562 to 1577.

We enter the town by a suspension-bridge over the Hérault. To the right is the *Cathedral* (12th cent.), with a crenellated roof which gives it the appearance of a castle from a distance. Below are large Romanesque arcades with small windows resembling loop-holes. The tower, which has no spire, is in a similar style. The W. portal has been built up and the choir transferred to the W. end of the church, while the entrance is now in one of the chapels of the original choir at the E. end.

The main street leads in the opposite direction from the church to an *Esplanade*, on which are remains of old fortifications, a *Fountain* with a marble statue of Agathè, and a *Bust of Cl. Terrisse*, a local benefactor.

To the S.E. of Agde rises an extinct volcano (360 ft.), which furnished the lava of which the town is built, and off the coast is the little *Ile de Brescou*, which, like the *Cap d'Agde* and the mouth of the Hérault, is fortified.

We next cross the canal and the Hérault and pass, on the left, the *Etang de Thau*, a salt lake 11 M. long and 5-8 M. wide, on the banks of which are large salt-works. The Canal du Midi euds here and is prolonged to the sea by the Canal de Cette. — Beyond (285 M.) *Les Onglous*, the line follows a tongue of land, about ¹/₂ M. wide, between the Mediterranean and the lake. On the opposite bank lies Mèze, a station on the Hérault line (see above). At the N.E. end are the baths of *Balaruc* (see *Baedeker's South-Eastern France*). Finally we cross the Canal de Cette, and reach —

296 M. **Cette** *(Buffet; Grand Hôtel, Hôt. Barillon*, Quai du Bosc 17 and 10), an ancient town of 36,540 inhab., situated on the *Mont St. Clair* (590 ft.; the *Mons Setius* of antiquity). Cette contains little of interest for the tourist, and even the commercial importance of the harbour has declined since its establishment at the end of the 17th century. The *Musée Municipal* contains a few good paintings. — For farther details and for the railway to Montpellier and Nîmes, etc., see *Baedeker's South-Eastern France*.

13. From Montauban to Montpellier viâ Castres.

Bédarieux. Paulhan. Lamalou-les-Bains.

187 M. RAILWAY in 7³/₄ hrs. (fares 30 fr. 45, 20 fr. 80, 13 fr. 35 c.). — This route is 18 M. shorter than that viâ Toulouse (RR. 10, 12).

Montauban, see p. 75. The line diverges to the left from the Toulouse line and ascends the valley of the *Tarn*, through an uninteresting plain on the left bank. — 3¹/₂ M. *Bressols*; 8 M. *Labastide-St. Pierre*; 10 M. *Orgueil*; 12 M. *Nohic*.

15¹/₂ M. *Villemur*, with 3929 inhab., lies on the right bank of the Tarn. — 19¹/₂ M. *La Magdelaine*; 23 M. *Bessières*. — Beyond (25 M.) *Buzet* we join the line from Toulouse to Limoges viâ Capdenac (R. 16b), on the right.

27¹/₂ M. *St. Sulpice* (Buffet). We cross the *Agout* and ascend the valley of that river, which we cross and recross several times, at Lavaur by a bridge 95 ft. in height. — 32 M. *St. Jean-de-Rives*.

36¹/₂ M. **Lavaur** *(Hôtel Bertrand)*, an ancient town with 6477 inhab., on the left bank of the Agout, was a stronghold of the Albigenses, sacked by Simon de Montfort in 1211. It was formerly the seat of a bishopric, held in 1685-1687 by Fléchier, before his translation to Nîmes. The *Cathedral*, a brick edifice of the 13th cent., contains two fine paintings, one of which is a Christ, by Ribera. The *Church of St. François* (14th cent.) has a richly decorated interior. The *Jardin de l'Evêché* is a public promenade with a *Statue of Las Cases* (1766-1842), who shared the exile of Napoleon I. and wrote the 'Mémorial de Ste-Hélène'. The rearing of silk-worms, silk-spinning, etc. are considerable industries at Lavaur.

41 M. *Fiac; Bravis;* 46¹/₂ M. *St. Paul-Damiatte,* two villages
on the Agout; 50 M. *L'Albarède;* 53¹/₂ M. *Vielmur-sur-Agout;*
55 M. *Semalens.* — Beyond *La Crémade* the line to Castelnaudary
diverges to the right.

61¹/₂ M. **Castres** (*Grand Hôtel,* Rue Thiers; *Hôt. du Nord,* Rue
Sabatier, R. 2-5, déj. 2¹/₂, D. 3 fr.), a town with 27,509 inhab., on
the Agout and the Durenque. Until 1625 it was one of the chief
strongholds of the Calvinists, but in that year it was forced to submit and was dismantled. The town has large manufactures of
textile fabrics.

The Avenue de Toulouse leads from the station to the centre of
the town, intersecting the boulevards and the Rue de l'Hôtel-de-
Ville, which ends, to the right, at the Agout, on the banks of which
are many picturesque houses. The *Hôtel de Ville* occupies the old
Bishops' Palace, built by Mansart, and incorporates a Romanesque
tower dating from an old Benedictine abbey, round which the town
sprang up. The old *Jardin de l'Evêché* (17th cent.), behind the
Hôtel de Ville, is now a public promenade. The *Church of St.
Benoît,* the former cathedral, opposite the Hôtel de Ville, was reconstructed in the 17-18th centuries. Farther on is the *Place Nationale,* embellished with a fountain. The town is connected by
two bridges with the suburb on the left bank, in which is the *Promenade du Mail.* The Rue du Temple leads from the Place Nationale to the pleasant promenades of the Boulevards, in which, to the
right, is the Collège, with the keep of a 12th cent. castle.

From Castres to *Castelnaudary,* see p. 87.

From Castres to Carmaux (*Rodez*) viâ Albi, 39¹/₂ M., railway in
2¹/₄ hrs. (fares 7 fr. 20, 4 fr. 85, 3 fr. 15 c.). — Beyond (9 M.) *Lautrec,* a
small decayed town, the line crosses the *Dadou,* a tributary of the Agout.
— 18¹/₂ M. *Lombers,* on the *Assou.* — 29¹/₂ M. Albi, *Gare d'Orléans* (branch
to Tessonnières, see p. 116). The line skirts the town to the right and
crosses the *Tarn* near the cathedral. 30¹/₂ M. *Albi, Gare du Midi,* in the
suburb on the right bank. — 39¹/₂ M. Carmaux, with 9580 inhab., has
important coal-mines. — The railway is to be continued to *Rodez* (p. 119),
and will be carried across the *Viaur,* a little beyond *Tanus* (10 M. from
Carmaux), by a viaduct even larger than that of Garabit (p. 265).

From Castres to Lacaune, 29 M. by the old road (carr. 25-35 fr.),
33 M. by the new road (diligence in 7-8 hrs.; 5 fr.). The old road, which
is more interesting but steeper than the other, leads viâ the *Sidobre,* a
granite plateau, and (15 M.) *Brassac* (Hotel), on the *Agout.* The new road
runs viâ the valley of the *Durenque* and (18¹/₂ M.) *Brassac.* — Lacaune
(*Hôtel Bastide; Moulon; de l'Etablissement*), picturesquely situated on the
Gijou, has a *Bath Establishment,* 3/4 M. to the E. (tramway), with thermal
and cold mineral springs. — Routes to *St. Pons* viâ La Salvetat, and to
Graissessac viâ St. Gervais-Ville and Murat-sur-Vèbre, see pp. 98, 269.

Beyond Castres our train crosses the Agout, crosses and recrosses
the *Thoré,* and halts at *Lostange.*

66¹/₂ M. *Labruyulère,* a manufacturing town (3450 inhab.), with
a ruined castle and a fine Romanesque tower. Then *Roubinarié*
and *St. Alby.*

73 M. **Mazamet** (**Hôtel Continental,* Rue de l'Hôtel-de-Ville),
a prosperous but uninteresting cloth-making town (14,361 inhab.),

situated on the Larue, to the N.W. of the Montagne Noire. Near the station is a *Promenade* with fine plane-trees. The *Church of St. Sauveur* has some curious paintings on its walls and vaulting. The scanty ruins of the *Château d'Hautpoul* occupy an eminence outside the town.

The two chief summits of the **Montagne Noire** may be ascended hence in 4-4^1/$_2$ hrs. (with guide): the *Pic de Nore* (3970 ft.), to the S.E., vià the valley of the Arnette; the *Pic de Montaud* (3350 ft.), to the S.W., by the new Carcassonne road.

76 M. *Alberts.* — At (79 M.) *St. Amans-Soult*, Marshal Soult (1769-1852) was born and died. — 82 M. *Albine*; 84^1/$_2$ M. *Lacabarède.* Then beyond a short tunnel (87 M.) *Labastide-Rouairoux*, a cloth-manufacturing town, with 2906 inhabitants.

A tunnel nearly ^{1}/$_2$ M. long takes us from the valley of the Tharé to that of the Salesse, and from the basin of the Atlantic to that of the Mediterranean. The scenery changes; fig-trees and olives appear. — 91^1/$_2$ M. *Courniou.*

95 M. **St. Pons** or *St. Pons-de-Thomières (Hôtel Pastré)*, a cloth-manufacturing town with 3247 inhab., about ^{1}/$_2$ M. to the left, in a valley at the head of which the Jaur rises. We pass under the railway and follow a fine avenue of plane-trees to the town. Near the other end of the town is the *Cathedral* (12th cent.; rebuilt in the 18th), which has a fine old portal behind the choir, and in the interior, handsome choir-stalls and choir-screen.

From St. Pons to St. Chinian *(Béziers)*, 14 M., public conveyance in 2^1/$_2$-3 hrs. (fare 2 fr.), thrice a day, from the Café du Commerce, near the church. — The route leads vià the deep *Defile of the Nourre* and down the valley of the *Vernaroobres*. — *St. Chinian*, see p. 96.

From St. Pons to La Salvetat, 13^1/$_2$ M., public conveyance in about 3 hrs. (fare 2^1/$_2$ fr.), starting daily at 1 p. m. from the little Hôtel Dauzat, at the end of the main street. — The route leads vià the *Col du Saumail* or *du Cabaretou* (3115 ft.) to (13^1/$_2$ M.) La Salvetat (3195 ft.; *Hôtel Calbérac*), with 3320 inhab., on the right bank of the Agout, a favourite summer-resort of the inhabitants of the plain of Narbonnais. Here are the mineral springs of *Rieumajou*. The neighbourhood is bracing, abounding in game and fish, and is a good centre for excursions. — *Lacaune* (p. 97) lies only 13^1/$_2$ M. to the N. of La Salvetat.

A small tunnel is traversed. — 97^1/$_2$ M. *Riols* has cloth-manufactures. Beyond (101^1/$_2$ M.) *St. Etienne-d'Albagnan* the Jaur is spanned by three bridges. The bare heights to the left are the *Monts de l'Espinouse* (3550 ft.). — 105 M. *Olargues*, situated on a crag on the right bank. We cross a long and lofty viaduct to (107^1/$_2$ M.) *Mons-la-Trivalle*. The Gorge d'Héric, see p. 99. Beyond another viaduct and two tunnels we enter the valley of the *Orb*, and halt at *Colombières* (Hotel), where are a double waterfall, a ruined château, and a huge chestnut-tree; the Gorge d'Héric may also be visited hence. To the left rise the lofty cliffs of the Caroux (p. 99). Beyond a tunnel is (113 M.) *Le Poujol.*

114 M. **Lamalou-les-Bains.** — Hotels. At Lamalou-le-Bas: Grand-Hôtel, R. from 3, B. 1, déj. 3, D. 3^1/$_2$ fr., Gr.-Hôt. des Bains, du Nord, these three of the first rank, 8-12 fr. per day. — Du Midi, de la Paix,

DE FRANCE, second class. — At Lamalou-le-Centre: GRAND-HÔTEL DU CENTRE. — At Lamalou-le-Haut: HÔTEL DE L'ETABLISSEMENT; TABARIÉ, R. from $1\frac{1}{2}$, B. $\frac{3}{4}$, déj. 3, D. $2\frac{1}{2}$ fr. — Numerous *Villas* and *Furnished Houses*.

Bath Establishments. At Lamalou-le-Bas: Bains de piscine $1\frac{1}{4}$-4 fr., douches $1\frac{1}{2}$-$1\frac{3}{4}$, plunge-bath 2 fr. At Lamalou-le-Haut: Bains de piscine $1\frac{1}{4}$-2, bain de baignoire 3, douche $1\frac{1}{2}$ fr. — At Lamalou-le-Centre: baths $1\frac{1}{2}$, douches $1\frac{1}{4}$-2 fr. — *Mineral Water*, 10 c. per glass.

Carriages. About 25 fr. per day; drives in the environs 10-40 fr. (tariff). — *Tramway Omnibuses* between the station, the three bath-establishments, and La Vernière, 15, 20, 25 c. — *Donkeys*, 5 fr. per day.

Casinos. *Casino-Théâtre* at Lamalou-le-Bas; *Casino Municipal*, new.

Post & Telegraph Offices at Lamalou-le-Centre.

Lamalou-les-Bains, a thermal station amidst the mountain-spurs that unite the Cévennes and the Montagne Noire (p. 98), consists of *Lamalou-le-Bas* or *l'Ancien*, *Lamalou-le-Centre*, and *Lamalou-le-Haut*, all near each other and at about the same elevation (590 ft.). The waters (61-114° Fahr.) are especially efficacious in rheumatic and nervous affections. The visitors are mostly from the S. of France and from Spain. Lamalou is very hot and dusty in summer, like all this part of southern France.

The ETABLISSEMENT DU BAS, to the left in the village, behind the casino, is pleasantly situated round a shady court, open towards the valley. On the hill-slope behind are a pretty *Park*, with the *Usclade* spring (118° Fahr.), one of the chief mineral springs, and a small *Botanic Garden* (adm. free). The *Lacets de Rhèdes* offer a picturesque walk with fine views. — The ETABLISSEMENT DU CENTRE, rebuilt in 1892, has a *Hydropathic Establishment* in connection with it. — The ETABLISSEMENT DU HAUT, $\frac{1}{2}$ M. farther on, is a well-equipped establishment in a pleasant *Park*, with a small stream and the buvette of the *Petit-Vichy*.

Excursions and Walks. BY TRAMWAY (25 c.) to the *Park of La Vernière* (adm. 25 c.), about $\frac{3}{4}$ M. to the S.S.E., on the bank of the Orb.

ON FOOT OR ON DONKEYS. To the N. W., to *Villecelle* (3 M.), a typical Cevenole village; to *Le Fraisse*, with its legendary chestnut-tree, 3 hrs. there and back; to the N.E. to the hermitage of *Notre-Dame-de-Capimont* (4 hrs.; fine view); to the S.W. to the priory of *St. Pierre-de-Rhèdes*, the foundation of which is attributed to Charlemagne; to the *Caroux*, see below.

BY CARRIAGE. Viâ *Hérépian* and the valley of the *Mare* to ($3\frac{1}{2}$ M.) *Villemagne*, said to have been endowed by Charlemagne (10 fr. there and back). The church dates from the 12th century. About $\frac{1}{2}$ M. farther is the picturesque *Pont du Diable*. To St. Gervais, see below. — To the *Valley of the Orb* and the *Gorge d'Héric*, 10 M., an interesting excursion requiring $\frac{1}{2}$ day. The route leads through a highly picturesque part of the valley viâ *Le Poujol* and (5 M.) *Colombières* (see below). The imposing rocky amphitheatre of the Gorge d'Héric lies to the left of the road, a little before the ($6\frac{3}{4}$ M.) *Pont de Tarassac*, a suspension-bridge over the Orb, commanding a beautiful view. This excursion may also be made by taking the train to Mons-la-Trivalle (p. 98), about $\frac{1}{2}$ M. beyond the Pont de Tarassac. — To ($8\frac{1}{2}$ M.; 20 fr.) *St. Gervais-Ville* (Hôtel Soulié), a village with 1780 inhab., picturesquely situated on a tributary of the Mare, viâ the plateau of *Taussac*, returning by the valley of the Mare viâ Villemagne ($12\frac{1}{2}$ M.; see above). — From St. Gervais to Graissesac and to Lacaune, see pp. 97, 263.

ASCENT OF MONT CAROUX ($3\frac{1}{2}$-4 hrs.). We drive to ($7\frac{1}{2}$ M.) *Douch* (there and back 35 fr.), $\frac{1}{2}$-$\frac{3}{4}$ hr. to the N.W. of the plateau; or walk viâ *Villecelle*, *Le Fraisse* (see above), *Le Logis-Neuf* ($1\frac{1}{4}$ hr. from Lamalou), and *Douch* (about 1 hr. from the top). **Mont Caroux** (3585 ft.; guide 8 fr.; from the inn 2 fr.), though not very lofty, commands an admirable view, embracing the plain of Bas-Languedoc, part of the Pyrenees, the Mediterranean, Mont Ventoux, and the beginning of the Alps, etc.

Beyond Lamalou the railway continues to ascend the valley of the Orb. — 116 M. *Hérépian*. To Villemagne, see p. 99. We cross the Orb, and join the main line from Neussargues to Béziers (R. 42).

118 M. **Bédarieux** (*Buffet*), see p. 269.

The Montpellier line follows that to Béziers as far as (124 M.) *Faugères*, the next station, where it turns to the E. It then passes through three tunnels. — 131 M. *Gabian*, a large village with a ruined château. — 133½ M. *Roujan-Neffiès*, in a coal-mining district. — 136 M. *Cauz* (1930 inhab.); 139 M. *Nizas*.

142 M. **Paulhan** (*Buffet*). Railway to Béziers and Pézenas, see p. 95.

From Paulhan to Lodève, 18½ M., railway in 1 hr. 10 min. (fares 3 fr. 25, 2 fr. 25, 1 fr. 45 c.). This line is a continuation of the line from Béziers through the valley of the Hérault. — 7½ M. *Clermont-l'Hérault* (*Hôt. du Commerce; de la Renaissance*), a small industrial town, with tanneries and manufactures of woollen cloth, mainly for the army. It contains a church of the 13-14th cent. and a ruined castle. About 5 M. to the S.W. is the small village of **Mourèze**, in a curious amphitheatre of dolomite rocks recalling Montpellier-le-Vieux (p. 275). A carriage (4-8 pers., 20-30 fr.) may be ordered in advance, through the station-master, for a visit to this 'cirque'. — A public conveyance (3 fr., with minimum of 12 fr.; places to be secured in advance) also plies to St. Guilhem-le-Désert, 15 M. to the N. E., viâ (11½ M.) *Gignac*, with two interesting churches, and (10½ M.) *Aniane*, an ancient little town beside an 18th cent. abbey, now a prison. St. Guilhem-le-Désert (*Inn*) occupies a curious site near the *Gorges of the Hérault*. It possesses a remarkable Romanesque-Byzantine *Church*, part of the *Cloisters* of the abbey to which it owes its origin, and some remains of fortifications, etc. — 18½ M. *Lodève* (*Hôtel du Nord*), the *Luteva* of the ancients, a finely situated town of 9080 inhabitants, was governed in the Middle Ages by viscounts, and then by bishops, who up to 1789 had the right of coining money. It is now a manufacturing town, specially engaged in making military cloth. The former *Cathedral* dates from the 13th and 16th centuries.

We cross the *Hérault*. — Between (144½ M.) *Campagnan* and (146 M.) *St. Pargoire* is a tunnel, and beyond (150½ M.) *Villeveyrac* another.

156 M. **Montbazin**, also a station on the line from Béziers viâ Mèze (p. 95) and connected by rail with Cette (8 M.), viâ *Balaruc* (p. 96). — 159 M. *Cournonterral*; 161½ M. *Fabrègues*; 165 M. *St. Jean-de-Vedas*.

167 M. **Montpellier** (for farther details and plan, see *Baedeker's South-Eastern France*).

Hotels. Nevet, Boulevard de l'Esplanade; Grand Hôtel, Rue Maguelone; Continental, Place de la Comédie; du Midi, Boul. Victor-Hugo; Delmas, Rue de la République; Maguelone, Rue Maguelone; Lebane, Boul. Victor-Hugo, unpretending. — Cafés in the Rue Maguelone, Place de la Comédie, Boulevard de l'Esplanade, etc. — Cabs, with one horse, per drive 1 fr.; with two horses 1½ fr.; per hr. 2 fr.

Montpellier, a town of 69,258 inhab., the capital of the department of the *Hérault*, is situated on a hill commanding a fine view,

with the *Lez* flowing below. From the square outside the station, with
a *Monument to Planchon*, late director of the Jardin des Plantes,
the handsome Rue Maguelone leads to the Place de la Comédie,
with the *Fontaine des Trois Graces* (1776) and the *Theatre*. To
the right of the Place extends the *Esplanade* with the *Musée*, containing one of the best provincial collections of paintings in France.
The *Boulevards*, beginning at the Place de la Comédie, make the
circuit of the old town. In the Boul. Victor-Hugo is the 12th cent.
Tour de la Babotte. The *Peyrou*, the higher part of the town, is
a fine promenade dating chiefly from the 17-18th centuries. The
Porte de Peyrou, a Doric triumphal arch, was erected in 1691. A
little below the Peyrou is the large *Jardin des Plantes*, the oldest
in France. — The *Cathedral*, founded in the 14th cent., has been
restored and enlarged in modern times. The various buildings of
the University Academy are also interesting.

14. From Périgueux to Tarbes (Pyrenees).

180 M. Railway in 9 hrs. (fares 33 fr. 70, 29 fr. 50, 14 fr. 90 c.). — From
Paris to *Tarbes* viâ Limoges, 495 M. in 23¹/₂ hrs. (fares 89 fr. 00, 60 fr. 50,
39 fr. 50 c.); viâ Bordeaux, 515 M., see R. 1 and p. 64. — From *Limoges* to
Tarbes, 247 M., in 12 hrs. (fares 44 fr. 80, 30 fr. 30, 19 fr. 75 c.).

Périgueux, see p. 43. The train passes near the ruins (left) of
Château Barrière (p. 45); to the right is the *Tour Vésone* (p. 45).
Beyond (7 M.) *Niversac*, the junction for Brive (p. 107), our line
ascends. 11 M. *Versannes*; 15¹/₂ M. *La Gélie*. — 21 M. *Miremont*.

About 3 M. to the E. of the station is the *Grotto of Miremont* or
Trou de Granville, the galleries of which measure altogether about 2¹/₂ M.
in length. The 'Grande Branche' is about 1100 yds. long, and contains
remarkable stalactites and stalagmites, fossil shells, etc. The guide, whose
attendance is necessary, lives close by. The entrance is narrow and the
ground almost everywhere slippery; the atmosphere cold and damp. To
see the whole would take eight hours, but curiosity may be satisfied in
two. The most interesting points are the *Cas de la Vieille*, a stalagmite;
the *Cake Room*, the *Sparkling Grotto*, the *Umbrella*, *St. Front*, a domed
chamber, the *Shell Room*, the *Table* and *Tomb of Gargantua*, the *Halle de
la Labenche*, and the *Foirail* or *Market Place*.

Beyond Miremont we cross two viaducts, pass through a short
tunnel, and cross the *Vézère*. — 25¹/₂ M. *Les Eyzies*, a picturesquely
placed village surrounded and overhung by magnificent rocks. These
rocks contain a large number of *Grottoes*, where remarkable dis-
coveries of bones of extinct animals and of implements of flint
and reindeer horn have recently been made.

The line now again crosses the Vézère. Beyond (30 M.) *Le
Bugue*, a commercial town with 2850 inhab., we cross for the last
time the tortuous Vézère, which joins the Dordogne a little farther
on. On the left is the ancient *Château de Perdigat*; to the right
the village of *Limeuil*, once a fortified town. We now enter the beautiful valley of the *Dordogne* and cross that river.

35¹/₂ M. **Le Buisson** (*Buffet*), the junction of the line from Bordeaux viâ Bergerac (p. 15).

About 3¹/₂ M. to the S. is *Cadouin*, which once possessed a celebrated abbey. The only remains are the church (12th cent.), with a fine painting of the 15th cent., and the magnificent *Cloisters, in the Flamboyant style.

From Le Buisson to St. Denis-près-Martel (*Aurillac*), 50 M., railway in 2 hrs. 40 min. (fares 8 fr. 95, 6 fr. 5, 3 fr. 95 c.). We follow the main line as far as (4¹/₂ M.) *Siorac*, the next station, and crossing the *Dordogne* ascend the beautiful valley of that river to the E. — 8¹/₂ M. *St. Cyprien*, a small town of 2134 inhab., on the left. To our left is a range of hills on which, beyond (13 M.) *St. Vincent-Bérenac*, the fine *Château de Beynac* (13th, 14th, and 16th cent.) comes into view and long remains in sight. We cross the Dordogne. The château (14th cent.) seen on the right before the bridge belongs to (14 M.) *Castelnaud*. Another château on a height comes in view lower down. The country is undulating; we recross the Dordogne and begin to ascend. — 16 M. *Vérac*. We now quit the river, traverse two tunnels (the first ¹/₄ M. long), and pass over a viaduct.

20¹/₂ M. **Sarlat** (*Hôt. de la Madeleine*, Rue de la République), a town of 6315 inhab., in a valley about ¹/₂ M. to the left of the station. The large building to our left as we arrive is a seminary. With the exception of the Rue de la République, the streets are narrow, crooked, and ill-built, but they contain several quaint old *Houses*, some even in the Gothic style. The most interesting are in the Rue Gambetta, to the right, where there is also a ruined church of the 14th century. A little farther on is a *Cathedral*, of the 11th, 12th, and 15th cent., with some fine wood-carving. The 16th cent. house near the entrance was the birthplace of La Boëtie (1530-1563), the author and friend of Montaigne, to whom a statue was erected in 1892. The lane ascending by the left of the church skirts an enclosure within which is a *Sepulchral Chapel*, a Gothic structure of two stories, belonging to a convent (visitors admitted). Farther up is a promenade known as the *Jardin Plantier*.

Beyond Sarlat the railway returns to the valley of the Dordogne; fine view to the right. — 25¹/₂ M. *Carsac*; 28¹/₂ M. *Calviac*. The line skirts the river, traverses a tunnel, ¹/₄ M. long, and crosses a bridge. 31 M. *Carlux*; 33¹/₂ M. *Caroulie*. We here join the line to Cahors and follow it to beyond the viaduct of Souillac, which now appears on the right. Fine amphitheatre of mountains; tunnel; two viaducts.

38 M. *Souillac* (p. 109). We cross the large viaduct and see another to the left, over which runs the line to Brive. Then, farther on, another viaduct and a tunnel, over ¹/₄ M. in length. — 41 M. *Le Pigeon*.

46 M. *Martel*, a little town to the left, has a curious 14th cent. Hôtel de Ville and an interesting church of the 15th century. — The railway now attains a considerable elevation (fine view to the right), traverses rock-cuttings and five tunnels, begins to descend rapidly, and joins the line from Toulouse viâ Capdenac (on the right). — 50 M. *St. Denis-près-Martel* (p. 107).

Beyond (40 M.) *Siorac* we quit the Dordogne valley, which diverges to the left (with the line to St. Denis-près-Martel), and skirt slopes planted with vines.

43¹/₂ M. *Belvès*, a small town of 2182 inhabitants. The country now becomes very hilly; the line crosses five viaducts and passes through a tunnel 1640 yds. long. 50 M. *Le Got*, with a large export of mushrooms (cèpes) gathered in the neighbourhood. 54¹/₂ M. *Villefranche-de-Belvès*, a small town on a hill rising from the *Allemance*, which we cross repeatedly farther on. 58 M. *Sauveterre*, with a ruined castle of the 13th century. — 60 M. *St. Front*, with a partly fortified Romanesque church. Then three bridges with a short tunnel between the first two. — 64 M. *Cuzorn*.

67¹/₂ M. **Monsempron-Libos** (*Buffet*). Monsempron, on a height to the right, has an interesting Gothic and Romanesque church.

From Monsempron-Libos to Cahors, 31 M., railway in 1³/₄-2 hrs. This branch ascends the picturesque valley of the *Lot*. 1¹/₄ M. *Fumel*, an industrial town of 3630 inhab., 5 M. from the well-preserved old castle of *Bonaguil*. The line then runs between the river and the steep heights on the left. At the foot of the hills on the right are the ruins of the old town of *Orgueil*. 5¹/₂ M. *Soturac-Touzac*; 8 M. *Duravel*, beyond which we cross the tortuous Lot; 11 M. *Puy-l'Evêque*, a town of 2200 inhab., situated on the left. Then another bridge over the Lot and a short tunnel. 15¹/₂ M. *Castelfranc*, with a castle situated on the right a little short of the station; 20 M. *Luzech*, with a ruined castle of the 13th cent., on a peninsula formerly defended by a Celtic fortress, of which some remains have been discovered. 22 M. *Parnac*. To the left is the château of *Grézelle*. 26 M. *Mercuès*, with an interesting castle of the 13th cent., on a hill to the right, belonging to the Bishop of Cahors. To the left are massive retaining walls, with arches. — 31 M. *Cahors*, see p. 110.

The Agen line skirts the Lot for some distance, passing (71 M.) *Trentels-Ladignac*. — Bridge over the Lot, and two short tunnels.

77¹/₂ M. *Penne*, on a hill 1¹/₄ M. to the N. of the station, with the scanty remains of a famous mediæval castle. At some distance, to the left, are the ruins of *Castel Gaillard*.

From Penne to Tonneins, 14¹/₂ M., railway in 1¹/₄ hr. (fares 4 fr. 80, 3 fr. 30, 2 fr. 10 c.). — 5¹/₂ M. *Villeneuve-sur-Lot* (*Hôtel Lamouroux*) is a town of 13,800 inhab., with a large trade especially in prunes, which it exports annually to the value of 120,000*l*. Part of the *Ramparts* of the 13th cent., especially on the left bank, and a bridge of the same period still remain. One of the squares is surrounded by arcades of the same date. — At (12 M.) *Ste. Livrade* (2844 inhab.) we cross the *Lot*. — 22¹/₂ M. *Clairac*, with 3560 inhab., embraced the Reformation with ardour and was captured by Louis XIII. in 1621. — 27 M. *Tonneins*, see p. 72.

We now traverse a pretty valley and a tunnel 1350 yds. long. To the left is the lofty *Tour de Hautefage* (15th cent.). 88 M. *Laroque*, with remains of fortifications. Beyond (90¹/₂ M.) *Pont-du-Casse*, we cross the *Canal Latéral à la Garonne* (p. 71) and join the Bordeaux line.

94 M. **Agen** (Buffet), see p. 73. To *Bordeaux* and to *Toulouse*, see R. 10.

We here quit the Orléans Railway and proceed by the Chemin de Fer du Midi (Toulouse line) as far as (3¹/₂ M.) *Bon-Encontre* (p. 74), we cross the Garonne by a fine viaduct and ascend the valley of the *Gers*. 101 M. *Layrac*, a small place with a Romanesque church; 104 M. *Goulens*; 106 M. *Astaffort*; 112 M. *Castez-Lectourois*.

116¹/₂ M. **Lectoure** (*Hôtel de l'Europe*, Rue Nationale, indifferent), an ancient town of 4994 inhab., on a steep and almost completely isolated hill. The principal *Church*, formerly a cathedral, to the right, at the end of the Rue Nationale, is a massive building of the 13th and 16th centuries. It contains side-chapels with galleries, a high-altar, and some modern stained glass. The fine pendentives of the apsidal chapels are noteworthy. Behind the church is a promenade commanding a fine view of the Pyrenees. At the end of the promenade is a *Statue of Marshal Lannes* (1769-1809), Duke of

Montebello, who was born at Lectoure of obscure parents. The Rue de Fontélie, which descends to the right of the old episcopal palace, near the church, leads to the *Fontaine Hondélie* or *Font-Elie*, which dates from the Roman period, when it is said to have been consecrated to Diana of Delos or to the Sun; it was partly rebuilt in the middle ages. It forms a grotto with pointed vaulting and two arches closed by a railing.

We now cross the Gers, and reach (123 M.) *Fleurance*, a small town on its right bank. Beyond (126½ M.) *Montestruc* the Gers is again crossed. 130 M. *Ste. Christie.* Beyond (133 M.) *Rambert-Preignan*, the line to Toulouse diverges to the left.

138 M. **Auch** (*Hôtel de France*, Place de l'Hôtel-de-Ville; *Georges*, Rue de Lorraine), the ancient capital of *Gascony*, and now the chief town of the department of the *Gers*, with 14,782 inhab., is situated on a steep hill rising from the river Gers. It was the capital of the *Ausci*, and was very flourishing under the Romans. Since the 9th cent. it has been the seat of archbishops, who formerly styled themselves the Primates of Novempopulania.

The town is entered by a street to the right of the station and the Avenue d'Alsace, which leads to a bridge over the turbid and yellowish *Gers*. The Rue de Lorraine, beyond the bridge, ascends to a small Place (right), with a *Statue of Admiral Villaret-Joyeuse* (1750-1812). Turning to the left into the Rue Gambetta, we soon reach the Place de l'Hôtel-de-Ville and the *Cours d'Etigny*, a promenade adorned with a *Statue of Meyret d'Etigny*, a governor and benefactor of the district in the 18th century. In the *Hôtel de Ville* is a small *Musée* of paintings, antiquities, etc. The building at the other end of the Cours is the *Palais de Justice*, a recent erection.

The ***Cathedral of St. Mary**, in the Place adjoining the Hôtel de Ville, rebuilt in 1483-1662, is one of the finest churches in the South of France. It is in the form of a Latin cross with a transept in the debased Gothic style; the classical portico is surmounted by two square towers of the composite order.

The Interior is more imposing than the exterior, which on the whole is somewhat heavy and cold. The *Choir* (closed) contains 113 beautifully carved **Stalls*, masterpieces of their period. The rood-loft between the nave and choir has given place to a pretentious modern *Choirorgan*, with panels on its sides adorned with paintings on a gold ground. The reredos at the *High Altar* is a huge and tasteless marble erection of the end of the 16th century. The chapels of the *Ambulatory* contain rich stained glass of the Renaissance, representing Patriarchs, Prophets, Apostles, and Sibyls. Some of the sculptures in the chapels are also noteworthy. Behind the choir are several bas-reliefs of the Renaissance.

Near the cathedral stand the *Archbishops' Palace* (18th cent.), with a *Tower* of the 14th cent., etc. A handsome flight of 232 steps descends hence to the left bank of the Gers, by which we may regain the bridge and the station.

From Auch to *Toulouse*, see p. 87.

142 M. *St. Jean-le-Comtal*; 151 M. *L'Isle-de-Noé*.

155 M. **Mirande** (*Hôtel Tartas*), a small town (4244 inhab.) with
the remains of fortifications, was built on a regular plan towards
the close of the 13th century. It contains an interesting church of
the 15th cent., with a belfry above the street.

160¹/₂ M. *Laas*; 165 M. *Mielan*; 171 M. *Villecomtal-sur-Arros*.
The Pyrenees, which have already been in sight for some time, are
now, in clear weather, very distinctly seen during the descent into
the valley of the Adour.

173 M. *Rabastens-de-Bigorre*, a small town to the left, at the
siege of which Blaise de Montluc, the famous and terrible opponent
of the Calvinists, received a frightful wound in the face, which
obliged him to wear a mask for the rest of his life (1570-77). In
revenge he ordered a general massacre, from which only four persons,
two of them Catholics, escaped.

The train now crosses the *Adour* and turns to the S. 178 M. *Vic-
en-Bigorre*, a town with 3650 inhab., the junction of a line to Morcenx
(p. 64); 179 M. *Pujo*; 180 M. *Andrest*.

186 M. *Tarbes* (see p. 135).

15. From Limoges (Paris) to Brive and Aurillac.

I. From Limoges to Brive.

a. Viâ Uzerche.

81¹/₂ M. RAILWAY in 3-3³/₄ hrs. (fares 11 fr. 20, 7 fr. 50, 4 fr. 90 c.).
The trains start from the Gare des Bénédictins.

Limoges, see p. 39. — The line passes below the town by a tunnel
1085 yds. in length, crosses the *Vienne*, and ascends the valley of
the *Briance*, to the S. E. Fine view of Limoges to the right. Then
a viaduct and a tunnel. To the left a modern château.

7¹/₂ M. *Solignac-le-Vigen*. The small town of *Solignac*, ¹/₂ M.
to the right, was formerly the seat of a Benedictine abbey, founded
in the 7th cent., rebuilt in the 18th, and now a porcelain manufactory. The interesting *Church* of the 12th cent. has a dome-vaulted
nave and fine 15th cent. stalls. Near *Le Vigen*, on an eminence on
the left bank of the Briance, is the *Castle of Chalusset*, the ancient
residence of the Viscounts of Limoges, which was built in the 12th
and 13th cent. and dismantled in 1593 during the Religious Wars.
Its triple walls were about 65 ft. in height. Two keeps and other parts
of the stronghold are still standing. This castle is seen from the
railway, to the right, beyond the next viaduct and tunnel.

13 M. *Pierre-Buffière*, with porcelain-manufactures, was the
birthplace of the surgeon Dupuytren (1777-1835), a statue of whom
has been erected near a bronze fountain presented by him to the
town. — The train then enters the valley of the Blanzou and crosses
the Briance. — 16¹/₂ M. *Glanges*; 20 M. *Magnac-Vicq*. The Petite-
Briance is crossed by a long and lofty viaduct. — 22¹/₂ M. *St. Ger-
main-les-Belles*; the little town lies 1 M. to the left. 26 M. *La*

Porcherie; 29 M. *Masseret.* — Beyond (31¹/₂ M.) *Malons-la-Tour*, where there is a ruined tower, we enter the valley of the Vézère.

36¹/₂ M. **Userche** (*Hôt. Pommarel*), a town of 4350 inhab., is picturesquely situated about ³/₄ M. to the S. of the station, on a steep hill washed by the *Vézère*. It contains an interesting Romanesque *Church* and several castellated *Mansions* of the 12-16th centuries. Uzerche claims to be the Uxellodunum of antiquity (comp. p. 107).

The railway next traverses a more undulating country, crosses three bridges (the third spanning the Vézère), and threads a tunnel. — Beyond (41¹/₂ M.) *Vigeois* (3266 inhab.) we enter a wooded rocky gorge in which there are eight tunnels, with a bridge after the first and a ruin, to the right, after the last. Between (46¹/₂ M.) *Estivaux* and (51 M.) *Allassac* there are four tunnels and a bridge, still in the gorge of the Vézère. We then quit that river.

54 M. **Donzenac** (*Hôt. du Commerce; des Voyageurs*), with 3240 inhab., picturesquely situated to the left, has an interesting *Church* (12-14th cent.) and several quaint houses.

57 M. *Ussac.* We cross the *Corrèze* and join the following railway, then that from Périgueux (see below). — 61¹/₂ M. *Brive* (R. 5).

b. Via St. Yrieix.

63¹/₂ M. Railway in 2¹/₂-3¹/₂ hrs. (fares as above).

Limoges, see p. 39. — This line diverges to the left from the preceding after crossing the Vienne (see p. 105). — 6¹/₂ M. *Beynac.*

12¹/₂ M. *Nexon* (3156 inhab.), with a church of the 12th and 15th cent., and a château in the style of the 16th century. Line to Périgueux, see p. 42.

18 M. *La Meyze*; 21 M. *Champseaux.* 26 M. **St. Yrieix** (*Hôt. du Faisan*), a town of 8700 inhab., where the first French quarries of kaolin or porcelain clay were discovered in 1765, possesses an interesting church of the 12-13th cent., with a single nave and three choirs. Tramway to Périgueux, see p. 46.

31¹/₂ M. *Coussac-Bonneval*, with a château of the 15-16th cent., to the left; 35 M. *St. Julien*; 38 M. *Lubersac*; 42 M. *Pompadour*, with a château presented by Louis XV., with the title of Marquise, to his mistress, Antoinette Poisson. The *National Stud Farm* here is one of the most important in Europe. — Then, after three viaducts (180, 120, and 60 ft. in height), the line descends, crossing several affluents of the Vézère, to (48¹/₂ M.) *Vignols-St. Solve.* At (52 M.) *Objat* we join the line from Thiviers (p. 42). Beyond (56 M.) *Le Burg* and (58 M.) *Varetz* we cross the *Vézère* and its tributary the *Corrèze.*

63 M. **Brive** (*Buffet; Hôtel de Bordeaux; de Toulouse*), an ancient town with 16,800 inhab., where Gundebald was proclaimed king of Aquitania in 585. It was the birthplace of Cardinal Dubois and Marshal Brune and has a statue of the latter. The chief local trade is in truffles. In the middle of the town stands the Romanesque and Gothic church of *St. Martin* (11-12th cent.), recently restored.

From Brive to *Tulle, Clermont-Ferrand*, etc., see R. 36 b; to *Thiviers*, p. 42.

From Brive to Périgueux (Coutras, Bordeaux), 45 M., railway in 1³/₄-3³/₄ hrs. (fares 8 fr. 10, 5 fr. 45, 3 fr. 55 c.). This line soon enters the valley of the *Vézère*, which it crosses and follows for a considerable distance. 13 M. *Terrasson*, a small commercial town with a Gothic church and the ruins of an abbey; 20¹/₂ M. *La Bachellerie*, a large village on a vine-clad slope, beyond which we quit the Vézère; 36¹/₂ M. *St. Pierre-de-Chignac*; 39 M. *Niversac*, where the line to Agen (p. 101) diverges. — 45 M. *Périgueux*, see p. 43.

II. From Brive to Aurillac.

84¹/₂ M. Railway in 2³/₄-4¹/₄ hrs. (fares 11 fr. 85, 7 fr. 95, 5 fr. 15 c.). From Brive to (17¹/₂ M.) *St. Denis-près-Martel* we follow the Capdenac and Toulouse line (p. 112); from St. Denis to (47 M.) *Aurillac* the route ascends the interesting *Valley of the Cère*.

Beyond Brive, where the most interesting and picturesque part of the route begins, the train passes through two tunnels; the second (1550 yards long), the *Montplaisir Tunnel*, is the longest on the Orléans Railway system. — At a distance, first on the left and then on the right, are the ruins of the Château de Turenne (see below).

73 M. *Turenne*, 1¹/₄ M. to the E. of the small and ancient town of that name. This was the capital of the 'vicomté' from which the celebrated Marshal Turenne (d. 1685) took his title. The ruins of his *Château* consist of two imposing towers situated on high and precipitous rocks; the older of the two (13th cent.) is round, the other (14th cent.) is square.

76 M. *Quatre-Routes*. Farther on, to the left, is the plateau on which stands the village of *Puy-d'Issolu*, the probable site of the Celtic town of *Uxellodunum*, taken by Cæsar B.C. 50 (see also pp. 106, 114, 236).

80¹/₂ M. St. Denis-près-Martel (*Buffet; Hôt. Vayssière*, at the station, moderate), a village in the valley of the Dordogne.

From St. Denis to *Capdenac* and *Toulouse*, see p. 112; to *Le Buisson* viâ *Sarlat*, see p. 102.

The railway to Aurillac ascends the valley of the *Dordogne*, then that of the *Cère*, which becomes highly picturesque beyond Bretenoux, where it is more than 1300 ft. above the sea-level. — 84¹/₂ M. *Vayrac*. Beyond (88 M.) *Puybrun* we cross the Dordogne by an iron bridge, to the right of which is a suspension-bridge. On the right also appears the château of *Castelnau* (see below). — 91 M. *Bretenoux*, a village, at one time fortified, on the left bank of the Cère.

The *Château of Castelnau (12-15th cent.) is a picturesque ruin on a steep rock, 1³/₄ M. to the S.W., commanding a fine view (key at the 'presbytère' of Castelnau). The village *Church*, dating from the 14th cent., contains stalls and an altar-piece of the 15th century.

A Diligence (1 fr.) plies from the station of Bretenoux to St. Céré, a small town, 6 M. to the S.E., dominated by the ruined *Tours de St. Laurent* (12th and 14th cent.).

Another Diligence plies to Beaulieu (*Hôt. de Bordeaux*), a little town on the right bank of the Dordogne, 3¹/₂ M. to the N., with a fine Romanesque *Church* of the 11-13th centuries. — Thence an interesting expedition may be made into the desolate upper valley of the Dordogne, which winds at the bottom of a deep ravine between wooded rocky heights.

After a short tunnel, the railway approaches the *Cère* and the valley contracts. — 93^1/$_2$ M. *Port-de-Gagnac*; 97 M. *Laval-de-Cère*. Then six tunnels and a bridge over the Cère. — Beyond (103 M.) *Lamativie* the valley becomes a wooded rocky gorge, 980 ft. deep, in which the railway passes through 17 tunnels before the next station. The gradients are steep and the sustaining-walls and other examples of railway engineering are interesting. Views to the left.

112 M. *La Roquebrou* (Hôt. Rieu), a small shoe-making town on the right bank, has a ruined castle and a Gothic church. A narrow-gauge line is to be constructed hence to Limoges (p. 39), viâ Tulle (p. 236).

The valley now expands. The line recrosses to the right bank by means of a viaduct 80 ft. in height, and gradually quits the river.

115^1/$_2$ M. *Miécaze* is the junction for the line from Aurillac to Montluçon viâ Eygurande (p. 228). In the distance, to the left, appear the mountains of Auvergne. Then the view opens on the right. A viaduct, 110 ft. in height, is crossed to the following station.

119 M. *Viescamp-sous-Jallès*. Thence to (146 M.) *Aurillac*, see p. 261.

16. From Brive (Limoges) to Toulouse.

a. Viâ Cahors and Montauban.

133 M. Railway in 4-6^3/$_4$ hrs. (fares 24 fr. 20, 16 fr. 35, 10 fr. 70 c.). — From *Limoges*, 197 M., in 6^1/$_4$-10^1/$_2$ hrs. (fares 35 fr. 60, 28 fr. 5, 15 fr. 70 c.). — From *Paris*, 445 M., in 13^1/$_2$-22^1/$_2$ hrs. (fares 80 fr. 30, 54 fr. 20, 35 fr. 35 c.).

The *New Railway to Toulouse viâ Cahors and Montauban*, built in 1880-91 at the cost of about 62,000l. per mile, the final link being the line between Limoges and Brive viâ Uzerche, not only supersedes the old line viâ Capdenac, but also shortens the route by 21 M., while its gradients and curves are much less abrupt than those of the older line. There are 19 tunnels (about 5^1/$_2$ M. in aggregate length), 11 viaducts, and 1 bridge, and about 30 M. of curves. The most interesting part of the line for engineers is near Souillac (p. 109). The work was executed for the French government by the engineers MM. Lantoirés and Pibler. The country traversed is not very fertile and is scantily wooded with chestnuts, and has no considerable elevations.

Brive, see p. 106. — The line to Cahors diverges to the right of those to Tulle and Capdenac and ascends towards the *Causse de Martel* ('causse', see p. 269), between the Corrèze and the Dordogne. Several tunnels (the first 1150 yds. long) and viaducts are traversed. — 5 M. *Noailles* (655 ft.), to the left, has given name to a well-known noble family. Fine view to the left. Before and after (8 M.) *Chasteaux* tunnels are traversed. The railway soon quits the basin of the Corrèze, and descends rapidly towards the Dordogne. Tunnels and viaducts follow each other in rapid succession, presenting constructions of considerable interest to engineers. The last viaduct is also used by the railway to St. Denis-près-Martel, which joins ours on the left. Fine view of the valley of the Dordogne.

23 M. **Souillac** (410 ft.; *Lion d'Or*), a manufacturing town with tanneries and 3218 inhab., lies ³/₄ M. to the left of the railway. Near the end of the main street is an ancient ruined church, and behind it a handsome *Parish Church*, formerly belonging to an abbey. The building is in the Romanesque-Byzantine style of the 12th cent., with domes and transept, and has an apse with semicircular apsides In the interior, beside the main portal, is a fine bas-relief, and some paintings on the vaults of the choir and transept.

To *Le Buisson* and *St. Denis-près-Martel*, see p. 102.

Two curved viaducts and a tunnel follow; view to the left. — At (26 M.) *Casoulès* (330 ft.) the line to Le Buisson diverges (p. 102), and soon afterwards we cross the *Dordogne* and begin to reascend. — 30 M. *Lamothe-Fénelon* (472 ft.) recalls the famous Périgord family, better known under the single name Fénelon. Archbishop Fénelon was, however, born at Lamothe-Salignac. — Tunnel, 700 yds. long. — 33¹/₂ M. *Nozac* (570 ft.).

36¹/₂ M. **Gourdon** (690 ft.; *Hôtel de l'Ecu*), with 4834 inhab., is situated to the right, on a hill commanding a fine view. The town is dominated by the *Church of St. Pierre* (14-16th cent.), with two W. towers. Another church dates from the 13th cent.; and the chapel of Notre-Dame-du-Majou is a pilgrim-resort. Remains of fortifications, an ancient gate, etc. may be seen.

Beyond a tunnel and a long and deep cutting lined with masonry, we begin to descend, but beyond (41 M.) *St. Clair* (555 ft.) we reascend. The *Tunnel de Marot* (1130 yds. long), before the next station, presented considerable difficulties in construction, as beds of quicksand were found here. The same also occurred in two tunnels immediately beyond (44¹/₂ M.) *Dégagnac* (740 ft.). — At (47¹/₂ M.) *Thédirac-Peyrilles* the railway reaches its highest point (1570 ft.), before passing from the basin of the Dordogne into that of the Lot, an affluent of the Garonne. The *Tunnel de Roques* (1 M. long) is the longest on the line, and also offered considerable difficulty in construction. It is followed by a deep cutting with massive retaining-walls, the sloping sides of which are 180 ft. high. — Beyond (52¹/₂ M.) *St. Denis-Catus* (685 ft.) are a tunnel and viaduct. — 56¹/₂ M. *Espère*. Farther on, to the right, is the fine 13th cent. *Château de Mercuès*, belonging to the bishopric of Cahors. A final tunnel now admits us to the valley of the *Lot*, which flows on the right. On that side also is the Monsempron-Libos railway, to which the line from Brive descends, traversing a stone embankment, ¹/₈ M. long, with 33 arches more than 50 ft. high. We now cross some old fortifications and enter —

62 M. *Cahors* (390 ft.; Buffet). Continuation of the railway to Toulouse, see p. 112.

Cahors. — Hotels. Des Ambassadeurs (Pl. a; B, 3), Boul. Gambetta, to the left from the Rue du Lycée, indifferent; de l'Europe (Pl. b; B, 3), near the end of the Rue du Lycée. — **Cafés** in the Boul. Gambetta. — **Post & Telegraph Office** (Pl. B, 3), Rue du Lycée, near the hospice.

Cahors, formerly more important, is now a town of but 15,369 inhab., to which the opening of the new direct line from Paris to Toulouse may perhaps restore some of its old prosperity. It was the old capital of the country of the *Carduci* and afterwards of *Quercy*, and it is now the chief town of the département of the *Lot*. It was occupied for a time by the English and taken by Henri IV., when king of Navarre. It formerly possessed a university founded by Pope John XXII. (Jacques d'Euse, 1244-1334), who was a native of the town. Clement Marot (1495-1544) and Léon Gambetta (1838-1882) were also born here.

Cahors is picturesquely situated on a peninsula on the right bank of the *Lot*, its E. side especially, away from the railway, being adorned with ruins and ancient monuments, which lend it much interest.

The station is in the new quarter Des Hortes (Hortus), where, however, some Roman remains have been found, including a theatre finally destroyed in 1851. We follow the avenue to the right, as far as the Rue du Lycée, which leads to the left to the town.

The *Pont Valentré (Pl. A, 3), to the right, at the beginning of the Rue du Lycée, is a remarkable monument of the 14th cent., with three towers, the two at the ends being machicolated. By means of gates, a barbican on the left bank, etc., it was converted into a strong fortification. It has recently been restored.

On the opposite bank are steep rocks. Beneath a rock about 300 paces to the left, behind a mill, is the **Fontaine des Chartreux**, a limpid spring, from which was derived the Roman name of the town, *Divona* ('holy fountain'). The water, when abundant, flows through three basins connected by cascades, and is finally conducted into the Lot. This spring supplies Cahors with drinking-water; near the bridge is the reservoir.

The Rue du Lycée, to the right, beyond the house (No. 11) in which Gambetta was born, leads past the Lycée Gambetta (Pl. B, 3), formerly a convent of the Cordeliers (Franciscans) and a Jesuits' college. The building, which has an elegant brick tower (17th cent.), also contains the *Municipal Library* (18,000 vols.).

The *Boulevard Gambetta*, a little farther on, marks the W. limit of the old town, as the Lot, parallel with it, marks the E. limit. In front is the *Hôtel de Ville* (Pl. B, 3), containing a small *Musée* of art, archæology, and natural history (open on Sun. and holidays from 2 to 4, and to strangers on other days also). It contains Gallo-Roman and Egyptian antiquities, a few sculptures, and some paintings, including: *Robert-Fleury*, Danaide; *A. de Pujol*, Sisyphus; *J. Leman*, Episode at Cahors during the Hundred Years' War; *H. Scott*, Obsequies of Gambetta.

Descending the Boul. Gambetta we pass, on the right, the *Monument of Gambetta (Pl. 7; B, 3), a large work by *Falguière*, with

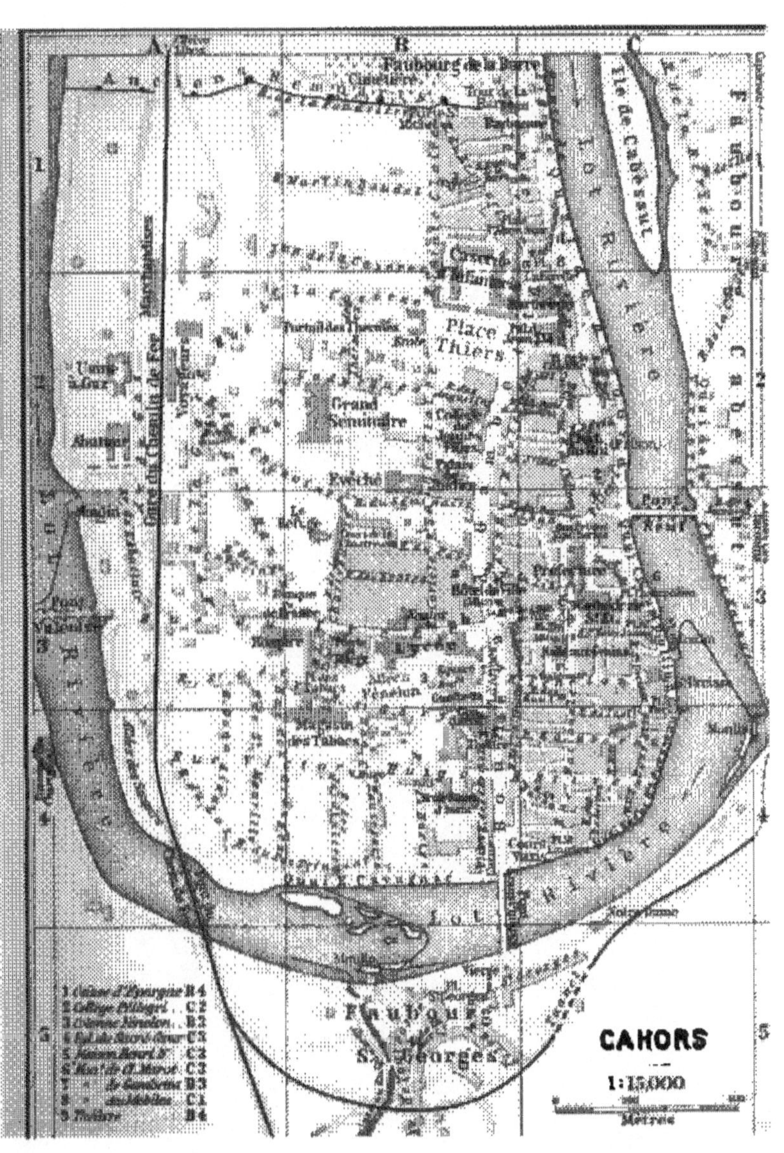
CAHORS
1:15,000
Mètres
Faubourg de la Barre
Cimetière
Place Thiers
Grand Séminaire
Évêché
Hôtel de Ville
Lycée
Ile de Cabessut
Lot Rivière
Lot Rivière
Pont Neuf
Faubourg St. Georges
Faubourg Cabessut
Chemin de Fer

a bronze statue of the dictator. Behind is a small square, with a *Fountain* adorned with a statue of Neptune. Farther on are the *Allées Fénelon*, with a *Bust of Fénelon*, who studied at the university of Cahors.

Farther down, the boulevard ends at the river and the *Pont Louis-Philippe* (Pl. B, C, 4, 5), built below a Roman bridge, the last remains of which lingered until 1868. On the opposite bank, in the suburb of St. Georges, is a *Statue of the Virgin*, by Pradier.

The old town is poorly built, but contains some picturesque corners and quaint old *Houses*; *e. g.* in the *Quartier des Badernes* (Pl. C, 4), near the Pont Louis-Philippe. — On the other side of this quarter, near the Lot and at the end of the Rue Fénelon, which begins opposite Gambetta's monument, is the *Church of St. Urcisse* (Pl. C, 3), of the 12-13th centuries. The Rue Fénelon runs between this church and the boulevard near the market-place, where also the Rue de l'Hôtel-de-Ville debouches.

The **Cathedral** (Pl. C, 3), to the right, belongs like those of Périgueux and Angoulême, to the Romanesque-Byzantine period, and has two domes. It dates from the end of the 11th cent., but has been much altered; the choir and some of the chapels having been in great part rebuilt in the 14-15th centuries. The *N. Portal*, on the left, unfortunately much dilapidated, is the most interesting part of the exterior; the tympanum contains fine sculptures. The most notable features of the interior, to which we descend by ten steps, are the paintings of the chapel on the right of the choir, and some restored paintings of the 14th century. On the right or S. side of the nave are remains of Gothic *Cloisters* of the 15th century.

The building to the N. of the cathedral-portal is the old bishops' palace, now the *Préfecture*. The street between the two descends to the quay, passing a small square with the *Monument of Marot* (Pl. 6; C, 3), in the Renaissance style, erected in 1892. The bust of the poet is by Turcan; the bas-relief by Puëch. The adjacent *Pont-Neuf* (Pl. C, 3), of the 13th cent., was so called in contrast to the old Roman bridge (see above). — In the suburb of Cabessut, on the opposite bank, is the fine ruined Gothic choir of a church (Pl. C, 3; 14th cent.) which belonged to a Dominican or Jacobin Convent, destroyed in 1580 by the Huguenot troops of Henry of Navarre.

On the right bank, above the Pont Neuf, are the curious remains of the *Collège Pélegri* (Pl. 2; C, 2), dating from the 14th century. Not far from this spot rises the square tower of the former *Château du Roi* (Pl C, 2; also 14th. cent.), now used as a prison; farther off is the Tour de la Barre (see below).

The Rue Pélegri, or the curious but dirty lane called Rue du Four-Ste. Catherine, beside the Collège, leads hence to the *Rue du Château*, which like the following streets, contains some curious old houses. At the end are the *Church of St. Barthélemy* (Pl. C, 2) and, on the left, the remains of the *Palace of John XXII.*, also of the 14th cent., with a large square tower. We here reach the upper part of the Boul. Gambetta and the Place Thiers, in front of a barrack. In the *Place Lafayette* (Pl. C, 1, 2), behind the church. is a *Monument to the Soldiers and Militia of the Lot* (1870-71), with sculptures by C. A. Calmon.

Farther on begins the Rue de la Barre, which leads to the *Barbacane*, a guard-house (15th cent.), beside the lofty TOUR DE LA BARRE or *Tour des Pendus* (Pl. B, C, 1), which rises on a sharp-pointed rock near the Lot, and is open on the side next the town. Since the 13th cent. Cahors has possessed *Ramparts*, shutting off the peninsula, and still intact but for the opening made for the railway. Near the Barbacane is the handsome *Porte St. Michel* (Pl. B, 1), now serving as the entrance to a cemetery. The massive tower a little farther on is used as a powder-magazine. — The Rue Ste. Claire, on this side of the cemetery, leads back to the Place Thiers, skirting the barrack-wall. In an enclosure on the right is a *Gateway* of Roman baths, known as the Porte de Diane.

Following the Boul. Gambetta to the Hôtel de Ville, we pass the new *College for Girls* and the *Palais de Justice* (Pl. B, 2). The Rue du Séminaire, a little beyond the Palais, and the Rue des Cadurques, on this side of the Collège, lead direct to the station, passing the Grand Séminaire.

Railway from Cahors to *Monsempron-Libos*, see p. 108; to *Capdenac*, see p. 114.

CONTINUATION OF THE RAILWAY TO MONTAUBAN AND TOULOUSE. — Beyond Cahors the line passes near the Pont Valentré (p. 110), on the right, crosses the Lot, and leaves the line to Capdenac on the left. We traverse a long curved viaduct. — 65 M. *Sept-Ponts*. Rock-cuttings; lofty viaduct; tunnel. — 67 M. *Cieurac*; 73 M. *Lalbenque*. — 77$\frac{1}{2}$ M. *Montpezat*, an ancient little town, fully 3 M. to the S.W. (diligence), with a fine 13th cent. church, rich in works of art of the 14-16th centuries. Beyond a tunnel and a large viaduct we reach (84 M.) *Borredon*.

87 M. **Caussade** (*Hotels*), to the left, a town of 3747 inhab., one of the fortresses of the Huguenots. Fine 14th cent. spire.

90$\frac{1}{2}$ M. *Réalville*. We cross the *Aveyron*. — 93$\frac{1}{2}$ M. *Albias*; 97 M. *Fonneuve*. To the left is the railway to Lexos. We cross the Tarn and join, on the right, the railway to Bordeaux.

101 M. *Montauban* (Ville-Bourbon; see p. 75). Hence to (32 M.) *Toulouse*, see p. 77.

b. Viâ Capdenac.

154$\frac{1}{2}$ M. RAILWAY in 5-8 hrs. (same fares). — The traveller should traverse the part of the line between Brive and Lexos by day.

To (17$\frac{1}{2}$ M.) *St. Denis-près-Martel*. see p. 107. — We now reach

the picturesque *Valley of the Dordogne*. The line crosses the river
and ascends the left side of the winding valley, overhung by rocks
more than 600 ft. high. The Buisson line (p. 102) runs on the other
side. Beyond (22 M.) *Montralent*, we reach the *Causse de Gramat*,
the rocky and barren plateau which separates the valley of the Dordogne from that of the Célé.

The Causse de Gramat is one of the most interesting plateaux in
France, from the point of view of hydrology. It contains numerous
'gouffres' or natural wells, which collect the rainfall and discharge it by
means of subterranean channels, which eventually return to the surface
and form the beginnings of rivers. The most important of these wells
is the *Gouffre de Padirac*, 120 ft. in diameter and 200 ft. deep, which lies
about 7½ M. to the N.E. of the station of Rocamadour (see below).

28½ M. *Rocamadour*. The village lies 2½ M. to the S. W.
(omnibus ½ fr., to the *Château* 1 fr.).

Rocamadour (*Hôt.-Rest. Ste. Marie; Grand-Soleil*, well spoken of; *Notre-
Dame*), romantically situated in a ravine, bounded by rocky walls 400 ft.
high, to which the houses cling, is one of the most ancient pilgrim-resorts
in France, especially frequented in mediæval times. Above the houses
are the church and chapels, and still higher is an ancient castle. The
name is derived from St. Amadour, a hermit who is said to have lived
here in the 1st cent., and is identified with Zacchæus, the Publican.

To reach the church from the lower town we climb two steep flights
of steps, with 143 and 51 steps respectively, and another of 75 steps
leads thence to the Chapel of the Virgin.

The *Church*, an early Gothic building, consists of two parts, the par-
ochial church, or St. Sauveur, and the subterranean church, or Chapel
of St. Amadour. The former has two aisles without transepts; the high-
altar stands in the middle of the apse, with a chapel on each side. The
walls are entirely covered with paintings, portraits, and inscriptions,
commemorating illustrious pilgrims, among them St. Louis, Charles IV.,
Louis XI., and other kings of France. The Chapel of St. Amadour is
smaller than the church above it, but is adorned in the same fashion.

The *Chapel of the Virgin* dates only from the 15th cent. and has been
partly rebuilt in our time. Its internal decoration is very rich. The
modern stained-glass windows are by Thévenot. On the altar is a small
black image of the Virgin, of wood, ascribed to Zacchæus.

There are three other chapels to the right as we ascend. — Opposite
the entrance of that of the Virgin are some ancient mural paintings and
a huge sword fixed to the wall. This sword is said to be an imitation
of Roland's famous 'Durandal', which according to tradition was vowed
by the Paladin to the Virgin, brought here after his death, and stolen in
the 12th century.

The *Castle*, which stands much higher up, was built in the middle ages
to defend the shrines, and has been partly reconstructed. It now serves
as a clergy-house. Fine view from the wall and the old tower.

A variety of interesting excursions may be made from Rocamadour:
to the numerous 'gouffres' in the vicinity; to several waterfalls; etc.

33½ M. *Gramat* (pop. 3867); 44 M. *Assier*, with an interesting
church and the remains of a 16th cent. château. Beyond (48 M.)
Le Pournel we descend by two tunnels and a viaduct into the valley
of the *Célé*, a tributary of the Lot.

56 M. **Figeac** (*Hôtel des Ambassadeurs*, near the market-place;
H. des Voyageurs, Allée des Platanes, on the left bank of the Célé),
an old town of 6660 inhab. on the right bank of the Célé, is badly
built, but possesses some interesting 13-14th cent. houses. The Avenue Gambetta leads from the station to the principal bridge and to the

Rue Gambetta, which ends at the Place du Marché. To the right of
the bridge is an *Obelisk* to the memory of *Champollion*, the Egyp-
tologist, a native of the town (1790-1832).

The *Church of St. Sauveur* (12-14th cent.) has a transept with a
central tower surmounted by a clumsy dome, and a modern W. tower.
Inside are two fine Corinthian capitals supporting holy-water basins,
the fonts, and, on the right, a large low chapel of the 13th cent.,
with aisles, and containing some fine bas-reliefs in wood.

In a narrow street on the left, at the beginning of the Rue Gambetta, is the *Old Palais de Justice* (14th cent.).

Notre-Dame-du-Puy, in the highest part of the town, beside
the college, is also a church of the 12-14th cent., with a modern
steeple. There is no transept, but the aisles extend all the way
round. Its chief attraction is a large and magnificent **Altar Screen*
of the latter part of the 18th cent., in perfect preservation and enclosing two pictures and two statues.

From Figeac to *Aurillac*, etc., see R. 40.

We now pass through two tunnels, the first 1350 yds. long, into
the beautiful valley of the *Lot*. On the right is the line to Cahors
(see below). Beyond another tunnel we cross the river.

59 M. **Capdenac** (*Buffet;* Hotels, near the station, small). The
town, which stands some way off, occupying a steep eminence on
the right bank of the Lot is another claimant to be the Roman
Uxellodunum (pp. 106, 107). In any case it was an important place
in the middle ages, and it still has remains of fortifications, pointed
gateways, a keep, etc.

From Capdenac to *Rodez* and *Béziers*, see R. 17; to *Aurillac*, see R. 40.
FROM CAPDENAC TO CAHORS, 45 M., railway in 2-4 hrs. (fares 8 fr. 5,
5 fr. 45, 3 fr. 55 c.). This line descends the interesting valley of the Lot,
at first on the right bank, at the foot of lofty pointed cliffs. — 8¹/₂ M.
Toirac. Tunnel ¹/₄ M. long. — 15¹/₂ M. *Cajarc*, a small town to the right,
with a ruined château. Then follow a tunnel (350 yds.), a bridge over
the Lot, two tunnels (600 and 120 yds.), and several rock-cuttings.
Fine views. — 20 M. *Calvignac*. To the right, farther on, the large *Château de Cénevières* (13th, 15th, and 16th cent.), on a cliff above the Lot.
Tunnel, bridge over the river. — 22¹/₂ M. *St. Martin-Laboural*. 25¹/₂ M.
St. Cirq-la-Popie, very picturesquely situated on the left bank of the river,
with a ruined castle (13th cent.) and a fine 15th cent. church. Tunnels
and bridges are numerous on the next part of the line, and the Lot is
bordered with steep heights. — 27¹/₂ M. *Conduché;* 33 M. *St. Géry;* 34 M.
Vers; 38 M. *Arcambal*, on a height to the left. — 42 M. *Cabessut* is an E.
suburb of Cahors, on the left bank of the Lot. Fine view on the right
of Cahors, which both railway and river now skirt. To the left is the
railway to Montauban. We cross the Lot, with a view of the Pont Valentré (p. 110) to the left. — 45 M. *Cahors*, see p. 110.

Beyond Capdenac the railway ascends considerably, traversing
several small tunnels and viaducts and affording a succession of
fine views. 64¹/₂ M. *Naussac;* 68 M. *Salles-Courbatier;* 71¹/₂ M.
Villeneuve. We now cross the *Aveyron*.

77¹/₂ M. **Villefranche-de-Rouergue** (*Hôtel Notre-Dame*), a commercial town with 9734 inhab., was a rich and important place in
the middle ages, when it distinguished itself in the wars with Eng-

land. In the 16th cent. it was noted for its devotion to Protestantism. Three times in the 15-17th cent. it was ravaged by the plague, and in 1643 it became the centre of the insurrection of the Croquants, or peasants who revolted against the exactions of the Intendants. The chief sights of the town are the *Church of Notre-Dame* (13-16th cent.), to the right on the way from the station, and an old *Carthusian Convent*, on the left bank, converted into a hospital, with pretty cloisters in the florid Gothic style.

The line next skirts the Aveyron, sometimes on one bank, sometimes on the other. At (84 M.) *Monteils*, the valley becomes highly picturesque, forming a rocky and wooded gorge in which no less than nine bridges and nine tunnels are passed. Then, to the right, we obtain a magnificent view of Najac and its castle.

88 M. **Najac** (*Hôt. des Voyageurs*), a small town on a height, with a *Castle, the remains of which are very striking as seen from the valley. To reach it we pass under the line, cross the river a little farther on, ascend by a path to the left, and turn to the right at the top ($^1/_4$ hr.). Founded in the 12th cent., the castle was rebuilt in the middle of the 13th. It stands on a bold cliff, washed on three sides by the Aveyron, commanding the valley. It was sold at the Revolution and has since been partly demolished to supply building materials. To inspect the interior we must obtain permission from the 'Frères' (to the left before reaching the castle). The chief part is the keep, which is 100 ft. in height and contains some fine rooms. The two enceintes are flanked with square and round towers, and afford pretty views. — The *Church* dates from the 13th century.

Recrossing the Aveyron and passing under the town by a tunnel, we obtain another very striking view of the castle on the left. Three more tunnels and three bridges are then traversed. At (94 M.) *La Guépie*, the ruins of a 16th cent. château are seen to the left. Beyond it the valley expands. — 100 M. *Lexos* (Buffet).

From Lexos to Montauban, 41 M., railway in 1 hr. 40 min. (fares 7 fr. 40, 5 fr., 3 fr. 25 c.). The line follows the rocky and picturesque valley of the Aveyron, crossing the river several times. Beyond (4 M.) *Peneyrols* is a short tunnel. 8 M. *St. Antonin* (*Hôtel Albouy*), an ancient town with 4137 inhab., has a curious *Hôtel de Ville* of the 12th cent. and a handsome modern Gothic *Church*. The Aveyron is here spanned by an ancient Gothic bridge. — $12^1/_2$ M. *Cazals*. 16 M. *Penne*, a picturesque town dominated by the ruins of a 15th cent. château. $20^1/_2$ M. *Bruniquel* has a château of the Middle Ages and the Renaissance, lately restored (visitors admitted). The valley now expands. 24 M. *Montricoux*, with remains of a 13th cent. castle. The train now quits the Aveyron. $28^1/_2$ M. *Négrepelisse*, a small town on the left bank of the Aveyron, devoted to Protestantism in the Religious Wars, was sacked by Louis XIII. in 1622. — 32 M. *St. Étienne-de-Tulmont*; 38 M. *Montauban-Ville-Nouvelle*. The *Tarn* is crossed. 41 M. *Montauban-Ville-Bourbon* (see p. 76).

Our route now ascends the valley of an affluent of the Aveyron. 106 M. *Vindrac*. In the distance to the left is the town of Cordes.

From Vindrac to Cordes, $3^1/_2$ M., diligence 50 c., free to travellers to or from Gaillac (p. 118), Albi, and places beyond. Vindrac being only served by a few slow trains, time may be saved by taking a private con-

veyance from *Lexos* to Cordes (7 fr.). — Cordes appears more and more
picturesque as we approach it. Below it, at the foot of the hill, is the
village of *Les Cabanes* (Hotel), whence we may ascend direct on foot. By the
road, which winds round the N. side of the hill (to the left), the distance
is nearly a mile. — Cordes (*Hotel*, near the church), with 1995 inhab.,
perched on an isolated hill, is an ancient and highly interesting town,
the general look of which takes us back to the middle ages. It still
retains its ramparts of the 13th cent. and several fine houses of the
13-14th centuries. The omnibus stops at the S. end of the town, not far
from the principal gate, which lies to the W. above Les Cabanes. The
street leading from the gateway to the right passes the *Maisons du Grand-
Ecuyer*, *du Grand-Veneur*, *du Grand-Fauconnier*, and other interesting
mediæval houses, with Gothic windows. The first two are adorned with
alto-reliefs, while the third, restored and converted into the Hôtel de
Ville, is specially remarkable for its trefoil and rose windows. The
Church, in the second of the streets which intersect the town from W.
to E., also dates from the 13-14th century. It has a fine nave and is decorated with polychrome painting and modern stained glass. We may walk
round the ramparts, which contain two ancient gateways and command
a fine view of the valley of the Cérou and the surrounding heights.

We now cross two more viaducts and pass through a tunnel
1640 yds. long. Beyond (112 M.) *Donnazac* there is a high viaduct
over the Vère, affording a pretty view. 115 M. *Cahuzac*, followed
by a tunnel 780 yds. long. On the right bank are two châteaux of
the 15-16th cent., and on the left bank is another. 117 M. *Tessonnières* (Buffet). Continuation of the railway to Toulouse, see p. 118.

From Tessonnières to Albi. 10 M., railway in 25-35 min. (fares 1 fr. 80,
1 fr. 30, 85 c.).
This line enters the valley of the *Tarn* and crosses that stream.
4 M. *Marsac*. To the left is the village of *Castelnau-de-Lévis*,
dominated by a 13th cent. tower, 160 ft. high. Farther on, also on
the left, we see the imposing cathedral of Albi.

10 M. **Albi** (*Hôtel Cassagnes*, Place du Vigan), an ancient town
with 20,900 inhab., the capital of the department of the *Tarn*, and
the seat of a bishopric, lies on the left bank of the Tarn, and gave
its name to the famous sect of the Albigenses and to the war which
deluged the South of France with blood from 1209 to 1229.

From the Gare d'Orléans, which is connected with the Gare du
Midi (p. 118) by a loop-line crossing the river, we enter the town by
the Avenue de la Gare and the Avenue Lapérouse, to the left, leaving
the Parc Rochegude (p. 118) on the right. The latter avenue ends at
the Place Lapérouse, in which stands a bronze *Statue of Lapérouse*,
the famous but unfortunate navigator, who was a native of Albi
(1741-88). — To the left of this Place is the *Palais de Justice*, with
ancient cloisters. Behind the statue a fine promenade leads to the
Lices and to the Place du Vigan (to the left; p. 117). We follow the
street to the left, on this side of the Palais de Justice, to the —

Cathedral of St. Cecilia, built between the end of the 13th
and the end of the 15th cent., and one of the finest and most remarkable churches in the S. of France. Its peculiar character is
due to the fact that it was constructed with the view of serving as

a fortress as well as a church, and to its being entirely of brick, with the exception of the porch. The works which defended the approaches have disappeared as well as the machicolations of the huge W. tower, but the latter, which is destitute of a spire and has no external openings in its lower part, still looks like a keep. The style of the church is Gothic, but its plan is Romanesque. It has a single nave, without aisles or transept, and two choirs. The exterior is very plain, the bare walls, 125 ft. in height, having neither turrets nor sculptures. The *S. Porch*, however, which is the principal entrance, is a magnificent structure of the 15th cent. approached by a double flight of steps and forming a kind of canopy with four arches, surmounted by rich open-work carving.

INTERIOR. After the general heaviness of the exterior, the interior of the church affords an agreeable surprise. The **Rood Screen* is a marvel of 15th cent. sculpture, considered to be almost without a rival. Its delicate lace-like forms are all the more remarkable from the fact that the stone of which it is made is hard and brittle. The ornamentation also includes statues under beautiful canopies, graceful pinnacles, etc. The *Ambulatory*, or *Cloister* surrounding the choir, is scarcely inferior in richness and beauty; its exterior is decorated with 72 exquisite statuettes of angels and with statues of prophets and other Bible characters. Above the doors are Constantine and Charlemagne, and inside are the Apostles. Both these splendid works were executed between 1473 and 1502, under the direction of a bishop (Louis I.) of the family of Amboise, who was noted for his love of art and good taste, while it was his nephew and successor (1502-13), who employed Italian artists to paint the scenes from the Bible which adorn the vaulting. The style of these paintings, however, is not quite in keeping with that of the building and the sculptures. The sadly damaged paintings in the second choir, representing the Last Judgment, date from the 14th cent., while some of the chapels contain others of the 15th century. The chapels, 28 in number, are inserted between the buttresses of the church in two stages. The pulpit, in stucco and marble, was made by Italians in 1776; the organ-case in 1736. In the chapel of the apse is a fine modern statue of the Virgin.

The *Archiepiscopal Palace* to the N. E. of the cathedral, by the riverside, is a vast building of the 14th cent., in the form of a fortified château with a keep. Higher up are an *Old Bridge* (13-14th cent.) and a modern bridge at the end of the Lices.

The Rue Mariès, behind the E. end of the cathedral, leads to the right to the *Church of St. Salvi*, dating mainly from the 15-16th cent., but standing on foundations of an earlier period. It has a tower of the 13th cent., over the N. transept, and a Romanesque cloister on the S. side, visible from the interior. Following the same street farther we reach the *Préfecture*; thence the street to the left leads to the Lices, the Rue Timbal, to the right, with two Renaissance houses, to the Place du Vigan.

The *Lices* form a boulevard descending to the left to the Tarn, passing the *Lycée* (on the left) and the *Post Office*, and ascending to the right to the allées beginning at the Place Lapérouse.

In the suburb of LA MADELEINE, on the opposite bank of the river, are the *Church of La Madeleine* (paintings), near the Old Bridge, and beyond it, the *Gare du Midi*, for the line to Carmaux (p. 97).

The *Place du Vigan*, skirted by the Lices, forms the centre of the town. Here begins the street in which is the *Hôtel de Ville*, containing a small *Art Collection* and a *Museum of Natural History*.

The Boulevard des Lices ends at the Place du Manège, near which, to the left, is the modern Romanesque *Church of St. Joseph*. The Avenue Gambetta, to the right, leads to the *Parc Rochegude*, embellished with a bust of Vice-admiral Rochegude, donor of the park, and with a curious 16th cent. *Fountain*, with bas-reliefs of the 13th cent., from Lisle-d'Albi (see below).

Railway from *Castres* to *Carmaux*, see p. 97. — Another line is to be constructed between Albi and *St. Affrique* (p. 269).

CONTINUATION OF RAILWAY TO TOULOUSE. Beyond Tessonnières we follow the valley of the Tarn for some distance. — 122 M. **Gaillac** (*Hôt. du Commerce*), a town of 7700 inhab., is situated on the right bank. The chief street, between the station and the river, passes near the Hôtel de Ville, in front of which is a *Statue of General d'Hautpoul* (1754-1807), then leads to the *Church of St. Pierre* (13-14th cent.) In the Place Thiers, embellished with an ancient *Fountain*, and to the *Church of St. Michel* (also 13-14th cent.). Gaillac also contains some quaint old houses; *e. g.* in the street to the left of St. Michel and in that to the right of the market (Place Thiers). — 121 M. *Lisle-d'Albi*, another little town to the left, has a 14th cent. church, with a brick belfry in the Tolosan style. The line crosses the Tarn. — 131$^1/_2$ M. **Rabastens** (*Hôt. Pongis*), a picturesque town with 4788 inhab., on the right bank of the Tarn, possesses a Romanesque and Gothic church decorated with frescoes of the 14-15th centuries. — We now cross the *Agout*.

136 M. *St. Sulpice-du-Tarn*, with a church, showing a façade of the 14th century. For the line to Montauban and Castres, see p. 96. Our line quits the valley of the Tarn and runs through a tunnel. Beyond (142 M.) *Gragnague*, the Pyrenees, which in clear weather have already been visible, come prominently into view. 150 M. *Montrabé*. — 154$^1/_2$ M. *Toulouse*, p. 78.

17. From Capdenac to Rodez and to Béziers or Montpellier.

RAILWAY to *Rodez*, 41 M., in 2-2$^1/_2$ hrs. (fares 7 fr. 50, 5 fr. 5, 3 fr. 30 c.); from Rodez to *Mende*, 68 M., in 6 hrs. (fares 12 fr. 65, 8 fr. 45, 5 fr. 50 c.). — From Rodez to *Béziers*, 120 M., in 6$^1/_4$-7$^1/_4$ hrs. (fares 21 fr. 85, 14 fr. 75, 9 fr. 55 c.).

Capdenac, see p. 114. This line, parts of which are interesting, ascends the valley of the *Lot*, commanding a series of pleasant views. Two tunnels. — 5 M. *St. Martin-de-Bouillac*. To the left, beyond another tunnel, are the ruins of the château of *La Roque-Bouillac*. — 7$^1/_2$ M. *Panchot*. We now quit the valley of the Lot by a tunnel and reach (9 M.) *Viriez*, a small industrial town with coal-mines and zinc works.

A branch-line runs from Viviez to (2½ M.) **Decazeville** (*Hôtel des Houillères*), a town of 8871 inhab., the centre of the coal-fields of the *Aveyron*, which occupy an area of 30 sq. M. and rank third among the coal-fields of France. Here and at *Firmy*, 3 M. farther on, are spots where the coal crops out on the surface of the ground and forms beds more than 130 ft. thick. With these important mines are connected smelting-works, blast-furnaces, foundries, and forges. The town owes its name to the *Duc Decazes* (1780-1860), a minister of Louis XVIII., and the chief promoter of these works, to whom a bronze statue, by Dumont, has been erected here.

The line now ascends considerably. 12 M. *Aubin*, a town of 9050 inhab., with coal and iron mines and iron-works. 13½ M. *Cransac* (Hôt. Sahut, etc.; 4773 inhab.), with mineral springs. About 5 M. to the S. is the handsome *Château de Bournazel* (15-16th cent.). We now traverse a busy district and pass through two short tunnels. 17½ M. *Auzits-Aussibals*; 22 M. *St. Christophe*; 27 M. *Marcillac*. At (30 M.) *Nuces* we reach a high plateau, commanding a fine and extensive view. We then cross a viaduct 115 ft. high and reach *Vanc* and (35 M.) *Salles-la-Source*, a large and picturesque village with fine cascades and grottoes.

41 M. **Rodez.** — Hotels. De France, Place de la Cité, R., L., & A. 3-5, B. ½-1, déj. 2½, D. 3 fr., omn. 40 c.; de l'Univers, Boulevard Gally-Birry, Boulevard Gambetta, R., L., & A. 1½-7½, B. ¾, déj. 2½, D. 3 fr., omn. 40 c. — *Buffet*, with R., at the station.

Rodez, a town of 16,122 inhab., the ancient capital of the *Ruteni* and later of the *Rouergue*, is the chief town of the department of the *Aveyron* and the seat of a bishop. It stands on an eminence, the base of which is washed by the Aveyron, ¾ M. from the station.

In the suburb below the town proper a fine *Church of the Sacred Heart* is being built. A street ascends to the left, a little farther on, to the boulevards surrounding the old town, which command fine views. We turn to the right on reaching the boulevards and pass between the Grand Séminaire and a view-point with a small garden, in which a bronze statue (by Puëch) was erected in 1889 to *Monteil* (1769-1850), the historian, a native of Rodez. The seminary-garden stretches from the left side of the boulevard to the ancient rampart. Farther on, near the cathedral, is the *Bishops' Palace* (17th cent.), which still retains a massive mediæval tower and a wall with Romanesque arcades.

The Cathedral or *Notre-Dame* of Rodez is an imposing fabric built between 1277 and 1535. As is the case with most of the churches of Southern France, the exterior is bare and severe in aspect. The W. front, flanked by two massive towers, is without a portal, but has a grand Flamboyant rose-window and a gallery in the same style, surmounted by a Renaissance pediment. The *Tower*, beyond the N. entrance, is square below but above consists of three octagonal stages remarkable for the richness of their decoration and flanked by four turrets with statues of the Evangelists. On the platform is a statue of the Virgin. The interesting side portals, in the Gothic style, are much dilapidated.

Among the chief points of interest in the interior are the *Gallery*, in the Renaissance style, extending into the aisles; the *Rood-Loft*, in the same style, now in the S. transept, but formerly at the entrance to the choir; the fine Gothic *Stalls*; the *Organ-Case* in the N. transept; on the same side, a *Sarcophagus* of the 5th or 6th cent., and a *Virgin* of the 14th cent. In the first chapel on the N. side of the choir, the *Tombs* of the bishops, from the middle ages down to our own time; an *Altar* with a fresco of the 6th cent. In the apsidal chapel, an *Alto-relief* of the Agony in the Garden, and a *Holy Sepulchre*, in the Renaissance style. In two chapels to the right of the nave, one of which is enclosed by a fine screen in the Flamboyant style.

The Rue Frayssinous, on the N. of the cathedral, and the following street lead to the Place de la Cité, in which is a bronze *Statue of Mgr. Affre* (1793-1848), archbishop of Paris, who was born in the district. — The Rue Neuve, to the right, connects the Place de la Cité with the Place du Bourg, before reaching which we pass, on the right, an old *House* with a corner-tower adorned with an Annunciation. Farther on, to the right, at the corner of the Rue d'Armagnac is the *Hôtel d'Armagnac*, a Renaissance edifice, also bearing an Annunciation and numerous medallions. — A little farther down as we come from the Place, is the *Church of St. Amans*, with a Romanesque nave, restored in the 18th century. The Rue d'Armagnac and the following street join the boulevards near the *Palais de Justice*, in which is a small musée. Thence we return to the cathedral viâ the Boulevards Gally and Gambetta (to the right). The former passes the *Lycée*, behind which is a *Fountain*, bearing a *Bust of Gally*, a benefactor of the town. — In the small square in front of the cathedral is a bronze statue of *Samson*, by Gayrard of Rodez.

A railway is being built from Rodez to *Carmaux* and *Albi* (p. 97). — A public conveyance plies to (16¹/₂ M.) *Espalion*, by an uninteresting route, except near Espalion (see below).

The line now ascends the valley of the *Areyron*, crossing the river several times and traversing a partly wooded district, with coal-mines. 46 M. *Canabols*; 47¹/₂ M. *Gages*. — 52 M. *Bertholène*, below the station, to the left, dominated by a ruin.

A Diligence plies hence to (11 M.) Espalion, viâ *Gabriac*, a large village halfway, on an eminence, near which is a pilgrimage-chapel. We join the road from Rodez about 1³/₄ M. before Espalion. The road descending in windings affords fine views of the *Valley of the Lot*, with its châteaux (see below), and of the Monts d'Aubrac (p. 268). — Espalion (*Hôtel de France*), a picturesque old town with 3667 inhab. and an ancient château, is situated in the deep valley of the Lot, above which rise the picturesque ruined châteaux of *Calmont-d'Olt* and *Roquelaure*. — Conveyance from Rodez, see above. — An attractive road runs from Espalion to (13¹/₂ M.) the station of Campagnac (p. 267) viâ the ravine of the Lot till beyond (2¹/₂ M.) *St. Côme*, and thence viâ (3 M.) *Lassouts* and (3 M.) *Ste. Eulalie*, 1³/₄ M. to the S.W. of St. Geniez-d'Olt (p. 267).

55 M. *Laissac*; 59¹/₂ M. *Lugans*, with a château, to the left; 61 M. *Guillac*; 64 M. *Recoules*.

At (69 M.) *Sévérac-le-Château* (p. 267) we join the direct line from Clermont-Ferrand (Paris) to *Béziers*, see R. 42.

18. From Bayonne to San Sebastian.

34 M. RAILWAY in 1³/₄-3³/₄ hrs.; fares about 6 fr. 25, 4 fr. 25, 3 fr. 75 c.;
to *Hendaye*, on the frontier, 22 M.; thence to *San Sebastian*, 12 M. — French
money is accepted at San Sebastian, the *franc* and *centime* corresponding
to the Spanish *peseta* and *centimo*.

Bayonne, see p. 66. — This route is highly attractive. The train
traverses a short tunnel, crosses first the *Adour* by a bridge commanding a fine view, and then beyond a second tunnel, the *Nire*.
To the left diverges the line to Pau (p. 127) and to St. Jean-Pied-de-
Port (p. 69). — 6 M. *Biarritz*, Station de la Négresse, nearly 2 M.
from the Baths (p. 68). To the right, a little farther on, we have a
view of the *Lac de Mouriscot* and the sea; and beyond another
short tunnel we reach (9 M.) *Bidart* and approach the coast, enjoying
a fine view of the sea. 10¹/₂ M. *Guéthary*, a small bathing-place,
beyond which the mountains dominated by the Rhune (p. 102) appear
to the left.

14 M. **St. Jean-de-Luz.** — Hotels. D'ANGLETERRE, on the beach, R.,
L., & A. 3-10, B. 1-1¹/₄, déj. 3, D. 4, pens. in summer 10-14 fr.; *DE FRANCE,
near the church, moderate; DE LA POSTE, Rue Gambetta 85; DE PARIS, at
the station. *Furnished Apartments* may also be obtained. — *Café Suisse*, in
the Maison Louis XIV. — *Post and Telegraph Office*, Rue St. Jacques, near
the Boulevard. — Sea-Baths. Bathing-box 25, costume 20, towel 6 c., etc.

English Church (*Ch. of the Nativity*); Chaplain, Rev. *Th. J. Cooper*, B.D.,
85 Rue Gambetta.

St. Jean-de-Luz, a quiet little seaport and bathing-resort, with
3856 inhab., is situated on a bay at the mouth of the *Nivelle*.

From the 14th to the middle of the 17th century, the town enjoyed
considerable prosperity, with at one time a population of 12,000, one fourth
of whom were engaged in the whale-fishery of the Bay of Biscay and in

The town itself is of little interest to strangers. Near the harbour, to the right as we arrive, is the Place Louis XIV., with the *Maison Louis XIV.*, in which the king lodged on the occasion of his marriage. The somewhat peculiar edifice, with its two square corbelled towers, dates from the 16th century. Farther on, to the left, is the *Château de l'Infante*, a large mansion of the 17th cent., with square towers at the corners, and a double tier of arcades on the façade. It contains two paintings by Gérôme, illustrating the marriage (visitors admitted). — On the left side of the Grande Rue or Rue Gambetta is the 13th cent. *Church of St. John*. Like all Basque churches, it has galleries in the nave for the men, the area being reserved for the women. In the interior is a large gilded reredos, in the Spanish fashion, adorned with twenty statues.

The Rue Garat, passing the E. end of the church, leads direct to the *Bay* with the *Bathing-Place*. The bay is almost circular in shape, partly enclosed by a breakwater and piers; it is bounded on the right by high cliffs, and on the left by the little harbour of Socoa. The beach is good, but slopes rapidly and is covered with shingle. There are two *Casinos*, one in the middle of the bay, the other at the end to the right, whence the Boulevard Gambetta (in which a picturesque *Moorish Villa* attracts attention) leads back to the Rue Gambetta.

Socoa may be reached by following the Route d'Espagne, between the Maison Louis XIV. and the station, and then turning to the right. Turning to the left at the little harbour of Socoa, we may proceed to the main breakwater.

From St. Jean-de-Luz to the Rhune, an easy and interesting excursion, via *Ascain*, 3¹/₂ M. to the S.E., in the valley of the *Nivelle*. The ascent takes 2¹/₂ hrs. and may be made on horseback. Beyond the village we ascend to the right for ¹/₂ hr., by the N. slope of the mountain; then turning to the right we reach (¹/₂ hr. more) a chalet; in another hour we turn to the left beyond a second chalet, and zigzag to the top. The Rhune (2950 ft.), the first mountain of any importance at the W. end of the Pyrenees, on the frontier of Spain, affords a splendid *View, extending over the valleys on the N. W. to the Atlantic and from W. to E. over a succession of mountains beginning with the Haya and ending in the Pic du Midi de Bigorre (p. 167), about 90 M. in a straight line. The Rhune, on which there are still remains of fortifications, was the object of desperate encounters in 1813, at the close of the Peninsular War. It was not taken, but General Clauzel had to abandon it when his position was turned on the E. by the Spaniards and threatened on the W. by Wellington.

The line next crosses the Nivelle, passes (15¹/₂ M.) *Urrugne* and runs through a tunnel, ¹/₄ M. long, into the valley of the *Bidassoa*, which affords a magnificent view. To the left, on Spanish territory, is the Haya, with its three peaks (see p. 125); to the right the mountain of Jaizquivel rising above a handsome modern château, the beach of Hendaye, the wide but sandy bed of the river, and the picturesque Fuentarabia (see below).

22 M. **Hendaye** (*Buffet; Hôtel de France, du Commerce*, both good but expensive; *Hôtel de la Gare*), the last station on French

soll, a large but uninteresting village. $1/_2$ M. to the left, below the station. The liqueur manufactured here is celebrated. The *Sea-baths* (Hotel & Casino) are situated $1^1/_4$ M. farther on, at the mouth of the Bidassoa. The beach is good, but not much frequented.

Excursion to Fuentarabia. It is shorter to start from Hendaye, crossing the Bidassoa, than from Irun, but we must ascend to the village to hire boats and there strike a bargain with the boatmen (1 fr. a head there and back is double the amount paid by the people of the place). The *Bidassoa* is here about $1/_2$ M. wide, and $2^1/_2$ M. at its mouth a little way off, near *Cap du Figuier*, which is in Spain. The navigation is, however, impeded by sand-banks. This river forms for 8 or 9 M. the boundary between France and Spain. Higher up, on the other side of the railway-bridge, is the *Ile des Paisans* or *de la Conférence*, on which various interviews between sovereigns and ambassadors of France and Spain have taken place, and the Treaty of the Pyrenees was concluded in 1659.

Fuentarabia (in French *Fontarabie*) is a decayed town of 3000 inhab., often a victim in the wars between France and Spain. It has not only a picturesque but also a thoroughly Spanish appearance, such as is not to be found in the modern San Sebastian. Its streets are very narrow and the roofs of its houses project considerably. The houses are large buildings with coats of arms and balconies of iron-work, which bear witness to the by-gone prosperity of the town. The population, of Basque origin, is equally interesting. In the upper part of the principal street is the *Church*, decorated with that lavish luxuriance which is characteristic of Spanish churches, and beside it the *Castle*, almost in ruins and presenting nothing noteworthy. The most ancient part, on the side of the river, dates from the 10th century. There is a fine view from the top (25 c.). A *Casino*, on the bank of the river, offers 'the same attractions as Monaco'. — The *Jaizquivel* (2230 ft.; fine view), which rises above the town, may be ascended in $1^1/_2$ hour.

Shortly after leaving Hendaye we cross the Bidassoa and the frontier.

$23^1/_2$ M. **Irun** (*Buffet*) is an old Spanish town with about 5500 inhab., $3/_4$ M. to the E. of the station. Repeatedly ravaged by war, it was bombarded by the Carlists in 1874, but relieved by General Loma. Its chief object of interest is the church of *Nuestra Señora del Juncal*, of the 10th century. — Luggage is examined here. Spanish time is 20 min. behind French time. Carriages are changed at Irun, as the gauge of the Spanish lines is nearly one third wider than that of the French lines. Travellers coming from Spain change at Hendaye. — To *Fuentarabia*, see above.

The **Haya** (3315 ft.; fine view) or *Trois Couronnes* (from its three peaks) may be easily ascended in 3 hrs. from Irun, viâ a valley to the S., whence after 40 min. we ascend to the left. The copper-mines on this mountain were worked by the Romans.

We next cross a tributary of the Bidassoa, and traverse a tunnel 630 yds. long, beyond which we enter a picturesque mountainous region. $28^1/_2$ M. *Renteria*, a decayed town, with a church with battlements. Beyond a bridge and another short tunnel we catch a fine view of the Bay of Passages, to the right.

$29^1/_2$ M. **Passages**, a picturesquely-situated little town, has a safe harbour, between the Jaizquivel and the Mont Ulia. The harbour, at one time important, was later silled up by the Oyarzun. Recently, however, the river has been diverted, and the bay dredged out to the depth of 25 ft., and Pasages is expected to become one of the centres of the wine-trade.

34 M. San Sebastian. — Hotels (all somewhat expensive). GRAND HÔTEL DE LONDRES, Avenida de la Libertad, first-class, R. 3-5, déj. 4, D. 5 fr.; INGLES Y DE INGLATERRA, a dépendance of the Londres, on the beach; HÔTEL CONTINENTAL, on the beach; GRAND HÔTEL ESCURRA, HÔTEL DE FRANCE, Calle del Camino 1 and 2; GRAND HÔTEL DEL COMMERCIO, Calle Reina Regente 4. — *Café Suisse*, on the Promenade, *Europa*, on the beach, both near the casino.

San Sebastian, with 27,800 inhab., is picturesquely situated on the Bay of Biscay, partly on a peninsula, and, though of ancient origin, now presents the appearance of an entirely modern town. Among the numberless hostile attacks and conflagrations from which the town has suffered, the most destructive occurred in 1813 when it was sacked and burned by the British under General Graham. Since then, however, it has been rebuilt on a regular plan, and the new quarters present a handsome appearance.

Turning to the right as we leave the station, we skirt the *Urumea*, which we cross by a bridge at the end of the *Bay of Zurriola*, not accessible to ships and recently largely curtailed by gigantic embankments. The *Avenida de la Libertad*, a handsome street, leads hence to the *Concha*, another bay on which is the *Harbour* and the much-frequented *Sea-baths*. This bay resembles that of Pasages in having no communication with the sea except by means of a narrow channel between the cliffs of *Mont Orgullo* (425 ft.), on the right, and *Mont Igueldo* (785 ft.), on the left. The former, terminating the peninsula on which the town stands, is crowned by a fort, to visit which a special permit is required. The ascent takes about $^3/_4$ hr., and is rewarded by a fine *View. A good view is also obtained from Mont Igueldo, on which rises a lighthouse.

The beach of San Sebastian is admirably adapted for bathing. Above is the *Villa Miramar*, recently built by the queen-regent of Spain who frequently visits San Sebastian in the season. At the end of the promenade, next the Mont Orgullo, a handsome *Casino has been erected; and farther on is the *Harbour*, of no great importance, but interesting to the stranger. The ascent to the fort begins near this point. In the same neighbourhood is the Renaissance *Church of St. Mary*, remarkable for the florid richness of its façade, and still more for its huge altars, in the Spanish taste. — The Calle Mayor, opposite, leads to the *Calle del Pozzo*, the promenade behind the casino, which is planted with trees, and in the evening lighted by electricity. — Farther on, to the left, is the Gothic *Church of St. Vincent*, dating from the 11th cent., with altars resembling those in St. Mary's, but otherwise not remarkable. To the left of the street leading to this church is the *Plaza de la Constitucion*, with the Casa Consistorial, or town hall. The arcaded houses which surround it have balconies on all their stories; while all the windows are numbered in view of the festivals celebrated in the square. — On the other side of the promenade are the *Plaza de Guipuzcoa*, with the Government buildings and a square, in the centre of the new quarter.

The *Amphitheatre*, outside the town, beyond the railway, is only remarkable as the scene of the favourite bull-fights. These are announced beforehand, even in the neighbouring parts of France. The spectators, excited almost to madness, are, to the stranger, a more curious sight than the fights themselves. It should not be forgotten that it is very difficult to obtain accommodation in San Sebastian on such occasions.

19. From Bayonne to Toulouse.

I. From Bayonne to Pau.

60 M. RAILWAY in 2¹/₄-3¹/₄ hrs. (fares 12 fr. 10, 8 fr. 10, 5 fr. 25 c.).

Bayonne, see p. 66. — This route is on the whole less interesting than might have been expected; it passes at too great a distance from the Pyrenees on the one side and on the other stretch fertile but monotonous plains, covered with fields of maize. Quitting Bayonne we follow the line to Spain (p. 123) through a tunnel and across the Adour; then, after a second tunnel, ascend the valley of that river, passing (3¹/₂ M.) *Le Gaz*, (7 M.) *Urcuit*, (10¹/₂ M.) *Urt*, (13 M.) *Pont de l'Arran*, and (15 M.) *Pont de la Bidouze*. Beyond (17¹/₂ M.) *Sames*, the valley of the Adour is exchanged for that of its tributary, the *Gave de Pau*, which is crossed shortly before (20 M.) *Orthevielle*. — 21 M. *Peyrehorade* is a small town with the ruins of a 15th cent. castle. To the right is the Pic d'Anie (p. 140). — 23¹/₂ M. *L'Eglise*; 26¹/₂ M. *Labatut*.

32 M. **Puyôo** (*Buffet*; *Hôt. des Voyageurs*, at the station) is the junction for a branch-line to Dax (p. 65). On the left bank of the river is (³/₄ M.; 3¹/₂ M. from Salies, see below) the village of *Bellocq*, overlooked by the ruins of a château.

FROM PUYÔO TO ST. PALAIS, 18¹/₂ M., railway in 1¹/₄-1¹/₂ hr. (fares 3 fr. 35, 2 fr. 25, 1 fr. 50 c.). — The line crosses the *Gave de Pau* and passes through a tunnel 785 yds. in length. 5 M. **Salies-de-Béarn** (*Grand Hôtel du Parc*; *de la Paix & Continental*; *de Paris*; *du Château*; *de France & d'Angleterre*; *Belleville*; *Beauséjour*; etc.), a town of 8240 inhab., owes its name to its salt springs, which have been utilised from a very early date and are among the richest in salt known. The springs are cold, and are used both for drinking and bathing. The new *Bath House* is much frequented and is open all the year round. — The line now crosses the *Gave d'Oloron* and ascends its valley. 12¹/₂ M. *Autevielle* is the junction for Mauléon (see below). — 18¹/₂ M. **St. Palais** (*Hôt. Habiague*) is a small place devoid of interest. A diligence-route leads hence viâ *Larceveau* to (18¹/₂ M.) *St. Jean-Pied-de-Port* (p. 70).

FROM PUYÔO TO MAULÉON, 28¹/₂ M., railway in 1¹/₂-2¹/₄ hrs. (fares 5 fr. 15, 3 fr. 50, 2 fr. 25 c.). As far as (12¹/₂ M.) *Autevielle*, see above. — 15 M. **Sauveterre-de-Béarn**, a small town with considerable remains of a château of the 12-13th cent., a church in the Romanesque and Gothic styles, and a ruined bridge with a tower of defence (14th cent.), affording a splendid view of the Pyrenees. — The line then ascends the valley of the *Saison*. — 28¹/₂ M. **Mauléon** (*Hôt. Habiague*), an uninteresting little town on the Saison. A diligence-route leads hence to (5 M.) *Tardets* (735 ft.; *Hôt. des Voyageurs*), whence the *Pic d'Orhy* (6615 ft.), affording a splendid view, may be ascended viâ (10 M.) *Larrau* in 3¹/₂ hrs., and thence to (18 M.) *Oloron* (p. 138).

Beyond (38 M.) *Baigts* the valley becomes picturesque. Then, to the right, the old bridge of Orthez, and, to the left, —

41 M. **Orthez** (*Hôt. de la Belle-Hôtesse*), a finely situated town of 6210 inhab. on the right bank of the Gave de Pau.

Orthez was in the 13th cent. the capital of Béarn, and until 1460 the residence of the viscounts. Afterwards it became a focus of Protestantism, under the protection of Jeanne d'Albret, who founded a Calvinistic college here, in which Theodore Beza was a teacher. One fourth of the inhabitants are to this day Protestants. Marshal Soult was defeated by Wellington on the neighbouring hills in 1814.

The only lions of Orthez are the mediæval *Bridge* across the Gave, with a tower at its centre, and the *Tour de Moncade*, a remnant of the château of the viscounts of Béarn. There is a fine view of the Pyrenees from the higher parts of the town. — The next stations are (46¹/₂ M.) *Argagnon*, (50 M.) *Lacq*, (53¹/₂ M.) *Artix*, (56¹/₂ M.) *Denguin*, and (58 M.) *Poey*.

62¹/₂ M. *Lescar*, though now it has only 1645 inhab., was a town of importance in the 16th cent., and long the seat of a bishop. The cathedral dates from the 12th and 16th cent., the castle partly from the 14th. Lescar perhaps occupies the site of the ancient *Beneharnum*, which gave name to the old province of *Béarn*.

66 M. *Pau* (Buffet, déj. 3, D. 3¹/₂ fr.), to the left.

Pau. — **Hotels.** Those of the first class are palatial establishments, admirably situated, and providing every comfort, at a corresponding tariff. HÔT. GASSION (Pl. a; D, 4), Place Gassion and Boul. du Midi, R. 3-20, L. & A. 1¹/₂, déj. 1¹/₂-2, D. 4-6, pens. from 12¹/₂, omn. ¹/₂-1 fr. (the Hôt. d'Angleterre at Cauterets is a dépendance of this house); HÔT. DE FRANCE (Pl. b; D, 4), Place Royale; HÔT. SPLENDIDE; BELLE-VUE, Boul. du Midi, next the Hôt. Gassion; BEAU-SÉJOUR (Pl. c; E, 4), Rue du Lycée, in the S.E. outskirts of the town; HÔT. DE LA PAIX (Pl. d; D, 4), Place Royale; GRAND-HÔTEL (Pl. e; D, 2), Avenue du Grand-Hôtel, with rooms looking to the S. The above are specially for families passing the winter at Pau. — HÔT. DE LA POSTE (Pl. f; C, 3, 4), Place de Gramont; DU COMMERCE (Pl. g; D, 4), R. 2¹/₂-8, B. 1, déj. 3, D. 3¹/₂, omn. ¹/₂ fr.; DE L'EUROPE & DE LA DORADE, Rue Préfecture (Pl. h, ; D, 4); HÔT. HENRI IV. (Pl. i; E. 3), Place de la Halle, R. 2¹/₂-4, B. ³/₄-1, déj. 3, D. 3¹/₂, omn. ¹/₂-³/₄, well spoken of; etc. — **Pensions:** *Barthé* (10-12 fr. per day), *Planté*, *Hattersley* (from 7 fr.), *Sarda*, *Guichard*, Rue Porte-Neuve (Pl. E, F, 2, 3); *Pitté*, *Beaulis*, Rue d'Orléans (Pl. C, D, 3); *Colbert*, 39 Rue Montpensier (Pl. C, D, 2, 3; 8-12 fr.); *Holf*, Passage Planté (Pl. D, 2, 3), etc.

Apartments and Furnished Villas in great number in the town and suburbs from 300 to 10,000 fr. for the season, which lasts from September to May or June. For further particulars apply to the *Syndicat*, Rue Lataple 21. Its information is impartial and gratuitous; and it is also charged with the settlement of differences between strangers and inhabitants. In hiring houses an inventory should be demanded.

Cafés-Restaurants: *Grand-Café*, Place Royale; *de la Dorade, du Commerce*, Rue Préfecture; *du Théâtre*, Place Royale, etc.

Cabs. (Night tariff after 10 o'clock)	With one horse		With two horses	
	Day	Night	Day	Night
Drive within the octroi-limits . . .	— fr. 75	1 fr. —	1 fr. —	1 fr. 25
„ of 3 kil. (2 M.) beyond the octroi	1 „ —	1 „ 50	1 „ 50	1 „ 75
Per hour within radius of 3 kil. . .	1 „ 50	2 „ —	2 „ —	2 „ 50
„ „ „ „ 8 „ (5 M).	2 „ —	2 „ 50	2 „ 50	3 „ —

Luggage. 1 trunk 25 c.; more, 50 c.

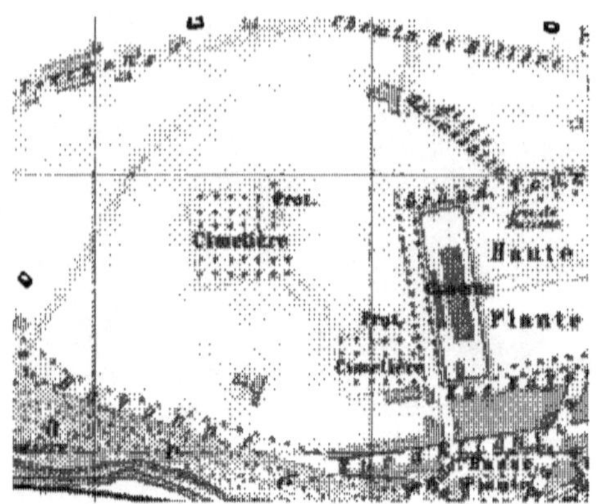
Prot.
Cimetière
Prot.
Cimetière
Haute
Caserne
Plante

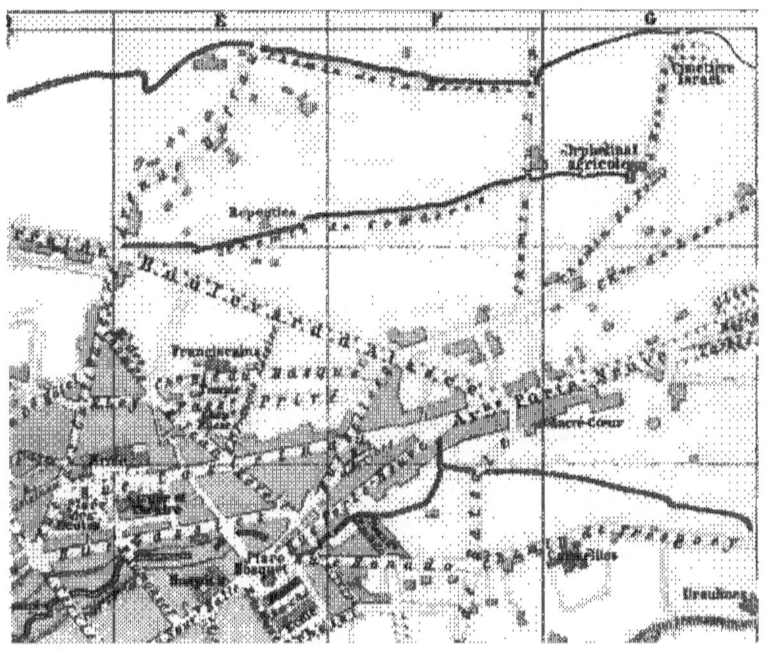
Cimetière Israël
Orphelinat agricole
Repos...
B.d.d.Terard.d'Alsace
Franciscains
Sacré-Cœur
Place Mosquet
Uraulinos

Carriages: '*Mylords*', 9 fr. per hr., 10 fr. a half-day, 20 fr. whole day; *Landaus*, 8, 12, and 20 fr. (to be hired in all parts of the town).

Post and Telegraph Office (Pl. E, 9), Rue des Arts 24.

Casino, near the Place Royale, below the side next the station. — *Club Anglais*, Place Royale, Hôtel de France (42 fr. per month); *de l'Union*, Place Royale; *National*, same Place; etc.

Concerts given by the municipal orchestra, at the kiosque in the Parc Beaumont or in the Casino.

Baths. *Grand Établissement Hydrothérapique*, Rue d'Orléans, 13 and 15; also at Rue Alexandre-Taylor 10, etc.

Reading Rooms. *Lafon*, Rue Henri IV.; *Carour*, Place Nouvelle-Halle; *Lescadé*, Rue Préfecture 17; *Ribaut*, Rue St. Louis 6.

American Consul: *Mr. J. Morris Post.* — **British Vice-consul**: *Mr. A. H. Foster-Barham*.

English Church Services. *St. Andrew's Church*, Avenue du Grand-Hôtel (services from October to May); chaplain: Rev. *R. H. Dyke Acland-Troyte*, M. A. — *Christ Church*, chaplain: Rev. *A. C. Manston*. — *Holy Trinity Church*, chaplain: Rev. *J. N. Soden*.

Pau (620 ft.), a town of 33,111 inhab., and the old capital of *Béarn*, is now the chief town of the department of the *Basses-Pyrénées*. It occupies a splendid site on the right bank of the *Gave de Pau*, and enjoys a delicious climate which renders it preëminent as a winter resort, high in favour with the English.

The mean temperature is 44° Fahr. in winter and 61° Fahr. for the whole year, *i. e.*, lower than the means of Rome, Hyères, Cannes, Mentone, and Nice, to all of which, however, Pau is superior in its freedom from chronic winds, especially the E. (except in summer), in the dryness of its air, and the equability of its temperature. Life at Pau is much quieter than at Nice, and its calm atmosphere and surroundings are no less beneficial to invalids. Pau is specially suited for those suffering from nervous affections, though it is also frequented by consumptive patients.

Pau sprang up round a castle of the viscounts of Béarn, dating originally from about the 10th cent. and rebuilt in the 14th by Gaston Phébus. It did not become a capital, however, until the 15th cent., but it attained great importance when its 'seigneur' François Phébus was made king of Navarre in 1479, and still more, when, in 1527, his third successor Henri d'Albret espoused Margaret of Valois, sister of Francis I. of France. This charming and witty princess gathered round her a brilliant court in which the Calvinists were well received. The successors of Henri and Margaret were Antoine de Bourbon and Jeanne d'Albret, under whom and their son, afterwards Henri IV. of France, the zenith of prosperity was reached. Jeanne d'Albret was no ordinary woman; she had 'l'âme entière aux choses viriles' and was able to sing a Béarnaise song while giving birth to her son, in order, as his father said, that he might be 'ni pleureur ni rechigné'. Antoine on his part carried off the infant to rub his lips with a clove of garlic, and to give him a taste of the local Jurançon wine. Jeanne had become a Calvinist, as was her son up to the time of his accession to the throne of France (1589); and Béarn had its share of suffering during the Religious Wars. Still, under the protection of Henri IV. and during the regency of his sister Catherine, the Calvinistic worship was maintained, but Louis XIII. put an end to the claims of the states of Béarn by personally interfering and annexing the country to the crown in 1620. Besides Henri IV., Pau counts among its natives Marshal Gassion (1609-47) and Bernadotte (1764-1844), who became king of Sweden.

The railway-station (Pl. D, 4) is at the foot of the plateau on which the town is built. Carriages have to make a long detour,

but foot-passengers ascend by a zigzag path which leads past the
Casino to the —

PLACE ROYALE (Pl. D, 4), a spacious square bordered by fine
buildings and adorned since 1843 with a marble *Statue of Henri IV.*,
by Raggi, with bas-reliefs by Etex. It is chiefly noted, however,
for the superb **Panorama* which it commands of the valley of
the Gave and the Pyrenees. The plain, through which the river winds,
is dotted with villages and villas, giving it a very animated appearance (the large building in the middle is the stud-farm of
(Iélos). Behind are eminences covered with vineyards and woods,
and the background is formed by the majestic chain of the Pyrenees,
visible for a length of about 60 miles. The most conspicuous of
the summits (the most distant of which are 50 miles away) is the
Pic du Midi d'Ossau (p. 147), in reality two peaks, 9465 ft. and
9150 ft. in height, presenting a bolder and more abrupt appearance
than the others in the advanced rank to the right. On the left, near
the other end of the chain, rises the conical Pic du Midi de Bigorre
(9440 ft.), and near the centre is the amphitheatre of the Vignemale,
with its glacier (10,820 ft.; p. 155), etc.

To inspect the town we follow the terrace and the Boulevard du
Midi to the W. from the Place Royale, passing behind the church
of St. Martin, and near the sumptuous Hôtel Gassion.

St. Martin's Church (Pl. D, 4) is a handsome modern edifice by
Boswillwald in the Gothic style of the 13th cent., with a stone
steeple on the façade. The high altar, the canopy, and the stained
windows after Steinheil deserve notice.

The *CASTLE (Pl. C, 4), rebuilt, as we have said, in the 14th cent.,
but considerably altered since, and recently restored, rises at the
W. end of the town, near the confluence of the Gave and the Hédas
rivulet. It is built in the form of an irregular pentagon with six
square towers. Entering on the side next the town, we cross a stone
bridge which under Louis XV. replaced the drawbridge over a
moat now filled by a fine row of trees. To the left is the *Chapel*,
built in 1840. The Renaissance *Portico*, farther on, dates from
1859-64. On the left again is the *Tour de Gaston-Phébus*, or
keep, 110 ft. high; to the right, the *Tour Neuve*, built under Napoleon III., and the *Tour Montauzet* or Monte-Oiseau, so called
because there was formerly no staircase, and in case of siege the
defenders ascended into it with ladders which they drew up after
them. The other towers are the *Tour Bilhère*, to the N. W., and the
Tours Mazères, to the S. W., one of which was erected under Louis-
Philippe. — The most interesting feature in the Cour d'Honneur is
the façade on the S. side, dating from the Renaissance, with three
tasteful dormer-windows.

The interior of the castle may be visited every day, in summer
from 10 to 5, in winter from 11 to 4. A guide accompanies the
visitor. The entrance is at the end of the court.   ..

GROUND FLOOR. — *Salle des Gardes:* fine antique vaulting; Renaissance chandelier; modern furniture; paintings. — *Salle à manger des Princes:* vaulting; statues of Henri IV. and Sully; time-piece in the style of Louis XIII. and Louis XIV., as in many of the other rooms. — *Salle à manger des Souverains,* successively Salle d'armes, Salle des Etats de Béarn, and a stable (in 1793); Flemish tapestry from the Château de Madrid in the Bois de Boulogne at Paris representing hunting-scenes in the reign of Francis I.; good statue of Henri IV., by Francheville. The *Grand Staircase* is an interesting work of the Renaissance.

FIRST FLOOR. — *Salle d'Attente,* Gobelins and Flemish tapestry, table of Francis I., with slab of Pyrenean marble, etc. — *Salon de Réception,* painfully associated with the massacre of six Roman Catholic nobles of Béarn by order of Montgomery, the general of Jeanne d'Albret; Renaissance chimney-piece; Flemish tapestry (continuation of the hunting scenes on the ground-floor); 16th cent. table, and a casket with a medallion of Henri IV.; table inlaid with mosaic of porphyry and Swedish agate, presented by Bernadotte; Sèvres vases, etc. — *Salon de Famille:* Gobelins tapestry, table with slab of Swedish rose-porphyry, another gift of Bernadotte. — *Chambre à coucher du Souverain:* fine mantelpiece, Flemish tapestry, antique furniture; statue of Henri IV. as a child, after Bosio; Gothic arm-chair and chest; ebony chest with medallion of Henri IV. (1607); very fine chest of the 15th cent. from Jerusalem, bought in 1838, etc. — *Cabinet du Souverain:* Brussels and Beauvais tapestries, Venetian glass, etc. — *Boudoir de la Reine:* pictures in Gobelins tapestry, Venetian glass. — *Chambre à coucher de la Reine:* antique furniture; magnificent Renaissance cabinet; pictures in Gobelins tapestry.

SECOND FLOOR ON S. SIDE. — *Rooms I-III.* Gobelins and Flemish tapestries; two chests of Henri II. (2nd R.) and one of Francis I.; cabinet of Louis XIII.; bronze fire-dogs of the 16th cent.; etc. — *Bedroom of Henri IV.,* shown as the one in which he was born, 14th Dec. 1553, and containing his cradle made of a large tortoise shell; Brussels tapestries; antique bed ornamented with 84 medallions and bust portraits and 12 small figures; crystal chandelier of the time of Francis I.; Gothic chest, upon which is a statuette of Crillon, the friend and comrade of Henri IV.; equestrian bas-relief of Henri IV., by G. Pilon. — *Chamber of Jeanne d'Albret,* Gobelins and Flemish tapestries, bed of 1562, etc. — The other apartments, not shown, are of little interest to strangers.

We now descend by the arcade near the keep. On this side, lower down, is the ruined Tour de la Monnaie. On the terrace behind the castle is a marble *Statue of Gaston Phébus,* by Triquety. A bridge leads hence to the *Quinconce de la Basse-Plante,* beyond which extends the *Park,* a charming promenade, much frequented by visitors. — In the Place Gramont (Pl. C, 3) is the *Statue of Marshal Bosquet* (1810-1861), by Millet and Mercilly, erected in 1894.

The *Church of St. James* (Pl. D, 3), on the N. of the town, beyond the small ravine of the Hédas, is an attractive building erected in 1866-68 by Loupot, in the Gothic style of the 13th century. It has two W. towers, and galleries above the aisles. The adjoining *Palais de Justice* (1847-55) is a heavy building in the classical style.

The Rue Serviez, a little farther to the right, ends in the Place de la Halle, not far from the Place Royale.

The *Musée* (Pl. E, 3), reached viâ the Rue de la Nouvelle-Halle, is open to the public on Sun. and Thurs. from 1 to 4 or 5, but is accessible on other days also.

GROUND FLOOR. Casts from the antique and some sculptures: *Etchelo,* Democritus; *Allouard,* The Infant Bacchus; *Oliva,* St. Theresa; *Barrias,*

Winter flowers. — On the staircase: 148. *Vafflard*, Henri IV. at Notre Dame, on the day of his entry into Paris.

First Floor. Paintings. Room I., to the left: 122. *Rigaud*, Singing to the guitar; 171. *Unknown Artist*, Guitar-player; 131. *Devéria*, after *Rubens*, Thomyris and the head of Cyrus; 152. *C. Vernet*, Sea-piece; 17. *E. Bordes*, St. Julian Hospitator; 118. *Bassano* (?), Christ with the reed; 163. *Zurbaran*, Portrait of a mitred abbot; 69. *Hoet the Elder*, Golden Calf; 115. *Oudry*, Stag-hunt; 142. *Teniers the Elder*, Landscape; 42. *Dehodencq*, Race of bulls; 147. *J. F. de Troy*, Mme. de Miramion, foundress of the order of Miramionnes; 108. *Hugues Merle*, Assassination of Henri III.; 97. *Largillière* (?), Portrait; 61. *P. Franceschi*, St. Jerome; 87. *B. van der Helst*, Portrait; 50. *Devéria*, Christopher Columbus before Ferdinand and Isabella (sketch); *Rubens*, 129. Thetis demanding arms for Achilles from Vulcan, 150. Death of Hector; 106. *Maratti*, John the Baptist; *Jordaens*, 92. Author meditating, 93. Woman with a ewer; 145. *Van Tulden*, Achilles at the court of Lycomedes; 15. *Bonvicino*, surnamed *Il Moretto*, Portrait. — Room II.: Engravings, drawings, coins, and faïence. — Room III.: 44. *Devéria*, Birth of Henri IV. (replica of the original in the Louvre); 112. *Monginot*, Duel; 18. *Bordes*, Attila consulting the augurs before the battle of Châlons; 138. *Schäffer*, Duchess of Nemours and Henri III.; 121. *Ribot*, Good Samaritan; 80. *L. Goupil*, Good Friday; 123. *Roll*, Hawker; *L. Capdevielle*, 55. Spanish card-players, 29. Marriage at Laruns; 155. *E. Duez*, St. Francis of Assisi; 16. *Bordes*, Concierge and tailor; 1. *L. Abbema*, Breakfast in the conservatory. — Room IV.: 2. *Em. Adam*, After mass; modern French paintings. — Rooms V. & VI.: Engravings and drawings. — Room VII.: Natural history collection; mummy; costumes from the Pyrenees, etc.

A little to the S.E. of the Musée lies the *Parc Beaumont* (Pl. F, 4), a fine public garden, commanding a view of the Pyrenees. Band several times a week.

From Pau to *Bordeaux*, see p. 65; to *Oloron* (Vallée d'Aspe), see R. 20; to *Eaux-Bonnes* and *Eaux-Chaudes*, R. 21.

10. From Pau to Toulouse.

134 M. Railway in 4½-7½ hrs. (fares 24 fr. 40, 16 fr. 50, 10 fr. 80 c.). — To *Lourdes*, 24 M., in 40-80 min. (fares 4 fr. 50, 3 fr., 1 fr. 85 c.). Best views generally to the right.

Tickets may be obtained at any of the stations, permitting the traveller to break the journey at Lourdes for not more than 24 hours.

Beyond Pau we continue to ascend the valley of the Gave de Pau. 71 M. (from Bayonne) *Assat*, beyond which the train stops at *Bezing*, *Baudreix*, and (76 M.) *Coarraze-Nay*. *Coarraze*, on the left of the line, is the place where Henri IV. was brought up in the simple fashion of the peasants, running about bare-footed and bare-headed. *Nay*, on the left bank of the Gave, is an industrial town with 3536 inhab., producing a large proportion of the bonnets worn by the inhabitants of the Pyrenees, and also Turkish fezes. 78 M. *Dufau*.

80 M. *Montaut-Bétharram*. *Bétharram* (Hôt. de France), ⅛ M. from the station, is a resort of pilgrims, dating from the time of the Crusades. It lies on the left bank of the Gave, which is here spanned by a picturesque ivy-clad bridge. On the other side are a *Seminary* and a *Monastery*, and to the right, the church and *Lestelle*, with the hotel. The *Church* (17th cent.) is remarkable for the richness and bad taste of its decoration. Beside it is a series of Romanesque *Chapels* (of ancient origin but restored in the 19th cent.), marking

the Stations of the Cross, and containing sculptured groups. On the top of the hill are a *Mt. Calvary* and a *Church of the Resurrection*. — About 1³/₄ M. to the S. is a fine grotto with stalactites.

The route now becomes for some distance very interesting. After passing (84 M.) *St. Pé* (St. Pierre), a small town to the left, we obtain a striking view to the right of the pilgrimage-churches, the grotto, and the town and castle of Lourdes.

90 M. Lourdes (**Buffet*). — Hotels (previous arrangement desirable): GR.-HÔTEL DU PALAIS ROYAL, D'ANGLETERRE, DU BOULEVARD, DE LA CHAPELLE, ST. MICHEL, NOTRE-DAME, all in the new street between the old town and the square in front of the pilgrimage-churches. — More in the town: HÔT. DE LA GROTTE, BELLEVUE, DE ROME; DES AMBASSADEURS, R. 3-5, L. ¹/₂, déj. 3, D. 4 fr.; ST. JOSEPH; CONTINENTAL; DU SACRÉ-CŒUR, R. 2-2¹/₂, B. ³/₄-1, déj. 3, D. 3¹/₂ fr.; all in the street leading from the station to the square (the two first with a view of the churches). — DU COMMERCE, near the parish church, R. 2¹/₂-3, B. 1¹/₂, déj. 2¹/₂, D. 3 fr.; DES PYRÉNÉES, DE FRANCE, near the Place du Marcadal.

Cabs, 2 and 3 fr. per hr.

Post and Telegraph-Office, behind the parish church, to the left.

Lourdes is a small town of 6876 inhab., on the right bank of the Gave du Pau, at the point where the river, descending from the valley of Argelès, turns abruptly W. towards the plain. It is built at the foot of a hill on which stands an ancient *Castle*, which formerly commanded the entrance of the valley and was often besieged in the middle ages, during the wars with England. This castle, to which visitors are admitted (gratuity), though uninteresting in itself, affords a beautiful view of the valley and the Pyrenees as far as the snowy slopes of the Vignemale. The entrance is in the interior of the town, to the E. Near it is the old *Parish Church*, which contains nothing remarkable. A new church has been begun farther E., but the work has been abandoned for want of means, since the death of the curé who undertook the enterprise (1877). Lourdes has some small manufactures, and in the neighbourhood marble and slate-quarries are worked.

The present importance and celebrity of the town are due to its *Pilgrimage*, dating only from 1858.

Bernadette Soubirous (who died in a convent in 1880), a peasant-girl, then about 14 years of age, alleged that the Virgin had several times appeared to her in a grotto and ordered that a shrine should be erected on the spot, to which many would resort for prayer. Lovers of the marvellous and pilgrims soon flocked thither, at first from the neighbourhood, then from all parts of France as well as from abroad, many of them, doubtless, drawn by the reports of the miraculous cures attributed to a spring issuing from the rock of the grotto. Now not a day passes in the season without pilgrims arriving either singly or in large organized parties. With the aid of the clergy, and by the admixture of a little of the political-religious element in the manifestations, the interest is so far kept up that from every quarter special trains are despatched (especially in summer) bringing thousands of passengers, ailing or not, to pay their devotions and to satisfy their curiosity. The pilgrims travel at greatly reduced fares and find themselves at Lourdes near one of the finest parts of the Pyrenees. — The tourist will do well to lay his plans to avoid sleeping at Lourdes when a train of pilgrims has arrived.

The Boulevard de la Grotte, a new road to the right of the exit
from the station, leads straight to the ($^1/_2$ M.) Grotto, crossing the
Gave on the way. A church has been built on the top and another
at the foot of the cliff in which it lies; the course of the Gave has
been diverted so as to make room for a promenade in front of the
grotto; while between the bridge and the churches lies a broad
square, adorned with statues of the Virgin and St. Michael, and
with a cross which is sometimes illuminated, etc. The left side and
the Boul. de la Grotte are occupied by *Shops* for the sale of mementoes,
religious articles, etc.

The *Grotto*, in the rocks beside the river, is a recess about
15 ft. deep and 15 ft. wide, now closed with a railing. On a rock
projecting above, to the right, is a statue by Fablsch, representing
the Virgin as Bernadette described her, in a white robe with a blue
scarf. The walls of the grotto are hung with crutches and other
votive offerings. To the left is the *Miraculous Spring*, now confined
by a wall garnished with taps, through which the water flows into
basins in which the pilgrims bathe. For certain ailments the remarkable coldness of the water renders it dangerous; sufferers from
these are warned by a notice that they bathe at their own risk.

The *Church of the Rosary* (1885-89) stands in front of the
Basilica, built above the grotto. It has the form of a rotunda in
the Byzantine style. Two flights of steps and two large inclined
planes, in the shape of horse-shoes, supported by arcades, give
access to the terrace above. Fifteen chapels in the interior of the
church radiate from the centre beneath the dome. — The *Basilica*,
about 60 ft. higher up, is a remarkable and richly ornamented building in the Gothic style of the 13th cent., designed by Hipp. Durand.
It was consecrated in 1876 in presence of thirty-five archbishops
and bishops, presided over by the Cardinal-Archbishop of Paris,
and the Papal Nuncio, who crowned the statue of the Virgin (by
Raffl). An elegant tower rises on the W. front. The interior, which
consists simply of a nave with side-chapels, is hung all over with
gold or gilded hearts, banners, medallions, inscribed tablets, and
other votive offerings. A crypt, with double nave, extends beneath
the whole length of the church.

On a hill (good view) to the S. of the Basilica stands a *Calvary*.
In the neighbourhood of the grotto are buildings for the use of the
pilgrims, *Convents*, an *Asylum for the Aged*, an *Orphanage*, etc.

There are a number of other and larger grottos in the mountain beyond the Basilica. In the ($^1/_2$ M.) *Spélugue* (now a chapel), articles made
of reindeer horn were discovered; $^1/_2$ M. farther is the *Grotte du Loup*,
of great depth.

Excursions are frequently made to the ($1^3/_4$ M.) *Lac de Lourdes*, a
moraine-lake about $2^1/_2$ M. in circumference, with erratic blocks in the
vicinity (café-restaurant). The route follows the road to Pau on the right
bank of the Gave as far as the church of *Poueyferré*, where it diverges
to the left.

From Lourdes to *Cauterets, St. Sauveur, Barèges*, etc., see RR. 22, 23, 24.

93 M. *Adé.* Beyond (96 M.) *Ossun*, a small town on the left, appears the Pic du Midi de Bigorre (p. 167). — Beyond (99 M.) *Juillan* the line to Bordeaux viâ Mont-de-Marsan diverges to the left (p. 64).

102 M. **Tarbes** (*Buffet*; *Hôtel de la Paix*, R. 3½-4, B. 1¼. déj. 3, D. 3½ fr., *des Ambassadeurs*, both Place Maubourguet; *de Strasbourg*, at the station, unpretending), with 25,087 inhab., the chief town of the department of the *Hautes-Pyrénées* and the seat of a bishop, is situated in a rich plain on the left bank of the Adour. Its importance dates from the middle ages, when it became the capital of the County of Bigorre. The English only occupied it from 1360 to 1406, but it suffered greatly during the religious wars of the 16th cent., in which it was taken and retaken seven times.

The town contains little to interest the tourist. Its centre is about ¾ M. to the S. of the station, and it extends nearly 1½ M. from W. to E., as far as the banks of the Adour.

A new street, a few yards to the left of the exit from the station, leads direct to the Place Maubourguet; while the street immediately to the right brings us to the *Cathedral* or *Sède*. The latter is a heavy but unimposing building of the 12-14th cent., the finest feature of which is the octagonal cupola (14th cent.) above the tran-sept. Over the high altar is a huge canopy supported by six co-lumns of red marble veined with white, with gilded pedestals and capitals. On each side of the nave is a double tier of noteworthy wood-carving, the upper tier adorned with tasteful iron railings.

The Rue Neuve-St. Louis, to the E. of the cathedral, leads to the *Place Maubourguet*, the centre of the town; and thence the Cours Gambetta, to the S., to the *Allées Nationales*. This fine promenade is embellished, in front of the cavalry barracks, with a statue in bronze (by Badiou de la Tronchère) of the surgeon *Larrey* (1766-1842), a native of the Hautes-Pyrénées.

The Rue Larrey diverges to the right and left before we reach the Allées. In its E. section is a handsome new *Theatre*. Turning to the right at the end of the W. section, we find ourselves in the Cours de Reffye, with a bronze bust, by Nelly, of *General Reffye*. The Rue Thiers leads to the left from the other end of the Cours to the Place Maubourguet.

Towards the E. end of the town are two other large squares, the *Place Marcadieu* or market-place and the *Forail* or place where the fairs are held. The latter presents a curious sight when the people from the mountains and also from Spain come to sell their commodities, horses, etc. Tarbes is the chief mart for the excellent horses of the Pyrenees.

The most interesting feature in Tarbes is the magnificent *JARDIN MASSEY, 550 yds. to the N. of the Place Maubourguet, and a short distance to the E. of the station. Though created and presented to the town by a former director of the Gardens of Versailles, it is laid

out in the style of an English park. It is planted with exotic
trees, and threaded by streamlets, and affords a delightful promenade. To the S. of a small lake here some 15th cent. *Cloisters*,
from St. Sever-de-Rustan, 13½ M. to the N.E. of Tarbes, have been
re-erected, unfortunately with some alterations. The 48 capitals
are covered with curious sculptures.

The garden also contains a small Museum, in an attractive brick
building, with a tower in the Moorish style. It is open on Sun.,
Thurs., and holidays, from 12 to 4 or 5; on other days for a gratuity.

Ground Floor. Plaster-casts from the antique and from mediæval
and Renaissance works; also, in the hall to the left: *Fr. Jouffroy*, Ariadne;
J. Coutan, St. Christopher. — Staircase. Fine Roman capitals; Gallo-
Roman votive altars and small antiquities; plaster-casts of sculptures
from the Parthenon; portion of the natural history collection.

First Floor. — Room I., to the right: 164. *J. L. Gérôme*, Innocence;
62. *Pietro Perugino*, Virgin and Child; 13. *Ann. Carracci*, Children;
33. *Everdingen*, Sea-piece; 102. *Zurbaran*, St. James of Compostella;
26. *Domenichino*, Cartoon for the fresco of the Martyrdom of St. Sebastian;
132. *School of Perugino*, St. Lawrence; 20. *Alonzo Cano*, Holy Family;
11. *After Ann. Carracci*, Reduced copy of the fresco of the Triumph of
Venus; 53. *Lazerges*, Kabyle reapers; 159. *Teniers*, Temptation of St.
Anthony; 6. *Baroccio*, Holy Family; 108. *Zurbaran*, Solomon and his
wives; 76. *Solimena*, Allegory. — R. II. Copies bequeathed by Lagarrigue,
a former curator of the Musée. — R. III.: to the left, 99. *Ad. Valentin* (?),
Musicians; 48. *J. B. Leprince*, Portrait of the artist; 79. *Sassoferrato*, St.
Margaret; 12. *Ann. Carracci*, Apollo; 39. *Guercino* (?), Lot and his daughters;
58. *Montero* (Spanish), Drunkenness of Noah; 108. *Hamd*, Holy Family;
180. *J. Laurens*, Ispahan; 14. *Alb. Cuyp*, Portrait; 9. *L. Boulanger*, Peace,
Agriculture, and Plenty; 184. *Dutch School*; 15. *A. Cuyp*, Portraits; 26.
Dourati, Cathedral of Toledo; 38. *Gérard*, Achilles finding the body of
Patroclus; 66. *Pordenone*, Adoration of the Magi; 60. *Lepoittevin*, Winter
in Holland; 92. *Watelet*, Tyrolese landscape; 160. *Snyders*, Animals; 64.
Parmeggiano, Judgment of Paris; 153. *Benj. Constant*, Hamlet and the
king. — R. IV. Religious and historical paintings by *M.* and *Mme. Latil*,
remarkable for their colouring. — R. V. Engravings; medals; bas-reliefs;
engraved portraits; Newfoundland dog of the Empress Eugénie; etc. —
R. VI. Ornamental designs; engravings (220. Loggie of Raphael); medals;
insects. — R. VII. Birds, shells, etc.

Fine view from the *Tower* of the Museum (25 c.).

From Tarbes to *Agen*, etc., see R. 14; to *Morcenx (Bordeaux)*, p. 64; to
Cauterets, St. Sauveur, Barèges, etc., RR. 22, 23, 24; to *Bagnères-de-Bigorre*,
R. 25; to *Bagnères-de-Luchon*, R. 26.

Quitting Tarbes we pass between the Jardin Massey and the
arsenal. Beyond *Marcadieu*, the line to Bagnères-de-Bigorre diverges
to the right. Beyond a tunnel, ¼ M. long, is (109½ M.) *Lespouey-
Laslades*, and beyond another tunnel, 700 yds. long, are (110½ M.)
Bordes-l'Hez, (113 M.) *Tournay*, and (116 M.) *Ozon - Lanespède*.
We next cross a curved viaduct from which there is a fine view to
the right, then another viaduct over a ravine, and ascend a steep
gradient. Among the mountains, to the right, the most conspicuous
are the Pic d'Ardiden, the isolated Pic du Midi de Bigorre, and the
triple summit of the Pic d'Arbizon.

122 M. **Capvern**, station for the *Baths* of that name, which lie
2 M. and 4½ M. to the N. (diligence; *Grand - Hôtel*; *Hôtel des*

Pyrénées, etc.; *Casino)* and have two springs, impregnated with sulphate of lime, resembling those of Bagnères-de-Bigorre (p. 171). The nearer and more important spring is that of *Hount - Caoudo*, the other that of *Le Bouridé*. There is a bath-establishment at each.

From (124½ M.) *Lannemezan* a diligence (fares 2 fr. 75, 2 fr. 20 c.) runs in 2½ hrs. to Arreau (p. 174), 16 M. to the S. A railway to this little town, viâ the valley of the Neste, is under construction. — 128 M. *Cantaous*; 131 M. *St. Laurent-St. Paul*: 133 M. *Aventignan* (Grotto of Gargas, see below). To the right, on a hill, is a ruin commanding the confluence of the Garonne and the Neste. We cross the Garonne and reach —

135 M. **Montréjeau** ('Mont-Royal'; *Buffet*; *Hôt. du Parc*, in the town; *de France*, at the station), a town of 3068 inhab., 1 M. from the station, on the edge of a plateau overlooking the Garonne and commanding a fine view.

From Montréjeau to *Bagnères-de-Luchon*, see R. 20.

About 5 M. to the S.W. of Montréjeau, beyond the village of (3 M.) *Aventignan* (see above), at which the custodian resides, is the Grotto of Gargas (adm. 1 fr., with illumination 1½ fr. and fee), with remarkable stalactites and stalagmites, and an arched roof more than 50 ft. high, etc. The name is said to be derived from a chieftain who used it as a prison. In the 18th cent. it was the haunt of a cannibal who killed and devoured more than thirty women of the neighbourhood.

The line now follows the valley of the Garonne and skirts the mountains for some time, affording a series of fine views. Beyond (139 M.) *Martres-de-Rivière* it crosses the river.

144 M. **St. Gaudens** (*Hôt. de France*; *Hôt. Ferrière*), a town of 7000 inhab., once very prosperous. situated on an eminence on the right bank of the Garonne, and commanding a fine view. Its chief building is the Romanesque *Church* of the 11 - 12th cent., with an imposing Gothic portal of the 15th century. The columns have curious capitals, and the interior is decorated with antique tapestry and modern paintings.

About 6 M. to the S. (omnibus in summer; 1 fr. 35 c.) is the village of **Encausse** (*Hôt. de Paris; de France*, etc.), the mineral waters of which are used both for drinking and bathing. Their effect is sedative and purgative. — Pretty neighbourhood.

Before (150 M.) *Laburthe-Inard*, we see on the right the picturesque ruins of the *Château de Montespan* ('Mont-Hispan') of the 13-15th centuries. We cross the Garonne. — 155 M. *St. Martory*, a place probably called, like others which bear the name Martres, after some martyrdom in the days of the Saracens. To the left the old *Château de Montpezat*. Farther on is another bridge over the Garonne, near which is the mouth of an irrigation canal, 40 M. in length, constructed with the object of watering the vast plain which extends lower down the river on the left.

At (159 M.) **Boussens** (*Hôtel Picard*) the Garonne becomes navigable. A visit heuce, to the S., to the ruins of the *Château de*

Roquefort (12-13th cent.), and the fine modern Romanesque church
of that village takes $1^1/_2$ hr., there and back.

From Boussens to *Aulus*, viâ *St. Girons*, see R. 23.

Near the little town of (161 M.) *Martres-Tolosane* (to the left)
the remains of a Roman villa were discovered in 1826, with 40
busts of Roman emperors, now in the Museum at Toulouse, and
various other antiquities.

165 M. *Cazères-sur-Garonne*, a small town. 169 M. *St. Julien-
St. Eliz.* St. Eliz, $1^3/_4$ M. to the N., has a Renaissance château.
The scenery becomes less interesting. The line recedes farther and
farther from the mountains, while wide and well-cultivated but
monotonous plains stretch on the left. — 174 M. *Carbonne*, a small
town; 179 M. *Longages*; 182 M. *Fauga*.

187 M. **Muret** (*Hôtel de France*, Place Lafayette), on the Garonne, with 4148 inhabitants.

The second turning on the right beyond the station leads to the
Place Lafayette, embellished with a statue of the Madonna, near
which is the church. A little farther on is the oblong Allée Niel,
in which are bronze statues (by St. Jean and Crauk respectively)
of the musician *Dalayrac* (1753-1809) and *Marshal Niel* (1802-69),
both natives of Muret. — The *Church* dates from the 14th and
15th cent., but the interior has been altered in the classic style
and recently adorned with mural paintings. To the left of the entrance is a cross from Bomarsund, presented by Marshal Niel.

In the neighbouring plain, to the N., the army of Dom Pedro,
king of Aragon, marching to the succour of Toulouse, was in 1213
defeated by Simon de Montfort the elder, the king with 15-20,000
of his followers being slain.

$192^1/_2$ M. *Portet-St. Simon*, at the confluence of the Garonne
and the *Arlège*, is the junction for Foix (R. 28). On the left, the
loop-line connecting the line from Auch and the St. Cyprien station
at Toulouse (see p. 78). Then, crossing the Garonne for the last
time and passing (198 M.) *St. Agne*, we cross the Canal du Midi,
and beyond *Pont-des-Demoiselles* and a short tunnel, we reach the
Gare Matabiau at —

199 M. *Toulouse* (Buffet), see p. 78.

20. From Pau to Oloron. Vallée d'Aspe.

From Pau to *Oloron*, $21^1/_2$ M., RAILWAY in $1^1/_4$-$1^1/_2$ hr. (fares 3 fr. 80,
2 fr. 85, 1 fr. 70 c.); thence DILIGENCE twice a day to $(25^1/_2$ M.) *Urdos* in
$4^3/_4$ hrs. (fare 3 fr. 20 c.). From Urdos to $(31^1/_2$ M.) *Jaca*, by Spanish
'Courrier', and railway thence to (69 M.) *Huesca* and to (44 M. farther)
Saragossa.

Pau, see p. 128. — This line, which coincides at first with that to
Laruns and Eaux-Bonnes (R. 21), crosses the Gave, ascends the valley
of the Nez to the S., and then turns to the W. — Beyond (5 M.) *Gan*

(2700 inhab.) on the left, the train mounts a considerable gradient,
and traverses successively a short tunnel, four viaducts (the second
of which, 100 ft. high, is curved), and two more tunnels, the last
being 620 yds. in length.

At (12 M.) *Buzy*, the branch to Laruns diverges (p. 142). —
15¹/₂ M. *Ogeu*, a small watering-place. — 18 M. *Escou*.

21¹/₂ M. **Oloron** (892 ft.; *Hôt. de la Poste*; *Loustalot*, at Ste. Marie,
near the station), the ancient *Iluro*, is an industrial and commercial town of 8760 inhab. including the suburb of Ste. Marie. It
is prettily situated at the confluence of the Gaves d'Ossau and d'Aspe,
which together form the Gave d'Oloron, and it was once the seat
of a bishop. The *Cathedral of Ste. Marie*, in the suburb of that
name, on the left bank of the Gave d'Aspe, is a Romanesque-
Gothic building of the 11-15th cent. with an interesting portal,
under a porch. The church of *Ste. Croix*, in Oloron itself, dating
from the 11th cent., has a gilded wooden altar of the 17th cent. in
the Spanish style, and some paintings by Romain Cazes. The town
has fine promenades and the remains of ramparts.

From Oloron to *Tardets*, see p. 127.

The **Vallée d'Aspe**, to the S. of Oloron, is traversed by a good
carriage-road, one of the best and most frequented of those which
cross the Pyrenees, and it is proposed to make a railway ('conceded'
as far as Bedous) also, which would shorten the journey from Paris
to Madrid by about 60 miles. The distance from Oloron to the
frontier at Somport is 33 M., and thence it is about 19 M. to the little
Spanish town of Jaca, via Canfranc. The valley is uninteresting
till beyond Asasp, 5 M. from Oloron, and its finest parts lie between
that point and Fort d'Urdos, about 18 M. higher up. In breadth it
hardly exceeds ¹/₂ M., while in many places it becomes a mere
gorge which the Gave has worn in the prevailing limestone.

The road follows the left bank of the Gave d'Aspe. At (1³/₄ M.)
Bidos, the road to (10 M.) St. Christau diverges to the left.

An omnibus plies in summer from Oloron to St. Christau (1 fr. 60 c.),
affording a convenient means of traversing the uninteresting portion of
the valley, St. Christau being only about 1¹/₄ M. from Asasp (see below).

St. Christau (*Hôtel de la Poste*) is a hamlet of Lurbe (see below), prettily situated and possessing sulphureous and other waters especially efficacious in skin-diseases. There are two bathing establishments. — To
the S. is *Mont Binet* (4020 ft.), which is easily ascended in 2 hours.

Passing (3 M.) *Gurmençon* and (4 M.) *Arros*, we reach (5¹/₂ M.)
the village of *Asasp*, beyond which on the left bank (bridge) is *Lurbe*
(Hôt. des Vallées), to which are attached the Baths of St. Christau,
1¹/₄ M. to the N. E. — We now leave on the right the valley of the
Lourdios, and soon enter the first gorge of the valley of the Gave.

From (10 M.) *Escot* a new route crosses the *Col de Marieblanque*
(3025 ft.) to (3 hrs.) the Vallée d'Ossau, joining the route to
Eaux-Bonnes at Bielle (p. 142). Another interesting route leads from
Escot to Arudy (15 M.; see p. 142).

Our road now crosses the Gave d'Aspe by the *Pont d'Escot*. To the left, on a rock, is a Latin inscription of doubtful authenticity, stating that the Duumvir L. Valerius Vernus twice repaired this route. Near the bridge are the small *Baths of Escot*, frequented by the natives only. -- We cross another bridge.

12 M. *Sarrance* (Inn), with a pilgrims' shrine and a ruined convent. As we continue to ascend the valley we pass successively a waterfall, the *Pont Suzon*, the *Cirque d'Ourdinse*, to the left (with the *Pic de Mousté*, 5235 ft., ascended from Bédous in 4¹/₂ hrs.), and a second gorge.

15¹/₂ M. *Bédous* (Hôt. de la Paix), situated in a basin which must have formed a lake before the waters of the torrent had sufficiently scooped out the gorge. The hillocks in this basin are composed of ophite, a volcanic product. A road, difficult in places, leads hence to Laruns (p. 142), viâ *Aydins* and the *Col de las Arques* (about 5600 ft.).

Farther on, in the valley of Aspe, is *Suberlaché*, a small watering-place, with chalybeate and sulphur springs.

18 M. *Accous* is supposed to be the *Aspa Lura* of the Romans. On a knoll is a column erected to the memory of the popular poet Despourrins (1693-1742). A path, affording fine views, leads hence in 4-5 hrs. to Eaux-Chaudes over the *Col d'Iseye* (about 6560 ft.).

The valley again narrows to a gorge, midway in which is the *Pont d'Esquit*, boldly spanning the torrent. Travellers bound for Urdos cross neither this nor the next bridge. — 20 M. *Pont de Lescun*, leading into the valley of that name.

The Gave de Lescun forms a picturesque waterfall, near a cottage, about ¹/₂ M. from the bridge (50 c.). The hamlet of Lescun (310 ft.; *Hotel*) is about ³/₄ M. farther on, and in the neighbourhood are the little *Baths of Laberou*, with warm sulphur-springs. The comparatively easy and interesting ascent of the *Pic d'Anie (8315 ft.; guide, Lonstallot) may be made from Lescun in 4-4¹/₂ hrs. We ascend the *Hourque de Lauga*, a valley to the right, and passing near the baths (see above), enter a wood, and beyond the huts of (2¹/₄ hrs.) *Atuns*, we climb alongside the streamlet that descends from the mountain, leaving on the right the (1 hr.) little *Lac d'Anie*, thus skirting the peak from E. to W. The magnificent panorama from the summit is one of the most striking in the Pyrenees, not only embracing the greater part of that chain but also extending to the ocean, 50 miles distant, and over the plains of Gascony as far as the Landes. The double Pic du Midi d'Ossan (p. 147), only 16 M. distant, specially attracts attention by its abrupt outlines.

Passing (20¹/₂ M.) *Cette-Eygun* and (22 M.) *Elsnut*, the road again crosses the torrent, by the *Pont de Sebers*, and enters a gorge at the end of which, on the left, rises (24 M.) the *Fort d'Urdos* or the *Portalet* (2805 ft.), presenting a striking and picturesque appearance. This fort, constructed in 1838-48, is to a great extent built on a rock overhanging the torrent, and is reached by no less than 506 steps. All that is visible is a frontage flanked by two turrets and some walls, only distinguishable from the rocks by their embrasures; but within there is accommodation for 3000 men.

Recrossing to the right bank by the *Pont d'Enfer*, at the foot of the fort, we enter another small basin about 3 miles long, and reach —

25½ M. **Urdos** (2493 ft.; *Hôtel Ferran*), the last French village.

From Urdos to Gabas, by a mule-track in 6, and by a footpath in 5 hours. The former passes to the N. of the *Pics de Lorry* (8170 ft.) and *d'Ayous* (10,865 ft.), and leads over the *Col d'Aas de Bielle* (7085 ft.; 4 hrs.), beyond which there is a splendid view of the Pic du Midi d'Ossau (p. 147); then past the saw-mill of *Bious-Artigues* (p. 147), whence Gabas is reached in an hour. — The footpath ascends to the S. of the *Pic Hourquette* (7820 ft.) to the (3 hrs.) *Col de Bious*, to the N. of the *Pic de Moines* (8012 ft.). Here, too, the Pic du Midi is in view. We descend by the saw-mill.

27½ M. a *Lazaretto*, in ruins; then another gorge, followed by a small basin and (28½ M.) the *Auberge du Peillou*, beyond which is (30 M.) a deserted *Foundry*. The road then separates from a path that continues to the right up the valley, at the end of which, on the left, the *Pic d'Aspe* (8880 ft.) is conspicuous. We pass two inns. The projected railway will cross the frontier by means of a tunnel, at the height of 3900 ft.

33 M. **Le Somport** or *Port d'Urdos* (5380 ft.), on the frontier, the *Summus Portus* of the Romans, through which passed the road from *Caesarea Augusta* (Saragossa) to *Iluro* (Oloron). A part of the army of Abd-er-Rahman, defeated by Charles Martel in 732, invaded France by this route. The view from the col is limited and the surroundings are bare and gloomy.

From Le Somport to Gabas, 4 hrs., by a path which passes to the S. of the *Pic d'Arnousse* (7020 ft.) and over the (1½ hr.) *Col des Moines* (7230 ft.), beyond which we descend, in view of the majestic Pic du Midi, and join the path from the Col de Bious (see above).

The road now descends in zigzags on the Spanish side, passing first the ruins of the hospital of *Santa Cristina*, and then an inn. — 40 M. *Chapelle St. Antoine*; 43 M. *Portalec*; 44½ M. *Spaluny*.

46 M. *Canfranc* (3410 ft.; Posada - Fonda Isuel), a small place on the right bank of the Aragon, above which rises an ancient castle. — Farther on are two highly picturesque gorges, between which, on the left, rises the *Peña-Collarada* (9460 ft.; ascended in 5 hrs.), the summit of which affords an extensive view. — 48½ M. *Villanua*; 52 M. *Castiello*.

57 M. **Jaca** (*Hôtel Mur-y-Bueno*), a walled town, with 3800 inhabitants. The interesting *Cathedral* dates from the 14-15th cent.; the *Citadel* (fine view from the top) from the 16th. — A railway runs hence to (69 M.) *Huesca*, the chief town of the province, and to (40 M.) *Saragossa*.

21. Eaux-Bonnes, Eaux-Chaudes, and their Environs.

I. From Pau to Eaux-Bonnes and Eaux-Chaudes.

Railway to (24 M.) Laruns in 1½ hr. (fares 4 fr. 35, 3 fr. 25, 1 fr. 90 c.); thence railway-omnibus to (4 M.) Eaux-Bonnes and Eaux-Chaudes, in

55 min. (fare 1 fr. 50 c.); other vehicles outside the station cheaper. Best view from seats in the banquette. Landau for 4 pers., 8 fr.

From *Pau* (p. 128) to (12¹/₂ M.) *Buzy*, see p. 139. — Leaving the line to Oloron on the right, we approach the Gave d'Ossau, and cross it by means of a viaduct, 100 ft. in height. — 16 M. *Arudy*, to the left, a place of some size.

The *Vallée d'Ossau begins here and extends S. to Gabas (p. 147), a distance of about 18 M. Sometimes, however, the name is restricted to the part between Arudy, where the Gave d'Ossau turns to the W. in the direction of Oloron, and Laruns (see below), where it descends from Eaux-Chaudes and is joined by the Valentin, which comes from Eaux-Bonnes. The valley of Ossau is one of the most picturesque in the Pyrenees, although the mountains which flank it have been to a great extent stripped of their woods since last century. At the upper end is the famous Pic du Midi d'Ossau; at the end of the lateral valley the Pic de Ger (p. 145), celebrated for its panorama, etc. The valley, in which are Eaux-Bonnes and Eaux-Chaudes, watering-places of the first rank, is only separated from the valley of Aspe (p. 139) by a minor chain of hills, easy to cross and affording fine excursions. The valley of Ossau, like that of Aspe, once formed a small commonwealth, which retained its privileges for a long time after its annexation to Béarn, and for still longer its peculiar manners and costumes. Traces of both still linger in the more sequestered parts of the valley. Curious costumes are still to be seen at Laruns on holidays, especially on the festival of the Assumption (Aug. 15th). The hoods worn by the women are characteristic.

At (17¹/₂ M.) *Izeste* the valley begins to form a picturesque gorge. Here there is a grotto interesting alike to geologists and to ordinary tourists (10 fr. for 1 or more persons). — 20 M. *Bielle*, the ancient capital of the viscounts of Ossau, has preserved its old archives. The Gothic church is partly built of ancient materials, and remains of Roman baths, with mosaics, have been discovered. Near the church are some curious houses of the 15th and 16th centuries.

We now reach the mountains, and traverse two short tunnels. To the left lie *Lourie* and *Soubiron*, noted for their quarries of Ossau marble.

24 M. **Laruns** (1650 ft.; *Hôtel des Touristes*, etc.), with 2200 inhab., has marble quarries of high repute.

Farther on to the right our road leaves the old road to Eaux-Chaudes viâ the Hourat (p. 144), recommended to pedestrians on account of the view. Beyond a bridge over the Gave d'Ossau we reach the (25¹/₂ M.) point where the *New Roads* to Eaux-Bonnes and Eaux-Chaudes diverge. For the latter see p. 145. That to Eaux-Bonnes leaves the old and steep road below on the left, and ascends the N.E. flank of the Gourzy (p. 144) in zigzags, affording fine views: behind, Laruns and its valley; on the left the valley of the Valentin and the Montagne-Verte; in front and on the right, the Latte de Bazen, the Pénémédaa, and the Pic de Ger (p. 145). *Eaux-Bonnes* is not visible until we are close to it.

II. Eaux-Bonnes.

Hotels. GRAND-HÔTEL DES PRINCES, DE FRANCE, CONTINENTAL, RICHELIEU, all first-class, round the Jardin Darralde; DE PARIS, D'ANGLETERRE &

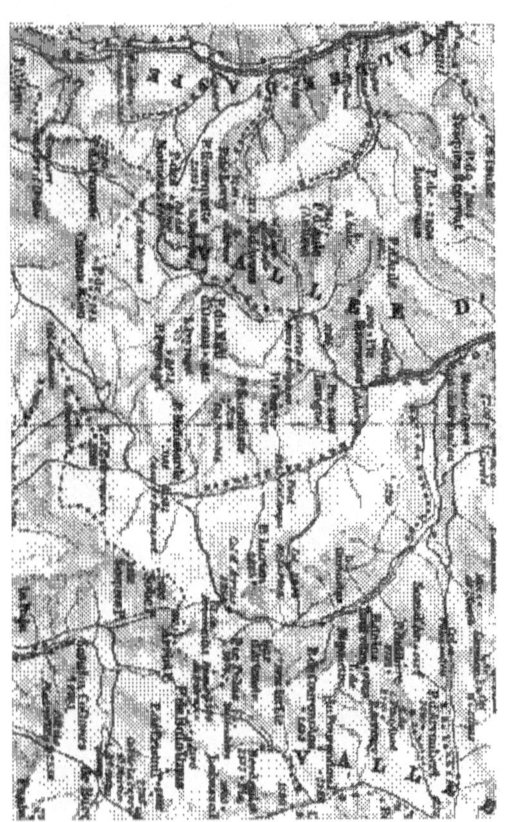

D'Espagne, de la Poste, des Touristes & de l'Univers, des Pyrénées, in the same place; de la Paix, Béarn, these last nearer the Thermal Establishment, etc. — **Furnished Houses and Private Pensions**. *Lanne-Lasar, Caraux aîné*, in the Promenade; *Bonnecaze, Pommé, Loubira*, in the Place de l'Hôtel de Ville; *Courtade, Tourné, C. Lamarque, Layouarre*, higher up and nearer the baths. — Charges vary considerably: R. 2 to 10, D. 5 to 8 fr.

Café and Club at the *Hôtel des Princes.*

Thermal Establishments, see below. Tariff for drinking and gargling, from June 20th to Aug. 20th, 20 fr.; at other times during the season, 10 fr.; family subscription, 50 fr. — Bath, from 7 to 10 a. m.: from June 20th to Aug. 20th, 2 fr.; at other hours and other seasons, 1 fr.; douche, 1 fr.; bath and douche, 2 fr. 50 or 1 fr. 50 c., etc. Tourists have the privilege of drinking once at the springs gratis.

Casino (see below): subscription for a fortnight, entitling to 7 representations, 10 fr., 2 pers. 15 fr., 3 pers. 20 fr., 4 pers. 25 fr.; per month, 15, 25, 35, or 40 fr.; for 3 months, 30, 55, 75, or 90 fr.

Horses and Mounted Guides: *Lanuse, Caillau, Casabonne*, etc. — There is no fixed tariff; charges vary from 7 to 12 fr. a day.

Guides. *J. Ortig, J. Soustrade, Esquerre, Navarrent.* — No tariff; 5 to 12 fr. a day.

Omnibus to Eaux-Chaudes, at 7 and 11 a. m., returning at 9 a. m. and 3 p. m. (fare 1 fr. 50, return 2 fr. 40 c.).

Eaux-Bonnes (2455 ft.), with 812 inhab., is situated at the confluence of two torrents, the Valentin and the Sourde, at the entrance to an extremely picturesque gorge between lofty mountains, which leave a very narrow space between them. Its chief importance, however, is due to the springs of sulphureous sodaic and calcareous waters, in which chloride of sodium is the chief ingredient. These waters are efficacious in throat and bronchial affections and in tubercular consumption. The climate is mild in summer, but in consequence of the altitude the season is short. There are not less than 6000 visitors a year.

The centre of Eaux-Bonnes is the *Jardin Darralde*, a small park planted with fine trees, in which a band plays in the afternoon and evening. Around it are the chief hotels, and at one end is the *Casino*, the terrace of which commands a fine view of the Pic de Ger (p. 145).

Ascending the Grande-Rue beyond the Jardin, we soon reach the principal *Etablissement Thermal*, of no great size, as the waters are seldom taken in baths. There are seven small springs, the most important being the Old Spring (Source Vieille; 89°26' Fahr.), which feeds only the tap of the pump-room. The water has a distinctly sulphureous odour but is less disagreeable to taste than to smell; it should be used with precaution. Farther up, at the end of the village, is a pavilion containing the pump-room of the *Fontaine Froide* (52°4' Fahr.). Opposite are some schools, and to the left, a Protestant Church. The mineral waters rise near here from the *Butte du Trésor*, on which is a kiosque. Near the bridge over the Valentin is the less important *Etablissement Ortig.*

Eaux-Bonnes has fine promenades. The *Promenade Eynard* leads round the Butte du Trésor, which may be reached from the interior of the Etablissement Thermal. The fine *Promenade de l'Impératrice* or *du Gros-Hêtre* diverges from the former behind the Butte, and runs beneath pleasant trees at a uniform height above the valley of the Valentin, for about $1^3/_4$ M. Above the *Cascade de Discoo* it crosses a bridge 80 ft. high, and joins another road, which leads to the fine *Cascade du Gros-Hêtre* (dairy), near a wooden bridge, about $2^1/_4$ M. from the village. We may return hence by the *Promenade du Valentin*, above the preceding, on the left bank of the stream, passing the pretty *Cascade des Eaux-Bonnes.*

On the other side of the village is the *Promenade Horizontale*, for pedestrians only, on the flank of the Gourzy (see below), which affords pretty views of the valley. Beginning at the terrace of the Casino, it extends at present for about a mile, but is to be continued as far as the Eaux-Chaudes road. The *Promenade Gramont*, also on the flank of the Gourzy, ascends in zigzags behind the Casino, as far as the Fontaine Froide. The *Promenade Jacqueminot*, diverging from the last-named, ascends to the first plateau, whence the view is very beautiful.

Excursions.

To EAUX-CHAUDES. (1) By Road, 5 M.; omnibus, see p. 143. We descend by the road to Pau as far as ($2^1/_2$ M.) the parting of the ways mentioned on p. 142. Beyond this point the *Route is one of the most picturesque in the Pyrenees. It is cut out in the rock on the left of the Hourat ('hollow'), the ravine in which the Gave d'Ossau frets 150 ft. below, and it is overhung by rocks of still greater height. At one spot there is a crevasse over which a bridge has been thrown between two rocks. On the other side of the torrent is the old road to Laruns, which descends very rapidly and joins the new road at the Pont Crabé or Pont des Chèvres. — For *Eaux-Chaudes* and excursions into the upper part of the valley see pp. 145-148.

(2) Vià the Gourzy, about $3^1/_2$ hrs., an interesting route which may be made on horseback, but for which a guide is desirable (4-5 fr.). We ascend through woods, in 50 min., to the first plateau to which the Promenade Jacqueminot (see above) leads. The second plateau is 40 min. farther. Here we leave on the left the path to the Pic du Ger (see below), and in 50 min. more reach the third plateau on the summit of the Gourzy (6033 ft.), whence there is a superb panorama, including the Pic de Ger and the majestic Pic du Midi d'Ossau. Thence we descend to the W. by a bad path, also through woods, which in 50 min. more joins the road to the grotto of Eaux-Chaudes (p. 146), about 1 M. from Eaux-Chaudes (p. 145).

To THE PIC DE GER. The usual route leads vià the Gourzy, and takes about 10 hrs. there and back. Part of this most interesting excursion may be accomplished on horseback, but the rest is laborious and the ascent should not be made without a guide (20 fr.) and provisions. Following the Eaux-Chaudes path as far as the second plateau ($1^1/_2$ hr., see above) we there turn to the left and reach (about 3 hrs.) the *Plateau d'Anouillas*, beyond the huts on which horses cannot ascend. Thence we proceed on foot to (1 hr.) the *Plateau de Cardoua* (des Chardons), where there is another hut, beyond which another hour's laborious climb by the *Pambassibé* brings us to the top. This last stage is not only remarkably steep, with a névé above a sheer precipice, but there is also a ridge which must be crossed partly on one's hands and knees and partly astride.

The *Pic de Ger* (8575 ft.), with its two peaks, the second of which is difficult to climb, affords a superb panorama presenting strong contrasts: to the S. a chaos of desolate mountains, and to the N. a sea of verdure in the midst of which are the towns of Tarbes and Pau. The most conspicuous summits visible, from east to west, are, in the foreground, the Latte de Bazen (6105 ft.) and the Pénemédaa (8165 ft.); farther away, to the right, the Pics de Gabizos (8680 ft. and 8805 ft.); then the mountains round the valleys of Gaube and Marcadaou, with the Vignemale (10,795 ft.), the Pic de Balaïtous (10,320 ft.), the Pic Palas (9785 ft.), and a succession of other peaks varying from 8500 to nearly 9000 ft. in height, extending to the famous Pic du Midi d'Ossau (9465 ft.), compared with which the peaks of the Vallée d'Aspe seem tamely uniform. Southwards, to the left of the Pic Amoulat (8515 ft.), which forms part of the Pic de Ger group, the large Lac d'Artouste is seen (p. 146).

To the Pic de Goupey, 7 hrs. there and back, easy, with guide. We follow the above route as far as the (3 hrs.) *Plateau d'Anoutilas*, where we turn to the right. From (1/2 hr.) the *Col de Lurdé* (6400 ft.) is seen the Pic du Midi rising in front, and in 3/4 hr. more we reach the top of the **Pic de Soupey** or *de Cézy* (7245 ft.). It affords a specially fine view, to the S., of the valleys of the Gave de Soussouéou, descending from the Lac d'Artouste (p. 146), and of the Gave de Brousset, as well as the valley of Gabas, with the Pics de Balaïtous, Palas, d'Ossau, etc.

To the Lac d'Anglas and Lac d'Uzious, etc., a fine excursion occupying a whole day (guide and provisions necessary), either viâ the gorge of the Valentin, partially practicable for horses, or viâ the gorge of the Sourde, the Coume d'Aas, etc. The **Lac d'Anglas** (6790 ft.) is a small round lake on a plateau between the buttresses of the Pénemédaa and the Sourins; the **Lac d'Uzious** (6955 ft.), oval in shape, lies a little farther to the S.E. Still higher up are the little *Lac de Laredan* and the *Col d'Uzious* (7325 ft.), whence a charming view is enjoyed.

To the Grand Pic de Gabizos, another fine excursion for one day which may be partly made on horseback (guide and provisions). The best route leads viâ the gorge of the Valentin, *Gourrette*, the *Rochers de las Néras* to the S. E., and the *Pastures of Bourroux*. The **Grand Pic de Gabizos** or *Pic d'Eras-Taillades* (8808 ft.), to the S., is the principal peak of a group in which the *Petit Pic*, or *Pic de Gabizos* properly so called (8680 ft.), ranks second in height. The magnificent panorama resembles that commanded by the Pic de Ger (see above).

To Arrens (*Cauterets*), 26 M. The very interesting carriage-road leads by the gorge of the Valentin and (6 M.) the *Col d'Aubisque* (5610 ft.), then across a desolate but striking tract, passing the *Col d'Arbate*, S. W. of the *Mont Laid* (6205 ft.), and the *Col du Couret* or *de Soulor* (4755 ft.) whence it descends to (13 1/2 M.) *Arrens* (hotel), the principal place in the pretty *Vallée d'Azun*, and thence by the valley of the *Gave d'Arrens*, in which are (20 M.) *Marsous*, (20 1/2 M.) *Aucun*, (21 1/2 M.) *Gaillagos*, (23 M.) *Arcizans-Dessus*, and (24 M.) *Arras*, with the ruined *Château of Castelnau-d'Azun* (14th cent.). *Argelès*, see p. 148. — A footpath, shortening the journey by 6 1/2 M., leads from the end of the gorge of the Valentin over the *Col de Tortes* (5000 ft.), rejoining the road a good 1/2 M. farther on. Another short-cut, at the descent into the Vallée d'Azun, follows the old road to the S.E., by the *Col de Saucède* (5015 ft.). — The easy and interesting ascent of the *Pic de Grum* (6155 ft.) may be made in 20 min. from the Col d'Aubisque.

Other excursions, see pp. 146, 147.

III. Eaux-Chaudes.

Arrival: from Pau, see p. 142; from Eaux-Bonnes, p. 144.

Hotels: de France; Baudot. Charges approximately the same as at Eaux-Bonnes. — **Furnished Houses.** *Caranx; Lanne; Reigbider; Nounuiz; Noguès; Abbadie.*

Café, on the Promenade Henri IV.

Thermal Establishment, see below. Fee for drinking the waters, 6 fr. from June 1st to Sept. 30th, 4 fr. at other seasons. Private bath or douche 1 fr. 25 c., in the general basin 50 c.; douche before or after a bath 1 fr. 75 c.; bath sheet 15, towel 10 c., etc. The above prices are the first-class tariff; the second class is for artizans, etc., the third-class for domestics and workmen.

Omnibus to Eaux-Bonnes, see p. 143. Another leaves Eaux-Chaudes for Eaux-Bonnes, every Sun. and Thurs. at 1 p. m., returning at 6 p. m.

Horse-Hirers and Mounted Guides. *Réchat, Labarthe, Larrouy, Ollivein.* — Guides on foot: *Grangé, Camy* (of Gabas), see below. — Charges, see Eaux-Bonnes.

English Church Service in summer (French Church).

Eaux-Chaudes (2215 ft.) is smaller, but perhaps even more grandly situated than Eaux-Bonnes. It is perched on the right bank of the *Gave d'Ossau* or *de Gabas*, which is so steep that the houses can hardly find standing-room. The waters, sulphureous like most in the Pyrenees, are very efficacious, though less patronised than those of Eaux-Bonnes. The average annual number of bathers is not more than 2000, and life is quieter than at Eaux-Bonnes.

The well-managed *Thermal Establishment*, standing just above the Gave, is a fine building partly constructed of Pyrenean marble. More attention is here paid to bathing than at Eaux-Bonnes; and a public basin ('piscine') has been fitted up. Three of the seven principal springs of Eaux-Chaudes are here in use, viz. the Esquirette which has a double source of supply (95 and 89° Fahr.), the Rey (92°), and the Clot (97°). They are much used in certain maladies of women and in cases of rheumatic neuralgia and chronic rheumatism. The attendants wear the local costume.

Eaux-Chaudes has some fine promenades: the *Promenade Henri IV.* near the baths; the *Promenade d'Argout* and the *Promenade Horizontale*, one above the other on the left bank of the Gave. Two bridges lead thither, one near the bath-house, the other higher up, to the right, outside the village; on this side also is a waterfall. There are two other promenades on the other side, the chief of which is the *Promenade Minvielle*, to the left and not far from the road, with the pump-room of the cold *Minvielle Spring*.

Excursions.

To the Grotto of Eaux-Chaudes, about 2 hrs. there and back. The custodian lives in the village ($1\frac{1}{2}$ fr. each pers., including lights). The rough path ascends to the left of the road to Gabas and for $\frac{1}{2}$ hr. is identical with that to Eaux-Bonnes by the Gourzy (p. 144); then it turns to the right. Prudence should be used in passing from the warm outer air into the very cold cavern. The **Grotto of Eaux-Chaudes**, which is about 1450 ft. deep, is specially remarkable for the torrent which runs through it and forms at its source a high cascade; the guide illuminates it with Bengal lights. There is a tavern at the entrance of the grotto.

To Gabas and to Bious-Artigues (*Pic de Biscaou*), an easy and interesting excursion; 5 and 3 M., carriage-road to Gabas, thence a bridle-path. — The road is a continuation of that from Pau and Eaux-Bonnes to the Spanish frontier (p. 141). It soon crosses the Gave d'Ossau and then steadily ascends the left bank along a most picturesque valley bordered by wooded mountains. After about 1³/₄ M., the path to Aceous over the Col d'Iseye (p. 140) diverges into a valley on the right. Farther on the valley narrows and the grand Pic du Midi d'Ossau comes into view on the right. To the left is one of the routes to the Lac d'Artouste (p. 148). — 5 M. *Gabas* (3090 ft.; *Hôtel des Pyrénées*, *Hôtel du Pic du Midi*, both good; guide, Camy), the last hamlet on French territory, lies at the confluence of the Gaves de Brousset and de Bious, which unite to form the Gave d'Ossau. It is a convenient starting-point for excursions in the upper part of the valley (see below). — Travellers should not fail to ascend the valley of the Gave de Bious to the right, as far as the saw-mill of (1¹/₂ hr.) *Bious-Artigues*, for the sake of the view of the Pic du Midi, the most striking and complete anywhere obtainable. The mountain rears its bare majestic peak in solitary grandeur from the midst of a wide meadow-land which offers a striking contrast to the gloomy pine-forests that clothe the mountain-slopes. — The Pic de Bisoaau (6460 ft.), to the W. of Gabas, is another splendid point of view by reason of its detached situation. The easy ascent (3¹/₂-4 hrs. there and back) is made partly by the road to the saw-mill, which we quit in the valley of Anie, and ascend to the E. The descent may be made in 2 hrs., by a 'couloir' on the N. side. — To *Urdos* and *Le Somport*, see p. 141.

To the Pic du Midi d'Ossau. This ascent, one of the most difficult in the Pyrenees, is only for experienced mountaineers. It occupies a full day and a good guide and provisions must be taken. The route lies by the valley of Gabas (see above) and by the valley of the Gave de Brousset or by that of the Gave de Bious, which skirt and isolate the mountain, the former on the E., the latter on the W. side. In the former case we follow the road to Spain for about 2 hrs. by carriage or on horseback, as far as the *Case de Brousset* (4835 ft.), a ruined inn, whence we ascend to the right for 2 hrs. more (riding still practicable) to the *Col de Pombie* or *de Suzon* (6890 ft.), between the *Pic de Saoubiste* (7245 ft.) on the right and the Pic du Midi on the left. Soon afterwards the difficulties of the ascent begin, but they have been lessened by the fixing of iron bars in the rocks of the three 'cheminées' by which we must climb, the last one overlooking a precipice. — The route by the valley of the Gave de Bious follows the road to Bious-Artigues as far as (¹/₂ M. from Gabas) the *Vallon de Magnabaigt*, to the left, ascends this valley for 1¹/₂ hr., and then mounts by the (1 hr.) *Plateau de Magnabaigt* to the *Col de Pombie* where the above route is joined. — The Pic du Midi d'Ossau (9465 ft.), which is thus attained in 5-6 hrs. from Gabas, is one of the most characteristic granite masses of the Pyrenees, rising precipitously from almost every side, like a gigantic pyramid in ruins, truncated and cleft by some convulsive agency. Its base is hardly more than a mile in diameter while the circle over which its débris are scattered is 10 M. in circumference. The prospect is very extensive, but more grand than beautiful. The principal features are, to the N., besides the *Pic d'Anie* (7910 ft.), which is very near, the Vallée d'Ossau and the plain as far as Pau; to the E., among the High Pyrenees, the Vignemale and Mont-Perdu; to the S., the mountains and plains of Aragon; to the W., the Pic d'Anie, etc. — The *Petit Pic* (9150 ft.), still more difficult than the Grand Pic, is reached by the Col de Peyreget, between the Pic du Midi and the *Pic de Peyreget* (8113 ft.), to the S.

To the Lac d'Artouste (*Pic Palas*, *Pic d'Arriel*, and *Pic de Balaïtous*). A great part of this excursion, which takes a day, is practicable on horseback, by the Col d'Arrius or the valley of the Gave de Soussouéou. By the former route we follow the road to Spain for about 1³/₄ hr. beyond Gabas, ¹/₄ hr. short of the Case de Brousset (see above), and ascend to the left through woods and by pasture ground, to the (1³/₄ hr.) *Col d'Arrius* (6060 ft.), whence the lake is visible below us, and is reached in ³/₄ hr. more. — The other route, a little longer and more laborious, diverges from the Gabas road 2¹/₂ M. from Eaux-Chaudes, crosses the Gave, and ascends by the right bank of the wild *Gorge du Soussouéou*, watered by a torrent that issues from the Lac d'Artouste itself. Halfway (about 3 hrs.) we reach a small plain entered on the left by a road coming from

Eaux-Bonnes viâ the Col de Lurdé (p. 145). Splendid views of the mountains are obtained, especially of the Pic Palas (9760 ft.), the Pic d'Arriel (9200 ft.), and the Balaïtous (see below), from the side of the lake. — The Lac d'Artouste (6445 ft.) is one of the largest in the Pyrenees, having an area of about 120 acres. It is hemmed in on all sides by rocks and mountains which, in combination with the solitude of these high regions, make the scene very impressive. A few huts are passed on the second of the above routes, about 1/2 hr. before reaching the lake; and the French Alpine Club has erected a refuge on the plateau of Arrémoulit. — The Pic d'Arriel (9200 ft.; fine view), rising to the S., on the frontier, may be easily ascended in 2¹/₄-2¹/₂ hrs. from the Col d'Arrius, viâ the (1/4 hr.) little *Lac d'Arrius* and the *Col de Sobe* (8020 ft.), 1 hr. to the W. of the summit. — The Pic Palas, or *de la Palas* (9760 ft.), nearer the Lac d'Artouste but also on the frontier, is difficult to climb, and is inferior as a point of view to both the Pic d'Arriel and the Balaïtous. — The Pic de Balaïtous, or *Bat-Laïtouse* (10,320 ft.), farther to the E., is another difficult peak, ascended in 8 hrs. from the Lac d'Artouste. The route leads viâ (2 hrs.) the *Col d'Arrémoulit* (8055 ft.), between the Arriel and the Palas, and then follows the ridge by a difficult 'couloir' and a dangerous ridge, between two precipices.

To the Baths of Panticosa (Spain), 3 days, allowing one day's visit; a fine excursion on horseback, viâ *Gabas* (p. 147) and the *Col du Pourtalet* (5890 ft.), called also *Col d'Anéou*, on the (13 M.) frontier; then viâ the beautiful *Valley of Roumigas*, the (2 hrs.) large Spanish village of *Sallent* (4105 ft.; Berga; Gonzales), and the poor village of (2 hrs.) *Panticosa*, 6 M. beyond which lie the Baths. The Baths of Panticosa (5575 ft.; *Hôt. d'Espagne*; *Franco-Espagnol*), celebrated for their thermal alkaline and sulphureous waters, are situated on the shores of a blue lake into which four cascades fall from the bare granite mountains which surround it. — The return journey may be made viâ the (2 hrs.) *Port de Marcadaou* (about 8200 ft.) and (7¹/₂ hrs.) *Cauterets* (p. 149), but the route is difficult and a guide is necessary.

22. Cauterets and its Environs.

I. From Lourdes to Cauterets.

19 M. Railway to (13 M.) *Pierrefitte* in 40-50 min. (fares 2 fr. 55, 1 fr. 90, 1 fr. 40 c.). Thence Diligence in the season to (6 M.) *Cauterets*, in 1³/₄-2 hrs. (return ³/₄-1 hr.), for 2 fr. 75 c. (inside or banquette); other vehicles, 1¹/₂ fr. Omnibuses from the larger hotels at Cauterets meet the trains at Pierrefitte (5 fr.). Carriages from the station for 4 pers. and 120 kilos of luggage 14 fr.

Lourdes, see p. 133. Tickets permitting the journey to be broken here, see p. 132. — The railway makes a wide circuit to the E., diverges to the right from the line to Tarbes, and approaches the Gave de Pau and Lourdes at the station of *Soum-de-la-Lanne*. The valley becomes more and more interesting as we proceed. Beyond (4 M.) *Lugagnan* and (7¹/₂ M.) *Bôo-Silhens* we cross to the left bank of the Gave and enter the fertile little plain of Argelès. On the right is a keep, dating from the 14th century.

9¹/₂ M. Argelès (1525 ft.; *Grand-Hôtel du Parc; de France*, well spoken of; *Beau-Séjour*) is a small town of 1733 inhab., prettily situated at the mouth of the Vallée d'Azun (p. 145). The sulphureous waters of Gazost were conducted hither and a *Thermal Establishment* erected in 1885. A handsome new quarter has sprung up beside the railway-station. English Church Service in summer.

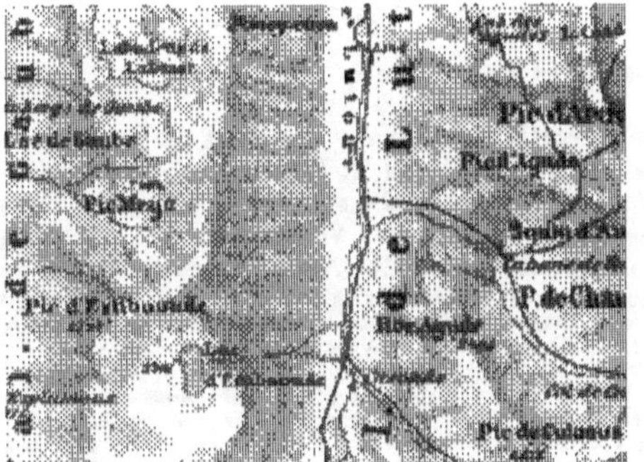

Numerous walks and points of view. Road to Eaux-Bonnes, see
p. 145.

Beyond Argelès we have on the right St. Savin and on the left
Beaucens (see below). — 13 M. **Pierrefitte-Nestalas** (*Gr.-Hôt. de la
Poste; Hôt. de France*, at the station), a village ¹/₂ M. to the S.W.,
where the road from Lourdes viâ Argelès forks, the right branch
going to Cauterets, the left to Luz-St. Sauveur and Barèges.

A road which diverges from the Lourdes route to the left at the end
of the village, leads in 25 min. to St. Savin, passing the little *Chapelle de
Piétat*, of the 16th cent., from which there is a fine view. — The village
of **St. Savin** (*Hotel*) is built round the celebrated abbey of that name
and should be visited on account of its fine Romanesque *Church*, which,
with the exception of the 14th cent. steeple, dates from the 11-12th centuries. It contains two noteworthy paintings of the 15th cent., in nine
compartments, representing the history of St. Savin, the hermit, and also
his tomb, of the Romanesque period, surmounted by a rich pyramidal
canopy of the 14th century. The chapter-house and other parts of the
abbey are also extant.

On the other side of the valley, also visited from Pierrefitte, is the
(³/₄ hr.) village of **Beaucens**, with a large ruined *Castle* of the 12-16th cent.,
and a small thermal establishment. The road thither diverges to the
left from the Barèges route, a good ¹/₂ M. from Pierrefitte.

The *Road to Cauterets, one of the finest in the country, is
admirably constructed, like all the roads in the Pyrenees. It leaves
the road to Luz-St. Sauveur and Barèges (RR. 23, 24) to the left,
in the valley of the Gave de Pau, and ascends in a wide and at first
steep curve to the valley of the *Gave de Cauterets*, affording a fine
retrospective view of Pierrefitte and the valley of Argelès. At the
top, to the right, is an argentiferous lead-mine. As we descend, the
Péguère, the height above Cauterets, soon comes into view. About
1¹/₄ M. from Pierrefitte we cross the Gave in order to avoid the
dangerous declivities of the right bank, along which the road originally led as far as the *Pont de Mediabat*, about halfway. Then
we thread a wild defile in which the road is at places cut out of
the rock and supported by walls on the side of the ravine along
which the torrent chafes. On both sides rise steep mountains, partly
clothed with wood. One of the most curious spots is the *Limaçon*,
a chaos of fallen rocks. Farther on the valley expands gradually
into a small cultivated plain.

II. Cauterets.

Hotels. Grand-Hôtel Continental, Gr.-Hôt. d'Angleterre, Boulevard
Latapie-Flurin, near the Esplanade, large and fine houses of the first class;
the latter is a dépendance of the Hôtel Gassion at Pau (same charges,
p. 129; omn. to Pierrefitte 5 fr.); Gr.-Hôt. du Boulevard, same Boulevard;
Gr.-Hôt. des Promenades, on the Esplanade, one of the best situated. —
In the town: Gr.-Hôt. du Parc; Hôt. de la Paix; de Paris, Place St.
Martin, well spoken of, R. 3-5, L. ¹/₂, B. 1, déj. 3¹/₂, D. 4, pens. 10-12 fr.;
Richelieu, Rue de la Railière, close by; Hôt. de France, Rue St. Louis
and Rue Richelieu; de Londres (8 fr.), des Ambassadeurs, Rue Richelieu;
de l'Univers, Rue de la Fontaine, beside the church, 7-8¹/₂ fr.; etc. —
Furnished Apartments are abundant, the town being able, it is said, to
accommodate 10,000 strangers at a time. Among others: *Chalet des Bains*,

near the Etab. des Œufs; *Villa Villeneuve, Maisons Pimerin, Toye, Bahy,
Genthieu*, Boulevard Latapie-Flurin; *Lannigran, Camman*, Avenue du Ma-
melon-Vert, parallel to the above Boulevard; *Amade*, Place de la Mairie;
Hôtel de Russie, Rue de Belfort, to the right beyond the Mairie; *Quellaien,
Duhourcau*, and *Marty*, Rue St. Louis, near the Place St. Martin; *Mayou,
Bérot, Byasson, Cabrols, Flurin, Danos, Dubertrand, Béry, Laborde, Vignau,
Bégué*, Rue de la Raillère, near the Place St. Martin; *Hôtel des Princes,
Fabères, Villeneuve, Bordenave, Lousteau*, etc., Rue Richelieu. — On the
whole prices are high, as much as 12 francs being charged for a room at
the first-class hotels during the height of the season (from mid-June to
mid-Sept.), 4 fr. for déjeuner, and 5 for dinner. Other hotels charge from
8 to 12 fr. a day (déj. 3-3$\frac{1}{2}$, D. 3-4 fr.).

Cafés. *Du Casino des Œufs; Café Anglais*, Boulevard Latapie-Flurin;
Grand Café, Place St. Martin; etc.

Thermal Establishments. *Drinking:* Subscription for 25 days from
June 1st to June 19th 5 fr., from June 20th to June 30th 10 fr., from July
1st to August 31st 15 fr., from Sept. 1st to Sept. 30th 6 fr., and from Oct.
1st to May 31st 3 fr. — *Baths and Douches:* 25 c. to 3 fr. according to the
time of year, the hour, and the establishment.

Cabs. Drive in the town, 2 pers. 1, 4 pers. 1$\frac{1}{2}$ fr.; ascent to La
Raillère, 3-4 fr.; to Mauhourat, Petit St. Sauveur, and Le Pré, 3$\frac{1}{2}$ and
5 fr.; to Le Bois 5 and 6 fr.; descent from La Raillère, 1$\frac{1}{2}$ and 2 fr. —
Per hour, in the town, 2$\frac{1}{2}$ and 3$\frac{1}{2}$ fr.; outside the town, 5 and 6 fr.
the first hr. and 3 and 4 fr. per hr. afterwards.

Omnibus. To Pierrefitte, see p. 148; to La Raillère, 75 c. up, and
25 c. down.

Carriages, Horses, and Donkeys for hire in large numbers. Carriage, per
day 20 to 25 fr. (bargaining necessary). — Tariff for horses indicated
below at the beginning of each excursion. Donkeys are usually 1/3 cheaper
than horses.

Guides. These number about 60 and are divided into two classes,
the first class having a white cloth crown above their badge. The best
mountain-guides are *J.-P.* and *Dom. Latapie, Dom. Pont, Pierre, Jean-Marie,*
and *Dom. Bordenave, Jos. Barrère, Paul Batan, Paul, Jean,* and *Math. Genthieu*. The charges are given at the head of each excursion. The usual
charge is 15 fr. a day, and the guide's provisions, except on the return
journey.

Casino, at the Thermes des Œufs. Subscription, including reserved
seats at entertainments: in the middle of the season, for 1, 2, 3 and 4 weeks,
23, 42, 60, and 75 fr.; cheaper at beginning and end of season (see bills).
Seats in the theatre: in the middle of the season, reserved, 4 fr.; front
row, 3 fr.

Post and Telegraph Office, at the Hôtel de Ville.

English Church Service in summer (French Church).

Cauterets (3055 ft.) is a small town of 1685 inhab., very beautifully situated in a valley encompassed by lofty mountains and on
the banks of the torrent of the same name. The town contains
nothing more noteworthy than the magnificent hotels in the new
quarter to the W., near the Esplanade, and this promenade itself
with the Etablissement des Œufs (view, see p. 152), to which perhaps may be added the new Gothic church. As a thermal station,
however, it ranks amongst the first not only in the Pyrenees, but in
the whole of France; while it is also one of the chief centres for
excursions in the High Pyrenees. Though the season only lasts
from June to October inclusive, the town is visited annually by
about 20,000 patients and tourists.

The centre of the town is the *Place St. Martin*, at the end of the

Rue Richelieu, the continuation of the Pierrefitte road, and the adjoining *Place de la Mairie*. These squares are the termini for the public conveyances. From the former diverge the streets leading to the chief bathing-establishments, except the Etablissement des Œufs, which is situated on the Esplanade, to the left of the farther side of the Place de la Mairie and of the Gave. The Mairie contains a new *Relief-Plan of the Central Pyrenees* (1 : 5000), by M. Wallon.

The WATERS of Cauterets contain chiefly sulphur and sodium, but there are also sulphate and alkaline waters. They are supplied by 24 *Springs*, several of which are very copious. They are, in fact, the most copious in the Pyrenees, yielding about 440.000 gallons per day. They vary greatly in temperature (61 to 131° Fahr.) and even in composition, though not so much in this latter respect as the waters of Bagnères-de-Luchon (p. 176). Cauterets possesses nine establishments, admirably arranged for the requirements of drinking, bathing, douches, inhalation, and pulverization.

The THERMES DES ŒUFS, called also simply *Les Œufs*, are the principal and the most remarkable of these establishments. This huge building was erected in 1867-69 at the foot of the wooded slopes of the Péguère and between the Promenades de l'Esplanade and des Lacets (p. 152). It is fed by the six *Sources des Œufs*, about 1¼ M. to the S., which supply no less than 132,000 gallons a day. It contains a swimming-bath of running water, 22 yds. long and 9 yds. wide. The waters of this establishment are principally used in the treatment of chlorosis, anæmia, and diseases of the skin and mucous membranes. The springs have a temperature of 131° Fahr., but at the buvette of the establishment the water is only 113"; at the buvette beside the springs (p. 150) 129°. The offices of the company that rents the waters are also at Les Œufs, while the first floor is occupied by the *Casino*, which comprises reading and card rooms, a café-restaurant, and a theatre.

The THERMES DE CÉSAR ET DES ESPAGNOLS, to the S.E. of the town, at the end of a street leading from the Place St. Martin, occupy a plain building in the neo-classic style, dating from 1844. The baths here are fed on the left by the *Source de César* (118° Fahr.), so named in remembrance of an alleged visit of Cæsar to Cauterets; on the right by the *Source des Espagnols* (116° Fahr.), both of which issue a little higher up from the Montagne de Peyraoute. These waters, the most powerful in Cauterets, are chiefly used in the treatment of chronic diseases of the respiratory organs and in scrofulous and syphilitic affections, skin diseases, and rheumatism. The establishment is open all the year round.

The NÉOTHERMES or *Bains du Rocher-Rieumisel*, constructed in 1863 and enlarged in 1879, are situated in a pretty garden, about 200 yds. to the N. of the preceding. They may be reached directly by a passage through the Hôtel du Parc. They are fed by three springs, viz. those of *César-Nouveau* (113° F.), *Le Rocher* (104° F.), which contains iron, and *Rieumiset* (61° F.). These waters are specially adapted to cutaneous and rheumatic affections for persons of nervous and irritable temperament.

Higher up, on the slope of the Montagne de Peyraoute, are the less important establishments of *Pauze-Vieux* and *Pauze-Nouveau* (the second closed at present).

The ETABLISSEMENT DE LA RAILLÈRE, the most important of all, is situated nearly a mile to the S. of the town on the road (omnibus, see p. 150) on the right bank, forming a continuation of the Rue de la Raillère; but there is a short-cut for pedestrians beginning on the Esplanade. The establishment has been rebuilt, with galleries and promenades. It is situated 3640 ft. above the sea-level (580 ft. above Cauterets), on a declivity of the mountain covered with fallen rocks (raillère). It is built over the three springs which feed it (103°, 100° and 91° Fahr.) and which are so abundant that even horses are treated. In the cure of diseases of the respiratory organs it vies with Eaux-Bonnes (p. 142). It is open from 6 to 11 a. m. and from 2 to 5 p. m. Beside it is now the *Etablissement du Bois Inférieur.*

The Raillère commands a good view, but a still finer prospect is enjoyed from the next buvette where two small waterfalls are in sight.

Still more distant are the *Buvette de Mauhourat* (122° Fahr.) and the *Burette des Œufs* (129°); the *Etablissement du Petit-St. Saureur* (111°), the *Etablissement du Pré* (108°), an unpretending establishment independent of the others (buvette gratis); the *Petit Mauhourat* (121°); the *Source des Yeux* (68°); and finally, higher up, the *Etablissement du Bois* (109° and 91°), the most remote (3670 ft.) but highly esteemed for the cure of rheumatism. The Cascade de Cérisey (p. 154) lies only ¼ hr. higher up.

Cauterets has fine promenades. The *Esplanade des Œufs* is the favourite resort of visitors during the concerts which are given at 1 and at 8.30 p. m., and it is flanked by little shops of all kinds.

The Esplanade is an excellent point from which to take one's bearings, before starting on excursions from Cauterets. The *Péguère*, to the S., behind Les Œufs, has already been mentioned. Beyond the *Raillère* is the *Pic de Hourmégas*, separated from the Péguère by the *Vallée de Jéret*, in which is the road to the Lac de Gaube, etc. To the left of the Hourmégas is the *Vallée de Lutour*, on the crest of the opposite side of which rise several bare peaks, with patches of snow even in summer. The chief of these is the *Pic d'Ardiden*, on the other side of which is St. Sauveur; then from E. to W., above the town, the *Pic de Pène-Nère*, the *Pic de Viscos*, the *Pic de Caballiros*, to the left of the valley of the Gave de Cauterets, and the *Monné*, separated from the Péguère by the *Vallée de Cambasque*, in which is the Lac Bleu, etc.

On the slope of the *Péguère* (ascent, see p. 156) extends the *Promenade des Lacets* or *de Cambasque*, which is not fatiguing and affords a fine view at the exit from the wood, about 25 min. from Les Œufs. The road leading to the Raillère route diverges to the left, about ¼ M. farther on.

The *Promenade du Mamelon -Vert* continues the avenue of the
same name down the valley. It is deficient in shade. At the end
we turn to the right, cross the Gave, and regain the town by the
Pierrefitte road. The *Mamelon -Vert* is the name given to the knoll
on the right, between the promenade and the Gave; it commands a
fine view of the head of the valley. — In the town itself, above the
Pierrefitte road and near the Néothermes, is a pretty and shady *Park*
now somewhat neglected, though still a resort of the visitors. —
Above this passes the road which leads, on the slope of the
Montagne de Peyraoute, to the (1³/₄ M.) hamlet of *Canséru*, well
shaded in the afternoon and offering beautiful views. We may
descend hence to the Pierrefitte road, which we reach near the
junction with the Mamelon-Vert road. — Still higher is the road
to the *Grange de la Reine Hortense*, issuing from the Etablissement de Pauze-Vieux. It is identical with that to the Col de Riou
(p. 158). The grange (barn), which is reached in ¹/₂ hr., owes its
name to the fact that Queen Hortense, when a visitor to Cauterets,
was once detained at it by a storm.

III. Excursions.

To THE MONNÉ, 3¹/₂-4 hrs., 6¹/₂ hrs. there and back; an easy
excursion, practicable on horseback; guide 12 fr., horse 12 fr.
Pedestrians turn to the left from the Avenue du Mamelon-Vert and
skirt the Péguère from E. to W., by the (³/₄ hr.) *l'allée de Cambasque*,
cross the torrent of that name, also called Paladère, and ascend
to the (1³/₄ hr.) *Plateau des Cinquets* (5725 ft.; refreshments),
1 hr. from the top. — The bridle-path follows the road to the
Raillère, and crossing the bridge, turns to the right and skirts the
flank of the Péguère until (³/₄ hr.) it joins the preceding path. The
horses must be left at the inn, about 450 ft. below the summit. —
The Monné or *Soum de Monné* (8935 ft.) is one of the nearest and
most conspicuous mountains seen from Cauterets, for which it
serves as a kind of barometer, the weather being foretold from the
state of the mists in which it is often enveloped. The S. side, towards the Val du Lys, is precipitous, but the N. side descends in
a gentle slope towards the valley of Labat-de-Bun, and ends in a
slaty crest, from which there is a wide view, extending W. to the
head of the Val d'Azun; N. over the flanks of the Cabaliros (see
below) to the plains of Tarbes and Béarn; E. to the Pic du Midi de
Bigorre, the Néouvielle, and Mont-Perdu; and S. to the Vignemale
and the Balaïtous. In the middle distance, to the S., is the Lac
Bleu or Lac d'Illéou (p. 154).

To the CABALIROS, 4 hrs., there and back 6 hrs.; guide 10 fr.,
horse (see below) 10 fr. We follow the Promenade du Mamelon-
Vert for about ¹/₂ M., then turn to the left behind the shed of a

(1 hr.) *Plateau d'Esponne* (refreshments). Thence we gain the (1/2 hr.) E. buttresses of the Monné, beyond which the ascent becomes more difficult. After passing a (1/2 hr.) slaty terrace we reach the (1 hr.) *Col de Contente* (6940 ft.; fine view), on which is an inn. Horses can ascend still farther, though the guides sometimes assert the contrary. The rest of the climb is easy. — The rounded **Cabaliros** (7655 ft.) is the principal summit to the N. of Cauterets. It is crowned by an ordnance-survey tower. The *Panorama from the top, one of the finest in the Pyrenees, resembles that from the Monné, but excels it as it includes the valley of Argelès.

To the Lac Bleu or Lac d'Illéou, 5 hrs. on foot, 4 hrs. on horseback, there and back; guide 10, horse 8 fr. We take the route to the Monné as far as the Plateau de Cambasque (see above); then, following the valley, we pass (3 hrs.) in front of the fine *Cascade d'Illéou* and farther on the little *Lac Noir*. — The Lac Bleu or *Lac d'Illéou* is 6515 ft. above the sea and covers nearly 30 acres. Its lonely situation and wild surroundings contrast strikingly with the deep blue tint of its limpid waters. To the E. rises the *Pic de Nets* (8025 ft.). The return may be made to the S.E. by the *Pont d'Espagne* (see below); it thus requires 4 1/2 hrs., and the guide is paid 5 fr. extra.

*To the Lac de Gaube *(Pic Péguère)*, 2 1/2 hrs. on foot, 4 1/4- 4 1/2 hrs. there and back; guide (not needed) 8, horse 8 fr. This is one of the favourite excursions from Cauterets, as far at least as the Cascade de Cérisey, and there is a carriage-road as far as the Pont d'Espagne, beyond which the road is continued in the valley of Marcadaou (p. 156). Passing the Raillère and the other establishments in the upper part of the valley, we reach the *Val de Jéret*, on the right, and skirt its torrent, the bed of which is almost blocked with huge boulders. The mountain on the opposite side is the Péguère (see below). Farther on, beyond the Etablissement du Bois and a small cascade, the roar of the (1 1/4 hr.) imposing **Cascade de Cérisey* (4050 ft. above the sea-level) becomes audible. The stream is split into two by a mass of rock from either side of which it falls into a deep abyss between two walls of rock. The best time to see it is between 10 o'clock and noon, when rainbows are formed above it by the sun. There are two more cascades of less importance farther on. We traverse striking scenery to (about 3/4 hr. beyond the Cascade) the *Pont d'Espagne* (4880 ft.; Hotel and Restaurant), a primitive bridge at which there is another cascade and where the torrent and valley of Marcadaou debouch. For this valley and the excursions in it see p. 156. — The path to the (3/4 hr.) Lac de Gaube, rather laborious for the first 1/4 hr., continues to ascend the left bank of the torrent. The scenery becomes more and more wild and at last there appears before us the Vignemale with its glacier. The **Lac de Gaube** (5865 ft.) is about 800 yds. long and 350 yds. wide, with an area of about 40 acres, in the middle of a wide and bleak basin formed by the bare sides of the *Pic Meya* (8080 ft.) on the E. and the *Pic de Gaube* (7540 ft.) to the W., etc. It abounds in trout and is fed by the glacier of the Vignemale, to the S. (see below). On the bank of the lake stand an inn (fixed tariff) and a monument in memory of a young Englishman and his wife who were drowned in the lake in 1832.

To THE PÉGUÈRE, 3¹/₂ hrs., there and back 6 hrs.; guide 8 fr. We follow the above route to (1¹/₄ hr.) the Cascade de Cérisey, a little beyond which is a bridge, with a placard, indicating the forest-path to the Péguère. This route ascends in zigzags above precipices 1650 ft. high, on the S. of the mountain, and reaches (¹/₂ hr.) the last spring (4395 ft.) on this slope. From the point (5250 ft.), ¹/₂ hr. farther up, where the road forks, we ascend the ravine of the *Lavune,* by means of paths, difficult to find without a guide, and which cease before the summit is reached. — The **Pic Péguère** (7175 ft.) is the wooded mountain which rises above Cauterets behind the Thermes des Œufs, and which appears in the vista of the valley as we come from Pierrefitte. A magnificent view is commanded by the paths at a height of 6500 ft. above the sea, or 3445 ft. above the town. To the E. and W. the view extends into the valleys of Jéret and Cambasque, but it is more or less limited by the higher peaks that bound these valleys, as well as by those of the chain to the S. of the Péguère.

To THE VIGNEMALE, 2 days (1 day from Gavarnie, see p. 164), the night being spent at the Lac de Gaube, whence it is ascended in 5-7 hrs. The ascent is laborious and only adapted to experienced climbers with good guides. A single tourist should take two guides. Rope and axe necessary. Guide, 30 fr. for one day or for two. Riding is practicable as far as the Hourquette d'Ossoue (col), and thence, on the return, to Gavarnie. — To the *Lac de Gaube,* see p. 154. Pedestrians may shorten the journey by rowing up the lake (1 fr. each). Thence we continue to ascend beside the torrent, which forms several cascades, the chief of which is the *Cascade d'Esplumous* or *de Splumouse,* 1³/₄ hr. from the inn on the lake. The ascent of the Pic de Chabarrou (p. 156), on the right, is usually made from the second cascade, beside which is a hut. Farther on we reach the *Oulettes du Vignemale* or *de Gaube* (7210 ft.), the last terrace in the valley, 1 hr. beyond the chief cascade. Hence we have a grand view of the N. glacier and the precipices of the mountain, which rears itself to a sheer height of more than 3000 ft. To the left rise the Pic d'Araillé and the Pic de Labassa, both ascended from this side (p. 157). From this point to the Vignemale there is a choice of two routes. One leads to the S.E. to (1 hr.) the *Hourquette d'Ossoue* or *Col du Vignemale* (8885 ft.), either by the base of the glacier or, which is much better, by the buttresses of the Araillé. Beyond the col the *Glacier d'Ossoue,* or E. glacier of the Vignemale, extends on the right upwards of 1¹/₂ M. in length and ¹/₂ M. in width. It is advisable not to cross this glacier, but to skirt it so as to avoid the most dangerous part, which will take 1¹/₂ hour. Finally we cross a little bit of it, using the rope; then the névé between the *Montferrat* or *Cerbillona* on the left, and the *Pique Longue* on the right, arriving in ¹/₂ hr. at the foot of the latter, the principal peak, which is climbed in 20 min. more across loose red slate. — The second route, longer by about 1³/₄ hr., but easier, leads to the S.W. over the (1 hr.) *Col des Mulets* or *des Oulettes* (7800 ft.), on the frontier, whence bending to the left, we continue at the same level for 20 min. as far as the *Clot de la Houet,* a ravine with a very dangerous glacier (falling stones) which should be avoided, whence we climb the (2 hrs. 20 min.) *Montferrat* and so reach the névé of the Glacier d'Ossoue; thence to the foot of the *Pique Longue* (¹/₄ hr.; see above). — The **Vignemale** (10,820 ft.) is the highest summit in the French Pyrenees,

the Monts-Maudits with the Néthou (11,160 ft.) and the Maledetta (11,005 ft.), the Pic Posets (11,045 ft.), the Mont-Perdu (10,660 ft.), and the Cylindre (10,920 ft.) being in Spain. It rises in nine peaks, the chief of which is the Pique Longue, separated by an impassable chasm from the *Petit Vignemale* (10,515 ft.), which may be ascended in 1½ hr. from the Hourquette d'Ossoue. The panorama from the Vignemale is most extensive, but it only includes a chaotic assemblage of mountains, hard to identify at this height, except those of the Marboré group. The Grottes Russell, near the *Col de Cerbillona* (10,500 ft.), 20 min. below the summit, have unfortunately been buried by the glacier, but they are to be restored, and a new grotto has already been excavated 260 ft. higher up. — The descent may be made on the Gavarnie side (see p. 164).

To the **Valley of Marcadaou** or *Marcadau*, 3½ hrs. on foot, 2½-3 hrs. on horseback as far as the Escalier de la Pourtère, there and back 6 or 5 hrs., 1 hr. more to the Cabane de Marcadaou; guide (not needed) and horse 12 and 15 fr. — To the (2 hrs.) *Pont d'Espagne*, see p. 154. We cross the bridge and ascend beside the Gave de Marcadaou as far as the (¾ hr.) *Plateau de Cayan* (5255 ft.), a charming and solitary region amidst lofty mountains, covered with woods affording a retreat to bears and heath-cocks. Path to the Lac Bleu, see p. 154. Farther on we leave to the left the *Vallon de Poueytrenous* or *Poueytrémous*, which ascends towards the Pic de Chabarrou (see below), cross the torrent, and reach the (¾ hr.) *Escalier de la Pourtère* (5510 ft.). We recross the torrent and reach in ½ hr. the *Cabane de Marcadaou* (5905 ft.), in the meadows of the *Pla de la Gole*. Hence the Som de Baccimaille (see below) is seen to advantage.

The hut, which has room for six persons, is an excellent starting-point for other excursions, especially for the tolerably easy ascent of the *Som de Baccimaille* or *Grande Fache* (9905 ft.), which requires 3¾ hrs., and for the difficult ascent of the *Pic d'Enfer*, or *Quijeda de Pandillos* (10,310 ft.), in Spain, which requires 4¾ or 7 hrs., according to the route taken from the Port de Marcadaou (see below), the shorter one leading by the glacier to the N., the longer by the Col de Sallent. These excursions should, of course, not be made without a guide.

The track along the valley is continued to the (2 hrs.) *Port de Marcadaou* (8370 ft.), on the frontier, whence the *Baths of Panticosa* (p. 148) may be reached in 2½-3 hrs., with guide.

To the Pic de Chabarrou, about 7 hrs., 4½ hrs. from the Lac de Gaube; guide 15 fr., or, including the return by the Valley of Marcadaou, 20 fr. Following the route to the Vignemale as far as the second cascade beyond the Lac de Gaube (p. 154), we there take a path to the right (W.) which leads to (1 hr.) the beautiful *Lac de Chabarrou* (7485 ft.). Thence we ascend straight to the summit in 1¾ hr., by a very steep slope, over debris, a short névé, and some precipitous rocks. The Pic de Chabarrou (8950 ft.) is one of the finest ascents in the neighbourhood of Cauterets, both on account of its situation and of its height. From the top the neighbouring Vignemale is particularly well seen, and beyond it the mountains of Spain. The view extends from the Pic d'Anie to Mont-Perdu and the Pic du Midi de Bigorre. — The descent may be made on the N. by the Valley of Marcadaou, viâ the (½ hr.) *Hrèche* (8920 ft.), the *Valley* and the (1½ hr.) *Cabane de Poueytrenous*, the (½ hr.) *Plateau de Cayan* (see above), and the (¾ hr.) *Pont d'Espagne* (p. 154).

To the Pic d'Araille and the Pic de Labassa, about 6½ and 8½ hrs.; guide 15 and 20 fr. We follow the Vignemale route as far as the (5¼ hrs.) *Oulettes de Vignemale*, where we turn to the left, between the slopes of the two mountains, ascending to the left for the first named peak, and to the right for the second. We pass through gaps, respectively 3/4 and 1 3/4 hr. from the Oulettes. The Pic d'Araillé (9000 ft.) is easily ascended in less than 1/2 hr. from its gap and commands a fine view, in which the Vignemale is conspicuous. — The Pic Labassa, *La Sède*, or *La Sèbe* (9780 ft.), is on the other hand a difficult ascent, in the higher part at least, which requires nearly 1 1/2 hr. from the gap. Its greater height commands a finer view than the Araillé; and even the col commands a beautiful survey. The descent may be made on the side next the valley of Lutour (see below) to the (1 - 1 1/4 hr.) Lac d'Estom.

To the **Valley of Lutour**, 3 hrs. to the Lac d'Estom, there and back 5 1/2 hrs.; guide (unnecessary) 8, horse 6 fr. This valley opens to the left at the Buvette de Mauhourat (p. 152), at the confluence of the torrents of Marcadaou and Lutour. A little higher up is a *Cascade*, where horses ford the stream, while pedestrians ascend straight on. The steepest part of the path is passed within 1 hr. from the confluence, and the footpath rejoins the bridle-path by means of another bridge. About 2 hrs. from Cauterets we pass a dairy, known as *La Fruitière*. The path by which the Pic d'Ardiden is ascended from this side (see below) diverges to the left; the scenery becomes striking. The slope on the right is well-wooded, while that on the left is seamed and scarred, and terminates in a rugged rocky crest, which culminates in the Pic d'Ardiden. We recross to the left bank at a triple *Cascade*, and the bridle-path ends shortly afterwards at the foot of a crag, which we must ascend to reach the lake. — The **Lac d'Estom** (6205 ft.) is a little smaller than the Lac de Gaube, but no less picturesque. It is colder and contains no fish. On the bank is an inn.

Farther up to the right is a path to the (1 hr.) *Hourquette d'Araillé*, by which we may ascend (with guide) the *Pic d'Araillé* (see above) or reach (about 4 hrs.) the *Lac de Gaube*, thence returning to Cauterets.

Still higher up the valley lie seven lakes of different sizes, known as the *Lacs d'Estom-Soubiran*. About 3 hrs. are required to reach the end of the valley, which is picturesque throughout. From the end we ascend in 1/2 hr. to the *Col d'Estom-Soubiran*, which commands a good view of the Vignemale. — To Gavarnie viâ this Col and the Col de Mallerouge, see below.

To the Pic d'Ardiden viâ Peyraoute, 5 hrs., there and back 8 hrs.; guide 20 fr. This expedition is well worth making. We ascend past the (1/2 hr.) Grange de la Reine Hortense (p. 153) and farther on, to the right (S.W.) towards the crest of the mountain, then turn to the S.E. to the (2 hrs.) *Cabane de Peyraoute*, to which point riding is practicable; and thence to the *Col d'Ardiden*. We next enter a gorge full of fallen rocks and containing the (1 hr.) *Lacs d'Ardiden*, the largest of which (1/2 hr.), the *Lac Grand* (7805 ft.), affords a magnificent spectacle. Thence, crossing some snow, we gain the N. slope of the peak, the ascent of which is toilsome, and in 1 hr. more reach the top of the Pic d'Ardiden (9805 ft.), which is composed, like its sides, of a chaos of rocks produced by the disintegration of the granite. There is a magnificent view of the plain, and the surrounding valleys, as well as of the Balaïtous, Vignemale, the mountains round Gavarnie, Néouvielle, etc. — The descent may be made to Cauterets viâ the *Valley of Lutour* (see above) in 3-3 1/2 hrs. The ascent is also sometimes made from this side. Another descent leads to (4 hrs.) Luz (p. 168), viâ the lakes mentioned above, the *Col d'Ardets*, and the *Vallée du Bernazaou*.

To Gavarnie by the Mountains (route viâ Pierrefitte and

St. Sauveur, see p. 148 and below). — 1. *Vià the Lac de Gaube*, about
10 hrs., guide 15 fr. (unnecessary), and as much for the return. The
whole expedition may now be made on horseback. We follow the
Vignemale route as far as the *Hourquette d'Ossoue* (about 6 hrs.;
p. 132) and thence descend to the S. towards the (¹/₂ hr.) *Gave
d'Ossoue*, the right bank of which we follow. To the left is the
Cascade des Oulettes, and farther on are the (¹/₂ hr.) *Bassin des
Oulettes* (6100 ft.), the *Pas des Oulettes*, the (¹/₂ hr.) *Plan de Millas*
(5715 ft.), and the (1 hr.) *Cabanes de Saussé* (5480 ft.). Thence
the path, which remains on the right bank, is practicable for
horses. It descends rapidly through wood, and crosses the torrent
¹/₂ hr. before *Gavarnie* (p. 162). — 2. *Vià the Valley of Lutour*,
about 11 hrs.; guide as above. There are two exits from the head
of the valley: (1) The *Col d'Estom-Soubiran* (6¹/₂-7 hrs.; see p. 157),
whence we descend into the *Vallée d'Ossoue* (see above). (2) The
Col de Mallerouge (9315 ft.), 1 hr. to the E. of the first Lac d'Estom-
Soubiran, and to the N. of the *Pic de Mallerouge* (9740 ft.). Thence
we keep to the S. vià the (¹/₂ hr.) *Col de Houle* (8860 ft.) and the
(¹/₂ hr.) *Cabane de Salent* (6510 ft.), and thence again to the E. by
the valley of the *Gave d'Aspe* (chaos), and finally once more to the
S. to *Gavarnie* (see p. 162).

To the Pic de Viscos, 3¹/₂ hrs., there and back 5¹/₂ hrs., a little less
on horseback; shorter from St. Sauveur (p. 160). Guide 10 fr. An ascent
of 2 hrs. takes us by the Grange de la Reine Hortense (p. 155) to the *Col
de Riou* (6375 ft.), on which there is a small inn, ¹/₂ hr. from the top of
the *Pène-Nère* (about 8560 ft.), whence also the view is very extensive. Thence
following to the N. the E. slope of the mountain, we reach in ³/₄ hr. the
foot of the peak and easily climb in a N.W. direction to the *Pic de
Viscos* (7025 ft.). The view is finest on the side next the plain, and
extends over the mountains as far as the Balaïtous, the Vignemale, Mont
Perdu, and Néouvielle. Among the nearer peaks, the Caballiros in the W.,
the Mound in the S., and the Bergons in the S.E. attract attention.

To Luz and St. Sauveur over the Col de Riou (by the road, see
p. 148 and below), about 4 hrs.; guide and horse, 8 fr. each as far as the
col, 15 fr. to Luz, 10 only for the guide if he is on horseback. As far
as the Col de Riou, see above. We descend by pasture-grounds and the
Granges de Cureilles (4185 ft.), to the little village of *Grust*, whence proceeding to the N.E. vià *Sazos* and *Sassis*, we reach Luz or St. Sauveur in
about ³/₄ hour.

23. Luz, St. Sauveur, and their Environs.

I. From Lourdes to Luz and St. Sauveur (Barèges).

Railway to (13 M.) *Pierrefitte-Nestalas* as for Cauterets (p. 148), thence
road (8-9 M.) and diligence (3 fr.) in the season in 1³/₄ hour. Carriages
also during the season as for Cauterets.

Our road leaves the Cauterets road on the right, beyond Pierrefitte, crosses the Gave de Cauterets to the village of *Soulom*, and
a short distance farther the Gave de Pau. Here, about 1¹/₄ M. from
Pierrefitte, begins the *Gorge de Luz, resembling that on the Cauterets road. It is about 5 M. long and the road in many places is cut

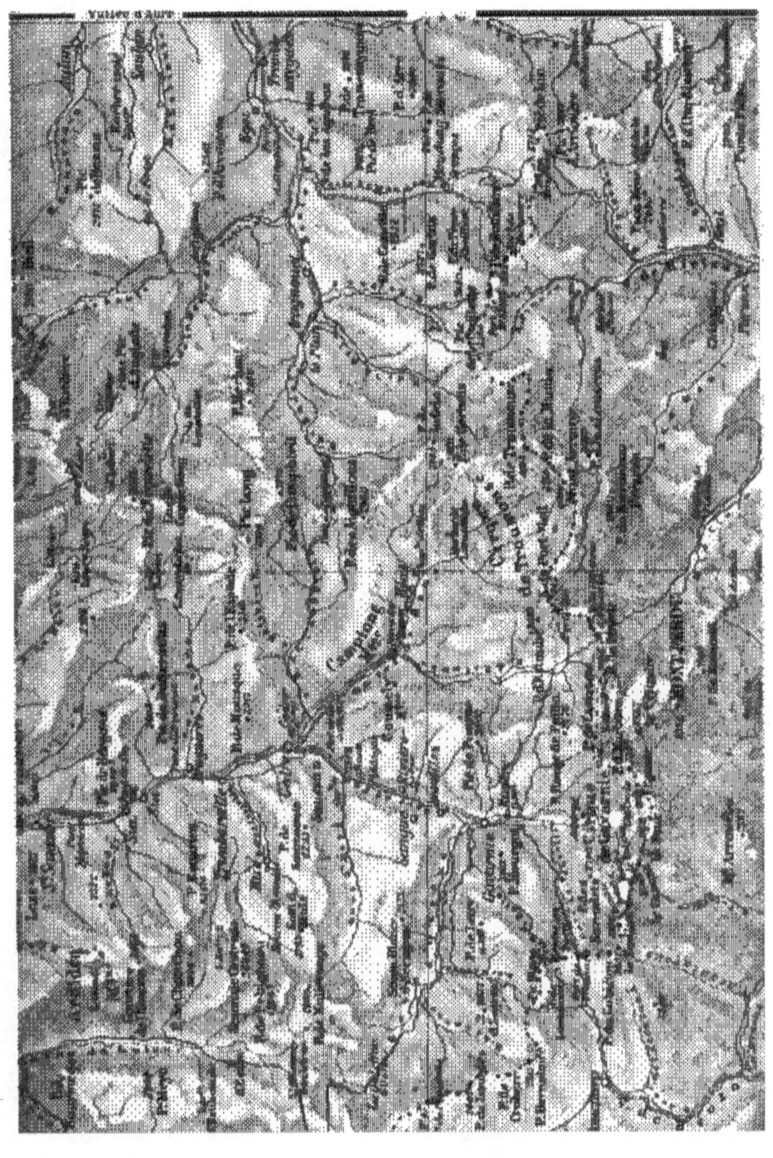

out along the rocks or supported on walls built at the side of the torrent. After about 2½-3 M. we pass, on the right, the *Pont de l'Echelle* and the *Pont d'Arsimpé*, neither of which we cross as the opposite bank is exposed to avalanches of stones. The road gradually ascends until it is about 260 ft. above the stream. — 4½ M. *Pont de la Crabe*, a lofty bridge over a ravine on the left, beyond which a tolerably wide grassy basin is entered. — We cross the (5½ M.) *Pont de la Hieladère* to the left bank, but in order to reach Luz recross by the (7 M.) *Pont de Pescadère*, beyond which the road runs under a fine avenue of poplars. To the left is the ruined *Château de Ste. Marie.* — *Luz*, see below.

Those who are bound for St. Sauveur continue straight on past the Pont de Pescadère, and ascend beyond the confluence of the *Gave de Gavarnie* and the *Gave de Bastan*, which unite to form the Gave de Pau. — *St. Sauveur*, see p. 160.

II. Luz and St. Sauveur.

Luz. — **Hotels.** *Hôt. de l'Univers*, where the public conveyances halt, R. 3½-4, B. 1¼, déj. 3, D. 4 fr.; Hôt. de France (*Esquièze*), at the bridge; des Pyrénées. — **Cafés.** *Diran*, at the Hôt. de l'Univers; *Globe*, at the Hôt. de France; *de l'Europe* (Club). — Etablissement Thermal. *Buvette*, 20 c. per glass of mineral water; subscription per month, 10 fr. from June 20th to Sept. 14th, at other seasons, half these charges; baths and douches from 1 to 2½ fr., etc.

Luz (2425 ft.), a small town of 1507 inhab., is situated on the Barèges road and on the Bastan, in a valley of which it was at one time the practically independent capital. It is much frequented in summer, both on account of its situation, and the vicinity of the dependent village of St. Sauveur, as well as on account of the *Thermes*, erected in 1881, when the waters of the *Bastan Spring* (81° F., resembling those of St. Sauveur) were conducted from Barèges to the town. The 'Etablissement' is situated to the left of the road to St. Sauveur, which diverges to the right from the road to Barèges, a little beyond the coach-office. The waters are specially adapted for nervous diseases. The *Church*, which is reached by the street to the left, at the beginning of the above-mentioned road, is a curious structure assigned to the Templars and possibly in parts as old as the 12th cent., but with many later additions. Not only is it embattled and fortified like many other churches in this part of the country, but it is also enclosed in a line of defensive works. The apse is flanked by two towers of which the one on the N. side is a kind of keep. The Romanesque N. portal is interesting. At the W. end, on the right, is a large 16th cent. chapel. In the Templars' tower there is a small museum of antiquities (½ fr.).

An interesting stroll (1 hr. there and back) may be made to the very picturesque ruins of the *Château Ste. Marie*, situated on a hill, beyond the Bastan.

To the S. of the town, charmingly situated on a knoll, in view of St. Sauveur, is the *Chapelle de Solférino*, a fine modern building in the Romanesque style on the site of one formerly belonging to a hermitage there.

The *Excursions* from Luz are practically identical with those from St. Sauveur.

St. Sauveur lies little more than 1/8 M. from Luz. The road passes the Thermes of Luz, and crosses the Gave de Gavarnie; there is also a short-cut for pedestrians, near the bridge.

St. Sauveur. — **Hotels.** Hôt. de Paris; de France, R. from 2, B. 1, déj. 3, D. 4, pens. 10 fr.; des Princes; des Bains, pens. 8-11 fr. — Furnished Apartments. *Villa Beau-Site; Padre; Villa Eugénie; Villa Ducente.* — *Restaurant de l'Hôtel de France*, with café; *Restaurant Français*.

Etablissements Thermaux. *Bains des Dames*, use of the water for drinking and gargling, 5 fr. for 30 days, between June 15th and Sept. 6th, 2 fr. at other seasons; baths 3/4-2 1/2 fr., according to hour and season. — *Thermes de la Hontalade*, baths 1 fr. 30 c.-2 fr.

Guides and Horse-hirers. *Henri-André Lons, Arnaud Noguès, Fr. Serp, Jean-Marie Thomas.* — Tariff given below for each excursion.

English Church Service in summer.

St. Sauveur (2525 ft.) is a prettily situated village of modern origin, consisting of a single street, running up the E. slope of the *Som de Lase* (6025 ft.), above the gorge through which rushes the Gave de Gavarnie. Many tourists visit it, especially those on the way to Gavarnie, but the place owes its chief importance to its warm sulphureous springs, beside which two 'Etablissements' have been erected. The principal of these, the *Etablissement des Dames*, fed by the spring of that name (93° F.), is situated in the middle of the village, to the left as we arrive. The mineral waters are chiefly used for maladies of women and for nervous diseases. Below the establishment is a fine public promenade, known as the *Jardin Anglais*, sloping steeply down to the stream, which is crossed by a bridge giving access to the direct road from Luz to the Pont Napoléon (see below).

The *Thermes de la Hontalade* are situated 820 ft. above St. Sauveur, on a plateau reached in 10 min. by an easy ascent beginning almost directly opposite the first-named establishment. The water of La Hontalade (70° F.) resembles that of Les Dames, but contains a considerably larger proportion of sulphate of soda. The *Plateau de la Hontalade*, which commands a fine view, is a favourite resort.

The *Church* of St. Sauveur, near the upper end of the village, is a modern Gothic edifice, with a tasteful spire. — A little farther on, on the road to Gavarnie, the *Pont Napoléon*, 220 ft. long, with a span of 150 ft., crosses the stream at a height of 212 ft. At a distance the bridge looks like a gigantic portal to the ravine, especially when viewed from the bank of the stream.

III. Excursions.

To Cauterets, over the *Col de Riou*, see p. 158; to the *Pic d'Ardiden*, see p. 157.

To the Pic de Viscos (7025 ft.), 3 1/2 hrs., there and back 5 1/2 hrs.; guide 10, horse 8 fr. This easy and interesting excursion follows the Col de Riou route to the N.W. as far as the (1 hr.) *Granges de Carrilles* (p. 158), then leads to the right in the direction of the Pic, which is scaled on the N.W. side (see p. 159).

To THE PIC DE BERGONS, from Luz, the path from St. Sauveur being very little shorter and impracticable for horses. This is a favourite and interesting excursion, 2¹/₂ hrs. on foot, 2 hrs. on horseback, there and back 4-4¹/₂ hrs.; guide (unnecessary) and horse. 6 fr. each. We leave Luz by the Barèges road (p. 165) and ascend to the S. viâ *Villenave* (2625 ft.), by a well-beaten track which presents no difficulty. The *Pic de Bergons* (6790 ft.), an almost isolated mountain, is one of the best points of view in the district. The panorama to the S., embracing the huge group of the Cirque de Gavarnie, is only inferior to that from the Piméné (p. 164); but even from this point the great waterfall is seen, more than 14 M. distant as the crow flies. From W. to E. the principal summits seen are the Balaïtous, the peaks of Monné, Viscos, and Ardiden, the Vignemale, the Gabiétou, Taillon, Fausse Brèche, Brèche de Roland, Casque, Tour, the Pic and the Cylindre du Marboré, Mont Perdu, the peaks of Estaubé, Munia, Bergons, Maucapéra, Piméné. Long, Néouvielle, Arbizon, Tourmalet, Midi de Bigorre, etc.

To THE PIC DE NÉRÉ, 3³/₄ hrs. from Luz, there and back 6¹/₂ hrs., a delightful excursion which can be made on horseback part of the way; guide 12, horse 10 fr.; adders abound. We leave Luz by the Barèges road and after 45 min. cross the stream. Beyond (1 hr.) *Sers* (3700 ft.) we continue to ascend to the N. to the (1¹/₂ hr.) *Cabanes d'Arbeousse* (5850 ft.), whence we bear to the W. to the (1 hr.) *Col d'Arbéousse* (7105 ft.; fine view). A climb of ¹/₂ hr. along the arête brings us to the summit of the *Pic de Néré* or *de Nère* (7875 ft.), which affords a fine view not unlike that from the Pic de Bergons (see above). — Ascent from Barèges, see p. 143.

To THE CIRQUE DE GAVARNIE, one of the principal excursions among the Pyrenees which should not be missed, 12 M. by road to Gavarnie, thence 1 hr. by bridle-path; guide unnecessary; carriage 20-30, horse 8 fr. By starting early the ascent of the Piméné (p. 164) may be included in the day's excursion. — The roads from Luz and St. Sauveur unite a short distance to the S. of the latter at the *Pont Napoléon* (p. 160). Thence we ascend the right bank to the foot of the Bergons (see above) and enter the *Gorge de St. Sauveur,* formerly fortified. — Near the (3 M.) *Pont de Sia* (3610 ft.) are a waterfall and a ruined bridge, beyond which the ravine expands into a little valley. — 4¹/₂ M. *Pont d'Arroucat* or *Deadou-roucat* (2840 ft.). On the left is seen the Piméné, concealing the crest of the Cirque de Gavarnie, which, however, comes into view at the end of the little basin which our road now crosses.

7¹/₂ M. **Gèdre** (3265 ft.; *Hôt. Polasset*, dear: *Hôt. des Voya-geurs*), a village at the junction of the Héas and Campbieil valleys, on the left, with the Gavarnie valley, on the right. Behind the hotel is an uninteresting 'grotto', or rather cutting, whence the Gave de Héas issues (50 c.). Excursions from Gèdre, see p. 164. Guide, Et. Theil.

The road next traverses the *Chaos*, formed of huge rocks fallen from a spur of the *Coumély*. The valley becomes arid and desolate. Farther on we begin distinctly to see the Cirque de Gavarnie.

12 M. **Gavarnie** (5085 ft.; **Hôtel des Voyageurs*; guides, see below), a small village originally formed around a hospice of the Templars.

The ****Cirque de Gavarnie** appears to be quite close to the village, but it is an hour's walk to its entrance and ¹/₃ hr. more to its head (horse 3, donkey 2 fr.). The illusion arises from the vastness of its proportions for which there is no standard of measurement. The entrance to the Cirque is readily reached (**Inn*), but to gain the foot of the highest waterfall is more difficult, and during the afternoon a wide berth should be given to the cliffs from which stones frequently fall. This superb amphitheatre, the head of whose area is 5380 ft. above the sea, is enclosed by limestone mountains, which rise in three stages to a height of 6900, 8500, and 9000 ft. The hollow thus formed is 2¹/₄ M. wide at the base of the mountains, whose crest-line, from the *Pic des Sarradets* (8990 ft.) on the W. to the *Pic de l'Astazou* (10,105 ft.) on the E., measures nearly 9 M. The summits between these peaks, beginning at the former, are the *Gabiétou* (9950 ft.); *Taillon* (10,320 ft.), to the left of which is the *Fausse Brèche* (9670 ft.) and the *Brèche de Roland* (9200 ft.); the *Casque* (9860 ft.); *Tour* (9900 ft.); *Epaule* (10,230 ft.); and the *Pic du Marboré* (10,670 ft.). The slopes between the successive stages are covered with perpetual snow and with glaciers, forming 13 cascades, of which two never dry up. The principal fall, the famous **Cascade de Gavarnie*, 1385 ft. in height, is the highest in Europe after the Dœrgerfos in Norway, which is 100 ft. higher. If there is plenty of water it forms a single fall, but in summer descends in two leaps, of 958 and 427 ft. respectively. The light-effects in the Cirque are singularly beautiful both at sunrise and sunset; and at about midday in summer the sun shines full upon the fall. Those who do not ascend the Piméné (p. 164) should ascend for ¹/₃ hr. on the S.W. of Gavarnie by the Port de Gavarnie route for the sake of the comprehensive view of the Cirque enjoyed thence.

The **Port de Gavarnie** or *de Boucharo* (7485 ft.), about 2 hrs. to the S.E. of Gavarnie, is the principal pass over this part of the Pyrenees. About 1¹/₄ hr. thence is the Spanish hamlet of *Boucharo* or *Bujaruelo* (4410 ft.), with barracks and an inn, situated on the Ara, which a little farther on enters a beautiful wooded gorge.

On the W. side of the Cirque is a break in the line of cliffs, known as the **Echelle des Sarradets**, which offers the only method of ascending from the bottom of the Cirque to its summits. The ascents are difficult and should be attempted only by experienced mountaineers with good guides, to be had at Gavarnie.

Guides. **Henri* and **Célestin Passet*, *Pierre* and *Henri Pujo*, *Math. Haurine*, *Henri Por*, *Fr. Bernat-Salles*, *Louis Junté*, etc. The first two are perhaps the best guides in the Pyrenees.

To the **Brèche de Tuquerouye**, 6¹/₂ hrs. there and back, or 8 hrs. if a horse be taken from Gavarnie to the Horse de Tuquerouye, 50 min.

on this side of the brèche. From Gavarnie we ascend to the S.E., viâ the (1¹/₂ hr.) *Cabanes de l'Espugnette*, to the *Brèche d'Allans* (8255 ft.), to the N.E. of the Cirque, and about 2 hrs. from Gavarnie. Thence we descend to the S.E. to (³/₄ hr.) the *Borne de Tuquerouye* (7790 ft.), to which horses may proceed, and to (25 min.) the *Echelle de Tuquerouye*, a couloir in which there is a kind of stair with iron clamps. From the (25 min.) *Brèche de Tuquerouye* (8775 ft.), between the Pic de Tuquerouye (9260 ft.), on the W., and the Pic de Pinède (9400 ft.), on the E., we enjoy a splendid *View of the Mont Perdu. At the Brèche is a shelter of the French Alpine Club. Thence to the Marboré, see below.

To the **Brèche de Roland and the Col du Taillon**, 4 and 4¹/₂ hrs., there and back 7¹/₂ hrs. from Gavarnie, guide (10 fr.) and axe necessary. We ascend by the Echelle des Sarradets (see above), and by the (1¹/₄ hr.) cornice reach the (¹/₂ hr.) *Sarradets Pastures*, and the (¹/₂ hr.) *Sarradets Spring* whence there is a fine view. The route now lies over terraces covered with snow during most of the year and we leave on our right a col leading to the Taillon glacier. In ³/₄ hr. we reach the *Glacier de la Brèche* which involves ¹/₂ hr. of difficult climbing, and in ¹/₂ hr. more the **Brèche de Roland** (9200 ft.), a cleft 130-190 ft. wide and more than 300 ft. deep which the famous paladin is fabled to have made with his sword Durandal to open a passage for his return from Spain. It is about 1000 yds. long and the traveller should follow it and descend to the **Col du Taillon** (9170 ft.), about ¹/₂ hr. from the entrance, in order to enjoy the magnificent view of the S. side of the Cirque and of Mont Perdu, etc. A refuge-hut has been built to the W. of the entrance of the Brèche. — The *Pic du Taillon* (10,320 ft.) may be ascended in 1¹/₂ hr. from the Brèche. Grand view.

To the **Pic du Marboré**. A. Viâ the **Brèche de Roland**, 8 hrs., there and back 10¹/₂ hrs. from Gavarnie; guide (25 fr.) and axe necessary. As far as the *Brèche de Roland* (3¹/₂ hrs.) see above. Thence we proceed to the S.E., passing in front of the *Tour* and the *Casque du Marboré*, which may also be ascended from this side, and gain in 1 hr. the *Col de la Cascade* (9840 ft.) between the Epaule and the Tour du Marboré, whence we enjoy a superb view into the abyss of the Cirque. Then we follow the crest (20 min.) and the glacier on the S. slope whence the summit of the *Pic du Marboré* is reached in 1 hr. 10 min. — B. Viâ the **Brèche de Tuquerouye**, returning viâ the Brèche de Roland, a fine expedition of the same character as the preceding. To the (3¹/₂ hrs.) *Brèche* (refuge-hut), see above. Thence the route passes to the E. of the *Lac Glacé du Mont-Perdu*, viâ the crevassed *Glacier du Cylindre*, and then, beyond a crevasse, leads by a cornice and over the (2¹/₄ hrs.) *Col du Cylindre*, between the Cylindre and the summit, which lies ¹/₄ hr. farther to the N.E. — The *Pic du Marboré* (10,670 ft.), the summit of which forms a huge platform, is perhaps the best view-point in the Pyrenees, after the *Cylindre du Marboré* (10,915 ft.), the ascent of which is dangerous. We complete the circuit by returning viâ the Brèche de Roland.

To **Mont-Perdu**. A. Via the **Brèche de Roland and the Marboré Terraces**, the shortest route, 8¹/₂ hrs., there and back 11¹/₂ hrs. from Gavarnie (the night being passed at the Brèche de Roland); guide (30 fr.), rope, and axe necessary. As far as the *Col de la Cascade* (4¹/₂ hrs.) see above. Turning to the E., we gain by terraces and snow-fields the foot of the Pic du Marboré Glacier, then the S. glacier of the Cylindre which we cross to the *Cheminée du Cylindre* (³/₄ hr.; refuge). Then leaving, on the left, this cheminée, which is difficult to scale, we gain without difficulty a gap by which we descend to the S.E. to the *Etang du Mont-Perdu* (10 min.; 8925 ft.) and thence in 1 hr. attain the summit of the *Mont-Perdu*. — B. Via the **Brèche de Tuquerouye**, same kind of expedition. To the (3¹/₂ hrs.) *Brèche de Tuquerouye* (shelter), see above. We continue to cross the glacier (1 hr.), but trend to the S., and then cross a crevasse and scale a rocky wall (¹/₄ hr.). Thence the (³/₄ hr.) *Col du Mont-Perdu* (10,185 ft.) is reached without difficulty, and the summit is gained either viâ the Etang (see above) or viâ a narrow crest between deep precipices. **Mont-Perdu** (10,995 ft.), the highest peak in the Pyrenees after the Pic de Néthou (11,170 ft.), Maladetta (11,005 ft.) and Pic Posets (11,045 ft.), is, like them, on Spanish territory. It forms part of the limestone mass of the Cirque de Gavarnie, but it lies out of the main chain of the Pyrenees and the view from the Pic du Marboré is finer. Together with the *Cylindre* (10,915 ft.) on the N.W. and the *Pic de Ramond* (10,760 ft.) on the S.E. it forms a group known by the Spaniards as the *Three Sisters*. On the S., as is almost universally the case on that slope of the Pyrenees, the mountains are barren and desolate.

To the **Vignemale** (10,820 ft.), *viâ Ossoue and Montferrat*, the shortest route (from Cauterets, see p. 155), a fine excursion, but laborious, 8 hrs., there and back 10 hrs. from Gavarnie; guide (30 fr.), rope, and axe necessary. We ascend the *Ossoue Valley* by the side of the Gave without difficulty as far as the (3 hrs.) *Pas des Oulettes-d'Ossoue* which is only feasible on the right bank. Then we leave on the right (1/2 hr.) the road to the Hourquette d'Ossoue (p. 155) and ascend to the S.W. in the direction of the *Montferrat* or *Cerbillona* (1/2 hr.) where it is necessary to proceed with care, especially on the glacier (comp. p. 155).

To THE **Piméné**, an easy and interesting ascent, 2¹/₂ hrs., there and back 4 hrs. from Gavarnie; guide 10 fr. From Gèdre the ascent takes 4¹/₂ hrs., there and back 7¹/₂ hrs. From Gavarnie we ascend to the E., through woods, to (³/₄ hr.) a terrace and (¹/₄ hr.) a spring. Thence we bear to the right up very steep slopes to (2 hrs. from Gavarnie) the *Col de Piméné* (8255 ft.) from which the view is already fine. Here we turn to the N. and, by a rather narrow arête, gain the summit of the **Piméné* or *Pic de Piméné* (9195 ft.), which affords a grand panorama, including the best view of the Cirque of Gavarnie, though the chief waterfall is not seen. The Vignemale and the Pic Long appear to advantage.

To THE **Cirque de Troumouse**, 6-8 hrs. there and back from St. Sauveur, 4¹/₂-5 hrs. from Gèdre; guide unnecessary; horse from St. Sauveur 8 fr. — *Gèdre* see p. 161. We take a stony path near the Hôtel Palassé to the *Valley of Héas*, which we ascend along the left bank of the torrent, where the road is better than on the right bank. Farther on, a short cut leads across meadows. On the other side is the *Valley of Campbieil*, by which the difficult and dangerous ascent of the *Pic Long* (10,480 ft.), the highest point in the granitic mass of Néouvielle (p. 169), is occasionally, though rarely, made. Then we cross at the foot of the Coumély, a *Chaos* similar to that on the Gavarnie road. In 1 hr. 10 min. from Gèdre we cross to the right bank by the *Pont de la Gardette*. On the left is the *Montagne de Camplong*. Then on the other side is the mouth of the *Val d'Estaubé*, which also ends in a 'cirque'. The valley of Héas is here still choked with blocks of rock, the result of a landslip in 1650, known as the *Peyrade* (4430 ft.), which dammed up the stream and formed a lake, in its turn destroyed by a flood in 1788. On the left is a huge block, known as the *Caillou de l'Arraylé*, on which the Virgin Mary is said once to have appeared; a statue was erected here in 1858. — About 40 min. from the bridge (4 M. from Gèdre) is *Héas* (4855 ft.), an insignificant hamlet. — 10 min. *Chapelle de Héas* (5075 ft.), dedicated to the Virgin and a place of pilgrimage for this district, particularly on Aug. 15 and Sept. 8. Adjoining it are some houses and the small *Hôtel de la Munia* (dear; kept by the guide Vict. Paget, surnamed Chapelle). — We next pass a pyramidal rock called the *Rocher* or *Tour de Lieussaoube* and enter a gorge beyond which, to the S., appear the peaks of Troumouse and the Munia. In ¹/₂ hr. more the valley forks. We take the path to the left and follow the right bank of a torrent which forms several waterfalls, notably the *Cascade de Mataras*, and in 1 hr. reach the **Cirque de Troumouse** (5816 ft.), less grand than that of Gavarnie but nevertheless of noble dimensions, 2¹/₂ M. in diameter and from 2500 to 4400 ft. in height. At its

head rises the *Pic de Troumouse* (10,125 ft.) with its glaciers and its two
pinnacles, called the Sisters of Troumouse. — On the right, the *Pic de la
Munia* (10,335 ft.), a superb point of view but involving a difficult climb
(2 hrs.). — On the other hand, the interesting ascents of the *Pic de la Géla*
(8345 ft.) and the *Pic des Aiguillous* (8710 ft.) to the S.E. and N.E. of Héas,
are easily made (with guide) in 4¹/₂ hrs. each.

24. Barèges and its Environs.
Comp. Map, p. 160.
I. From Lourdes to Barèges.

RAILWAY to (13 M.) *Pierrefitte-Nestalas* as for Cauterets and Luz-St. Sauveur
(p. 148); thence a carriage-road (12 M.) and diligence during the season
(fare 4¹/₂ fr.). The diligence takes 3¹/₂ hrs., besides ¹/₂ hr. halt at Luz. The
'voiture du courrier' is quicker, taking only 3 hrs., with no stoppage.
Carriages also in the season, 25 fr. for 4 travellers and 200 lbs. of luggage.

To (8 M.) *Luz*, see p. 159. The road then makes a considerable
ascent to the N.E. into the *Valley of the Bastan* or Gave de Barèges,
so that the diligence takes 2 hrs. from Luz to Barèges. At first we
have, left and right, the wooded slopes of the Pic de Néré and Pic
de Bergons, but the country soon changes its character and the
mountains become bare and furrowed. The journey is interesting
and the road itself excellent, especially since the last improvements
were made, involving the construction of two bridges over the torrent in the Pontis ravin e(p. 166), about 1¹/₄ M. from Barèges.

II. Barèges.

Hotels. DE L'EUROPE; DE FRANCE & DES PYRÉNÉES, R. 2-5, L. ¹/₄, A.
¹/₂, B. 1¹/₂, déj. 3¹/₂, D. 4¹/₂, pens. 8-12 fr.; RICHELIEU, etc. Houses and
lodgings to let.
Cafés. *De Paris, Richelieu, de l'Union*, in the Grand' Rue.
Bath Establishment. Fee for drinking the waters between June 15
and Sept. 5, 10 fr. for 30 days; rest of the season, 2 fr. — Baths ¹/₂-2¹/₂ fr.
according to the kind, the hour, and time of year, usual tariff 1 fr. 70
and 2 fr. 50 c.; baths in public basin 30 c.-1¹/₂ fr.
Casino, at the entrance to the village; subscription per month 35 fr.,
fortnight 22 fr., week 12 fr.; reserved seat in theatre 3 fr.
Guides. *Bern. Anclade, Ant., Jean, Pierre*, and *Laurent Caranx-Pais,
Marc Honta, Jean-Marie Honta-Pontis, Pierre Menvielle, Ant.* and *Clem.
Verges*. All these are of the 1st class, and shew the tariff (see the separate excursions) when requested.

Barèges (4040 ft.), a village consisting almost entirely of one
long street running up the left bank of the Bastan, has long been
noted for its warm sulphur springs. Owing to its altitude the place
is scarcely habitable in winter, when the cold is extreme. Its climate is very variable and the upward limit of trees is only 2000 ft.
above the village. Nevertheless it attracts many visitors in summer
and is often crowded. The re-planting of the hill-sides with trees
and grass has already considerably altered the appearance of the
valley, which is very pleasant in summer.

and are all highly charged with a peculiar nitrogenous substance, called 'barégine' or 'glairine', which renders them oily to the touch. Their temperature varies between 91,4° Fahr. (Chapelle) and 111,2° (Tambour), roughly corresponding with the amount of sulphate of soda they contain. They are used for baths and drinking, in the treatment of surgical cases, the healing of wounds, ulcers, etc., and for scrofula, gout, rheumatism, skin diseases, syphilis, chlorosis, anæmia, and certain nervous affections. There are thirteen springs whose united yield is about 60,000 gallons per diem.

The *Bath Establishment*, rebuilt between 1861 and 1864, is a handsome building of marble at the top of the village, on the right of the street descending the latter. All the springs are here brought together and the bathing arrangements are very complete. — To the left of the baths is a *Military Hospital*, founded in 1760, but recently rebuilt. — On the right, behind and at some distance above it, is the *Hospice Ste. Eugénie*, set apart for ecclesiastics and nuns from June 15 to Sept. 1, while the poor are admitted before and after those dates.

The *Promenade Horizontale*, the principal promenade of Barèges, begins at the Hospice and runs westward below the Ayré (see below) and above the village as far as the Rioulet ravine (see below). There are also walks higher up in the *Forêt de Barèges* or *Bois d'Artigou*, which protects the baths from avalanches and the ravages of the Mouré torrent. Among these is the *Allée Verte* (about 5900 ft.), a clearing in the forest, 3 M. distant, between the valleys of the Lienz and the Rioulet. The *Héritage à Culas*, beyond the Rioulet, 1¹/₂ M. from the Promenade Horizontale, is another pleasant promenade.

Avalanches and the rush of waters from the neighbouring mountains are the two special dangers against which the authorities of Barèges have to contend. Avalanches of the most destructive character gather on the flanks of the mountain of Labas-Blancs on the N. and rush down by four ravines into the valley and over the stream to the other slope. Masses of snow etc. of more than 100,000 cubic yds. have thus been hurled upon the village. On spots liable to be overwhelmed in this manner only wooden buildings are erected and these are annually removed before the winter. The most dangerous spot was the *Ravin du Midsou* or *de Cap*, behind the Military Hospital. To some extent the exertions of the Forest Department of the government have succeeded in arresting or lessening the avalanches, by planting the hill-sides with trees and by making embankments or small terraces. The works are interesting and from them there is a good view (2 hrs. there and back). — The *Rioulet Ravine*, on the left bank below Barèges, is traversed by a torrent which in times of thaw and after heavy rain used to carry away everything before it that was not solid rock, and even destroyed the main road; but it too has to a great extent been rendered harmless by planting trees and by the construction of embankments and channels which distribute its waters higher up. The *Postis Ravine*, lower down the valley, now calls for works of a like nature. The alteration in the course of the road mentioned at p. 165 was necessitated by the risks to which its previous course was exposed.

III. Excursions.

To the **Pic de Néré** (from Luz, see p. 161), 3³/₄ hrs., there and back on foot 6¹/₂ hrs.; guide, 10 fr., horse 6 fr. (adders abound). We cross the Bastan about 550 yds. below Barèges, near the Source de Barzun (p. 159), and proceed to the W. to (³/₄ hr.). *St. Justin*, once the site of a hermitage, commanding a fine view. Thence we go N. to the *Cirque de Sers* (¹/₂ hr.) and again turn W. a little farther on, descending into a little valley and ascending the exceedingly steep slopes on the other side to the plateau on which are the *Arbéousse Huts* (about 1 hr.). There we join the route from Luz (p. 161).

To the Pic du Midi de Bigorre, an easy excursion which should not be missed, 3¹/₂ hrs., there and back 5¹/₂-6 hrs.; guide (unnecessary) 10, horse 7 fr. The night may be spent in the small hotel near the top of the mountain, in order to see the sunrise, but it is advisable to secure a bed beforehand as otherwise the visitor may have to sleep in the public room. In any case an early start should be made so as to reach the summit before noon, as mists often hide the lower ground during the afternoon. We follow the road above Barèges on the left bank of the Bastan, crossing the stream by the (¹/₂ hr.) *Pont de Tournabout* (4755 ft.), and then ascend to the E. along the flank of the Labas-Blancs, passing in ¹/₂ hr. the point where the path to the Lac Bleu (see below) diverges to the left. Shortly afterwards our route turns to the N. and reaches the *Cabanes de Toue* (6370 ft.), where a small obelisk commemorates the Duc de Nemours, who promoted the opening of the road in 1839, then the only one and still the shortest by which to reach (to the right) Bagnères over the Col du Tourmalet (¹/₂ hr.; p. 169). A well-beaten path leads from the Cabanes to the summit; a short-cut for walkers ascends directly to the N. The greyish dome of the Pic du Midi and its observatory are now in sight. We cross a brook (¹/₂ hr.) and mount to a considerable height to the E. of the *Lac d'Oncet* (7340 ft.) from which it flows. This lake, about 550 yds. long by 330 yds. wide, lies in a basin shut in by abrupt heights. — In 2¹/₂ hrs. from Barèges we reach the *Hourque des Cinq-Cours* or *de Sencours* (7780 ft.), a col where the route from Bagnères is joined, and on which is the *Hôtellerie du Pic du Midi*.

The hotel has several good bedrooms with 2 beds in each and a public bedroom, fitted with camp-bedsteads. Tariff: admission merely 50 c.; bed in the public room, 1 fr., in one of the bedrooms, 3 fr. for the first night, 2 fr. for the second; déj. 2¹/₂, D. 3¹/₂ fr. without wine which costs 80 c., 1 fr., and 2 fr. per litre; café noir, 60 c.; café au lait 1¹/₂ fr.; petit verre, 30 c. Charges of 25 c. table money and 25 c. for putting up the horse are also made, and visitors are expected to fee the attendants.

In 1 hr. more we reach the summit of the mountain by many zigzags practicable for horses, passing the *Col du Laquet* (8530 ft.) from which there is a fine view of the plain.

The ****Pic du Midi de Bigorre** or *de Bagnères* (9440 ft.), although

in altitude it only ranks 40th among Pyrenean summits, is one of
the first in respect of the view it affords of nearly the whole chain.
This it owes to its isolated position, like that of a watch-tower on
the side of the plain over which the view extends almost without
limit, and at times as far westward as the Atlantic Ocean. The
contrast between the plain and the countless snow-capped summits
on the S. is its great charm; the latter looking like the billows of
a stormy sea suddenly petrified. — The summit ends on the W. in
a small platform which has precipices on its N. side not to be care-
lessly approached. On the E. side an *Observatory* was built between 1878 and 1881 and is connected by telegraph with Bagnères-
de-Bigorre (p. 169). The house is in a little cleft facing the S.; the
public are not admitted. — By reason of its isolation, the Pic du
Midi is not snow-clad in summer though snow often falls on the
summit.

To the **Lac Bleu** (from Bagnères, see p. 172), 3½ hrs., there and back
about 8 hrs., guide 10, horse 7 fr. For the first hour our route follows
the Pic du Midi road (see above). We then turn to the left and ascend
in ½ hr. to the *Cabanes d'Aoube* (5965 ft.) from which we gain in 1½ hr.
the *Col d'Aoube* (about 8200 ft.), which commands a fine view, particularly
of the Néouvielle. A descent of ¾ hr., to the W., takes us past a little
lake, also blue, to the *Lac Bleu* (p. 173).

To the **Pic d'Ayré**, 3½ hrs., there and back 8 hrs.; guide and horse
8 fr. each. Visitors generally only go to within ½ hr. of the top which
is difficult to scale; in that case a guide is not necessary. On horseback
we take the bridle-path through the forest of Barèges (p. 166), traverse
the *Allée Verte* (p. 166), and ascend by a circuitous path to the pastures
above the Rioulet ravine. The same point may be reached direct by
a steep footpath along the torrent. Thence we proceed W. to a fine
View-point, 2½ hrs. from Barèges; then, retracing our steps for a short
distance, we ascend in ¾ hr., by zigzags, the flower-decked slopes to the
Col d'Ayré, whence the view extends to the Pic de Néré and the Néouvielle. Another ½ hr. brings us from the Col to the summit of the
Pic d'Ayré (7095 ft.), but the climb is laborious and should not be undertaken without a guide.

To the **Pic de Néouvielle** (*Lac d'Orridon*), an easy and interesting
excursion, 6 hrs., there and back 10 hrs.; guide 20 fr.; horse as far as
the Lac d'Escoubous (2 hrs.) 5 fr. We follow the road beyond the Baths,
leave on the left the bridge crossed by the Pic du Midi route, and beyond
a bridge over the *Escoubous* or *Escougous* torrent (40 min.) turn to the
right up the valley of that name. We ascend through a chaos of granite
blocks, pass the (¾ hr.) mouth of the *Vallon d'Aigue-Cluse* on the left,
recross the torrent, and reach the (35 min.) *Lac d'Escoubous* (6395 ft.).
This lake is little larger than the Lac d'Oncet on the Pic du Midi, but
its environment of shattered mountains makes it an interesting object for
an excursion, particularly if we proceed on foot ⅜ hr. farther up to
the *Lac Blanc*. The latter is on our way to the Pic de Néouvielle, on
which we leave the *Lac de Tracens* on the left, reaching (¾ hr.) the *Lac
Noir* (7200 ft.) and following its left bank. Thence an ascent of 25 min.
brings us to the *Col d'Aure* (8200 ft.), where we obtain a very fine view
of the Néouvielle, Pic Long, the Gavarnie mountains, etc. — If we descend hence to the left, towards the lakes of *Aubert* and *Aumar*, which
are in sight from the col, we may reach in 1 hr. 10 min. the *Lac d'Orridon* (6135 ft.). This lake (130 acres in area) is well worth a visit; it
is dammed up in order to supply water to the Aure valley (p. 174) in
summer, by means of the Neste de Couplan. Refreshments are usually
to be obtained from the reservoir-keeper. — Continuing our route to the

Néouvielle we descend from the col on the right and enter another chaos
of rocks, and cross higher up from S. to W. a snow slope, free from
risk, but very steep towards the end. In 2¹/₄ hrs. from the col, we reach
the summit of the *Pic de Néouvielle* or *Néouvielle*, also called *Pic
d'Aubert* (10,145 ft.), which commands a magnificent panorama of the
Pyrenees from the Balaïtous to the Monts Maudits, with a fine view of
the Gavarnie mountains, Mont-Perdu, Pic Posets, and, much nearer, of
the peaks Long, Campbieil, Méchant, etc., and a remarkable survey
of the numerous lakes of this district, of which 37 may be counted. —
We may return viâ the *Brèche de Chaussenque*, the lakes and valley of
Gloire, parallel, on the W., to that of Escoubous, but this difficult
route takes an extra hour.

To BAGNÈRES-DE-BIGORRE VIÂ THE COL DU TOURMALET, 25 M., by
carriage road in 4 hrs., on foot 7 hrs.; carriage 40-60 fr., horse 12 fr. per
day, to the col 5 fr. The road follows the left bank of the Bastan;
pedestrians and riders may shorten the distance by taking the Pic du
Midi road (p. 187) by which they reach the col in 2 hrs. — 8 M. Col du
Tourmalet (6960 ft.), between the *Pic du Tourmalet* (6985 ft.), on the left,
and the *Pic d'Espade* (8075 ft.), on the right, one of the highest carriage-
passes in Europe. The view is limited except on the W. The road
descends by wide zigzags towards the valley of the Adour; the old road
is a short-cut for pedestrians and horsemen. — At (12¹/₂ M.) *Tramesaygues*,
we obtain a very fine view of the Pic du Midi. Then traversing wooded
hills we reach the bank of the Adour, which forms the *Cascades d'Artigues*
or *de Gripp*, one of which is very pretty. There is a good Inn (*Hôt. des
Pyrénées*; guide to the Pic du Midi 10 fr.). — 15 M. *Gripp* (3495 ft.;
Hôt. des Voyageurs). — At (17¹/₂ M.) *Ste. Marie* we enter the Campan
valley (p. 173). — *Bagnères-de-Bigorre*, see below.

25. Bagnères-de-Bigorre and its Environs.

Comp. Map, p. 160.

I. From Tarbes to Bagnères-de-Bigorre.

13¹/₂ M. RAILWAY in ¹/₂-1 hr. (fares 2 fr. 45, 1 fr. 85, 1 fr. 10 c.).

Tarbes, see p. 135. — We follow the Toulouse line to *Marcadieu*
and turn to the right into the fine and fertile valley of the *Adour*.
The best view is on the right. — 4¹/₂ M. *Salles-Adour*; 7 M. *Ber-
nac-Debat*; 8 M. *Vielle-Adour*; 10 M. *Montgaillard*; 11 M. *Ordi-
san*. — 12¹/₂ M. *Pouzac*, with a fortified church containing a reredos of the 18th cent. and other works of art. On the hill are the
remains of an earthwork known as *Caesar's Camp*. — To the right
as we reach Bagnères is the Mont du Bédat, crowned by a statue of
the Virgin (p. 172).

II. Bagnères-de-Bigorre.

Hotels. GRAND-HÔTEL DE PARIS, R. 3-12, L. ¹/₂, A. ¹/₂-1, B. 1¹/₂, déj.
3¹/₂, D. 4¹/₂, pens. in summer from 11 fr.; BEAUSÉJOUR, DE LONDRES ET
D'ANGLETERRE, Nos. 18, 23, and 5 Promenade des Coustous; DE FRANCE,
Boulevard Carnot; FRASCATI, Rue Frascati, both near the Baths; DU BON
PASTEUR, Rue de l'Horloge, near the tower; DURAU, Rue de Tarbes, near
the promenades. — Numerous *Villas* and *Apartments*, those to let being
commonly indicated by the window-shutters being closed; room 2-3 fr.
per day.

Bath Establishments. *Thermes* and *Néothermes*; 'buvette', 10 days,
4 fr., season 8 fr.; private baths 1-3 fr.; baths in the great basin of the

Néothermes, 1-1½ fr., 25 fr. per month, 40 fr. for the season. *Thermes de Salut*, 'buvette' 5 fr. in July and August, 3 fr. during the rest of the season; baths ½-2½ fr. — A list of *Physicians* is displayed in the bath-establishments.

Cabs, for 2 pers. per drive 75 c. during the day, 1½ fr. at night; per hour 2 and 2½ fr., 3 fr. in the country; for 4 pers., per drive 1 and 2 fr., per hour 3 and 3½ fr. — *Calèches* and *Landaus*, 30-40 fr. per day. — *Horses*, ride of 4 hrs., 5 fr., per day 10 fr.

Guides. *Arnauné*, *J. M. Courtade*, *Idrac*, *Noguès*, *Aug. Védère*, *Arn. Verdour*. For tariff, see the separate excursions.

Casino, per season. 1 pers. 90 fr., husband and wife 140 fr., each additional member of a family 30 fr. Per month 50, 75, and 30 fr.; for 3 weeks 40, 60, and 20 fr.; for 10 days, 20, 30, and 10 fr. Admission on special occasions, 3 fr.

Protestant Churches. *Anglican*, Rue des Pyrénées; *French*, Avenue du Salut.

Post and Telegraph Office, Place Ramond, not far from the Thermes.

Bagnères-de-Bigorre or simply *Bagnères* (1805 ft.) is a town of 8638 inhab., in a pretty situation on the left bank of the *Adour*, at the point where this river issues from the fine Campan valley into the plain of Tarbes. It is one of the leading thermal stations of the Pyrenees and enjoys, what many others do not, a mild climate. It is frequented annually by about 20,000 bathers and tourists. The Romans were acquainted with its waters, which they called *Aquae Bigerrionum Balneariae,* and they erected here various bath-houses and a temple of Diana.

The railway-station lies to the N. of the town. The avenue beginning opposite the exit leads towards the centre of the town, viâ the handsome *Square des Vigneaux*, a quiet and well-shaded promenade. A little farther on is the curious *Church of St. Vincent,* dating from the 14-15th cent.; the façade is formed by a great wall, square at the top, with fourteen Gothic arcades, while on the right it is flanked by a Gothic turret. On the S. side is a tasteful portico of 1557. The interior presents a broad and short nave, flanked by chapels, decorated with modern marble altars. There is a fine statue of the Virgin, by Clésinger, above the high altar. Some of the windows have good stained glass.

The *Promenade des Coustous,* near this church, is shaded by trees, as far even as the centre of the town. This street and the Place Lafayette and Place des Pyrénées, at either end of it, contain the principal hotels and cafés and form the usual evening rendezvous of the visitors. The part of the town lying to the E. or left of this promenade is uninteresting. It is bounded by the Adour, which is spanned by a bridge at the end of the street skirting the side of St. Vincent's church.

The Bath Establishments and the Casino are situated to the W., the principal street, the Boulevard Carnot and Boulevard du Casino, beginning at the place Lafayette. On this side also, in the old town, is the *Tour des Jacobins* or *Tour de l'Horloge*, the remains of a church of the 15th century. This curious edifice is octagonal in shape and is crowned by a receding story, with a gallery and platform.

The MINERAL WATERS of Bagnères are now supplied by 30 *Springs*. The chief are characterized by the presence of sulphate of lime; but they vary much in their composition and in the uses to which they are applied. The springs are usually divided into three groups: 23 are warm springs containing sulphate of lime, and also sulphate of magnesia and soda; 3 are warm sulphur-springs; and 4 are cold chalybeate springs.

For rheumatism the waters of the springs known as Le Dauphin, La Reine, Le Foulon, Le Platane, and Le Petit-Barèges are usually prescribed; for nervous affections, those of Le Salut, Le Platane, Le Grand Pré, and St. Roch; for feminine ailments and diseases of the skin, those of Le Foulon and Salles; for diseases of the digestive organs, those of Labassère, La Reine, and La Rampe; for diseases of the urinary canals those of Salles and Le Salut; for diseases of the respiratory organs, those of Labassère and Salles; and for anæmia, general diseases, and surgical cases, those of the two last and of La Rampe.

Bagnères has still 10 bath-establishments, and formerly had more. The chief are the *Thermes* and the *Néothermes*, which, as well as those of Théas, belong to the town. The others are private establishments.

The THERMES are situated in a square of the same name, to the left as we follow the boulevards, and at the foot of the bare mountains whence issue the streams that supply the baths. The building is a plain structure, dating from 1824, but the bathing arrangements and equipments are excellent. The baths of this establishment are fed by the springs of *Le Dauphin* (120° Fahr.), *La Reine* (115°), *St. Roch* (105°), *Le Foulon* (95°), *Le Platane* (91°), *Marie-Thérèse* or *Les Yeux* (91°), *Le Roc-de-Lannes* (118°), and *St. Barthélemy* (118°). — Adjoining the Thermes, on the N., is the *Buvette de Salles*, so called from the *Salies* spring (124°), one of the chief in Bagnères, which is conducted hither, along with the waters of *Labassère* (64°) and *La Rampe* (100°). The Buvettes de la Reine and du Dauphin are also here. — A tasteful *Fountain* has been erected in front of the establishment, in memory of A. Soubies, to whom Bagnères owes much of its prosperity. — Not far from the Buvette de Salles are the *Baths of Cazaux* and of *Théas*, each supplied by a special spring (114-124°).

The NÉOTHERMES lie somewhat farther to the N., occupying the ground-floor of the right wing of the casino. They contain large basins, supplied with running water from the *Source de la Tour* (113° reduced to 86°), which yields nearly 220,000 gallons per day. The *Casino*, a handsome edifice, built in 1881-84, contains ball-rooms, recreation-rooms, a restaurant, café, etc. Its park is open daily to the public until 6 p. m.; concerts frequently take place in the afternoon.

Among the other bath-establishments are those of *Bellevue* (114°), behind the Thermes (higher up are two chalybeate springs);

Mora (100°), Rue du Théâtre, opposite the Thermes; the *Petit-Prieur* (96°), under the hospice, a little farther to the S.; *Versailles* (96°) and the *Petit-Barèges* (91°), farther off, to the right and left; and the *Grand-Pré* (98° and 89°) to the S.E., in the Allée de Salut, a fine avenue which leads also to the *Thermes de Salut*, about ¹/₂ M. from the town (omn. 40 c. there, 20 c. back).

At the Thermes are a small *Musée* and a *Library*, open during the season from 9 a. m. to 12, and from 1 to 5 or 6 p. m.

Bagnères has many pleasant walks. The *Allées de Maintenon*, at the S. end of the town, are reached viâ the Rue des Pyrénées. The *Allée du Montaliouet*, on the mountain-slope behind the Thermes, ascends to the chalybeate springs; and by the *Allées Dramatiques*, to the S. of the Montaliouet, near the Thermes de Salut, we may proceed, to the right, to the *Mont du Bédat* (2890 ft.; ³/₄ hr.), on which there is a bronze statue of the Virgin. The hill contains some large caves.

In the valley of Campan (p. 173), and elsewhere in the neighbourhood of Bagnères are *Marble Quarries*, which yield many varieties of valuable marble; and the town contains several important *Marble Works*, manufacturing chimney-pieces, table-tops, etc. Bagnères is also noted for its woollen knitted goods.

III. Excursions.

To the Monné, 2¹/₂ hrs., 2 hrs. on horseback; guide (unnecessary) 6, horse 8-10 fr. We ascend first by the Allées Dramatiques, then to the right along the hills, skirting the mountain from E. to W. The Monné or *Monné de Bagnères* (4125 ft.) is the highest summit in the immediate vicinity of Bagnères. It affords a wide view of the Tarbes plain on the N., while to the S. the eye ranges from the Vignemale to the Maladetta, the Montaigu opposite Bagnères being prominent; to the left is the Pic du Midi and farther off in that direction the Pic d'Arbizon. The descent may be made viâ Beaudéan (see below).

To the Pic de Montaigu, 5¹/₂-6 hrs., there and back 8-10 hrs., a fatiguing expedition; guide 12 fr. We follow the Monné road for 1¹/₂ hr., then cross on the right the *Plaine d'Esquiou*, turn to the left, skirting the *Courré* (4285 ft), climb the steep path of the *Échelles de Pilate*, skirt *La Peyre* (5710 ft.), on the left, follow a rocky crest, and finally skirting the mountain to the right gain the top. The Pic de Montaigu (7880 ft.) affords a very wide view to the N., over the neighbouring valleys and the plain, but the view to the S. is limited owing to the vicinity of the Pic du Midi and its W. neighbours. The return may be made by the Lesponne valley (see below).

To the Lesponne Valley and the Lac Bleu, 3¹/₂ hrs. to the Cabanes de Chiroulet, 5 hrs. to the lake. The visit to the latter is best made when the dam of the lake is open. Riding is practicable as far as the lake and driving as far as the Cabanes. Guide (unnecessary) 8, horse 10, carriage 25-30 fr. We ascend to the S. by the Adour valley, leaving *Gerde* and *Asté* (p. 173) to the left, and *Médous*, with its old convent, to the right. At (1 hr.) *Beaudéan* Larrey, the celebrated surgeon (1766-1842), was born. Near the pretty house called *Prieuré de St. Paul* we quit the Campan valley (see below) and turn to the right up the Lesponne Valley, which is shut in right and left respectively by spurs of the Montaigu and Pic du Midi. Cultivation soon ceases. In 1 hr. we reach *Lesponne*; ³/₄ hr. farther is the *Hospital*, and, on the right, a ravine with the pretty *Waterfall of Aspi*. At the head of the ravine appears the Montaigu, which may be ascended hence. About 1/2 hr. farther on, to the left, is another ravine with a view of the Pic du Midi, which also is accessible on this side, and 20 min. more bring us to the *Cabanes de Chiroulet* where refreshments may be obtained. Beyond them we leave, on the right, the road leading to Argelès (p. 148), viâ the Hourquette de Haraué and the Izaby valley, and ascend on the left by a considerable slope, to (1 hr. 10 min.) the dam and (1/4 hr. more) to the Lac Bleu (6455 ft.), shut in by a vast environment of rocks, and fully justifying its name by its fine blue colour. The lake is about 125 acres in area and 350 ft. deep, but a tunnel has been made on the N., 200 yds. long (closed), for the purpose of augmenting the Adour in dry seasons. This reduces the level of the water about 65 feet.

To the **Pic du Midi de Bigorre**, 1 or 1 1/2 day, see p. 167. — The ascent on this side is best made by starting from (3 1/4 hrs.) *Gripp* (p. 169), where guides and horses are more conveniently obtained. Thence the ascent requires 4 1/2 hrs., viâ the *Vallon d'Arizes* and the *Gorge de Sencours*, beyond which we join the road from Barèges, at the *Lac d'Oncet* (p. 167). The route viâ the Tourmalet (p. 169) is longer, but a great part of it, as far as the *Cabanes de Tous* (p. 167), 1/2 hr. from the col, and 1 1/2 hr. from the top, may be made by carriage.

To *Barèges* viâ the *Tourmalet*, see p. 169.

To the **Pène de Lhéris**, 3 hrs., guide 5 fr., 2 fr. extra if the return is made by Ordincède; horse to the inn, 10 fr.; an excursion of special interest for botanists. We follow the Adour valley to the S., cross the (1/2 M.) *Pont de Gerde*, and proceed to (1 1/4 M.) *Asté*. Thence we ascend to the left for about 1 hr. in the ravine of the Lhéris brook, whence we climb the mountain to the right, viâ a wood, some pastures, and the *Col du Tillet* (4210 ft.; fine view) to the (1 hr.) *Auberge de Tournefort*, whose name reminds us of the great botanist's (1656-1708) explorations in this neighbourhood. On the right towers the *Casque*, a rocky wall which affords a remarkable echo. From there we scramble direct to the peak by the *Pas du Chat*, or, longer but easier, climb to the left by the *Puits d'Arris* or *des Corneilles*. The Pène de Lhéris (5225 ft.) commands only a limited view in the direction of the mountains but a very fine one over the plain, similar to that from the Pic du Midi but more detailed owing to the lower elevation. — The descent is often made by the *Col de Lhéris* (4825 ft.) and the *Cabanes d'Ordincède* (4415 ft.) on the S., whence there is a splendid view of the Campan Valley (see below), by which we return to Bagnères.

To **Bagnères de Luchon via the Col d'Aspin** (*Campan Valley, Gripp Waterfalls, Arreau*), 49 M., open carriage, 100 fr., sometimes return-carriages may be had for less. This fine excursion should be made at least as far as the Col d'Aspin. Beyond (7 M.) Arreau, a public conveyance plies to Lannemezan (see pp. 114, 137). — To *Beaudéan* (3 M.), see above. We then follow the delightful **Campan Valley** which is bordered by green hills with bright pastures on the right and on the left by sterile rocks. It takes its name from the *Campani*, who inhabited it during the Roman period. — 5 3/4 M. *Campan* has given its name to a well-known kind of green marble, shaded with red and white, which is quarried higher up the valley (see below). — At (7 1/2 M.) *Ste. Marie*, the road from Barèges, over the Col du Tourmalet, joins our route. On this route, 2 1/2 M. from the junction, is Gripp, with its fine waterfalls (p. 169).

The Luchon road now ascends the Séoube valley, which is a continuation of the Campan valley. — 11 M. *Paillole* (3040 ft.), a tavern in a hollow still covered with pastures but surrounded by forests which indicate our approach to the higher mountains. The *Pic d'Arbizon* (9285 ft.), to the S., may be ascended in 1 day from Paillole; the ascent is difficult and should not be attempted without a good guide. — 12 1/2 M. *Espiadet*, a hamlet, with the Campan *Marble Quarries*. — The road now zigzags up through pine forests. — 15 1/2 M. Col d'Aspin (4910 ft.) from which, and still better from the height on the left, there is a magnificent *View

of the *Aure Valley*, which we now descend. This very fertile and thickly
peopled valley, abounding in mineral springs for the most part little
known, is separated from the valley of Luchon by a range of mountains
which is connected with the Mont Maudit group, the loftiest of the Pyrenees. — The road descends by great zigzags (short-cuts for walkers) and
passes to the left of *Aspin*. — 22¹/₂ M. **Arreau** (*Hôt. de France; d'Angleterre*),
a small town of 1077 inhab. and the chief place in the valley, is situated
at the confluence of the Neste d'Aure, the Neste de Louron, and the
Lastie. A railway is being built to join the Tarbes line at Lannemezau
(p. 137), whither in the meantime a public conveyance plies daily, leaving
Arreau at 8.30 a. m. About 1¹/₄ M. to the S. is *Cadéac*, with two bath-
houses supplied with cold mineral springs very rich in sulphuret ofsodium,
and used in cutaneous diseases. About 4¹/₂ M. to the N. is *Sarrancolin*,
celebrated for its red marble veined with grey or yellow.

From Arreau our route ascends the Louron valley to the S.E., leaving
right and left *Couret* and *Cazaux-Debat*, where there are mineral springs. —
26 M. *Bordères*, with the ruins of a castle. Then the valley expands and
becomes thickly peopled. — At (28 M.) *Avajan* we cross the Neste and
leave the old and longer road on our left. — 29¹/₄ M. *Fréchet-Casaux*. —
31 M. *Loudervielle*. We now leave the Louron valley and ascend on the
left by a ravine and forest to the (34 M.) *Col de Peyresourde* (5085 ft.), where
the view is limited. The descent into the *Arbourt Valley* is made viâ
(39¹/₂ M.) *Casaux*, which lies 4¹/₂ M. from *Luchon* (p. 175).

26. Bagnères-de-Luchon and its Environs.

I. From Montréjeau (Tarbes) to Bagnères-de-Luchon.

22¹/₂ M. RAILWAY in ²/₃-1¹/₂ hr. (fares 4 fr. 5, 2 fr. 70, 1 fr. 75 c.).

Montréjeau, see p. 137. — We leave on the left the Toulouse
line and enter the Garonne valley. — 3³/₄ M. *Labroquère*.

About 2 M. to the S. is **St. Bertrand-de-Cominges** (*Hôt. de Cominges*),
the ancient city of the Convenae (*Lugdunum Convenarum*), a place of
importance under the Romans but reduced to ruins towards the end of
the 6th cent. after the overthrow of Gondovald, the rival of King Guntram,
who had taken refuge here. At present it is a small town of 718 inhab.,
which owes its name to one of its best known bishops. Its situation
upon an isolated rock renders it conspicuous from a distance. The old
*Cathedral is one of the most interesting in the S. of France and particu-
larly worth seeing. In part it dates from the time of St. Bertrand (1062)
but it is chiefly the work of Bertrand de Goth, who was its bishop (1295-
1299) and later became Pope (Clement V). The façade is flanked by a
square tower with a modern spire. Its portal has columns with curiously
decorated capitals and other sculptures including an antique head of Jupiter. Several Roman inscriptions are also built into the façade. The
interior has a fine Gothic nave, over 80 ft. in height, with eleven side
chapels. The most conspicuous features, however, are the *Rood-loft and
the *Choir-screen, superb examples of early Renaissance woodwork, completed in 1536 and forming as if were a second edifice within the church,
of which the choir occupies the greater part. They are equally remarkable
for the richness and for the variety of their carving, though in this respect
surpassed by the 68 *Stalls to be found within. The *High-altar has also
some remarkable carvings representing the lives of the Virgin and of
Christ, and at the side of the entrance of the church is a dilapidated
organ-case also of the Renaissance period. Behind the choir is the tomb
of St. Bertrand (1432). In the 1st chapel on the left is the *Tomb of
Bishop Hugh de Châtillon, of the 15th cent. The sacristan who shows
the choir (ring the bell thrice) also shows the fine Romanesque cloisters
(23 arcades) on the S. of the church and now in ruins, and the sacristy
where are preserved two copes, the mitre, ring, and ivory pastoral staff

of St. Bertrand, etc. Visitors make a small offering to the church, but no gratuity is expected.

About 1/2 M. to the E. of St. Bertrand, in the fields, on the way to (35-40 min.) *Loures*, where the train can be rejoined (see below), is the *Church of St. Just*, in a burial-ground entered by a Romanesque doorway into which an antique inscription has been built. The church, also in part of ancient materials, is a somewhat clumsy building in the Romanesque style, with a side portal and ciborium of the 13th cent., both worth notice.

For the *Grotte de Gargas*, 5 M. to the N. of St. Bertrand, see p. 197.

We cross the Garonne a little beyond Labroquère. — 5 M. *Loures*, 1 1/4 M. to the N.E. of which is *Barbazan* with a mineral spring (sulphate of lime) and a 16-17th cent. castle commanding a good view. — 7 1/2 M. *Galié*. — 9 1/4 M. *Salechan*, the station for the baths of *Ste. Marie*, 3/4 M. to the N.W., and for those of *Siradan*, 3/4 M. farther to the W. Their waters are similar to those of Barbazan. — The mountains at the head of the valley now begin to appear and we again cross the Garonne. — 11 1/4 M. *Fronsac*, to the left, commanded by a keep of the 12th century. We once more cross the Garonne, which descends on the left from the Spanish *Valley of the Aran*, a railway in which is proposed. — 13 M. *Marignac-St. Béat*. St. *Béat* (Hôt. du Commerce), a small town of 1000 inhab. at the entrance of a picturesque defile on the bank of the Garonne, has a church and a castle partly of the 11th cent., with a statue of the Virgin on the principal tower. The quarries of grey and white marble here were worked even in the time of the Romans. To the N. are the *Pic du Gars* (5765 ft.) and the *Pic Saillant* (5860 ft.) whence there is a very fine view. — The line now ascends, traverses a short tunnel, and crosses three bridges. — 16 1/4 M. *Lège*; 18 M. *Cier-de-Luchon*. We now enter the Luchon valley and have a good view of the snow-crowned mountains at its head. — 19 1/4 M. *Antignac*. — 22 1/2 M. *Bagnères-de-Luchon*: the station is 3/4 M. from the centre of the town (omnibus 60 c.; luggage 40 c. each trunk).

II. Bagnères-de-Luchon.

Hotels. Gr.-Hôt. de Honnemaison, déj. 4, D. 5 fr.; Grand-Hôtel, open all the year round, R. 2-15, B. 1 1/2, déj. 3 1/2, D. 4 1/2, pens. 10-25 fr.; Gr.-Hôt. des Bains, R., L., & A. 3-8, B. 1-1 1/2, déj. 4, D. 5, pens. 12-15 fr.; Sacaron, déj. & D. 10 fr.; d'Etigny & d'Europe, déj. 3 1/2, D. 4 fr.; Broc-Verdeil; d'Angleterre, déj. 3, D. 4 fr.; Continental, same charges; de la Poste-Sacail, de la Paix, Pardeillan, déj. & D. at these 7 fr.; de Bordeaux, déj. & D. 6 fr.; de France, all in the Allée or Cours d'Etigny. — Gr.-Hôt. Richelieu, Rue d'Espagne et des Thermes, near the Baths and of the 1st class, 15-20 fr. per day; Gr.-Hôt. des Thermes, Rue des Thermes, beside the preceding, déj. 4, D. 5 fr.; Hôt. Canton, Hôtel de Paris, Rue d'Espagne, behind those in the Allée d'Etigny, déj. & D. 7 fr. — Gr.-Hôt. de Luchon et du Casino, at a distance from the centre of the town and the baths, R., L., & A. 4-10, B. 1 1/2, déj. 4, D. 5, pens. 12-20 fr. — Déjeuner usually at 10.30 a.m., dinner at 6.30 p.m.

Villas, Apartments, and Rooms to Let. In the Rue d'Espagne beyond the Quinconces, the *Villas* or *Maisons Monteil*, O. Gleye, Vignaux, Cantaloup; Huguet, Florida, and Mirens; in the Allée d'Etigny, very numerous: *Lafon*, (bookseller), *B. Gascon, Gasquet, Lasbs, Perrotin, Colomb*, etc.; in the Allée des Bains, *Baqué*, well spoken of, *Maison Dorée*; in the Rue de Piqué, near the Allée d'Etigny, *Dubos*; in the Avenue du Casino, *Bonnette, Raymaud, Estrujo*, etc. — Ladies travelling alone are recommended to the *Couvent de l'Espérance*, Route de St. Mamet.

Living at Luchon is expensive during the season, which is at its height from the end of June to the end of August.

Café-Restaurants. *Armaïve, du Parc, Dicon*, Allée d'Etigny, etc.

Bath-Establishment. *Drinking*, subscription for 1 month, 10 fr. between July 1st and Sept. 15th, 15 fr. for the season. *Baths*, 60 c.-5 fr. according to the time of year and the hour. *Douches*, 50 c.-3 fr. — The list of Luchon *Physicians* is exhibited in the entrance-hall of the Establishment.

Cabs for drives outside the town (no tariff; bargain), with one horse 3-4 fr., with two horses 4-5 fr. per hour. — *Private Carriages for Excursions*, with 2 horses 20-35 fr., according to distance; with 4 horses, 25-40 fr. — *Brakes* start for the Vallée du Lys and the Lac d'Oo daily at 12 noon; fare 3 or 4 fr. each, or more, according to number of passengers; the fares and times are posted up in the Allée d'Etigny. The brakes do not always go to the Lac d'Oo; enquire at one of the offices, Nos. 26 and 52 in the Allée.

Guides and Horses are numerous and regulated by tariff (see excursions), but it is always prudent to ascertain charges beforehand. Admission fees, tolls, and horses for the guides are at the cost of the traveller. Most of the guides merely let horses or act as conductors for parties on horseback; the chief mountain guides are *Bert. Courrège, Bertrand*, nicknamed *Traqué, Hourillon*, nicknamed *Odo*, and *Bern. Lafont*, nicknamed *Bernatet*.

Casino, open from June 1 to Sept. 30: 1 day, 1 fr. 50 c., ten days 10 fr., month 30 fr., season 60 fr. *Theatre* at the Casino: reserved seat 2½ or 3 fr.; season-ticket 25 fr. Family tickets at a reduction.

Post and Telegraph Office, Rue Sylvie at the E. end of the Allée d'Etigny.

English Church Service in summer at *M. Corneille's Chapel*.

Bagnères-de-Luchon or simply *Luchon* (2065 ft.) is a town of 3528 inhab., charmingly situated at the end of the valley of the same name. It is the nearest town to the central Pyrenean range and has been celebrated for its baths from the time of the Romans, to whom it was known as *Balneariae Lixonienses*. Frequently ravaged during the middle ages and in later centuries, this thermal station, like many others, was at one time almost completely deserted; but since the close of last century it has revived, and has for many years been one of the most prosperous watering-places in the Pyrenees, visited annually by about 36,000 patients and tourists. It has the advantage of its rival Cauterets in possessing a greater variety of thermal saline and sulphureous springs and a milder climate, owing to its lower altitude. Its climate is, however, more variable.

Luchon consists of two distinct quarters, the old town and the new. The old town, the nearer to the station, whence it is reached by a grand avenue of plane trees, dating from 1788, is a small collection of mean houses, with narrow and tortuous streets, on the left bank of the One and at the mouth of the Arboust valley. The modern Romanesque *Church*, decorated with mural paintings by Romain Cazes, is the only edifice worthy of note.

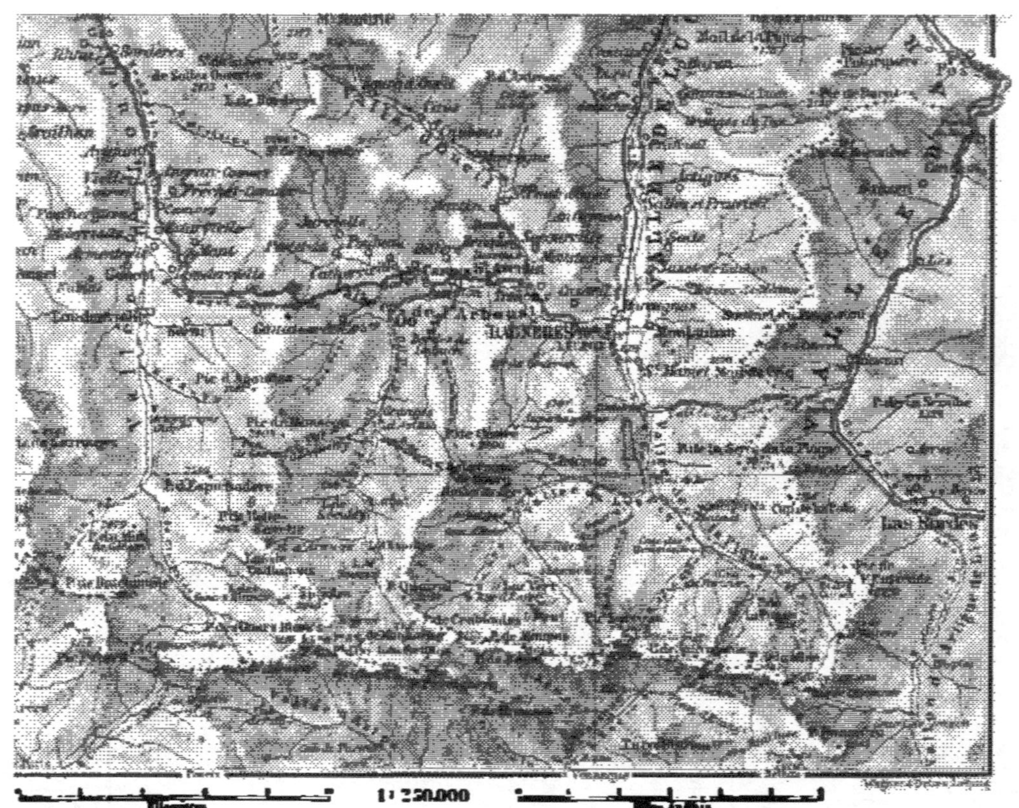

1 : 250.000
Kilomètres
Milles Anglais

The new town, on the other hand, is farther from the station, lower down, between the One and the Pique. It is about five times as large as the old town and is handsomely laid out with pleasant buildings, villas surrounded with gardens, good streets, and fine promenades. The *Allée or *Allées d'Etigny*, which we enter immediately beyond the old town, is an avenue planted with four rows of old lime-trees, which extends to the Bath Establishment. It is the centre of the town and takes its name from Meyret d'Etigny, who came to Luchon after 1751 as magistrate, induced the chemists Bayen and Richard to examine the waters, had the Montréjeau and Bigorre roads made, and laid out this promenade in 1765. At the end of the valley appear the three summits of the Pic Sacrous, Pic de Sauvegarde, and Pic de la Mine (pp. 184, 183).

At the end of the Allée is a *Statue of M. d'Etigny*, by Crauk.

The BATH ESTABLISHMENT, adjacent on the W. to the Superbagnères mountain, from which the springs rise, is a large building with nothing remarkable in its exterior save its peristyle of 28 pillars, each a monolith of white St. Béat marble. In the interior the entrance-hall (Salle des Pas-Perdus) is a fine chamber decorated with mural paintings by Romain Cazes, representing the springs, oreads, etc. Two transverse galleries lead to the halls for baths and douches; and a staircase at the end to the drinking places, and to the curious subterranean galleries. An annexe is allotted to vapour baths and to 'graduated moistenings' under a special system. The establishment at Luchon is considered to be one of the best organised in existence; it is open all the year round.

The MINERAL WATERS contain chiefly sulphate of sodium. One of the advantages of Luchon as a health-resort is the great choice presented by its 48 springs, which vary much in their composition, in amount of sulphuration, and in temperature (62° to 151° Fahr.), and thus allow of a great diversity of treatment. They are, however, especially employed in skin affections, rheumatism, scrofula, lymphatic cases, catarrhs, syphilis, and surgical cases. The waters are drunk and inhaled, but chiefly taken in baths. They change rapidly on exposure to the air, becoming milky and precipitating sulphur. The principal springs, all sulphureous, are known by the following names: *Reine* (126° Fahr.), *Bayen* (151°), *Azémar* (102°), *Richard Nouvelle* (122°), *Grotte Supérieure* (137.5°), *Blanche* (117°), *Ferras Ancienne* (100°), *Ferras Nouvelle* (105°), *Enceinte* (120°), *Etigny* (118°), *Bosquet* (109°), *Senges* (106°), *Bordeu* (120°), *Richard Inférieure* or *Ancienne* (100°), *Grotte Inférieure* (126°), and *Pré I, II,* and *III* (145°; 108°; 95°). The remaining springs either differ but little from these, or are used as 'sources alimentaires', *i. e.* in a combination of springs of small outflow. The annual yield of the warm sulphur springs is over 132,000 gallons per day. There is also a *Saline Spring* (62°).

In front of the Baths stretches the fine *Promenade des Quin-*

ronces, where concerts are given in the morning from 10 to 11 (in the
Casino in the evening). Chair 10 c. during the day, 20 c. for the
concerts, or by subscription.

Adjoining the promenade is a *Jardin Anglais* with a small
lake, the *Burette du Pré*, and a *Fruitière* for the whey-cure. Higher
up is the *Bosquet*, a much frequented promenade at the foot of
Superbagnères (p. 157), with the *Fontaine d'Amour* and several
restaurants. Behind the Buvette du Pré is a *Mountain Railway*
(opened in 1893), which ascends the slope of Superbagnères to the
Café-Restaurant de la Chaumière; it affords pretty views. The
Allée des Bains, extending from the Quinconces to the bank of the
Pique and along that river, forms a promenade in the town itself.

The *Grand Casino* is in the new town between the Allée des
Bains and the Boulevard du Casino. It is a handsome building of
recent erection and situated in a park of about 9 acres. The rooms
are extensive and richly ornamented, including a concert room, ball
room, theatre, reading, billiard, and refreshment rooms, etc.

On the first floor are some *Relief-models* of much interest, executed by
Lézat, the engineer. One represents the whole chain of the Pyrenees on
a scale of 1 to 40,000, and another, a master-piece of patience and accuracy
modelled on the spot, the central range of the same mountains on 1 : 10,000
horizontal, and 1 : 5000 vertical scale. There are also geological and botanical collections, an exhibition of paintings, etc.

The principal points of interest in the immediate vicinity of Luchon
are *Castelvieil* and the *Waterfalls of Juzet* and *Montauban*. — Juzet lies
about 2 M. to the N.E., on the right bank of the Pique, and is reached
by crossing first the railway and then the river, not far from the station.
The fall is about 120 ft. high; 1/2 fr. is charged for visiting it, but it
can be well seen from the opposite side of the valley. — Montauban,
1 1/2 M. to the E. of Luchon, along the road prolonging the Rue de Pique,
may also be reached from Juzet in 1/2 hr. The fall is at the top of the
village and the usual approach is through the curé's garden (50 c.). —
Castelvieil is a ruined tower (14th cent.) on an isolated hill (2450 ft.)
about 2 M. up the valley, to the left of the road leading into Spain. It
commands a fine view up and down the valley of the Pique and of the
valley of Burbe to the E. (50 c.). In making the excursion into the Val
du Lys (p. 181) we pass the tower. Not far from it is a chalybeate spring.

III. Excursions.

To St. Bertrand-de-Comings, 22 M., carriage 30-35 fr.; railway route viâ *Loures*, see p. 174.

*To the Lac d'Oo, 10 M., of which 8 M. are practicable for
carriages; brakes, see p. 176; guide (unnecessary) and horse 6 fr.
each; carriage and pair 25 fr., with 4 horses 30 fr. An early start
is advisable, to avoid the heat. After passing through the old town
and along the *Allée des Soupirs*, we follow the Bagnères-de-Bigorre
road, which first ascends sharply and then descends into the *Valley of the Arboust*. — 2 3/4 M. *Chapelle-St. Aventin*, at the mouth
of the Ouell valley (p. 180). — 3 3/4 M. *St. Aventin*, a village with
a Romanesque church into which some ancient altars and carvings

have been built. — 4¹/₂ M. *Cazaux-de-l'Arbousi*, where the church has some rude but interesting frescoes of the 15th century. Here we leave the Bagnères road (p. 174), turn to the left, and skirt the right side of the huge moraine, deposited by the glacier which once filled the Oo valley, descending more than 5000 ft. lower than those of to day. The tourist will observe many erratic blocks due to this glacier. — 5¹/₂ M. *Oo* (guide, J. Brunet), at the mouth of the narrow valley of that name, which is also known as the *Val d'Astau* (toll for each horse 20 c.). — At (8 M.) *Granges d'Astau* the carriage-road ends, and the excursion must be continued on horseback (2-3 fr.) or on foot. To the left opens the *Vallon de Médassoles*, interesting to botanists; to the right is the *Val d'Esquierry*, which is also rich in flowers. The latter valley, at the entrance to which is the *Cascade de la Chevelure de Madeleine*, forms the first part of the difficult but interesting ascent (2 hrs.) of the *Pic des Gours-Blancs* (Gouffres Blancs; 10,220 ft.). The ascent leads past the *Lac de Caillaouas*, on the bank of which is a hut with sleeping accommodation. — The Lac d'Oo road now ascends in zigzags among huge rocks, to the left of the torrent which descends from the (³/₄-1 hr.) *Lac d'Oo, or *de Sécutéjo* (4920 ft.; Inn; each pers. and horse 25 c.). The lake is nearly ¹/₂ M. long and about ¹/₈ M. broad and has an area of 95 acres with a depth of 180-210 ft. Its waters, which are full of trout, are steadily shrinking and there is little doubt that, like many others, the lake will ultimately disappear. The scene is wild and impressive. The lake is surrounded by bold and lofty rocks, above which appear the snow-clad summits of the Quairats (left), the Montarqué (in front), and the Crête de Spijoles and the Pic de Nère (right; nearer). At the head of the lake a fine * *Waterfall* (890 ft.) descends in three successive leaps to the rocks below, while not the least charm of the picture is the changeful mirror afforded by the greenish waters of the lake. Ferry across the lake, 1 pers. 1 fr. 75 c., 2 pers. 2 fr., 3 or more pers. 75 c. each; boat round the lake 2¹/₂, 3, and 4 fr., each addit. pers. 75 c. To reach the waterfall on foot takes 35 min. (rough path).

To the Port d'Oo (*Pic Quairats*), 8 hrs. from Luchon, 5¹/₄ hrs. from the Lac d'Oo; guide 10-12 fr., horse to (12¹/₂ M.) the Lac de Saousat 8 fr. — From the Lac d'Oo (see above) we ascend to the left and in 1 hr. pass the *Lac d'Espingo* (8160 ft.), whence the difficult ascent of the *Pic Quairats* (10,035 ft.) may be made in 4 hours. In 25-30 min. more we reach the *Lac de Saousat* (8395 ft.), where we leave the path to the Portillon d'Oo (see below) on the left. The pyramid in front is the Tuc de Montarqué (see below). We take the right hand path, which is very steep, and, 1¹/₂ hr. farther on, skirt a small lake and the *Pic de Spijoles* (10,000 ft.). Another 1¹/₂ hr. brings us to the *Lac Glacé d'Oo* (8780 ft.) beyond which we enter on perpetual snow. The ascent now becomes easier and it is only ³/₄ hr. to the Port d'Oo (9850 ft.), the col between the *Pic du Port d'Oo* (10,215 ft.), on the right, and the *Néil de la Baque* (10,040 ft.), on the left. The view is striking; on every side are mountains covered with snow and glaciers, the chief summits being the Pic Posets in front of us, the Gours-Blancs to the W., the crest of the Spijoles to the N.W., and to the E. the Cra-

bioules. — The descent on the other side of the col brings us in 4 hrs. to
Vénasque (p. 183).

To THE PORTILLON D'Oo (*Tuc de Montarqué, Pic de Crabioules, Pic de
Perdighero*), about 8 hrs.; guide and horse as above. The road is the
same as the above as far as the (5½ hrs.) *Lac de Saousat.* Thence we
ascend to the left between the Tuc de Montarqué and the Pic Quairats
and pass the *Michot Waterfall* and to the right of the (2 hrs.) *Lac Glacé
du Portillon* (8860 ft.). The last part of the ascent is difficult. The Portillon d'Oo (9885 ft.) is the highest of the Pyrenean passes; the view is
similar to that from the Port d'Oo (see above). — From the Lac Glacé
du Portillon the *Tuc de Montarqué* (9885 ft.; 1 hr., easy), to the N.E., the
Pic de Crabioules (10,230 ft.; 1½ hr.), to the E., and the *Pic Perdighero*
(9585 ft.; 2½ hrs.), to the S.E., may be ascended. The two last are difficult; the views from all three are fine.

To THE PIC DE CÉCIRÉ, 4-4½ hrs.; guide and horse 8 fr. each. We
proceed to *Cazaux* (p. 179) and then take an easy bridle-path to the S.,
which beyond (40 min.) *Bordes-de-Labach* leads direct to the peak, by
the *Col de la Coume-de-Bourg.* A shorter but more fatiguing route leads
via Superbagnères (see p. 181) and thence to the W. by the arête of
a spur of the mountain. The *Pic de Céciré* (7875 ft.) affords a wide
view, one of the finest to be had in the Luchon district. To the S. it commands a grand amphitheatre of snow-clad peaks from those of the Lys
valley to the Pic Posets. — The descent, by the Lys valley, takes 3½ hrs.

To THE PIC DE MONSÉOU, 4½ hrs.; guide and horse 6 fr. each, or
7 fr. if the return is made by the Esquierry valley (5 hrs.). To (4½ M.)
Cazaux, see p. 179. We follow the same road for 1½ M. farther, passing
Garin, then diverge to the left, by the route to (1 M.) *Gouaux-de-l'Arboust.* Thence we ascend through meadows, a wood, and pastures to
a slate-quarry where we turn to the left and, passing a small lake, reach
(1¼ hr.) a little col with a spring. From here to the summit, 1¼ hr. more.
Travellers intending to return by the Esquierry valley dismount, ½ hr.
from the spring, and send the horses to the Pas de Couret, on the S.
side of the mountain. The Pic de Monséou (7880 ft.) affords a very fine
view of the central chain of the Pyrenees, with its glaciers, from those
of the Gours-Blancs to those of the Monts-Maudits. At the foot of the
truncated cone forming the summit is an echo which repeats eight syl-
lables. — The descent to the *Pas de Couret,* to the S., takes 1 hr.; thence
the Val d'Esquierry branches to the E. to the Vallée d'Oo (p. 179).

To THE MONNÉ, 4½ hrs.; guide (unnecessary) and horse, each 7 fr.
by day, 10 fr. by night, when the ascent is made in order to see the
sunrise; carriage to (9¼ M.) Bourg-d'Ouell and back 20-25 fr. —
We follow the Lac d'Oo road as far as the (2¾ M.) *Chapelle St.
Aventin* (p. 178), where we turn to the right into the pretty *Ouell
Valley,* in which we pass a succession of small villages, well situated but otherwise uninteresting: *Benqué-Dessous, Benqué-Dessus,
Maylin,* (2¾ M.) *St. Paul-d'Ouell, Mayrègne, Caubous, Cirès,*
and (3½ M.) *Bourg-d'Ouell* (Inn). Beyond this village we ascend
to the right to (1½ hr.) the summit of the Monné or *Monîne*
(7045 ft.), a view-point situated between the plain and the highest
range and commanding the Pyrenees from Mont-Perdu to the Pic de
Montvallier, a sweep of 50 M., distant from the Monné from 25 to
30 M. in a direct line. The glaciers of the central mass as far as
the Monts-Maudits are also well seen. The ascent of the Monné
is most frequently made in order to enjoy the sunrise, which from
June to the end of August, owing to the sun then rising to the N.
of the mountains, lights up their snows and glaciers.

To the Pic d'Antenac, 3-4 hrs., there and back 6 hrs.; guide (not indispensable) and horse 6 fr. The route is identical with the one just described as far as (5½ M.) *St. Paul-d'Oueil.* Thence we ascend to the right by a steep bridle-path into a bare valley and across the *Col de la Serre.* The Pic d'Antenac (about 6560 ft.) affords a view embracing the Monts-Maudits and the glaciers of Crabioules and of the Cours-Blancs, etc., but more especially in the direction of the Garonne valley. — In returning we may follow the crest of the mountain southward and descend either into the Oueil valley at *Sacourville,* opposite Benqué-Dessous (see above) or, farther on, into the Arboust valley at *Trébons,* a little before the Chapelle St. Aventin.

To Superbagnères, 2½-3½ hrs.; guide and horse, 6 fr. each. Pedestrians may ascend either directly from the town (using the mountain-railway at first; p. 178) or by a path to the left at the first bridge (Pont de Mousquérès), on the Lac d'Oo road (p. 178); but both routes are hard to find. Riders proceed to (3½ M.) St. Aventin (p. 178) and thence ascend to the left, by meadows and a shaded bridle-path in the direction of the (¾ hr.) *Granges de Gourron.* Crossing the brook beyond the hamlet they mount to the left, and traverse a pine wood to the (¾ hr. more) pastures and plateau of Superbagnères (5900 ft.; Inn). The plateau forms a kind of terrace of the *Pic de Céciré,* which rises 1970 ft. above it, requiring 2 hrs. more for the ascent (with guide; see p. 180). The view from the plateau is delightful in the direction of the Luchon valley, but even finer looking towards the glaciers of the Cirque du Lys. The descent may be made to the E. into the Vallée du Lys.

*To the Vallée du Lys and the Rue d'Enfer, a most interesting excursion; road to the (8 M.) head of the valley, then paths practicable for horses (1½ hr.). Carriage and pair, 20 fr., with 4 horses 25 fr.; guide (unnecessary) and horse 5 and 7 fr. each.; brakes, see p. 176. We follow at first the road to Spain, passing the tower of Castelvieil (p. 178) and crossing a bridge over the Pique, but a little farther on leave this road to the left (to the Port de Vénasque, see p. 183) and return to the left bank by the (3 M.) *Pont de Ravi.* At this point begins the *Vallée du Lys,* or *Lis,* one of the finest in the Pyrenees. The valley is at first narrow and flanked by wooded heights, while the torrent, skirted by the road, forms several cascades, the chief of which is the *Trou de Bounéou* or the *Estranguillé,* between huge rocks which demand caution. [A visitor, to whom there is a monument, met his death here in 1876.] The valley soon expands and we see in front of us the *Cirque du Lys,* shut in by noble mountains clad with glaciers among which that of the Crabioules is conspicuous. Of the three inns here, the best is that at the head of the valley, on the left beyond the torrent (about 3600 ft.). A few minutes more bring us to the Cascade

d'Enfer, a massive fall in a gloomy channel, worn in the rocks by
the torrent. It is not possible, however, to obtain a single comprehensive view of the entire fall. To the left, on the other side
of the inn, is a much smaller waterfall, named from its shape the
Cascade du Cœur. It is most conveniently visited on the return by
the S. side of the Lys. A zigzag path to the right, before the great
waterfall is reached, leads in 25 min. to a bridge beyond this smaller
fall. From the latter we reach, in about 15 min. more, the grand
*Gouffre d'Enfer, which should be viewed from the foot of the flight
of steps leading down into it. About 10 min. farther on there is another bridge, beyond which we continue to skirt the torrent. The
gorge slightly expands. In 40 min. more we reach the *Rue d'Enfer,
a striking chasm in a mountain of slate, of which the end and top
can scarcely be seen. A path has recently been constructed by which
we may penetrate to the end of the ravine in about $^3/_4$ hr.

To THE LAC VERT (*Pic de Maupas, Pic de Boum*), 4 hrs., carriage-road
to the head of the Val du Lys, thence a bridle-path; guide (unnecessary
for the road) and horse, 8 fr. each. From the last inn we turn to the
S.E., in the direction of the Cascade du Cœur (see above), and ascend
through the wood to the (25 min.) *Cascade de Solage*. Farther on we
pass the *Cascade de Trigon* on the left, and reach ($1^1/_4$ hr. from the inn)
the *Cirque des Graouès*, an ancient lake-bed, and ($^1/_4$ hr. more) the beautiful, horse-shoe shaped Lac Vert (6490 ft.), bordered on the E. by high
rocks. The lake receives, by a cascade on the S., the waters of the *Lac
Bleu*, which lies 40 min. higher up. — From the Lac Vert the difficult
ascents (about 4 hrs.) of the *Pic* or *Tuc de Maupas* (10,200 ft.) and the *Pic
de Boum* (10,040 ft.) may be made. Fine views.

To THE PIC DE BACANÈRE AND THE PIC DE BURAT, 4-5 hrs.,
9 hrs. there and back; guide and horse, 8 fr. each; a fine excursion.
We proceed first to *Juzet* (p. 178) and thence ascend to the N.E.
to (3 M.) *Sode* (3000 ft.). Through woods we reach (5 M.) *Artigues*
(4070 ft.) and ($1^1/_4$ hr. farther to the E.), the *Rochers de Cigalère*,
a fine view-point. We next skirt the mountain to the left, and in
$1^1/_4$ hr. more gain the summit of the Pic de Bacanère (7200 ft.), the
view from which includes the valley of Luchon and its side valleys,
as well as the Aran valley, the Port de la Glère, Port de Vénasque,
and Port de la Piquade (see below), the Monné and the Pic du
Midi, on the sky-line, the Superbagnères plateau, the cone of the
Quairats, the Monts-Maudits, etc. — About $^1/_2$ hr. to the N. of the
Pic de Bacanère rises the Palas or Pic de Burat (7050 ft.; Inn)
which affords a splendid view resembling those from the Monné
and the Pic d'Antenac (p. 181). — The descent may be made to
the W. to Gouaux-de-Luchon, whence the Luchon road may be
reached, to the left.

To THE POUJASTOU, $4^1/_2$ hrs., there and back 8 hrs.; guide and horse
(as far as the Col), 8 fr. each. The route leads viâ (20 min.) *Montauban*
(p. 178), a small wood, the ($1^1/_2$ hr.) *Prairies d'Erran* (fine view), and the
(10 min.) *Forêt de Sésartigues*, where we turn to the right. We next reach
the ($1^1/_2$ hr.) *Fontaine Rouge*, a chalybeate spring, near the little *Grotte
du Chat* (1 fr.; uninteresting), and ($^1/_2$ hr. more) the *Col des Courets* (6990 ft.).
Thence the ($^1/_2$-$^3/_4$ hr.) summit of the *Poujastou* (6925 ft.) is reached on

foot, over slippery turf. Here, on the side next the Aran valley, which is
well seen, we are on Spanish territory. The glaciers of the Val du Lys
are in sight, but not those of the Monts-Maudits.

*To the Port de Vénasque and the Port de la Piquade
(Pic de Sauvegarde), a very interesting excursion, but long and
fatiguing, requiring a whole day. It may be made on horseback
throughout and even a carriage may be taken as far as the (6 M.)
Hospice. Guide and horse to the Hospice 5, to the Port 8 fr.; carriage and pair to the Hospice, 25 fr., with 4 horses 30 fr.; toll
at the frontier 50 c. — We take the road to Spain described as far
as the *Pont de Ravi* on p. 181. Thence we continue the ascent, to
the left, of the Pique valley, passing (^{3}/$_4$ M.) the *Granges de Labach*
or *de Castaing*, whence a road diverging to the right (the old road
over the Col de la Glère, p. 184) leads to (20-25 min.) the *Cascade
des Demoiselles* (about 4920 ft., see below). Our road continues
straight on through the *Bois de Charuga*.

6 M. **Hospice du Port de Vénasque**, *de France*, or *de Luchon*
(4460 ft.), a large and good inn where the carriage-road ends and
three paths diverge respectively to the Port de Vénasque, the old
Port de la Glère, on the right, and the Ports Mounjoyo and de la
Piquade, on the left.

Crossing a bridge in front of the Hospice and following the left bank
of the Pique we come to a fork of the footpath. The left branch leads
to (10 min.) the *Cascade du Parisien*, issuing from an exceedingly narrow
gorge and descending by five leaps. — The right-hand path at the fork
leads to the (25-30 min.) *Cascade des Demoiselles* (see above), at the end
of a gloomy gorge shut in between wooded cliffs.

Beyond the Hospice the valley divides at the foot of the *Pic de
la Pique* (7850 ft.), the ascent of which is dangerous. The valley
to the left is the *Val de la Frèche*; that to the right is the sterile
and desolate *Val du Port de Vénasque*, through which a toilsome
bridle-path leads to the (3^3/$_4$ M.) Port. — 7^1/$_2$ M. *Le Culet*, a spot
covered with detritus brought down by avalanches in the spring;
here there are two little waterfalls. — 8^3/$_4$ M. *Vallon de l'Homme*,
so named from the rude monument to a French custom-house of-
ficer who was murdered by a smuggler. Farther on, to the left, is
the *Trou des Chaudronniers*, where nine tinkers were buried in the
snow. Then above five small lakes, on the right, the path mounts
in zigzags to (9 M.) the *Port de Vénasque (7930 ft.), a dip in the
frontier ridge between the *Pic de la Mine* (8880 ft.) on the left, and
the *Pic de Sauvegarde*, on the right. The view of the Monts-Maudits which here suddenly opens is superb; but the prospect is even
finer from the *Pic de Sauvegarde (8975 ft.; ^{3}/$_4$-1 hr. from the Port)
which may be easily ascended even on horseback. There is a path
to the summit (1 fr. for its use).

On the other side of the Col is a small Spanish inn. Bearing
to the left along the *Peña Blanca*, we pass the springs of *Peña
Blanca* and *Coustères*, and, always in view of the Monts-Maudits,
reach (1^1/$_4$ M.) the **Port de la Piquade** or *Picade* (7950 ft.), from

which the view is equally fine. The difficult bit we now enter on,
to the left, over slippery rocks, is the *Pas de l'Escalette* (7870 ft.),
whence we may descend to (5 M.) the Hospice du Port de Vénasque
viâ the *Pas de Mounjoyu* (which leads, on the right, into the Aran
valley), by a route presenting some difficulty at places, and finally
descending to the left, into the Val de la Frêche (p. 183).

To the Col de la Glère (*Pic Sacrous*), 4 hrs; guide and horse (to the
lake) 8 fr. each. The old road diverges to the right at the Granges de
Labach, in the Pique valley (p. 189); the new road starts from the Hospice
du Port de Vénasque; the two unite in the *Cirque de la Glère*, from which
an easy ascent mounts to the Col de la Glère (7815 ft.), an old 'port' or
pass into Aragon. The view from the col is somewhat limited, but from
the *Lac de Gorgutes*, 10 min. below it on the Spanish side, there is a very
wide prospect. — The Pic Sacrous (8785 ft.), to the W., may be ascended
from the col in 3/4 hr. The view includes the Monts-Maudits and the
glaciers of the Vallée du Lys.

To the Pic de l'Entécade, 4 hrs.; guide (not indispensable) and
horse, 6 fr. each. The route follows the road to Spain as far as the
Hospice (p. 183) and thence for 3/4 hr. more the bridle-path to the
Port de la Piquade. Then, turning once more to the left, we cross
the pastures to the (1/2 hr.) *Cabane de Pouylane*, inhabited by
Spanish shepherds. Passing next the little *Etang des Garees*, we
reach (10 min.) a col affording a view of the Maladetta, and (20 min.)
another col whence we see the Aran valley. The summit of the Pic
de l'Entécade (7285 ft.) is gained in 10 min. more. The view is
magnificent, finer if possible on the Monts-Maudits side than from
the Port de Vénasque. It includes moreover the summits on this
side and extends westward as far as the Pic du Midi, the Vignemale,
and Mont-Perdu; eastward over the Spanish summits beyond the
Aran; and northward to the plains of Gascony.

To the Pic de Néthou. This expedition, fit only for practised climbers, is long and expensive, especially to the single traveller, but with
ordinary prudence it is without danger. The best season is between
July 20 and Sept. 1, and it requires two days. If the Rencluse route be
taken two guides are required, with ice-axes and ropes; but one guide
is sufficient for the ascent by the Maliblerne valley. In the former case
riding is practicable as far as the (7 hrs.) Rencluse; in the latter case,
as far as the (10 1/2 hrs.) Ribereta hut. Guides and horses, each 15 fr.
per day; provisions must also be taken. The night is spent at the Spanish
inn beyond the Port du Vénasque (moderate) or better at the Rencluse
(10 fr.), or in the Ribereta hut, unless the traveller prefers to bivouac
in the open air. — To the *Port de Vénasque*, see p. 183.

A. Viâ the Rencluse. We follow the Port de la Piquade route as far
as the *Peña Blanca Spring*, then turn to the right to the (1 hr.) *Plan des
Etangs*, and, farther on, to the right again to (1 hr.; 7 hrs. from Luchon)
the *Rencluse* (6970 ft.). This hut is situated at the foot of a rock near
the *Gouffre de Turmon*, where the *Esera*, the torrent fed by the Maladetta
glacier, becomes subterranean only to reappear in the Vénasque valley.
The torrent of the Néthou glacier also disappears at the *Trou du Toro*,
1/2 hr. from the Rencluse route, near the top of the Plan des Etangs. —
A very early start is made on the second day so as to ensure, if possible,
a clear view from the summit of the Néthou. We ascend in a S.S.E.
direction to (2 1/2 hrs.) the *Portillon* (9510 ft.), between the *Maladetta
Glacier*, on the right, and the *Néthou Glacier*, on the left. Then (using
the rope) we ascend the last-named, the main one (2 1/2 by 1 M.), from

N.W. to S.E., as far as the (1 hr.) *Lac Coroué* (10,410 ft.) at the foot of the *Dôme du Néthou*, which we ascend, with difficulty, in 1/2 hr. The next part of the ascent, the (1/2 hr.) *Pont de Mahomet*, is the most trying point for those who are subject to giddiness, as it is a ridge about 80 ft. long and only 3 ft. wide, with an abyss on each side. This accomplished, we are on the Pic de Néthou, or *d'Aneto* (11,170 ft.), the highest summit of the Pyrenees, and the centre of the Monts-Maudits, a nearly isolated group of granite peaks, to the S. of the principal range, in Spanish territory. The group has been compared to Mont Blanc, but it is 4600 ft. lower. The other summits are, to the W., the *Maladetta* (11,015 ft.), a name often given to the whole group, and also known as the *Pic du Milieu*, the *Pic Occidental de la Maladetta* (10,885 ft.), and the *Pic d'Albe* (10,780 ft.). The range which links this mass to the main chain on the N. includes the peaks of *Les Sallanques*, *Moutlères*, *Fourcanade* (9485 ft.), *des Harrances*, and *Pouméro* (8810 ft.). — The summit of the Néthou, a plateau of 75 ft. by 26 ft., is surrounded by precipices on all sides, except the N. by which the ascent is made. The view is very extensive but is often obscured by mist and always indistinct on account of the elevation. The peaks best seen are those mentioned above, those on the frontier to the N.W., the Pic Posets to the W., and the Pic Maliblerne (10,475 ft.) and Pic Castaness (9405 ft.) to the S. There is a register on the summit in which the traveller writes his name and he is also desired to read the thermometers fixed there. — The descent may be made by the Col de Coroué (see below), and thence over the (2 hrs.) *Col de Querigueña* (9000 ft.) to the (3/4 hr.) *Lac de Querigueña*, *Cregueña*, or *Gregonio* (8710 ft.), one of the largest in the Pyrenees (200 acres), and by the *Gorge de Querigueña* to the *Bains de Vénasque*, 5 hrs. from the summit. The horses should be ordered to meet the traveller here or at any rate at the Hospice de Vénasque. — The *Pic de la Maladetta* (41/2 hrs.) and the *Pic d'Albe* (3 hrs.) are also ascended, through seldom, from the Reneluse.

B. Vià THE MALIBIERNE VALLEY (*Bains de Vénasque*). — From the *Port de Vénasque* (p. 183) we descend to the right in 1 hr. to the *Hospice de Vénasque* (5895 ft.; toll). Thence we follow the Vénasque (or Esera) valley, crossing several torrents, one of which, the (1/2 hr.) *Romeno*, forms a fine waterfall. About 2 hrs. from the Port, 20 min. to the left, are the *Bains de Vénasque* (moderate), with warm sulphur springs similar to those of Luchon. In 1/4 hr. more, on the left, is the Gorge de Queriguaña (see above), and in another 1/2 hr. we turn to the left from the road to *Vénasque*, a small fortified town, 11/4 hr. farther on. We now ascend the *Malibierne Valley*, wooded at first and then pastoral, to (31/2 hrs.) the *Ribereta Hut* (6855 ft.), 101/2 hrs. from Luchon. — On the second day, we follow the same track in the valley, first on the right and afterwards on the left bank of the torrent, passing (11/4 hr.) a fine waterfall. We then ascend to the left (N.), leaving on the left the *Lac Inférieur d'Erloueil* and the *Lac Glacé d'Erloueil* and reach the (1/2 hr.) *Lac Supérieur d'Erloueil* (9070 ft.), which is also frozen. Thence we command a grand view of the *Glacier de Coroué* and of the massive precipices of Néthou and Maladetta. We ascend for some time to the W. of the glacier and then cross it (no crevasses), to the (13/4 hr.) *Col de Coroué* (10,475 ft.), where we join the route described above.

To THE PIC POSETS, a toilsome but unhazardous expedition, seldom made. It takes 3 days, the nights being spent at the Turmes hut (to which riding is practicable), or at the Astos hut. Guides and horses, each 15 fr. per day. We follow the route last described, up the Vénasque valley, and beyond the divergence of the Malibierne valley, to the (71/2 hrs.) *Pont de Cubère*, 11/2 M. on this side of Vénasque (see above). Crossing the bridge we ascend to the N.W. in the *Astos Valley*, with its fine waterfalls, to the (11/2 hr.) *Turmes Hut* (5510 ft.) and the (11/2 hr. more) *Astos Hut* (5900 ft.). At least an hour may be saved by leaving the Vénasque road opposite the Baths and proceeding to the W. into the Val de Lilayrolles and so direct into the Astos valley, below the Turmes hut. — The hut lies 51/2 hrs. below the summit. We turn first to the

S. and then to the S.W., mounting a succession of rocky terraces to the
glacier, which is gained in 3 hrs., at the *Col de Paoul* or *Pasi* (about
6510 ft.). Crossing the glacier, which is free from danger, we reach (about
1 hr.) a sheer rocky wall, the scaling of which (20 min.) is the chief difficulty in the expedition. The *Pic Posets* or *des Posets* (11,045 ft.), the
second summit in the Pyrenees, forms, like the Néthou, its neighbour on
the E., the centre of a nearly isolated mass. It commands a finer view
because it is more central: to the W., Mont-Perdu, the Vignemale, and
the peaks of Balaïtous, Ger, Gabizos, and Midi d'Ossau; to the N.W.,
the Neouvielle and the Pic du Midi de Bigorre; to the N. the peaks of
Clarabide, Gours-Blancs, Port d'Oo, Perdighero, and Sauvegarde; to the
E., the Monts-Maudits; and to the S., the Pic d'Eristé. — The return may
be made on foot viâ the Port d'Oo (p. 179), 3¹/₂ hrs. from the Astos hut;
there is no path and the descent to the Lac d'Oo is fatiguing, but the
view to the N. is very fine.

27. From Boussens (Toulouse or Tarbes) to Aulus
viâ St. Girons.

41 M. Railway to (20¹/₂ M.) *St. Girons*, in 1 hr. (fares 3 fr. 70, 2 fr. 50,
1 fr. 85 c.). Diligence in the season from St. Girons to (20¹/₂ M.) *Aulus*
in 3 hrs.; fare, 3 fr.; another public conveyance 1¹/₂ fr.; carriages, to
hold 4 pers., 25 fr.; the hotels also send carriages to meet the trains. A
'courrier' also leaves St. Girons at 4 a. m. and at 1 p. m.

Boussens and the Château de Roquefort, see p. 137. — Our line
diverges to the left from the Tarbes line, crosses the Garonne, and
ascends the *Salat* valley. 3¹/₂ M. *Mazères-sur-Salat.*

6 M. *Salies-du-Salat* (Hôt. Feuillerat), a small town dominated
by the ruins of a castle (13-14th cent.) and possessing some unimportant saline and sulphur springs. — 8 M. *His-Mane-Touille*
is the station for three villages. — 10 M. *Castagnède*; 13 M. *Prat-
et-Bonrepaux*; 16 M. *Caumont.* The valley contracts.

16 M. **St. Lizier**, a decayed little town of 1411 inhab., picturesquely situated on a hill to the left, is the ancient *Lugdunum Con-
soranorum* and was formerly the chief town of the Couserans. It
still retains a large part of its *Roman Walls*, with twelve towers. The
ancient *Cathedral* (12-14th cent.) has a cloister of the 12-13th
cent., etc. — About 1¹/₄ M. to the E. (omnibus) is *Audinac*, a
hamlet with baths supplied by two considerable mineral springs.

41 M. **St. Girons** (1350 ft.; *Hôtel de France* or *Ferrière*), an
industrial town of 5448 inhab., at the confluence of the Salat, the
Lez, and the Baup, contains one modern and two ancient churches,
of which one is in ruins. It is a convenient starting-point for some
interesting excursions among the neighbouring parts of the Pyrenees. The railway is to be extended to Foix (R. 28).

The Road to Sentein (15¹/₂ M.) ascends the Lez valley, to the S.W. —
At (2¹/₂ M.) *Aubert* there is a fine bone-cavern, with stalactites. 3 M.
Moulis has a ruined castle. 5 M. *Engommer*; 8 M. *Castillon* (Inn). 10 M.
Les Bordes, at the opening of the fine valley of (3 M.) *Bethmale*, whose
inhabitants retain their peculiar costume. — In the next valley, the
Vallée de Biros, one of the finest in the district, there are zinc and lead
mines. — 11 M. *Bonnac.* — 12¹/₂ M. *Sentein* (2480 ft.; *Inn*) contains a fortified
church of the 14th century. — About 12 M. to the S. is the *Port d'Urets*

(8355 ft.), leading into the Aran valley in Spain, and commanded by the *Pic de Maybermé* (9450 ft.), the highest summit in this part of the Pyrenees.

The ROAD TO FOIX (p. 189), to the E., viâ the Baup valley and (1¹/₄ M.) *Ludiaac* (p. 186), forks at (6¹/₄ M.) *Lescure*, one branch leading to (28¹/₂ M.) *Pamiers* (p. 189). About 11 M. from Lescure and 1¹/₄ M. before the little town of *Mas-d'Azil* (Hôt. du Grand-Soleil) is a gorge, containing the bold Roche du Mas, pierced by a large cavern through which run the river Arize and the road. The cavern is ¹/₄ M. long and 200 ft. high by 180 ft. wide at the entrance, but less in the middle and at the other end. Various side-galleries may be examined on application to the keeper at the entrance.

The ROAD TO AULUS (Couflens) ascends the valley of the Salat which gradually narrows and forms a defile at the entrance to which are the ivy-clad ruins of the *Château d'Encourtiech*. — 3³/₄ M. *Lacourt*, with the remains of a 14th cent. keep and of a castle (16th cent.). The gorge now passes between wooded heights. — 7¹/₂ M. *Pont de Kercabanac*, at the confluence of the Salat and Arac.

The ROAD TO TARASCON (28 M.), also interesting, crosses the bridge and ascends the valley of the Arac. — Beyond (2¹/₂ M.) *Castet*, we thread a (¹/₄ M.) rocky defile. 8³/₄ M. *Biert*. 9¹/₄ M. *Massat* (2130 ft.; *Hôt. Lapène*), a decayed town of 3700 inhab., with bone-caverns in the vicinity. — 15 M. *Rieupregous*. — 20 M. *Le Port* (4100 ft.; fine view), the col between the *Tuc de l'Homme-Mort* (5490 ft.). on the left, and the *Pic d'Estibat* (5475 ft.), on the right. — 23¹/₂ M. *Saurat*, with 3124 inhab., whence a public conveyance plies to Tarascon. — 25 M. *Bédeillac*, with a ruined *Castle* and two large and very interesting stalactite caverns. These may be visited from *Tarascon* (p. 190).

The road now turns to the S. and traverses a short tunnel. — 8 M. *St. Sernin*. — 9 M. *Soueix*.

The ROAD TO COUFLENS (8³/₄ M.) diverges to the right from the Aulus road a little farther on and continues to ascend the Salat valley. About 2¹/₂ M. from Soueix is *Seix* (Hôt. *Broussel*), an ancient town of 3000 inhab., with *Baths* and marble quarries. Above it rises a hill (3965 ft.) on which are the ruins of the *Château de Mirabal*. — From (2 M. farther) *Couflens-de-Betmajou* the ascent of the Montvallier, to the W., may be made in 7-7¹/₂ hrs. (with guide from Seix). The route leads up the *Estours* valley to the (4 hrs.) *Cabanes d'Aula*, where the night may be spent, and thence viâ the (2¹/₂ hrs.) *Col de Peyreblanque*, and by a dip where we have to pass below a rock, the only point of any difficulty. The Pic de Montvallier (9314 ft.) is a nearly isolated cone commanding a wide prospect, extending from the Monts-Maudits to the Montcalm. — The road beyond Couflens-de-Betmajou traverses a gorge, dominated by the ruined *Château de la Garde*, and ends at (8³/₄ M.) *Couflens*, an unimportant town, 17¹/₂ M. from St. Girons.

The valley again expands. The Aulus road crosses the Salat and ascends the valley of the Garbet, to the right of which rises the Montvallier (see above). — 10 M. *Vic*, with an interesting Romanesque church. — 10¹/₂ M. *Oust* is a place of early origin ('Augusta'), with remains of its ancient walls. — 15¹/₂ M. *Ercé*, with 2630 inhabitants.

20¹/₂ M. Aulus. — Hotels. GRAND HÔTEL, near the chief Bath Establishment, R. 1-5, B. 1, déj. 3¹/₂, D. 3¹/₂, pens. 10-13 fr.; HÔTEL DU PARC, near the Casino; HÔTEL DU MIDI or MINOS, GEORGE, DES BAINS, at the entrance of the village; HÔT. DE FRANCE; SOUQUET. — FURNISHED APARTMENTS: *Francis Rougé, Théoph. Crouzat, Hôtel de l'Europe*, etc. — Bath Establishments. Fee for drinking the waters, 10 fr. for 3 weeks at the old, 5 fr. at the new; baths and douches, 2 fr. at the old, 75 c. at the new.

Aulus (2500 ft.) is a well-situated village on the Garbet, in a
little valley enclosed by mountains covered with pastures and
woods. Its warm mineral *Springs* (sulphate of lime and iron) were
probably known to the Romans and still enjoy a considerable reputation. The waters are strongly charged with soda and magnesia
and are actively purgative and diuretic. They have long been used
for a special treatment of serious cases of syphilis. There are two
Bath Establishments, both on the left bank of the river, to the right
of the village proper. The *Etablissement Lombard*, the older, with
four warm springs, is situated in an attractive little park, at the end
of which is a *Casino*. The newer *Etablissement Lacoste* has only
one spring (55° Fahr.), the water of which is heated for bathing.

EXCURSIONS. — To the **Montbéas** (6240 ft.), the mountain overlooking
the valley on the N., an easy climb of 2 hrs. The view is fine and extends to the plains of Toulouse. Halfway up, from the *Bertrone* (4595 ft.),
there is also a good view of the valley and of a large number of the
mountain peaks on the frontier. — *To THE CASCADE D'ARSE, a delightful
walk of 1½-2 hrs., up the valleys of the Garbet and the Arse, the latter
of which begins about 1½ M. to the S.E. of Aulus. We follow the left
bank of the torrent, traversing a defile known as the *Trou d'Enfer*. The
*Cascade d'Arse is one of the largest and finest in the Pyrenees. The
total height of the fall is about 360 ft., divided into three leaps of which
the second has a breadth of more than 160 ft. — To THE LAC DE GARBET,
2 hrs. The road ascends the stream to the huts of *Castel-Minier*, where
we turn to the S., still following the beautiful valley of the Garbet,
which also forms a fine waterfall. The Lac de Garbet (5480 ft.) is of considerable size, and is surrounded by pastures. Not far from it is another
and smaller lake. — To VICDESSOS, 4½ hrs. We take the carriage-road
via *Castel-Minier* (see above), and thence over the (2½ hrs.) *Port de Saleix*
(5910 ft.) and via (1¾ hrs.) *Saleix* (3520 ft.), whence there is a pretty
view. — *Vicdessos*, see p. 190.

28. From Toulouse to Foix, Tarascon, Ussat, and Ax.

77 M. RAILWAY all the way. To (51½ M.) *Foix*, in 2-2½ hrs. (fares
9 fr. 30, 6 fr. 25, 4 fr. 10 c.). — To (61 M.) *Tarascon*, in 2½-3¼ hrs.
(fares 11 fr. 10, 7 fr. 40, 4 fr. 85 c.). — To (63 M.) *Ussat*, in 2½-3½ hrs. (fares
11 fr. 50, 7 fr. 70, 5 fr. 5 c.). — To (77 M.) *Ax*, in 3-4 hrs. (fares 14 fr.,
9 fr. 35, 6 fr. 10 c.).

Toulouse, see p. 78. — The train leaves the *Gare Matabiau*
and follows the Tarbes line as far as (7½ M.) *Portet-St. Simon*
(p. 138). — Beyond (8½ M.) *Pinsaguel*, turning to the S., we cross
the Garonne, and ascend the valley of the *Ariège*. — Beyond (11 M.)
Pins-Justaret we cross the *Lèze*. — 14 M. *Venerque-le-Vernet*;
17½ M. *Miremont*; 21 M. *Auterive*, a town of 2800 inhab.; 25 M.
Cintegabelle (2500 inhab.), with an interesting church with a 16th
cent. spire.

30 M. *Saverdun*, to the right, an old town of 3466 inhab., and
one of the chief places in the county of Foix during the middle
ages, was the birthplace of Benedict XII., the third of the Avignon popes (1334-1342).

Beyond Saverdun we cross the Ariège and passing (35 M.) *Le Vernet-d'Ariège* reach —

40 M. **Pamiers** (*Grand Soleil*, Rue des Nobles; *Catala*, Rue Major, R., L., & A. 2, B. ¹/₂, déj. 2¹/₂, D. 3 fr.), an industrial town of 11,143 inhab., on the Ariège, and the seat of a bishopric. The iron of the Pamiers foundries enjoys a high repute.

The town sprang up around an abbey and castle of the 12th cent. which no longer exists. Its founder, Roger II. of Foix, named it after the Syrian city Apamea as a memorial of the First Crusade. It often suffered from the chronic rivalry between the Counts of Foix, the abbots, the bishops, and the townsfolk. In 1563 it was ravaged by the plague; and in 1628, having become Protestant, it was taken and sacked by Condé (Henry II. of France). The abbey had already (1586) been destroyed, like many others, by the 'Casaques Noires' of the Sire d'Audon.

The Rue Ste. Hélène, beginning at the station, traverses the entire town and passes through the market-place. From the latter, the Rue Major leads, to the right, to the partly modern Romanesque church of *Notre-Dame-du-Camp*, with a fortified brick façade of the 14th century. The church of *Notre-Dame-des-Cordeliers*, farther to the N.E., has a curious small ruined tower. — The Rue des Nobles, behind the market to the left, leads by a small vaulted passage to the *Cathedral*, also largely rebuilt in modern times. It has a Transition portal, concealed by a modern brick tower in the Tolosan style, and other portions are in the Greco-Roman style of the 17th century. The interior is decorated with modern mural paintings by Bénezet and Baduel. Behind the cathedral is the *Palais de Justice*, and in front of it, to the right, are the *Seminary* and the *Bishop's Palace*. The ascent in front leads up to the *Castellat*, a promenade on the site of the old castle, with a fine view.

43 M. *Verniolle*; 46 M. *Varilhes*. The valley now contracts and the line recrosses the Ariège. — Beyond (48¹/₂ M.) *St. Jean-de-Verges* the scenery improves. To the right is a handsome modern château. The Ariège is again crossed.

51¹/₂ M. **Foix** (*Hôt. Rousse*, *Hôt. Lacoste*, near the bridge), a town of 7588 inhab., formerly the capital of the Counts of Foix and now the chief town of the department of the *Ariège*, is admirably situated at the confluence of the Ariège and the Arget. It is overlooked by its picturesque castle, but the town itself is badly built and unimportant.

Foix during the middle ages was the capital of the Counts of Foix, one of whom, Raymond (1188-1223), successfully resisted Simon de Montfort's attack upon his castle during the Albigensian crusade. Having thrown off the suzerainty of the lords of Toulouse, the Countship of Foix passed in 1229 under that of the kings of France; but nevertheless, owing to the differences between Roger Bernard III. and Philip the Bold, the countship was invaded in 1272 by the latter, who only became master of the castle on its becoming evident that he was determined to undermine the rock on which it stood. The territory was afterwards united to Béarn and annexed to France under Henri IV.

The CASTLE, or rather what is left of it, presents a very picturesque appearance from a distance. It stands on a rock, 180 ft. high,

on the N.W. of the town, and still retains two square towers, of
different sizes, dating in part from the 12th cent., and one round
tower, 136 ft. high, forming an interesting specimen of 14th cent.
architecture. To enter the castle (gratuity) we skirt the rock to the
right. The buildings are now unoccupied and contain little or
nothing of interest; they were used last as a prison. In the lowest
and oldest of the towers, originally the keep, are a chamber once
used by the Inquisition and some of its dungeons. The main tower
affords a fine view.

At the foot of the rock is *St. Volusien*, the principal church,
dating from the 12th cent., but with some older work. It has been
restored in recent years, and contains some fine altars and modern
paintings. — In 1882 a *Statue of Lakanal*, a member of the National
Convention of 1792, by Picault, was erected in the Promenade
Villotte, on the other side of the town.

About 5½ M. to the E., near the village of *Herm*, is the large *Grotte
de l'Herm*, a bone-cavern interesting to geologists; there are also other
caves, see below.

The railway now passes under the bridge of Foix and ascends
the right bank of the Ariège. The best views are to the right. —
55 M. *St. Paul-St. Antoine*. Beyond a tunnel we command a view
of the gorge of the Ariège, spanned by an ancient fortified bridge.
Lofty and barren mountains now appear. — Shortly after (58 M.)
Mercus, the Ariège is crossed.

61 M. **Tarascon** (*Hôtel Francal; Arnaud*), a small though very
ancient industrial town, at the confluence of the Ariège and the Oriège.
Tarascon-le-Vieux, to the left of the road, is built round a picturesque rock, surmounted by a *Tower*, now the only relic of a castle
destroyed in the 17th century. The iron-furnaces and foundries of
Tarascon are well-known.

About 3 M. to the N.W., on the St. Girons road, is *Bédeillac*, where there
are some interesting caves (see p. 187). Similar caves abound in the limestone mountains of this district, among others the *Grotte du Pounchut*, in the
Montagne de Sabart, a short distance from Tarascon, beyond the confluence of the Ariège and the Oriège; besides those mentioned below, the
cavern at the Roche de Mas (p. 187), etc.

From Tarascon to Vicdessos (*Montcalm* and *Pic d'Estat*), 8½ M.;
diligence from the station, 1 fr. The road leads to the S., up the narrow
valley of the Oriège, or of Vicdessos, which is flanked by bare mountains.
— 2½ M. *Niaux*, with the celebrated stalactite *Grotte de la Calbière*, in which
are two small lakes. — 3½ M. *Capoulet*, near the ruined *Château de Miglos*.
— 8½ M. **Vicdessos** (*Hôt. des Voyageurs; de la Renaissance*), a village to
the S.E. of which is the *Montagne de Rancié* with the richest iron-mines
in France. The ore yields 70⁰/₀ of excellent iron. Visitors to the mines
proceed to the village of *Sem*, about 2 M. from Vicdessos, and thence
ascend in about 1 hr. — From Vicdessos to *Aulus*, see p. 188.

Vicdessos is the point whence the Montcalm and the Pic d'Estat are
ascended in about 7¼ hrs. to the first summit, 8 hrs. to the second (guide
necessary). Part of the ascent may be made on horseback. We continue to ascend the Oriège valley, via (¼ hr.) *Auzat*, and the (¾ hr.)
large and fine *Cascade de Bassiès* (on the right), to (1 hr.) *Marc*. There
we enter the lateral valley on the right, making direct towards the
Montcalm, and ascend steeply via the (2 hrs.) *Cabanes de Pignol* (5590 ft.) to

the (1/2 hr.) *Cabanes de Subra* (6285 ft.), beyond which the horses cannot proceed. Thence a climb of 2 hrs., toilsome at first, brings us to the crest (9335 ft.) between the valleys of Subra and Rioufred; and in 3/4 hr. more we reach the top of the **Montcalm** (10,105 ft.), which repays us with a glorious view extending W. to the snowy peaks beyond Luchon and E. to the Canigou. On the S. the view is partly blocked by the Pic d'Estax or *Pique d'Estats* (10,300 ft.), whose summit may be gained in less than 1/4 hr. from the Montcalm.

The railway recrosses the Ariège, and continues to ascend its valley.

63 M. **Ussat-les-Bains.** — **Hotels.** Gr.-Hôt. des Bains et du Parc, on the right bank, near the chief Bath Estab.; Gr.-Hôt. Chaumont, farther to the right; Cassagne Fils, Merville, beyond the Establishment; Hôt. de France, Bonc, de la Renaissance, on the left bank, nearer the station. — *Furnished Apartments.* — Baths, 70 c.-1 1/2 fr.; douches, 60 c.-1 fr. — Small Casino beside the Hôtel des Bains, and *Café* close by. — *Telegraph Office* in the season.

Ussat-les-Bains (1590 ft.), which takes its name from *Ussat-le-Vieux*, the neighbouring village on the right bank of the Ariège, is a hamlet widely known on account of its abundant thermal springs (bicarbonate of lime), supplied by a subterranean lake situated below the rocks which border the valley. These waters, which are almost solely used for baths and douches, are extremely soothing and efficacious in certain female and nervous complaints. Their temperature varies from 103° to 89.6° Fahr., according to the distance of the bathing-places from the outflow. The principal *Etablissement Thermal* is situated on the left bank of the Ariège, beyond a small park, which forms the only promenade of the place. The *Thermes Ste. Germaine*, and the *Bains St. Vincent* (closed for several years) are on the right bank.

About 1 1/2 M. from Ussat is the **Grotte de Lombrive**, one of the most interesting caverns in the district, the mouth of which may be seen on the hill on the left bank, opposite the station. Intending visitors apply at the ground-floor of the lodging-house Pujo; adm. 5 fr. each, bargain for a party. The cavern consists of a series of chambers on different levels, connected by narrow passages. It contains stalactites, bone-deposits, and a small pool, and it may be followed for nearly 3 M. into the heart of the mountain, which also contains other caverns possibly communicating with the Grotte de Lombrive. Several Albigenses who had taken refuge in this cavern were buried alive by the troops of the Inquisition who built up the entrance.

The valley now expands a little. At (67 1/2 M.) *Les Cabannes* (1745 ft.; Hôt. d'Espague) is a château on a hill to the right, and at the head of a little valley rises the *Pic de Riex* (8485 ft.). We cross a bridge, traverse a short tunnel, and again cross a bridge. To the left are the Pic St. Barthélemy (p. 192), and, on a cliff, the picturesque ruins of the *Château de Lordat*, which was in existence as early as the 10th century. — 71 1/2 M. *Luzenac-Garanou.*

77 M. **Ax.** — **Hotels.** Royal, Rue de la Gare; Sicre, at the Establishment of the same name; Bordeaux, in the town, plain. — *Maison Meublée Tardieu*, Place du Couloubret. — Numerous *Furnished Apartments.* — *Cafés*, Place du Couloubret. — Baths, 80 c.-1 fr. 25 c.; douches, 40 c.-1 fr. 25 c. — Glass of the water, 5 c.

Ax (2350 ft.), an ancient and ill-built town with 1609 inhab., is

well-situated at the confluence of three streams. The warm sulphur
springs, for which it is noted, were known to the Romans, as is indicated by the name of the town, derived from *Aquae*. Ax has
no fewer than 61 springs, which vary in temperature (63°-171°
Fahr.), mineral constituents, and medicinal uses, like those of
Luchon and Cauterets. The opening of the railway and the quiet-
ness of the place as compared with the fashionable life at other
spas, have largely contributed to the prosperity of Ax. The waters
are used both for drinking and for bathing, and are specially efficacious in rheumatism, skin diseases, scrofula, and catarrhs; while
they are also used for domestic purposes. The springs are so numerous and so thickly strewn that it has been conjectured that the
town is built above a natural reservoir of thermal mineral water.

There are four bath establishments in the town, each fed by a
different group of springs; *viz.* the *Couloubret*, to the left, at the
end of the square of the same name, reached directly viâ the street
ascending from the station; the *Etablissement Thermal Modèle*, on
the bank of the stream skirting the right side of the same square;
the *Breilh*, a little farther on, in a square of the same name, in the
shady court of the Hôtel Sicre; and the *Teich*, on the other side of
the town, reached by the Rue du Coustou. Behind the Teich is a
pretty park, and higher up are the ruins of a castle, on which a
statue of the Virgin has been erected. — The *Hospital*, in the Place
Breilh, was founded for leprous soldiers by St. Louis in 1260. The
neighbouring *Church* is dedicated to St. Udant, 'conqueror of Attila
and martyred at Ax in 452'. — The temperature of Ax is very
variable, and the evenings are generally cool.

Excursions. — The Pic St. Barthélemy may be ascended in about
5¹/₂ hrs. (with guide) from the small village of *Lassur* (to which we
may drive), about ³/₄ M. beyond the station of Luzenac (p. 181). The excursion is interesting and easy. We cross the Ariège at Lassur and ascend
to the N.E., viâ (1 hr.) *Lordat* (p. 191), to the (3 hrs.) *Col de la Peyre*
(5080 ft.), which, however, we do not cross, but bear to the W. and pass
to the left of the (³/₄ hr.) *Lac Tort*. Then skirting the *Pic de Soularac*
(7645 ft.), we descend to (¹/₄ hr.) a little col, and finally ascend once
more to the (¹/₂ hr.) summit of the Pic St. Barthélemy (7705 ft.), which
affords a famous view, from the Pic du Midi to the Canigou and from the
mountains of Andorra to the plains of Toulouse.

To Quillan (p. 105), to the N.E., an easy and interesting excursion
occupying one day. The route leads viâ the (3 hrs.) *Col d'El Pradel*
(about 5400 ft.) and the *Vallée du Rabenty*, in which the scenery is remarkably picturesque as far as Joucou, about 4 hrs. from the col. —
The ascent of the Puy de Carlitte (9580 ft.; with guide), to the S.E., may
be made viâ the *Lac Lanoux* (p. 193) in 2 days from Ax (1 day from
L'Hospitalet); but it is more conveniently undertaken from Les Escaldas
(6 hrs. from Ax; see p. 204).

To Puycerda and Bourg-Madame (*Les Escaldas*), 31 M., diligence daily
in about 10 hrs.; fare 8 fr. The road leaves the valley of the Oriège to
the left, and ascends to the S. in the narrow and rocky valley of the
Ariège. — 5 M. *Mérens* (3640 ft.; Hotel), with little-used warm springs
(93° to 154° Fahr.; sulphur). — 8¹/₂ M. *Soillens*, with a cold sulphur
spring. About ¹/₂ M. farther on we pass a bridge and a waterfall.
10¹/₂ M. L'Hospitalet (4930 ft.; *Astrié*) lies at the point of divergence
of the Andorra road (p. 193). — To make the ascent of the *Puy de*

Carlitte (p. 192) we return towards Ax as far as the bridge near Salllens and then ascend to the E. to the (3¹/₂ hrs.) *Col de Bésines* (7710 ft.), on the N.E. of the *Pic Pédroux* (9290 ft.). From the col we descend in about 1 hr. to the *Lac Lanoux* (7085 ft.; fishermen's hut), the largest lake in the Pyrenees (about 270 acres), and thence reach the summit of the mountain (p. 204) in 2¹/₂ hrs.

Beyond L'Hospitalet the road proceeds in windings, at one place making a detour of 3¹/₂ M., which pedestrians may avoid by means of a well-marked path. — 16¹/₂ M. *Col de Puymorens* (6290 ft.). — 19¹/₂ M. *Porté* (5325 ft.) is another starting-point for the ascent of the Puy de Carlitte (1 day) vià the Lac Lanoux. To the right, farther on, are the defile and tower of *Cerdane*. 22¹/₂ M. *Porta* (4950 ft.; Inn), from which the *Pic de Campcardos* (9580 ft.; fine view) may be ascended in 4¹/₂ hrs. (7 hrs. there and back). We soon perceive the two *Tours de Carol*. — 23¹/₂ M. *Courbassil*. — Beyond the (27¹/₂ M.) village of *La Tour-de-Carol* (4070 ft.; Pellegrin), a road diverges to the left to *Les Escaldas* (5 M.; p. 204). — 28¹/₂ M. *Vignole*. We now cross the Spanish frontier to (30¹/₂ M.) *Puycerda* (p. 209), but soon re-enter France to reach (31 M.) *Bourg-Madame* (p. 203).

To ANDORRA (Andorre) vià the Port de Saldeu, the shortest and easiest route, about 12 hrs. Carriages can go as far as (4 hrs.) L'Hospitalet, where it is well to sleep, and the road is practicable for horses for the rest of the way. A guide, not necessary in fine weather, may be useful as an interpreter. The charge is 10 fr. a day for horse and man from L'Hospitalet in addition to food for both. — To (10¹/₂ M.) *L'Hospitalet*, see p. 192. The Andorra road continues for some time to ascend the Ariège valley, and in less than ¹/₂ hr. crosses a brook on the frontier and turns to the W. where it is indicated by a kind of landmarks. After 1 hr. more a path vià the *Port de Framiquel* (about 8200 ft.), also leading to Andorra but 1 hr. longer, diverges to the left from our route. About 2 hrs. beyond we gain the *Port de Saldeu* (8200 ft.), which affords only a limited and monotonous view, and we then descend vià (1 hr. 20 min.) *Saldeu* (Inn), (1 hr. 20 min.) *Canillo*, the *Mérixell Chapel* (a resort of pilgrims), a (1 hr.) defile commanded by the remains of a fort, and (¹/₂ hr.) *Les Escaldas*, with warm sulphur springs, situated in a valley planted with olives and tobacco. Thence Andorra is reached in ¹/₂ hr. more.

Andorra (3540 ft.; *Calounes's Inn*, tolerable), a village of 700-800 inhab., is of importance only as the chief place of the little republic of that name. It is well situated at the foot of the Anclar and above a small and fertile plain, but it is ill-built and, beyond the primitive manners of its inhabitants and the organization of its petty government, the only object of interest is the modest *Palais*, with three irregular windows in the façade, and a tower pierced with loopholes. The meetings of the Conseil Général are held in this building, and the members and their steeds are lodged in it. It also serves as the Palais de Justice, the Hôtel de Ville, the school, and the gaol. The Council Chamber, an unadorned apartment, surrounded with oak benches, and the kitchen, with a huge fireplace, should be visited.

Andorra is a little independent Republic lying amidst the mountains between the territories of France and Spain. In no direction does it measure more than 18 M. across and its total population is less than 10,000. Tradition asserts that Charlemagne granted independence to the Val d'Andorre in return for assistance lent him in his wars with the Moors. It is certain that the little state was from 1278 to 1793 under the joint rule of the Bishops of Urgel (in Spain) and the Counts of Foix (and their successors the Kings of France), while since the French Revolution it has been almost wholly independent of its two suzerains. — The government is vested in a council of 24 members, 4 for each of the 6 parishes comprized within its territory, who appoint a Syndic Procureur Général, a President, and two coadjutor syndics. The French government and the bishop of Urgel, on their part, each nominate a viguier or provost, the former for life, the latter for 3 years, and the Spanish government appoints a viceroy. The executive authority is wielded

by the vigniers, through an official known as the 'bayle', subject to the
usages and customs of the country. The French viguier resides at Prades
(p. 201). — Life is still patriarchal among the Andorrans; the law of
primogeniture prevails; every man is a soldier at his own charges; taxes
are levied on an income-tax basis; public education is free. The people
devote themselves to cattle-rearing, but still more to smuggling.

29. From Carcassonne to Quillan.

Upper Valley of the Aude. Valley of the Rebenty.

34 M. Railway in 2 hrs. (fares 6 fr. 75, 5 fr. 5, 3 fr. 70 c.). The line is
to be continued towards Axat (p. 195) and Rivesaltes (p. 197).

Carcassonne, see p. 88. The line ascends the valley of the Aude
and crosses the river between (4½ M.) *Madame* and (6½ M.) *Couf-
foulens-Leuc.* From (8 M.) *Verzeille* a diligence (½ fr.) plies to
(3 M.) *St. Hilaire*, where there are the remains of a famous abbey,
with a church of the 13th cent. containing the tomb of St. Hilary,
with bas-reliefs of the 11th century. The cloisters date from the
14th cent.; the abbot's house is adorned with paintings, etc. —
Beyond (10½ M.) *Pomas* we cross the Aude for the second time
and beyond (13 M.) *Cépie* for the third time. Before the last bridge
the church of Notre-Dame-de-Marceille comes into view on the left.

16½ M. **Limoux** (*Hôt. du Commerce*), an industrial town with
6371 inhab., on the Aude, is surrounded by vine-clad hills, which
produce a white wine of good quality, known as 'blanquette'. — A
little to the N. is *Notre-Dame-de-Marceille*, a pilgrim-resort of considerable local repute, with a black marble statue of the Virgin and
a fine altar-screen, etc. Fine view of the valley and the mountains.

Beyond Limoux the valley contracts, and the line passes through
four short tunnels and crosses the Aude for the last time.

22 M. **Alet** (*Établissement Thermal*, moderate), a decayed
town, called *Electra* by the Romans, who made use of its mineral
waters. It was a place of some importance during the middle
ages when it possessed a Benedictine Abbey and was the seat of
a bishopric. Its *Cathedral*, founded in 873 and rebuilt in 1018,
is now in ruins, but the pentagonal apse, the most interesting
part, is standing. This is adorned on the outside by four large
columns in the Corinthian style and an elaborate cornice. — The
Établissement Thermal possesses two warm springs (bicarbonate
of lime; aperient; 68° and 82° Fahr.) and a cold chalybeate spring.
There are gardens and a well shaded promenade on the Aude.

Two more tunnels are passed. — 27 M. *Couiza-Montazels.*

From Couiza-Montazels a diligence (1¼ fr.) plies daily in summer
to the village of **Rennes-les-Bains** (*Grand Hôtel; Reine*), 6½ M. to the S.E.,
with five mineral springs (chalybeate and saline), known to the Romans.
There are three bath-establishments, the *Bain Fort, Bain de la Reine*, and
Bain Doux. The environs are interesting. Rennes is the starting-point for
the ascent of the *Pech de Bugarach* (4040 ft.; 4 hrs.; extensive view), viâ
(3½ M.) *Bugarach*.

28 M. *Espérasa.* — 30¹/₂ M. *Campagne-sur-Aude* possesses a bath-establishment with two mineral springs (76° and 82° Fahr.).

34 M. **Quillan** (*Hôt. des Pyrénées*), an industrial town of 2410 inhab., on the Aude, with the ruins of a castle, is the centre of an important forest district. A statue of the *Abbé Armand* commemorates his services in procuring the construction of the road in the upper Aude valley. About ³/₄ M. to the W. is the Établissement Thermal of *Ginoles*, with three springs.

An interesting excursion, 7 hrs. there and back (carriage-road), may be made to the S.E. to the fine **Forêt des Fanges** (firs; 2700 acres). One road, leading about 1¹/₄ M. to the N. of Quillan, skirts the heights (3150 ft.) occupied by the forest. We quit this road at the (9 M.) *Col de St. Louis* (2250 ft.), to the S.W. of the Pech de Bugarach (p. 194), and return through the forest by a road which descends in zigzags into the valley of the Aude near Axat, and thence through the Pierre-Lis defile (see below) back to

short tunnels. Beyond these the waters have worn the rocks on the right bank into a kind of huge colonnade. The stream and road now wind round a projecting bluff and, above a mill, enter the *Able Defile* which is even wilder than the previous one. About 1 hr. from Joncou is *Belfort*, 1/4 hr. beyond which is the striking and magnificent *Niort Defile*. The village of *Niort* (Inn), 1³/4 hr. from Belfort, was formerly the chief town of the Sault or Forêts district. The upper part of the valley is also interesting; it contains the hamlets of (1/2 hr.) *Mériel* and (1/2 hr. more) *La Fajole*. In 2¹/2 hrs. from the latter we reach the *Col d'El Pradel* (about 5400 ft.), whence we descend to Ax (p. 191).

30. From Narbonne to Perpignan.

39¹/2 M. Railway in 1-2 hrs. (fares 7 fr. 15, 4 fr. 85, 3 fr. 15 c.).

Narbonne, see p. 91. The line is at first the same as that to Carcassonne, skirting the left side of the town. Beyond (5¹/2 M.) *Mandirac* it keeps along the *Robine Canal* and passes between the *Étang de Bages et de Sijean*, on the right, and the *Étang de Gruissan*, on the left, the former 11 M. long by 2 to 4 wide, the latter 8 M. long, with an average width of 2 M., communicating by two channels with the *Mediterranean*, which is now visible for some distance. The hills on the right are the Corbières (p. 90). — 10 M. *Ste. Lucie*. To the left are salt-marshes.

13 M. **La Nouvelle** (*Hôt. St. Michel; d'Italie*), a modern seaport town with 2445 inhab., at the mouth of the Robine and of the channel from the Sijean lagoon. Its present importance is due to its relations with Algeria. There are sea-baths at the end of the channel, about 1 M. from the town. Route to the Corbières, see p. 90.

The railway now keeps close to the sea, skirting on the right the *Étang de la Palme*, and crossing its mouth, called *Grau de la Franqui*, where there are sea-baths.

20¹/2 M. *Leucate*, station for the large village of that name, 1³/4 M. to the S.E., near *Cape Leucate*, so called from its white rocks. — We next skirt on the left and then cross the *Étang de Leucate* or *de Salces*, about 9 M. long with an average width of 5 M. (14,000 acres). — 22¹/2 M. *Fitou*.

28¹/2 M. *Salces* (*Hôt. Baillayre*), a town of 2207 inhab., owes its name to two salt-springs in the neighbourhood. It is an ancient stronghold, of which the *Castle* (to the right) remains, built by Charles V. and now used as a powder-magazine. Salces is within the ancient province of *Roussillon*, and produces one of the most highly esteemed white wines, known as Macabeu.

The line, now at a considerable distance from the sea, crosses a wide and very fertile plain, where two or three annual crops are grown by means of irrigation. Above the last offshoot of the Corbières appear the imposing Canigou and other Pyrenean heights. At Rivesaltes we cross the wide and often dry bed of the *Agly*.

35 M. *Rivesaltes* (Hôt. du Commerce), a town of 6016 inhab., famous for its Muscat wine, though the vineyards have suffered

from the phylloxera. This is the junction for the new line from Carcassonne viâ Quillan (p. 194).

About 9¹/₂ M. to the E. is the small town, with some old fortifications, of **Estagel** (*Hôt. Gary*), the home of the *Arago* family. There is a statue, by Oliva, of François Arago, the astronomer, the best known of the seven brothers (see below). Estagel is pleasantly situated on the right bank of the Agly, which separates the Corbières from the Pyrénées. Route to the Corbières, see p. 90. Estagel will be a station on the above-mentioned new line.

39¹/₂ M. **Perpignan.** — **Hotels.** GR.-HÔT. DE PERPIGNAN, HÔT. DE FRANCE, Quai de la Préfecture; *DU NORD ET DU PETIT-PARIS, Place d'Armes, near the cathedral, R., L., & A. 3, B. ³/₄, déj. 2¹/₂, D. 3 fr., omn. 30 c.; CENTRAL, Place Arago, R. 2¹/₂-3¹/₂, no table-d'hôte, pens. 8¹/₂ fr.; DE LA LOGE, Place de la Loge, with a good restaurant, R. 2, déj. 3, D. 3¹/₂ fr.; HÔT.-RESTAUR. DU HELDER, near the station. — *Cafés,* chiefly in the Place de la Loge. — *Omnibus-tramway* from the station to the town, 15 c.

Perpignan, a town of 33,878 inhab. and formerly the capital of Roussillon, is now the chief town of the department of the *Pyrénées Orientales*, the seat of a bishopric, and a fortress of the first class, on the right bank of the *Tet*, a river almost dry in summer, 7 miles from its mouth in the Mediterranean.

Its importance, now much diminished, dates from the 12th and still more the 13th cent., when it was the residence of the kings of Majorca. On the extinction of the kingdom, Perpignan reverted to Aragon, to which it had been ceded by its last count in 1172, and it remained faithful to its new masters until the middle of the 17th century. Louis XI. besieged it during his disputes with the king of Aragon in 1475, and only obtained possession of it with difficulty. Francis I. failed to capture it in 1542; but a century later, when the Spanish governor had violated its privileges, Richelieu was called in to its assistance, and annexed it definitely to France. Owing, however, to its vicinity to and long dependence on Spain, Perpignan still displays more of the Spanish character than any other town on the frontier.

The town, which is about ¹/₂ M. from the station, is divided into two unequal parts by the *Basse*, a tributary of the Tet. The old town, which lies on the farther side of the river and contains all the objects of interest, is poorly built and consists of a perfect labyrinth of narrow streets which, however, are kept clean and are cool in summer. We enter the town by a handsome square with a promenade along the river, embellished with a bronze statue, by A. Mercié, of the astronomer *Fr. Arago* (1786-1853; see above). Opposite is the small modern *Palais de Justice*.

The Quai de la Préfecture, at the opposite end of the square, on the small tributary of the Tet, ends at the *Castillet*, a small but massive brick structure, with battlements and a cupola, built in 1319 by Sancho, the second king of Majorca, restored and now used as a prison. At the side is the *Porte Notre-Dame*, and beyond it, the *Promenades des Platanes*.

The Rue Louis-Blanc leads from the Porte Notre-Dame to the right to *La Loge* (Spanish, 'lonja', or market), originally constructed at the end of the 14th cent., and now occupied partly as the 'mairie' and partly as a café. The exterior presents a singular mixture of the Gothic and Moorish styles, while the arcades of the court are Romanesque.

Recrossing the Place de la Loge we continue straight on by the Rue St. Jean, pass the Place d'Armes, and reach the —

CATHEDRAL OF ST. JEAN, at the extreme N. E. of the town. Its foundation dates from the year 1324, in the reign of Sancho, but the E. end was only finished at the end of the 15th cent. during the French occupation, while the nave, not begun until the 16th cent., has remained without a portal.

There is nothing to be noticed in the exterior, except the iron frame of the tower (18th cent.); but the interior is remarkable for the bold proportions of its nave, 230 ft. long, 60 ft. wide, and 90 ft. high, and still more for the gorgeous decoration of its altars in the Spanish taste. The *Reredos of the high altar (1620) is of white marble with scenes from the life of St. John, etc., by Soler of Barcelona. In the left transept is the black and white marble tomb of Louis de Montmor (d. 1695), the first French bishop of Perpignan. A chapel opening from this transept to the left of the choir contains a curious altar-screen of painted wood, dating from the 15th or 16th century. The stained-glass windows, the organ-case, the paintings on the walls of the chapels, and a Gothic chapel near the porch to the right, are worthy of notice.

n returning we follow the Rue Fond-Froide, to the left of the Place d'Armes, then the Rue des Trois-Journées to the right, and another small street to the left, and reach the *Place de la République*, the largest and finest open space in the town, ornamented with trees and a white marble fountain, and used as a market for the excellent fruit which is produced in the neighbourhood.

To the E. is the theatre, to the right of which we pass, and then turn to the right to the *Place au Blé*, in which a bronze statue, by G. Farraill, was erected in 1890 to *H. Rigaud* (1659-1743), the painter, a native of Perpignan.

The Rue St. Sauveur leads farther in the same direction to the *University*, founded in 1349, which contains the civic *Library* and the *Museum* (open Sun. and Thurs. from 1 p. m., or noon in winter, to 5 p. m.). Visitors are also admitted on other days.

GROUND FLOOR. Room I, to the right: 118. *School of Perugino*, Virgin with saints and donor. — Chief Room: to the left, *Turchi* (?), Marriage at Cana; *H. Rigaud*, 71. Portrait of himself, 70. Christ, 69. Cardinal Fleury; 65. *Ingres*, Duke of Orléans; 62. *Jordaens* (?), Head of Silenus; 60. *N. Maes*, Portrait; 59. *Correggio* (?), Head of Christ; 57. *Tiepolo*, St. Roch; 43. *Procaccini*, Mary Magdalen; 31. *Ribera*, Portrait of a scholar. — *B. Constant*, 'Too late'; 1. *Rigaud*, Cardinal de Bouillon; 5. *Cignani* (?), Mary Magdalen. — Three Rooms to the left of the entrance contain drawings, paintings, and sculptures.

FIRST AND SECOND FLOORS. *Museum of Natural History*; photographs of the principal thermal establishments in the Eastern Pyrenees and a few sculptures.

A little farther, to the S. of the town, is the *Citadel*, in which little of interest remains (no admission without special permit). The keep is the ancient castle, entirely transformed, of the kings of Majorca; the chapel, which is used as an arsenal, has retained its Romanesque portal and Gothic arcades.

From Perpignan to *Port-Bou* (Barcelona), see below; to *Prades* and *Puycerda*, etc. see p. 201; to *Amélie-les-Bains* and *La Preste*, see p. 204.

From Perpignan to Canet, 6¼ M. The road leads to the E. To the left, about half-way, lies the hamlet of *Castell-Rossello*, with its conspicuous mediæval tower, 65 ft. in height. This was the site of the town of *Ruscino*, afterwards called *Rousكino* and *Rousceillio*, whence the name *Roussillon* came to be applied to the surrounding district. Here Hannibal made a treaty with the Gauls for the free passage of his army. Ruscino was at that time near the sea, at the mouth of the Tet. — About 1¼ M. beyond the village of Canet are *Sea-baths* (Hotels), on a sandy beach. About 1¼ M. to the S. of the village, and ½ M. to the S. W. of the baths, is the *Etang de Canet et de St. Nazaire*, about 2½ M. long and 1 to 1½ M. broad.

31. Excursions from Perpignan.

I. From Perpignan to Port-Bou (*Barcelona*).

26½ M. Railway in 50 min. - 2 hrs. (fares 4 fr. 65, 3 fr. 35, 2 fr. 15 c.); an interesting line. — To *Barcelona*, 131½ M., Railway in 7¾-10½ hrs. (fares about 28 fr. 20, 19 fr. 35, 12 fr. 60 c.). Best views to the left.

Perpignan, see p. 197. The railway to Spain, leaving the line to Prades on the right, passes under an aqueduct, constructed by the kings of Majorca, and crosses the Réart. Beyond (5½ M.) *Cornella* we obtain a fine view of Elne, to the left.

8 M. **Elne** (*Hôt. du Commerce*), a decayed and poorly - built town of 3230 inhab., has remains of fortifications and a fine view. The sea, now 3 M. distant, formerly washed the foot of the little hill on which the town stands.

Elne is the ancient *Illiberis*, an important city of the Sardones, under the walls of which Hannibal encamped after crossing the Pyrenees (B. C. 218). It was named *Helena* by Constantine in memory of his mother, and was the scene of the assassination of the emperor Constantius (A. D. 350). Elne was destroyed by the Moors in the 8th cent., by the Normans in the 11th, and by the kings of France in the 13th and 15th centuries. The bishopric was removed to Perpignan in 1602.

The old *Cathedral* is a Romanesque building of the 12th cent., altered in the 14th and 15th. The plain battlemented façade is flanked by two square towers, that on the right being of stone, of the latter half of the 12th cent., that on the left of modern brick. On the N. side is a small *Cloister in white marble, of the 12th-15th cent., containing some remarkable sculptures and inscriptions, and three fine ancient sarcophagi. — Hence to Céret, Amélie-les-Bains, and La Presta, see p. 206.

The line crosses the *Tech*. — 10 M. *Palau-del-Vidre*. — Beyond (13½ M.) *Argelès-sur-Mer* (Hôt. Llobet), with 3400 inhab., now 1¼ M. from the coast, we again approach the sea, in order to round the outliers of the *Monts Albères*, the E. extremity of the Pyrenees. The first tunnel is soon reached.

17 M. **Collioure** (*Hôt. Fontano*), the ancient *Cauco Illiberis*, a small seaport with 3400 inhab., is picturesquely situated. It possesses an old castle, and the *Fort St. Elme* on the S. E. side, the chief remaining fortification, was built in the 16th cent., under

Charles V. General Berge and General Riéra, two famous natives
of the town, are commemorated by monuments. Good Roussillon
wine is grown here. Trade in cork, important fishing industry, etc.

Excursions. To the S.W., to *Notre-Dame-de-Consolation*, by a shaded
valley, ³/₄ hr. there and back; to the W. to the *Tour de Madeloch* or *du
Diable* (2160 ft.), the view from which embraces the whole Gulf of Lions,
4 hrs. (descent to Banyuls, 1 hr., see below); to the ruins of the abbey
of *Valbonne*, 5 hrs.; to the tower and the cork-forest of *La Massane*, 6 hrs.
with a guide.

We now traverse a second tunnel, 920 yds. long.

18 M. **Port-Vendres** (*Hôt. Durand*), the *Portus Veneris* of the
Romans, a small town of 3050 inhab., is important both as a commercial and a military harbour, being one of the safest on the
Mediterranean. Its extensive roadstead, with a depth of 40 ft., can
accommodate the largest vessels. There are sea-water baths. To
the S.E. (¹/₂ M.) is the *Cap Béar* (665 ft.), with a first-class lighthouse and a semaphore; fine view.

Steamers leave for *Algiers* every Tues. and Thurs. evening; passage
24-26 hrs.

Before reaching the next station three tunnels are passed through.
Between this point and the frontier fine glimpses of the Mediterranean are obtained, though in spring and autumn it is liable to be
obscured by fog.

21 M. **Banyuls-sur-Mer** (*Hôt. Roussillonnais*), with 3120 inhab.,
is noted for the best Roussillon wine. The modern *Church*, elaborately ornamented but somewhat dark, contains a statue of the Virgin,
by Oliva, a Pyrenean sculptor. Banyuls is situated on a small bay
of the Mediterranean, with pleasant sea-water baths, and enjoys a
mild climate. Visitors may inspect the *Laboratoire Arago*, a lab-
oratory of marine zoology, at the S. end of the bay, about ¹/₂ M.
from the town.

Excursions. To the N.W., to the *Valley of Banyuls*, planted with orange
trees, 3 hrs. there and back; to the *Tour du Diable* (see above), viâ the *Vallon
de Cosperons*, where the famous Vin de Ranclo is produced, 4 hrs., or
5 hrs. there and back, making use of the short-cuts in descending; to the
Col des Balistres, on the frontier (see below), a very pleasant walk, by a
mule-track, 4 hrs. there and back; from the Col to the *Pic Jouan*, 2 hrs.
there and back.

We pass through a tunnel (³/₄ M. long) between two fine bays
and reach (25¹/₂ M.) *Cerbère* (Buffet-hotel), the last French station,
on a bay of the same name, 1 M. from *Cap Cerbère*, which has marked
from ancient times the frontier of France and Spain. The station
is on a lofty embankment supported by a wall with two tiers of
arches. We pass through a tunnel (1200 yds. long) under the *Col
des Balistres* (850 ft.), and enter Spanish territory.

26¹/₂ M. *Port-Bou* (Buffet; custom-house), where our line joins
that to (104 M.) Barcelona, viâ (16 M.) *Figueras* (p. 204), at the end
of the main route over the Col du Perthus (p. 204).

II. From Perpignan to Prades and Puycerda.

Le Vernet. The Canigou. Molitg. Montlouis. Les Escaldas.

RAILWAY to *Prades*, 25¹/₂ M., in 1¹/₂-1¹/₂ hrs. (fares 4 fr. 60, 3 fr. 10 c., 2 fr.); thence carriage-road to (35 M.) *Puycerda*. The railway is to be opened in 1895 as far as (3¹/₂ M. beyond Prades) *Villefranche-de-Conflent*. DILIGENCE from Prades to (22 M.) *Montlouis* in 5 hrs. (fares 5 fr. 40, 3 fr. 60 c.); from Prades to (8 M.) *Olette* in 2¹/₂ hrs. (fares 2 fr. 25, 1 fr. 60 c.). Public conveyance also from Montlouis to (12¹/₂ M.) *Bourg-Madame*.

The line ascends the fertile valley of the Tet. — 5 M. *Le Soler*; 8 M. *St. Féliu-d'Aval*; 8³/₄ M. *St. Féliu-d'Amont*; 9³/₄ M. *Millas*, with 2460 inhab., formerly a fortified place.

14 M. *Ille*, with 3340 inhab., is situated in a plain noted for its fruit. — 16¹/₂ M. *Bouleternère*, with a ruined castle. The valley contracts. — 20 M. *Vinça* (Hôtel St. Pierre), a small town, 1¹/₄ M. to the N.W. of which are the baths of that name, with thermal sulphur springs. — Beyond a short tunnel and a small viaduct we have a view of the Canigou to the left. — 22 M. *Marquixanes*.

25¹/₂ M. **Prades** (*Hôt. January*), a town of 3760 inhab., in a fine situation, is the starting-point for several important routes. The *Church* contains several altars in the Spanish style, notably the high-altar, a pretentious if not very tasteful work by Jos. Sunyer (14th cent.), formerly at St. Michel-de-Cuxa (see below). The railway is to be continued to Olette (p. 202), and is to be opened in 1895 as far as Villefranche (p. 202). Route to Puycerda, see p. 202.

In the charming valley of the Taurinya, 2 M. to the S., are the ruins of the powerful abbey of *St. Michel-de-Cuxa*, founded in 878, with some fine portions still remaining, including the Romanesque cloister-arcades in pink marble, the Romanesque church with a Gothic choir, the marble portal of the abbots' house with sculptures of the 11th cent., etc.

FROM PRADES TO LE VERNET (Canigou), 7¹/₂ M., with regular service of carriages (1 fr.), in 1895, probably from Villefranche (p. 202). — As far as (3¹/₂ M.) *Villefranche* (see p. 202) we follow the road to Puycerda, then turn to the right into a narrow valley, descending from the Canigou, which soon appears on the left. — 5¹/₂ M. *Corneilla-de-Conflent*, the Romanesque church of which possesses a fine white marble porch, and a stone altar-screen of the 14th century.

7¹/₂ M. **Le Vernet** or *Vernet-les-Bains*. — Hotels: *Grand-Hôt. du Portugal*, 12¹/₂ fr. per day; *du Parc*, 8 fr.; *Ibrahim-Pacha*; *de la Préfecture*, attached to the establishment; *Hôtel du Canigou*, family hotel; *de la Poste*. — *Furnished Villas*. — *Baths* 1-1¹/₂ fr. *Douches* 50 c.-1 fr. 50. *Glass of Mineral Water* 5 c. — *Casino* with theatre, etc.

Le Vernet (2035 ft.), famous for its thermal waters, is a beautifully situated village in a mountain-valley, the E. side of which is formed by a shoulder of the Canigou (see below). The *Etablissement Thermal* is situated in a fine park on the bank of a stream, a little outside the village. The sulphur waters are supplied by 10 principal springs with a temperature varying from 46° to 138° Fahr. They are used especially for affections of the respiratory organs, the climate being such as to allow invalids to remain during the winter. A *Sanatorium* has recently been constructed on the slope of the Canigou above the park, for the open-air cure. The entire establishment has also been newly altered and improved; a large and fine new hotel (Portugal) has been built in the park; and the huge new *Casino* is designed, according to a special notice, to become 'el centro de la high life internacional'.

An interesting excursion (³/₄ hr.) may be made to the S. viâ (1 M.)

Castell to the ruins of the abbey of *St. Martin-de-Canigou*, where there is a Byzantine church with monolithic white marble columns.

The ASCENT OF THE CANIGOU (10 hrs. there and back; guide, *Jacques Noe* of Castell, *Carol* of Le Vernet, 10 fr., advisable; horse 10 fr.; provisions must be taken) is best made from Le Vernet. Riding is practicable to within 1 hr. of the summit. We proceed to *Castell* (see above) and continue by a valley to the right to the (1 hr.) *Cascade Anglaise*. Ascending thence to the (1¹/₄ hr.) *Col du Cheval-Mort*, and leaving to the right a path to Prats-de-Mollo (p. 208), we reach the (¹/₄ hr.) *Randots Hut* and the (¹/₂ hr.) *Serrat de Marialles* pastures. We then descend into the valley of a tributary of the Castell, ascend to the (¹/₂ hr.) *Col Vert*, descend again into a ravine to reach the (¹/₂ hr.) *Granges de Cadi*, and mount again to the (¹/₂ hr.) *Plateau de Cadi*, the farthest point to which horses can ascend. The last part of the ascent is by a tiresome climb over débris, and through a fissure or cheminée, in which natural steps are formed by the schist. The Alpine Club has supplied a railing. The *Canigou (9135 ft.), the top of which forms a platform, 26 ft. long by 10 ft. wide, with a hut, is the last of the high mountains at the E. end of the Pyrenees. It forms a huge mass, the buttresses of which radiate to distances of 7 to 12 miles as the crow flies, and form exceedingly steep arêtes on the N. and N.E. sides of the summit. The view is superb, embracing from the S.E. to the N.E. beyond the Albères and the Corbières, the coast of the Mediterranean from Barcelona to Montpellier, 100 M. distant; to the N. the Corbières, and the plain extending to the mountains of the Aveyron; to the W. the mountains of the Ariège; and to the S. those of Catalonia.

FROM PRADES TO THE BATHS OF MOLITG (pron. 'Mollieh'), 5 M., diligence (1 fr.) during the season. The road diverges from that to Villefranche outside the town, descends to the right, and crosses the Tet. 2 M. *Castlar*, beyond which we ascend the valley of the Castellane, crossing the stream several times. 5 M. *Baths of Molitg* (1475 ft.; *Thermal Establishments; Marty*, etc.), in the narrow gorge of the Castellane, in which it has been difficult to find room for the three thermal establishments. The latter are supplied by 12 sulphur springs (77°-100° Fahr.), which are used for drinking and for bathing in the treatment of mucous and skin diseases, rheumatism, etc.

Beyond Prades the Puycerda road continues to ascend the valley of the Tet, which gradually becomes narrower. To the left is a lofty railway-viaduct; farther on is another to the right, crossing the stream. — 26¹/₂ M. (from Perpignan) *Ria*, with an iron and marble factory.

28 M. **Villefranche-de-Conflent** (1425 ft.), a small town at the confluence of the Tet and the stream descending from the valley of Le Vernet (see above), fortified on the plans of Vauban to command the valley of the Tet, which is here very narrow. The *Château*, or fort, commands both valleys. The extensive caves which are used as casemates and magazines for the citadel cannot be visited without special permission. The situation is wild and picturesque.

The Tet is crossed. To the left is a ruined tower. — 32 M. *Serdinya*; 32¹/₂ M. *Joncet*.

34¹/₂ M. **Olette** (2010 ft.; *Hôtel Gaillarde*), a market-village, beyond which there was until lately only a path with steps or 'graus' (Lat. gradus). — The road now passes through a tunnel and over a fine bridge. About 2¹/₂ M. from Olette a path to the left descends to the (¹/₄ M.) baths of the *Graus des Canareilles*, supplied by 10 sulphur springs (95°-130° Fahr.), similar to those described below. To the right is *Jugols;* to the left the towers of *La Bastide.* — 38 M. *Les Graus d'Olette* or *Bains de Thuès* (about 2460 ft.), a modern establishment with 42 copious sulphur springs, from 80° to 172° Fahr., *i. e.* only a few degrees less than the waters of Chaudesaigues in the Cantal (p. 265). They are chiefly employed in the treatment of rheumatism, neuralgia, and diseases of the urinary organs.

We recross to the left bank shortly before reaching (39 M.) *Thuès-de-Liar.* The valley continues to be shut in by high mountains. On the right bank are the *Gorges de Carença*, rising to the *Lake of Carença* (about 6 hrs.; 7430 ft.), with some exceedingly picturesque spots in the first two-thirds of the way.

42 M. *Fontpédrouse* (3210 ft.; Inn). Considerable engineering works have been necessary for the continuation of the road, which makes wide circuits and crosses two ravines by means of viaducts.

48 M. **Montlouis** (5260 m.; *Hôtel de France; Jambon*), the old capital of the French Cerdagne, is a small town once important as a fortress, situated upon a plateau, the S. side of which is steep, while the E. and N. sides are perpendicular. It is commanded by the neighbouring heights, especially the *Pic de la Tausse* (6685 ft.), to the N.E., on which a new fort has been built. The cool climate of Montlouis attracts numerous Spanish visitors. The winter is very cold.

To the S.E. is (3 M.) **Planès**, where there is a very curious church, perhaps of Arabic construction. It forms an equilateral triangle with a semicircular apse on each side and a dome in the centre.

About 5 M. to the W. is the **Hermitage of Font-Romeu**, a pilgrim-resort and a summer-residence, with a Mt. Calvary on a height commanding an admirable view of the Cerdagne. Cheap accommodation may be obtained from the hermit ('paborde'). The pilgrimages are interesting sights for strangers, and are invariably accompanied with dancing and other amusements. The chief pilgrimage occurs on Sept. 8th.

The road ascends for about $2^{1}/_{2}$ M. more to the *Col de la Perche* (5320 ft.; Inn), which affords a fine view. We then descend into the (3 M.) valley and then into the (2 M.) fertile plain of the Cerdagne. — 55 M. *Saillagouse* (4295 ft.; *Cousinet*), on the Sègre.

The ascent of the **Puigmal** (9045 ft.; 7 hrs. up, 5 hrs. down), on the frontier to the S.E., may be made from Saillagouse without difficulty (with guide). We ascend via ($3/_4$ hr.) *Lio*, the ($2^3/_4$ hrs.) *Cirque de la Culasse*, the ($1^3/_4$ hr.) *Col de Lio* (8395 ft.), and (1 hr.) the *Pic de Sègre* (9170 ft.). The view is extensive to the S. and towards the sea.

The route now leaves to the right a more interesting but badly kept road, and traverses an isolated portion of Spanish territory, about $4^{1}/_{2}$ sq. M. in area. In the latter is (3 M. from Saillagouse) *Llivia*, a dirty village of ancient origin with some ruins remaining. Our road passes (57 M.) *Ste. Léocadie* and (60 M.) *Hix*, and reaches —

61 M. **Bourg-Madame** (3740 ft.; *Hôtel du Commerce*), a small town at the confluence of the Sègre and Raur, the last place on French territory, with the custom-house. To *Les Escaldas*, see p. 204.

$61^{1}/_{2}$ M. **Puycerda** (4075 ft.; *Hôtel de Europa*), with about 2000 inhab., was the ancient capital of the Spanish Cerdagne, and a fortress several times taken by the French. The church is curiously decorated in the Spanish style. Custom-house.

From Bourg-Madame to Les Escaldas (*Puy de Carlitte*), 4 M.; during the season carriages, 1 fr. per head. — Les Escaldas (*Aguas caldas*, or Hot-Springs; 4430 ft.; Hotel at the *Thermal Establishment*) is a French hamlet with 10 sulphur, chalybeate, and other springs (62° to 107° Fahr.), chiefly frequented by Spaniards from the neighbouring districts. The establishment is well managed, and is surrounded by shady walks in which there are fine points of view. — Guide (with mule): Jean Durand of Dorres, 1/2 M. to the W.

Puy de Carlitte. The ascent is best made from Les Escaldas (5 hrs.; 8 1/2 hrs. there and back) without difficulty, and for the greater part of the way on mules. We ascend first to the N., and then to the W. to the pastures of the (1/2 hr.) *Coma Armada*, and passing an irrigation canal, reach (1 1/4 hr.) a col to the left of the *Casteilla* (6850 ft.). We then cross the *Désert de Carlitte*, studded with ponds, and passing (1 1/4 hr.) a hut, and (1/2 hr.) a spring, arrive in 1/2 hr. more at the base of the peak. The mules must be left at this point. A fatiguing climb of 1/2 hr. now takes us to the *Col de Carlitte* (8550 ft.) and 20 min. more to the exceedingly narrow crest of the Puy de Carlitte (8580 ft.), the highest summit of the Eastern Pyrenees. The view is magnificent, including the whole of this part of the chain from the Central Pyrenees to the Mediterranean, which, however, is not always visible, and from the plains of Languedoc to the most distant summits of Catalonia. — Descent to *L'Hospitalet* (Ax; Andorra), see p. 189.

III. From Perpignan to Amélie-les-Bains and La Preste.

To Amélie-les-Bains, 27 M. The Railway, open at the beginning of 1895 only as far as (23 M.) *Céret*, whence a diligence plies, will perhaps be completed before the end of the year. — From Céret to (29 1/2 M.) *La Preste*, diligence daily in summer (7 fr. up, 5 fr. down, return-fare 10 fr.).

From *Perpignan* to (8 1/2 M.) *Elne*, see p. 199. The line diverges to the S. W. and ascends the valley of the *Tech*, bounded on the S. by the *Monts Albères*. To the right, towards the head of the valley, is the *Canigou* (p. 202). — 13 M. *Brouilla*; 15 M. *Banyuls-des-Aspres*.

18 1/2 M. Le Boulou (*Hôt. Lefèvre*), about 1 M. to the S. of which are the *Baths of Le Boulou*, with several chalybeate and other springs, chiefly employed for diseases of the liver. General Dugommier here inflicted a decisive defeat on the Spaniards who had invaded Roussillon in 1794.

A Diligence (1 fr.) plies hence to the frontier-village of *Le Perthus* (Hotels), 5 1/2 M. to the S., situated on the *Col du Perthus*, and commanded by the *Fort de Bellegarde*, on an isolated height (1380 ft.). The road (Barcelona road) passes the Baths of Le Boulou, and affords fine views of the Canigou, to the right, etc. — The Col du Perthus (950 ft.) is said to have been Hannibal's route across the Pyrenees; and was possibly the site of the 'Trophées de Pompée', a tower erected to commemorate the conquest of Spain. — About 5 M. farther is the Spanish village of *La Junquera* (custom-house; Inn), 5 M. beyond which is *Figueras* (Hotels), a town of 10,000 inhab., commanded by a *Citadel* of no military importance. Figueras is a station on the railway from Perpignan to Barcelona (p. 200).

20 1/2 M. *St. Jean - Pla - de - Corts*. We next cross the Tech by means of a lofty and long viaduct, to the left of which is the old *Pont de Céret*, with an arch of 150 ft. span, rising to the height of over 95 ft. This bridge is said to be of Roman origin, dating from the 3rd cent. of the Christian era.

23¹/₂ M. **Céret** (*Hôtel de France*), 1¹/₄ M. to the S. E. of the station, is an ancient town with 3830 inhab. noted for its fruit, with some remains of fortifications (two *Gates* and four *Towers*). It contains also a 14th cent. *Fountain*, and a 12th cent. *Church*, with a marble Gothic portal.

The valley contracts and takes the name of *Vallespir* ('vallis aspera'). The railway crosses to the left bank of the Tech, traverses a lofty viaduct over a tributary stream, and again crosses and re-crosses the Tech, on the last occasion by a large bridge at Amélie-les-Bains. Fine view of the Canigou to the right. On the right is *Palalda* (see below), and on the left, the fort of Amélie, on a height commanding the valley.

28 M. **Amélie-les-Bains** (800 ft.; *Thermes Pujade; Thermes Romains; Martinet; Bocassin*, all moderate; bath, 1 fr.; English Church Service in summer), formerly *Arles-les-Bains*, received its present name under Louis Philippe in honour of Queen Amélie. It is a prosperous town, finely situated at the confluence of the Tech and the Mondony, and at the foot of the *Fort-les-Bains* (1225 ft.), constructed in the time of Louis XIV. Though an important thermal station, it is not expensive. There are 20 copious sulphur springs (68°-145° Fahr.), which have been in use since the time of the Romans. Owing to the mildness of the climate the baths, which are used mainly for affections of the lungs, are open throughout the year and are considerably frequented even in winter.

There are two public bath-establishments and a military hospital. The last is at the lower end of the town; the others in the Rue des Thermes, to the left from the main street.

The *Thermes Romains*, to the right, still retain some parts of the ancient establishment, including the 'lavacrum', a large vaulted hall at the entrance, 66 ft. long, 40 ft. wide, and 37 ft. high, and another room on the left, containing a piscina. The baths are well equipped and are reached by a gallery from the hotel in connection. In front is a fountain with thermal water.

The *Thermes Pujade*, at the end of the street, on the left bank of the Mondony, are better situated, but the bathing arrangements are less complete. Behind the establishment is an attractive little park on the verge of a gorge, from which the Mondony descends in a cascade, above a dam, called 'Hannibal's Wall'.

A short distance below these baths the Mondony is crossed by a high *Foot-bridge*, leading to a shady promenade in which is the *Military Hospital*, the largest military thermal establishment in France, with accommodation for 500 patients.

WALKS AND EXCURSIONS. — To *Palalda* ('Palatium Dani'), a picturesque village on the slope of a hill on the left bank of the Tech, which we cross by a bridge of ancient origin at the entrance to Amélie. — To *Montbolo* (1890 ft.; fine view), 3 M. to the N. — To *Arles-sur-Tech* and the *Gorge de la Fou*, see p. 206. — To the *Serrat-d'en-Merle* (about 1840 ft.; fine view), a height about ¹/₂ hr. below the Military Hospital. — To *Montalba*,

3½ M. to the S., viâ the pretty valley of the Mondony. — To the *Roc de France* (4700 ft.), on the frontier, about 4 hrs. by a path for which a guide is advisable. Splendid view.

30½ M. **Arles-sur-Tech** (907 ft.; *Hotel*), the Roman *Arulae*, a quaint little town with a remarkable Romanesque *Church* and *Cloisters* in the Transition style, the remains of a Benedictine abbey. The old Catalonian manners and customs, fêtes and public dances, are preserved here perhaps better than anywhere else in this part of the French Pyrenees.

About 1¼ M. beyond Arles a road diverges to the right, skirting the (½ hr.) *Gorge de la Fou*, a fissure in the limestone rock nearly 1 mile long, with its two sides, 525 ft. in height, at the most only 15 or 18 ft. apart, while the channel at the bottom, through which the torrent dashes, is but 3 ft. wide. The road leads viâ the plateau on the right, to (1 hr. more) the village of *Corsavy* (2579 ft.; view).

From (33½ M.) *Pont-du-Loup* a road leads to the left into Spain viâ (10½ M.) *St. Laurent-de-Cerdans* (Hotel) and (3 M.) *Coustouges* (Custodia), a village ¾ M. to the W. of the frontier, with a pretty 12th cent. church.

The road to La Preste ascends a picturesque defile. 37½ M. *Le Tech* (Inn), picturesquely situated.

42 M. **Prats-de-Mollo** (pron. 'Moyo'; 2620 ft.; *Hotel*), a small walled town on a mountain-slope commanded by the *Fort de la Garde* (2810 ft.), constructed after plans by Vauban, and by an interesting Gothic and Romanesque *Church*, with good altar-pieces.

A mule-path leads hence into Spain, viâ the (2 hrs.) Col d'Ares (about 4820 ft.), perhaps the pass crossed by Cæsar, in which case the name might be derived from the altar ('ara') erected by him to commemorate the defeat of Pompey's lieutenants. The route leads to (2 hrs. more) the small Spanish town of *Camprodon* (3215 ft.).

Beyond Prats the road is highly picturesque. On an eminence (5050 ft.) to the left (S.) rises the 14th cent. *Tour de Mir*; to the right lies the hamlet of *St. Sauveur*; to the left the *Cascade de Graffouil* (80 ft.); to the right the hamlet of *La Preste*.

46 M. **La Preste-les-Bains** (3705 ft.; *Thermal Establishments*) lies partly on a plateau between the ravines of the Tech and the Llabane. There are two establishments, open throughout the year, with abundant sulphur springs (113° Fahr.), which have been long known and are used especially for calculus. There are beautiful shady walks in the neighbourhood.

About ½ hr. to the N.W. is the attractive *Grotte de Can-Brixot*, rather difficult of access. — The *Col Pragon* (5805 ft.) is 1¼ hr. to the S.; ½ hr. beyond it lies the Spanish village of *Espinabell*; then (½ hr.) *Mollo* and (1 hr.) *Camprodon* (see above).

The ascent of the frontier-summit Pic de Costabonne (8085 ft.; 5 hrs.; with guide), to the W., is easily made. We follow the valley and round the mountain to the N. to reach the *Col de la Pale*, which lies about ½ hr. to the W. of the top. *View superior even to that from the Canigou. — About ¼ hr. below the col is the *Source of the Tech*.

III. CENTRAL FRANCE. AUVERGNE. THE CEVENNES.

32. From Paris to Lyons viâ Nevers.

321 M. *viâ Roanne and Tarare*, RAILWAY in 14¹/₄ · 15¹/₂ hrs. (fares
58 fr. 00, 38 fr. 45, 25 fr. 10 c.); or 346 M. *viâ Roanne and St. Etienne* in
12²/₃ · 13¹/₄ hrs. (fares 62 fr. 60, 42 fr. 30, 27 fr. 60 c.). — For the route
viâ Dijon, see *Baedeker's South-Eastern France*.

I. From Paris to Nevers viâ Montargis.

157 M. RAILWAY in 5-8¹/₂ hrs. (fares 28 fr. 45, 10 fr. 20, 12 fr. 60 c.).
For details of this route, and for the alternative route viâ Orléans and
Bourges (187 M. in 8³/₄ - 11¹/₄ hrs.; higher fares), see *Baedeker's Northern
France*. The trains start from the Gare de Lyon.

Paris, see *Baedeker's Paris*. — As far as Montargis (see below)
there are two alternative routes. The main line runs viâ (28 M.)
Melun, (36¹/₂ M.) *Fontainebleau*, (41¹/₂ M.) *Moret* (where we quit
the line to Lyons viâ Dijon), and (54 M.) *Nemours* (4526 inhab.),
with an ancient ducal château. The other line, with two expresses
daily in summer, runs viâ the little towns of (20¹/₂ M.) *Corbeil*,
(47¹/₂ M.) *Malesherbes*, and (63 M.) *Beaune-la-Rolande*.

73 M. (by the main line) **Montargis** (*Buffet*), with 11,600 inhab.,
has a *Church* of the 13 - 16th cent.; a *Statue of Mirabeau*; and a
modern *Hôtel de Ville*, with a small Musée.

96 M. **Gien** (*Buffet*), with 8519 inhab., has an ancient *Château*
(15th cent.), commanding the *Loire*. — 120 M. *Cosne* (8672 inhab.);
140 M. *La Charité* (5443 inhab.).

157 M. **Nevers** (*Buffet; Hôtel de Paix*, etc.), a town with 26,436
inhab., at the junction of the Loire and the Nièvre. The **Palais
de Justice*, formerly a ducal château, the **Cathedral* (13-15th cent.),
the church of *St. Etienne*, in the Auvergnat Romanesque style, the
Porte du Croux (14th cent.), etc. are interesting.

II. From Nevers to Lyons.

a. Viâ Roanne and Tarare.

183 M. RAILWAY in 8-12 hrs. (fares 32 fr. 85, 24 fr. 65, 18 fr. 10 c.).

Nevers, see above. — We cross the Loire and, turning to the W.,
leave its valley for that of the Allier. Farther on we cross the Canal
Latéral, which has itself been carried over the Allier by the Guétin
aqueduct. Beyond a tunnel we reach (6 M.) **Saincaize** (*Buffet*), the
junction of the line from Bourges (p. 225). — 12¹/₂ M. *Mars*. —
16¹/₂ M. *St. Pierre-le-Moutier*, which has an interesting church,
chiefly of the 12-13th centuries. Beyond another tunnel we see, on
the left, a tasteful modern château and further on, to the right, on
the left bank of the Allier, a larger one. — 22¹/₂ M. *Chantenay-St.
Imbert; 28¹/₂ M. *Villeneuve-sur-Allier*. The bed of the Allier is
very wide and, like that of the Loire, almost dry in summer.

36¹/₂ M. **Moulins** (*Buffet*). — Hotels: HÔTEL DE PARIS, Rue de Paris,
R., L., & A. 2¹/₂-3¹/₂ fr., H. 30 c. - 1 fr., déj. 2¹/₂, D. 8, pens. 7¹/₂, omn. ¹/₂ fr.;
DU DAUPHIN, lately rebuilt, Place de l'Allier; DE L'ALLIER, Place de
l'Allier, R., L., & A. 2·5, déj. 1 or 3, D. 3 fr., omn. 30-50 c.¹

Moulins, a town with 26.665 inhab. and the capital of the department of the *Allier*, is of no great antiquity and was of importance as capital of *Bourbonnais* only from 1368 to 1527. In the latter year Francis I. confiscated the duchy in consequence of the treason of the Constable Bourbon, who had entered the service of Charles V.

A fine avenue of plane trees, facing the station, leads to the centre of the town. To the left is the theatre, to the right the Boulevard Crolay and the Boulevard de la Préfecture, which turns to the left to join the Rue de Paris (see below). Passing to the left of the theatre we gain the Rue de la Flèche, and turning to the right reach the *Tour de l'Horloge*, a square belfry of the 15th cent., the upper part of which, a fine gallery surmounted by a lantern, was restored in the 17th century. Opposite is the *Hôtel de Ville*, containing a library of 25,000 vols., the chief treasure of which is the Bible of Souvigny, a splendid MS., dated 1115 and containing 122 miniatures. The library is open every day except holidays and during vacations from noon to 4 p. m.

The CATHEDRAL, a little farther to the left, has its façade, embellished with two fine towers, on the opposite side, in the Place du Château. The nave is Early Gothic in style and was built from the plans of Viollet-le-Duc, who has here imitated the combination of black lava and white stone which characterizes many churches of Auvergne. The choir, which internally is loftier than the nave, dates mainly from the latter half of the 15th cent. and was originally the chapel of the château. It has been restored since 1885. The chief points calling for notice are the fine 15-16th cent. glass; a gilt wooden canopy (modern) over the high altar; a Holy Sepulchre (16th cent.), in the crypt behind that altar; a tasteful winding staircase on the right of the choir; and a small monument, representing a corpse devoured by worms, in the chapel before the staircase just mentioned. The chief artistic treasure, however, is a *Triptych by Ghirlandajo*, in the sacristy, on the left of the choir. This fine work, recently restored, represents on the outside the Annunciation (grisaille) and on the inside the Virgin and Child surrounded by angels, with the donors Pierre II. de Bourbon (d. 1503) and his wife Anne of France (d. 1522; daughter of Louis XI.) attended by their patron saints.

The *Château* of the Dukes of Bourbon stood opposite the cathedral, but the only portions left of it are a square tower (14th cent.), now used as a prison, and the buildings (of later date) of the Gendarmerie, to the right.

A little beyond, on the same side, are the Place de Paris and the Rue de Paris, at the entrance of which stands the *Palais de Justice*, formerly a Jesuit college. It contains an *Archaeological Museum*, composed chiefly of local antiquities (open to the public twice a month, but at all times to strangers).

A short distance from this point, to the left, is the *Lycée*, originally the Convent of the Visitation, in which, on applying to the porter, visitors are shewn the *Mausoleum of Duke Henry II. of Montmorency, beheaded for treason at Toulouse in 1632. It was erected by his widow, the Princess des Ursins, who rests beside him. The design is by François Anguier (d. 1669), who also worked at it as a sculptor, with Regnaudin and Thibaut Poissant.

In the middle, on a black marble sarcophagus, is the white marble statue of the Duke, in a reclining posture with his wife seated by him overcome with grief. The latter statue is a fine work. To the left, Strength, symbolized by a figure of Hercules, and to the right, Charity. The base, also of black and white marble, has four columns, between which are three niches, the middle one containing an urn which two angels are wreathing with flowers, the others with statues of War and Religion. Above is a fine pediment and the Montmorency coat of arms.

Returning to the Rue de la Flèche and descending to the right by the Rue d'Allier, we enter the *Place d'Allier*, at the end of which is the Church of the Sacred Heart (*du Sacré-Cœur*), a fine modern building in the early Gothic style, designed by Lassus. The ornamentation of the exterior is somewhat poor, but the interior is noteworthy and consists of nave and aisles and a transept, with only one side portal, and galleries below the rose-windows. This church has some very fine glass, by Lobin.

The Rue Régemortes, the second on the left of the façade, leads to the banks of the Allier, here crossed by a fine stone bridge. — The church of *St. Pierre*, in the Rue Delorme, partly in the Gothic style of the 15th cent., has some good modern stained glass.

From Moulins to Montluçon (Limoges), 50 M., railway in 2¹/₂-4 hrs. (fares 9 fr. 20, 6 fr. 20, 4 fr. 5 c.). — The line crosses the Allier and skirts the town to the left. Farther on, to the right, appear the *Château de Chartilly* and the *Château de Chassagne*, both of the 16th century.

8¹/₂ M. Souvigny (*Hôt. du Lion-d'Or.* good). is a little town. once famous

cuttings. — Beyond (19 M.) *Tronget* the line descends rapidly through a district intersected by many valleys. — 26½ M. *Charenon*, beyond which are the extensive ruins of the *Château de Marat* (13-14th cent.). — 32 M. *Villefranche-d'Allier*, the terminus of the line from La Guerche-Sancoins viâ Cosne-sur-l'Œil (see below). — We soon enter the coal-basin of Commentry. — 30 M. *Doyet-la-Preste*, the junction for (3½ M.) *Bézenet* (3389 inhab.), with important coal mines, and (45 M.) *Varennes* (p. 213). — 41½ M. *Commentry*. For this town and the rest of the journey see p. 227.

From Moulins to Bourbon-l'Archambault (Cosne-sur-l'Œil), 18 M., railway in 1-1¾ hr. (fares 2 fr. 15, 1 fr. 45 c.). — This line follows that to Montluçon until the Allier is crossed and then diverges to the right. — 10½ M. *St. Menoux* possesses an interesting abbey-church of the 11-15th centuries. — 13 M. *Agonges*, with another interesting church.

16 M. **Bourbon-l'Archambault** (*Hôt. du Parc; Montespan; de France*, etc.), a town of 4000 inhab., noted for its thermal mineral springs, the *Aquae Borvonis* of the Romans, is commanded by the extensive ruins of the castle (13-15th cent.) of the Sires de Bourbon. The two springs, the *Source Chaude* (124° Fahr.) and the *Source Jonas* (72° Fahr.) belong to government, and supply a *Civil* and a *Military Establishment*. The waters are efficacious in cases of scrofula and chronic rheumatism. The environs are pleasant. — *Souvigny* (p. 211) lies 8 M. to the S.E. of Bourbon, viâ *Autry*, with its curious 12th cent. church, and only 4½ M. to the S. of St. Menoux (see above).

This railway proceeds viâ (26 M.) *Buxières-les-Mines* (3184 inhab.) to (35 M.) *Cosne-sur-l'Œil* (2180 inhab.), junction for the line from La Guerche to Villefranche-d'Allier (p. 225).

From Moulins to Mâcon, 90 M., railway in 4-5 hrs. (fares 16 fr. 35, 11 fr. 5, 7 fr. 15 c.). — 17½ M. *Dompierre-Sept-Fonts*, an industrial town with 3113 inhab., on the *Bèbre*, 2 M. to the N.E. of which is the abbey of *Sept-Fonts* (founded in 1132), now belonging to the Trappists. — 22 M. *Diou*, on the banks of the Canal Latéral and the Loire. 25 M. *Gilly*, junction of a line to Auxerre viâ Cercy-la-Tour (see *Baedeker's Northern France*), with marble quarries. — Beyond (20 M.) *St. Agnan* we cross the *Arroux* and the *Canal du Centre*. — 36 M. **Digoin** (*Hôtel de la Poste*), an old industrial town with 4880 inhab., on the Loire, at the mouth of the *Canal du Centre* and the Canal Latéral. — The railway now leaves the Loire, and skirts the Canal du Centre.

41½ M. **Paray-le-Monial** (*Buffet; Hôtel de la Poste; Drago*, for pilgrims; *de Bourgogne*, moderate), a town of 3815 inhab., which takes the latter part of its name from an ancient Benedictine monastery, and is still to some extent famous by reason of its convent of the Visitation, or rather from the fact that one of the nuns of this house, Marie Alacoque (d. 1690) brought into prominence the worship of the Sacred Heart of Jesus. The *Church* is a fine building erected in the 12th cent. by Cluniac monks; the *Hôtel de Ville* dates from the 16th cent. — For the line to Chagny and Roanne, see *Baedeker's South-Eastern France*.

58 M. **Charolles** (*Buffet*), a very ancient town of 3246 inhab., prettily situated at the confluence of the Saône and Loire, and formerly capital of Charolais, once belonged to Burgundy and from it Charles the Bold took his title of Count of Charolais. — Farther on we ascend the valley of the *Semence*. — 61 M. *Les Terreaux-Verosvres*, beyond which the line passes through a tunnel from the valley of the Loire to that of the Rhone. — Several small stations are passed.

76 M. **Cluny** (*Buffet; *Hôtel de Bourgogne; de l'Étoile*), a town of 4073 inhab., once of world-wide repute on account of its great Benedictine abbey founded in the 9th cent., which was at the height of its glory in the 12th. It had some 2000 religious houses dependent on it and was the intellectual capital of Europe until its wealth led to a relaxation of discipline and the preëminence passed to the Cistercian order under St. Bernard. The prodigality of the Cluniacs was especially shown in the superb churches which they built. Unhappily but little is left of their *Abbey Church*

which furnished the type. The other buildings of the abbey have to a great extent been rebuilt and now contain an *École Normale* and an *École de Contre-Maîtres*. The *Abbot's Palace*, now converted into the *Hôtel de Ville* and *Museum*, dates from the 15-16th centuries. The latter contains fragments of the old abbey, a model of the church, and about 80 unimportant pictures. The visitor should also note *Notre-Dame*, of the 13th cent.; *St. Marcel*, which has a Romanesque steeple of the 12th cent.; some old houses, remains of fortifications, etc. The *Chapel of the Hôtel-Dieu* contains two fine statues of the early part of the 18th cent., intended for the mausoleum of the Duke and Duchess of Bouillon, which, however, has never been erected.

[From Cluny a RAILWAY runs to Roanne ($53^1/_2$ M. in $2^1/_2$-3 hrs.; fares 9 fr. 15, 6 fr. 50, 4 fr. 25 c.) viâ (8 M.) *Clermain*, (26 M.) *La Clayette-Baudemont*, (32 M.) *St. Maurice-Châteauneuf*, and several other small stations. — 38 M. *Charlieu* (*Lion d'Or*), a town of 6247 inhab., originated in an ancient Benedictine abbey, of which the chief feature remaining is the very beautiful church-porch (11-12th cent.). — At ($41^1/_2$ M.) *Pouilly-sous-Charlieu* we join the line from Montchanin and Paray-le-Monial to *Roanne* (p. 214).]

Returning for a short distance by the same line we ascend to the left, pass through a tunnel nearly 1 M. long, and, after a view of the old fortress of *Bertd*, also on the left, reach (83 M.), *St. Sorlin-Milly* (Buffet). Milly, $1/_2$ M. to the right, was the home of Lamartine (d. 1809). — 90 M. *Mâcon*, see *Baedeker's South-Eastern France*.

Beyond Moulins the main line continues to ascend the valley of the Allier, passing (45 M.) *Bessay* and (49 M.) *La Ferté-Hauterive*, with its large modern château farther on, to the left. — $54^1/_2$ M. *Varennes-sur-Allier*.

FROM VARENNES TO COMMENTRY, $48^1/_2$ M., railway in $3^3/_4$ hrs. (fares 9 fr. 60, 5 fr. 25 c.). — 8 M. *St. Pourçain-sur-Sioule*, an ancient town with 5000 inhab., and an interesting church. — At (18 M.) *Chantelle* is a ruined castle of the dukes of Bourbon, dismantled by Francis I. in 1527, after the treason of the Constable Bourbon (p. 210). Adjoining is a Romanesque church, with cloisters of the 11th and 15th centuries. A branch-line runs hence to ($17^1/_2$ M.) *St. Bonnet-de-Rochefort* (Ébreuil; p. 227). — The line ascends the pretty valley of the *Bouble*. 34 M. *Montmarault*. 41 M. *Béranet*, and thence to ($48^1/_2$ M.) *Commentry*, see p. 212.

58 M. *Créchy*. Farther on, to the left, is *Billy*, with the picturesque ruins of its feudal castle, a favourite excursion from Vichy.

$61^1/_2$ M. **St. Germain-des-Fossés** (*Buffet*), where the lines to Clermont-Ferrand (R. 34) and Vichy (R. 33) diverge to the right. The former priory church of St. Germain, above the village, probably dates from the 11th century.

The Lyons line bends to the left towards the valley of the Nèbre, passing through a pretty, undulating country. $66^1/_2$ M. *St. Gérand-le-Puy*. 73 M. *Lapalisse*, a town with 2900 inhab., $1^1/_4$ M. to the left, with a castle of the 15-16th centuries. Beyond ($77^1/_2$ M.) *Arfeuilles*, the *Montagnes de la Madeleine* appear on the right. We pass several viaducts and a tunnel more than $3/_4$ M. long. 88 M. *St. Martin-d'Estréaux*.

An OMNIBUS ($1^1/_2$ fr.) plies hence in summer to ($3^1/_2$ M.) *Sail-les-Bains* (*Hôtel de l'Établissement*), the mineral waters of which were known to the Romans. These waters, believed to be the most highly charged with silicate in existence, are efficacious in infectious diseases and in skin-

After another viaduct and a short tunnel comes (89¹/₂ M.) *La Pacaudière.* — 95¹/₂ M. *St. Germain-l'Espinasse.*

St. Germain lies 1¹/₄ M. to the E. About 1³/₄ M. to the N.W. is **Ambierle** (*Hôt. Dallerie*), a picturesquely situated town with a handsome Benedictine *Church* (15th cent.), which has twelve windows with ancient stained glass, and an altar-piece, presented in 1466, attributed to Rogier van der Weyden.

103¹/₂ M. **Roanne** (*Buffet; Hôtel du Nord*, Rue de la Sous-Préfecture), an industrial town of 31,400 inhab., on the left bank of the Loire, the *Rodomna* or *Rhidomna* of the Romans, offers few attractions to the tourist. The Cours de la République, to the right as we quit the station, and the Rue de la Côte, at the end on the left, lead to the Rue Nationale, which descends towards the Loire, passing the modern *Hôtel de Ville*, and, farther on, running near to *Notre-Dame-des-Victoires*, a fine modern church in the style of the 13th century. The second main thoroughfare of the town passes in front of the Sous-Préfecture, on the right, at the end of the Rue de la Côte, and is continued, to the left, towards the *Collège* (recently rebuilt) and *St. Etienne* (13-14th cent.), the principal church. The cross-street before the church is reached leads back to the station. Roanne has important spinning-mills and cotton factories.

About 8 M. to the W. (omnibus, 1 fr.) is **St. Alban** (*Hôt. St. Louis*, etc.), a village with cold mineral springs (aërated chalybeate), long famous as table-waters. There is a well-managed *Establishment* and a *Casino*. A variety of excursions may be made in the Monts de la Madeleine, which command fine views of the Loire valley.

From Roanne to *Paray-le-Monial, Montchanin*, and *Chagny*, see *Baedeker's South-Eastern France.*

Passing to the right of Roanne, the line crosses the *Loire* at a point where the bed of the river has been changed. — 105 M. *Le Coteau*, a suburb of Roanne, whence the line to St. Etienne diverges to the right and that to Paray-le-Monial to the left. The Tarare line ascends the valley of the Rhins, which it crosses several times. — Beyond (109 M.) *L'Hôpital* are four short tunnels. 113¹/₂ M. *Régny*, an ancient village on the Rhins, which had a Cluniac priory. Fine modern church and some remains of fortifications. Then between two tunnels, to the left, the pencil manufactory founded by the celebrated Conté. 117 M. *St. Victor-Thizy.*

A branch-line runs hence to (4¹/₂ M.) *Thizy*, a town with 4878 inhab., picturesquely situated to the N.E., and to (8 M.) *Cours*, a cloth-manufacturing town, with 6000 inhabitants.

The engineering difficulties of the line increase and the country becomes more broken as we approach the mountains of Lyonnais. Beyond two more tunnels is (121 M.) *Amplepuis*, with 7113 inhab., and cotton and muslin manufactories. The line now makes a considerable ascent, passes through a tunnel 1³/₄ M. long, and rapidly descends into the basin of the Rhone. The scenery is picturesque and a good view of Tarare is obtained, to the left. Another tunnel, ¹/₂ M. long, is passed through.

129¹/₂ M. **Tarare** (*Buffet; Hôtel de l'Europe*), a modern industrial town of 12,387 inhab.. in the narrow valley of the Turdine. surrounded by mountains. It is an important centre for the manufacture of plain and embroidered muslins, and of silk plush for hats.

132¹/₂ M. *Pontcharra-St. Forgeux;* 135 M. *St. Romain-de-Popey.* Two short tunnels. 139 M. *L'Arbresle,* an ancient town, with 3576 inhab., and the remains of a fortress. of which the keep has been restored. — We traverse four more short tunnels. 143¹/₂ M. *Lozanne;* 146¹/₂ M. *Chazay-Marcilly;* 148 M. *Les Chères-Chassel.* — At (153 M.) *St. Germain-au-Mont-d'Or* (small buffet) we join the line from Paris viâ Dijon.

165 M. *Lyons,* see p. 216.

b. Viâ Roanne and St. Etienne.

180 M. RAILWAY in 8¹/₄-8¹/₂ hrs. (fares 37 fr. 55, 28 fr. 15, 20 fr. 70 c.).

To (103¹/₂ M.) *Roanne,* see p. 214. The direct line is quitted beyond (105 M.) *Le Coteau.* The country becomes very broken, and the line beyond (110¹/₂ M.) *St. Cyr-de-Favières* passes through three tunnels, and beyond (114 M.) *Vendranges-St. Priest* through cuttings and two more tunnels. Near (117 M.) *St. Jodard* we reach the banks of the Loire, whose bed is here shut in between the hills of the Forez, which extend as far as Roanne. — Beyond (123¹/₂ M.) *Balbigny* the valley expands to the right, on which side it is sprinkled with pools and still bordered by the Forez mountains, dominated to the S.W. by the *Pierre-sur-Haute* (5370 ft.). — 129 M. *Feurs,* a town with 3492 inhab., was formerly the capital of the Forez. Its decorated Gothic church is partly modern.

136 M. **Montrond** (*Gr.-Hôt. du Forez; Mallière*), with the imposing ruins of a castle of the 14-16th cent., overlooking the Loire. The *Source du Geyser,* a mineral spring of considerable value, was discovered here in 1881, and a thermal establishment erected. — Line to Montbrison (p. 232), see *Baedeker's South-Eastern France.*

142 M. **St. Galmier** (*Hôt. Lamounery; du Commerce; des Voyageurs*), a town of 3257 inhab., 2¹/₂ M. (omn. 45 c.) to the left, is celebrated for its mineral waters which are largely exported. The *Church* (15-17th cent.) contains a remarkable tabernacle of the 16th cent., and a painted altar. A diligence plies hence to *Bellegarde,* 4¹/₂ M. to the N.

146 M. *La Renardière.* — At (146¹/₂ M.) *St. Just-sur-Loire,* we join the line from Clermont-Ferrand (p. 232).

FROM ST. JUST-SUR-LOIRE TO FIRMINY (*Annonay*), 12 M., railway in ³/₄-1 hr. (fares 2 fr. 15, 1 fr. 45, 95 c.). — The valley of the Loire is gained by a tunnel 170 yds. long, beyond which is (9¹/₂ M.) *St. Just-St. Rambert,* the station for the little town of **St. Rambert-sur-Loire,** which has remains of fortifications. We next cross three viaducts, 55, 100, and 90 ft. high, the second after three short tunnels and before a fourth ¹/₄ M. long. — 6¹/₂ M. *St. Victor-sur-Loire.* Viaducts, the first 95 ft. high, and tunnels follow in rapid succession. — 10¹/₂ M. *Fraisse-Unieux,* also on the line

from Le Puy to St. Etienne (R. 40) which we follow as far as the next
station. — 12 M. *Firminy* (p. 254).

Continuation of the railway viâ (152¹/₂ M.) *St. Etienne*, see pp.
230, 229.

190 M. **Lyons** (for farther details, see *Baedeker's South-Eastern
France*).

Hotels. Gr.-Hôt. Collet & Continental, Gr.-Hôt. de Lyon, Rue de
la République 69 and 10; Gr.-Hôt. de Bellecour, Place de Bellecour;
Gr.-Hôt. de l'Europe, 1 Rue de Bellecour; de Rome, 4 Rue de Peyrat;
des Beaux-Arts, 75 Rue de l'Hôtel-de-Ville; des Etrangers, 5 Rue Stella;
du Globe, 21 Rue Gasparin; des Négociants, 1 Rue des Quatre-Chapeaux;
*des Archers, 15 Rue des Archers; Bayard, 47 Rue de l'Hôtel-de-Ville;
de Russie, 6 Rue Gasparin; de Milan, 8 Place des Terreaux; de Paris
& du Nord, 16 Rue de la Platière. — Gr.-Hôt. de l'Univers, Cours du
Midi 27; d'Angleterre, de Bordeaux & du Parc, both Place Carnot; de
Toulouse, Cours du Midi 23; Hôt.-Restaur. Dubost, Place Carnot 19.

Restaurants. *Maison Dorée*, Place Bellecour; *Maderni, Casati*, Rue de
la République 19 and 8; *du Helder*, Rue de l'Hôtel-de-Ville 88; *Au Roabif*
(cheaper), various establishments; *Bouillon Montesquieu*, Place Carnot. —
Cafés. *Maison Dorée, Casati*, see above; *Anglais, du Dix-Neuvième Siècle,
de Madrid*, Rue de la République 24, 97, and 1; *Morel, de Lyon*, Rue de
l'Hôtel-de-Ville 108 and 49.

Cabs. With seats for 2 pers. 1 fr. 50 c. per drive, 2 fr. per hr.; for
4 pers., 1³/₄ and 2¹/₂ fr.; 50 c. extra between midnight and 6 a. m. Each
trunk 25 c., 75 c. for three or more.

Post Office, Place de la Charité and Place Bellecour. — **Telegraph
Office**, Place de la République 53 (open day and night).

American Consul, *Frank K. Hyde, Esq.* — **British Vice Consul**, *Robert
Ottley, Esq.* — **English Church Service**, *Holy Trinity Church*, Quai de l'Est.

Lyons, the ancient *Lugdunum*, with 438,000 inhab., is the
second city of France both for size and industrial importance, and
occupies a magnificent site at the confluence of the *Rhône* and
Saône. These rivers divide Lyons into three distinct parts, *viz.* the
town proper between them (with the Gare de Perrache); the quarter
on the right bank of the Saône, including *Fourvière* and *Vaise;*
and the quarter on the left bank of the Rhone, including *La Guil-
lotière* and *Les Brotteaux*.

In front of the Gare de Perrache are the broad Cours du Midi
and the Place Carnot, with the *Monument of the Republic*. Nearer
the centre of the town are the *Church of Ainay*, the oldest in Lyons
(10-11th cent.), and the Place Bellecour with an *Equestrian Statue
of Louis XIV*. Thence the Rue de Bellecour leads to the right bank
of the Saône on which are the *Cathedral* (12-15th cent.) and the
church of *Notre-Dame-de-Fourvière*. — The church of *St. Nizier*
(15-16th cent.), in the Rue de l'Hôtel-de-Ville, between the two
rivers, is the ancient cathedral. In the Place de l'Hôtel-de-Ville is
the *Palais des Arts*, containing important collections of paintings,
sculptures, antiquities, and natural history. — The *Hôtel de Ville*
dates in its present form from 1702. — The *Palais de la Bourse*,
in the Rue de la République, is one of the most striking buildings
in Lyons; it contains an interesting *Museum of Textile Industry*.
To the N.E. of the town is the *Parc de la Tête-d'Or*, at the entrance

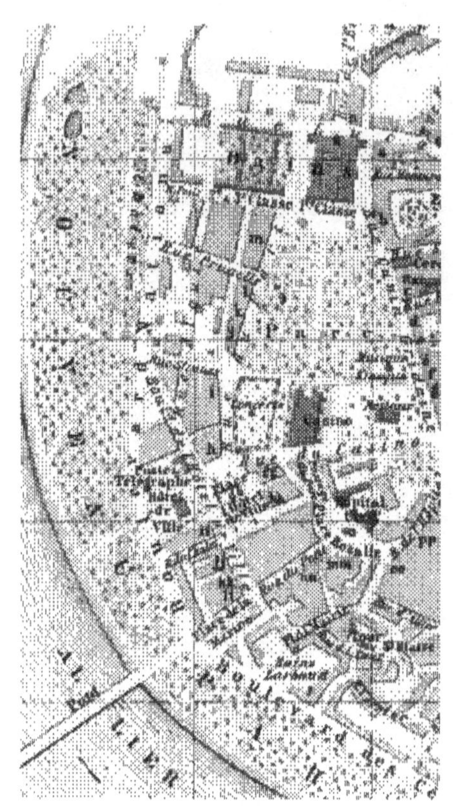

33. From Nevers (Paris) to Vichy and Thiers
(St. Etienne).

92¹/₂ M. Railway to (69 M.) *Vichy* in 2-4³/₄ hrs. (fares 12 fr. 55, 8 fr. 45, 5 fr. 50 c.). From Vichy to (23¹/₂ M.) *Thiers*, Railway in 1³/₄-2 hrs. (fares 4 fr. 70, 3 fr. 50, 2 fr. 25 c.). — From Paris to Vichy, 227 M., Railway in 8¹/₂-13¹/₂ hrs. (fares 40 fr. 95, 27 fr. 75, 17 fr. 85 c.).

To (63 M.) *St. Germain-des-Fossés*, see p. 213. — The Vichy line continues to follow the valley of the Allier. To the right (fine view) the line to Clermont-Ferrand (R. 34) diverges. — 69 M. *Vichy*.

Vichy. — Hotel-omnibuses (2 fr. or less) meet the trains. Railway-omnibus, 30 c. by day, 50 c. by night. Cabs, see below.

Hotels. In the Rue Cunin-Gridaine (Pl. C, 2-4), on the E. side of the Park, beginning at the Establishment: Grand-Hôtel des Bains (Pl. a); Nouvel Hôtel (Pl. b); Hôt. de l'Amirauté (Pl. c); Velay et des Anglais (Pl. d); Royal Hôtel (Pl. e); Molière et du Casino, united (Pl. f, f), pens. 10-20 fr. per day; Hôt. Bonnet et de la Restauration (Pl. g). — In the Rue du Parc (Pl. B, 3, 4), on the other side of the Park, beginning at the Casino: Grand-Hôt. des Ambassadeurs (Pl. h), elegantly fitted up, R., L., & A. 4-18, B. 1-2, déj. 4, D. 6, pens. 11-20, omn. 1 fr. (trunk 50 c.); des Thermes (Pl. i); de Cherbourg (Pl. j); des Princes et de la Paix (Pl. k, l), open all the year round; du Parc et Grand-Hôtel (Pl. m). All the above are of the first class (at least 10-20 fr. per day). — Richelieu (Pl. n; B, 2), Rue de l'Etablissement. — Britannique (Pl. o; C, 2), de la Source Lucas (Pl. p; C, 3), both in the Rue Lucas; Gr.-Hôt. Maussant et de Madrid (Pl. q; C, 2), in the Rue de Ballore. In the Rue de Paris (Pl. D, 3): to the right as we go to the station, Hôt. du Louvre et de Reims (Pl. r); Gr.-Hôt. de l'Univers (Pl. s), Dubessay (Pl. t), du Rhône (Pl. u), de la Couronne (Pl. v), du Beaujolais (Pl. w); to the left, Hôt. de la Suisse (Pl. x), de Rome (Pl. y), etc. — Rue de Nîmes (Pl. C, 4, 5): Hôt. de Rouen (Pl. z), second-class; Hôt. de Nice (Pl. bb), near the church of St. Louis, de l'Europe (Pl. cc), d'Orléans (Pl. dd), de Milan (Pl. ee), not far from the Park, Hôt. du Palais (Pl. ée), de Genève (Pl. ff), farther on. — Hôt. Molière (Pl. gg; B, 4), Rue du Casino, well situated, open all the year. — Place and Rue de l'Hôtel-de-Ville (Pl. B, 4, 5), also well-placed: Hôt. de Narbonne et d'Espagne (Pl. hh), de Londres & du Chalet (Pl. ii, kk), de Rivoli (Pl. ll), all of the second class. — Near the Source de l'Hôpital (Pl. B, 5): Hôt. de Russie (Pl. mm), de l'Union (meublé, Pl. nn); Gr.-Hôt. du Centre (Pl. pp); Hôt. de la Porte de France (Pl. oo), etc. — Hôtel Belle-Vue (Pl. ss), R., L., & A. 3¹/₂-5 fr.; Gr.-Hôt. du Palais-Royal (Pl. tt), des Célestins (Pl. uu), two second-class houses in a quiet street behind the Parc des Célestins (Pl. C, 5). — In the Rue de Paris, nearer the station (Pl. D, 3): Côte d'Or, de Castille, de Brest, Heurtparlant, de la Poste, du Globe, the last two unpretending but good. There are also a great number of furnished houses and smaller hotels, especially in Old Vichy, amongst which may be mentioned a new '*Hôtel de Famille*' in the Pavillon de Sévigné (p. 220). Living is not so dear at Vichy as one might expect considering the reputation of the place. There are, at any rate, hotels to suit every purse.

Cafés. *La Restauration*, also restaurant, in the Park, to the left of the Casino; *Gr.-Café de la Perle*, *Café Riche*, *Grand Café*, all in the Rue de Nîmes; *Grand Café Neuf*, Square de l'Hôtel-de-Ville; etc.

Cabs. From the station to the hotels, with or without luggage by day (6 a. m. to 8 p. m.), with 1 horse, 1¹/₂, with 2 horses 2¹/₂ fr., by night 1 fr. extra; same scale from the station to lodgings. — Per drive, by day, 1¹/₄ and 2 fr.; night 2 and 3 fr. Per hour, by day, 3 and 4 fr.; night, 4 and

Thermal Establishment, open all the year (see below). The mineral water drunk on the spot is gratis; sent to a special address, 30 c. per litre. For the *Baths*, visitors enter their names at the office, in the Grande Gallerie of the 1st class. Tariff: baths or douches de luxe, 5 fr.; mineral baths. 1st cl., 2 fr. 50 c.; 2nd cl., 1 fr. 50 c.; 3rd cl., 60 c.; bath in the common basin, 2 fr., etc., according to tariff posted up in the establishment. The season reaches its height in July and August.

Physicians. A complete list of consulting physicians is posted up in the galleries of the Establishment, with their addresses.

Casino (see p. 219), admission, 2 fr. per day, 25 fr. per month. The subscription admits to all rooms except the theatre, and includes the use of chairs in the promenade and the public parks. Admission to the *Theatre*, with numbered stall, 4 fr.; to Casino and Theatre, 5 fr.; subscription for both, 60 fr., etc. An introduction is requisite.

Club. CERCLE INTERNATIONAL (Pl. C, 3), at the corner of the Rue Cusin-Gridaine and the Rue Sornin. Admission only granted to members of existing clubs, or on presentation. — *Eden Theatre*, behind the Nouvel Hôtel (3 and 2 fr.).

English Church Service in summer (June-Sept.).

Vichy (850 ft.) is a town of 10,870 inhab., prettily situated on the right bank of the *Allier*, and enjoying a healthy and temperate climate. It is the principal watering-place of France and even of Europe, for it is visited by nearly 50,000 foreigners annually. Except its old quarter, which dates from the middle ages, the town is entirely modern. Its waters, though well known to the Romans, who named the town *Vicus Calidus*, only came into favour towards the end of the 17th cent., when Madame de Sévigné made them known at the court of Louis XIV.; and they did not become really fashionable until the Second Empire. The celebrity of the Vichy waters, however, is not solely due to the favour of Napoleon III., who was a frequent visitor, nor to the transformation which the town partly owes to him, but also to their intrinsic virtues. The place is also indebted for its prosperity to the admirably managed Establishment, which is the property of the state and is leased by a company. The waters are chiefly used for drinking, and yet such is the influx of strangers at the height of the season that the company is called on to provide 3500 baths a day.

The long Rue de Paris leads from the station to the centre of the new town. Thence the Rue Lucas, almost straight on, passes between the *Military Hospital*, on the right, and the *Sources Lucas* and *Prunelle*, on the left, the former used chiefly for baths, the latter private property. — Farther on the Rue Cusin-Gridaine strikes away to the left, skirting the Thermal Establishment and the Park and containing many of the chief hotels.

The **Thermal Establishment** (Pl. B, 2, 3) consists mainly of a vast square structure with an arcade of round arches of massive design built in 1820, to which a yet larger annexe, on the W. side, was added in 1853. The first block, in which are the offices, is reserved for baths of the 1st class, which are only distinguished from the two others, in the annexe, by their elegance and comfort. Here, too, are several of the principal springs: the *Puits Chomel* (113°

Fahr.) at the end of the gallery as we come from the Park, where
the water is raised by a pump; the *Grande Grille* (111° Fahr.), the
most celebrated of the Vichy springs, the water of which bubbles up
naturally at the E. end of the cross gallery at the back of the building; the *Source Mesdames* (59° Fahr.), at the other end, brought
hither from the Cusset road; and the *Puits Carré* (113° Fahr.), the
most abundant spring (55,000 gallons per day), which is in the basement. The total daily supply from all the springs is about 64,000
gallons. The water of the Puits Chomel is especially effective in
maladies of the digestive organs; that of the Grande Grille for liver-
complaints, and hepatic affections; that of the Source Mesdames
for chlorosis and other female diseases; while that of the Puits Carré
is used solely to supply the baths. For the other springs, see below.
Behind the Establishment are the *Bâtiments d'Exploitation* (visitors admitted), in which are produced the salts, pastilles, and barley-
sugar of Vichy. About 7,000,000 bottles of the water are annually
exported from Vichy.

The **Park** (Pl. B, C, 3, 4), between the Thermal Establishment
and the Casino, is a promenade shaded by fine trees, planted in the
time of Napoleon I. It is the centre of Vichy, and the rendezvous
of the visitors during the *Concerts* (8.30 to 9.30 a. m., and 2.30 to
3.30 p. m.). It is still more frequented in the evening. On the right
as we come from the Establishment is the *Source du Parc* (71.6°
Fahr.), which is little used, though in certain cases it is to be preferred to the Sources de l'Hôpital and des Célestins (p. 220). —
Farther on, to the right of the Casino, is the Concert enclosure; to
the left the band-pavilion and the Café 'La Restauration' (p. 217).

The **Casino** (Pl. B, 4) is a fine building in the style of the Renaissance, erected 1860-65, by Badger. The façade, in front of
which is a small garden, forms a verandah in the middle, and on
each side a pavilion, with a large window between two colossal
caryatides, and a circular pediment. The caryatides, representing
the Seasons, are by Carrier-Belleuse. On the back of the building is a colossal high-relief, by the same artist, representing 'The
Springs of Vichy'. Within are to be found all the means of re-
creation usual in establishments of this kind. These include a
large Salle des Fêtes, a reading-room, well provided with French
and foreign newspapers, a ladies' saloon, a billiard room, a card
room, and a theatre. The Casino is open from May 15th to Sept.
30th, but the real season only lasts from June 1st to Sept. 15th.
Admission, p. 218.

To the right of the Casino, beyond the Park, is the *Hôtel de
Ville* (Pl. A, 4), a small plain building with a pretty fountain in
front of it. At the side are the *Post* and *Telegraph Offices*. Behind
the Casino and on the left side are large *Bazaars*. — The Passage
du Parc leads to the *Place Rosalie* (Pl. B, 5), in front of the *Hôpital
Civil*. Here is the *Source de l'Hôpital* (88° Fahr.), similar in char-

acter to the Grande Grille. The water is chiefly used for gastric
disorders. It has a separate bathing establishment in the Place

The Rue du Pont, which descends from this spring towards the
Allier, crosses the **New Park**, a splendid promenade formed since
1861 by the construction of an embankment, nearly a mile long,
protecting land which the Allier used often to overflow. It extends
almost the whole length of the town by the river-bank, and has an
area of nearly 30 acres. There is a fine view of the valley and the
eminences on the opposite bank. The bridge dates from 1866.
Lower down the stream is a weir.

Old Vichy, skirted by this park on the left side of the Rue du
Pont, has little or nothing to interest the visitor. The *Tour de
l'Horloge* is a relic of a 15th cent. château. In the lower part of Old
Vichy are the private *Bains Larbaud* (Pl. D, 5), with a gratuitous
drinking-room, and a little higher up is the *Pavillon de Sérigné*,
so named from its having been in 1676 the residence of Madame de
Sévigné, who then spent a season at Vichy, and speaks of it in her
letters. The latter has been restored and is now a hotel (p. 217).

Farther on are the *Sources des Célestins* (Pl. C, 6), named after a
convent of Celestines which existed here down to the last century.
They are three in number: the Source de la Grotte (57.2° Fahr.),
the Old Source (53.6° Fahr.) farther away and scanty, and the New
Source (53.6° Fahr.), the most frequented. Their waters are pleasant
to drink, but must, it is said, be used with caution. They are
efficacious in cases of gout, gravel, and diabetes. Above the springs
is a pretty park which, on the other side, communicates with the
Route de Nîmes.

The Boulevard des Célestins joins, at the end of the New Park,
the Avenue des Célestins, which skirts the town, passing in front
of the private establishment of the *Bains Lardy* (Pl. D, 6) and an
establishment of *Bains Thermo - Résineux* (pine - cone baths;
Pl. D, 6).

Turning to the left beyond the Parc des Célestins, we re-enter
the town by the Rue de Nîmes. In this street, not far from the park,
is the *Church of St. Louis* (Pl. C, 4), built in 1861 in the Romanesque style, and decorated inside with polychrome paintings.

Excursions. — To Cusset, 1³/₄ M. to the E., beyond the railway.
Omnibus-railway, 20 c., gratis for bathers at the establishment Ste. Marie.
An alternative route leads by the *Allée des Dames*, a pleasant promenade
skirting the *Sichon*, a small tributary of the Allier, and reached by the
Rue de Ballore. Cusset (*Hôtel et Villa des Bains*) is a small and ancient
town (6454 inhab.), with its own *Bath Establishment*, having two cold springs.
Both the establishment and the hotel are situated a little on this side of
the square, in which the cars stop. In the square is a third mineral
spring. — About 2¹/₂ M. farther, on the left, is *Les Malavaux*, in a somewhat dull valley.

To the Ardoisière, a continuation of the preceding route, 7 M. from
Vichy; one-horse carriage, 10 fr., two-horse, 15 fr. there and back including halt of 1 hr. About 1³/₄ M. from Cusset, in the valley of the Sichon,
is the village of *Les Grivats*; 1³/₄ M. farther, in a picturesque gorge, the

Gour Saillant, a pretty little cascade, and 1¾ M. beyond it the *Ardoisière* (slate quarry), less interesting than the road to it. There is an expensive restaurant (déj. 5, D. 6 fr.).

To the Château de Bourbon-Busset, a continuation of the preceding route, 8 M. from Vichy. There is also a road viâ *St. Yorre* (see below), but it is to be preferred for the return, unless we go by train (see below) from Vichy to St. Yorre and walk thence (2½ M.). One-horse carriage 15 or 18 fr.; two-horse, 20 or 23 fr., according to the route chosen; public conveyance from the Place de la Marine, 4 fr. each. An ascent of little more than a mile from the Ardoisière beings us to the plateau on which stands the Château de Bourbon-Busset, with the large village of *Busset*. This château (visitors admitted) became in the 18th cent. the property of a branch of the Bourbon family, but the building dates from the 14th century. It is a very remarkable feudal castle, entered by a draw-bridge between two large modern round towers. The block in the rear, the only old part, though restored in recent times, presents a severe but picturesque appearance, with its massive machicolated tower. On this side is a terrace commanding a superb *View of the valley of the Allier, the Limagne (p. 222), the Monts Dôme, and the Monts Dore (pp. 243, 245, 250), as well as of the Forez group (p. 215). To the left of the court is a small chapel, rebuilt in the style of the 13th century. Some of the rooms have been judiciously restored in the original style. — In returning by (2½ M.) St. Yorre, we obtain splendid views of the valley of the Allier and the mountains.

To the Springs of Vesse and Hauterive. The former is an intermittent spring near Vichy (about 1 M.), on the left bank of the Allier, by the bridge. The hours at which it flows are posted up at the Thermal Establishment (adm., 50 and 25 c.). — *Hauterive*, 2½ M. farther (carriage, 7 or 10 fr.), possesses, within a fine park, one of the chief mineral springs worked by the Company. The water, of the same character as that of Les Célestins (p. 220), is only used for exportation.

To the Château de Randan, 10 M., viâ the *Bois de Randan*. One-horse carriage, 15 fr., two-horse, 20 fr., with return viâ Maulmont (see below) 18 and 24 fr.; public conveyance from the Place de la Marine, 3½ fr. The Château de Randan is of very ancient foundation, but was entirely rebuilt in 1822 by Mme. Adélaïde d'Orléans, sister of Louis-Philippe, and now belongs to the Comtesse de Paris. It is open to visitors from July 1st to Oct. 15th on Thurs., Sun., and holidays, from noon to 5. The return is usually made by the hunting-lodge of *Maulmont* (5 M.), also a modern edifice. Thence we may either proceed by *Hauterive* (see above), or, better, cross the Allier by the Pont de Ris (1¾ M., see below).

The *Côte St. Amand*, 2½ M. to the S.E. of Vichy, on the left of the road to Thiers, and the *Montagne Verte*, 2½ M. to the N., are especially visited for the sake of the views, similar to that from Busset (carr. 7 or 10 fr.). — The ruins of the *Château de Billy*, mentioned on p. 213, are also visited; they are 2½ M. from the of station of St. Germain-des-Fossés (p. 213).

The railway now follows the right bank of the Allier, passing on the left the municipal hospital of Vichy. — 74 M. (from Nevers; 5 M. from Vichy) **St. Yorre** (*Hôtel Gay*) has a copious cold mineral spring, in a fine park to the right of the line a little before the station. The water is only used for drinking purposes. Excursion to Busset, whose château is seen on the left, see above.

78½ M. *Ris-Châteldon*. *Ris*, near the confluence of the Allier and the Dore, has a fine suspension bridge over the Allier (to Randan, see above). *Châteldon* (Hôt. Dassaud), 1¾ M. to the S.E. at the foot of rocky heights, is an ancient town of 2099 inhab., with

remains of fortifications and an old castle. It has also a small
Mineral Water Establishment. To the right of the *Dore*, which
the line now skirts, are the Monts Dôme (pp. 243, 245). 82 M.
Puy-Guillaume; 86½ M. *Noalhat.*

At (92 M.) *Courty* (Buvette) our line joins that from Clermont-
Ferrand to Thiers and St. Etienne, see p. 234.

34. From Nevers (Paris) to Clermont-Ferrand and Le Puy.

103 M. and 91 M. RAILWAY in 3¼-4½ hrs. and in 6½ hrs. (fares
18 fr. 80, 12 fr. 75, 8 fr. 25 c.). — From Paris to Clermont-Ferrand, 261 M.,
RAILWAY in 8½-14 hrs. (fares 47 fr. 15, 31 fr. 85, 20 fr. 30 c.). — Line to
Clermont-Ferrand viâ Bourges and Montluçon, see R. 35; to Le Puy viâ
Lyons and St. Etienne, RR. 3? and 34.

To (63 M.) *St-Germain-des-Fossés,* see p. 213. — The railway
turns to the W. and crosses the Allier. Beyond (66½ M.) *St. Remy,*
the line steadily ascends, affording a fine view of the basin of the
Allier and the mountains of the Forez (p. 215), bounding the horizon
to the left. The Monts Dôme are also in view (pp. 243, 245). —
74 M. *Monteignet-Escurolles.*

77½ M. **Gannat** (*Hôt. de la Poste; *Railway Restaurant*), a
town of 5760 inhab., on the *Andelot,* with an interesting church of
the 11th and 14th centuries. — Line to Montluçon and Bordeaux,
R. 36. — We next traverse the *Limagne,* a fertile basin of the Basse-
Auvergne, covering an area of about 90 sq. miles, watered by the
Allier and bounded by the Monts Dôme on the W. and the Forez
range on the E.

84½ M. **Aigueperse** (*Hôt. St. Louis*), a town of 2340 inhab., with
a fine Gothic church of the 13-15th cent., lately restored. It possesses
a painting by A. Mantegna, one by Ben. Ghirlandajo, and some good
carving. — 90 M. *Pontmort.* To the right is the chain of the Monts
Dôme, dominated by the Puy de Dôme (p. 245).

95 M. **Riom** (*Gr.-Hôt. Place Desaix; Hôt. de Paris*), a town of
11,189 inhab., long the capital of Auvergne and a rival of Clermont,
is well built, but of dark stone or Volvic lava. The chief churches
are *St. Amable* (11-14th and 18th cent.); *Notre-Dame-du-Mar-
thuret* (15th cent.), with a dome; and *Ste. Chapelle* (14-15th cent.),
with fine windows of the 15th century. There is a *Museum* with
200 pictures, a large *Prison* of the 17th cent., and some ancient
houses of the 15th and 16th cent., including the *Hôtel des Consuls,*
opposite the Hôtel de Ville.

The church of *Morat,* 1 M. to the N., contains two valuable reliquaries
of the 15th and 16th cent. respectively.

About 3 M. to the N.W. (omnibus in 35 min., 4 times a day, 75 c.)
is *Châtelguyon* (*Splendid Hôtel; Grand Hôtel des Bains; Barthélemy,* etc.), a
village of about 1000 inhab., noted for its mineral-springs, with a well
managed *Establishment.* The church contains a gilded altar-piece (18th cent.)
and there is another of the same kind in the church of the neighbouring

village of *St. Bonnet.* — The church of *Usson-la-Tourelle* contains two alabaster altar-panels in the Gothic style (13-14th cent.), attributed by some authorities to Flemish artists.

Public conveyances also leave Riom twice a day in the season (2 and 3 fr.) for (17¹/₂ M. to the N.W.) **Châteauneuf-les-Bains** (*Hôt. St. Cyr; Bresle; Chassard; La Rotonde; Petit Rocher*, etc.), on the *Sioule*, also with mineral springs. The 13th cent. *Château* contains various collections.

A Branch Railway runs from Riom to (6 M.) **Volvic** (*Commerce*), at the foot of the *Puy de la Bannière*, with a considerable trade in lava-stone. About 1 M. to the N. are the interesting ruins of the *Château de Tournoël*, dating partly from the 12th century. Farther on is the *Gorge d'Enval* or *Bout-du-Monde.* — The railway goes on to join the (11 M.) Clermont and Limoges line (R. 36), thus cutting off about 10 M.

Besides the Puy de Dôme on the right, we now see, on the left the Mont Rognon, with a ruined tower, and the Plateau of Gergovie (p. 246). Beyond (99 M.) *Gerzat*, on the right, is *Montferrand*, with large new barracks.

A branch-line runs from Gerzat to (12¹/₂ M.) *Maringues*, a small industrial town, viâ (8¹/₂ M.) *Joze*, with mineral springs.

103 M. Clermont-Ferrand (*Buffet*). For this town and Auvergne, see pp. 238 seq.

Keeping in view for a long time the Puy de Dôme, Mont-Rognon, and the Plateau of Gergovie, we pass (108 M.) *Sarlière-Cournon* and (109 M.) *Le Cendre-Orcet*, and reach the banks of the Allier. Undulating country; best views to the right. Beyond (112 M.) *Les Martres-de-Veyres* we have on the right the *Puy de Monton* (1925 ft.) on which is a modern statue of the Virgin, 65 ft. in height. We cross the Allier. — 114 M. *Vic-le-Comte*, the little town of which name lies 3 M. to the S.E. The old part of its church, the Ste. Chapelle, is remarkable as a rich example of the end of the Gothic period and the beginning of the Renaissance.

Farther on, to the left, near Coudes, are the imposing ruins of the *Château de Buron*, an ancient stronghold of the Counts of Auvergne. This country abounds in old castles and ruins, most of them on 'puys' (p. 243), as the singularly formed peaks are called. To the right, beside the Allier, are the ruins of a toll-tower. Above Coudes, on the right, is *Montpeyroux*, dominated by a 13th cent. tower.

118¹/₂ M. Coudes (*Hôt. du Commerce*, at the station; *Dumon*), on the right bank of the Allier.

A diligence in connection with the first morning train plies hence to (13¹/₂ M.) *St. Nectaire* (p. 258) in about 3 hrs., and thence to (3 M. farther) *Murols* (p. 259), returning from Murols at 3 p. m. and from St. Nectaire at 4 p. m.

Another diligence plies also to (19 M.) *Besse* (p. 251) viâ (11¹/₂ M.) *Montaigut-le-Blanc* and (13¹/₂ M.) *Le Cheix*, near which are the *Grottes de Jonas* (p. 251).

To the right and left are rocks and picturesque eminences. We recross the Allier and see on the horizon to the right the Monts Dore (p. 250).

124¹/₂ M. Issoire (*Buffet; Hôt. de la Poste*), a town of 6182 inhab., to the right, on the *Couze*, was the scene of many excesses

both by Calvinists and Catholics in the 16th century. The fine
Church of St. Paul, in the Auvergnat-Romanesque style, resembles
Notre-Dame-du-Port at Clermont.

The country now becomes less interesting. To the left, at a
distance, is the *Château de la Grange*; farther off, to the right,
St. Germain-Lembron, a considerable village on an eminence; then
the ruins of the *Château de Châlus*. — Passing (130 M.) *Le Breuil*
and (132½ M.) *Le Saut-du-Loup*, we cross the *Alagnon* and note
on the left another castle in ruins. Then, after a short tunnel,
(136½ M.) *Brassac*, the centre of a small coal-field.

At (140 M.) **Arvant** *(Buffet)* the Aurillac branch (p. 259) diverges to the right.

To the right, on an eminence, is the *Château de Paulhac* (15th
cent.); to the left, a fine mountain amphitheatre.

146½ M. **Brioude** *(Hôtel du Nord)*, an ancient town of 4928 inhabitants. The *Church of St. Julien*, well seen from the railway, is
a remarkable monument of the 12-13th cent., Gothic in its details.
but still Romanesque as a whole. It has a tower at each end, both
rebuilt in modern times, that over the portal without a spire. The
Chapel of St. Michel contains some valuable mural paintings. —
La Chaise-Dieu (p. 234) lies 24 M. to the E. of Brioude (carriage-road).

Recrossing the Allier 1½ M. farther on, we pass (153 M.) *Frugières-le-Pin*. On the right, the picturesque ruins of the *Château
de Domeyrat* (15th cent.), overlooking the village of the same
name. — 157½ M. *Paulhaguet*. — At (16 M.) *St. Georges-d'Aurac*
diverges the line to Nîmes (R. 41). — Hence to *Le Puy*, see p. 259.

35. From Orléans (Paris) to Clermont-Ferrand.

a. Viâ Bourges and Saincaize.

204 M. Railway in 10¾-11½ hrs. (fares about 36 fr. 85, 24 fr. 90, 16 fr.
25 c.). — From Paris, 298 M. in 13¼-16½ hrs. (fares about 50 fr. 40,
34 fr. 5, 22 fr. 25 c.). For details of this route as far as and including
Bourges, see *Baedeker's Northern France.*

Orléans, see p. 3 and *Baedeker's Northern France.* — To (49 M.)
Vierzon, see p. 34. — The railway crosses the *Yèvre* and the *Canal
du Berry*, and traverses a tunnel, beyond which diverges the line to
Limoges (R. 5). We continue to skirt the S. side of the canal.

55 M. *Foëcy*. — 58 M. *Mehun-sur-Yèvre*, a town of 6572 inhab.,
with some remains of a castle in which Charles VII. starved himself to death in 1461, from fear of being poisoned by his son, afterwards Louis XI. Mehun also contains a remarkable Romanesque-
Gothic church. — Beyond (63½ M.) *Marmagne* (p. 225) the line to
Montluçon (p. 227) diverges on the right. We recross the Canal du
Berry and the Yèvre.

69 M. **Bourges** (**Buffet*); for farther details, see *Baedeker's
Northern France*.

Hotels. BOULE D'OR, Place Gordaine; DE FRANCE, Place Planchat, of
the same class, R. from 3, déj. 3, D. 4 fr.; JACQUES-CŒUR, Rue des Arènes
35. — Cafés. *Grand Café*, Rue Moyenne 14; *Beaux-Arts*, near the Ecole des
Beaux-Arts. — Cabs. Per drive 1 fr. 50; 1st hr., 2 fr. 50 c., afterwards
2 fr. 25 c. per hour. — *Post and Telegraph-Office*, Place Berry.

Bourges, a town of 45,342 inhab., the old capital of Berry and
now the chief town of the department of the *Cher*, stands in the midst
of flat meadows at the confluence of the Yèvre and the Auron. Its
principal attractions for tourists are the **Cathedral of St. Etienne*
(13-16th cent.), one of the most beautiful churches in France, and
the **Hôtel de Jacques Cœur*, now the Palais de Justice. Bourges
also contains several other quaint and interesting buildings and has
a large arsenal with a cannon foundry.

From Bourges to (43 M.) *Nevers* and to (84 M.) *Beaune-la-Rolande* and
to (35 M.) *Laugère*, see *Baedeker's Northern France*.

For some distance beyond Bourges the railway ascends the valley
of the Yèvre. To the left is the new line to Sancerre. Between
(75 M.) *Moulins-sur-Yèvre* and (78½ M.) *Sarigny-en-Septaine*
the Yèvre is crossed thrice. — At (82 M.) *Avor* are a camp for
military manœuvres and a school for non-commissioned officers.
— 88 M. *Bengy*. — Beyond (91½ M.) *Nérondes* (2481 inhab.) the
railway threads a tunnel and crosses the *Aubois* and the Canal
de Berry.

98 M. *La Guerche* (3515 inhab.), on the Aubois, with blast-
furnaces and a quarry of lithographic stone.

Branch-Lines run hence to (33½ M.) *St. Amand* (p. 226) and (45½ M.)
Villefranche-d'Allier (p. 212), diverging from each other at (9½ M.) *San-
coins*, a small town on the Canal de Berry. The St. Amand line runs
thence to the S.W. viâ (24 M.) *Laugère*; the other turns to the S. and joins
the Moulins line (p. 212) at (58 M.) *Cosne-sur-l'Œil*.

103½ M. *Le Guétin*. The railway then crosses the *Canal Latéral à la Loire* near the point where the canal is carried across
the Allier by an *Aqueduct*, over ¼ M. in length. The *Allier* itself
is crossed.

105 M. **Saincaize** (*Buffet*) and thence to Clermont-Ferrand, see
p. 209.

b. Viâ Montluçon and Gannat.

198 M. RAILWAY in 10-11½ hrs. (fares about 35 fr. 40, 23 fr. 90,
15 fr. 60 c.). — To *Montluçon*, 128 M., in 4-7¾ hrs. (fares 23 fr. 40, 15 fr. 80,
10 fr. 35 c.); thence to *Gannat*, 42 M., in 2-3 hrs. (7 fr. 75, 5 fr. 20, 3 fr. 40 c.).
— This line is very interesting beyond Montluçon. — From Paris to Clermont-Ferrand, 270 M., in 12¼-16½ hrs. (fares about 48 fr. 95, 33 fr. 5, 21 fr.
60 c.).

To (63½ M.) *Marmagne*, see p. 224. The morning-express proceeds hence by the direct line, while other trains go on to *Bourges*
(see above), 5½ farther, and thence rejoin the main line by a loop-
line viâ *La Chapelle-St. Ursin*. — 74 M. (from Orléans) *St. Florent*,
a small town on the Cher, with iron-mines and manufactories in the

neighbourhood. Branch to Issoudun, see p. 35. — We next skirt
the right bank of the Cher, and soon cross it. — 78 M. *Lunery.*

84¹/₂ M. *Châteauneuf-sur-Cher,* a little town with a beautiful
castle of the Renaissance, on the right bank, and a modern Gothic
church with a stone spire. Continuing to skirt the Cher, we reach
(89¹/₂ M.) *Bigny,* with manufactories and a castle, and (93 M.) *La
Celle-Bruère.*

About 2 M. to the S. is the old *Abbey of Noirlac,* of the 12-13th cent.,
converted into a porcelain manufactory; and 4 M. to the N.E. is *Meillant,*
with a magnificent Renaissance *Château* in the same style as the Hôtel
de Jacques Cœur at Bourges.

99¹/₂ M. **St. Amand-Mont-Rond** (*Hôtel de la Poste*), a town of
8673 inhab., situated on the *Marmande,* between the Cher and the
Canal du Berry. It has a Transition church; and on a hill a little
higher up are the ruins of the *Château de Mont-Rond,* which was
taken by the great Condé and dismantled during the wars of the
Fronde.

Noirlac lies nearly 2 M. from this town, and Meillant 4 M. (see above).
About 2¹/₂ M. to the S. is *Drivant,* a village with the remains of a Roman
fortified enceinte and theatre, and other Roman antiquities.

From St. Amand-Mont-Rond to *La Guerche* (Nevers), see p. 235. —
This line is continued to (21 M.) *Châteaumeillant* (p. 38) viâ (19 M.) *Le
Châtelet,* a small town with a ruined château.

103¹/₂ M. *Ainay-le-Vieil* has a Renaissance castle, to the left, a
little before the station. We now skirt the Canal du Berry, which
has crossed the Cher and runs parallel with it on the left bank. —
The next stations are (107¹/₂ M.) *Urçay,* (114 M.) *Vallon,* (120 M.)
Magnette, and (123¹/₂ M.) *Les Trillers,* whence an industrial branch-
line diverges to the left, and the line to Tours and Châteauroux
(p. 37) to the right. We then join the line from Guéret (p. 228),
cross the Cher, and reach (128 M.) **Montluçon** (*Buffet*). For this
town and the journey thence to (170 M.) *Gannat,* see p. 227; from
Gannat to (198 M.) *Clermont-Ferrand,* p. 222.

36. From Lyons to Bordeaux.

a. Viâ Roanne, Montluçon, and Limoges.

392 M. Railway in 15-16¹/₂ hrs. (fares about 70 fr. 65, 54 fr. 75, 31 fr.
15 c.). — The trains start from the Gare de Perrache.

Lyons, see p. 216. — To (98 M.) *St. Germain-des-Fossés,* see
pp. 215-213. — From St. Germain-des-Fossés to (15 M.) *Gannat,*
see p. 222. — Beyond Gannat we follow the Orléans line and return
for a short distance in the direction of St. Germain, then ascend to
the left, with a fine view to the right. The line re-descends and
passes through three tunnels between two viaducts, the latter of
which spans the *Sioule.* The district traversed is varied, with a
succession of picturesque valleys and plateaux, more or less well-
wooded. — 119 M. (from Lyons) *St. Bonnet-de-Rochefort* has a fine
15th cent. château.

Branch to (7¹/₂ M.) *Chantelle*, see p. 213. This branch is continued in the opposite direction to (4¹/₂ M.) **Ebreuil** (*Hôt. du Commerce; de la Poste*), picturesquely situated on the Sioule, with an ancient abbey-church. About 4¹/₂ M. beyond Ebreuil is the *Château of Veauce.*

To the right, as we once more ascend, is the *Château of Lignat.* 125 M. *Bellenave*, with a château of the 16th cent. and a church, mainly Romanesque. Beyond (130¹/₂ M.) *Louroux-de-Bouble* we pass through a short tunnel, quitting the valley of the Allier and entering that of the Cher. 135 M. *Lapeyrouse.*

A Branch Line runs hence to (5¹/₂ M.) **St. Eloy** (3895 inhab.), with important coal-mines. An omnibus plies from St. Eloy to the baths of *Châteauneuf* (p. 229).

Railway to *La Guerche* and *Cosne-sur-l'Œil* viâ Villefranche-d'Allier, see p. 225.

The view on the right is extensive. Two viaducts are crossed. — 143 M. *Hyds.*

145 M. **Commentry** (*Hôtel du Bourbonnais*) is a modern town with 12,618 inhab., engaged in the large coal-mines and iron-works of the vicinity.

From Commentry to Marcillat, 15¹/₂ M., railway in continuation of the line from Varennes, and to be prolonged to (7¹/₂ M. farther to the W.) *Franz* (p. 229). — *Marcillat* has a 15th cent. château.

Branch-line to *Moulins*, see p. 211; to *Varennes-sur-Allier*, see p. 213. Our line now descends and passes through a short tunnel.

147¹/₂ M. *Chamblet-Néris.* Omnibus to (3 M.) Néris (1 fr.), see below. The line descends a picturesque valley, at first well-wooded but farther on flanked by bare and rocky heights. To the right appears the large convent and school of the *Dames de St. Maur.*

154 M. **Montluçon** (*Buffet; Hôtel de France*, Place de l'Hôtel-de-Ville; *Grand Cerf*), an industrial town with 27,878 inhab., is situated on the *Cher.* It contains an important mirror-factory, besides glass-works, large iron-works, etc., but is of little interest to tourists. The ancient *Castle* (15-16th cent.), which rises above the old town, is better seen from a distance than from near at hand. It is now used as barracks. A handsome avenue leads from the station to the boulevards that skirt the old town. To the left lies the new town, the workmen's quarter, on the left bank of the Cher; to the right we reach the ancient *Hôtel de Ville*, formerly a convent, the cloisters being still recognizable. The Rue de la Comédie ascends behind this building to *Notre-Dame*, an uninteresting and much mutilated church of the 13-15th centuries. In the interior are some old paintings of interest: above the side-entrance is a large Adoration of the Magi; to the left of the organ, Jesus appearing to Thomas; between the door and the organ, seven small panels of the early Flemish school, representing scenes from the life of the Virgin, with the donors.

About 5 M. to the S.E. is **Néris** (*Gr.-Hôt. de Paris; Rochette; des Bains;*

From Montluçon to Aurillac, 142 M., railway in $6^3/_4$-$8^1/_2$ hrs. (fares 25 fr. 85, 17 fr. 50, 11 fr. 45 c.). This line is a continuation of that from Bourges in the valley of the Cher. Best views to the left. — 14 M. *Budelière-Chambon*. The little village of *Chambon*, 3 M. to the S.W. (diligence 60 c.), possesses a pretty Romanesque and Transition church. We next cross the *"Viaduc de la Tardes*, 300 ft. high, spanning the picturesque gorge of an affluent of the Cher. $17^1/_2$ M. *Evaux* (*Hôt. de l'Établissement*, R. 2-3, pens. $6^1/_2$, omn. $1/_2$-$^3/_4$ fr.; *Lépine*; *de la Fontaine*), a town (3040 inhab.), $1^3/_4$ M. from the station, possessing thermal springs, known to the Romans. — $28^1/_2$ M. *Auzances*, to the left of the line. Beyond (39 M.) *Lètrade*, the Monts Dôme appear more and more distinctly. Several small stations are passed, and the line reaches a height of 1800 ft. above Montluçon. It then descends to (58 M.) *Eygurande-Merlines* (p. 235), where it joins the railway from Limoges to Clermont-Ferrand (p. 238). — Our line continues hence to the S. in the valley of the *Charanon*, an affluent of the Dordogne. — 63 M. *Savennes-St. Étienne-aux-Clos*; $68^1/_2$ M. *Singles*. We here enter the valley of the Dordogne. — $75^1/_2$ M. *Mialet*. To the left is the *Château de Vals*. — 80 M. *Bort* (*Hôt. des Messageries*), a picturesquely situated town with 3858 inhab., near which are the curious columnar basaltic formations known as the *Orgues de Bort*, and the *Saut de la Saule*, a fine cascade on the Rue. — $85^1/_2$ M. *Saignes-Ydes* (Hotels), the station for *Ydes* (Hotels), a small watering-place with cold mineral springs. — 90 M. *Largnac*. — The railway now ascends, in wide curves, round the W. extremity of the *Monts du Cantal*. On a height to the right appears the 16th cent. *Château de Charlus*, ruined in 1633. — 93 M. *Vendes*, on the *Sumène*. — 103 M. *Mauriac* (*Écu de France*), an ancient town (3631 inhab.), with a Romanesque church of the 12th century. — The railway soon begins to descend viâ ($109^1/_2$ M.) *Drugeac*, whence a diligence ($1^1/_4$ fr.) plies to ($8^1/_2$ M.) the quaint little town of *Salers* (*Hôtel*). — Beyond (113 M.) *Drignac-Ally* we descend to the valley of the *Maronne*; and beyond ($116^1/_2$ M.) *Loupiac-St. Christophe*, we cross the valleys of the Maronne and the *Doire*, and ascend a third valley, where many engineering difficulties have been overcome. — About 7 M. from (124 M.) *St. Illide* lies *St. Cernin* (Hotel), on the *Doire*, with a Romanesque church. — At (131 M.) *Miécase* we join the line from St. Denis-près-Martel (p. 107) to (142 M.) *Aurillac* (p. 261).

From Montluçon to *Châteauroux and Tours*, see pp. 37, 38; to **Bourges**, p. 235.

Beyond Montluçon we cross the Cher. $157^1/_2$ M. *Domérat*. 161 M. *Huriel* has a château of the 12th and 15th cent., with an interesting keep. $168^1/_2$ M. *Treignat*. From (172 M.) *Lavaud-Franche*, a branch-line runs to ($23^1/_4$ M.) Champillet-Urciers (p. 38). $188^1/_2$ M. *Cressat*. We cross the *Creuse* by a handsome trellis-work viaduct, 184 ft. high and 320 yds. long. 193 M. *Busseau-d'Ahun* (Buffet).

From Busseau-d'Ahun to Felletin, $22^1/_2$ M., railway in $1^1/_2$ hr. (fares 4 fr. 40, 3 fr. 30, 2 fr. 45 c.). The line ascends the valley of the Creuse, crossing first the great viaduct of Busseau, and then a curved stone viaduct, 80 ft. in height. 5 M. *Lavaveix-les-Mines*, with coal-mines. 10 M. *Fournaux*. $15^1/_2$ M. *Aubusson* (*Hôtel de France*; *Notre-Dame*), with 6671 inhab., picturesquely situated, was the birthplace of Pierre d'Aubusson, grandmaster of the order of St. John of Jerusalem, who distinguished himself by his successful defence of Rhodes against Mahomet II. in 1480. Aubusson is noted for its carpets, the manufacture of which occupies about 2000 hands. — $22^1/_2$ M. *Felletin* (*Notre-Dame*), with 3380 inhab., is also engaged in the carpet-industry.

200 M. *Ste. Feyre*. — 204 M. *Guéret* (*Buffet*, very plain; *Hôt. de la Paix*), with 7800 inhab., was the former capital of *Marche*. The Rue des Chers diverges to the right near the end of the Avenue de la Gare to the Place du Palais and Place Bonnyaud. The street on the opposite side leads to the *Préfecture*, enlarged in 1893 by

the incorporation of a private mansion (15-16th cent.), erroneously
said to have belonged to the counts of Marche. The Grande Rue
descends thence to the Place du Marché, with the Hôtel de Ville,
containing a small *Musée* of paintings and textile fabrics. — Branch-
line to *St. Sébastien*, see p. 39.

We traverse a short tunnel. — 209 M. *La Brionne*, 3 M. to the
N.W. of which (diligence) is *St. Vaury*, with a church containing
five beautiful bas-reliefs, in wood, of the Passion (15th cent.).
214 M. *Montaigut*; 219 M. *Vieilleville*.

A branch-line runs from Vieilleville to (12¹/₂ M.) **Bourganeuf** (*Hôtel
Bayard*), an industrial town with 3863 inhab., manufacturing porcelain,
hats, paper, etc. It contains the remains of a priory, including a *Tower*
in which Zizim (d. 1495), brother of Bajazet II., was imprisoned for several
years.

230 M. *Marsac*. Then a tunnel 600 yds. in length.

232 M. **St. Sulpice-Laurière** (*Buffet*) and thence to *Limoges* and
Bordeaux, see pp. 39 seq.

b. Viâ St. Etienne, Clermont-Ferrand, and Tulle. Auvergne.

I. From Lyons to Clermont-Ferrand.

121 M. R**AILWAY** in 7¹/₂-9¹/₄ hrs. (fares about 22 fr., 14 fr. 85, 9 fr. 60 c.).
The trains start from the Gare de Perrache.

Lyons, see p. 210. — The train follows the Paris line to beyond
the bridge over the *Saône*, then returns by a line not entering the
station, and traverses the S. end of the peninsula of Perrache, crossing the Saône once more near its confluence with the Rhone. Beyond a short tunnel *La Mulatière*, with 3377 inhab., appears on
the right. Fine retrospect (on the left) of Lyons. The line follows
the right bank of the Rhone.

3 M. *Oullins*, a picturesquely situated town with 8327 inhab.,
with three old castles and numerous country-houses. Fine view
of the Rhone to the left. — 3¹/₂ M. *Pierre-Bénite*; 6 M. *Irigny*;
8¹/₂ M. *Vernaison*. The little towers seen here and there on the
banks of the river are used for cable-ferries. — 10 M. *La Tour-de-
Millery*; 10¹/₂ M. *Grigny*; 11 M. *Le Sablon* (2136 inhab.). Farther
on a branch crosses the Rhone and joins the line on the left bank
(see *Baedeker's South-Eastern France*).

13 M. *Givors-Canal* (Buffet) is the junction for the line on the
right bank to Le Teil and Nîmes (see *Baedeker's South-Eastern
France*), under which we pass, after crossing the *Canal du Gier* or
de Givors.

13¹/₂ M. **Givors** (*Hôtel de Provence*), an industrial town with
10,850 inhab., at the junction of the Rhone and the *Gier*. The whole
of the irregular valley of the latter river, which our line now ascends,
is the scene of a busy and varied industry, fostered by one of the chief
coal-fields in France. Lofty chimneys rise in all directions, and the
district is blackened by smoke. — Beyond (16¹/₂ M.) *St. Romain-de-*

Gier we traverse five tunnels; and beyond (19 M.) *Trèves-Burel*, two more. — 21¹/₂ M. *Couzon.* Then a tunnel 600 yds. long.

22¹/₂ M. **Rive-de-Gier** *(Buffet; Hôtel du Nord)*, with 13,134 inhab., is situated on the Gier and the Canal du Gier. It has upwards of fifty coal-mines, noted glass-works, iron-works, and considerable silk-factories. Steam-tramway to St. Chamond (see below).

Beyond (24 M.) *Lorette* (4144 inhab.) Mont-Pilat (p. 231) appears at the head of a lateral valley. 25¹/₂ M. *La Grand-Croix*, with 4535 inhabitants.

28¹/₂ M. **St. Chamond** *(Hôtel de la Poste; Lion d'Or)*, with 14,963 inhab., has coal-mines, active manufactures of silk, ribbons, laces, and nails, iron-works, etc. An excursion may be made hence to Mont-Pilat, which again becomes visible to the left a little farther on. Steam-tramway to Rive-de-Gier (see above) and St. Etienne (see below).

32 M. *Terre-Noire*, with 4944 inhab., has iron-foundries and iron-furnaces. A tunnel, ³/₄ M. long, now carries the line from the basin of the Rhone to that of the Loire.

36 M. **St. Etienne** *(Buffet).* — **Hotels.** De France, Place Dorian, high charges; du Nord, Rue de la République 7; De l'Europe, Rue de Foy, etc. — **Cafés** in the Place de l'Hôtel-de-Ville. — **Cabs.** For two pers., per drive 1¹/₄, per hr. 2 fr.; for four pers., 1¹/₂ and 2¹/₂ fr.; at night, after 11 p.m., ¹/₂ fr. more. — **Steam Tramways** from *La Terrasse* to *Bellerue* viâ the long street traversing the town from N. to S. (see below); to *St. Chamond* in 50 min. from the Place Fourneyron, at the end of the Rue de la République next the station; to *Firminy* in ³/₄ hr., from the Place Bellevue, to the S. of the town, etc. — **Post & Telegraph Office** in the Place Marengo.
American Consul. *Mr. Charles W. Whiley.*

St. Etienne, an important manufacturing town with 133,443 inhab., has been the chief town of the department of the *Loire* since 1856. St. Etienne has developed more rapidly than any other modern French town, due largely to its situation in the midst of the largest coal-field in the S. of France, yielding annually over 3,000,000 tons of coal. Weapons, ironmongery, cutlery, ribbons, etc. are among the chief manufactures. For the tourist the busy, well-built, modern town is comparatively uninteresting. The Rue de la République diverges to the right from the end of the avenue leading from the station, and passes behind the modern Romanesque-Byzantine church of *Ste. Marie*, the portals and interior of which are elaborately carved. Farther on this street ends in the Place Dorian, to the right of which rises the *Hôtel de Ville*, a modern edifice with a heavy cupola surmounted by a lantern, and a platform decorated with cast iron statues of Metallurgy and Ribbon-making, by Montagny. Behind it is the large and handsome *Place Marengo*.

Another main thoroughfare, traversing the city from N. to S. for a distance of 2¹/₂ M., crosses the Rue de la République at the Place Dorian. In this to the N. is the immense *National Arms Factory* (no admission), in which rifles and revolvers are made (10,000 workmen).

On the left of the Rue des Jardins, the continuation of the Rue de la République, is the *Palais de Justice*, a large modern building, the façade of which has a portico of ten Corinthian columns, and is surmounted by an allegorical group, by L. Mertey. In a street to the right as we return from the Palais de Justice, is *St. Etienne*, a parish church of the 15th cent., with an interesting interior.

Farther to the S., to the right of the main thoroughfare mentioned above, on the slope of a hill, is the *Palais des Arts*, containing various *Museums*, open to the public daily (except Mon.), 10-12 and 2-4, 5, or 6 and to strangers at other times also. The *Library* is open on week-days 10-12 and 5-10 p. m.

On the GROUND FLOOR is a historical Museum of Artillery, some of the exhibits being richly ornamented (explanatory labels). — On the staircase are The Triumph of Strength and an Episode from St. Bartholomew, paintings by *Gloire* and *Fragonard*. — The principal room on the FIRST FLOOR is occupied by a Gallery of Paintings, consisting mainly of modern pictures, though with a few noteworthy older canvases: no number, *Alb. Fourie*, Etienne Marcel and the Dauphin; 111. *Sal. Rosa*, Christ in Gethsemane; 100. *Ribera* (?), Jacob's blessing; 35. *Cervex*, Reminiscence of the Siege of Paris, 1870-71; 2. *Alb. Aublet*, Nero testing poisons on a slave; 14. *Chazal*, Queen of Sheba visiting Solomon; 139. *Van de Velde*, Sea-piece; 106. *Moucheron*, Landscape; etc. — Five of the other rooms are devoted to an Industrial Museum, containing collections illustrative of *Ribbonmaking*, *Goldsmith's Work*, *Silk-weaving*, *Pottery*, and *Furniture*. On this floor also is a *Library* (see above). — On the SECOND FLOOR is a *Natural History Collection*, including a fine mineralogical collection.

The Rue de la Radouillère leads from the front of the Palais des Arts to the *Jardin des Plantes*. — In this neighbourhood is an important *School of Mines*, in which nearly all the engineers and chiefs of industry of the district have been educated. It contains some interesting collections.

From St. Etienne to *Roanne*, etc., see p. 232; to *Annonay* viâ Firminy, see pp. 232, 254; to *Le Puy*, etc., R. 40.

EXCURSION TO MONT PILAT, 16 M. to the Ferme du Pilat, and thence 1/2 hr. to the Crêt de la Perdrix. Omnibus 4 times a day in summer from the Place du Peuple to (4 1/2 M.) Rochetaillée, and on Sun. and Wed. at 5 a. m. from the Place Dorian to (11 M.) Le Bessat. — The road leads to the S.E. viâ the suburb of *Valbenoîte*, whence it skirts the left bank of the *Furens*, a stream descending from Mont-Pilat. 4 1/2 M. *Rochetaillée*, a village picturesquely situated on an isolated rock and commanded by a ruined castle. About 3/4 M. farther on, in a wild gorge, is the interesting *Reservoir du Gouffre-d'Enfer*, constructed in 1861-68 to supply St. Etienne with water. It is formed by a huge dam, 330 ft. long, 130 ft. high, and 130 ft. broad at the base, connected with a rock rising in the middle of the channel of the Furens. It is estimated to contain about 1,600,000 cubic mètres of water. 7 M. *Reservoir du Pas-du-Riot*, a similar construction nearly as large. — 11 M. *Le Bessat* (Inn). The road leads thence to the (1/2 M.) col of the *Croix de Chabouret*, and beyond a wood the Crêt de la Perdrix lies to the right. — 16 M. *Ferme du Pilat*, where refreshments and a bed, if desired, may be obtained, lies at the foot of the Crêt de la Perdrix.

Mont Pilat is one of the chief summits of the *Northern Cévennes*. Its lower slopes are covered with forests, its top with pastures. Three sum-

mits are distinguished: the *Crêt de la Perdrix* (4705 ft.), the *Crêt de l'Aillon*
(4530 ft.), and the *Pic des Trois-Dents* (4475 ft.). The legend that Pontius
Pilate killed himself here in despairing remorse is related of this mountain just as it is of the Pilatus above the lake of Lucerne in Switzerland, and both mountains serve as barometers for the surrounding districts. A popular saying in this district runs 'When Pilate puts on his
hat, put on your cloak'. A similar remark is made with reference to the
mists settling on the Puy de Dôme. — The summit commands a splendid
view, ranging to the Alps on the E., to the Rhône valley and Southern
Cévennes on the S., to the Mts. of Auvergne on the W., and on the N. to
the continuation of the Cévennes, the Mts. of Lyonnais, to which Mont
Pilat belongs, and the Mts. of Beaujolais and Charolais. The other two
summits, though lower, also command fine views. — The Gier, which
rises on the Crêt de la Perdrix, near the farm, forms lower down a beautiful waterfall, 100 ft. high, known as the *Saut du Gier*.

Beyond St. Etienne our line trends to the N.W. and skirts the National Arms Factory to the left. 37³/₄ M. *La Terrasse*, a suburban
station of St. Etienne. 39¹/₂ M. *Villars*; 41 M. *La Fouillouse*;
42 M. *St. Just-sur-Loire*, junction of the lines to Roanne (p. 215)
and Firminy (p. 254). At (46 M.) *Andrézieux* we cross the bed
of the *Loire*, frequently dry in great part. 47¹/₂ M. *Bonson*.

A branch-line runs from Bonson to (17 M.) St. *Bonnet-la-Château* (*Hôt.
du Commerce*), a picturesquely situated and ancient little town, with remains of fortifications, and a church of the 15-16th cent., containing some
fine ancient mural paintings in the crypt. The château is no longer in
existence; but several quaint old houses still remain. This line is to be
continued towards La Chaise-Dieu (p. 234).

The line now turns towards the E., in the direction of the mountains of the Forez (p. 233), which it afterwards skirts for a considerable distance, commanding an extensive view over the valley of the
Loire, on the right, bounded by the mountains of the Lyonnais. —
49¹/₂ M. *Sury-le-Comtal* has a late-Gothic church and a Renaissance château, richly decorated in the interior. — 52¹/₂ M. *St.
Romain-le-Puy*, with a ruined priory, of the beginning of the 11th
century.

57 M. **Montbrison** (*Hôtel de la Poste; Lion d'Or*), an ancient
town of 7086 inhab., the former capital of the Forez, is situated on
the *Vizezy*, at the foot of a hill surmounted by a Calvary. The principal church, *Notre-Dame-de-l'Espérance*, is a handsome Gothic
edifice of the 13-15th cent., with modern decorations in the interior. Behind the church is an ancient chapter-house, known as the
Diana (Decana), founded about 1300, but restored in 1866. It now
contains the libraries of a learned society and of the town. In the
public *Jardin Allard* is a bronze statue of *Victor de Laprade*
(1812-1883), the poet, a native of Montbrison. About 1¹/₂ M. to the
S. of Montbrison is *Moingt*, with Roman remains and a feudal
keep. — From Montbrison to *Lyons* viâ L'Arbresle and Montrond,
see p. 215 and *Baedeker's South-Eastern France*.

60 M. *Champdieu* has a fortified church in the Auvergnat Romanesque style, dating from a Benedictine priory, and a 15th cent.
hospital, with a tall decagonal turret. Both the priory and the town
had fortified enceintes, and remains of the former are still to be

seen. To the right is the isolated volcanic hill of *Mont-d'Uzore* (1770 ft.). 64 M. *Marcilly-le-Pavé*, with a fine Gothic *Château*, recently restored. 67¹/₂ M. *Boën*; 3 M. to the E. is the mediæval *Château de la Bâtie*, still inhabited. The railway now enters the mountains, ascending first the valley of the *Lignon*, then the picturesque valley of the *Auzon*.

70 M. **Sail-sous-Couzan**, or *Couzan*. The village (Hôt. des Roches; du Midi), 1¹/₂ M. to the S., has two mineral springs, with a well-managed bath-establishment.

An interesting route leads hence viâ the valley of the *Lignon* and (5 M.) *St. Georges-en-Couzan* (Hotel) to (9¹/₂ M.) *Chalmazel* (Hôt. des Voyageurs), with a château of the 13th and 16th centuries. Chalmazel is a good centre for excursions among the *Monts du Forez*, including the ascent of the *Pierre-sur-Haute* (5380 ft.; 3 hrs.; p. 234).

Farther on, to the left, are the well-preserved ruins of the *Château de Couzan* (11-16th cent.). 72¹/₂ M. *L'Hôpital-sous-Rochefort*, with remains of a fortified Benedictine priory; 76¹/₂ M. *St. Thurin*; 84 M. *Noirétable*. The railway turns to the S.W. and enters the valley of the *Durolle*. 89¹/₂ M. *Chabreloche*; 94 M. *St. Remy-sur-Durolle*. Eight tunnels and four bridges are passed between this point and Thiers. As we emerge from the last tunnel we have a fine view, to the left, of Thiers, the wide plain of the Limagne (p. 204), and the distant mountains of Auvergne.

97¹/₂ M. **Thiers** (*Hôtel de l'Univers, de Paris*, both in the Rue des Grammonts), a town with 16,814 inhab., is an important seat of the cutlery and paper manufactures. It consists of two distinct parts: the new town, beside the station, and the mediæval town, on the steep bank of the *Durolle*, ill-built but highly picturesque, with many old houses of the 15th cent. or older, blackened by time.

Beyond a square in the Rue des Grammonts we descend to the right to the Hôtel de Ville. The Rue des Barres, to the left of the latter, enters the old town. In the Place du Prioux is a curious old timber house, and a few yards to the left, in the Rue de la Vaur, are two others. The ground-floors of nearly all the houses in this part of the town are occupied by small cutlers' workshops, the workmen generally working in their own homes.

The *Church of St. Genès*, to the right, a little above the Place du Prioux, in the Romanesque and Gothic styles of the 11-12th cent., contains a tomb of the 13th cent. under the porch on the left side. In the interior the capitals and the modern stained-glass windows should be noticed.

The Rue Durolle, to the right as we leave the church, leads down to the *Durolle*, from the picturesque banks of which the most attractive view of the town is obtained. Here are numerous papermills, workshops for polishing scissors, knives, etc., and other industrial establishments. Farther down, on the left, is the Romanesque *Church of Moûtier*, founded in the 7th or 8th cent., but largely rebuilt in the 11th. It also has curious capitals, and at the end, two high-reliefs in stone. — The valley up the river is also interesting.

To the N.E. rises the **Puy de Montoncel** (4255 ft.), connected with the Forez mountains. The ascent takes 5 hrs. on foot, viâ (5 M.) *St. Remy* and (8 M.) *Paladus*, to which point there is a carriage-road. The summit commands a beautiful and extensive prospect, including the Monts Dore.

Beyond Thiers we traverse two tunnels, and descend by wide curves to the valley of the *Dore*, a tributary of the Allier. Fine views to the left. At (98¹/₂ M.) *Courty* the line to Vichy diverges (p. 222). We cross the river. — 100 M. *Pont-de-Dore.*

From Pont-de-Dore to Arlanc (*La Chaise-Dieu*), 40 M., railway in 2-2³/₄ hrs. This line ascends the valley of the Dore to the S. — 6 M. *Courpière* (3884 inhab.), beyond which lies the most picturesque part of the route. — 13¹/₂ M. *Giroux*; 16¹/₂ M. *Olliergues*. — About 1¹/₂ M. to the S.E. of (21¹/₂ M.) *Vertolaye* lies *Job* (Hôt. des Voyageurs), whence the *Pierre-sur-Haute* (5380 ft.), the chief summit of the *Monts du Forez*, may be ascended in 2¹/₂-3 hrs. Descent in 1¹/₂ hrs. to Chalmazel (p. 233). — 30 M. *Ambert* (*Tête d'Or; de Paris*), an ancient town of 7900 inhab., with an interesting church of the 15-16th cent., and manufactures of paper and of bunting for flags. — Beyond (35 M.) *Marsac* we cross the Dore for the last time.

40 M. *Arlanc* (*Hôt. du Prince; Rérol*), a poorly-built town of 3500 inhab., on a hill between the Dore and its affluent the Dolore. — A public vehicle (2 fr.) plies daily from Arlanc to (10¹/₂ M.; in 2¹/₂ hrs.) *La Chaise-Dieu* (carr. for 1-4 pers. 8 fr.), short-cuts for walkers. The road ascends through picturesque wooded gorges, beyond (3 M.) *Le Procureur*.

10 M. **La Chaise-Dieu** (*Lion d'Or*), a village with 1631 inhab., situated on a hill (3575 ft.), owes its name to a celebrated Benedictine abbey, the *Casa Dei*, founded about 1036 by St. Robert. Amongst its abbots and nominal rulers have been Roger de Beaufort, afterwards Pope Clement VI., Mazarin, Richelieu, etc. The vast buildings of the *Abbey* were surrounded in the 14-15th cent. by fortifications, parts of which still remain, notably the *Tower of Clement VI.*, at the side of the church. There are few traces of the *Cloister* which dates from the 14-15th cent., to which time also belongs the present *Church*. The façade is approached by a grand flight of steps and is flanked by two towers, which have, however, lost their spires. The wide nave and aisles are uniform in height, with galleries. The rood-loft and the organ-case (at the W. end) date from the 17th century. In the choir, which has a stone-screen, is the mutilated tomb of Clement VI., some magnificent stalls, tapestries of 1501-1518, and, on the left, in the ambulatory a remarkable but very dilapidated Dance of the Dead (p. 255) by an unknown artist of the second half of the 15th century. — From La Chaise-Dieu to (15 M.) *Darsac*, see p. 230; to (31 M.) *Le Puy*, see p. 258.

We are now in the Limagne (p. 222). 106 M. *Lezoux* (3500 inhab.) manufactures earthenware.

113¹/₂ M. *Pont-du-Château*, a small town ¹/₂ M. to the N., on the left bank of the Allier, has a ruined château, and bitumen-wells.

A branch-line runs hence to (5¹/₂ M.) *Billom* (*Hôtel des Voyageurs*), an ancient town with 4380 inhab., formerly celebrated for its school. The church of *St. Cerneuf* (10th, 11th, and 13th cent.) contains a fine tomb of the 14th cent., etc. — About 5 M. to the S.E. are the considerable ruins of the *Château de Mauzun* (13th cent.).

We cross the Allier. 118 M. *Aulnat.* To the left appear the Plateau de Gergovie and Mont Rognon (p. 246), to the right the Monts Dôme (pp. 243, 245). — 121 M. *Clermont-Ferrand* (Buffet), see p. 238.

II. From Clermont-Ferrand to Tulle. Northern Auvergne.

107 1/2 M. RAILWAY in 6 hrs. (fares 18 fr. 15, 13 fr. 85, 8 fr. 55 c.). — From the Place de Jaude (p. 233) it is shorter to catch the train at Royat.

This line makes a wide circuit to the S. of Clermont, of which it affords a fine view as far as the second station; it then skirts the N. side of the Monts Dôme. — 3 1/2 M. *Royat* (p. 242), of which there is also a fine view, especially from the viaduct, 70 ft. high, which is crossed beyond the station. After passing (5 M.) *Durtol* and going through 4 short tunnels, with the Puy de Dôme, the Puy de Pariou, etc. on the left, it reaches (9 1/2 M.) *Chanat* and (12 1/2 M.) *Volvic*. The latter, 2 M. to the right, is more conveniently reached by a branch-line from Riom (p. 223), which here joins the Clermont-Ferrand railway. On each side of the railway are large quarries of lava, used for building. Fine views all the way to (17 M.) *Vauriat* and (20 M.) *St. Ours-les-Roches*. To the right and then to the left, rise the Monts Dore.

23 1/2 M. **Pontgibaud** (*Hôtel Johannet*), a small town, has argentiferous lead-mines and a 13th cent. *Château* containing a choice and valuable collection of paintings (visitors admitted). The *Church* (15-16th cent.) contains two paintings of the Adoration, by Guido Reni, and an Assumption by Parrocel. One of the town-gates dates from 1444. There are two mineral springs in the environs, and in the neighbouring valley of the Sioule are those of *Châteaufort*.

The line now rounds the end of the Monts Dôme and ascends the valley of the *Sioule*, in which the view is limited. 25 1/2 M. *Les Rosiers-sur-Sioule*; 28 M. *La Miouse-Rochefort.*

Rochefort, which has a *Castle in ruins, is 6 1/2 M. to the S. and 5 M. from Laqueuille (see below). About 1 1/2 M. to the E. of Rochefort is *Orcival*, the church of which, with a black statue of the Virgin, is one of the chief resorts of pilgrims in Auvergne.

At (55 M.) *Bourgeade* the view opens in the direction of the Monts Dore; to the left is the truncated Pic de la Banne-d'Ordenche, and in the distance to the right the Puy de Sancy (p. 250).

38 1/2 M. **Laqueuille** (3235 ft.; *Buffet*, déj. 3, D. 3 1/2 fr.). The village lies on a hill, 1 3/4 M. to the E. To La Bourboule, Mont Dore, etc., see R. 39. — The line now passes into the basin of the Dordogne. The Monts Dore and, afterwards, the Monts du Cantal occupy the horizon on the left.

Beyond (47 1/2 M.) *Bourg-Lastic-Messeix* we descend the picturesque valley of the *Clidane*, crossing the stream eight times before (51 M.) *La Celette*, the old convent of which is now a lunatic asylum. The line now passes at a great height above the stream and enters a tunnel. — 52 1/2 M. **Eygurande-Merlines** (*Buffet*, mediocre; *Hôtel Tixier*, at the station, moderate), station for two villages, 1 1/2 and 1 M. distant.

From Eygurande-Merlines to *Montluçon* and to *Aurillac*, see p. 228.

57 1/2 M. *Aix-la-Marsalouse.*

64¹/₂ M. **Ussel** (*Hôtel de la Gare*), a town of 4832 inhab., built on
a hill, ¹/₂ M. to the S. of the railway. Here on a modern fountain
is a *Roman Eagle* in granite, measuring 2 yds., found in an old Roman
camp in the neighbourhood. Ussel is, perhaps, the *Uxellodunum* of
the ancients (see pp. 106, 107).

Beyond a short tunnel is (72¹/₂ M.) **Meymac** (*Hôtel de la Gare*),
with 4112 inhab., and an interesting church of the 11-12th cent.,
formerly belonging to a Benedictine monastery. The *Puy de Meymac*
(3220 ft.) is adjoined on the N. by the *Plateau de Millevaches*, important as the watershed between the Loire and the Dordogne. Line
to Limoges, see p. 42.

The line to Tulle here turns to the S.W., with a view of the
Monts du Cantal (p. 250) on the left. — 76¹/₂ M. *Lapleau-Maussac*;
81 M. *Soudeilles*; 84¹/₂ M. *Egletons*; 88¹/₂ M. *Roslers-d'Egletons*;
90¹/₂ M. *Montagnac-St. Hippolyte*. Beyond (93¹/₂ M.) *Eyrein* we
enter the valley of the *Montane*. 96 M. *Corrèze*, a small village at
the S. end of the *Monédières* (2950 ft.).

98¹/₂ M. *Gimel*, a village below which the Montane forms a
celebrated cascade nearly 400 ft. in height, often rather scanty and
divided into several falls, but imposing after heavy rains. — Then
come four short tunnels and a bridge over the *Corrèze*.

106 M. **Tulle** (*Hôt. de la Comédie*, R., L., & A. 1¹/₂-3 fr., B. 60-75 c.,
déj. 2¹/₂, D. 3 fr., omn. 15 c. and 15 c. per trunk), a town of 18,964
inhab., the capital of the department of the *Corrèze*, is picturesquely
situated on the Corrèze, near its junction with the Solane. The
Avenue Victor-Hugo, crossing the Corrèze, leads direct from the
station to (¹/₄ hr.) the centre of the town. The chief object of interest, farther on in the same direction, is the *Cathedral*, of the 12th
cent., with a fine tower of the 14th cent., but script of its choir and
its transepts in 1793. At the side is a cloister of the 12th century.
Houses of the Renaissance and even of the Middle Ages are still to
be seen in the town, one of the most interesting being the *Maison
de l'Abbé* (15th cent.), to the N. of the cathedral. The government
Fire-Arms Factory (no admission) is in the suburb of Souilhac,
watered by the Solane, to the W. of the station.

III. From Tulle to Bordeaux, viâ Périgueux.

140 M. RAILWAY in 6³/₄ hrs. (fares about 25 fr. 40, 17 fr. 20, 11 fr. 25 c.).

The first part of the way is through the deep-set valley of the
Corrèze, which is crossed several times before reaching Brive. Two
short tunnels, beyond which is (5 M.) *Cornil*. — 15 M. *Aubazine*.
The village, 1³/₄ M. to the left, grew up towards the close of the
11th cent., round a Benedictine *Abbey*, of which some interesting
remains are still extant. The *Church* contains the splendid 13th
cent. *Tomb of St. Stephen*, founder of the abbey.

18 M. **Brive** (*Buffet*), on the line from Limoges to Aurillac
(R. 15). Thence to *Périgueux* and *Bordeaux*, see p. 107.

37. From St. Etienne to Annonay and St. Rambert-d'Albon.

62 M. To *Annonay*, 50 M., Railway in 4-4¹/₂ hrs. (fares 9 fr. 5, 6 fr. 10 c., 5 fr.). From Annonay to *St. Rambert*, 12 M., Railway in ³/₄-1 hr. (fares 2 fr. 25, 1 fr. 50 c., 1 fr.).

This line, of special importance from an industrial point of view, has 38 tunnels, of a total length of about 7 miles, ¹/₉ of the whole distance; 19 viaducts of medium length but varying in height from 30 to 100 feet, and numerous deep cuttings. At Bourg-Argental it makes a very sharp curved loop, with a spiral tunnel, similar in character to those on the St. Gotthard line.

To (12 M.) *Firminy*, see p. 254. — The 'Ligne d'Annonay' runs S. and at first ascends the valley of the *Demène*, by considerable gradients. To the E. (left) is Mont Pilat (p. 231). Five tunnels and three viaducts are passed before (17¹/₂ M.) *Pont-Salomon*, and two viaducts and two tunnels after that station. — 23 M. **St. Didier - la - Séauve** (2415 ft.; *Hôt. Verdier*), a town with 5346 inhab., beyond which we quit the valley of the Demène. Beyond (27 M.) *St. Pal-St. Romain* are a tunnel 650 yds. long, and a viaduct 115 yds. long and 100 ft. high (the loftiest on the line), closely followed by a tunnel of 265 yds. and a viaduct of 175 yds. (60 ft. high), the longest of all. Beyond (31 M.) *Dunières - Montfaucon* we ascend the valley of the *Dunières*, in which our direction changes to N.E. 32 M. *Riotord* (2835 ft.; *Hôt. Souvignet*) is the centre of the timber-trade (pit-props, etc.) of the district. We now traverse the longest tunnel (1¹/₂ M.), and descend to the E. by the unusual gradient, for an ordinary line, of 1 in 33. Beyond (35¹/₂ M.) *St. Sauveur-en-Rue*, a viaduct, and 5 tunnels, we reach the beginning of the **Loop of Bourg-Argental,* where the line describes almost a complete circle with a radius of only 315 yds.

44 M. **Bourg - Argental** (1755 ft.; *Hôt. de France*), a town of 4560 inhab. on the *Déome*. Its *Church* has an interesting 11th cent. portal, but is otherwise modern.

The loop ends a little farther on with a tunnel 1050 yds. long. We now descend the valley of the *Déome*. — 47¹/₂ *St. Marcel-lès-Annonay*. — 49¹/₂ M. *Boulieu*. View of Annonay to the right.

62 M. **Annonay** (**Hôt. du Midi*), an industrial town of 17,626 inhab. at the junction of the deep valleys of the Déome and the *Cance*, has glove-leather factories and paper-mills. In the Place de l'Hôtel-de-Ville a monument (by H. Cordier) was erected in 1888 to the *Brothers Montgolfier*, who in 1783 made their first balloon ascent from the Place des Cordeliers. The Champ-de-Mars contains a bronze statue of *Boissy-d'Anglas* (1756-1826), president of the Convention, by Hébert.

Annonay and its manufactories obtain their water-supply from a reservoir of the same character as those at St. Etienne, Rive-de-Gier, and St. Chamont, and constructed at the same period. This lies 5 M. to the N.W. and is formed by the *Barrage du Ternay*, a dam more than 100 ft. high, 80 ft. thick, and nearly 200 yds. long at the summit.

Beyond Annonay we thread a tunnel, 200 yds. long. At (55 M.) *Midon* the line turns once more to the N. E., and then rapidly descends through 4 tunnels, the first 700 yards long, and over two lofty viaducts. Fine view of the Rhone valley. 61 M. *Peyraud*, on the line from Lyons to Nîmes viâ the right bank of the Rhone. We cross the Rhone at a point where it forms an island. — 64¹/₂ M. *St. Rambert-d'Albon*, see *Baedeker's South-Eastern France*.

38. Clermont-Ferrand, Royat, and the Puy de Dôme.

a. Clermont-Ferrand.

Hotels. GRAND-HÔTEL DE LA POSTE (Pl. a; A. 3), R., L., & A. 4-9, B. 1-1¹/₂, déj. 3, D. 4, omn. ¹/₄ fr., luggage ¹/₄ fr. each trunk; °DE L'UNIVERS (Pl. b; B, 4), R., L., & A. from 2³/₄, B. 1, déj. 3, D. 3¹/₂ fr., omn. 50 and 25 c., view of the Puy de Dôme; GRAND-HÔT. DE L'EUROPE (Pl. c; A, 4); HÔT. DE LYON (Pl. d; A, 4), unpretending; all these are in the Place de Jaude, about 1 M. from the station; DE LA PAIX, Boulevard Desaix (Pl. e; B, 3); °HÔTEL DU LOUVRE, behind the theatre; DES VOYAGEURS, opposite the station, R. 2, déj. 2¹/₂, D. 3 fr.

Restaurants. *Hugon*, Rue Royale (Pl. B, 3); and in most of the hotels.

Cafés. *De Paris, Lyonnais, de l'Univers, Glacier*, Place de Jaude; etc.

Cabs. In the town, by day, 1 fr., by night (9 p. m. to 5 a. m.) 1 fr. 50; to the station and from the Place de Jaude to Royal, 50 c. extra; luggage 50 c. extra, 1 fr. to the hotels at Royat; per hr., 3 and 4 fr., etc. — *Omnibus* from the Place de Jaude to Royat; 25 c.

Electric Tramways (on the aërial or 'trolley' system) ply from *Montferrand* and from the *Station* to the *Place de Jaude* (Pl. A, 4), viâ the *Place Delille* (Pl. D, 2); and from the *Place de Jaude* to *Royat*. Fares from Montferrand to the Place Delille 10 c.; thence to the Place de Jaude 10 c.; from the station to the Place de Jaude 15 c.; thence to Royat 20 c. (40 c. after 10 p. m.).

Post Office (Pl. B, 2), Rue du Poids-de-Ville. — **Telegraph Office** (Pl. B, 4), Square d'Assas; also at the Post Office and the Station.

Theatre. Place de Jaude (p. 240). — EDEN CONCERT, near the Place de Jaude.

Churches. *Protestant*, near the Rue Sidoine-Apollinaire (Pl. B, 2); *Evangelical*, Rue St. André, N. of the Rue Blatin (Pl. A, 4).

Clermont-Ferrand (1320 ft.), the former capital of *Auvergne* (p. 243), and now the chief place in the department of the *Puy-de-Dôme*, is a town of 50,119 inhab., the head-quarters of the 13th army corps, the seat of a bishopric, as well as of a university, etc. It is built on a slight eminence rising from the wide and fertile basin of Limagne on the E. and at the foot of the remarkable range of extinct volcanoes known as the Monts Dôme on the W. The chief summit in this range is the Puy de Dôme, which rises to a height of 4805 ft. (p. 245), in full view of the Place de Jaude. In general appearance the town does not correspond with the beauty of its situation. Its streets are, as a rule, narrow, and the houses, built of lava, have a gloomy and forbidding look.

The town has superseded the Celtic *Nemetum*, which itself succeeded Gergovia (p. 248) as the capital of the Arverni, after the overthrow of Vercingetorix by Cæsar, at Alesia in B. C. 52. It was in particular favour with Augustus and for that reason named *Augusta Nemetum*. After being

repeatedly ravaged by the barbarians, it took in the 10th cent. the name of *Clarus Mons*, whence its present name *Clermont*. To this was added in the 17th cent. the name of *Ferrand* on the occasion of the annexation of the little town of *Montferrand*, situated 1 M. to the N. Here at a council summoned by Pope Urban II. in 1095 the first crusade was arranged. Since that time the history of the town has been uneventful. Whether Gregory of Tours was a native of it, is uncertain, but it was the birthplace of Pascal (1623-1662) and of Delille (1738-1813), the poet.

From the station we reach the town by the Avenue Charras, which traverses a suburb (with the handsome new church of *St. Joseph*) and leads to the *Place Delille* (Pl. D, 2, 3), ornamented with a fountain. The Rue du Port, beginning near the middle of this square, passes a little farther on to the S. of —

Notre-Dame-du-Port (Pl. C, D, 2), a church founded in the 9th cent., rebuilt in the 10th, and recently restored. Archæologically it is the most remarkable church in Clermont, being the typical representative of the Auvergnat Romanesque style, of which there are several fine examples at Nevers (p. 209) and Issoire (p. 224). The most interesting part of the exterior is the choir, which is covered with patterns formed of black lava and white stones and has three fine chapels, with rich modillions and pillars with capitals of elaborate workmanship, radiating in a semicircle, and alternating with buttresses. The transepts are decorated in the same manner and flanked by small apses. The south transept contains a side-portal with low-reliefs representing the Annunciation, the Nativity, and the Adoration of the Magi, and is also decorated with statues of the Apostles. From the crossing rises a good modern tower, the base of which is in the Auvergnat Romanesque style. The plain façade has a Gothic 14th cent. doorway. The first bay of the nave and the aisles are surmounted by small round-vaulted galleries with a triforium of round arches on the left and trefoil-headed on the right. Under the chancel is a fine crypt with a small black statue of the Virgin.

A small street to the N. of this church leads to the *Place d'Espagne* (Pl. C, D, 2), oblong in shape, so called because in 1692 Spanish prisoners of war were employed upon it. From this square and from the *Place de Poterne* (Pl. B, C, 2), a little farther on, fine views are obtained of the Monts Dôme. Lower down, in a square which bears his name (Pl. B, 2), is the bronze *Statue of Blaise Pascal* (1623-62), the philosopher, by Guillaume (1880).

We now re-enter the town, passing along the Square Blaise-Pascal and the Place de la Poterne. The second street on the right passes in front of the *Hôtel de Ville* and the *Palais de Justice* (Pl. C, 3), which together form one huge building in the neo-classical style. Farther to the S. is —

The **Cathedral** (Pl. B, C, 3), a fine Gothic building, the construction of which was begun in 1248 from plans by Jean Deschamps, but has been interrupted and resumed several times. In the 15th cent. the side portals with their unfinished towers were added; then the building was once more abandoned till the present period which has witnessed the completion of the façade with its two towers after the plans of Viollet-le-Duc. The interior is distinguished by its harmonious proportions. The choir, with its plain aisles, apses, and side chapels, is in the early Gothic style; the nave with double aisles and chapels, is in a later Gothic style. The windows, below which is a fine triforium with pointed gables, contain good stained glass of the 13-15th cent., the rose windows in the transepts being specially fine. The high altar, of copper, the bishop's throne, and the railings of the choir are all modern, designed by Viollet-le-Duc. In the second chapel to the right of the choir is a painted wooden reredos of the 16th cent., representing the Life of St. Crispin and St. Crispinian. In the left transept is a 'Jacquemart' (clock figure), taken in the Religious Wars of the 16th cent. at Issoire.

To the S. of the cathedral we cross the Place de Clermont, in which stands the *House of Pascal*, indicated by a bust. We proceed to the S. by the Rue Royale (Pl. B, 3), and descend to the right by the Place de Sugny, on the left side of which is the *Préfecture* (Pl. B, 4). In this square rises a *Monument du Centenaire de 1789*, with a bronze allegorical statue by Gourgouillon.

The **Place de Jaude** (Pl. A, 4), a little farther on, is the centre of Clermont, though situated to the W. of the town proper. It is 300 yards long and 90 yards wide and is adorned at its S. end by a bronze statue, by Nanteuil, of *Desaix* (1768-1800), the distinguished general, a native of Auvergne.

The Rue Blatin, in the direction of the Puy de Dôme, leads from the W. side of the Place de Jaude to Royat (p. 242).

In the N.W. angle of the same Place is the *Church of St. Pierre-des-Minimes* (Pl. A, 3, 4), dating from the 17th century. — Opposite is the *Théâtre*, constructed in 1893 from the old cloth-market.

On this side of the town, but farther on (direction-placards) are the *Fontaines Pétrifiantes de St. Alyre* (Pl. A, 1; mineral baths), of little interest. Visitors are expected to make some small purchase or to give a gratuity.

In a small open space near the Place de Jaude, to the right beyond the statue of Desaix, is the *Eden Concert*, recently built in the Moorish style.

We return viâ the Centenary monument (see above), and crossing the *Square d'Assas* (Pl. B, 4) we keep straight on along the Rue du St. Esprit, at the bottom of which is the *Lycée Pascal* (Pl. C, 4). There we turn once more to the right, along the wide Rue Ballainvilliers, passing in front of the *Halle au Blé* (Corn Market), and reaching the *Fontaine Desaix* (Pl. C, 5), surmounted by an obelisk.

The building to the left at the corner of the Boulevard du Taureau and the Avenue Vercingetorix, which is adjoined by the Palais de l'Académie (p. 241), contains the library and the **Musée** (Pl. C, 5). The latter is open to the public daily from 10 to 12 and 1.30 to 4, except Mon. and Frid., and on those days also to strangers.

Ground-Floor. — This part of the museum contains fragments of Roman sculpture, mediæval and modern sculptures; model of a statue of

Vercingetorix (p. 248), by *Bartholdi*, design for a monument to be placed
probably on the site of the former theatre at Clermont, near the cathedral; Hope deceived, a bronze by *Barrand*: Hero and Leander, group in
marble by *Diébolt*; Lesbia's toilette, marble statue by *Chevallier*; Roman
mosaic; antique bronzes; medals and coins (including a unique silver
denier of Lothair), etc.

STAIRCASE. — 20. *School of Valentin*, A good story; 19. Attributed to
Ph. de Champaigne, Diogenes looking for a man; 73. Attributed to *O.
Vaenius*, Susannah.

FIRST FLOOR. — Room I. Weapons, furniture, coffer of embossed
leather, of the 15th cent.; faïence; door of a sacristy with 13th cent.
paintings; works in copper; Chinese ornaments. — Room II. Portraits,
including, to the left: 116. *Holbein*, Ant. Duprat, chief minister of Francis I.; 104, 106. *H. Rigaud*, The artist, P. Puget; 71 (near the Holbein).
Flemish School, St. Jerome; 186. *L. Leloir*, Jacob wrestling with the angel;
177. *F. Ehrmann*, Vercingetorix. — In the central glass-case: bas-reliefs,
enamels, caskets; Pascal's calculating machine; mediæval cross; despatch-
box of the 13th cent.; reliquary of the 13th cent. and other enamelled
bronze works; Russian Ikon. In the glass-cases at the sides, beginning
at the entrance: medals, seals, combs with cameos, pottery, etc. Between
the windows on the left side is a series of small painted terracotta reliefs
(16th cent.), reproducing the Dance of Death at Bâle. — Room III contains principally pictures. On the right, 42. *D. Romekkof*, Fairy ring;
18. *C. Dolci*, Head of the Virgin; 17. *Géricault*, Study for the picture of
the Wreck of the Medusa, at the Louvre; 75. *Fr. Pourbus*, Kitchen; 26. *O.
Vaenius*, Infant Bacchus; 194. Copy of *Guido*, Martyrdom of St. Andrew;
24. *Phil. de Champaigne*, Annunciation; 39. After *G. Romano*, Battle of Constantine, a fine old copy of a picture no longer extant; 26, 27, 29. *Callot*,
The Miseries of War; 3. *Rombouts*, Dentist; 318. *Ribera*, Adoration of the
Shepherds; 5. *Teniers the Younger*, Fair at Florence, a reversed reduction,
by the artist himself, of a picture which is now in the Old Pinakothek at
Munich; 526. *Garofalo*, Holy Family; 100. *G. Franck*, Mt. Calvary; 196. *Dutch
School*, Old Man; 14. *Poelenburg*, Bathers; 385. *Flemish School*, Interior of
a tavern; 193. *Fyt*, Game; 30. *J. Parrocel*, Attack of cavalry; 121. *Drog-
loen*, Scene during war; 21. Copy of *Rubens*, Death of Cleopatra; —
Berthon, Procession at St. Bonnet, Puy-de-Dôme; no number, *Sain*, End
of autumn; 8. *Schenck*, Torrent; several landscapes and other modern
paintings; 136. *Debat-Ponsan*, A gate of the Louvre during the massacre
of St. Bartholomew. — In the centre, two shields of repoussé work in
silver and iron, representing scenes from Paradise Lost and The Pilgrim's
Progress, by *Morel-Ladeuil*, of Clermont. A glass-case contains a small
ethnographical collection. — Room IV. Paintings of inferior interest;
antique vases, drawings, engravings, etc.

The *Library*, with upwards of 55,000 vols. and 1100 MSS., is
open daily, except Sun., 12-5, and (in winter) 7.30-10 p.m.

The *Palais de l'Académie* (Pl. C, 5), in the Avenue Vercingetorix,
a tasteful modern erection, is the seat of the university academy,
which has faculties of science and literature.

Between the Museum and the Académie is a *School of Pisci-
culture*, open to visitors daily from 2 to 6 p. m.

The **Jardin Lecoq** (Pl. C, 5, 6), in the vicinity, is a fine public
promenade, with a Botanical Garden; a military band plays here
in summer. At the entrance stands the bust of *H. Lecoq* (d. 1871),
the naturalist, formerly the director of the garden.

At the E. end of the small Place du Taureau, near the entrance
to the garden, is the *Musée Lecoq* (Pl. C, 5), bequeathed by Lecoq to
the town, containing a natural history collection, especially rich in

specimens illustrating the geology and mineralogy of Auvergne. The museum is open to the public on Sun. and Thurs. from 10 to 3, and on other days also to strangers.

We now retrace our steps by the Rue Ballainvilliers. Behind the Lycée is the *Church des Carmes* (Pl. C, 4), a fine Gothic structure of the 14-15th cent., without aisles. Its large windows have modern glass.

A little farther on we reach a square, whence a street leads to the right to the Boulevards, in the centre of which is the **Grande Fontaine** (Pl. D, 4), or *Fontaine de Jacques d'Amboise*, a tasteful monument in Volvic stone, dating from 1515. It consists of three basins, one above the other, richly sculptured and adorned with statuettes. The whole is surmounted by a statue of Hercules, with the arms of the Amboise family.

The Boulevard Trudaine ascends hence to the Place Delille and the Avenue Charras (p. 239).

b. Royat.

From Clermont to Royat, 1¼ M. to the W., by the Rue Blatin, which begins at the Place de Jaude; 3½ M. by rail. Electric tramway, see p. 238; railway, p. 236. By the road we turn to the left before reaching Chamalières (p. 244), ascend the valley of the Tiretaine, and pass under a railway-viaduct. — The station is above us, to the left.

Hotels. Splendid-Hôtel; Continental, above the park of the Thermal Establishment, with a fine view, R. 3-10, L. 1, A. 1, B. 1½, déj. 4, D. 5, pens. 12-20 fr.; Grand Hôtel, a little higher, R. 2-10, L. 1, A. 1, B. 1½-2, déj. 4, D. 5, pens. 10-20 fr. — Grand-Hôtel de Lyon, still higher. — Grand-Hôtel Richelieu (hôtel-meublé), below, near the Baths; Grand-Hôtel Bristol, behind the Baths; Hôtel Central, Grand-Hôtel du Parc, du Louvre, César, de France et d'Angleterre, des Sources, etc., farther off in the valley; Hôtel St. Mart, de la Paix, de Paris, de l'Europe, in an elevated situation; Hôtel de l'Univers, near the station, etc. Numerous *Furnished Houses*. Pension, 10 to 30 fr. per day. Royat is considered expensive.

Restaurants. *Du Casino*, in the Parc, déj. 4, D. 5 fr.; *du Parc*, near the new casino.

Baths, 1½ fr., 2 fr., and 2½ fr. according to the month and the hour at which they are taken. — Douches, same charges. — Inhalation. 1-1½ fr.

Mineral Water. Subscription (obligatory), 10 fr.; then, 5 c. a glass.

Casinos. *Casino Municipal*, open from May 15 to Sept. 30; admission, 2 fr., with seat in the theatre, 5 fr.; subscription for 25 days, 20 fr., season 40 fr., including the theatre 40 and 80 fr.; seat in the park during the music, 15 c. (day), 25 c. (evening); subscription, 5 fr. for 25 days. — *New Casino*, adm. including theatre 3-4 fr.; subscription for 25 days, 25 fr.

Band daily in the Park of the Casino Municipal from 9.30 to 10.30 a. m., from 3.30 to 5, and 8 to 9 p. m. — At the New Casino, 3.45-5.45 and at 7.45 p. m.

Post and Telegraph Office in the Park. — Cabs, see p. 238. Carr. to the Puy de Dôme 20 fr., etc.; see the tariff posted on the bridge.

English Church Service in summer.

A list of *Physicians* and other useful information is given in the *Guide du Baigneur*, which is distributed at the Etablissement.

Royat (1450 ft.), together with *St. Mart*, the part nearest to Clermont, is a place of 1560 inhab., in a beautiful valley watered by the

Tartaret, and overlooked on the N. by the Puy de Chalet
and on the S. by the Puy de Grosmanoire (2700 ft.). It com-

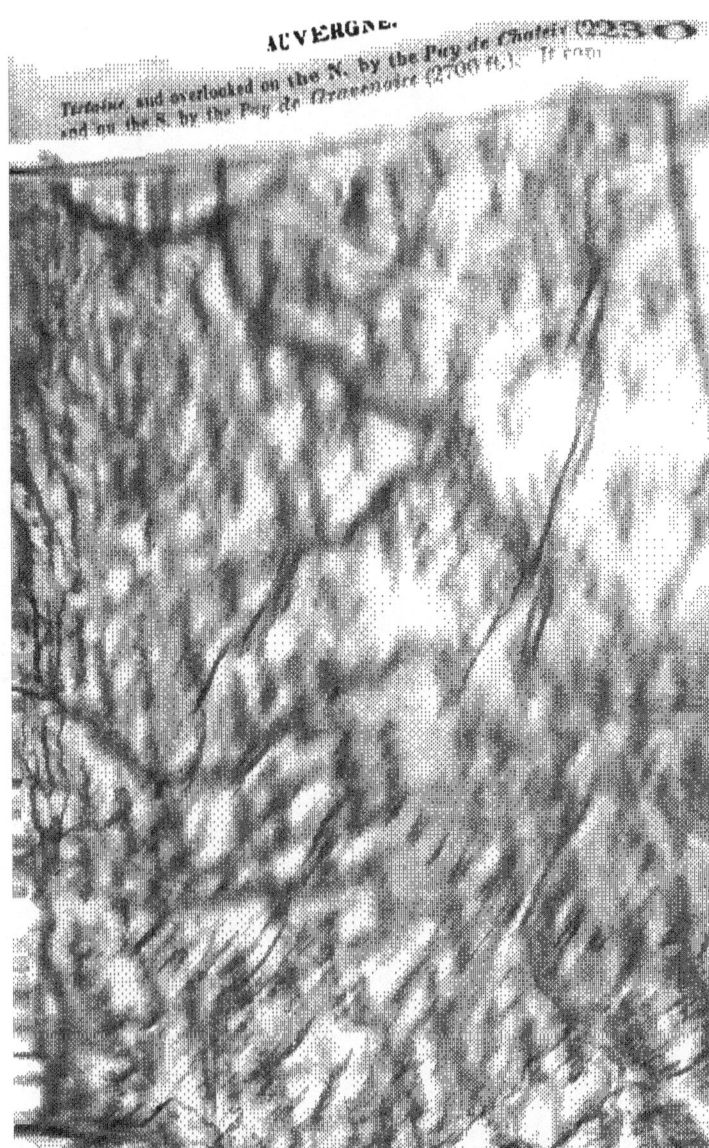

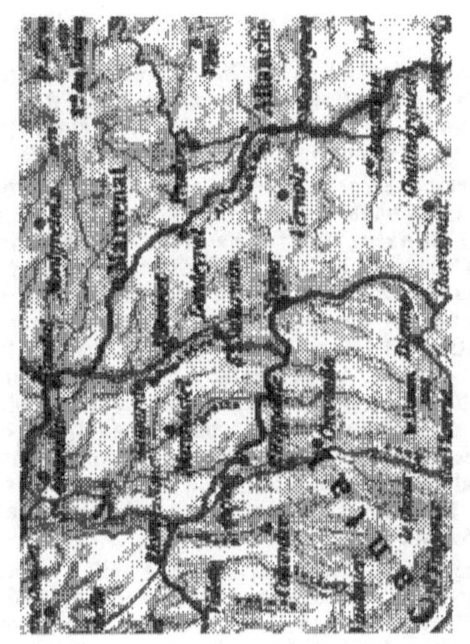

rlaine, and overlooked on the N. by the *Puy de Chatelr* (2230 ft.)
.d on the S. by the *Puy de Gravenoire* (2700 ft.). It commands
slendid views of the valley from which rises the Puy de Dôme, to
ie W., and of Clermont and the Limagne, to the E.

The *Thermal Establishment* is at St. Mart, at the end of the
alley and on the bank of the river. It has four mineral springs,
ised both for drinking and for bathing. These are the springs of
St. Mart (55° Fahr.), *St. Victor* (68°), *César* (84°), and *Eugénie*
(98°), all grouped round the Establishment. The last-named, which
is open throughout the year, and especially frequented between
May 15 and Oct. 15 (about 5000 visitors annually), has 94 private
bath-rooms, besides large basins, pulverization and inhalation
rooms, douche-cabinets of all sorts, etc. The maladies which are
successfully treated here are rheumatism, gout, and other arthritic
diseases, affections of the respiratory organs, and chlorosis and anæmia. Royat claims to rival Vichy and in certain cases to be preferable. In the Park are remains of *Roman Baths*, to the right, behind
the Establishment.

The village proper lies farther up the valley. The church (10-
12th cent.) presents a picturesque appearance, viewed from the left
bank of the Tirtaine. Below it, on the bank of the river, is a grotto,
in which seven springs rise, partly used for the water-supply of
Clermont. — Excursions, see below.

e. The Puy de Dôme.

AUVERGNE, *Arvernia*, an old province of France, was divided
into *Basse-Auvergne*, to the N. and E., and *Haute-Auvergne*, to the
S., the two together corresponding to the present departments of
Puy-de-Dôme and Cantal and a part of Haute-Loire. Haute-Auvergne
and the environs of Clermont-Ferrand in Basse-Auvergne are especially interesting from a geological point of view, and, for the tourist, rank amongst the most interesting regions of France. Nowhere
can the results of volcanic action be better studied. The shape of
the mountains reveals their origin at a glance. They are in general
rounded. presenting a succession of isolated cones, the outcome of
volcanoes extinct before the dawn of history, but whose craters are
still easily recognizable. Many of these mountains bear the name
of *Puy*, derived from the Latin *podium*. They may be divided into
three systems. The first chain is that of the *Monts Dôme*, in which
are 60 puys, from 2500 to 4000 ft. in height, descending in steps
right and left of the Puy de Dôme (4805 ft.; p. 245). The second
chain, more to the W., includes the *Monts Dore* and the *Monts du
Cantal*, of which the culminating point is the *Puy de Sancy*
(6185 ft.), near Mont Dore (p. 250), the loftiest summit in the interior of France. The third chain, to the S., culminates in the *Plomb
du Cantal* (6095 ft.; p. 260).

The distance from Clermont-Ferrand to the top of the Puy de Dôme is from 8 to 10 miles, which may be accomplished by carriage in about 4 hours, except the ascent of the cone, and in 7 hours on foot, there and back, besides halts. A carriage costs not less than 20 to 25 fr. Omnibuses occasionally ply in the season to the Col de Ceyssat (see below), leaving Clermont about 7.30 a. m. and the col about 4 p. m., enquiries should be made beforehand. — The air at the top of the Dôme is always cold. There is a café-restaurant (déj. 3½ fr.), and the custodian of the Observatory has rooms for the accommodation of tourists.

a. Viâ Royat. — *Carriage Road.* — *Royat,* see p. 242. From the Bath Establishment, where the tram-cars stop, we cross the river and ascend by the street on the left. We leave on the right the footpath (see below), nearly opposite the church and near a small cascade formed by the Tirtaine under a bridge. Farther on, towards the end of the village, we turn to the left, cross the river, follow for a short distance a street in the upper part of the village, and turn to the right at the second cross-street. After that there can be no mistake. The new road ascends through meadows, with very little shade, a defect shared by most roads in this region and materially detracting from the tourist's enjoyment in summer. About 1 hr. from Royat we reach the poor hamlet of *Fontanat* (two small restaurants), a little short of which the road twice crosses the Tirtaine, leaving the village on the right. About 20-25 min. farther on we join the La Baraque road, and a post on the other side indicates the road to the Col de Coyssat and the Puy de Dôme, across a flat succeeded by a strip of wood at the foot of the cone. To the left, on a hill, are the scanty remains of the *Château de Montrodeix,* the foundation of which dates back at least to the 8th century. The *Col de Ceyssat* (3535 ft.), on which are an inn and some huts at which the carriages stop, is 2½ M. from the above mentioned point, to the S. of the Puy, whence a good zigzag road ascends for 1½ M. more to the Observatory on the top of the mountain.

Pedestrian Route from Royat. This route, which is particularly to be recommended for the return on account of the view of the valley and in the direction of Clermont, ascends, as stated above, to the right at Royat, crosses some vineyards, turns to the left, and skirts the valley all the way to Fontanat, through which it passes to join the carriage-road.

b. Viâ Villars. — This is a less interesting route than either of the preceding, but as compensation it offers remnants of a Roman

will only be followed in returning by those who descend by the side
of the Puy de Pariou (p. 246). It leaves the Royat road on the
left and passes through *Chamalières* (p. 244). Fully 1/2 M. farther
it joins the Tulle road at a point where a turn is made to the left and
zigzags up to La Baraque. (A path cutting off the last curve diverges
half-way.) *La Baraque* is a hamlet, 4 M. from Clermont, built on
a lava-stream from the Puy de Pariou, the road to which branches
off 1 1/4 M. farther to the right of the Tulle road, which is the way
to the Col de Ceyssat mentioned above.

The *Puy de Dôme* (4805 ft.) is formed of a white siliceous limestone, here and there tinted with yellow and red, which is peculiar
to this mountain and therefore called *domite*. It is scantily clothed
round its base by wood, and elsewhere by coarse grass. The top is
a fairly extensive plateau sloping towards the S. Upon it are an
observatory and some ruins, but the view is naturally the chief
attraction.

In clear weather the *PANORAMA* is vast and magnificent: to the
E. the valley of Royat, Clermont, and the Limagne; to the S. a
number of naked volcanic cones, attaining a height of from 3600 to
4100 ft. above the sea; farther away, the Lac d'Aydat, to the left of
which are the Monts Dore, dominated by the Puy de Sancy, and still
farther, the heights of the Cantal; westward, a broken plain; to the
N., other volcanic cones, forming a continuation of those to the S.,
amongst which we may single out the Petit Puy de Dôme, a buttress
of the chief mountain; then the two Suchets: to the left, the Puy de
Côme; to the right, the Puy de Pariou, etc. (see below). In clear
weather it is said that the Pelvoux, 175 M. distant, and Mont Blanc,
190 M. distant, are visible.

The RUINS which cover a part of the plateau are those of a *Temple
of Mercury*. The foundation and a few courses of masonry alone remain. It was built of enormous stone blocks bound together by iron
clamps. Several platforms are still recognizable, and on the last of
these are some small apartments, looking towards the S., and ending
in semicircular form, nearly all provided with stone seats. This temple
dates from the Roman period and is mentioned in Cæsar's Commen-
taries. Besides the fragments of stone sculptures scattered by the side
of the path, similar fragments in marble of various kinds have also
been discovered, as well as bronze articles, Roman coins, etc.

The OBSERVATORY, at the upper end of the plateau, was opened
in 1876. It consists of a tower for observations at the highest point
of the mountain and a main building lower down, sheltered from
the north and connected with the tower by an underground passage.
It communicates with Clermont by means of a special telegraph. —
Pascal made his first experiments to ascertain the weight of the
atmosphere on the Puy de Dôme in 1648.

Sure-footed pedestrians who wish to save time may descend
in about 1 hr. straight from the summit to the road by which they

ascended, by following the direction of the telegraph.   Footpassengers or those who send down their carriage by this road generally descend on the N. side towards the *Petit Puy de Dôme* (4160 ft.), to which there are two paths, the left one being shorter but steeper than the right.   On the left there is a complete crater called the *Nid de la Poule*.   Farther on, in front, is the *Puy du Petit-Suchet* (3950 ft.), and to the left the *Grand-Suchet* (4070 ft.).   Passing to the right of the former, we may reach the *Puy de Pariou* (3970 ft.) in about 2 hrs. from the top of the Puy de Dôme.   It has a crater over 1000 ft. in diameter and about 300 ft. in depth, and a '*Cheire*' or lava-stream on the side next Clermont.   The *Puy de Côme* (4150 ft.), the second to the W., has a double crater; on the *Puy de Chierson* (3965 ft.), between the two, are curious caves, especially on the S. side (torch or candle required).   The descent is made to the N.E. to the road to Pontaumur, which joins the Tulle road at *La Baraque* (p. 245), about 2¹/₂ M. from the foot of the Puy de Pariou. It skirts the lava-stream of that mountain.

From Clermont-Ferrand to Mont-Rognon and the Plateau de Gergovie, 4 and 6 M., 4-5 hrs. walk there and back, carriage about 15 fr. We follow the Bordeaux road, by the Rue Gonod, to the S. of the Place du Jaude (Pl. A, B, 5, 6).   This road, bordered by trees, leads through fine orchards and vineyards.   A short-cut for pedestrians diverges to the right at the first bend, rejoining the road ¹/₈ M. farther on, to the right of *Beaumont*, a village with about 1400 inhab. nearly 2 M. from Clermont. Another short-cut, to the left, may be made from the next curve, leading direct to *Ceyrat*, another large village nearly 2 M. from Beaumont, at the foot of the *Puy du Mont-Rognon* (1980 ft.).   The top of this mountain, which, like all the neighbouring puys, is of volcanic formation, is reached in ¹/₄ hr. by a steep ascent to the left.   It commands fine views of Clermont to the N., the Puy de Dôme and its satellites to the W., and the Plateau de Gergovie to the S.E.   On the summit are the ruins of a *Castle* which dominate the country round.   They consist of two towers one of which has partly fallen in.   This castle, built about 1160, has been in ruins since 1634.

The *Plateau de Gergovie* (2440 ft.) lies about 2 M. to the E. of Mont-Rognon.   It is reached either by a direct footpath or by a longer carriage-road, passing *Clémensat* and the *Gorge d'Opme* to the S.   This plateau, which measures about 1600 yds. by 650 yds., is the site of the Gallic town of *Gergovia*, which Cæsar besieged after occupying Bourges, and where he was defeated by the famous Vercingetorix.   After the submission of the Gauls Augustus tried to efface the memory of this defeat by transporting the inhabitants to Nemetum, now Clermont, which he loaded with his favours, whilst Gergovia was suffered to fall into ruin.   The present scanty remains consist of heaps of stones lying by the sides of the roads which cross the fields, and which are said to indicate the course of the streets of the town.   Excavations have from time to time been undertaken, with abundant results, especially on the E. side.   The view from the plateau is still more extensive than from Mont-Rognon.   A statue of Vercingetorix is to be erected here, after Bartholdi's design (p. 241). The shortest route for returning descends to the E. to the Issoire road, which the pedestrian may join by a path to the N. at (2¹/₂ M.) *Aubière*, a place of 3265 inhab., about 1³/₄ M. from Clermont.

39. La Bourboule, Mont Dore and its Environs.

I. La Bourboule.

Comp. the Map, p. 243.

From Laqueuille to La Bourboule. — Omnibuses ($4^1/_2$, $3^1/_2$, 2 fr.) ply in the season from the station of Laqueuille to (8 M.) *La Bourboule* in $1^1/_2$ hr. Carriages also for hire (10-12 fr. for 4 pers.). A railway is under construction.

Laqueuille, see p. 235. — The road first crosses an uninteresting plain in the direction of the valley of the Dordogne. After $2^1/_2$ M. the road to the Mont Dore diverges to the left (see p. 248). — $4^1/_2$ M. *St. Sauves,* a village of 2374 inhab., has a modern Romanesque church, superseding an earlier Renaissance church, the portal of which stands in a small Place. — The road runs high above the picturesque wooded valley of the Dordogne, and then descends to La Bourboule, which it reaches opposite the baths. The omnibus-office lies a little nearer the Hôtel de Ville.

La Bourboule. — **Hotels.** Most of the hotels are new and comfortable, but it is advisable to ascertain the charges beforehand. HÔTEL DES ILES-BRITANNIQUES, on the left bank, pens. 11-19 fr.; GRAND-HÔTEL, GR.-HÔT. DES ETRANGERS, DE L'ETABLISSEMENT, PERRIÈRE, DE PARIS, all of the first class and on the right bank; BRISTOL; SPLENDID-HÔTEL; BEAUSÉJOUR ET DU CASINO; DE FRANCE, less pretentious; DE LONDRES, R. 4-5, A. $^1/_2$, pens. from 10 fr.; DU PARC, DES DEUX-MONDES, RICHELIEU, DU GLOBE, DE L'EUROPE ET DES BAINS, DE L'UNIVERS; ALGER ET DES DEUX-MONDES, R. 3-10, L. & A. 1, B. $1^1/_4$, déj. $3^1/_2$, D. $4^1/_2$, pens. 6-15 fr.; BOURBOULE, POSTE, RUSSIE, BELDER; LOUVRE, R. 3-6, L. $^1/_2$, B. $1^1/_2$, déj. $3^1/_2$, D. $4^1/_2$, pens. 6-15 fr.; DES AMBASSADEURS, CONTINENTAL; DES SOURCES, DES ANGLAIS, DE VEILDE, BELLEVUE, second class. Numerous *Villas* and *Furnished Houses.*

Cafés, in the parks; *Café-Restaurant des Thermes,* at the theatre, déj. 3, D. 5 fr.; *Café Français,* opposite the chief Establishment.

Thermal Establishments. Drinking, 12 fr. per season. Baths 1 fr. 30 c.- 5 fr. according to class, establishment, season; douche 1-3 fr.; together $2^1/_2$-8 fr.

Carriages dear, bargaining desirable. *Public Conveyance,* to Laqueuille, p. 248; to Mont-Dore, $1-1^1/_2$ fr. — *Saddle-horses,* 6-10 fr. per day; *Donkeys,* $^1/_2$-1 fr. per hr.

Casinos. *Casino de la Bourboule,* Parc Chardon; *Casino de la Compagnie,* Parc de Fenestre. Subscription for the former, 3 fr. per day, 10 fr. per week, 20 fr. for three weeks. — *Théâtre des Thermes,* 2-3 fr.

La Bourboule (2790 ft.), formerly an insignificant hamlet, had 1708 inhab. in 1891, and is rapidly developing into a small town, owing to the growing popularity of its thermal mineral springs, which are said to attract about 7000 visitors annually. There are three thermal establishments and two casinos. The chief springs, rising on the *Rocher de la Bourboule,* a height above the town, are the *Source Choussy* and the *Source Perrière,* with a temperature of 60° Fahr., used in cases of anæmia, rheumatism, lymphatic affections, diseases of the skin and the respiratory organs, diabetes, and intermittent fevers. La Bourboule has the character of a health-resort for families and children, though complaints are made of its expensiveness.

Excursions. The excursions from La Bourboule are practically the same as those from Le Mont-Dore. — The *Mont-Dore Road* ($4^1/_2$ M.; carr. see above) ascends the right bank of the Dordogne and joins the road from Laqueuille (p. 235) after about 2 M. Cross-roads, see p. 251. Near the junction of the roads are the *Cascades de la Vernière* and *du Plat-à-Barbe*, often visited from La Barboule. The former is visible from the road (p. 251). They may also be reached viâ the right bank.

The **Roche Vendeix** (3845 ft.) is nearer to La Bourboule than to Mont-Dore. It lies about 2 M. to the S.E. of the former, viâ the valley of the *Fenestre*, beyond the park of that name. In the middle ages it was surmounted by a castle, of which no traces now remain. The fine view to the N. includes the wooded heights and the valley of the Dordogne, above which rise the Puy Gros and the Banne-d'Ordenche. — At *Pragnour*, farther down to the N., obsidians are found. — A route descends on the S. to (5 M.) Le Mont-Dore.

The heights to the E., in the direction of the valley, are the *Puy Gros* and the *Banne-d'Ordenche* (p. 252). Nearer lies *Murat-le-Quaire* (see below), presenting a most picturesque appearance.

II. Le Mont-Dore.

From Laqueuille to Mont-Dore. — An omnibus plies in the season from the station of Laqueuille (p. 235) to (9½ M.) Le Mont-Dore in 1¾ hr. Carriages also for hire (see p. 247). Best views to the right.

Laqueuille, see p. 235. The road, like that to La Bourboule, crosses the plain, then turns to the left, and ascends and descends alternately. The mountains become more clearly defined; to the left is the Banne-d'Ordenche, mentioned above; to the right the Puy de Sancy (p. 250), recognizable by its three peaks.

4½ M. *Murat-le-Quaire*, the halfway village, from which La Bourboule is only about ½ M. distant in a straight line. After about 7 M., a road diverges on the right to La Bourboule. We next reach the banks of the *Dordogne*, ascend its picturesque valley, turning to the right, and find ourselves in front of the mountains which close the valley, particularly the Puy de Sancy. We descend by a zigzag road. The diligence office is near the casino.

Le Mont-Dore. — **Hotels.** Most of the hotels are new and comfortable, but it is advisable to ascertain the charges beforehand. Near the Bath Establishments: Hôtel SARCIRON-BAIKALDY; NOUVEL HÔTEL, next the preceding, and HÔTEL DE LA POSTE, same proprietor; DE PARIS; DU PARC; all these are first-class houses in the Place Michel-Bertrand; DE FRANCE et DE L'UNIVERS, Rue Favart; RAMADE AÎNÉ, DES BAINS ET DE LYON, Rue Rigny, second-class. — Near the church and the Casino: BARDET, GRAND HÔTEL, first-class; BEAU-SITE, Rue Ramond; DE LONDRES, first-class. — In the Rue Rigny, beyond the three above-named: DE LA PAIX; behind, GR.-HOT. DES ÉTRANGERS, R., L., & A. 4-8, B. 1, déj. 3½, D. 4, pens. 9-12 fr. — In the Rue Favart, below the Hôtel de France: BAUGIRAS AÎNÉ, small; BARADUC-LAUDOUZE, DES THERMES, etc. — Numerous *Furnished Houses* and *Villas*.

Cafés. *Du Casino*, *du Pont*, *de la Rotonde*, all near the Promenade, on the left bank; *de Paris*, higher up, on the banks of the Dordogne.

Thermal Establishment. Drinking and gargling, 12 fr. for 20 days; baths ¾-3 fr.; in the common basin, free (except in July); douches ¾-3 fr.; baths with douches 3 and 5 fr.; porters 40 and 50 c., there and back 75 c. and 1 fr. The tariff and a list of *Physicians* are exhibited in the Establishment.

Carriages, generally dear, about 20 fr. per day (bargaining necessary). — *Public Conveyances* to Laqueuille, see p. 240; to La Bourboule 1¼ fr., 2 fr. there and back. — *Horses and Donkeys*, 3-6 fr. per day; no tariff.

Guides, scarcely required for the ordinary excursions, with the details given below; 3-10 fr. for half a day, 5-12 fr. per day.

Casino. Admission per day 1 fr.; subscription for 20 days, 15 fr., including chairs in the park; theatre 1/2-4 fr.

Post and Telegraph Office, Rue Favart, at the corner of the Issoire road.
Protestant Service on Sun. at 1 p. m. in the Bath-Establishment, first floor.

Le Mont-Dore (3440 ft.), a little town of 1758 inhab., on the *Dordogne,* which rises a few miles higher up, lies in a beautiful valley surrounded on three sides by the loftiest heights of the Monts Dore. To the charm of situation it adds the advantages afforded by very important mineral waters, which have been known from the days of the Romans and at present attract about 6000 invalids annually. They are used both for drinking and bathing in cases of diseases of the respiratory organs, incipient pulmonary affections, rheumatism, chlorosis, etc.

The place itself is fairly well built but has no specially interesting feature. It consists chiefly of one main street, ascending in the direction of the valley, named Rue Favart below and Rue Rigny above the Place Michel-Bertrand. The *Thermal Establishment,* in the Place, was partly rebuilt in 1893, and is now an attractive and well-managed institution. Within may be seen fragments of Roman architecture and sculpture, discovered in rebuilding the establishment in 1817 and later. Remains of a Roman Pantheon lingered till 1793 in the Place. The Establishment is built with its back against the *Montagne de l'Angle,* from which issue the mineral springs, and has an annexe to the N., containing the vapour-baths. The springs, ten in number, are in the order of their copiousness, as follows: *Source Bertrand* or *de la Madeleine* (113° Fahr.), *César* and *Caroline,* combined (113°), *du Pavillon, Grand-Bain* or *Bain St. Jean* (111°), *Ramond* (108°), *Rigny* (109°), *Boyer* (113°), *Pigeon* (112°), *Ste. Marguerite* (54°), and a *New Spring.* These yield together about 90,000 gallons of water daily. There are 'buvettes' for the César, Ramond (the most chalybeate), and Bertrand springs. The aërated water of the cold Ste. Marguerite spring has an agreeable taste. The Bath Establishment is open 4-10 a. m. and 2-5 p. m.; visitors may inspect it in the interval.

The treatment at Mont-Dore is peculiar. It consists chiefly in very hot baths (104-113° Fahr.), douches, vapour-baths, inhalation of vapour, and equally hot foot-baths for the reaction. It requires the supervision of a specialist. The patients are frequently carried to and from the establishment in litters or beds (porter, see p. 248). A special flannel costume is worn. The season, nominally from June 1st to Oct. 1st, only extends in reality from June 15th to Sept. 15th, the climate at this altitude being severe, the more so from the fact that the valley is exposed to the N., and closed to the S. by the great wall of the Puy de Sancy.

A little way from the Establishment, at the end of the street that fronts it, is the *Casino,* a fine building erected in 1881, with a small park on the right bank of the Dordogne.

III. The Environs of Mont-Dore.

A number of interesting excursions may be made from Mont-Dore, most of them by carriage or on horses or donkeys (see p. 248).

To THE PUY DE SANCY viâ the valley, 2¹/₂ hrs., or 4 hrs. there and back, by a road and path practicable for horses to within ¹/₄ hr. of the summit. We ascend the right bank of the Dordogne, from the end of the main street, with the object of our excursion in front of us. After about 550 yards a path diverges to the left to the *Grande Cascade*, which is seen at a distance. It falls from a sheer rock of trachyte to a depth of more than 100 ft.

We may also proceed from the fall to the Puy de Sancy, or return past it at the expense of ³/₄-1 hr. extra. Ascending to it in 25 min. we find a flight of steps in the rock with a handrail leading in ¹/₂ hr. to the *Plateau de Durbise*, over which we follow for ¹/₄ hr. the route to the valley of Chaudefour (p. 252), and then turn to the right along the path to Les Crêtes (fine views), above the *Roc de Cuzeau* (5855 ft.) and the *Pic de Cacadogne* (5895 ft.), between the valley of Le Mont-Dore on the right, and the *Vallée de Chaudefour*, on the left. The latter may be visited from this side (p. 252). About 3¹/₂ M. farther we rejoin the path which ascends from the valley.

To the right of the valley rises first the *Pic du Capucin* (4800 ft.; see below), which more or less resembles a head covered by a cowl; then the *Puy de Cliergue* (5470 ft.). Behind, opposite the Puy de Sancy, is the *Puy Gros* (4860 ft.). The carriage-road ends 7 M. from the village; ¹/₂ M. farther is a bridge; and ³/₄ M. farther we keep straight on, avoiding the descent to the left. To our right lies the wild *Vallon de Lacour*, with its streamlet. After about 1 hr. we cross the *Dore* and then the *Dogne*, which descend from the Puy de Sancy and unite to form the *Dordogne*, 2³/₄ M. from Le Mont-Dore. The Dore descends in a cascade from the Puy, the summit of which is hidden by the black peaks bordering the *Gorge d'Enfer*, to the right. About 7 min. farther the long *Cascade du Serpent* is seen among the trees, descending from the Puy de Cacadogne. Thence the ascent is continued by a fairly good zigzag path to the left over pastures to the (1 hr.) *Col de Sancy*, where we leave the horses (50 c.), and find refreshments in the season. Thence it is a short ¹/₄ hr's ascent to the top of the *Puy de Sancy (6185 ft.), the highest mountain in the centre of France. A cross marks the summit.

The *PANORAMA is very grand and extensive, comprising to the N., the valley of the Dordogne and the Monts Dore, *i. e.* the mountains already named, several lower peaks to the right, farther away, the Puy Marbler (5870 ft.), Puy de Frigoux (5825 ft.), Puy de la Tache (5470 ft.), etc.; the Lac de Guéry, overlooked by the Roche Sanadoire (4225 ft.; p. 252); to the left, the Puy Gros (4860 ft.) and the Banne-d'Ordenche (p. 252), and on the horizon the Monts Dôme; to the W. forests, pasture-lands and smaller Puys; to the S., near at hand, another Puy Gros (5820 ft.), the Puy Ferrand (p. 251), the Puy de Paillaret (5680 ft.) etc., the Lac Chouvet and the Lac de la Landle, a wide stretch of pasture and the Monts du Cantal; to the E., the Lac Chambon, in the valley of Chaudefour, on this side of Murols (p. 253). — The view on this side is finer and more complete from the Puy Ferrand (6065 ft.), which can be reached in ¹/₂ hr. from the Sancy.

This excursion may be agreeably prolonged by descending on the other side of the Puy de Sancy. In 3 hrs. we reach the hamlet of *Vassivières* (inns), a celebrated pilgrim-resort, with a church containing a black statue of the Virgin, which is transported to Besse for the winter. About ³/₄ hr. farther on, to the right of the road, is the *Lac Pavin* ('pavens'; 3840 ft.), an ancient crater half-filled with water, over ¹/₂ M. long and nearly as broad. Its precipitous banks, on which rises the *Puy de Montchal* (4840 ft.), and the solitude which reigns all around, have given rise to many weird traditions. About 2¹/₂ M. hence lies Besse ("*Cheval Blanc*, 9 fr. per day), a curious and very ancient little town, with remains of fortifications including a 15th cent. belfry-tower. — The *Grottes de Jonas*, 5¹/₂ M. from Besse, are among the chief curiosities of Auvergne. They form an entire village, now abandoned, the dwellings being hollowed out of the volcanic rock. There are 64 of these abodes, at various elevations, connected with one another by winding staircases. Similar dwellings are to be seen at St. Nectaire (p. 253). The road leads on to *Coudes* (p. 223), 19 M. from Besse (omnibus). Another road, to the left, halfway between Besse and the grottos, leads to (5¹/₂ M. from Besse) *Murols* (p. 253).

To the Capucin, about 2¹/₂ hrs. on foot there and back. Horses may be taken to within 10 min. of the top. The Plateau du Capucin is one of the principal promenades of Mont-Dore. After crossing the Dordogne we follow a steep path through the wood which clothes the greater part of this mountain, and in 45 min. reach the *Salon du Capucin*, a forest clearing, where refreshments are to be had in the season. Turning to the left, we skirt the Pic du Capucin (4630 ft.) in order to ascend it on the W., the only accessible side. The summit is bare and affords a fine view of the valley of the Dordogne, etc.

To La Bourboule. The carriage route to La Bourboule follows the road to Laqueuille as far as the divergence mentioned on p. 248 (about 2 M.), where it takes the left branch (2 M.). On horseback or on foot it is much more interesting to take the somewhat longer cross-roads, in the valley to the left. In the latter case we cross the Dordogne, and turning to the right, follow the left bank of the river until we are behind the hamlet of *Rigolet-Haut* (on the left are considerable beds of tufa); or we may take the shorter path which diverges to the left near the beginning of the route and ascends to Rigolet-Haut, afterwards rejoining the route. Thence we descend straight to *Rigolet-Bas*, turn to the left, and follow the banks of the *Cliergue* streamlet. About 1¹/₂ M. higher up is a saw-mill. Near the hamlet is the fine *Cascade du Plat-à-Barbe* (fee), so named from the shape of the ravine into which it falls from a height of 55 ft. The *Cascade de la Vernière* (fee), 10-15 min. lower down, is even finer, though only 25 ft. in height. In a wood to the right is a (1¹/₂ M.) clearing, much visited by pedestrians, called the *Salon de Mirabeau*, from the fact that Mirabeau-Tonneau, brother of the famous orator of the Revolution, made it a rendezvous of pleasure parties when he visited Le Mont-Dore in 1787. The path along the right bank of the streamlet leads to the Dordogne, on the other side of which, at the above-mentioned fork, the road to La Bourboule is joined. This point may also be reached by the left bank of the Dordogne.

To the N. of the Valley. — About ¹/₂ M. from Mont Dore, on
the road to Laqueuille, is the hamlet of *Queureilh*, whence we ascend
to the right viâ the hamlet of *Prends-t'y-Garde*, to the *Cascade de
Queureilh* (100 ft.; fee), 400 yds. above the road to Murols (see below).
About ³/₄ M. farther on in the valley, near a saw-mill, is the *Cascade
du Rossignolet*; and 1 M. farther (5 M. from Mont Dore) is the *Lac
de Guéry*, oval in shape, surrounded by pasture-lands and with a
cascade. About 20 min. farther, to the right, the *Roche Sanadoire*
(4225 ft.), to the left, the *Roche Tuillière* (4250 ft.), two masses of
basaltic rock, very steep and composed of very curious columns. A
fortress which once stood on the Roche Sanadoire has disappeared,
after being besieged for three weeks in the 14th cent., to dislodge a
band of 400 English adventurers. — Hence we proceed to the N.
to (2 hrs.) Orcival (p. 235) and (2¹/₂ hrs.) Rochefort (p. 235).

The *Puy Gros* (4860 ft.) may be ascended in 2 hrs. from Mont
Dore or La Bourboule, by a path (guide-post) to the N. of the road,
leading viâ the hamlets of *Legal* and *Tamboine*. Fine view from
the top. — Thence a climb of ¹/₂ hr. brings us to the summit of the
Corne or *Banne-d'Ordenche* (4975 ft.), another fine point of view.

To Murols and St. Nectaire (Issoire). 12¹/₂ and 15¹/₂ M.; carriage road. The road ascends to the right of the post-office and skirts
the Plateau de l'Angle, whence there is a magnificent view of the
valley and the mountains already mentioned. As we round the
Rocher de l'Angle we see before us the valley of Guéry. We next
cross the steamlet which forms on the right, at about 1¹/₂ M. from Le
Mont-Dore, the *Cascade du Saut-du-Loup* and ¹/₄ M. lower down
the *Cascade du Queureilh* (see above). The road turns to the left
and, ¹/₂ M. farther, forks.

The road to the left leads to Clermont-Ferrand (27 M. from Le Mont-
Dore). Near the fork, to the left, by the side of a saw-mill, is the *Cascade
du Rossignolet* (see above); ¹/₂ hr. farther, to the right of the road, the *Cascade du Pré-du-Barbier*. About 1¹/₂ M. thence, 5 M. from Le Mont-Dore,
is the *Lac de Guéry* (see above).

The road to Murols and Issoire crosses, about 2¹/₂ M. beyond the
fork, the *Col de Dyanne*, between the *Puy de la Tache* (5455 ft.), on
the right, and the *Puy de la Croix-Morand* (4960 ft.), on the left.
It descends, viâ the hamlet of *Dyanne*, over a high plateau, partly
planted with pines, at the end of which we see Murols, its castle, and
the Lac Chambon. To the right are the peaks of the Monts Dore.
About 1¹/₂ M. beyond Dyanne a road leads to the left, saving about
³/₄ M. and passing the hamlet of *Bressouilleile*.

10 M. *Chambon*, a village on the *Couse*, which descends to the
S.W. of the Monts Dore. Besse (p. 251) lies 6 M. from Chambon.

The Couse issues from the *Valley of Chaudefour, the upper part of
which is extremely picturesque. From it we can easily join the paths
to the Puy de Sancy (p. 250), 4-5 M. from Chambon.

About ¹/₄ hr. farther on, the Murols road passes to the N. of the
Lac Chambon, through which the Couse flows, and then skirts the

base of the *Tartaret* (3155 ft.), a pine-clad volcanic cone separating
it from Murols.

12¹/₂ M. **Murols** (*Hôtel Nidrat*), a village famous for its *Castle
of the 13-15th centuries. The imposing ruins, perched on a mound
to the left, attract attention from a distance. The château was once
an extensive and splendid manor-house, and its ruins are among
the finest extant. One of its towers has been restored and commands
a very fine view. The guide (in the village) expects a gratuity.

A road leads from Murols to (7¹/₂ M.) *Besse* (p. 251) viâ *Besolles*, before
which a road diverges to the left to Le Chelx (p. 221), and *St. Victor-la-
Rivière.* — Diligence from Murols to *Condes* (Clermont-Ferrand), see p. 223.

The road, turning then to the N.E., enters the valley of the *Fredet*.

15¹/₂ M. **St. Nectaire**, a village on the *Fredet*, consisting of St.
Nectaire-le-Bas (*Grand-Hôtel des Thermes; de Paris; Maudon
Jeune; Madeuf;* etc.) and St. Nectaire-le-Haut (*Hôtel du Mont
Cornadore; de la Paix; de France*). St. Nectaire has about a dozen
thermal mineral springs, and three thermal establishments: the *Bains
Romains* and the *Bains Boëtte* in St. Nectaire-le-Bas, and the *Etablissement du Mont-Cornadore*, the most important, in St. Nectaire-
le-Haut. The Romanesque *Church* (11-12th cent.) is interesting and
has lately been restored.

Interesting walks may be taken in the *Gorge of the Fredet*, both above
and below St. Nectaire. — To the S. of St. Nectaire-le-Bas rises the *Puy
d'Ersigne* (2935 ft.; fine view). — About 1³/₄ M. in the opposite direction
is the pretty *Cascade des Granges*, near the village of that name, on the
Couse; and 1¹/₂ M. to the E. are the stalactite *Grottes du Mont-Cornadore*.
— To the N.W. rises the *Puy de Châteauneuf* (3065 ft.) with some shapeless
ruins, and nine grottos near the top resembling the Grottes de Jonas
(p. 251). — From St. Nectaire to *Condes* (Clermont-Ferrand), see p. 223.

40. From Lyons to Toulouse viâ Le Puy and Aurillac.
Southern Auvergne.

348 M. Railway interesting, but no through trains. The best plan
is to sleep at Le Puy, whence there is a morning train with connections
(fares about 63, 42¹/₂, 28 fr.). — From Lyons to *Le Puy*, 90 M., railway in
5¹/₄-6³/₄ hrs. (fares 16 fr. 35, 11 fr. 5, 7 fr. 25 c.). — From Le Puy to
Toulouse, railway in about 15¹/₂ hrs.

From Lyons to Toulouse viâ *Tarascon* and *Nîmes*, 357 M., in 10⁵/₄-19³/₄
hrs. (fares 64 fr. 85, 43 fr. 80, 28 fr. 60 c.). See *Baedeker's South-Eastern
France* and R. 12.

To (36 M.) *St. Etienne*, see p. 230. — The line to Le Puy skirts
the town on the W., passing the arms manufactory, to the right, and
crossing a curved viaduct. Beyond (38 M.) *Le Clapier* are two short
tunnels; and beyond (40 M.) *Bellevue* another, nearly 1¹/₄ M. long.

41¹/₂ M. *La Ricamarie*, an industrial place of 7044 inhab.,
producing shoe-nails and bolts. In the neighbourhood are coal-
mines, one of which has been on fire since the 15th century.

43¹/₂ M. *Le Chambon-Feugerolles*, with 9016 inhab., has iron-works and coal-mines. About ¹/₂ M. to the S. is the interesting *Château de Feugerolles* (11-17th cent.).

45¹/₂ M. **Firminy** (*Buffet*; *Hôtel du Nord*), another industrial town with 14,511 inhab., the centre of a coal and iron district.

Lines to *St. Just-sur-Loire* and *Annonay-St. Rambert-d'Albon*, see p. 216.

46¹/₂ M. *Fraisse-Unieux* is the junction for St. Just-sur-Loire (p. 197). After a tunnel we reach the banks of the *Loire*, which flows between very picturesque mountains. — 47¹/₂ M. *Pertuiset*. The aspect of the country changes. A busy industrial region, black with smoke and coal, is succeeded by a peaceful valley with picturesque and verdant landscapes. On *Mont Cornillon*, to the left, are the ruins of a fortress of the 12-16th cent., including within its walls a church of the 12th and 15th cent., with some good wood-carving, etc. We traverse a tunnel, a viaduct 65 ft. high, and another tunnel, and beyond (51¹/₂ M.) *Aurec*, two more tunnels and another viaduct. To the right, beyond the stream, is the ruined *Château de Roche-baron*. 58 M. *Bas-Monistrol*, the station for *Bas* (pron. 'Bass'), with 3040 inhab., 2¹/₂ M. to the W., and *Monistrol*, with 4720 inhab., 2 M. to the E. From Bas we visit the ruins of Rochebaron, and Monistrol also has a castle of the 15th century. Farther on are three tunnels and a bridge over the Loire. — 61¹/₂ M. *Pont-de-Lignon*. Beyond two more tunnels we cross the Loire twice.

69 M. *Retournac*, with 4013 inhabitants. Beyond it another bridge and tunnel and, on a hill to the right, the ruins of the *Château d'Artias*. Beyond (71¹/₂ M.) *Chamalières* we pass a bridge and three tunnels. 77 M. *Vorey* and (80 M.) *St. Vincent* are each followed by a short tunnel. 82 M. *Laroûte-sur-Loire*. The *Château de Laroûte* is visible from the railway, to the left a little farther on. It is dominated by a modern castle.

From Lavoûte-sur-Loire to Yssingeaux, 14 M., railway in 1¼ hr.; fares 2 fr. 60, 1 fr. 95, 1 fr. 40 c. — *Yssingeaux* (*Hôt. Lavocat*), with 7800 inhab., is an old manufacturing town, producing tulle and lace.

Farther on follow several other bridges and tunnels and a viaduct.

89¹/₂ M. **Le Puy** (*Hôtel Garnier*, Boulevard St. Louis 17; *de l'Europe*, Place de l'Hôtel-de-Ville; etc.), the Roman *Podium*, a town of 20,308 inhab., was the ancient capital of the *Velay* and is now the chief town of the department of the *Haute-Loire*. It is, taken as a whole, ill-built, but it is picturesquely situated between the *Borne* and the *Dolezon* on the slope of *Mont Anis*, on which rise the remarkable cathedral and a colossal statue of the Virgin.

Quitting the station we cross a suburb and, turning to the left, viâ the Boulevard St. Jean, reach the large and fine PLACE DU BREUIL, the centre of the lower town. In the middle is the *Fontaine Crozatier, presented by M. Crozatier, a bronze-founder, who was a native of Le Puy (1796-1855). The imposing structure was designed by Pradier of Le Puy, the bronze sculptures by Bosio, the

nephew. The latter consist of a statue of the town of Le Puy, on
the top of the monument, and of seated statues of the Loire, the
Allier, the Borne, and the Dolezou, four rivers of the department,
and of genii, grouped round four basins at the foot of the fountain.

On the other side of the Place is the *Préfecture* and, on the left
the *Palais de Justice*.

At the back of the Préfecture is a public garden, at the foot of
which is the *Musée Crozatier*, a fine modern building, also due to
the munificence of M. Crozatier. It is open free on Sun. and Thurs.
from 9 to 12 and from 2 to 4; on other days for a small gratuity.

GROUND FLOOR. In the vestibule, sculptures and inscriptions; Charity,
by *Outine*; plaster-casts. Rooms to the left, small museums of mechanics
and geology. Rooms to the right, remains of Roman monuments; mediæval
and Renaissance sculptures; prehistoric antiquities; furniture, miniatures,
arms, ivories, tapestries, antique vases, mummies. Room at the foot of
the staircase, Roman antiquities. On the staircase, copies of mural paintings in Le Puy and its environs.

FIRST FLOOR. Paintings. Room I: 82. *P. Pourbus* (?), Henri II.; 42. *School
of Goltzius*, Smell; 58. *Van Orley*, Vow to the Virgin; 74. *Perréal* (?), Virgin
on a gold ground; *Wencker*, St. John Chrysostom and the Empress Eudoxia;
A. Dumont, Rescue; *Bin*, Birth of Eve. — Room II, on the right: *Cerquozzi*,
Battle-field; *Terburg*, Portrait; 14. *Umbrian School*, Virgin; *Brisset*, Arrest
of Conseiller Broussel (1848), by order of Anne of Austria; 72. *Terburg*,
Karel du Jardin; 8. *Lombard School*, Study of a head; 43. *D. de Heem*,
Flowers, fruit, and birds; 4. *Badalocchio* (?), St. Jerome; *Barrias*, Helen
taking refuge at the altar of Vesta; 50. *N. Maes*, A Protestant minister;
Hyon, The flag; 92. *L. Rousseau*, Still-life; 94. *Blondel*, Triumph of Religion
over Atheism; 188. *Renoux*, Landscape; *Verhulst*, Court dame of the First
Empire; 212. *School of Fra Bartolommeo*, Holy Family. — 167. *Le Nain*,
Old woman; *Roux*, Thomas Aquinas; 189. *Rigaud*, Louis XIV. — *Glaize*,
The Foolish Virgins; 44. *Huysmans*, Forest; *Lair*, Punishment of Prome-
theus; *Drolling*, Parting of Hecuba and Polyxena; 41. *Franck the Elder*, Por-
traits, supposed to be of himself and his family; 60. *Van der Plas*, Portrait
of himself; 54. *Van Mieris*, Bacchante and satyr; 40. *Van Falens*, Start for
the hunt; *Ulmann*, Etienne Marcel and two other victims of the partisans
of the Dauphin in 1358, lying assassinated at the door of a church in
Paris; 68. *Rubens*, Departure of Adonis (the landscape by Brueghel); 29.
Ribera, Death of Cato of Utica; *J. Vernet*, Italian landscape; 39. *Van Dyck* (?),
Study of a head; 58. *Van Miereveit*, Portrait; *H. Motte*, Vercingetorix. —
Room III. Natural History collection, specially rich in birds. — Room IV,
on the other side: 21. *Tintoretto*, Annunciation; *Grateyrolle*, The Semailles.
— *French School*, Mdlle. de la Vallière; *Dagnan*, Boulevard St. Martin at
Paris; *Renoux*, St. Etienne-du-Mont at Paris; 139. *Huet*, Landscape; 12. *G.
Poussin*, Flight into Egypt; 69. *Teniers the Younger*, Portrait; *J. Ouvrié*,
Château of Pierrefonds; 106. *Daurats*, Interior of the Cathedral at Albi;
5. *Guercino*, Dædalus and Icarus; *Van Craesbeke*, 34. Beggar, 35. Portrait;
64. *Early School of Rubens*, Martyrdom of St. Catharine; 72. *Van der Werff*,
Queen Henrietta of England; 10. *Carlo Dolci*, Angel holding a lily; 45.
Hobbema, Landscape; 194. *Santerre*, Girl at a window; 87. *Le Brun*, Portrait; *De Troy*, Jason and the bull; 37. *Van Dyck*, Pietà; 61. *C. Poelenburg*,
Amazon asleep; 157. *Largillière*, Portrait of La Bruyère; 18. *Giulio Romano*,
The armed dwarf. — There are also some sculptures, including the Battle
of the Centaurs and the Lapithae, in bronze, by *Barye*; a Virgin, also in
bronze, the last work of *Crozatier*. — Room V: rich collection of lace-
work, guipures, etc. The manufacture of lace is the chief industry of
the district, employing upwards of 100,000 women.

The Rue Porte-Aiguière, opposite the Fontaine Crozatier, leads
to the *Hôtel de Ville*, an uninteresting building of the 18th century.

Continuing straight on from the other side, we reach a small square, whence we see on the right, at the end of a steep street, the —

CATHEDRAL OF NOTRE-DAME. This church is very singular in its general character, and particularly so in its arrangement, certain peculiarities in which are quite unique. It dates chiefly from the 11th and 12th centuries. The church is approached by a grand staircase which has 60 steps outside, 42 under the great vaulted porch beneath the actual nave of the church, and 32 on the side, to the right. Formerly this staircase went straight on, crossing the pavement of the nave and joining the transept, in front of the choir, in such a way that the faithful might see the officiating priest, it is said, from the steps outside. The great *Portal* comprises three semicircular arches opening to the *Porch*, above is some smaller arcading; then three windows, at the end of the nave, and three gables, those at the sides extending beyond the roof and open. Noteworthy, too, in this church is the mixture of white and black stone which is a characteristic decoration of the churches of Auvergne. Under the porch is a small chapel with traces of paintings. Two of the steps bear the following inscription of the 11th cent.: 'Ni caveas crimen, caveas contingere limen; Nam regina Poli vult sine sorde coli'. The flight of steps to the left, under the porch, leads to the *Cloister*, by visiting which at once we avoid retracing our steps. It is partly enclosed by a fine Romanesque railing, which the verger will open, though it may be sufficiently well seen without his aid. The most ancient part of this fine erection dates from the 9th or even the 8th cent. and has lately been restored. Its chief features are the little columns and the splendid cornice, adorned with heads of men and beasts. The building to the W., with machicolations, is the remnant of a 13th cent. fortress.

The *Interior* of the Cathedral presents a nave and aisles with six domes in the Byzantine style, a small transept with a lantern over the centre, galleries, and small double chapels at the ends, a square choir, and a kind of apse under the tower (see below). On the high altar is a small modern black statue of the Virgin, not less venerated than the one that preceded it, destroyed in 1793. The votive offerings hung up on the pillars of the choir indicate the character of the prevalent devotion. At the farther side, on the wall of the tower, is a noteworthy fresco of the end of the 13th cent., removed from the cloister (see above) and restored; its chief subject is Christ between the Virgin and St. John.

Making our exit by a door at the end of the left aisle we find ourselves under the *N. Portal*, with a very slightly pointed arch.

The *S. Portal (Porche du For)*, on the other side of the tower, is very remarkable. It forms a curious kind of porch, each side presenting a round arch, connected with the others only at three points. The *Tower*, one of the rare examples of Transitional clock-towers still extant, has seven stages with Romanesque arches, plain and

trefoil-headed, intermingled with pointed arches. It dates mainly
from the end of the 13th century.

Adjoining the S. portal is the *Bishop's Palace*. From the small
square in front of it there is a fine view.

Beside the N. portal are a *Baptistery* of the 11th cent., including
some remains of a Roman edifice, and a *Renaissance Chapel* ('So-
cietas Gonfalonis', 1584), decorated in the interior by artists of the
district (apply to concierge of the Bishop's Palace). A lane which
passes between them leads to the approach to the Rocher de Corneille
(10 c.).

The **Rocher de Corneille**, which forms the summit of Mont
Anis, is a mass of volcanic breccia, rising to a peak 420 ft. above
the lower town and 2480 ft. above the level of the sea. We reach
it by a succession of stairs hewn in the rock. At the top was erected
in 1860 a *Statue of Notre-Dame de France*, 52 ft. in height, on a
pedestal of 20 ft. It was designed by Bonnassieux, and is made
with more than 200 Russian cannons, taken at Sebastopol, like those
which lie around it on the platform. The Virgin is represented
standing erect, and holding the child Jesus who is blessing France.
Notwithstanding its colossal size, it is not in keeping with the
rock on which it stands. Visitors may ascend inside the statue to
the head. The openings made at various places permit us to enjoy
the splendid view afforded by the environs, with their grand amphitheatre of mountains, consisting chiefly of the Cévennes, amongst
which the Mézenc and the Gerbier-de-Jonc (p. 258) are specially
conspicuous to the S.E. In the suburb of Le Puy, to the N.W., rises
the Rock of St. Michel (see below). Farther away, to the left, is
Espaly and its Orgues (p. 258); to the right, the ruins of Polignac
(p. 258), etc. — On the platform of the Rocher de Corneille is the
bronze *Statue of Mgr. de Morlhon*, Bishop of Le Puy (d. 1862), also
by Bonnassieux.

In descending it is better to pass again by the cathedral than
to entangle oneself in the winding and ill-paved streets which
surround it.

The street at the foot of that which ascends to the cathedral
leads towards the western Boulevards, where we note, on the left as
we arrive, the low, massive *Tour Pannessac*, with machicolations,
forming the remains of a town-gateway of the 13th century. On the
next Boulevard is a *Statue of La Fayette* (1757-1834), by Iliolle.
— We descend by the Boulevard at the side of the tower.

St. Laurent, a church of the 14th cent., in the lower part of the
town, near the Borne, contains the *Tomb of Bertrand du Guesclin*
(d. 1380), with the statue of the famous warrior. To the left of the
entrance are some Gothic fonts.

The street on this side of the church leads to the base of a rock
(280 ft.), similar to the Rocher de Corneille but even more picturesque, on which stands the *Church of St. Michel-d'Aiguilhe*. It is

reached by a succession of stairs with 277 steps (10 c., paid to the 'lessee'). This church, or rather chapel, is an architectural curiosity. dating from 962-84. The plan is very irregular. It forms a sort of oval, the chancel occupying the end to the right of the entrance, while in front of this chancel is a small central aisle, inclosed with very low pillars and surrounded by a small aisle. The portal is adorned with curious bas-reliefs. Opposite to the entrance stands an isolated tower, of the same style as that of the cathedral; the upper part is less ancient than the church.

In the suburb, a little way off in front of the rock, is an old 12th century chapel of the knights-templar, baptistery, or funeral chapel called the *Temple of Diana.*

Excursions. — The following are the principal of the numerous excursions that may be made in the neighbourhood of Le Puy.

To Espaly, Polignac, etc. Espaly lies fully 1/2 M. to the W., Polignac 3 M. to the N.W. The road crosses the Borne beyond the Church of St. Laurent and ascends for a considerable distance, leaving on the right. halfway, a direct path to Polignac, by which we may return. — Espaly, to which another road on the left leads, is a large village, above which we may see from the road, a curious mass of basalt, showing fine columns, called from their arrangement the *Orgues d'Espaly.* — Polignac, situated farther to the right of the road to St. Paulien and La Chaise-Dieu, is celebrated for the imposing ruins of the **Castle* of the same name, on a rocky plateau which overlooks it and on which are found Roman remains, seen in the midst of the other ruins. The plateau is encircled by a battlemented enceinte in a tolerably good state of preservation. The road which ascends to it begins near the church. The remains of the castle, properly so called, dating from the 12-15th cent., are scanty. The guide (gratuity) gives the necessary explanations. The principal parts are the keep, square and very high (14th cent.), and a round tower (13th cent.), which together give to the whole a picturesque appearance.

The second route mentioned above is in the valley on the other side of Polignac; it skirts the high ground on the right.

The road is continued across a very broken country. At 8 1/2 M. it is joined by the road from Darsac (p. 259) and 2 M. farther reaches *Nolhac.* — 13 M. *St. Paulien,* a small town near which is the site of *Ruessium,* the capital of the Vellavi or Velauni. The *Church* (11th cent.) occupies the site of an antique building, and other antiquities have been found. To the left is seen the *Mont de Bar* (3825 ft.), a volcanic mountain, ascended in 1/2 hr. from *Allègre,* 8 M. from St. Paulien, whence it is reached by a good road which joins our road 8 M. farther on, 4 M. from La Chaise-Dieu. — 20 M. *St. Just-près-Chomelix.* Here, and again at (26 1/2 M.) *Chomborne,* our road bends to the left. — 31 M. *La Chaise-Dieu* (p. 234).

To the Mézenc via Le Monastier. A carriage-road leads from Le Puy to (23 M.) Les Estables; thence a bridle-path to the (1 1/2 hr.) Mézenc. A public conveyance plies from Le Puy to (13 M.) Le Monastier (3 hrs.; fare 1 fr. 60 c.). — We proceed to the E. At (2 1/2 M.) *Charensac* we cross the Loire. The Mézenc road turns to the right at (3 M.) *Brives.* To the left is the *Mont-Dore* (2740 ft.), on which stands an old 12th cent. abbey of the Premonstratensians. Farther on, to the right, on another eminence is the fine *Château de Bouzols,* the oldest part of which dates from the 11th century. — 7 1/2 M. *Arsac.* At (8 M.) *La Terrasse* are some artificial grottoes, once used as dwellings. — 13 M. Le Monastier (*Hôt. Ponsonnaille*), with 3759 inhab., owes its name to a monastery of which the church remains, partly Romanesque in style. — The road (carr. 10 fr.) proceeds to the S.E. via *Freycenet-la-Tour* to (23 M.) *Les Estables* (Testud, etc.), a village of some size, on the W. side of the Mézenc. — The Mézenc (5750 ft.) is a volcanic mountain, isolated and precipitous, except to the W.,

the side next Les Estables. Its slopes afford excellent pasturage. From the
top there is a fine panorama extending westwards to the mountains of
the Cantal, northwards over the mountains on both sides of the Loire,
and the valley of that river, eastwards to the mountains of Dauphiné
and Savoy, as far as Mont Blanc, and southwards to the Cévennes, amongst
which the Gerbier-de-Jonc (see below) is conspicuous, and to the western
extremity of the Alps, where, on the horizon, Mont Ventoux rears itself.
— About 4½ hrs. from the Mézenc is the *Gerbier-de-Jonc*, another volcanic
mountain on which the Loire rises. Its height has been only 5090 ft.
since a landslip which occurred in 1821; before that it was 5610 ft.

Beyond Le Puy the railway turns to the S., commanding on the
right a fine view of the picturesque town. We cross the Borne and
ascend its valley for some distance. From (98 M.) *Borne* an omnibus
plies to (3 M.) St. Paullen (p. 258), and from (102 M.) *Darsac*, an
omnibus plies to La Chaise-Dieu (see p. 234). We traverse a tunnel,
1⅛ M. long, in the Monts du Velay, beyond which the line attains
its highest point (3680 ft.), afterwards descending into the valley of
the Allier, with magnificent views to the right, extending as far as the
Monts Dôme (pp. 243, 245). — 107 M. *Fix-St. Geneys*; 110 M. *La
Chaud*, beyond which are a tunnel and a wide sweep to the S., round
the *Mont-Briançon* (3420 ft.). — 118 M. *Rougeac*; 122 M. *St. Georges-
d'Aurac*. Here we join the line from Nîmes to Clermont-Ferrand,
which we follow viâ *Paulhaguet*, *Frugières-le-Pin*, and *Brioude*,
to (143 M.) **Arvant** (see p. 224).

The line which crosses the Cantal is also very interesting and
its construction has demanded much engineering skill. It attains
an elevation of 3800 ft. in the tunnel of Le Lioran (p. 260). The
best views are to the right. — 146 M. *Lempdes*, on the *Alagnon*. The line
ascends the picturesque and in places very narrow valley of that river,
with an extensive retrospect to the right. Seven bridges and five
tunnels are passed. 154 M. *Blesle*, on the right, at the foot of columnar basaltic rocks ('orgues'). — 158 M. *Massiac*; 162 M. *Molom-
piae*. Fine view into a valley on the left. The river frets along on
the right; and on the same side are the ruins of a castle. Before
and after (167 M.) *Ferrières* are tunnels. Beyond a rocky gorge appear
some ruins on the right; to the left is the line to St. Flour, etc.

173 M. **Neussargues** *(Buffet-Hotel)*. Line to *St. Flour*, *Millau*,
and *Béziers* (Causses de la Lozère), see R. 42.

We next perceive, at a distance on the right, the ruins of the
Château de Merdogne. On the same side there is a fine view. We
recross the Alagnon.

178½ M. **Murat** *(Hôtel Gauvain)*, an ill-built town with 3200
inhab., at the foot of a basaltic rock (⅛ hr.; view) crowned by a
colossal statue of the Virgin. — *Bredons*, opposite Murat, on the
other side of the line, has a fine Romanesque church (11th cent.)
on a rock.

On the left the Plomb du Cantal appears (p. 260): on the
right, the *Château de Massebeau*. The valley contracts as we enter
the region of the *Monts du Cantal* and the line rapidly ascends,

crossing a dozen bridges or viaducts, running through a short tunnel, and overlooking deep valleys, with rocky or wooded gorges, torrents, and cascades (best views on the right). The nearest large peak is the *Puy Griou*; farther to the right, the *Puy Mary*, etc. (see below).

186 M. *Le-Lioran* (Hôt. du Cantal), a good centre for excursions.

The PLOMB DU CANTAL may be ascended hence in less than 2 hrs., 3 hrs. there and back; guide 5 fr. We follow the high road as far as a tunnel, where we take the stony path to the right, which bends to the left before a wood. We then direct our course towards a 'buron' or herdsman's hut which we reach in less than 1 hr.; and thence scale the summit on the N. side.

The *Plomb du Cantal (6095 ft.) is volcanic, like all the mountains of Auvergne, and culminates in an isolated cone, whence radiate a number of valleys. The view from the summit is said to command a circumference of 150 M. In the neighbourhood, to the S., is the *Puy Gros* (5245 ft.), to the N.W. the *Puy Griou* (5680 ft.), farther off, the *Puy Mary* (5800 ft.), the *Puy Chavaroche* (5720 ft.), the *Puy Violent* (5280 ft.), etc., all forming part of the same group. To the N. are the Monts Dore (p. 250), with the Pic de Sancy, and the Monts Dôme (p. 245); to the E. the Cévennes and the Alps; to the S.S.E. the Pyrenees.

The *Puy Mary* (5800 ft.), the peak most frequently visited next to the Plomb, may be ascended in 4 hrs. from Le Lioran. — The ascent of the *Puy Griou* (5600 ft.), which commands the most interesting view of the Cantal group, takes only 1-1^1/$_2$ hr., by the old route through fine pine-woods, to the W. of the Signal du Lioran (4490 ft.).

Beyond a viaduct we now enter the *Tunnel du Lioran*, 1^1/$_4$ M. long, in which the line attains its culminating point (3800 ft.), and by which we pass from the basin of the Loire to that of the Garonne, where we descend the valley of the *Cère*. Above the railway is the *Col de Sagnes* (4100 ft.), between the *Puy Lioran* (4660 ft.) and the *Plomb du Cantal* (see above). A road also passes through a tunnel here, nearly 1 M. long, always lighted. — We cross a viaduct, 100 ft. high, and beyond a short tunnel, three more viaducts, nearly as high. To the right is the Puy Griou, to the left the Plomb du Cantal. — 190 M. *St. Jacques-des-Blats* (3250 ft.). The village (Inn) lies ^{1}/$_2$ M. distant in the valley.

The Plomb du Cantal may be ascended from this point also, in 5-6 hrs. there and back; guide 5 fr. We cross the Cère and the railway above the station, and ascend towards the N.E. (short-cuts by the footpaths) over pastures, with herdsman's huts ('burons'). In 20 min. we reach the huts of *St. Erral*, and in 35 min. more the *Grange du Sarret*. Thence we proceed to the left to the (50 min.) 'buron' of the *Pré Delbos*, which we leave on the right (fine view), and in 1 hr. more we reach the 'buron' of *Prossdal* at the base of the crest, by which we climb in ^{1}/$_2$ hr. to the summit of the Plomb (see above).

Beyond St. Jacques the route is not less interesting. The Cère flows through splendid gorges, along which the railway is carried by works of great engineering skill, including six viaducts and two short tunnels, with a fine cascade between the first and second. Behind us, to the right, appears the Puy Chavaroche, while on the left we skirt the Puy Gros. — Beyond (194 M.) *Thiézac*, we pass through three more tunnels, and traverse fine wooded gorges, after which the valley widens. Extensive view to the right.

196½ M. **Vic-sur-Cère** (*Hôtel du Pont*, near the station; *Coutel*), beautifully situated, with remains of fortifications. In the environs are chalybeate and aërated springs, used chiefly for drinking. — 190½ M. *Polminhac* with an old castle to the right, and a modern château to the left. Farther on are several other old castles. We now enter the plain. Beyond (206½ M.) *Arpajon* the line turns to the N. On the right is Aurillac.

209 M. **Aurillac** (*Buffet*; *Hôtel St. Pierre*, at Le Gravier, far from the station; *de Bordeaux*, pens. 7½-8½ fr., *des Trois-Frères*, Place du Palais-de-Justice), on the *Jordanne*, with 15,824 inhab., is the chief town of the department of the *Cantal*.

The street which descends from the station leads to the Place du Palais-de-Justice, whence is seen, on the right, the pretty Renaissance tower of *Notre-Dame-des-Neiges*. Hence the Avenue du Pont leads to *Le Gravier*, a square decorated with a bronze *Statue of General Delzons* (1775-1812), with bas-reliefs (1883), and, farther on, a *Statue of Gerbert* (Pope Sylvester II.), of Aurillac, also in bronze and with bas-reliefs, by David d'Augers.

The *Church of St. Géraud*, which we reach by turning to the right, into the Rue du Buis, is a 15th cent. building, recently continued and with a still unfinished tower. It was dependent on an abbey founded in the 9th cent. by its patron saint, born in the château of Aurillac. It has finely reticulated vaulting. In a chapel on the left are some paintings of the 16th cent., and behind the pulpit a Death of St. Francis Xavier, attributed to Zurbaran.

From the door of the church we may see, on an eminence, the *Château*, in great part rebuilt and transformed into a normal school. — The Rue du Monastère and the Rue du Consulat, on the right, lead into the middle of the town. At the end of the Rue du Consulat is the *Hôtel des Consuls*, a 16th cent. house, with turrets and a fine Gothic gateway in the street on the left.

The *Collège*, in the vicinity, contains a small *Museum*, open to the public on Sun. and Thurs. from 1 to 4, and on others days also to strangers.

A single large room, on the first floor, contains paintings and sculptures. On the right. 0. *Dutch School*, Landscape; 35. *Gourdet*, The Steward; 73. *School of Giotto*, Crucifixion; 80. *Syrouy*, Prodigal son; 71. *Gennari*, Virgin suckling the Infant Jesus; 84. *Cassolini*, Virgin and Child; 85. *Manetti*, Saint; 68. *Lagrende*, Fidelity of a Satrap; 82. *Vagrez*, Education of Achilles; 12. *Monginot*, The Rent; 83. *Callias*, Devotion of the Chevalier d'Assas; 70. *Sir Peter Lely* (*Van der Faes*), Portrait; 14. *Largillière*, Portrait; etc. In the middle, *Manglier*, Fortune, in bronze; *Boisseau*, Daughter of Celuta mourning for her child, in marble.

Returning to the Rue des Consuls, we proceed to the right, by the Rue Marchand, to the Place de l'Hôtel-de-Ville, and straight on thence to the Palais de Justice.

From Aurillac to *Montluçon* (Paris), see p. 228; to *Brive*, p. 229.

214 M. *Ytrac.* On the right the view extends as far as the Monts Dore, dominated by the Puy de Sancy (p. 250).

217¹/₂ M. *Viescamp-sous-Jallès* is the junction for the line to St. Denis-près-Martel (p. 107). Railway to Montluçon, see p. 108. — 219 M. *La Chapelle-Viescamp*, beyond which is a high viaduct, the last over the valley of the Cère. On the right the view is fine and extensive. — 224¹/₂ M. *Le Rouget*, whence we descend into the wild gorge of the *Moulègre*, in which we successively come to four bridges, four tunnels, and three more bridges. Beyond (231 M.) *Boisset* we pass a viaduct, cross the Moulègre three times, and pass by a tunnel into the valley of the *Rance*, where a fine view presents itself to the left. Then follow rocky gorges, two viaducts, a tunnel, and four bridges. — 237 M. *Maurs*, a small commercial town, beyond which is another bridge and a viaduct over the Rance, whence we pass through a short tunnel into the pretty valley of the Célé, crossing the stream twice. — 241¹/₂ M. *Bagnac*, followed by another bridge, a short tunnel and a last bridge over the Célé. To the right is —

249 M. *Figeac*, on the line from Paris and Limoges to Toulouse (p. 113).

41. From Clermont-Ferrand to Nîmes,
viâ the Cévennes.

189 M. RAILWAY in 8¹/₂-12 hrs. (fares 34 fr. 25, 23 fr. 15, 15 fr. 15 c.). — This interesting route, which forms part of the direct line from Paris to Nîmes, should be taken by day. The views are for the most part better on the right than on the left. This line traverses 108 tunnels and 32 viaducts. — From Paris to Nîmes viâ Nevers and Clermont-Ferrand, 450 M., RAILWAY in 17¹/₂-24 hrs. (fares 81 fr. 30, 55 fr., 35 fr. 85 c.); viâ Lyons and Tarascon (see *Baedeker's South-Eastern France*), 482 M. in 12¹/₂-26 hrs. (fares 68 fr. 90, 60 fr. 5, 39 fr. 20 c.).

Clermont-Ferrand, see p. 238. — Thence to (58 M.) *St. Georges-d'Aurac*, see p. 224. The railway again approaches the Allier, which it crosses. At (62¹/₂ M.) *Langeac* (4318 inhab.) travellers from Nîmes change carriages for the Le Puy line (R. 35). We now follow the river, the valley of which increases in interest, and the tunnels and viaducts are both numerous and remarkable. Beyond (66¹/₂ M.) *Chanteuges* on both sides are basaltic mountains, though afterwards granite becomes the prevailing rock. Then follow a tunnel and a viaduct, and after (71 M.) *St. Julien-des-Chazes*, 2 viaducts, 3 bridges (one of them over the Allier) and 10 tunnels. 77 M. *Monistrol-d'Allier* (10 viaducts and 12 tunnels); 83 M. *Alleyras* (12 tunnels and 6 viaducts); 92¹/₂ M. *Chapeauroux* (7 tunnels and 3 viaducts); 97 M. *Jonchères*, with a ruined 15th century castle, on the left (5 tunnels and 5 viaducts).

104 M. *Langogne* (Buffet; Hotel), a town with 3650 inhab., ¹/₂ M. to the S.

An OMNIBUS plies hence to Mende, 31 M. to the S.W., in 4³/₄ hrs. (fares 9 fr. 75, 8 fr. 50 c.); see also below under Villefort. The country traversed is mountainous, but monotonous, barren, and bare. We pass near (12¹/₂ M.) *Châteauneuf-de-Randon*, a small town, during the siege of

which Bertrand du Guesclin was killed in 1380. The English governor,
who had promised to surrender, kept his word and placed the keys upon
Du Guesclin's coffin. — *Mende*, see p. 266.

About 8½ M. to the N. E. of Langogne (no public conveyance) is the
little watering-place of *Montbel* (Hotel).

Then again five bridges, the second and the last across the Allier,
and two tunnels; and beyond (112 M.) *Luc* the Allier is again crossed
twice. — 116½ M. *La Bastide* (Hotel), which is to be connected
by rail with Mende (27½ M.; p. 266).

About 5½ M. to the N.E. is *St. Laurent-les-Bains*, a small town surrounded by mountains. It possesses two thermal mineral springs, known
to the Romans, and two bath-establishments. The road thither passes
near the *Trappe de Notre-Dame-des-Neiges*, which is worth a visit.

We now cross the Allier for the last time, and entering a tunnel
(½ M. long) under the watershed of the *Cévennes*, pass from the
basin of the Loire into that of the Rhone. The route here attains
its summit-level (3375 ft.), having risen over 1600 ft. between this
point and Langeac (54 M.). It then descends still more rapidly through
eight tunnels, between which we obtain fine glimpses of the country.
— Beyond (122½ M.) *Prévenchères* we traverse twelve tunnels and
galleries (the third nearly 1 M. long) and six viaducts or bridges.
The last viaduct, 230 ft. high, over the Allier, consists of two stories,
across the lower of which runs the road to Mende (see below). —
129 M. *Villefort* (1980 ft.; Buffet; hotels; guide).

An Omnibus plies twice a day to *Mende* (p. 266), 36½ M. to the W.N.W.,
in about 7 hrs. (fares 8 fr. 75, 7 fr. 75 c.). For pedestrians Villefort is a
better starting-point than Langogne (see above). The road first runs to
the N., but beyond a short tunnel turns to the W. into the valley of the
Allier, where it crosses the viaduct mentioned above. To the N. is the
Montagne du Goulet (4890 ft.), to the S. *Mont Lozère* (see below). We pass
some groves of old chestnut-trees and two hamlets.

7½ M. *Allier* (Inns), with an old castle. We then mount to the *Col
du Bleymard* (3855 ft.) from which we descend into the valley of the Lot.
Near *Le Bleymard* (3470 ft.; Inn), a village with 865 inhab., which we leave
to the left, we cross the track ('draye'), used from time immemorial by
the flocks of Provence on their way to their summer-pastures on the
central plateau. To the Pic de Finiels, see below. — 19½ M. *St. Jean-de-
Bleymard* (Hôtel St. Jean; Teissier, clean; carriages for hire), a hamlet,
about 500 yds. from the village, on the *Lot*, whose source is 2½ M. to the
N. We descend the right bank to (22½ M.) *St. Jean-du-Tournel*, with a
ruined castle, under which the road passes by means of a tunnel. —
23½ M. **Bagnols-les-Bains** (1810 ft.; *Grand-Hôtel; Hôtel des Bains*, etc.), a
village on the Lot, with six mineral springs (68°-107° Fahr.), known to
the Romans, as is shown by the remains of various buildings. Numerous
excursions may be made in the neighbourhood. — Beyond (30 M.) *Ste.
Hélène* we cross the Lot, and beyond a small col rejoin the route from
Langogne (p. 262). — 32 M. *Badaroux*. — 36½ M. *Mende* (p. 266).

An easy and interesting excursion (2 days) may be made from Villefort to the S.W., to the **Mont Lozère** group, including the *Roc de Malpertus*, the *Pic de Finiels*, and the *Signal des Laubies*. The first day's expedition takes 8 hrs., the second, 7½ hrs. An early start should be made
on account of the heat. From Le Bleymard we may return to Villefort
or go on to Bagnols and Mende.

1st day. We pass below the railway and proceed to the S. along the
right bank of a brook which we cross at (1¾ M.) *Palhères*. Beyond this
village we turn to the left into a bridle-path which leaves to the right
two cart-roads, and runs parallel to the ravine, which it overlooks. From

the (2 hrs.) poor village of *Costeilades* (3435 ft.) a child or herdsman should be taken as guide at least as far as the *Source of the Tarn*, 1¹/₄ hr. higher up. There we turn to the W., and in ³/₄ hr. reach the *Roc de Malpertus* (5520 ft.) which affords a fine view, including the Aigoual to the S., the mountains of Aubrac and Margeride to the N., and the valleys of the Lot and Aveyron to the W. We descend to the S.W. (not too much in the direction of the Tarn), viâ *Camarquès*, *l'Hôpital*, and *Le Masel*, to *Pont-de-Montvert* (Hôtel des Cévennes), a market-town on the Tarn, and on the road from Genolhac (18 M.; see below) to Florac (15 M.; p. 271). Here in 1703, after the revocation of the Edict of Nantes, broke out the Protestant insurrection known as the War of the Camisards, from the shirts ('camise') worn over their clothes by the insurgents. The town is still almost entirely Protestant.

2nd day. We ascend first to the N. of Pont-de-Montvert, by a ravine, to (1³/₄ M.) *Champlong-de-Lozère*, (¹/₂ M.) *Pré-Soulayran* (3908 ft.), and (1 M.) *Finiels*, about 1¹/₂ hr. from Pont and halfway to the *Col de Finiels* (short-cut for walkers). To the W. is the *Pic de Finiels* (5585 ft.), whence there is a fine view to the S. and E. From the *Signal des Laubies* (5445 ft.), ³/₄ hr. to the W., the view includes not only the whole chain of the Cévennes, but also the plateaux and the gigantic ramparts of the Causses. We return to the col to gain the new Bleymard road, or we may descend direct to the N. by the sheep-track ('draye'; see p. 263). — *Le Bleymard*, see p. 263.

Beyond Villefort the country is still very broken, and we enjoy beautiful glimpses of the Cévennes. Tunnels and viaducts are still numerous. — 131 M. *Concoules* (6 tunnels). Beyond (138 M.) *Genolhac* are four viaducts, the third of which is curved and 150 ft. high, and commands a fine retrospective view to the right, and six tunnels. — 142 M. *Chamborigaud*, followed by three tunnels, the first of which is nearly a mile long. Beyond (144 M.) *Ste. Cécile-d'Andorge* we pass through four more tunnels, and then quit the Cévennes, and enter the region of the mulberry. — 147¹/₂ M. *La Levade* and (150 M.) *La Pise* belong to the *Grand' Combe*, a commune of 13,140 inhab., engaged in the important coal-mines of the district. — Before and after (156 M.) *Tamaris*, with its briquette-works, we traverse a tunnel.

158 M. **Alais** (*Buffet*; *Hôt. du Luxembourg*), to the right, a town of 24,356 inhab., on the left bank of the Gardon. It is the centre of an important coal-field, and carries on an extensive trade in silk, glass, bricks and tiles, etc. In the Place St. Sebastien, to the right of the Avenue de la Gare, is a bronze statue by G. Pech, of the celebrated chemist *J. B. Dumas* (1800-1884); and in the *Bosquet*, or public park is a bust of *La Fare-Alais* (1791-1846), the Cevenole poet. The 18th cent. *Cathedral* includes some remains of the 12th century.

FROM ALAIS TO QUISSAC (*Le Vigan*), 19¹/₂ M. This branch-line diverges from the Nîmes line at *Mas-des-Gardies* (see below), and enters the valley of the Gardon d'Anduze. — From (10¹/₂ M.) *Lezan* a branch-line runs to (3¹/₂ M.) *Anduze*, an old town with 3900 inhabitants. — 19¹/₂ M. *Quissac*, etc., see *Baedeker's South-Eastern France*.

From Alais to *L'Ardoise*, 35 M., see *Baedeker's South-Eastern France*.

161 M. *St. Hilaire*; 164¹/₂ M. *Mas-des-Gardies*. Branch-line to Quissac, see above. — 166¹/₂ M. *Vézenobres*; 167 M. *Ners*. To the right is a 12th cent. keep. 170 M. *Bourdiran*; 171¹/₂ M. *Nozières*. Branch-line to Uzès. 173 M. *St. Géniès*; 177 M. *Fons*; 182 M.

Mas-de-Ponge. Farther on, to the right, is the Tour Magne on a hill beneath which we pass by means of a tunnel. Our line joins the railways from Tarascon and from Le Teil, and the train backs into the station.

189 M. **Nîmes** *(Buffet)*, see *Baedeker's South-Eastern France.*

42. From Clermont-Ferrand to Béziers,
viâ St. Flour and Millau.

240 M. Railway in 11 hrs. (fares 43 fr. 55, 39 fr. 45, 19 fr. 20 c.). — From Paris to Béziers the distance by this line is 500 M. (express in 20¹/₂ hrs.) while it is 532 M. viâ Limoges and Rodez and 553 or 575 M. viâ Limoges and Toulouse. — This route will be still farther shortened by the opening of a direct section beyond Arvant (see the map). At present, however, there is no express train on this route, and no through connection except by the morning train from Clermont.

To (37 M.) *Arrant,* and thence to (30 M.; 67 M. in all) *Neussargues,* see p. 259. — The railway leaves the valley of the Alagnon and ascends rapidly to the S. E., entering a tunnel over ³/₄ M. long. To the right are the mountains of the Cantal (p. 260). — 71¹/₂ M. *Talizat* (3265 ft.); 76¹/₂ M. *Andelat.*

79 M. **St. Flour** (2900 ft.; *Hôtel de l'Europe* or *Aurlac*), a poorly-built town of 5308 inhab., occupies a remarkable situation on the verge of a plateau, which presents a steep face rising many hundred feet above the valley in which the railway runs. The road (2 M.; short-cuts for pedestrians) leads to the W. from the station, and skirting a height partly composed of basaltic pillars, ends in the square with the chief hotel. The seat of a bishopric, St. Flour contains a *Cathedral* of the 14-15th cent., dedicated to St. Florus, the apostle of the district. In the interior are fine modern stained-glass windows and other works of art.

An Omnibus (3-4 fr.) plies hence in 3¹/₂ hrs. to (20¹/₂ M.) **Chaudesaigues** *(Hôtel du Midi* or *Ginisty)*, a small watering-place to the S., in the valley of a tributary of the Truyère. It has five thermal springs and three cold chalybeate springs. The former, though not highly charged with mineral ingredients, are probably the hottest springs in France (above 177° Fahr.), and one of them is so copious that its water is used even to warm the houses in winter. Chaudesaigues is only 16¹/₂ M. from the station of St. Chély (see below), viâ (8 M.) *Fournels.*

We cross a viaduct. To the left appears the *Montagne de la Margeride* (5100 ft.). — About 2³/₄ M. beyond (86¹/₂ M.) *Ruines* we cross the famous Viaduc de Garabit.

The *Garabit Viaduct, spanning the gorge of the *Truyère,* one of the largest constructions of the kind, is 607 yds. long and 400 ft. high. Its central span of 542 ft. was at one time among the widest in the world, but it has been far out-distanced by the Forth Bridge (1890), with two spans of 1710 and 1700 ft., and the Brooklyn Suspension Bridge (1888), with a span of 1596 ft. The two widest spans of the Britannia Tubular Bridge are 460 ft. each. The Garabit Viaduct,

constructed by Boyer and Eiffel, should be viewed from below. It
is built of iron, with five reticulated piers, more than 200 ft. high,
supported on huge bases of solid masonry.

89 M. *Viaduc de Garabit Station*. The railway crosses the
broken plateaux of the Lozère and attains its highest point (3465 ft.)
before reaching St. Chély. Views to the right. — 92½ M. *Louba-
resse*; 97½ M. *Arcomie*. Then a tunnel.

101½ M. *St. Chély-d'Apcher* (3255 ft.; Hôtel Bardol), a little
town on an eminence to the left, unsuccessfully besieged by the
English in the Hundred Years'War (1362).

A DILIGENCE (3 fr.) plies in the season, in connection with the
10 a. m. train, to (18 M.) *Chaudesaigues* (p. 265). Another plies in the
season to (15½ M.) *La Chaldette*, a hamlet with a thermal establishment,
in a wooded district to the E. The road leads viâ (8½ M.) *Fournels*,
which is only 8 M. to the E. of Chaudesaigues (p. 265).

Farther on is a viaduct. To the right appear the *Monts d'Aubrac*
(4825 ft.).

108 M. *Aumont*; 113 M. *St. Sauveur-de-Peyre*. The best views
are now to the left. We pass a tunnel, over ¼ M. long, and the
stone *Viaduc de la Crueize*, 200 ft. high, beyond which are several
more tunnels and viaducts.

122 M. **Marvejols** (2234 ft.; *Hôtel de la Paix*), a town of 4672
inhab., on the Colagne, rebuilt in the 16th cent. after having been
almost entirely destroyed in the Religious Wars. Three gateways
still remain, though the rest of the fortifications have been converted
into a handsome boulevard. Dr. Prunières of Marvejols possesses a
valuable collection of pre-historic antiquities.

124 M. *Chirac*. — 125½ M. *Le Monastier*.

FROM LE MONASTIER TO MENDE, 18 M., railway in 50-55 min.
(fares 3 fr. 35, 2 fr. 25, 1 fr. 50 c.). The railway to Mende which is
to be extended to meet the main line from Clermont-Ferrand to
Nîmes (La Bastide, p. 263), crosses the *Colagne*, passes through a
tunnel, and ascends to the E. the winding gorge of the Lot, crossing
the stream before and after another tunnel. To the S., on the left
bank, is the *Causse de Sauveterre* (p. 270).

3 M. *Le Villard-Satelles*; 6 M. *Chanac*, a little town with a
ruined castle. Beyond (10½ M.) *Barjac* are two bridges, a tunnel,
a viaduct, and another tunnel. — 14 M. *Balsièges*. Routes to Ste.
Enimie and Ispagnac, see p. 272. Beyond Balsièges we·cross the
Lot twice more, on each side of a tunnel. To the right are the
ramparts of the Causse de Mende (see below), on which, above the
town, is the Hermitage of St. Privat (p. 267).

18 M. **Mende** (2425 ft.; *Gr. Hôt. de Paris*, Rue de la République,
R., L., & A. 2-3, B. ¾, déj. 2½, D. 3, omn. ¼-½ fr.; *Manse*, at
the entrance of the town), a badly built but pleasantly situated
town with 7878 inhab., was formerly the capital of the *Gévaudan*,
and is now the chief town of the department of the *Lozère* and the

seat of a bishopric. It stands on the left bank of the Lot, at the foot
of the *Causse de Mende* (3475 ft.), which raises its perpendicular
ramparts 1000 ft. above it. The *Cathedral*, originally of the 14th
cent., was rebuilt between 1600 and 1620, after having been partly
destroyed by the Calvinists. It has two towers dating from 1508-
1512, which are 280 and 210 ft. high respectively, the former having
an elegant spire. On the N.W. side is the *Préfecture*, an attractive
modern building. In front of the cathedral is the bronze statue, by
Dumont, of *Urban V.*, the 6th of the Avignon Popes, and a native
of the district. The Salle d'Asile contains a small *Musée Archéolo-
gique.* Above the town is the *Hermitage de St. Privat*, an ancient
and much frequented pilgrim-resort. We ascend (about $^3/_4$ hr.) by
a road diverging to the right from the upper part of the boulevard
passing in front of the Place de la Cathédrale.

Diligence to *Langogne* and *Villefort*, see p. 263; fares 3, 4 fr.; to *Bay-
nols* (p. 263), 1 fr. 70 c., 3 fr. — Routes to *Ste. Enimie*, see p. 272.

The main line to Béziers descends the winding gorge of the *Lot*,
which it crosses four times, passing through five tunnels. To the left
are the Causse de Sauveterre (p. 270), a lofty bridge, and a ruined
château. — 131$^1/_2$ M. *Banassac-la-Canourgue* (Inn). Hence to the
Cañon of the Tarn, see p. 273. — 137 M. *St. Laurent-d'Olt.* Two
short viaducts and a tunnel $^3/_4$ M. long. — 139$^1/_2$ M. *Campagnac.*

A diligence (1$^1/_2$ fr.) plies hence to (6 M.) St. Géniez, viâ the road
passing the N.E. end of the *Causse de Sévérac*, from which there is a fine
view of the Monts d'Aubrac (p. 377). Farther on we approach the *Gorges
du Lot.* — St. Géniez-d'Olt (*Hôtel Rouquette*), an important cloth-making
town of 3325 inhab., is picturesquely situated on the Lot. Mgr. de Frayssinous (1765-1842), orator and politician of the Restoration, a native of
the district, is commemorated by a monument in the church, erected
by the Comte de Chambord, whose tutor he was. — From St. Géniez
to (10$^1/_2$ M.) *Espalion*, see p. 120.

The railway crosses the W. end of the Causse de Sauveterre,
passing through two tunnels. 142 M. *Tarnesque.* Tunnel, $^1/_2$ M. long.

146$^1/_2$ M. **Sévérac-le-Château** (*Buffet; Hôtel Sévénié*), a town
with 3168 inhab., is commanded by a ruined castle, which existed
in the 13th century. — Railway to *Rodez* and *Capdenac*, see R. 17.

We now cross the *Aveyron*, which rises not far off, ascend an
incline, with a tunnel $^1/_2$ M. long, and descend again towards the
valley of the Tarn, through four tunnels and over a viaduct. —
159 M. *Quezayuel.* We skirt, on the left, the gorges of the Tarn
(p. 271). — 152 M. *Aguessac.* Road to Peyreleau (Tarn Cañon), see
p. 275. A 'courrier' meets the midday train.

166 M. **Millau.** — *Hotels.* Du Commerce, Place Mandarous, with café,
R., L., & A. 2$^1/_2$-5, déj. 3, D. 3$^1/_2$ fr.; De France, Boul. de la République,
R., L., & A. from 1$^1/_2$, déj. 2$^1/_2$-3 fr. — Diligences, see below.

Millau, the *Æmilianum Castrum* of the Romans, is a town with
17,429 inhab., situated to the left of the railway, on the right bank
of the Tarn. It is the capital of the arrondissement of Aveyron, the
richest in the entire Cévennes region. Having been in the 16th cent.

one of the principal strongholds of the Calvinists, it lost ground
after the Revocation of the Edict of Nantes. Its production of kid
gloves is considerable. The town itself is badly built and contains
little of interest beyond *Notre-Dame*, a church in the Romanesque
and Renaissance styles, with galleries in place of aisles, and a tower
(16-17th cent.) in the Tolosan style; the *Place de l'Hôtel-de-Ville*,
with galleries dating from the 12-15th cent.; a Gothic *Belfry*; and
the modern Romanesque *Church of St. François*.

For the route to *Peyreleau, Meyrueis, Montpellier-le-Vieux* (Gorges of
the Tarn; Causses), etc., see p. 276.

FROM MILLAU TO LE VIGAN (*La Roque-Ste. Marguerite*), 47 M., public
conveyances daily at 4 a. m. and 3 p. m., in about 4 hrs. (4 fr.) to St. Jean-
du-Bruel, where we change carriages for the second stage of the journey
(also 4 hrs.). On the return the conveyances start from St. Jean about
5 a. m. and 2 p. m. — To La Roque-Ste. Marguerite, 1³/₄ hr., back in 1 hr.
(fare 2 fr.). The road follows the *Valley of the Dourbie* (p. 276), which is
very picturesque. — 8¹/₂ M. *La Roque-Ste. Marguerite* (p. 276), at the foot
of the rocks of *Montpellier-le-Vieux* (p. 275). 12¹/₂ M. *St. Véran*, picturesquely situated among the rocks of the Causse Noir, at the end of the
grand *Ravine of St. Véran*. — 15¹/₂ M. *Gardies*, a hamlet with lignite
mines. 18¹/₂ M. *Cantobre*, curiously built against dolomite rocks resembling ruins.

20¹/₂ M. Nant (about 1570 ft.; *Hôtel Bousat*), a little town in a well-
watered and fertile valley, overlooked on the N. by the *Roc Nantais*
(2775 ft.), on the S. by the *Roc de St. Alban* (2630 ft.), and on the W. by
the Larzac heights. — 24¹/₂ M. St. Jean-du-Bruel (1705 ft.; *Hôtel Fassas*),
a bright little town, in a fertile valley. Walks to the *Moulin Bondon*, the
Château d'Algue, etc. — We here quit the valley of the Dourbie, which
turns to the N.W., and ascend along the Larzac. — 29¹/₂ M. *Sauclières*,
where we join the railway now being built from Tournemire (see below)
to Le Vigan. The road next descends in zigzags and crosses a valley. —
35¹/₂ M. *Alzon*, a village on the Vis, beyond which we pass through a
tunnel. — 39¹/₂ M. *Les Trois-Ponts*. About 2 M. to the left is *Aumessas*, in
a wooded valley. — 41¹/₂ M. *Arre*, a manufacturing village. — 42 M.
Bez-et-Esparon, at the mouth of a ravine, at the head of which is the
Château d'Assas. — 44¹/₂ M. *Molières*, on a hill. We cross the *Arre*. —
46¹/₂ M. *Arrée*, a picturesque summer-resort, near which are the *Bains de
Cauralet*. — 47 M. Le Vigan (*Hôtel des Voyageurs; du Midi*), a town of 5374
inhab., on the Arre, has hosiery and silk factories, and coal-mines. The
old *Gothic Bridge* and the bronze statues of the *Chevalier d'Assas* (d. 1760)
and of *Sergeant Triaire* (d. 1800), who blew up the fort of El-Arish (Egypt),
are noteworthy. — Railway from Le Vigan to (57¹/₂ M.) *Nîmes*, see *Baedeker's
South-Eastern France*.

We continue to follow the valley of the Tarn for a short distance
viâ the station of *Peyre*. The line crosses the Tarn, which it then
quits for the valley of the Cernon. To the left are the cliffs of the
Larzac, more extensive and wilder than the preceding causses. —
172¹/₂ M. *St. Georges-de-Luzençon*; 177 M. *St. Rome-de-Cernon*.

181 M. *Tournemire* (two small hotels), picturesquely situated
below the high cliffs of the Larzac.

About 1¹/₂ M. to the N.W. is **Roquefort**, celebrated for its cheeses.
These are mostly made in the environs of the place, of goats' and sheep's
milk, but acquire their excellence in the grottoes and rocky caves under
the village. The mould on the cheese is due to musty bread powdered
and mixed with the curds. The smell in the grottoes is rather strong.
Roquefort exports about 13 million lbs. of cheese, worth about 250,000*l*.

The *Larzac* is accessible from Tournemire by several paths, the best being that through the *Boulinengue Ravine*. There is a magnificent view from the plateau, of the valley of the Cernon and the Rouergue. This plateau is crossed by the line which is being constructed to Le Vigan.

A branch-railway runs from Tournemire to (9½ M.) St. Affrique (*Cheval-Vert*), a manufacturing and commercial town with 7223 inhab., on the Sorgues, overlooked by a curious rock. This town was one of the strongholds of the Calvinists, who successfully sustained a siege here in 1628. The line is to be prolonged to Albi (p. 118).

The gradients on the line are abrupt. 185 M. *St. Jean-et-St. Paul*; 188 M. *Lauglanet*; 191½ M. *Montpaon*. A tunnel a mile long. — 196½ M. *Ceilhes-Roqueronde*; 199½ M. *Les Cabrils*. Another tunnel of a mile, followed by two viaducts, between which is a short tunnel. On the left we overlook the valley of a tributary of the Orb. — 202½ M. *Joncels*; 205½ M. *Lunas*. Traversing a short tunnel, we enter the *Valley of the Orb*. Olive, almond, and fig trees begin to appear. — 207 M. *Le Bousquet-d'Orb*. Beyond (210 M.) *Latour* we traverse a tunnel. To the left is a long viaduct over the Orb, no longer traversed by passenger-trains.

212 M. **Bédarieux** (*Buffet; Hôtel du Midi*), a commercial town (6578 inhab.), with cloth-factories and tanneries, on the Orb.

Railway to *Castres* (Montauban) viâ *Lamalou, St. Pons*, etc., and continuation to *Montpellier*, see R. 13.

From Bédarieux to Graissessac (*Lacaune*), 8½ M., by a branch-railway diverging from the Neussargues line at (3½ M.) *Latour* and crossing a viaduct 165 ft. in height. — 5½ M. *Espace*. — 8½ M. *Graissessac* (*Hôtel du Commerce*), about 1 M. from the station, with 3000 inhab., has considerable mines of coal, iron, copper, and argentiferous lead. — An interesting road (public conveyances; 60 c.) leads from the station to (5½ M.) *St. Gervais-Ville* (p. 99) viâ the valley of the *Mare*, and thence to (23½ M.) *Lacaune* (5 fr.; p. 218), viâ *Murat-sur-Vèbre* (Hotel), a town on the Agout, with an old château.

Beyond Bédarieux the Béziers railway diverges to the left from that to Castres and from the valley of the Orb, and traverses a viaduct and three tunnels. — 219 M. *Faugères*. Line to Montpellier viâ Paulhan, see R. 13.

Three more short tunnels. — 224 M. *Laurens*; 228½ M. *Magalas*; 230 M. *Espondeilhan*; 232½ M. *Bassan*. — 233½ M. *Lieuran-Ribauté*, a station which owes the latter part of its name to the *Château de Ribauté* ('Ripa alta'), to the left. We pass beneath the line from Montpellier viâ Mèze, and, on the E. side of the town, join the Cette line.

240 M. *Béziers* (p. 93).

43. The Causses and the Cañon of the Tarn.

The Causses are, as their name indicates (Latin 'calx'), plateaux of Jurassic limestone, occurring in the Lozère and the neighbouring departments. The principal are the *Causse de Sauveterre*, *Causse Méjean* ('du Milieu'; p. 211), *Causse Noir* (p. 276), and the *Larzac* (see above). They are bounded by the valleys of the Lot, Tarn, Jonte, Dourbie, some of their tributaries and those of the Hérault. As plateaux they are not remarkable but are merely bare uplands 2500-3700 ft. above the sea, without water, and almost treeless, where scarcely anything beyond a little barley and oats will grow, and with a very scanty population. Here and there the general level is broken by 'Couronnes' ('crowns') or mounds; and at certain spots, particularly on the Causse Méjean, are 'avens' or chasms into which the rainfall sinks, to issue again in the copious springs of the gorges. There are also a number of dolmens or table-stones. — The gorges worn by the rivers are, on the contrary, exceedingly interesting, especially the *Cañon of the Tarn* (p. 271).

The Causses and the Cañon of the Tarn are now most conveniently explored from *Mende* or from *Banassac-la-Canourgue*, from which points a series of diligence-routes in connection with the trains have been organized for the summer months by the Midi Railway Co. Twenty-four hours' notice (reply paid advisable) must be given to the station-master, together with an indication of the route selected, and a preliminary instalment of 5 fr. Circular tickets may be obtained on application. — Little luggage should be taken on a visit to the Causses, but warm clothing should not be forgotten. — The most interesting part of the Cañon and Montpellier-le-Vieux may also still be visited from *Millau*.

a. From Mende to Ste. Enimie, Le Rozier (Montpellier-le-Vieux), and Millau.

The expedition from Mende to Millau viâ the Cañon of the Tarn may be made in a single day if an early start be made and all detours avoided. The digression to Montpellier-le-Vieux requires fully 1/2 day more.

Besides the railway-omnibuses, *Post-cars* ply from Mende to Ste. Enimie (2-3 fr.), Florac, Ispagnac & Ste. Enimie, Meyrueis, etc.; and *Carriages* may be hired for little more than the omnibus-fare. An *Omnibus* also plies to Florac (2 fr.).

I. From Mende to Ste. Enimie.

a. Viâ Sauveterre, 17 1/2 M., in 4-6 hrs. at the travellers' option; carriage for 2 pers. 13, for 4 pers. 19 fr., 5 fr. extra in each case for an additional person on the box. Carriages start between 5 and 7 a. m., or between 11 a. m. and 1 p. m.

Mende, see p. 266. — The road at first follows the valley of the *Lot*, which it crosses about 1 3/4 M. from the town, passes the station of (4 1/2 M.) *Balsièges* (p. 266), and ascends in curves to the barren plateau of the *Causse de Sauveterre* (see below), across which it runs. Fine view as we ascend. At the top the road viâ Ispagnac (see below) diverges to the left; to the right is the *Chazal*, an old château, now a farm. About 7 1/2 M. from Balsièges is the little village of *Sauveterre* (3420 ft.), and farther on is the hamlet of *Bac*. The road then winds down into the Cañon of the Tarn, opposite the lofty cliffs of the Causse Méjean. — 17 1/2 M. *Ste. Enimie* (p. 272).

b. Viâ Ispagnac, 20 M., in 7-9 hrs., fares 18 or 24 fr.; details as above.

This route is the same as the preceding until the *Causse de Sauveterre* is reached. Here it diverges to the left, by the E. end of the causse, and it descends to the S. E., affording a fine view of the Tarn Cañon. Instead of going as far as Ispagnac, we may turn to the right before the village is reached, at the point where the Ste. Enimie road diverges. — 15 1/2 M. *Ispagnac* (p. 271). Continuation of route, see p. 272.

SAUVET
La Capelle
La Fraite

c. Viâ the Col de Montmirat, Florac, and Ispagnac, 43¹/₂ M., in 12-14 hrs., including 3 hrs.' halt at Florac; fares 25 or 45 fr. etc. (see p. 270). Time is saved by omitting Florac and following the Ispagnac road 4¹/₂ M. before Florac is reached.

d. Viâ Lanuéjols, the Col de Montmirat, and Ispagnac, 41¹/₂ M., same times and fares as the preceding, 3 hrs.' halt being made at the inn of Molinette before the Col. This route is very much the same as the preceding, Lanuéjols being visited instead of Florac.

Mende, see p. 288. — Route c. leads viâ (4¹/₂ M.) *Balsièges*, like the two first, but there enters a valley between the Causse de Sauveterre and the Causse de Mende, and passes (6¹/₂ M.) *Rouffiac*. It joins the following route about 12¹/₂ M. from Mende, before the Col.

Route d. leads to the E. of the Causse de Mende and passes (5¹/₂ M.) the village of *Lanuéjols*, with a Roman tomb of great size. — Beyond *St. Etienne-du-Valdonnès* (1103 inhab.), at a point about 11 M. from Mende, we join the preceding route, and ascend to the (2¹/₂ M.) *Col de Montmirat* (3430 ft.) whence there is a very fine view. Beyond (3 M.) *Noxières* we enter the valley of the Tarn, where the road to Ispagnac diverges 4¹/₂ M. before we reach Florac.

Florac (2290 ft.; *Hôtel Melquion; de Paris*) is a town of 1976 inhab., at the foot of the *Causse Méjean* or *Méjas* and on the left bank of the *Tarnon*, a tributary of the Tarn. Its principal object of note is the *Source du Pêcher*, which, rising in the Causse above the town, forms fine cascades after heavy rains. A monument was erected here in 1890 to *Boyer* (d. in Panama), the designer of the Viaduc de Garabit (p. 265).

A road leads hence to the E. to (16 M.) *Pont-de-Montvert* (p. 264), whence excursions may be made among the Lozère mountains.

From Florac to Meyrueis (22 M.). This route is a continuation of the preceding into the Tarnon valley, dominated on the right by the escarpments of the Causse Méjean, more than 1600 ft. high. — 6 M. *Salgas*, with a fine château. Beyond (8 M.) *Vébron* we quit the valley. — From (11 M.) *Fraissinet-de-Fourques* the road ascends to the Col de Perjuret (3380 ft.; but). This is the only point where the Causse Méjean is not isolated; a neck of land connecting it with the Aigoual (p. 277). We descend into the valley of the *Jonte*, which bounds the Causse on the S. — 17 M. *Gatuzières*. — 22 M. *Meyrueis* (p. 276).

Ispagnac (1740 ft.; *Hôtel Laget*), a picturesquely situated and straggling village, 10¹/₂ M. from Ste. Enimie, on the right bank of the Tarn and at the mouth of the Cañon. Ruins of the Château de Rocheblave, see p. 272. Opposite the village the Tarn forms a peninsula, on which is *Quézac*, connected with Ispagnac by a 14th-17th cent. bridge.

The *Cañon du Tarn*, or *Gorges du Tarn*, still more beautiful beyond Ste. Enimie or rather St. Chély, and particularly so between La Malène and Le Pas-de-Souci, begins at Ispagnac and extends as far as Le Rozier, a distance of more than 31 M. It is the most curious of the gorges produced in the Causses by the erosion of the streams, which were much more abundant during the glacial epoch in the Cévennes. As the name indicates, it has suggested comparison with the celebrated Cañon of the Colorado in the United States. To the right and left the sheer rocks of the Causses de Sauveterre and Méjean rise to a height of from 800 to 1100 ft., the

distance between their summits varying from $^1/_2$ to $^3/_4$ M. It is difficult to imagine a more impressive gorge. Gigantic ramparts and
perpendicular cliffs at one time overhang the river, at others retire
in terraces, formed of the several strata of the limestone and as
varied in outline as they are in colour. Here the rocks are shivered
into a thousand different shapes and there appear yellow limestone,
black schistous marl, and pink and brown dolomite. In addition
there is abundant vegetation (vines and fruit trees), affording a
charming contrast to the rocks, as well as clear, full springs and
many caverns. The windings which the gorge describes in its 30 M.
course contribute to its beauty and provide a series of pleasant
surprises for the traveller. Even when the end is reached, we have
still to explore the very curious gorges of the Jonte and the
Dourbie and *Montpellier-le-Vieux* (p. 275). It is impossible to
describe these natural curiosities. There is scarcely anything at
all equal to the Tarn Cañon in Europe except perhaps the Romsdal
and other fjords in Norway.

The ROUTE FROM ISPAGNAC TO STE. ENIMIE (about 4 hrs. on foot)
follows the right bank of the Tarn, passing the picturesquely situated *Château de Rocheblave* (16th cent.), recently restored. A little
farther, on the left bank, is a mill worked by one of the numerous
springs formed by the rains which filter through the limestone of the
Causses. 10$^1/_2$ M. *Montbrun*, also on the left bank. The road then
passes the hamlets of *Poujols* and *Blajour*. On the other side are
the ruins of the *Château de Charbonnières*, and farther on *Castelbouc*,
where there is another ruin. This is the most remarkable point between Ispagnac and Ste. Énimie and one of the prettiest parts of the
gorge. In a neighbouring grotto is a very copious spring. — 13$^3/_4$ M.
Prades, on the right bank. The ramparts of the Causses, already very
high, approach the river more and more closely at *Les Ecoutas* (echo).

17 M. **Ste. Énimie** (*Hôtel Parisien*, R. 1, déj. 2$^1/_2$, D. 2$^1/_2$ fr.;
du Commerce, same charges; boats, see below), a town of 1070 inhab., owes its origin to a monastery, founded about 630, of which
a few uninteresting remains are left. It occupies a curious position, at one of the great angles formed by the gorge and in a kind
of huge well, 1650 ft. deep. Above issues the beautiful *Fontaine
de Burle* and below is the *Source du Coussac*. The river is spanned
by a bridge, across which passes the road vià the Causses from Balsièges (p. 266) to Meyrueis (15$^1/_2$ M. from Ste. Énimie; p. 276).

II. From Ste. Énimie to Le Rozier.

26 M. By boat on the Tarn (included in the excursion-tickets), in
8-13 hrs., at the travellers' option, starting between 5 and 8 a. m. or
between 11 a. m. and 1 p. m.; fare 42 fr. for 1-5 persons with fee of 8 fr.
Boats are changed several times, and the distance from Pas de Soucy
to Les Vignes (p. 274), about 1$^1/_4$ M., is performed on land (carr., ordered
beforehand, 10 fr.). Luggage is transported without extra charge, but
large packages should not be brought if the traveller proposes to walk
from Pas-de-Soucy to Les Vignes. — Some travellers may prefer to make

the entire expedition on foot, both because they can thus examine the gorges more at their leisure, and because the boat-journey, though not dangerous, presents various difficulties that distract attention.

Boats take about $3^1/_2$ hrs., excluding baits, to perform the distance from Ste. Enimie to La Malène. There is also a footpath (4-$4^1/_4$ hrs.) on the right bank. By either route the every-varying scenery steadily increases in grandeur and interest beyond St. Chély. — At ($1^1/_4$ hr.) *St. Chély-du-Tarn*, a village on the left bank, the gorge forms a second elbow or angle, and again turns soon afterwards at *Les Pougnadoires* (inhabited grottoes), where there is a dam. Many minor windings are also passed, each revealing some unexpected beauty. To the right is the *Château de la Caze*, partly dating from the 15th cent., before which the path ascends to cross the *Pas de l'Escalette*, a flight of steps protected by a railing. In 1 hr. from Les Pougnadoires we reach the dam of *Hauterive*, a village with a ruined castle, affording a very fine view of our road.

At *La Malène*, 1-$1^1/_4$ hr. from Hauterive, we meet the road from Banassac (p. 267). Hence to *Le Rozier* and to *Millau*, see below.

b. From Banassac-la-Canourgue to La Malène, Le Rozier (Montpellier-le-Vieux), and Millau.

The Cañon of the Tarn, or at least its finest parts, may be visited from this side in a single day, even by travellers not quitting St. Flour or Millau until the first train in the morning.

I. From Banassac to La Malène.

16 M. in $3^1/_2$-5 hrs. at the traveller's option; carriage for 2 pers. 12, for 4 pers. 20 fr., 5 fr. extra for additional passenger on the box. The start is made between 9 and 10 a. m.

Banassac (station, p. 267) is a large village on the left bank of the Lot, at its confluence with the Urugne. We ascend the valley of the latter viâ the little town of ($1^1/_4$ M.) *La Canourgue*, beyond which we reach the desolate plateau of the *Causse de Sauveterre* (p. 270). Crossing the causse we descend a gorge into the *Cañon of the Tarn*, opposite the imposing *Causse Méjean* (p. 272).

La Malène (*Hôtel Monginoux*, déj. $2^1/_2$ fr., good wine), a considerable village, with a bridge, lies near the finest part of the Tarn Cañon. Here also are a château belonging to the family of Montesquieu du Tarn; an abundant spring; and several grottoes.

II. From La Malène to Le Rozier.

$16^1/_4$ M., by boat in 5-8 hrs., starting between 5 and 7 a. m. or between 11 a. m. and 1 p. m. (fare 27 fr., included in excursion-tickets, etc., comp. p. 270).

We skirt on the left the *Rocher du Planiol* with the ruins of a castle. Beyond the *Source de l'Angle*, to the right, we pass the *Rocher de Montesquieu*, on which also are ruins, to the left, and reach the entrance of the Détroit.

The *Détroit*, also called *Les Etroits*, 40 min. from La Malène and about 3 M. long, is the most remarkable part of the Tarn Cañon. The gorge here contracts to a width of less than $1/_8$ M. between the summits of its flanking rocks, which exceed 1600 ft. In height. As the gorge winds the rocks seem to bar the passage, and sometimes they over-hang so much that they appear to form a gigantic bridge across the river. The whole effect is majestic, without any approach to the grotesque, while the picturesqueness is enhanced by the rich colouring of the cliffs. The climax of the whole scene is reached when we emerge from the Détroit, at *La Croze*, into the *Cirque des Baumes, a sort of gulf at an angle of the cañon, the most remarkable spot in the whole gorge. Here are the hamlets of *Les Baumes-Vieilles* and *Les Baumes-Basses* and the pilgrimage *Chapel of St. Hilaire*, perched on the sides of the cirque. A splendid *View is commanded from the *Point Sublime* (1960 ft.), a cliff rising above the cirque and ascended in $^3/_4$-1 hr. by a very rocky path. At *Les Baumes-Claudes*, to the N., is a grotto with three stories. Farther on we pass through another magnificent defile, before reaching the Pas-de-Soucy.

The Pas-de-Soucy, $2^1/_4$ hrs. from La Malène, is a chaos of fallen rocks, where the Tarn disappears from view, and boat navigation is interrupted (carr., see p. 273). A road starting from Les Baumes, follows the right bank, in front of the *Sourde*, one of the largest rocks, and dominated also on the right by the *Aiguille*, 260 ft. high.

$1^1/_4$ M. *Les Vignes* (Solanet's Inn, small) and on the opposite bank *St. Préjet-du-Tarn*. Here we find the fourth of the Tarn bridges in the cañon crossed by the roads over the Causses. The boat journey onward is still very interesting, but it presents serious difficulties in the shape of rapids and rocks in mid-channel. The descent to Le Rozier is made in 2 hrs., whilst for the ascent 8 hrs. are ne-cessary. By the footpath on the right bank it takes $2^1/_2$ hrs. We pass *Villaret* and (3 M.) *Cambon*. On the other bank are some ruins, the *Pas de l'Arc*, *La Sablière*, and the *Pic de Cinglegros* (3280 ft.). On the right bank are the cirque and hermitage of *St. Marcelin*. Then on the same side, the *Mas-de-la-Font* ; on the left *Plaisance*, beyond which the cañon widens to form the basin of Le Rozier.

To the left is Le Rozier (1290 ft.; *Hôtel Rascalou*, déj. or D. $2^1/_2$ fr., well spoken of), a little village at the confluence of the Tarn and *Jonte*, with a bridge over each river, and opposite *Peyreleau* (p. 275). The *Rocher de Capluc* ('caput lucis'; 2000 ft.; fine view). dominating the village, may be ascended in $^3/_4$ hr., at the top by iron ladders. — Excursion to the valley of the Jonte, see p. 276.

III. From Le Rozier to Millau.

a. Via Aguessac. $13^1/_2$ M., carriage in $2^1/_2$-3 hrs., starting between 5 a. m. and 8 p. m. (fare 10 & 15 fr.). The station of *Aguessac* is reached $^1/_2$ hr. before Millau (carr. same fare). A 'courrier' (1 fr.) also plies twice

(1825 ft.) and the enormous *Ruines de Peyrelade* (2780 ft.), where the caverns are used in the manufacture of Roquefort cheese (see p. 268). 9¹/₄ M. *Aguessac* (p. 267). 13 M. *Millau* (p. 267).

b. Viâ Montpellier-le-Vieux, 23¹/₂ M., carriage in 7-12 hrs., fare 30 fr. Not more than 3 pers. can be conveyed in a single carriage, owing to the nature of the road. Passengers alight on reaching the plateau and rejoin the carriage at La Roque-Ste. Marguerite, beyond Montpellier. On foot, Montpellier may be reached in 2 hrs. from Peyreleau; carriages take 3 hrs. and mules (6-10 fr.) 2¹/₂ hrs. — To La Roque-Ste. Marguerite we may use the public conveyances mentioned on p. 270. — It is advisable to take provisions.

We cross the *Jonte* and traverse the village of *Peyreleau* (Hôtel Blanc-Costecalde), situated on the left bank, with an ancient château. Thence the route ascends in zigzags to the S., to the *Causse Noir*, which owes its name to the dark colour of its weird and stunted pines. A footpath offers a short-cut. Fine view of the Tarn Cañon. We quit the route near the summit, when it turns finally to the E.

The Ravines of Les Paliès and the Riou-Sec, towards which this road leads, are well worth a visit. We soon pass *Aleyrac*, and then the *Hermitage of St. Jean-de-Balme* (11-13th cent.). Thence a path leads to the N. to the *Ravine of Les Paliès*, which descends towards the Jonte. In the ravine is a magnificent view-point from the top of a precipice, on the other side of which are the ruins of the *Hermitage of St. Miquel*, on some isolated rocks, difficult of access (1 hr.), whence there is also a very fine view over the Jonte valley. The head of the ravine, the *Cirque de Madaus*, is also very interesting. In 2 hrs. thence, we reach the *Riou-Sec*, a ravine to the S. which descends towards the Dourbie. On the side are the *Roques-Altes* ('high rocks'; 160-200 ft. high), a sort of natural fortress, seen also from the route. About 1¹/₂ hr. is required to descend into the ravine and ascend on the other side to *Maubert* (see below).

The path continues in a S. direction and passes the hamlet of *Maubert* (2675 ft.; accommodation at the 'Ferme Robert'; guide 3-5 fr.). About ¹/₄ M. farther we reach Montpellier-le-Vieux at the *Cirques de la Millière* and *du Lac* (see below).

*Montpellier-le-Vieux (perhaps from 'mont pelé', bald mountain) is not an inhabited place, but a spot covered with huge rocks and blocks of the strangest forms, a fantastic ruined city, with imposing monuments. It remained unknown till 1883. The plateau occupied by this natural curiosity is about 2 M. long and 1¹/₄ M. broad. In order to gain an idea of the whole and its general arrangement it is better not to descend at once into the cirque, but to continue straight on to the rocks which block on the S. the road by which we approach, and to mount those on the left, called the *Ciutad* from their resemblance to a citadel. Thence we have a really marvellous *View of the Cyclopean city. The corridor by which we arrive and its continuation beyond the rocks very nearly divide the town in two parts, one to the left or E., the other to the right or W. In the first are 4 cirques or amphitheatres: to the S., the *Rouquettes*; to the N., the *Lac*; and beyond, to the E., the *Amats* and the *Citerns*. In the second the walls are 380 ft. high. Near the Amats the '*Porte de Mycènes*'. In an isolated rock, an alley of 'obelisks', etc., are pointed out. A striking *View is obtained from the top of the rocks, in the direction of the Dourbie. An 'aven' (p. 270) separates the Millière from the Rouquettes. — We may thence descend directly to the (1³/₄ M.) —

Valley of the Dourbie, between the Causse Noir and the Larzac. This is the finest gorge of the Causses next to the Tarn Cañon, at least in its lower part near Millau. — *La Roque-Ste. Marguerite* (1310 ft.; Parguel's Inn; guide, Froment) is the nearest village to Montpellier-le-Vieux, 1¹/₄ hr. to the S. of Maubert, and 8 M. from Millau. Ravine of St. Véran, see p. 268. Downstream, the prettiest part is the *Val Nègre* ravine, 2 M. from La Roque. In this part also is the *Grotte d'Aluech*. — 5¹/₂ M. *Le Monna*, with the château of the Bonald family, and the tombs of the cardinal and the philosopher of that name. — 6¹/₄ M. *Massebiau*. — 8 M. *Millau* (p. 267).

Excursion from Le Rozier to the Valley of the Jonte, Bramabiau, etc. From Le Rozier to Meyrueis, 13¹/₂ M., omnibus twice daily (2 fr.), in 3-3¹/₂ hrs. This route may also be included in an excursion-ticket to the Tarn Cañon: from Le Rozier to Millau, viâ Meyrueis, 41 M. in 8-10 hrs., fares 30 or 35 fr.; to Millau, viâ Meyrueis and Bramabiau, 48¹/₂ M., in 12-16 hrs., fares 45 or 50 fr. — This route ascends the very interesting *Valley of the Jonte*, which at first forms a gorge between the Causse Méjean and Causse Noir, having almost the character of the Tarn Cañon, on a small scale. At about 1¹/₂ hr. from Le Rozier is *Le Truel*; ³/₄ hr. farther *Les Douzes*, at the mouth of a ravine; and 2 hrs. farther, *Meyrueis*.

Meyrueis (2510 ft.; *Hôtel Lévéjac*; *Boulet*; *Parguel*) is a little town on the Jonte, near the end of the Causse Noir. Among the *Grottoes* in the neighbourhood, the chief is the fine stalactite cavern known as the *Grotte de Dargilan*, discovered in 1880 in the Causse Noir, about 3¹/₂ M. before the town is reached. A guide (5 fr.) and a special costume (2 fr.) are required for a visit to this grotto. The charge for admission is 2 fr., and for the guide's lunch 2¹/₂ fr., so that the visit costs 11¹/₂ fr., besides the cost of the magnesium lights provided by the guide, etc. On the other side of the Jonte is the *Grotte de Nabrigas*, noted chiefly for its old world frelics and the great quantity of bones of cave-bears which have been found in it. — From Meyrueis to Florac, see p. 383. — A 'courrier' plies hence to (43 M.) *Le Vigan* (p. 268) in 7-8 hrs. (9 fr.) viâ (7 M.) *Lanuéjols*, (13 M.) *Trèves*, and (20 M.) *St. Jean-du-Bruel*, where we join the road from Millau (p. 267).

About 3³/₄ M. to the S. of Meyrueis is *St. Sauveur-des-Pourcils*, with mines of silver-lead and copper. In the neighbourhood, to the E., is the curious *Source de Bramabiau ('bellowing ox'), a cascade, 48 ft. high, formed by the *Bonheur*. This stream, which formerly fell from a limestone cliff 500 ft. in height, has now bored for itself through the rock a subterranean channel, more than 500 yds. long. It issues from the channel like a torrent, into a gorge 650 ft. deep, hollowed out by its waters. Only the channel is accessible. The entrance on this side is about ¹/₂ M. from *Camprieux* (3900 ft.; Philippine Inn; guide, Emile Michel), 11¹/₂ M. from Meyrueis (8 M. by short-cuts).

The ascent of the **Aigoual** or *Signal de la Hort-Dieu* (5140 ft.), to the S.E., may be made from Meyrueis partly by carriage (20 M.; 30 fr.) viâ *Camprieux* (see above) and the (16 M.) *Col de Sérepréde*. On foot the ascent is made in about 4-5 hrs. viâ the beautiful valley of the Bulézon, one of the tributaries of the Jonte. An observatory and a refuge-hut have been built on the summit, which commands a very fine panorama. The descent may be made to Le Vigan (p. 268).

INDEX.

INDEX.

Brive
Rouère
St Denis
Beaumont
Gramat
le Pournié
Cajarc
74
Cahors
St Cirq la Popie
Villa

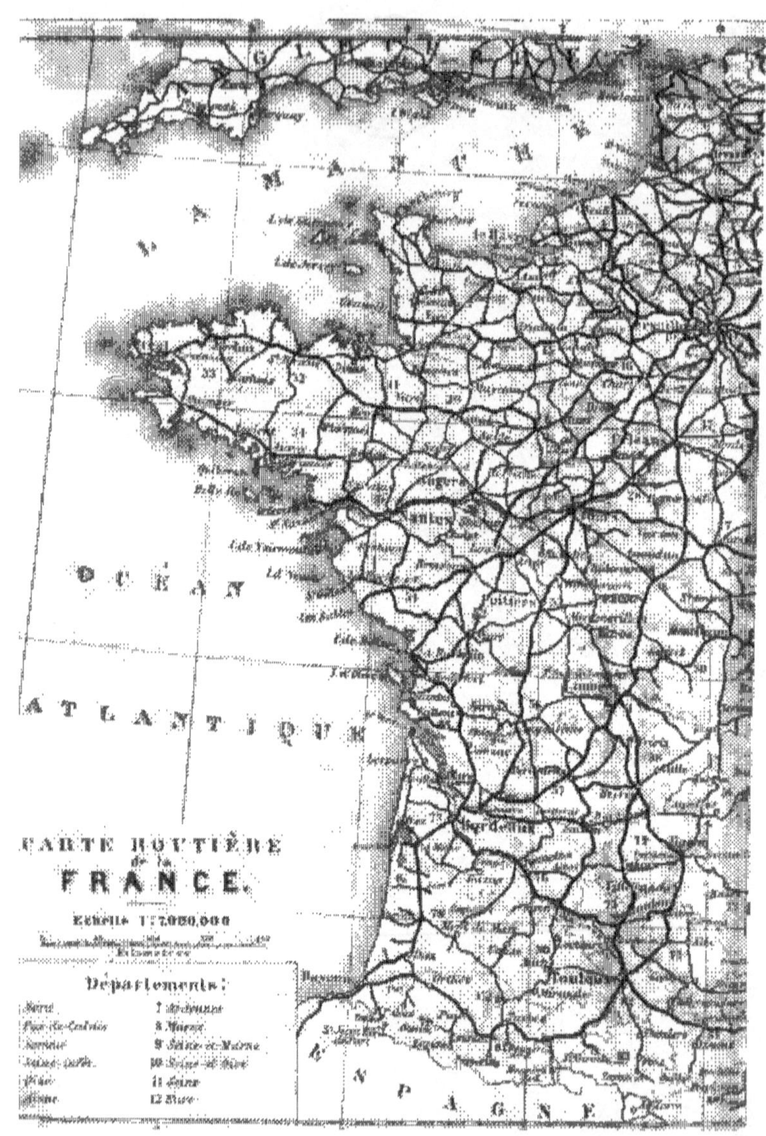
LA MANCHE
OCÉAN
ATLANTIQUE
CARTE ROUTIÈRE
de la
FRANCE.
Échelle 1:7.050.000
Kilomètres
Départements:
1 Charente
2 Mayenne
9 Seine-et-Marne
10 Seine-et-Oise
11 Seine
12 Eure
ESPAGNE